SOARING

A MAGDALENE NOVEL

KRISTEN ASHLEY

ROCK CHICK
P R E S S

NEW YORK TIMES BESTSELLING AUTHOR

KRISTEN ASHLEY

Soaring

―A MAGDALENE NOVEL―

License Notes

First ebook edition: March 2015

Latest ebook edition September 2022

First print edition: March 2015

Cover Art and Interior Graphics: Pixel Mischief Design

PROLOGUE

START ANEW

$\mathcal{I}$ stood in the middle of the huge room, the long, high wall of windows showing a grayed view of the Atlantic Ocean foaming against the cliff rock, my furniture (mostly) where I wanted it, the rest of the space was taken up with boxes stacked high.

I'd brought too much stuff.

I should have gone through it. Weeded things out. Dumped stuff.

Started anew.

That's what I needed.

That was why I was there.

To start anew.

The problem with that was, to do it, I needed to backtrack and rectify past mistakes.

As if the biggest mistake of all could be conjured by my thoughts, I heard my doorbell ring.

In buying the house long-distance without looking at anything but photos, I'd obviously not heard my doorbell. Hearing it then, I was surprised it was just as stunning and elegant as the rest of the house. Muted chimes that rang dulcetly through the space as if they were precisely what they were, carefully crafted to belong right there.

I looked to the door with its curving slash of extraordinary stained glass just as a loud banging that was not dulcet in the slightest came on the heels of the bell.

I couldn't see anything but a shadow through the blues, purples and pinks of the stained glass, but I still knew that body shadowed through the glass. I'd know the lines of that body anywhere.

"*Amelia! Open the fuck up!*"

There it was.

Conrad.

Angry.

Actually, very angry.

As he had been now for years.

I hurried to the door for several reasons.

One was that he was still banging and I liked my door. It was custom-made to fit the house. I didn't want him damaging it. And I knew he was angry enough to keep banging and doing it that hard might cause harm to the door.

Two was that I didn't want him to wait. He was angry and I didn't want him angrier. Though how that could be, I couldn't imagine. I'd spent years plumbing the depths of his wrath. However, as I did, I found those depths were unending.

And three was that he had a right to be angry and I didn't want to do anything to give him more of a right.

I arrived at the door, flipped the lock, opened it and looked up at my ex-husband.

God, so beautiful. So…very…*beautiful.*

My heart shriveled.

"You fucking did it," he snarled, his eyes slits, his fury so visible, so palpable, I could taste it.

I was used to the taste. It was acrid, it burned my tongue. I hated it but somewhere along the way I had become addicted to it.

"Con," I whispered.

"Couldn't leave well enough alone," he bit out.

"Please, just—"

"We're fine. We're good. We're finally far from you and happy, and you…" He shook his head furiously, "Fuck, *you…*" He drew in a massive breath then shouted, "*Gotta show and fuck everything up!*"

Oh yes. Very angry.

"That's not my intention, Con," I replied soothingly. "I know that you won't believe that, but—"

"*You know I won't believe that?*" he bellowed. "You know? Fuck yeah, you know, you bitch! Of course you fucking know!"

I lifted my hands in a pacifying gesture. "Really. Give me time. I promise—"

"*You* promise?" he thundered. "*You?* A promise from you? *What a fucking joke!*"

"If you give me time, Con—" I tried again, softly.

I stopped when he leaned into me, coming close.

"*Time?* You stupid, *fucking bitch!* So full of *shit!* Time? I'm not giving you time. I'm not giving you fucking *shit.* Amelia, you fuck this up for me, for my wife, for my kids, *again*, I'll make you *fucking pay.* You hear me? *I'll make you fucking pay!*"

I opened my mouth to say something. Something about the fact they weren't *his* kids but *our* kids.

However, before I got it out, I heard a deep voice demand, "Step back. Now."

Conrad jerked around.

I looked beyond him and the world suspended.

This was because, five feet away from Conrad, standing on my front walk, was a tall, muscular man with dark hair clipped short to his skull and the most beautiful blue eyes I'd ever seen in my life.

Those eyes were on Conrad. They were irate.

But I didn't take that in.

I took *him* in.

His blue khakis hanging on narrow hips and covering long legs with noticeably meaty thighs. His matching blue t-shirt that fit snug at his wide chest and bulky biceps. A t-shirt that had a recognizable cross insignia over his heart with "MFD" in the middle and "fire" at the top, "rescue" at the bottom. His strong jaw covered in a dark five o'clock shadow that had hints of salt in it, those whiskers matching his thick, cropped hair.

And those eyes. Those eyes that were angry now but I knew with one look they could be many different things. They could be warm. They could laugh. They could be frustrated. They could be impatient. They could be determined. They could be joyful.

They could be heated.

And I knew with that one look I wanted to see those eyes every way they could be.

Yes, I wanted that but I also wanted more.

I wanted to *make* him feel all the things those eyes could communicate to me. I wanted to *make* him happy. I wanted to *make* him laugh. I even wanted to make him annoyed.

But most of all, in that moment, I found myself wanting, in a myriad of ways, to make those beautiful blue eyes *heated*.

Yes, standing in my brand new house facing off with the love of my life, my ex-husband, the man who I lost, a man I didn't think I could get over but knew I had to find a way—for him but mostly for our children—that was what I thought.

I wanted it all from this stranger.

And I wanted it immediately.

"Who the fuck are you?" Conrad asked irately, jolting me out of these thoughts.

"I'm a man who doesn't like it when another man shouts at, threatens and curses at a woman. Now, I said, step back," the stranger replied.

"This isn't any of your business," Conrad informed him.

"Man sees another doin' what I just saw you doin', 'fraid you're wrong. It *is* my business." He delivered that and didn't even pause before he said, "I'll say it one more time, step back."

Conrad turned to me. "You know this asshole?"

Before I could answer, Conrad was no longer standing at my front door.

He was off the front walk, several steps into the yard, and I had the back of the stranger to me as he'd positioned himself in my door between Conrad and me.

I'd seen him move, I had to. Yet it happened so fast, it almost seemed like I didn't.

But it happened and there he was, this stranger, unknowingly standing between me and my gravest mistake.

Protecting me.

I'd never had that. Not in my forty-seven years of life.

I didn't know if it was right to like it, I just knew I did.

Okay, yes.

Absolutely, one hundred percent yes.

I didn't know him but I knew I wanted it all from this man.

"Go somewhere. Cool off," the stranger ordered. "You know this woman and got somethin' to say to her, you do it a lot more calm and with a fuckuva lot more respect. Am I understood?"

I looked beyond his back (which was a difficult endeavor, the t-shirt clung to his shoulders and lats and it was a pleasant visual) to see Conrad was even more livid after the man had pushed him into the yard.

However, Conrad wasn't stupid. He was tall and lean, fit because he worked at it. But he was no match for this man and he knew it.

"You obviously don't know her," he spat.

"Don't need to know her to know you never got call to treat a woman like that," the stranger returned. He waited the barest of moments before he continued, "You're still standin' there."

Conrad scowled at him then turned that scowl to me. "This isn't done."

The stranger moved, leaning forward an inch, and Conrad instantly (and wisely) turned his attention back to him. It was wise because I only got the back of it, but I still knew that inch was a significantly threatening inch.

He glared at the stranger for a second before he turned and stalked to the drive where he'd parked his Yukon.

I stood and watched.

The stranger stood and watched.

Only after Conrad got in, reversed out too quickly and took off even more quickly, did the stranger turn around to face me.

I looked up into his eyes realizing that it hadn't been a figment of my imagination just minutes before.

They were the most beautiful eyes I'd ever seen.

"You okay?" he asked.

The honest answer to that was that I wasn't. I hadn't been for years. Decades. Perhaps my entire life.

"Yes," I answered.

His eyes moved over my face. The sensation was pleasant at the same time disconcerting.

Before I could get a lock on how both of these could be, he shoved a hand my way. "Mickey Donovan."

I looked at his hand and so as not to appear rude, I didn't study it like I wanted to. The squared off fingers, the closely clipped nails, the roughness, the strength, the sureness.

Instead, I took it, raised my eyes to his and said, "Amelia Moss...I mean, Hathaway."

His fingers remained warm and strong around mine in a way I liked before he let me go and asked as if to confirm, "Amelia Hathaway?"

"Yes. I, well...I was Amelia Moss. I've recently changed it back to my maiden name. That was my ex-husband." I tipped my head to the drive and went on hesitantly, "We have a...somewhat rocky history."

He nodded once, doing it shortly, taking that in as understood without making a big deal of it or asking anything further, something that brought me relief and made me like this Mickey Donovan even more.

"I'm really sorry you had to step in on that," I said.

"No problem," he replied, shaking his head and flipping out a hand. "Woulda done it just if I saw it but," he grinned a highly attractive, somewhat roguish grin that made my stomach flip, "I'm your neighbor."

He twisted his torso and threw a long arm out toward the street to indicate an attractive, somewhat rambling, one-story, weathered, gray shingle-sided house with pristine white woodwork around the windows, eaves and front door.

I stared at the house he occupied, a house that was right across the street, feeling a number of emotions. Elation and terror, however, reigned supreme.

He turned back to me. "We have to look out for our neighbors."

Although I agreed, it was then I rather tardily became embarrassed by that scene. So much so, for the first time in years, I felt heat in my cheeks.

I looked to his shoulder and murmured, "This is true. However, I'll do my best to make certain you don't have to do that again."

"Amelia."

Startled by the gentle way the rough velvet of his deep voice enveloped my name, and my extreme reaction to it, my gaze darted to his.

"I'm divorced," he declared bluntly. "Shit happens. Sometimes it isn't pretty. I get it. I hope I don't have to do that again too, just because I don't want it to happen to you again. But if it does, and you can't handle it, I'm right across the way. That isn't an offer I'm makin' just to make it. I mean it. Whatever happened between you and that guy happened. Now this is your home and a home should be a safe place. Even if you weren't at your home, he should respect you. You demand that, and he doesn't agree, I'll be there to make him agree or make it stop. And I mean that."

He wasn't lying. He meant it. I could tell by looking in his eyes. He was a nice man. He was a good neighbor. He believed women should be shown respect. He was the kind of man who would step in and do what he could to make that so if need be.

He also didn't know me. If he did, if he knew what I'd done, he might no longer believe in that so thoroughly.

And that was when I knew he wouldn't know me.

I'd be a nice neighbor. A good one. If he had a dog and went on vacation, I'd watch it. I'd do my best to keep my ex-husband from shouting obscenities at me in my front door, disturbing the neighborhood. I'd keep my yard nice. I'd put attractive, but not outlandish or overwhelming, holiday decorations out. I wouldn't play loud music. I'd wave if I saw him driving by or mowing his lawn. And if he needed a cup of sugar, I would be his go-to girl.

But other than that, he would not know me.

He didn't need me in his life.

I didn't even like me in my life.

Alas, I couldn't escape me.

"I don't know what to say," I told him. "Except to thank you again."

He gave me another grin, which also gave me another stomach curl, then he looked beyond me into the house.

"You need help with anything?" he offered.

I did. Absolutely. I had hours of unpacking, cleaning, arranging, organizing, hanging, shoving furniture around. All of this and I was not handy in any way. I might be relatively adept with a screwdriver, but I'd had several go-arounds with a drill and not a one of them was pretty.

Back in La Jolla, after Conrad left me, I'd had a handyman. I'd also had landscape and cleaning services. I'd even had a young woman who made extra cash for college by running errands for me, like getting my groceries and picking up dry cleaning. The only thing I did was pay my bills.

Now I had none of that.

This was me starting anew.

This was me creating a new me.

I didn't think Mickey wanted to hear any of this and he'd already been kind enough to come over and intervene when Conrad was shouting at me, so I decided not to ask him to help me unpack boxes and hang pictures.

"I'm good," I told him.

He clearly didn't believe me and he didn't hide the fact he didn't. It was not only written on his face but right there in his eyes.

He wasn't wrong.

I kept silent and didn't amend my statement. That was part of me keeping myself to me. Being a nice guy who would intervene when a man was shouting at a woman, he didn't need the mess I'd made of my life to touch his in any way. And I was going to see that didn't happen.

"You do, you know where I live," he replied.

I nodded. "Thanks. That's very kind."

And again I got his grin. Seeing it, *feeling* it, I wondered how it would affect me if he actually smiled.

"Welcome to the neighborhood, Amelia," he said quietly.

I forced my lips to smile. "Thanks, Mickey."

When I said that, he gave me more. His eyes warmed and that did things to me I'd never experienced. I wasn't sure why. Perhaps it was the genuineness I saw there. The friendliness that was just real and nothing else.

Whatever it was, it did a number on me and I wanted to crawl into it, into *him*, burrowing deep, wrapping myself in that warmth and doing it so tight it would seep into my bones and force out the cold that lay in my marrow since I was able to understand how to feel.

He lifted a hand in a casual way and dropped it. "See you around."

"Yes," I replied, my voice strange, husky, like I was about to start crying. "Yeah. See you around."

He studied me for another second before he did a short nod, turned and walked down my front walk that was also jagged, inlaid here and there with interesting pieces of glass, edged in a thick line of travertine.

I stood and took in the way he walked, how comfortable he was with his bulky frame. I also fully took in his clothing.

He was a firefighter.

That was not surprising.

Then it struck me that I was standing in my doorway watching him, and if he caught me, what that might say, so I quickly jumped back and closed the door.

I turned to my living room.

Upon arriving in Magdalene the day before, I'd picked up the keys and the garage door openers and done the first walk-through of my house.

I'd been thrilled to find that it was even better than the pictures. It was a newish build by the award-winning Scottish architect, Prentice Cameron. I knew his work because he'd designed a home in La Jolla that I'd loved so much when I saw it, I'd done something I'd never done before. I'd looked it up and then researched him on the Internet. When I did, I'd found all of his designs were breathtaking.

They were all modern without looking space-age, instead seeming timeless. Unusual. Multi-level. Spacious. Open. With generous use of windows, in my case one whole side of the house—the one that faced the Atlantic Ocean—was floor to tall ceilings *view*. A view that was such a view, it was almost like you were floating over the sea.

It was amazing.

So when Conrad, Martine and the kids had moved from La Jolla to the small coastal town of Magdalene in Maine and my world imploded, after which I'd made my decision to move out, I'd found to my glee this Cameron home was for sale. So I'd jumped on it.

It was only five years old but the couple who'd had it built had split. It was not amicable (oh, how I understood that) and they'd fought bitterly over the house. In the end, the judge had forced them to liquidate.

Their loss.

My gain.

That was what I thought yesterday.

Right then, staring at what was already stunning, and I hoped by my hand I could make exquisite, I worried.

I worried if I did the right thing following Conrad and Martine and moving to Maine. I worried if my children were as angry as Conrad. I worried if I had it in me to show them all I'd changed. I worried if I could win my children back. I worried if I could create a safe place for them; a comfortable home, a happy, extended family.

I worried if I could do what I should have done three years ago but didn't. Beat back the bitterness, the loss, the anger. Give my children a mother they could love, be proud of, not be ashamed of and hate. Build a new life for myself and find some contentment.

I worried I didn't have that in me. I worried with all I'd done—even while doing it knowing it wasn't right—that I couldn't beat back that part of me that was pure Hathaway. That was selfish and thoughtless and sour and vindictive.

I didn't believe in me. I'd lost it all. My husband. Custody of the kids except every other weekend, which changed to once a month when Conrad and Martine moved to Maine. My self-respect.

Heck, I didn't even *know* me so there was no *me* to believe in.

That thought drove me around the edge of the sunken living room, my bare feet silent on the beautiful gloss of the wood floors. I hit the doorway off to the side and walked down the short hall to the flight of four steps that guided me up the elevation of the cliff the single-story house rambled along. One side of the hall all windows, open to the sea, the other side my three car garage.

I continued down that hall and up two more steps into the master bedroom that was gigantic. So big you could fit bed, dressers, nightstands, armoires and jewelry cabinets in there, plus couches, day beds, club chairs, a TV, whatever I decided. There was even a luscious, staggered stone fireplace, freestanding, delineating what I envisioned would one day be the bed area at the back (and currently was, as my big king was there) from a seating area (to be created) at the front.

I walked through it to the bathroom that ran the width of the room. It included two walk-in closets and a large, oval, sunken bath at the end that had windows all around, butting up to the sea so you could take a bath and gaze at the ocean, feeling you were bathing and floating. There were also double-bowled sinks (and the sinks were beautiful *bowls*). The entire room was paneled in a rich, knotty wood, bringing together a rustic and elegant feel in a way that was astonishing.

I didn't see any of that.

I walked by the huge mirror over the basins and into one of the closets where there were wardrobe boxes and suitcases.

Something in me drove me straight to a box. I ripped off the tape and the front panel fell away.

I reached in and pulled out the clothes randomly. Strewing them over the tops of other boxes, I pulled out more and did the same. Some of them landed on the boxes. Some on the floor. All haphazard. Messy.

It was wrong to do. They were designer. They were expensive. Many women would want their whole life just to own one piece of what I had many, but they'd never be able to afford it.

And they were all—every garment—something my mother would wear.

It had happened. I knew it in the heart of me. I hadn't fought it. Not even a little bit. And I knew it before the movers had packed those boxes.

Every stitch should have been left behind. Sold. Discarded.

So I could start anew.

I walked out of the closet and to the basins. There were several boxes on the floor with labels on them that said "vanity." I bent to them, ripped them open and pulled things out. Putting some on the floor, some on the countertop. I did this until, in box two, I found it.

My perfume.

"Every woman should have a signature scent," my mother had told me.

Mine was Chanel N° 5. I loved it. It was everything a woman should be.

But I had this niggling feeling it wasn't all that was me.

I had this feeling because sometimes I felt more flowery.

And sometimes I felt more musky.

Then there were times I felt more summery.

I'd been taught that was wrong. You were what you were, *only* what you were, and you stuck with that.

As for me, I was the daughter of J.P. and Felicia Hathaway, which meant I was a *Hathaway*. Upper class. Moneyed. Well-educated. Appropriately dressed. Conservative. Mannered. Superior. Aloof. Privileged. Elite.

That was what I was and I was given no choice to be anything else.

So that was what I became.

And thus I buried the fact that sometimes I wanted just to go with the Amelia of the Day, whoever she might be, and grab whatever scent that defined her that day.

Then the next, I could be something different.

Whatever I wanted to be.

Not what *she* wanted me to be. Not what *they* demanded I be.

I glanced in the mirror but immediately looked away and walked out, through the bedroom, down the hall, the steps. I turned right into the large, open kitchen that looked down to the sunken living room, across to the cozy landing, all with views to the frothy sea. Calmly, I tore open boxes until I found them.

My dishes. Stoneware that was very pretty but cost forty dollars a plate.

My mother had picked it. She did it in a way that seemed she was encouraging me to pick it. But in reality, *she* picked it.

Suddenly, I had the nearly overwhelming urge to scoot the entire box out to the deck and, piece by piece, throw it into the sea.

I didn't.

That would be a waste and those dishes could be put to good use.

I was starting anew. I didn't need to do it being wasteful.

I was going to do something else with those plates.

I was going to do something else with all my stuff.

I was going to make it worth something. Something *real*.

Because that was what I was going to be. I was going to stop being what I was, the Felicia Hathaway mini-me all grown up.

I was going to be me.

I had absolutely no idea what that me would turn out to be.

I just knew whoever she was, for the first time in her life, she'd be real.

THEY'D SEE

*B*y that weekend, the weekend the kids would normally fly out to California to spend a day and a half with me, they were instead coming to their new home.

I'd been in Magdalene for three days.

In that time, thankfully, I had not seen Mickey.

In that time, I'd also been through every box, mostly repacking things and lugging them to walls, stacking them up.

I had a plan.

But first, I had to start reparation work with my children.

I could say that due to my activities since Conrad and I separated—when joint custody turned to every other weekend, which then turned to the judge awarding Conrad custody of the children as he moved across the country, allowing me one weekend a month—along the way the visitations with my kids had deteriorated.

In the beginning I had cause. It was just. My neurosurgeon husband had cheated on me with a nurse at his hospital, a woman fifteen years younger than me. He then left our family in order to divorce me so they could be married.

Conrad and I signed our divorce papers on a Wednesday.

Conrad and Martine had a massive beach wedding that next Saturday, where my son was his father's best man and my daughter was a junior bridesmaid.

Then, as the months passed into years, the extremity of my antics increasing, my cause was no longer just.

No, and not only because the extremity of my antics was extreme, but because I'd done what no mother should do.

I'd dragged my children right along with me.

I didn't involve them, oh no. Never that.

But I didn't hide it from them.

Therefore, that first Friday in Magdalene with the kids imminently arriving, I was a nervous wreck.

Auden, my sixteen-year-old son, drove. A month after his sixteenth birthday, his father and stepmother bought him a car. It was used. It was okay, not great. Through stilted reports from my boy, I learned what it was and knew that it ran (which was all he needed) and was relatively trendy (which was all he wanted).

I would have bought him his heart's desire, even if that were a Porsche or a Mercedes.

Conrad would have attempted to educate me about the fact that if we gave everything to our children, they would become spoiled and wouldn't know how to work for things themselves.

Conrad would have been right.

I still would have bought Auden the car he wanted, brand new with all the bells and whistles. And if Conrad and I had still been married, I'd have done it without thought, without discussion, giving it to Auden so Conrad would have had two choices: be the bad guy and take it away or give in and let him have it.

Now that I didn't have that say in my son's life, at three thirty on that Friday, that car drove up and parked in my drive.

A red Honda Civic.

I stood in my open front door and watched my children alight from it. They didn't look at the house. They didn't look at me.

Auden and Olympia Moss just grabbed small bags from the trunk of the car and trudged up to the house like they were walking into a classroom at eight o'clock on a Saturday morning to take their SATs.

I watched them approach me.

Auden looked like his dad, tall with a straight nose, light brown eyes and rich brown hair that had a subtle reddish cast to it. My son was bulkier than his father, maybe an inch or two shorter, but he was still growing.

As if our lives were golden and the fates shined their smiles on us and gave us the perfect family, Auden got his looks from his father, but Olympia was just like me, petite but slightly curvy (or in Pippa's case, her curves were filling out). Brunette hair that was several shades darker than her brother's and father's, with no reddish cast, but it had a natural shine that said someone up there liked my baby girl and me. She also had my hazel eyes that popped due to the darkness of our hair.

My boy was already handsome, like Conrad.

My girl was far, far prettier than me.

When they got close, my throat feeling clogged, I forced out, "Hey, honeys."

Auden looked up. My beautiful boy who got all I loved from his dad (and then some), his eyes on me emotionless, my throat completely closed.

My fourteen-year-old daughter, Pippa, flinched at the sound of my voice.

That slashed through me.

I took that cut and it sliced deep as I moved out of their way and they walked by me, Auden averting his eyes, Pippa never even looking at me.

I followed them in and closed the door, seeing they'd stopped and were taking in the view.

Hoping they liked what they were seeing, I moved to their sides, wanting to hug them, touch them, kiss their cheeks, draw in their scents. I hadn't seen them in weeks.

But I'd learned affection from me was not wanted.

Not anymore.

So I didn't do this.

I stood not far, not close, and said, "This is it, kiddos. Our new place."

Auden had a curl in his lip.

Olympia looked bored.

That cut deep as well but I forged ahead.

The new me.

The new *us*.

No matter the wounds they inflicted, I had to keep going. Never fall back. Never retreat. I couldn't allow any of my weaknesses to delay me in restarting my family.

"Your rooms are that way." I pointed to the opposite end of the living area from where the kitchen was. "I had the movers put your furniture in the two rooms that had sea views. If you want different—"

"Whatever," Auden muttered, talking over me and starting the way I indicated. "It'll work."

Olympia followed him silently.

I did the same, not silently, instead calling, "I haven't unpacked your stuff. I had an idea. I thought...new house, fresh start. You two might want to have a look at your things. Decide what you want to keep. What you don't. We can get rid of what you don't, go out and get you new. You can decora—"

"Only got two years with this crap, not worth the bother," Auden cut me off to say.

Pippa said nothing. She just followed Auden around the lip of the sunken living room and into the hall that, opposite to the one on the other side of the house, had stretches of straight and steps that led down the cliff rather than up.

I chose the front sea view room for Pippa and thinking Auden, as a boy, would want more privacy, the back room for him.

I considered putting him in the room that ran the length of the far end, which was large and could be anything, a den, a family room, an office. I decided against it because the two front rooms had their own baths and the back room only had a half-bath.

The two bedrooms opposite shared a Jack and Jill. I wanted my kids to see the ocean, to have access to the deck right from their rooms. But I also thought they were too old to share a Jack and Jill.

I stood at the mouth of the hall as they moved down it and said, "You can drop your bags in your room. Then I'll give you a full tour."

"We can look around," Auden replied as he stopped and looked into the first room then kept going and disappeared in the second.

Pippa looked in the first room and walked in, out of sight.

I stood there, waiting, thinking this wasn't going well but knowing it wouldn't.

Patience.

Perseverance.

This was going to take time and I had to put in the time. Take my licks. Endure the cuts. Bleed inside. Give them what they needed to take it out on me because I deserved it.

Then I'd show them this was different. This time it was a promise I wouldn't break. This time we really were going to rebuild our family.

And they'd come to me. They were my babies. We'd once been close. We'd once been affectionate.

We'd once been happy.

They'd come to me.

At that moment, they didn't come to me.

Auden came out of his room mere seconds after he entered it and he called, "Pippa!"

Immediately she came out of hers.

They both moved along the hall, toward me then past me and right to the front door.

"Pip's curfew is eleven o'clock on weekends," Auden stated as they walked. "I'm dropping her off at her friend's. Leave a key under the mat or something. She'll be home then."

I stared, my insides frozen, my throat burning from the chill.

"You're leaving?" I asked.

Auden opened the door and Pippa walked right through, never looking at me.

But my son looked at me.

Or through me.

Though, his words were directed at me.

"Goin' out with the guys. My curfew is midnight. Pip'll leave the key somewhere for me. Later."

With that, he went through the door and closed it behind him.

I stood immobile, allowing the vicious feel of the fact my children had walked into their new home they would be sharing with me (not often, but they'd be doing it), dropped their bags and walked out. They didn't greet me. They didn't look around. They barely looked at me. My daughter didn't even speak to me.

And then they were gone.

I stared at the door and whispered, "I deserved that. I deserved it. Take it. Bury it. Move on. Move on, Amelia."

I didn't know how I did it but I forced my body to move. I went to the kitchen counter and grabbed the keys I'd had made for them. I found some notepaper. I wrote their names on two sheets. Under that, on each sheet, I wrote, "Welcome home. These are yours to keep."

I went to the front door and lifted the mat, put the papers down side by side, laid the keys on top and dropped the mat.

Then I closed the door, took in a deep breath and decided against dinner that night. I had the groceries to make one of the few dishes that was a favorite of both my children.

Maybe I'd get to make it the next night.

———— • ————

I stayed up but I did it in my room with the door open.

I heard them both come home, safe and sound.

Even though the light was on in my room and down the hallway, neither of them came to say goodnight to me.

———— • ————

The next morning, late, I stood in the kitchen sipping coffee out of a twenty dollar mug that I would soon be replacing, when my daughter came out.

I did not take it as a good sign that she was dressed to face the day.

"Hey, sweetheart, you want some breakfast?" I called.

She skirted the living room toward the door.

And the first words my daughter said to me in our new home were, "Polly's here with her mom. We're going to the mall and to a movie. Then pizza tonight. I'll be home by curfew."

She was out the door before I could say another word.

I hurried to the door, opened it and looked out just in time to see a Chevy SUV, the woman in the front seat looking my way, smiling, giving me a wave, but reversing out of my drive then rolling away.

I endured that and decided on what was next, knowing from experience that Auden was not an early riser on weekends.

So I chanced a shower.

It was a bad decision.

I came out to a note on the kitchen counter that simply said, "Out. Be back later."

Even though I knew I had no right, the mother in me boiled inside that my teenage son (and incidentally, daughter) felt they could take off giving me very limited information as to where they were going and who they were with. Heck, Pippa's friend's mother should have gotten out, walked up to my house and introduced herself to me.

But I had to suffer the boil. Let it cool. Give them what they needed. Take it and move on.

So I did.

Through that day.

And through the next, where they didn't leave their rooms except to go and raid the fridge with nary a word to me.

Until it was five o'clock. Time to leave and go back to their father's.

Auden said, "Later," on his way out the door.

Pippa said nothing.

I died inside and hoped to God I had the strength to revive myself because I had long weeks yawning ahead of me of nothing. They wouldn't return calls. They wouldn't return texts. They wouldn't do anything.

And I determined I'd use those weeks to show them things were different.

I would not go to their father's and stepmother's work and cause a scene. I would not go to their home and get into it with Martine. I would not go to their school activities and embarrass them, aiming my acid publically at their dad and stepmom (though it was summer, but *when* they had school activities, I wouldn't do this).

I would be what I promised them I would be when I emailed them to tell them I was moving to Maine and things would change.

Yes, that and only that was what I'd be.

They'd see.

God, I hoped they'd see.

THEY DIDN'T REPLY

I was driving down Cross Street, the main street of Magdalene, that next day on an errand of going nowhere and doing nothing, just getting the lay of the land of my new home.

I'd been born in California, and although Conrad had moved to a practice in Boston and we'd lived there for two years (and then to Lexington, Kentucky for two more), I'd never been to Maine.

From what I could see, I liked it. It was pretty. Quiet. Sparsely populated. Restful.

There was a chill in the air even though it was early June, which I wasn't used to, and I worried that the bloom would go off the rose of not having everything you could possibly want in the form of shopping, restaurants and movies within easy driving distance. But I liked the change.

And the fact there was practically no traffic was a major plus.

For a woman who needed to reinvent herself, a relatively sleepy coastal Maine town seemed the perfect place to focus inwards without any distractions.

These were my thoughts when my phone in my purse rang.

My children had not phoned me of their own volition in over a year.

I still held hope. I was there. Close. Not in California when they were in Maine like it had been for the last ten months.

Maybe they felt badly about ignoring me all weekend.

Maybe they liked the new house (because who wouldn't? it was fabulous) and wanted to ask if they could show their friends around.

And maybe I was insane to hope.

But the idea of losing hope terrified me to extremes.

So I hoped.

I saw a road with a sign that said Haver Way, turned off and turned right into a parking lot. I pulled into a space, put my car in park and grabbed my purse.

I yanked out my phone and stared at it.

It was unsurprisingly not my children.

It was my mother.

Since I'd left California, this wasn't the first time she'd called. She'd called once a day starting the day I got in my car with my suitcases to drive across the country.

And this was only once per day, regardless if I didn't return her calls. She would not be so ill-bred as to phone more than once, even if her only daughter, who had been ravaged by divorce then took that out on her family, was driving across a continent for the first time in her life to launch an all-out effort to save her family...and herself.

Even if only once a day, I had not taken a single call.

This, I knew, was not going over well. I also knew she'd call the next day. And perhaps the next. She would not get angry at me. Her voicemails would not become heated.

No.

The day after that, my father would call.

He would bring the heat but he'd do it using a chill.

I wondered if I'd have the courage not to take his call.

The truth was I was surprised I hadn't caved and taken one of my mother's.

But I hadn't and I hadn't because, during my long drive across country, I'd figured out at least one thing about me: she was a trigger. So was my father. They were triggers that sent me down a path of feeling entitled at the same time feeling small. A path where, for some reason, I had no control of my actions. I did what was ingrained in me. I did what was expected of me. They flipped the switch and anything that could have been me disappeared and all that was bred in me turned on and took over.

Because of this, for the past three years I'd done all I could to be certain that any person involved in putting a blight on the Hathaway name paid, to extremes.

Divorce was a blight. My brother had been living with the coldest bitch the west coast had ever seen for the last twenty years. In that time, she'd drained every ounce of joy out of my once fun-loving, teasing, sweet older brother, leaving him a zombie without the decaying flesh but with a working-way-too-much habit. All this, and he would no sooner leave her than cut off his own arm.

Divorce for a Hathaway wasn't *done*.

Ever.

Mom and Dad didn't blame me for Conrad leaving me. They blamed him. No one would leave a *Hathaway*.

And thus, they backed every selfish, thoughtless, insane move I'd made to make his and Martine's lives a misery.

On this thought, the phone stopped ringing.

I dropped my hand to my lap and looked up. It was only then I saw that I'd parked in front of what looked like a store, but on the window, in gold with black on the edges, it said "Truck's Gym."

I looked beyond the sign and inside I saw it wasn't any old gym. It was a boxing gym.

This intrigued me, but what caught my attention was a large placard leaning against the inside of the window beside the door that proudly declared, "Home of the Magdalene Junior Boxing League."

My son, Auden wrestled.

The instant he started doing that, my parents had lost their minds (quietly), horrified that he didn't turn his attention to something like polo, archery or sailing.

Conrad, an athlete his whole life, had been beside himself with happiness.

As for me, I didn't like watching other boys trying to pin my son to a mat. I found it distressing. And unfortunately, I was not good at hiding that.

In the end, Auden got very good. He also got to the point he didn't like me at his matches, and not just because I usually took that opportunity to confront Conrad and/or Martine, but because I tried to be supportive. However, since I really wished he'd chosen baseball, I'd failed in demonstrating that support.

But staring at that placard, I knew that youth athletics programs were always needing money, doing fundraising drives, selling candy bars or moms setting up bake sales.

And I intended to have a massive house sale. Sell all the old in order to bring in the new. And since both sets of my grandparents, and my parents, had all given me substantial trust funds on which I could live more than comfortably, I didn't need money.

I'd intended to give the house sale proceeds to charity.

Looking at that sign, I tightened my hold on my phone, grabbed my purse and threw open the door to my car. I got out, walked to the door of the gym, and before my courage could fail me, I pushed through.

I barely got in when I heard, "Nice ride."

I looked to my left to see a man in track pants and a loose fitting tank top that had openings that hung low down his sides almost to his waist, this exposing the muscled ridges of his ribs. He was staring out the window toward my car.

I had a black Mercedes SLK 350. A beautiful car. A car I loved. A car that was ridiculous for a mother of two and in a few months might be ridiculous for a winter in Maine.

"Thank you," I replied.

"Need help?"

This came from another direction and I turned my head again to see a man approaching me.

He was tall, taller than Conrad, taller than Mickey (who was also taller than Conrad). He was built. He was rough.

And he was gorgeous.

Men from Maine.

Who knew?

"Hello," I replied as he kept coming my way. "I'm looking for someone who knows something about the boxing league."

"Which one?" he asked.

In this sleepy town, there was more than one?

"The junior one," I answered.

He stopped several feet in front of me and crossed his arms on his chest. "That'd be me."

"Oh, excellent," I mumbled, staring at him, thinking he was almost as handsome as Mickey (but not quite), which was a feat.

"You got a kid you wanna enroll?" he queried.

"No, my son wrestles," I told him, straightening my shoulders proudly. A mom's reflex action, the kind any mom should have (in my opinion), even if she wasn't all that thrilled with his chosen endeavor.

He grinned. It, as well, was almost as devastating as Mickey's. But not quite.

"Wrestling works," he muttered.

"Yes," I agreed. "Anyway, I was just wondering if the junior boxing league takes donations?"

"If you mean money, then fuck yeah," he said, surprisingly coarsely. "If you mean equipment, and it's new, then another yeah. But if you mean equipment that's used, I'd have to take a look. Kids need good shit. Don't like them sparrin' in somethin' that's supposed to protect 'em but could end up hurtin' 'em."

I thought this was a good policy, but he obviously already knew that so I didn't share my thoughts.

I said, "I mean money. In a way. Or not in a way, as it would definitely be money. What I mean is…in the future. You see, I just moved to Magdalene and I'm having a house sale. I thought, perhaps, the league could use the proceeds."

At that, he smiled, which was also attractive, and he did this as he uncrossed his arms from his wide chest, planted his hands on his hips and decreed, "Great idea." He then turned, started walking away from me and kept talking, "Come to the office. I'll get you Josie's number. Bet most the moms have shit they'd sell off. You get with Josie, you can make it a thing."

"Josie?" I asked, deciding it best to follow him, something I did, the heels of the flats I wore that I was pretty sure my mother also had (in every color) making muted sounds against the wood floors.

"My wife," he said, turning his head to look over his shoulder at me. "She's taken charge of fundraising."

Taken charge?

That gave the impression she didn't get involved before, and I thought that was strange.

I thought this because no matter what Conrad was involved in, what he needed, I did it. For instance, me to give a fabulous dinner party, or show at a business dinner in an appropriate dress and be charming, or become involved on the board of a charitable organization.

I didn't just do it. I gave it my everything.

"Oh, right," I said to the man's back.

We entered a tidy office and I did it surprised boxers could be tidy. Then I forced myself to stop being surprised because I didn't know any boxers and that was judgmental, a reaction my parents would have. And I forced myself to stop thinking about it at all when I halted as he continued walking to the desk.

He bent at the waist (a trim waist, I could see that through his well-fitting t-shirt), scribbled on a piece of paper, turned and came to me.

He held out the paper. "Josie's number," he declared. "I'll give her the heads up you're callin'. You wanna leave yours, I'll give her your number too." He grinned again and said, "And by the way, I'm Jake Spear. Owner of Truck's Gym and the man behind Magdalene's junior boxing league."

I took the paper, shoved it into my purse with my phone and held out my hand, "Nice to meet you, Jake. I'm Amelia Hathaway."

He took my hand, and much like when Mickey did it (with obvious differences, seeing as he wasn't *quite* as attractive, not to mention the significant fact he was married), the strength and warmth of his fingers around mine communicated something I liked.

Deeply.

"Good to meet you, Amelia," he replied, squeezing my fingers lightly and briefly before letting me go. "Real good to meet you, you raise some cake for my kids."

I had a feeling, considering my plan, how much stuff I was selling and how nice it was, I'd definitely raise some *cake* for his *kids*.

I smiled at him then looked to his desk before moving my gaze back to him. "Shall I write down my number for your wife so we can introduce ourselves and make plans?"

"Absolutely," he said while walking back to the desk.

I followed and did what he did, bending and writing my name and number on a sheet of paper.

I straightened and looked up to him. "I'll give her a call today or tomorrow, if that's okay."

"You don't, she'll call you," he told me. "A lot of the equipment is shot and enrollment is up. We need cash to cover the expansion. The last gig she did she wasn't pleased with the results. Put her all into it and we made dick. She's a dog with a bone now. So you might get a call before you even have time to drive home."

I wouldn't mind that. I hadn't been there a week but I needed to settle in. Get the lay of the land. Sort out my home. Win back my family.

But I also needed to start a life.

That was what I'd failed to do when Conrad left. My life had been him. I should have licked my wounds, found a way to let them heal and moved on.

I didn't do that.

Now, I had to do that. My thought: a healthy mom means a healthy home, which ends in a healthy relationship with my children.

My goal. What I was living for.

And although this Jake Spear didn't hesitate to curse in front of a stranger who was also a female (my mother *and* father would lose their minds at that, genteelly, of course), he ran a junior boxing league. At least that said good things about him and a good man (sometimes) meant a good woman as his wife.

I needed to know good people.

And I needed friends.

This Josie might not be one but at least she was someone calling me that was not thousands of miles away and better, not my mother.

"Babe."

At the word, a trill raced down my spine, exploding along my lower back and cascading over my bottom. I experienced this swift, surprising and alarmingly pleasant sensation and slowly turned to the door.

One syllable. He'd said one syllable and I'd met him once and I knew who would be there. I knew who made me feel that feeling.

I was right.

In the office doorway stood Mickey Donovan in loose fitting, navy track pants and a short-sleeved, skintight white workout shirt.

And he was smiling, doing it warmly, looking pleasantly startled (likely at my being in a boxing gym) and very welcoming.

I was startled he was there at that precise moment, but I wasn't surprised he was at a boxing gym.

"Not where I expected to run into you," Mickey remarked.

"Well...no," I replied. "How are you, Mickey?"

"Doin' good," he told me, leaning a shoulder against the doorjamb, a casual stance I found oddly devastating to my peace of mind. "You?"

"Just fine," I lied.

"You know Amelia?" Jake asked and Mickey's eyes went to him.

"She's my new neighbor," Mickey shared then added, "The Cameron place."

I felt Jake's gaze and tore mine off Mickey to look up at him.

"The Cameron place?" he asked when he got my gaze, then noted, "That's a fuckuva score."

"You're right," I agreed, even though I wasn't entirely certain how he meant that. I took a guess and remarked, "It's an amazing property."

He nodded. "It is. No way me, Josie and the kids'd ever leave Lavender House, but the realtor had an open house for Cliff Blue so we went and we all loved it. The place is phenomenal."

I liked that he agreed with me but I was confused.

"Cliff Blue?" I asked.

"Your house, darlin'," Mickey stated, and I had to control a jump since his voice was a lot closer than before.

I managed that and looked up at him to see he *was* close. Not as close as I would have liked but could never have, but a lot closer than before.

"My house?" I asked.

"Cameron called it Cliff Blue. It stuck. And it works," he explained. "Folks who had the lot before had an old house on it. Two generations of women who liked the feel of their hands in the dirt tended that property for nearly seventy years. Place was covered in bluebells. Planted some, they took off, went everywhere. Even jumped the street and now they're all over my lot, and that's not a complaint. Cameron liked 'em too, used them in the design, the color, the stained glass, the walk, and was careful not to disturb them if he didn't have to. Went so far as to plant a bunch more to replace any they killed during construction. 'Cause of that, March and April, your house looks like it's floating by a cliff on a cloud of blue."

"Oh my God," I whispered, his words filling my head with a wondrous image, making me wish for another reason that I'd been able to move in several months earlier. "The realtor should have put a picture of that on the Internet. If I saw it, I would have probably paid full price."

I couldn't contain my jump when Mickey's laughter filled the room, not only because it was an exceedingly handsome sound, but because it came as a surprise.

Before I could ask what was funny, he told me.

"Glad you didn't, babe. The couple who built that place were pieces of work. She was a raging bitch and that was only capped by how huge of a dick he was. Place was on the market forever because neither would agree on an offer and actually got into it with the buyers so bad they'd pull out. They kept screwing around, the price on your place dropped three times, which is a shame 'cause that house is that house. Not a shame 'cause those two assholes got screwed in the end. But it's a pain in the ass because that house is in my neighborhood and that kinda shit affects the values of all the properties around it. Figure the only way they could sell was to someone like you who the realtor could keep those two piranhas away from."

"That sounds unpleasant," I noted and the residual grin from his laughter turned into a smile.

"Suffice it to say, I don't know you too well and I like you a whole lot more than I liked them," he replied.

And one could say I liked *that*.

But I shouldn't like that. I shouldn't *anything* that.

Even so, I needed to make a response so I did it mumbling, "That's good."

"Yeah," he agreed. "Bad neighbors suck."

Considering our first meeting he had to rescue me from my infuriated, foul-mouthed ex-husband, I decided not to respond to that.

Mickey didn't stick with that subject either.

Instead, he prompted, "Still got no idea why you're here, Amelia." His blue eyes twinkled and my stomach fluttered. "But if you're a female fighter, that'd shock the shit out of me."

"Oh, right," I mumbled then cleared my throat and carried on, "I'm selling a few things and thought I'd donate the proceeds to the junior boxing league."

Another smile from Mickey. "Fantastic."

"House sale. Josie's gonna help," Jake put in and Mickey looked to him then to me.

"Got some shit I could put in. Tell me when you're havin' it. I'll lug it over."

This was not conducive to me steering clear of Mickey Donovan, but if the young boxers needed decent equipment, the more was definitely the merrier. So at least for that, I'd have to suck it up.

"Of course. I'll make sure you know," I replied.

"And you need help, I'm across the way," he offered.

That wasn't going to happen.

"Thanks," I said, swiftly looked to Jake, stuck out my hand and continued, "It was nice meeting you. I'll call your wife soon."

He took my hand, squeezed it and returned, "Same meetin' you. Sure I'll see you again soon."

"Yes." I nodded and forced my attention back to Mickey. "Good to see you again, Mickey."

Another grin. "You too, babe."

I dipped my chin, averted my eyes, murmured, "Good-bye, gentlemen," and walked to the door.

This got me a, "Later," from Jake and a, "'Bye, darlin'," from Mickey.

As I swiftly made my way through the gym, I sent a hesitant smile to the boxer still training, doing this now not punching a bag as he had been when I walked in, but jumping rope.

He smiled back distractedly but I got the impression he did it only because we met eyes.

I kept moving through the gym as his attention drifted away and something about this stung.

He was not unattractive, though he wasn't gorgeous like Mickey and Jake. I couldn't fathom his exact age but I guessed both Mickey and Jake were around mine, and although the rope-jumping boxer looked younger, he was nowhere near his twenties so he was not *that* far off.

What he was was not interested in me.

I was a woman in a boxing gym. I had breasts. I had a booty. I had long hair and it was thick and shiny.

But to him, a man perhaps in his mid-thirties, who, depending on a woman's preferences, might not turn heads but was not a man you'd dismiss, I was a nonentity.

I'd been married to Conrad for sixteen years. We'd been together for three before that. And the three after, I'd had nothing on my mind but resentment and revenge. I hadn't thought of a man looking at me because I hadn't looked at a man.

Then came Maine.

And the day after I arrived...Mickey.

And it hit me then with that boxer paying absolutely no mind to me that I had no idea what a man would think of me. I had no idea if men looked at me.

Until then when I knew they didn't.

Mickey disturbed me in a pleasant way I couldn't allow myself to feel and I hoped I hid.

But either he was phenomenally good at hiding it himself or I didn't disturb him in the slightest.

I figured it was the latter.

Jake was married but he didn't even look past my eyes to my hair.

And I had good hair.

Further, the rope-jumping boxer barely glanced at me.

My *ride*, yes.

Me, no.

I got in my car and didn't waste time pulling out of the spot, getting away from Mickey, burying the sting of these realizations, how deep they bit, how they made me feel—old and past my prime, insignificant, a body passing through a gym who was not female or male or *anything*.

I drove, resolutely turning my mind to heading home (which, alas, was across the street from Mickey).

And as I drove, I forced myself to think about the fact that I was happy I'd found a local organization that would put the money I made off my old life to good use.

I drove also troubled this involved Mickey.

And when I was getting out of my car in my garage, I was surprised when my phone rang.

The garage door was folding down as I dug my phone out of my purse, doing this with some trepidation.

I, not officially (but unofficially for certain), was severing ties with Robin, my best friend back in La Jolla. This was because she was much like my mother, spurring me on to random acts of bitchery in order to make Conrad's (but mostly Martine's) life a misery.

Along with coming to the understanding my mother and father were triggers, on my drive across country I'd also decided Robin was a bad influence.

She had called too and I'd texted her back. I'd email her when I had my computer set up. And according to my plan, if I couldn't manage to adjust our friendship to something that was far healthier for me, we'd eventually become acquaintances. Something, if she brought it up, I'd blame on the distance.

I did not take this in stride and I didn't take it lightly. Just the thought of losing Robin hurt and I hated it. Robin and I had been friends for years. We'd met at a party when Conrad had joined her husband's practice. She was beautiful and funny and she loved my kids like I loved hers. We spent a lot of time together. We shared everything with each other. We trusted each other completely. In forty-seven years, she was the only woman I'd met who'd become the absent sister I'd always needed.

Over the past years, the rest of my friends had shied away as my random acts of bitchery carried on (and on), so Robin was the only one I had left.

But her husband had left her two years before mine did and not for a nurse, for a Pilates instructor. Thus Robin had random acts of bitchery down to an art as she'd been honing her skills way before I entered the game.

She'd been my mentor, a very good one, and we'd carried on with our shenanigans, doing it with a glee that I only very recently realized hid our despair.

She was still there and living her bitterness while spurring mine on, nowhere near coming to a place in her life where she'd reflect on this, move past it and take back her life.

But to save my family, I had to do just that. And to do that, I had to cut her off (semi) cold turkey.

Which, to start anew, was what I was doing.

So the call could only be from Mom, something that would be out of her usual modus operandi.

Or, if she jumped the gun, it would be from Dad, angry with me that I hadn't taken Mom's calls and not only willing but very able to share that with me, cutting me to the bone with his precisely aimed ice daggers, reducing me to nothing.

I didn't know what to make of the fact that the screen had nothing but a number I didn't recognize.

Mom would not play games. She wouldn't get to me through subterfuge. And Dad never phoned me on anything but his cell because that would require the effort of looking up my number, which he would not bother to memorize. He would never make that effort, even to allow himself his relished pastime of laying into me.

Though, it could be Robin. She had a variety of ways of getting to people who didn't want to hear from her.

Even thinking this, I took the chance of taking the call, putting my phone to my ear and saying a cautious, "Hello."

"Hello. Is this Amelia?" a woman (not Robin, thankfully) asked.

"Yes," I answered, pushing through the door from the garage that led into the dining area portion of the landing of the open-space great room.

"This is Josephine Spear," she announced and I stopped, eyes unfocused on the blue sea beyond my windows, my mind on the fact that Jake hadn't lied. His wife must be a dog with a bone because, as he predicted, I'd barely made it home before she contacted me. "You met my husband at the gym. Jake Spear?"

"I did, Josephine," I confirmed. "And I'm pleased you phoned."

"Head gear is crucial in boxing," she declared strangely. "We have thirty-seven boys in the league and only gear enough to fit twelve boys appropriately." Her voice started filling with excitement. "Jake told me what you were wishing to do and a house sale is just the thing! I don't know why I didn't think of it myself."

I almost had the opportunity to agree as I heard her pull in a quick breath, but I didn't get that chance when she went on.

"Now, I don't want to pressure you but the season will be on us before we know it and our bake sales and magazine subscription efforts are not exactly thriving. But everyone has items in their homes they no longer want that another *will* want. So, if you're amenable, I'll call Alyssa. She's my friend and a fighter mom. We'll activate the mom phone tree. We'll get more items donated and make plans to get the word out, far and wide."

"That's wonderful, Josephine, I think the bigger this is the better it can be. But just to warn you, I do have a great deal of stuff I'll be needing to sell," I told her. "I've also got a plan of designing fliers, putting an ad in the paper, going to local businesses and asking if I can put notices up on public bulletin boards and in staff rooms—"

I wasn't quite finished when she declared, "Excellent! And I'll speak with the schools. They email newsletters to parents, even in the summer. They can add that as a news item. We'll also need volunteers…" She hesitated before she said, "There's a good deal to go over. Perhaps we should meet. Iron all this out face to face. I'll ask Alyssa to join us. Do you work? Should this be lunch or dinner or coffee?"

Yes, Jake had not lied. His wife was very keen.

"I…don't work," I admitted, feeling another new feeling, that being ashamed of that fact, not to mention the fact that I never had worked. Ever. Not in my life. I pushed past that and finished, "So, I could do anything at your schedule."

"Fabulous. I'll speak with Alyssa and phone you back. How does that sound?"

I started moving toward the kitchen to dump my purse on the counter and replied, "Sounds great."

"Jake says you're new to Magdalene?" she remarked.

"I've been here just under a week," I shared.

"Well then, welcome to our home that is now your home and I look forward to meeting you."

"Same, Josephine."

"Josie," she said. "Please, call me Josie."

"All right, Josie."

"I'll phone shortly after I speak with Alyssa."

"Wonderful."

"Take care, Amelia."

"You too, Josie."

She rang off and I dumped my purse and phone on the counter. I went to the fridge, opened it, stared in and, even though I'd skipped breakfast, forgot about lunch and had a fully loaded fridge since the kids had been there that weekend, I couldn't see anything in it that interested me.

So I closed the door to the fridge and jumped when my phone rang.

I grabbed it from the counter, saw the same number on the screen and took the call.

"Josie?" I asked as greeting.

"Is Wednesday at lunchtime good for you?" she asked back.

I stared at the counter thinking she wasn't keen, she was *raring*.

"Yes, that's fine," I told her.

"Excellent. Noon. Weatherby's Diner. We'll be the two blondes in a window booth."

"Well, if there are two other blondes, so you know me, I'll be the short, middle-aged brunette," I informed her.

"Petite," she stated as reply.

"I'm sorry?" I asked.

"Women are not short. They're petite. They also are never middle-aged. They're mature."

I didn't know how to reply to that true but firmly declared statement except to say, "Oh. Right."

She sounded vaguely flustered when she backtracked, "You can, of course, refer to yourself however you wish."

I felt the need to smooth her fluster and did this saying, "Petite is a nicer word. So is mature."

"They are, indeed," she agreed. "Though I also am not overly fond of mature. Why a woman needs to qualify that, I cannot fathom."

I couldn't help but agree.

"So I'll be the petite, mature brunette," I told her, trying to make a joke. "However, the mature part is just for you and me."

"And Alyssa and I will be the not-petite, mature blondes," she returned, and thankfully I could hear the smile in her voice. "Further, you should be aware that as it's summer, I may have my son, Ethan, with me. And as Alyssa and her husband, Junior, are kind, good-hearted people, they've wisely made the decision to copiously populate Magdalene with their offspring. Therefore, she could have a bevy of children with her. They'll be the ones causing mayhem. I'll do my best to be certain Ethan doesn't join in, but he has a mind of his own and his father and I like to encourage exactly that."

I grinned at the counter. "That'll be good then as you all will be hard to miss."

"Indeed," she again agreed. "Now, do we have a plan?"

"Yes, Josie, we have a plan. I'll see you and Alyssa Wednesday at this Weatherby's place."

"You can't miss it," she told me. "It's in town and town's not that big. It's right on Cross Street. But if you have troubles, simply call me."

She seemed oddly formal, which was quite a contradiction to her cursing, but friendly and totally informal husband.

"I'll find it," I assured her.

"Good. We'll see you then, Amelia."

"Yes, Josie. See you Wednesday."

She rang off and I put the phone to the counter.

Lifting my head, I looked at a beautiful space that didn't look that fabulous with boxes stacked against the walls.

However, apparently, if Josie Spear had anything to do with it, this house sale would happen quickly and I could get started on creating a home I loved that my children were comfortable in.

Until I had that clean palette, though, I wasn't going to start that project.

Which meant, home from my meanderings to nowhere doing nothing that actually bore fruit as I'd met some people and had plans for lunch on Wednesday, at that exact time, I had nothing to do.

Nothing.

No friends.

No housework.

No job to get to.

No children coming home imminently.

The cable and Internet were scheduled to be installed the next day so I didn't even have that.

All of sudden, I had the strange feeling of being crushed.

Crushed by the weight of all that was new that was around me.

Crushed by the weight of all that I had to do to make my house a home.

Crushed by the weight of all my mistakes and the effort I knew it would take to remedy them.

Crushed by loneliness. Loneliness that in all my years of being alone I hadn't even begun the work to make the change from feeling that to feeling *aloneness* and being comfortable with it.

Crushed by the fear of the specter of my parents who were remaining aloof, but they'd tire of that and then they'd invade in insidious ways that could obliterate the fragile embryo of what I was trying to create.

It took effort. It took time. I stood in my beautiful open plan kitchen with its views of blue sea as I expended that effort and took that time.

Then I made a plan.

I grabbed my phone, pulled up the app that found places that you needed that were close, hit the map to let the GPS guide my way and I went back out to my car.

I pulled out of my garage and headed to the home improvement store. There, I gathered so many paint chips I could set up a display in my house.

I then drove to the closest mall, not only so I would know where it was, but so I could buy a few books.

Only then did I go home.

I put the paint chips in a kitchen drawer. I'd go through them after the house sale and when I'd lived at Cliff Blue awhile so I knew what the walls needed (and incidentally, I *loved* that name and determined to refer to my house by its name even on the address labels I would order when I had the Internet).

Instead, I did something I'd never done in my life (though part of it I couldn't do as in La Jolla I had a house on a golf course, not by a beach). Something I'd never even considered doing.

I spent time with me.

I did this lying on my couch with a glass of wine. I sometimes read. I sometimes stared at the sea.

I then had another glass of wine.

And then another.

As I did it, I realized I liked doing it, reading, sipping, staring at the sea. So much so, I didn't think to have dinner.

And finally, I fell asleep on the couch and when I woke up there hours later, I didn't do what I would have done simply because my mother would decree it wasn't appropriate to sleep in your clothes on your couch.

I didn't drag myself to bed.

Instead, I closed my eyes and went back to sleep in my clothes on my couch.

I didn't sleep great and woke up with a pain in my shoulder.

Regardless, for some reason, I woke up feeling satisfied.

I WAITED UNTIL TUESDAY AFTERNOON TO TEXT THE KIDS AND LET THEM know I was doing a house sale to get rid of some of the old in order to start anew. I invited them to come over and go through their things should they wish to get rid of anything. And I shared the proceeds would go to the local junior boxing league.

I didn't want to text them the day before, the Monday after they left, because I didn't want them to get the feeling with me again being in the same town, I'd suffocate them with pathological communication. Nor that I'd pester them with good intentions.

I just wanted to seem normal.

And I hoped that was normal.

———— • ————

IT MIGHT HAVE BEEN NORMAL, IT MIGHT NOT.

I didn't know.

Neither of them replied.

———— • ————

ON WEDNESDAY, I HAD LUNCH AND MADE GRAND SCHEMES FOR A BLOWOUT house sale to benefit the Magdalene junior boxing league with the yin and yang of breathtakingly beautiful blondes.

First, there was the classy, sophisticated Josie, who scarily reminded me of my parents at first. Then I saw her interact with the dazzling but brash, take-me-as-I-come-or-kiss-off Alyssa, who my parents would detest.

After watching that, even if Josie still seemed somewhat formal, it clearly was only part of a complicated personality and the rest was all good.

They'd come without children, which was a little disappointing. They'd also told me there was no way we'd get through this without roping in all the children (apparently, all the junior boxing moms had tons of stuff they wanted to unload and most of them were willing to help).

So blowout house sale it would be.

And two possible friends I would have.

That was good.

———— • ————

IT WAS BAD THAT I WAITED UNTIL SUNDAY TO TEXT MY OWN CHILDREN again to remind them I was having a house sale, it would be that next Saturday, and they had the opportunity to unload old stuff and jump on new. I shared that it'd make me happy if they replied sooner rather than later as plans were in full swing (and they were, both Josie and Alyssa had jobs, but they also both had more energy than I felt was natural, coupled with a driving desire to make huge amounts of money).

I also invited Auden and Pippa to come to the house sale if they felt like it.

I did this, but again, neither of them replied.

———•———

THE NEXT WEEK AND A HALF I DESIGNED, HAD PRINTED, PUT UP AND GAVE out fliers, put ads in various papers, opened my door and accepted a multitude of drop offs from a variety of moms of budding boxers. I even talked the local radio station into sharing the event and made plans to offer refreshments (for sale, of course) in order to make this house sale all it could be.

When Alyssa came by to drop off her items and she caught sight of some of the things I was letting go, I also sent Alyssa home with two boxes of free stuff she *had to have*. We had a good-natured fight over the fact I wouldn't let her pay for any of it but she only gave in because she left three filled boxes that she intended to pick up on the big day and pay for, which she'd marked on the sides with a Sharpie, "Alyssa's, touch and you'll be hunted! Dig me?"

During this time, I let my children be.

———•———

TWO DAYS BEFORE THE HOUSE SALE, I TEXTED THE KIDS TO REMIND THEM IT was happening and again to invite them to come if they wanted.

———•———

THEY DIDN'T REPLY.

3

CLEAN PALETTE

The evening before the house sale, I was in my kitchen, running on empty.

I was ready...mostly.

There were items all over the place with some stacked at the doors to put out in the front yard and on the deck. These items were arranged (and then rearranged, and in some cases re-rearranged) so they were displayed attractively. They all had price tags. There were signs directing folks to rooms with more stuff for sale.

And I was in the kitchen baking.

I'd found some cute plastic bags with happy designs on the sides at a craft store that I'd decided to put my snickerdoodles in and then tied them with big, bright extravagant bows. Same with my chocolate chip cookies. Also with peanut butter cookies with mini Reese's cups shoved in. They were lying all over the countertop, on tiered plates (plates that were for sale) or on platters (also for sale).

They were all bagged, tagged and ready.

And I was currently working on my meringue-frosting-topped cupcakes with pastel flower sprinkles. Cupcakes that were delicious, but with that glossy dollop of white icing decorated with sprinkles, they were also kid magnets.

I'd sell out of those in fifteen minutes.

Guaranteed.

I'd made big vats of lemonade and iced tea I was going to put in my fancy crystal (for sale) and not-as-fancy-but-still-fancy glass (also for sale) drink dispensers. I had bottles of water chilling in the fridge in the garage with bags of ice in both my freezers that I was going to put into attractive buckets and also sell.

Now, it was eight o'clock and I'd been going nonstop since the day before—no, actually for the last week.

I'd dropped into bed the night before at midnight. But I needed to go to bed that night and I'd needed to do that two hours ago.

Instead, I was arranging glossy frosting blobs on cupcakes and I had a dozen more in the oven baking.

Those were the last ones.

Then I'd get a glass of wine, a shower and hit my bed.

If after that last dozen I had all that in me.

On this thought, my doorbell rang and for once, I didn't exult in the beautiful chimes.

No, I fought the urge to throttle whatever late-arriving mom of a budding boxer who was going to dump a load of crap that I had to tag and arrange after eight o'clock the night prior to the big day that we'd advertised I was opening my doors at seven in the morning.

I dropped the spoon in the bowl and made my way to the door, seeing through the shadowed panes there was more than one body out there and one of them was not a mom of a budding boxer, but the dad of one.

That figured and I should have known.

Men didn't know any better.

I flipped the locks, opening the door arranging my features so they were pleasant, not murderous, and then completely arrested.

"Hey," Mickey Donovan greeted, standing at my door looking unfairly attractive in a pair of faded jeans, a beat up chambray shirt with the sleeves rolled up his sinewy forearms, another five o'clock shadow adorning his strong jaw.

He had two other beings with him, two beings I didn't take in because first, Mickey was grinning, second, he looked unfairly attractive in his casual clothing, and third, he was holding a huge box filled with stuff I knew I would need to tag and arrange, which meant wine and shower were out. It was going to be tag, arrange and *bed*.

"Jesus, did heaven crash into your living room?"

I moved but only to blink.

"I'm sorry?" I asked.

"Amelia, darlin', whatever you're doin' in there smells like it could only come from the hand of God."

Wow.

That felt good. So good. Unusually good.

Abnormally good.

And it felt good because I loved to bake. I'd fallen in love with it all the way back in junior high school home economics class.

However, when I'd taken over my parents' vast kitchen in order to enjoy my newfound hobby, my mother moved immediately to curtail these activities.

"We have staff to do that kind of thing, Amelia," she'd rebuked. "Not to mention, a lady should do all in her power to shy away from sweets."

Unfortunately, years later, when these tethers were severed and I might have been freed to bake at my leisure, more were tied because Conrad had felt the same.

"You're gonna give me a gut, little bird," he'd told me after the second time I'd baked him cookies. He'd then given me a meaningful look. "And you want to avoid getting one too."

I thought, when the kids came, I could indulge, kids being kids and liking cookies and glossy, frosting-topped cupcakes with sprinkles.

But I'd been wrong. Conrad had acted like any sugar they consumed was akin to feeding our children poison.

In fact, he told me it *was* poison, "And should be avoided at all costs, pookie."

Thus I'd been reduced to sneaking them cupcakes, cookies, pies and cakes when their dad was away at conferences.

Other than that, I'd buried that part of me.

And I had to admit, when I'd started baking hours ago, no matter how tired I was, I'd lost myself in it.

It was just that now the fatigue had settled deep, I wasn't enjoying it as much.

Regardless, Mickey was right. The house smelled like a bakery. Sugary and sweet.

And heavenly.

Thus I decided right then I was going to bake again. For me. For the kids.

In fact, the next time they came maybe I'd get them to stay home and in my presence for more than five minutes, bribing them with cupcakes.

"Earth calling Amelia. You there, babe?"

I shook my head sharply and focused on Mickey, who was calling me, laughter in his deep voice, that and his saying my name with that laughter doing things to me I refused to feel.

"Sorry, it's been a long day."

"I bet it has," he murmured, his eye on me dancing (something I refused to see). He hefted the box in his arms an inch. "Junior called, said the big day was tomorrow. You didn't tell me."

I didn't and not because I was avoiding him (which I also was) but because I completely forgot.

"I didn't, Mickey," I admitted. "I'm so sorry."

He kept grinning. "No apologies, babe. Not lost on me your house has been a hub of activity the past week. But the kids and I had a troll through our place and thought we'd pop these by to do our bit."

"And to get a cupcake."

This came from one of the beings with him and I finally gave my attention to the boy and girl that were standing on either side of Mickey. Taking them in, I saw that Mickey and his ex-wife had flip-flopped what Conrad and I had created.

This included his daughter clearly being the oldest and looking a lot like her father, except female, shorter and very curvy to the point of being a little plump, still carrying what was probably some pre-adolescent baby fat.

His boy had dark blond hair, but luckily got his father's blue eyes. He also had a body that had yet to declare its full intentions seeing as, at a guess, Mickey's daughter was around thirteen or fourteen and his son was maybe ten or eleven.

"My girl, Aisling," he said, jerking his head to the girl. "Said starting with the Ash, but spelled Irish with an a, i and s." This came out practiced and I knew he'd given his girl a beautiful name but one many messed up. "Cillian, also spelled Irish," he stated, jerking his head the other way, to the boy. "Spelled with a c not a k."

"Got it," I mumbled. "Ash with an a, i, s and kill. I'll be certain to get that right on your Christmas card." This made Mickey smile, Cillian grin and Aisling's blue eyes twinkle like her dad's. "How about the three of you come in, drop that and get a cupcake?" I invited.

"*Awesome,*" Cillian decreed and raced in, straight to the kitchen, something that caused a pang around my heart, most likely because I wished just one of my own children had done that.

"Thanks, uh...Miz..." Aisling said, allowing that to hang.

"Miz nothing," I replied on a smile to her, moving out of the way. "I'm Amelia."

She looked to her father as he shifted into the house, then nodded to me and followed him.

I closed the door behind them and repeated my invitation. "Help yourself to a cupcake. Or a bag of cookies if you prefer."

Aisling wandered toward the kitchen.

"Just sayin'," Mickey started and I looked to him to see he'd put the box on the floor at the lip of the top step to the sunken living room. "My kids aren't allowed to call adults by their given names."

"Oh," I murmured, feeling rattled, thinking I'd put my foot in it.

"Not a big deal," he said quietly and quickly, then came another of his easy grins. "She wouldn't have called you Amelia anyway. She woulda probably avoided calling you anything until the go-ahead was given to call you *Aunt* Amelia, which is how they address their elders that they're tight with."

It would seem that Mickey was kind of strict with his kids.

I didn't know how to take this outside of reminding myself it wasn't mine to take in any way. So I just nodded.

"And also just sayin'," he went on, talking lower, "you've worked your ass off, that's plain to see." He tossed a hand toward the room. "So we'll unload this and tag it. Not cool for us to dump last minute shit on you."

It felt good he noticed.

I still didn't think it was healthy for him to hang around (this being healthy *for me*), so I assured him, "That's very nice but I'll be okay. Your box is small, it won't take too long."

He didn't look assured and he didn't look this for a while and this was because he did it studying me.

Then he asked, "You doin' okay?"

I thought that was an odd question so I answered, "Sure."

He kept studying me as he continued, "You eatin'?"

It was then I realized I hadn't had anything except licking the spatula of cupcake batter since I had my Cream of Wheat that morning.

"I'm fine, Mickey," I told him.

He didn't stop studying me for several moments before he looked to the kitchen, murmuring, "It'll be good this sale gets done, you can settle in and then relax."

He was wrong.

I had been relaxing a good long while.

Now I needed to kick my own behind for a variety of reasons.

"Yes, it will," I fibbed and kept on doing it. "When tomorrow's done, it'll all be good."

"Help with that," he stated. "Sunday, I'll get in the food and the booze and you come over. I'll fire up the grill, cook some brats, some chicken. You kick back with a beer and shoot the shit with me and my kids, get as loose as you want." He awarded me another grin with dancing blue eyes, something I wanted at the same time I wished fervently he wouldn't keep giving them to me. "You need me to pour you into my truck to drive you across the street at the end of the night, won't be any skin off my nose."

As good as his comment about my house smelling like heaven felt, that invitation felt the same amount of bad.

A bad I wasn't allowed to feel.

A bad that I felt because no man who was interested in a woman in a certain way would bring his kids over to her house on the spur of the moment then invite her over for a Sunday cookout to "kick back" and "get loose."

A man who was interested in a woman would carefully time and meticulously plan such meetings with progeny, and they would happen only after he knew he wanted the woman he was inviting to be invited again.

And again.

Until she stayed, maybe forever.

Or, at least, that was what I would do with my kids.

And that was what Conrad did with them. Unfortunately, when he started these endeavors, he'd still been married to me.

"Jesus, Amelia, you asleep on your feet?" Mickey asked and again I jerked to attention and focused on him.

"Sorry," I said. "So sorry. I've got my mind on a million things."

Before Mickey could reply, "I don't know what to pick!" was shouted from the kitchen.

We both turned that way to see Cillian standing amongst the sprinkled cupcakes and bags of cookies looking like he'd just been let into Willy Wonka's Chocolate Factory but hadn't been given the go ahead to make a glutton of himself.

"Take whatever you want, Cillian," I called.

Cillian's eyes grew so huge at this offer I nearly burst out laughing.

"Miz...uh...hey!" Aisling called back to me. "You want me to finish frosting these?" She pointed at the unfrosted cupcakes.

"She's good at that shit," Mickey muttered, his voice sounding further away and I turned then tucked my chin to see him crouched by his box. He tipped his head back to catch my eyes. "Let her do it."

"I..." I looked to Aisling and suggested, "How about we do it together?" She beamed.

With nothing for it, I moved that way.

Cillian shoved a cupcake in his mouth, peeling back the wrapper expertly with his lips as he did it.

I'd never seen anyone do that so I noted on a smile as I made my way to the kitchen, "You got a special skill with that, kiddo."

"Toad-ag-lee," he said with his mouth full and kept going, "Prag-dis."

My smile got bigger.

"Keister over here, boy, help your dad unload this stuff and tag it," Mickey ordered.

Cillian dashed by me and toward his father.

At that moment, the oven binged.

"You do those, honey," I said to Aisling, moving into the kitchen. "I'll grab the last batch."

Aisling nodded and nabbed the spoon from the bowl.

As I pulled the tray out of the oven, Mickey called, "Babe? Tags?"

An unusual-when-it-came-to-Mickey unpleasant sensation slithered down my spine.

Conrad called me "babe." Conrad called me every endearment he could think of.

I'd later learned none of them were special since I'd heard him call Martine some of the same things.

And I knew the casual way Mickey said them was the same way, but worse. Any woman was "babe" to him. Or his other, "darlin'."

It wasn't just me.

It wasn't special.

I'd never been special.

I just *was*.

With all the rest, I pushed that aside, put the tin on the cooling rack and looked his way, answering, "Up here."

"Go get 'em, son," he said to Cillian.

Cillian darted back my way.

I got the tags and markers out of their drawer and gave them to Mickey's boy. He raced back to his dad. Thus began a lot of activity, which included Mickey and Cillian pulling stuff out of their box, tagging it and calling to me to ask where to put it, as well as Aisling and me frosting and sprinkling cupcakes while we tidied the kitchen.

As tired as I was, as much as I was fighting my attraction to Mickey, I couldn't help but admit that it felt good to have company. To feel activity around me. To hear the murmur of voices. To exchange words or shuffle by a body and get or give a smile as you did it.

I hadn't had that in a while. Not on a regular basis in three years and not even frequently for the last ten months.

I liked it.

And Mickey had good kids, though that part wasn't surprising.

We were done in no time and when we were, I found that I wished we weren't.

This was because the second we were, Mickey said, "Time to get outta Miz Hathaway's hair."

To which Cillian instantly replied, "Can I have a bag of Reese's cookies before we do it?"

Mickey grinned at his son. "You're costin' me a fortune in food, kid."

Cillian grinned back, unrepentant, probably because he knew he was but he also knew his dad didn't care in the least.

"Just to say," I butted in and got two sets of blue eyes, "for neighbors, the goodies are free."

"Not gonna raise cash for the league, you do that," Mickey told me, wandering my way, his son doing the same and doing it close to his dad.

He made it to the opposite side of the counter, scanned the signs I already had set up to announce the prices of treats, and he did this pulling out his wallet.

"Really, Mickey," I said. "Aisling helped me frost and clean up. Goodies are payback."

He looked to me. "Really, Amelia, Cill's in that league so we're chippin' in."

With his eyes on me, warm and friendly, I could do nothing but agree so I did this on a nod.

He tossed a five dollar bill on my counter, declaring, "Junior says this gig starts at seven. We'll be here at a quarter to."

My insides clutched in fear at this offer, but before I could get it together to politely decline, Cillian shouted in horror, "In the morning?" His face was wreathed in that horror as he finished, dread dripping from each syllable. "*On a Saturday?*"

Mickey looked down at his son. "You want new head gear, shoes and gloves next season?"

"Yeah," Cillian muttered like he wished he didn't have to.

"Then we're up early and over here to help Miz Hathaway sell all this crap tomorrow," Mickey decreed.

"That really isn't—" I started but stopped when Mickey's eyes sliced my way.

Point taken. Absolutely.

I'd seen Mickey Donovan's eyes friendly, smiling, laughing, thoughtful, assessing.

But the look in them right then said that when Mickey talked, his children listened and no one said a word to the contrary.

The problem was I didn't *want* Mickey over at my house first thing. In fact, Josie, Jake, Junior, Alyssa and their families were going to be there at six thirty so I didn't actually *need* Mickey and his kids there.

I stared into his blue eyes and decided not to share that.

Mickey broke contact and looked from his boy to his girl. "Now, say goodnight to Miz Hathaway and then let's get home."

I got two goodnights, one disgruntled (Cillian), one quiet (Aisling) and gave them back as they headed to the door.

Mickey did too.

So I did as well.

At the door, Mickey stopped just outside of it and ordered his children, "Careful of the street, I'm right behind."

"'Kay, Dad," Cillian muttered, starting to trudge across my yard.

"Boy, path," Mickey directed.

"Oh, right," Cillian looked to me, changing direction and heading toward my front walk. "Sorry, Miz Hathaway."

I wanted to tell him I didn't think his feet would damage my grass simply treading on the turf and he could take the more direct path to his house, but I didn't.

I said, "It's okay, kiddo."

He grinned at me.

Aisling silently put her hand between her brother's shoulder blades and guided him down the path.

Mickey stood watching.

I did too.

When they'd crossed the street safely and Cillian was racing up their yard while Aisling meandered behind him, Mickey turned to me.

"Their mother drinks."

At his blunt honesty and the fact it came from left field, I could do nothing but stare.

"I'm tellin' you that because, for the most part, she's functioning," he went on. "But those other parts, she's sloppy so everyone in town knows it and that means you eventually will too."

"Oh God, Mickey," I whispered. "I don't know what to say."

"Nothin' to say," he replied matter-of-factly. "Time will tell if it was right or wrong I ended that nightmare so my kids would have one home where they had a parent who was all there all the time, they need them or not, rather than a parent who was takin' care of his kids half the time and coverin' shit for his wife the other half. And the good news is the functioning parts are when she has our kids. So it's bad and somethin' I hate for my kids instead of bein' *bad* and I gotta keep my kids away from their mom."

I pressed my lips together, shocked at his sharing, saddened by what he was sharing and unsure what to say or do.

Mickey wasn't unsure. He continued sharing.

"I'm also tellin' you that because Aisling loves to bake, to be with her family, to take care of us in a lotta ways. But not when she's next to a woman who's got a wineglass soldered to her hand who's slurrin' her words and droppin' the flour and forgettin' how much sugar she put in."

Oh God.

Poor Aisling.

"Right," I said softly. It was lame, far from enough, didn't cover a smidgeon of what I felt or wished I had it in me to say, but it was the only thing I could force out.

Mickey kept going.

"It sucks for me, but I'm strict 'cause she's not. Somewhere deep, she knows she's gotta make shit up to them and she does it by lettin' 'em get away with a load of shit that she shouldn't."

That struck close to the bone but obviously I said nothing, which was a good call because Mickey still wasn't done.

"It also sucks that I gotta lean on the village with my kids," he continued and his blue eyes grew intent. "And you're in that village, darlin', right across the street. It doesn't take much with my Ash. She's the best girl there is and not just because she's fourteen and smart enough to know the simple things in life can bring the most joy. That means she dug slappin' frosting on some cupcakes with you, even if she spent 'bout fifteen minutes doin' it. She'll also dig helpin' you out tomorrow. And I'll say now, I appreciate you lettin' her."

"I..." I stopped speaking because I was worried I'd start weeping. I pulled in a deep breath, controlled the urge and blurted, "I'm across the street for her or Cillian anytime you or they need me."

Now, why did I do that?

Why?

They were Mickey's and would come with Mickey. I couldn't exactly avoid him and befriend his children at the same time.

Still, I knew I was going to and in doing so probably fail spectacularly at the avoiding Mickey part.

This gave me the feeling I was in trouble and with all the other feelings I was burying, that was really not good.

He reached out and touched his finger in a whisper against the back of my hand. That fleeting touch raced a tingle up my arm, over my shoulder and down my chest, right to two specific targets.

I stood still and let it, liking it—no, loving it—at the same time stunned by it as I'd never experienced anything like it my entire life.

And through this profound experience, Mickey made it more profound by saying softly, "Thanks."

My voice was low and had a husk that I hoped he put down to emotion for his children and not the fact that he could touch the back of my hand for less than half a second and it had the power to make my nipples get hard when I replied, "Don't mention it."

He nodded to me. "See you in the mornin', Amelia."

I fought back a defeated (or possibly aroused) sigh and forced a smile. "Yes, Mickey. See you in the morning. And thanks for introducing me to your kids."

He started moving even as he threw a return smile over his shoulder at the same time he shot an arrow straight through my heart.

"Look forward to you returnin' that favor."

At this juncture the way things were he'd meet my kids when I was on my deathbed and they were making their guilt trip visit to say good-bye and make sure I put them in my will.

I kept the smile pinned to my face even knowing it now looked totally fake.

Luckily he'd turned his back to me and was walking away.

Not to appear rude, I waited until he was halfway down the drive before I closed the door.

And so he wouldn't hear me doing it, I waited until I knew for certain he was well out of earshot before I locked it.

And when the only thing I wanted to do was curl up somewhere and let loose all the feelings I was feeling, all the things I kept burying, everything I continued to push aside, even if doing that allowed them to destroy me, I didn't do that.

I went to the kitchen, made sure everything was covered, decided against a glass of wine and hit the shower.

Then I hit the bed.

I fell asleep slowly and once asleep did it fitfully.

And when I woke, not refreshed in the slightest, I knew this had happened for a variety of reasons.

But I didn't allow myself to feel any of them.

"WHEN ARE YOUR KIDS GETTIN' HERE?"

I turned my head at Mickey's voice.

It was nearly noon the next day and clearly my decision not to pay for simple notices but place ads not only in Magdalene's weekly newspaper but every paper in the county with a short list of the items for sale (and the brands) had made the day an unqualified success.

We'd been overrun.

In fact, there were cars lining the street before six o'clock.

This meant good things, including us making wads and wads of money and all my stuff heading out the door.

It also meant that I'd been way too busy to fret about spending time with Mickey.

But now, most of the stuff had been picked over, the dregs were remaining (which meant all of my stuff that I had on sale was gone and even some of it I didn't intend to sell but sold anyway) and the crowd was waning.

Which meant Mickey could get to me and do it sharing the fact that he'd noticed my children hadn't shown.

His had and they'd worked their behinds off. Alyssa and Junior's had and they'd done the same. Jake and Josie's Conner, Amber and Ethan had also arrived with their parents.

Though, only Ethan was Josie's and she'd only recently adopted him after recently marrying Jake. A long story she'd shared amongst planning sessions, but one that explained why she'd also only recently taken over league fundraising.

Not to mention, several other budding boxers and their parents had shown, with brothers and sisters.

It meant the crush hadn't been overwhelming and the day had been a winner. I had no idea the ongoing tally but I knew we'd made thousands. Josie and Alyssa had started beaming at around eight o'clock and were now walking on air.

I had been too. I felt wonderfully free watching my old life walk out the door in the hands of people who were delighted to get a screaming bargain and who would enjoy my stuff far more than I ever had. And I just felt plain wonderful doing what I was doing to give good to a bunch of boys who wanted to learn how to box.

But right then, at Mickey's question, both of these feelings fled instantly.

"They're with their dad," I mumbled, rearranging some of our wares (none of them mine) on the kitchen counter for better visibility.

"You got a big gig like this goin' on, their dad doesn't let them show?" Mickey asked incredulously.

I looked at him.

He took in my look and noticeably flinched.

This meant he read my look completely.

Seeing that, I decided the time was nigh to share with Mickey Donovan—my attractive neighbor who did not look at me like I looked at him, but even if he did he didn't deserve to be saddled with the likes of me —some of why he might wish to keep distance from his neighbor.

"Their father would not be pleased if they came because he doesn't want our children around me. But Auden and Olympia not being here is not their father's choice. It's theirs. My kids and I aren't very close. We were. We aren't any more. And that's my doing."

"Sorry, babe," Mickey murmured, holding my eyes. "Wasn't my business. Shouldn't have said anything."

The evening before, he'd given me his honesty.

I gave mine back.

"I don't know what to say to that because it is and it isn't. It would become your business because you live across the street. You'd notice I have them infrequently and when they're here, they do their best to find reasons to leave."

"Amelia," he said gently.

I waited for more but that was all he had.

Then again, there wasn't anything to say.

And anyway, he was speaking with his eyes. He was feeling my pain. He was feeling how it would feel if his children did the same.

And I could read the agony.

Looking at how I felt blazing out of his eyes, I knew why I buried everything.

Because if I didn't, it would consume me in such a way that I would cease to be.

So that was it.

I'd used up my honesty.

Therefore, I shrugged. "It is what it is. I'm here now. We'll see. Now, do you want a sandwich? I had some delivered from Wayfarer's and I don't know if you know, but they arrived half an hour ago. They're in the fridge."

He looked to the fridge as if he knew I needed a break from his scrutiny before looking back at me, his gaze shuttered but gentle. "I'll get what I need."

I nodded and turned away.

"Amy."

I stuttered to a halt and looked back at him, knowing no one by that name was in my house, and being startled when I looked at him to see he was addressing me.

Did he forget my name?

"This," he stated, throwing out a hand to the house sale carnage that was now my great room. "You did good, babe, and you gotta know it's appreciated."

I allowed that to feel good for a nanosecond.

Then I mumbled, "Thanks," and moved away.

"JESUS H, YOU GOT NOTHIN'," ALYSSA ANNOUNCED, STANDING ON THE landing with me and staring into my living room.

It was three thirty. The sale was over. The remaining items had been boxed and were right then being carted away by Junior and Jake, some to Goodwill, some to be stored for a possible later sale.

The rest of us were in my house, tidying.

But there wasn't a lot to tidy.

I had a couch. A standing lamp. A single end table (the other one had sold even though it wasn't for sale).

I didn't even have any barstools (those had actually been on sale).

The rest was history.

Most of the moms of budding boxers were gone. A few remained, including Josie and Alyssa and their families (save Jake and Junior who had just taken off, Conner and Ethan going with them to help).

And Aisling was there. Mickey was outside hauling the end table that I wasn't expecting to sell, which was the last thing that sold, to a buyer's car with Cillian spotting.

"This is good, a clean palette," I replied, also surveying the cavernous space that looked like no one lived there.

But it still looked better than it looked when there were boxes stacked everywhere.

And I was determined it would one day (soon) look *amazing*.

"A what?" Alyssa asked and I looked to her.

"A clean palette," I repeated. "Now time to decorate."

She grinned devilishly. "You need help with that, sister, I got a way with spending money."

I had not been to her home. I *had* seen how she dressed. She took some chances (with hair, makeup *and* clothes) and it was admittedly not nice (but true) to say she skirted the skank side.

I still wanted her to help me decorate because I didn't care what side she skirted. I liked her a lot.

"I'm ready when you are."

Her grin turned excited.

"I know of a local interior designer who does very good work," Josie joined our conversation, a can of Pledge and a dusting cloth in her hand, even though I had no idea what she could possibly be polishing since I'd sold my dining room table (that had been for sale) and she'd been nowhere near the end table.

"I want whatever I create here to be all me," I replied carefully, not wanting to hurt her feelings and also not sharing that I had no idea who that *me* would turn out to be.

She tipped her head to the side as her lips curved up. "Then that's what it'll be."

Alyssa threw her hands in the air shouting, "Girlie home décor shopping trip!"

More like fifty of them. I had a big house, and except for the kids' rooms that were still untouched, it was now a clean slate.

On this thought, while Alyssa still had hands in the air and was celebrating, Josie turned concerned eyes to her friend. "Amelia will not want her home to look like a bordello."

I sucked in an audible breath at what this might mean but more, how Alyssa might take it.

I let it out when Alyssa dropped her arms, burst out laughing, allowing herself to do that with abandon for a few moments before pushing out words while still doing it, "Are you sayin' my place looks like a whorehouse?"

"I'm saying you decorate heavily in *scarves*," Josie replied.

"Every girl knows lighting is everything," Alyssa returned.

"Agreed. Thus those who have that ability provide light bulbs of a multitude of different wattages and finishes in order to offer us a variety of lighting opportunities," Josie retorted.

Alyssa turned to me and jerked a thumb at Josie. "Ain't this bitch a kick?"

She was.

However, I wasn't sure Josie knew *how* she was and thus shared in the amusement making it okay to be amused so I decided to say nothing.

"Babe!"

I stiffened then turned at hearing Mickey's voice.

With the women as well as kids that were female in my house, there were currently eight "babes" he could be speaking to.

Upon catching his eyes, eyes that were aimed my way, I found this particular "babe" was me.

"Two o'clock tomorrow good for you?" he asked when he got my attention.

"Sorry?" I asked back.

"Brats, chicken, you kickin' back," he reminded me.

Oh...*shit*.

I'd totally forgotten.

"Uh...well..."

"Two," he stated firmly. "And don't even think of offerin' to bring anything. Just come over. We'll have you covered." Before I could come up with a suitable way to decline his invitation, he looked to his daughter and called, "Ash, baby, you ready?"

"Yeah, Dad," she called back quietly and I looked her way to see her eyes come to me. "It went awesome, Miz Hathaway."

"Partially thanks to you, blossom," I told her.

She lifted her shoulders, dropped them, tipped her head to the side, looked to the ground and made no reply, doing all of this while heading toward the door.

I watched, feeling my eyes narrow, not certain why those brief, subtle movements made by Aisling troubled me, just certain that they did.

"Two."

I jumped and looked at Mickey who'd repeated himself and again did it firmly.

How to get out of this?

How?

"Two, Mickey," my mouth said.

Well, that was how *not* to get out of it.

Shit.

He nodded, swept his eyes through the room and called a general, "Later."

Then he disappeared, closing the door behind him and his daughter.

It barely clicked before I found my body shifting an inch to the right at the same time I felt a piercing pain in my ribs, all because Alyssa had elbowed me and did it hard.

I looked her way in surprise.

She waggled her eyebrows, saying, "Mickey?"

"I like this," Josie said softly and I looked to her to see she did like it. A lot.

"I don't like it, I love it," Alyssa declared, and my eyes went back to her. "Mickey Donovan. The Irishman. Total score," she decreed.

If this was that, she would not be wrong.

However, this was absolutely not that.

"We're neighbors," I told them both.

"Neighbors where one of you has boy parts and one of you has girl parts," Alyssa pointed out suggestively and unnecessarily.

"Yes," I agreed, also unnecessarily. "But his kids will be there."

Alyssa's grin got big. "All the better. Though, not about the boy-girl parts. Just about the invitin' you over with the family part."

"No, Alyssa," I said softly. "I'm a neighbor. Just a neighbor. Sure, a female one, but this is how it goes," I began to explain. "You'll never know it because you and Junior look at each other like you're passing in the halls in high school on a Friday afternoon and you have a hot date planned that night so you'll never have to do this. But if this was a neighbor with boy parts and one with girl parts scenario, I'd meet his kids

probably in six months after we spent six weeks planning for that particular meeting."

"This is, unfortunately, true," Josie murmured.

I nodded, even though I wasn't fond of her confirming. She didn't
need to. "So this has nothing to do with boy and girl parts. This is just
Mickey being a good guy."

"Bet, you go over there with cleavage, his good guy will get better,"
Alyssa suggested.

I shook my head but did it grinning.

Josie snapped, "It's hardly appropriate for her to wear cleavage in front
of Mickey's children."

Alyssa looked to Josie, raising her brows. "Why? I wear it front of my
kids."

"They're *your* children, Alyssa, with *your* children you can do what you
wish," Josie pointed out. "And if something were to happen between
Amelia and Mickey, and the children got used to her and she became a
part of their family, *then* she could do what *she* wishes."

"Oh…right," Alyssa muttered.

"Anyway," I cut in. "It's nothing to get excited about. Just brats, chicken
and relaxing with a new neighbor."

"Bummed," Alyssa kept muttering. Then she perked up. "Though,
means you're good to go on the prowl, which means we can go on the
prowl with you."

On her *we*, she elbowed Josie, who didn't shift an inch to the side, but
she did glare at Alyssa.

"You're kinda *very* married," I reminded her.

"I'm definitely *very* married," she agreed with me. "That doesn't mean I
don't get to go out. Junior knows I wouldn't stray. He doesn't care." She
turned to Josie. "You in?"

"I'm always in for something that would allow me to dress up," Josie
announced.

I was uncertain about this, therefore told them, "I'm not sure I'm
ready."

"Okay, then don't be ready," Alyssa gave in instantly. "First, we pimp
your house. Then, we go on the prowl. You call it. We're there. Lunch
wore off about half a minute after they ate it so now I gotta get my brood

home or they're gonna start eating your couch and that's the only thing you got left to sit on."

I looked to her brood, which was expansive. Every one of them was crashed on my large sectional, looking cranky.

She corralled them out of the house and into her SUV while I said good-bye to them along with Amber, who took off with her two friends, both named Taylor (though one was a boy and one was a girl) as well as handing out hugs and giving and receiving thanks from the last moms who left.

This left me with Josie, both of us standing at the door.

"I delayed because I wanted to be certain you're okay," she explained her lollygagging.

"I'm good. I have a couch. I have a bed. And unless someone sold it, I have a bottle of wine," I replied on a smile.

"No, Amelia, I dawdled because I wanted to be certain *you're okay.*"

I pulled my lower lip between my teeth.

Josie's eyes dropped to watch.

Then she said softly, "I see."

I let my lip go and whispered, "I need to decorate."

It made no sense, couldn't make any sense to anyone but me.

Somehow, when Josie lifted her gaze to mine, I knew it made sense to her too.

"Then we shall be certain to get on that immediately."

Why was that such a relief?

"I love it that you and Alyssa are helping," I told her honestly. "I—"

"I love it you want us to help," she cut me off and I felt more relief that she understood and I didn't have to say it. "A very short time ago, I was new here too. And I had many who embraced me. I know how it feels. So I might love it more, seeing as you're giving me the opportunity to return that to somebody."

I couldn't say we'd gotten to know each other very well in the time it took to pull this house sale off. There were certain things you shared just because you were communicating but nothing had been that deep.

I could say, although she was an unusual woman, I knew she was one I liked.

Now I could say I'd been right in doing that.

I took a chance, reached out a hand and grabbed hers.

I squeezed briefly and let it go. "I'll call you. Set something up. We'll get Alyssa and start Cliff Blue Project, Phase Two."

She nodded as she reached out, grabbed my hand, but she didn't squeeze it briefly and let it go.

She held it tight and didn't let go.

"And I'll look forward to your call and think of wonderful places to take you that will inspire you."

"Thanks," I whispered.

"My pleasure," she whispered back, her hand tightening.

I tightened mine too.

We held on as she said, "All you gave today, I cannot say. Jake did a preliminary count, Amelia, and we're stunned at what we raised but not surprised," she threw out a hand to my empty space, "given your generosity. That money will most assuredly cover new equipment plus gym time, something Jake always took a hit on, which meant the gym's bottom line suffered, rather drastically. But he never even considered letting the league go, and now, for the first time, that won't be an issue. He might even be able to afford to get the boys into a better ring for their matches with decent seating for parents, something the league's never been able to do. You'll need to come and see the boys when the season is on so you can witness what you've done for them and how much they enjoy it."

"You're on for that."

She smiled.

I smiled back.

She let me go on a warm squeeze and said, "Farewell, Amelia, see you very soon."

"Very soon, Josie."

She turned to leave and I lifted my hand and waved as she did.

She waved back.

I made sure she was safely on the road before I closed and locked the door.

I turned back to the room, the light feeling I had escaping me completely as the cavernous space suddenly didn't seem like an invitation to create beauty, but instead with the quiet after a busy day, a crushing emptiness that could never be appropriately filled.

"Clean palette," I murmured to myself, moving to the kitchen and finding that my last bottle of wine had not been sold.

I opened it, poured a glass in a plastic cup (for I no longer had wine-glasses) and opened the fridge.

I stared at the picked over sandwiches and curled my lip.

I hadn't even had breakfast, what with everyone lining the street so early. All I'd had time for was wolfing down a small bag of chips.

But none of that mess looked appealing.

I closed the fridge.

I briefly considered texting my kids to tell them the house sale was a huge success. Something they couldn't care less about. A fact that, if I'd actually had an appetite, would have completely erased it.

Then I decided taking my first bubble bath in my fabulous bathroom in my fabulous tub overlooking the sea, doing this with a plastic glass of wine by my side, something my mother would never do and would actually find abhorrent (starting with the tub that had windows all around exposing her to the sea, though no neighbors, but definitely including consuming wine out of plastic), was just the thing.

So I did that.

4

THE DANGER ZONE

*T*he next afternoon, not allowing myself to wish I was walking down my lawn toward Mickey's house for reasons other than just being a neighbor coming over for a barbeque, I walked down my lawn toward Mickey's house.

I'd spent the day doing the minimal clean up left from the house sale and unpacking Auden and Olympia's rooms. Since they didn't take the opportunity, I'd also gone through their things. Anything I hadn't seen them wear in some time, or I thought might not fit anymore, or they didn't use, I put in piles with notes asking if I could add it to the next sale the league might put on.

In other words, I stayed busy, mostly so I wouldn't think on things, however, this only partially worked.

It allowed me not to think of my impending *kicking back* with Mickey and his children.

But it forced me to think about my children and how lost they were to me.

I powered through this, finished with the kids' rooms, took a shower and got ready, donning some of the Felicia Hathaway clothes I didn't sell (but only because I needed something to wear).

Now I was standing at Mickey's door.

I drew in a deep breath, let it out and hit the doorbell.

I could hear it ringing inside and it was a normal bell, not dulcet and uncommon, like mine.

As I listened to it ring, I allowed myself to hope for two seconds that the Donovan family had forgotten about my visit and had taken a spur of the moment trip to Disneyland.

These hopes were dashed when the door was flung open.

"Hey, Miz Hathaway!" Cillian cried, beaming up at me. Then he declared, "We're in the kitchen," turned and started walking into the house.

I took that as what it was, my invitation to follow him, so I did, closing the door behind me.

I wanted to take time to study Mickey's house but Cillian was moving at a good clip down a short hall toward the back of the house so I didn't get the chance.

I still took in as much as I could get. And with what I took in I knew that either Mickey had put a goodly amount of effort into making his post-divorce house a home for his children or he'd gotten the house in the divorce.

It was dark, not due to lack of windows, there were a lot of them, nor due to the plethora of wood and wood paneling, but instead due to the fact that Mickey had a number of mature trees on his lot and many of them were close to his home.

The outside of the house made me think the inside would scream *Home in Coastal Maine*.

I was slightly surprised it didn't.

When I looked left to take in the living room, above the stone fireplace, there was a beautiful seascape with an old-fashioned boat on it. There were also some of those colorful glass things that were suspended in webs of ropes hanging on the walls.

That was it.

The rest was comfortable, cushiony furniture, some in attractive tweed (the armchairs), some in worn leather (the couch). The tables were topped in everything from what appeared to be an old baseball ensconced in a glass block, bronze figurines (two, both art deco, one that looked like an angel without wings, arms out, head back, as if ascending to the heavens, the other an elephant) to multi-paned standing frames filled with photos from a variety of eras, sepia to color.

To the right was a long hall I suspected led to bedrooms and bathrooms.

As I followed Cillian, I saw on the walls of the hall an expertly scattered display of frames that were mostly pictures of Mickey's kids, from babyhood to recently. These were interspersed with pictures of what, to my fascinated eyes, appeared to be Mickey from a baby through adolescence and even into adulthood.

These included Mickey (possibly) lying in nothing but a diaper on a fur rug in front of a fire, head up, doing a baby giggle at the camera. Also Mickey in a Little League uniform, posing with cap on, wearing a grin that would mature from the cute in that picture to the heart-stopping of today, bat on his shoulder. And another with Mickey, perhaps in his late twenties, leaning back against the front of a fire rig.

There were also framed pieces of art, none of them good because all of them were done by a child's hand, some of them signed "Aisling" others "Cillian."

And last, there were empty spaces that didn't fit the careful arrangement. Empty spaces that laid testimony to this being the Donovan family home considering they were at some point more than likely filled with pictures of Mickey's wife, perhaps their wedding, them together, the family together, but now they were gone.

I knew what those empty spaces felt like in real life so by the time I made it to the back of the house, my heart was heavy.

Once I moved through the mouth of the hall, I gave myself the quick opportunity to take in the long great room that was open plan.

There was a large kitchen with gleaming, attractive wood cabinets and granite countertops to the right, delineated by a bar from the family room to the left that had a big sectional that faced a wide, flat-screen TV mounted on the wall above another, smaller and less formal, stone fireplace.

This space, too, was not imposing. It was all family, with thick rugs over the wood floors, the sectional an attractive, very dark purple twill with high backs, deep set cushions, throw pillows and afghans tossed around for maximum lounging potential.

Around the couch there were a variety of standing lamps that could offer bright lighting, say, should you wish to lounge and read, or subtle lighting, say, should you want to watch a horror movie and get in the mood.

A long, wide, carefully distressed dark wood, rectangular coffee table with drawers on the sides ran the middle of the sectional. It held a lovely globe filled with burgundy-colored sand in which a fat candle was positioned that had tiers of blue, purple and forest green.

Staring at that candle, I knew, in leaving, the ex-wife forgot it. I knew it because a man would not buy that glass globe, pour sand in it and find the perfect candle to stick in.

Her one stamp. The last of her.

In my limited perusal of the house, except empty spaces where her image and history with her family occupied the wall, that candle was the only physical evidence that I'd seen of her.

Seeing it, I wondered if, when she went, she left it just to remind them she'd been there and now she was gone.

I didn't know what to make of this, except to think that if she left it on purpose, it was a cruelty, plain and simple. Conrad had left us in our home and when he'd gone, he'd taken every vestige of himself with him. Yes, including the pictures off the walls and out of frames on shelves and tables.

And when he went, this caused me profound grief that only dug the pit of his departure deeper.

Now I saw it as something else entirely.

As a kindness.

Staring at the candle, I also wondered why Mickey kept it.

Perhaps, as a man, he didn't even see it. It had been lit, but it was far from burned low and he didn't strike me as a man who lit candles to provide a relaxing atmosphere.

Perhaps he wanted a reminder of his wife, the family they shared, the hopes he'd had, these being things he wasn't ready to let go.

I would get no answers to these questions and not only because I'd never ask them.

No, it was because Mickey called, "Hey, babe."

I stopped staring at the candle and turned his way.

Cillian was up on a barstool opposite Mickey, who was wearing another unfairly attractive shirt, this in lightweight cotton the color of mocha, sleeves again rolled up over muscular forearms, doing something beyond the elevated portion of counter where the tall barstools sat.

Both pairs of blue eyes were on me.

"I'm completely unable to come to a home for a meal without bringing something," I blurted, lifting up my empty hands. "I feel weird. Like I'm going to get a Good Guest Demerit or something."

Mickey grinned and Cillian asked, "What's a demerit?"

"A bad mark, son," Mickey explained to his boy then looked to me. "Come in. Take a seat. Want a beer?"

I didn't often drink beer; it wasn't a beverage of preference. I drank wine and if I had a cocktail it could vary, but it usually had vodka in it.

However, I keenly remembered Mickey saying his children's mother had a wineglass soldered to her hand so I nodded.

"Beer sounds good," I replied, moving further into the room in the direction of the bar.

I arrived, took my own barstool and noted that Mickey had a plethora of stuff all over the counter and appeared to be creating a smorgasbord of salads ranging from spinach to Asian noodle to macaroni. There were bowls, small packets of slivered almonds, used packs of ramen noodles, bottles of mayonnaise and mustard, cutting boards covered in residue and the waste parts of pickles, carrots, tomatoes, onions.

It struck me how long it'd been since my countertop looked like that and when it struck me, that feeling fell down the hollow well left after my family disintegrated, and it kept falling, that pit a bottomless pit of agony.

"Get Miz Hathaway a beer, boy," Mickey ordered, thankfully taking me out of my thoughts, and Cillian jumped off his stool and raced to the fridge.

I failed to note the first time I met Cillian that he seemed to have an overabundance of energy.

I did not fail to note this same thing the day before when he stuck to his father's, or Jake's, or Junior's sides like glue, helping with anything that needed help with, dashing around getting packing materials, dragging boxes, but most specifically manly things, like lifting and carrying.

Even if what he was lifting and carrying was too big, which sent him grunting and making hilarious faces at which I would never laugh because he was so serious in doing whatever he was doing, and I didn't want him to see me and hurt his feelings.

I saw then, although getting a beer was not an onerous task, this was his nature for he didn't delay and delivered the fastest drink I'd ever received.

"Thanks, honey," I murmured when he put it on the bar in front of me.

"No probs," he replied, moving around me then pulling himself back into his barstool, still talking, albeit briefly. And this was to demand of me, "Get this."

I swiveled my stool his way to look at him.

"What?" I asked on a grin.

"I just figured out today that when I'm a fighter pilot for the Air Force, they don't have to give me a call sign," he declared and finished excitedly, "They can call me Kill since Kill is an *awesome* call sign but it's also my name!"

He was clearly ecstatic about this.

But I stared at him in utter fear.

"You want to be a fighter pilot?" I asked.

"Totally," he answered.

"*Top Gun,*" Mickey stated and I turned concerned eyes to him. "Cill caught it on cable a few years back. Made me buy him the DVD. He's seen it a million times."

"Two million," Cillian contradicted proudly, and I turned my attention back to him. "It flipping *rocks!*"

I couldn't agree or disagree. I'd seen it several times myself, including when it came out. Back then it was the best thing going.

However, I wasn't certain it had aged well.

"The pilots in that movie fly for the Navy," I informed him.

"Yeah, I know, but who wants to land a jet on a boat?" Cillian asked but didn't allow me to answer. He shared his opinion immediately, "Not me. Plus, there are no babes on boats."

"About a year after Cill saw *Top Gun,*" Mickey started and my eyes went to him, "he became aware there were girls in this world."

"Isn't that young?" I asked Mickey.

"I'm advanced," Cillian said cheekily.

I grinned at him but even if he was being funny, the mother in me came right out.

"Being a fighter pilot is kind of a dangerous job, Cillian," I shared hesitantly.

"I *know!*" he cried exuberantly, doing it sharing that danger was a big draw for that particular occupation.

I looked to Mickey, eyes wide.

He gave me one of his quick grins. "Not gonna talk him outta it, darlin'. Before he entered the highway to the danger zone, he wanted to be a firefighter, like his dad, a cop, a lawyer, which I also blame on Tom Cruise seein' as that stretch, thankfully brief, came after Cill saw *A Few Good Men*. Then he was back to firefighter, moved on to Navy SEAL, then latched onto fighter pilot. Not one of 'em is a desk job that would make a mother's heart settle, 'cept bein' a lawyer, which would make his father's head explode. But with this last one, it's been years. I'm thinkin' this one's here to stay."

"And get this!" Cillian butted in. "Dad's got a friend who's an instructor at Luke in Phoenix and we're goin' there for Christmas and we're goin' on the base *and* Uncle Chopper thinks he can get me in the flight simulator!"

"Do or die," Mickey muttered and when I looked at him questioningly, he explained, "Luke's an Air Force base. And Chop is gonna show us around. Cill sees and does, he either knows he's gotta work at that, and it isn't easy, or he'll have to explore other options."

I turned to Cillian. "How old are you?"

"Eleven," he told me.

"You do have some time to figure it out," I remarked.

"Not if I wanna get in the Air Force Academy, which is the *only* way to go, so I wanna get in the Air Force Academy. And I gotta have it together to do that," Cillian replied with hard to miss determination.

I was astonished at his maturity that mingled naturally with his childish effusiveness.

Astonished by it and charmed by it.

"I'll bet you do," I murmured, falling a little in love with Cillian Donovan.

"Go get your sister, son," Mickey ordered.

"'Kay," Cillian agreed and again jumped off his stool and raced away.

I wrapped my fingers around my beer and took a pull before looking to Mickey and asking, "Can I help?"

"As I said, not lost on me you've run yourself ragged since you got to Magdalene, so no. Let me and my kids do the work, babe. You just relax."

Relaxing would be good, but in Mickey's presence, I figured it was highly unlikely.

But at that moment, what I really wanted was to find a nice way to ask him not to call me "babe."

I wanted this because it reminded me of Conrad calling me that and it not meaning anything.

I also wanted it because I wanted it to mean something when Mickey said it, but it still didn't.

I couldn't figure out a nice way to say that so I just nodded, took another sip of cold beer and let my eyes wander his kitchen.

His ex was gone from there, totally. I knew it through my eye sweep.

There was a standing KitchenAid mixer that was in a neutral cream that would normally say a woman lived there, but I suspected this was on the counter because Mickey's daughter liked to bake and Mickey clearly liked his daughter.

Other than that, there was a crock with a gravely lacking selection of cooking utensils stuck in it. Beside the rather nice stainless steel stove were salt and pepper shakers that didn't match the crock (or the butter dish), and the salt shaker was chipped. There was also a truly unattractive, purchased solely because it did the job, wooden bread box. And although there was a good deal of counter space in the u-shaped kitchen, which also included a large pantry and more counter space separated from the rest against the opposite wall, all of it was taken up with appliances, none of them matching, none of them high quality.

I knew from experience that a family of the age of Mickey's needed more, and if not the best, at least they needed ones they'd purchased to work and for a good long time, rather than shoddy brands that would break frequently, making you wonder why you didn't invest wisely in quality in the first place.

You cooked for your family. Your kids had sleepovers and birthday parties that you needed to prepare for. You had friends over. You had family over. You had barbeques and special breakfasts that were about nothing. There were holidays to consider.

This was a man's kitchen. Although the actual kitchen was highly attractive, it was not tidy and any woman knew the accoutrements had to be copious, carefully selected, and perhaps most importantly, fit the aesthetic.

At the end of my perusal, on the counter against the opposite wall, I spied a big chocolate cake on what appeared to be an antique glass cake plate.

"Aisling's contribution to our barbeque," he stated and I moved my gaze to him. "Said we couldn't have someone over for food without offering dessert." The easy grin came as he tipped his head sideways, toward the cake. "That's one she does a lot 'cause her dad and brother fuckin' love it. She's hopin' you will too."

"I'm sure I will," I replied quietly.

His eyes lit with pride. "Be crazy not to, it's fuckin' amazing."

I loved his unhidden pride in his girl so much I couldn't help but smile back.

"And to answer the question you're too good-mannered to ask, I got the house. But Rhiannon got the kitchen," he declared.

I blinked. "Rhiannon?"

"Ex-wife," he stated. "It's my house since I grew up in it. My folks moved to Florida, sold Rhiannon and me this place for a song. No way I could afford to live in this neighborhood, raise my kids in it, if they didn't. She was decent enough not to make a play for it or fuck things up by pickin' over shit, takin' furniture, altering her kids' home in a way that would freak them out more than they were already freaked their parents were splitting. She did that for me and the kids, I let her pick over everything else she could get and she took everything else she could get."

This meant she left the candle. I just hoped she did it because she wasn't overly fond of it.

"MFD has got one employee, our fire chief, and he's only paid part-time. Town can't afford more," Mickey told me.

I nodded, uncertain at the flow of our conversation, so I decided not to reply.

"The rest of us, we volunteer," he shared, grabbing one of his many bowls and turning toward the fridge, still talking. "Would do that for a job if I could. I can't and I grew up in Magdalene, love it here, great place for a kid to be, good people, got all the seasons, safe, beautiful, don't want to leave. I wanted to settle here, find a woman here, raise my kids here, so I had to find a way to do what I love doin' and still put food in my kids' mouths."

He put the bowl in the fridge and turned back, walking my way, continuing to speak.

"I work for a local company, does roofing and construction. Job sucks, my boss is an asshole. Wanna strike out on my own but with two kids fast approaching college, can't take that risk. Gotta eat his bullshit and get a paycheck. But they work seven days a week and the only way my boss isn't an asshole is that he doesn't want his house to burn down without local volunteer firefighters to stop it. So he lets me adjust my schedule so I can take some shifts at the department during weekdays, as well as doin' nights and some weekends."

"I'm sorry you don't like your boss but it's good you get to do what you like to do," I told him, even though I didn't actually think him being able to be a firefighter was good.

In this climate, I could imagine fires weren't as prevalent as in other, drier climates. But fires happened everywhere and I wasn't really big on Mickey taking his life in his hands to go out and fight them.

However, this had nothing to do with me and would be an unwelcome (and rude) opinion to share, so I didn't share it.

He put his hands on the counter, his attention still on me. "Life is life. You're smart, you take what you can get."

All of a sudden, that feeling of being crushed came back, thinking Mickey, a nice guy, a good father, a handsome man, had this philosophy.

He wanted to stay in his hometown and that was his prerogative.

He wanted to be a firefighter so he made that work.

That was commendable.

But I hated the idea that he felt with the rest he had to take what he could get.

I wanted him to be fulfilled. Happy. If not having it all (because who did?), at least having as much as he could get. Loving his family, his home, his job...his *life*.

Not taking what he could get.

"Hey, Miz Hathaway."

I turned at Aisling's greeting and smiled when I caught her beautiful blue eyes.

"Hey, blossom. Thanks again for all your help yesterday."

Mickey had not been wrong. She'd loved helping. She'd worked hard, this mostly being, as the stuff quickly disappeared, running around rearranging so the other items for sale would be attractively displayed and not looked picked over or like the dregs since the early birds got the good stuff. She also sold beverages, the goodies, and when each drink dispenser was purchased, she'd helped me empty them out and clean them up so they could go out the door.

"No probs," she repeated her brother's words of earlier, moving into the kitchen and looking up to her father. "Want me to do the spinach?"

"Closer to, beautiful," he said softly, gazing at her the same way. "Make sure it's fresh. Got a lot of grillin' to do."

"'Kay, Dad," she mumbled, shifting around him, eyes to the counter, eyes that assessed the situation immediately as she saw what Mickey had done, what needed to be done, and thus she left what was still needed while clearing away what no longer was.

Yes, she was a good girl who liked to take care of her family and I liked that, thus I started to fall a little in love with quiet, sweet Aisling Donovan too.

"Son, you wanna start the grill, get it ready for your dad?" Mickey offered.

"Totally!" Cill accepted loudly.

Mickey gave his grin to his boy. "Fire it up."

Cillian raced away.

Mickey went to the fridge and came out with his own beer.

When he turned, he caught my eyes. "Let's move this outside."

"Sounds good," I agreed.

He reached out and nabbed a packet of tortilla chips that were sitting on the counter and said to Aisling, "Grab the guac from the fridge before you head out, yeah, darlin'?"

"Yeah, Dad," she replied.

We went out and I saw that when Rhiannon left the furniture, she also left the patio furniture. Further, I noted this was an outdoor family.

I knew this because there was a colossal shining grill against the side railing of the deck—a deck that spanned the living room and kitchen areas of the long house. Further, there was a four-seater, wrought iron table with umbrella and chairs that I knew would be comfortable because they had fluffy taupe cushions, high backs and they rocked. There were also two matching lounge chairs with matching cushions, angled toward the view of Mickey's backyard, which was mostly trees. And last, there was a coordinating loveseat at the opposite end of the deck from the grill that had an ottoman in front of it and tables at each side.

All this, and in the densely wooded backyard that had a narrow wedge of grass close to the deck, I saw a tire swing in a tree. There were Frisbees lying in the grass (three, to be precise). And to one side, what appeared to be a narrow baseball pitcher plate set up, beyond it a tall, wide net to catch pitched balls.

I followed Mickey out but he went to the grill to survey Cillian's activities.

I decided on the table, where we could all sit, eat chips and guacamole, and chat.

Mickey and Cillian joined me, Mickey opening the chips after he sat, tossing them on the table.

Aisling came out with the guac, which was homemade, had the perfect hint of cilantro, a nice tang of garlic and minimum tomatoes, making it sublime (Mickey's creation, which made me look forward to dinner). She also saw the chips, rolled her eyes at her father and went back in, coming out with a bowl in which she dumped the chips (budding hostess, and a good one, for certain).

And we all sat, munching, sipping, Cillian doing most of the talking with Mickey and I interjecting.

Not long after, Mickey got up and went in to get the meat.

He started grilling.

At their father's good-natured demand, without complaint, the kids got up and grabbed outdoor table stuff, including nice plastic plates, and set the table.

When it was time, Aisling went in to make the spinach salad.

In the end, I ate more than I had in weeks (and my stomach protested, but I didn't listen because it was all so delicious) and surprisingly in Mickey's company, did exactly what he wanted me to do.

I kicked back, drank beer, ate good food, sat with a nice family on the deck during a comfortable summer day in Maine, and relaxed.

"Babe."

I was in the danger zone.

"Hey." A hand was on my hip.

Highway straight to the danger zone.

That hand gently shook me. "Amy."

My eyes fluttered open and I saw dark purple twill.

I knew exactly where I was.

I was in a home with a family that liked me.

A home where we sat in the sun on the deck and ate three different salads (all excellent), superbly grilled brats and chicken breasts slathered in barbeque sauce. This being followed by a heavenly chocolate cake that made my meringue-frosting-topped cupcakes seem like sawdust topped with pillow foam.

A home where I told a fourteen-year-old girl I felt that way about her cake, and she handed the world to me when her blue eyes started shining.

A home where we chatted and laughed and ended our meal playing Frisbee.

A home where I could run around the backyard with kids who enjoyed my company, demonstrating my Frisbee prowess because I was an awesome Frisbee player, seeing as my brother and I would go to the beach as often as possible (it was what you did, we grew up in La Jolla, we had a beach, we used it) and we'd play Frisbee. And being good at Frisbee was apparently a skill you didn't lose.

A home where, during Frisbee, an eleven-year-old boy told me I was "da bomb" because I was an awesome Frisbee player.

A home where, after Frisbee, we camped out on a big cozy sectional to watch Tom Cruise and Val Kilmer play volleyball (amongst other things) and with beer, a full belly and wonderful company, relaxed and at ease, I'd fallen asleep curled into a corner of that big, cozy, purple couch.

Right then, still half-asleep, I turned my head and looked into Mickey Donovan's amazing blue eyes.

This didn't make me shake the dream.

No, the dream took hold of me and I stayed in the danger zone because I *liked* it.

And I liked it because I was in a home with a handsome man who protected me, fed me, laughed with me, was open, honest, loved his kids, didn't hide his admiration of my Frisbee abilities, and who looked after me.

"Kids are in bed," this handsome man in his comfortable home murmured to me words a handsome father, a handsome husband, a hand-some *lover* would say to his woman. "You needed to crash, so I let you sleep. Now we both need to hit our beds, Amy."

We did. We needed to hit our beds.

But half-asleep, staring at the most beautiful man I'd ever seen, having the only really good day I'd had in three years, spending time with him, being a part of his life, a part of his family, I decided first that I needed to *hit him.*

So I did, blinking at the dream that still had hold of me, unwilling and maybe unable to let it go, I leaned up and in, doing it deep. At the same time, I lifted a hand to curl around the side of his strong neck, feeling the muscle there and also feeling the thrill of knowing that hardness was probably everywhere.

And without delay, I pressed my lips to his, wanting nothing more, nothing else, nothing in my whole life, *caring* about nothing but living that dream.

Mickey jerked away.

I jerked fully awake.

"Amy," he whispered.

Oh God, had I just kissed Mickey?

I stared at him, immobile, no, *frozen,* completely mortified, taking in the look in his eyes.

Surprise.

Remorse.

Aversion.

Oh God.

I'd just kissed him.

I flew off the couch, aiming sideways to miss him where he was leaning over me, mumbling humiliatingly, "God, sorry. So, so sorry. I was half-asleep."

"Amy," he called but I was on the move.

"Gotta go," I kept mumbling, now walking and doing it swiftly. "I'm sorry I fell asleep. A lot has been happening, I guess I let it..." I trailed off, hit the mouth of the hall, turned to him and saw he'd straightened but hadn't moved. I aimed my eyes at his chest. "Anyway, thanks for a great day. It was just what I needed. You gave me that, I wore out my welcome. Another demerit and I'm so, so sorry."

Then I turned and I wanted to walk casually down his hall like nothing had happened.

But my feet had a mind of their own.

They ran, taking me down his hall, out his door, across his lawn, the street and to my house, one desperate step after the other, until I was behind my closed door.

I locked it and made another dash through my empty, dark house, straight to my bedroom then to my bath.

I closed that door and locked it too, as if Mickey would come for me, break down my door, demand an explanation for me touching him without invitation, *putting my mouth on his* when he didn't want that.

Surprise.

Remorse.

Aversion.

Oh God, I'd kissed Mickey!

I put my back to the bathroom door and slid down it until my behind was on the floor. I bent forward, resting forehead to my knees, my heart slamming in my chest, my breaths coming fast and uneven, my skin burning.

The dulcet tones of my doorbell sounded.

I didn't move, didn't even lift my head.

I didn't know how late it was but it was summer and dark so I knew it was late.

This meant that could be nobody but Mickey. Mickey being a nice guy and trying to make me feel better after I'd embarrassed myself *and* him, putting us both in an untenable situation that had no escape.

I was forty-seven years old. I should be old enough, brave enough, to get up and go to the door. Talk to my neighbor. Open myself to him (slightly) the way he seemed perfectly okay with opening himself to me, and sharing that I'd lost my husband, my family, and I'd been alone for a long time. And that day I got lost in him and his family, I liked it, and I was half-asleep. I didn't think.

I didn't think.

But sitting on my bathroom floor, it didn't matter that I should be old and brave enough to do it.

I didn't move.

The doorbell sounded again and I heard my whimper whisper through the knotty wood paneled room of my rustic, elegant, fabulous bathroom.

And I didn't move.

I stayed in that position, the mortification burning through me, as minutes passed, listening hard and not shifting an inch.

The doorbell didn't ring again.

After what felt like hours, lifetimes, I crawled on hands and knees to the towel rack. I grabbed a pink towel that looked great in my master bath in La Jolla but did not fit at all in that rustic, elegant bathroom in Maine.

And right there, I curled on my side on the floor, pulled the towel over me, up to my neck, where I tucked it in and closed my eyes.

I knew in that moment I'd hit bottom.

I knew in that moment I could sink no lower.

But I feared with everything that was me, that being me, I'd find new ways to fuck everything up even worse.

I had a talent with that.

It was the only talent I had.

And I didn't want it.

I just had no idea how to get rid of it.

It was the only part of me I knew was real.

So I lay on the floor in my bathroom, covered in a towel, and thought (maybe hysterically) that perhaps I didn't need to find me.

And thus I fell asleep on the floor of my bathroom fearing that was the only me that there could be.

THE NEXT EVENING, I WAS SITTING ON MY COUCH IN THE SUNKEN LIVING room, feet to the seat, arms around my calves, chin to my knees, eyes to the darkening sky over the sea that had been gray all day, and stormy (reflecting my mood), thinking, priority: since I'd sold mine (all four of them), I needed to get a new TV.

Immediately.

I had not had dinner (or lunch, or breakfast for that matter). And I didn't have a glass of wine beside me (though I wanted one, I just had an empty stomach and Mickey's ex made me worry I wasn't consuming much anymore, but I was going through wine like crazy).

So I was sitting there alone, as always, in a way that felt like it would be forever, wondering where the day went.

The only thing I'd done was make plans to go out with Josie and Alyssa to begin Cliff Blue Project: Phase Two on Wednesday, Alyssa's day off from her salon.

That's all I'd done.

Except wallow in my misery.

The doorbell rang.

I stiffened, feeling every sinew tighten inside me, and closed my eyes.

Shit.

Mickey.

"You're a big girl, Amelia, you've gotta grow the fuck up," my mouth told me.

I was right.

I had to grow up, get up, and go to the door.

I thought moving to Maine was the first step to the new me.

It wasn't.

Walking to the door to face Mickey was.

Shit.

As hard as it was, I uncurled, got off the couch, headed to the door and I did this swiftly. Not because I wanted to get to the door. Not because I was smart enough to go fast in order to get something unpleasant, harrowing and utterly mortifying over and done with as quickly as possible.

Because I didn't want to leave Mickey waiting.

I allowed myself slight relief that I'd at least had a shower and changed clothes that day before I unlocked and opened the door.

I lifted my eyes and put every effort into not wincing when I caught his.

Then I said, "Hey."

"Hey, Amy," he replied gently.

"I'm sorry," I said quickly. "I'm sorry you had to come over here and I wasn't big enough to go to you and apologize. I'm even sorrier I did what I did. I was half-asleep but that's no excuse. You shouldn't have anyone touching you who you don't want touching you. I don't know what came over me. But I do know, and want you to know, I'm really so *very* sorry."

"It isn't that, darlin'," he said quietly. "You're very…"

He trailed off but kept his eyes pinned to mine and I knew in that instant he did it so they wouldn't wander. They wouldn't become assessing.

But his next word and the hesitation said everything.

And it destroyed me.

"Attractive."

I fought back another wince.

"It's just that you don't shit where you live," he went on. "And, babe, you live right across the street and we both got kids."

That was a lie. A kind one. But it was a total lie.

He didn't want me, plain and simple.

I was just his…"attractive" neighbor.

I gave him that because he needed to give it to me and I needed to let him.

"You're right," I agreed.

"You're a good woman, Amelia."

God, that was completely lame.

But worse, I wasn't even that.

"I…I'm…" I shook my head. "I can't say how sorry I am. You're a good neighbor. You're a good guy. You've been so very kind to me. And you've got great kids. Can we," I shrugged, hoping it was nonchalantly, "forget this even happened?"

That's when the grin came but it killed that it wasn't easy.

"Absolutely."

I swallowed before I nodded and said, "Thanks, Mickey." I drew in a breath and let it out finishing, "And again, I'm really sorry."

"Nothin' to apologize for. It didn't happen."

A good man. A kind man.

A man with great kids, all of whom I'd now go out of my way to see extremely rarely.

It was wave from the car or haul my behind into the house if I had the bad fortune to be out when they were out time.

"Right," I said, injecting a firm thread in my voice. "I'd ask you in for a glass of wine but I don't have glasses and I'm kinda in the middle of something."

His grin got easier. "I'd say I appreciate the offer but I don't drink wine and I also got shit to do."

He was lying.

Then again, so was I.

It was over.

This should have caused me relief but instead, it dug deep then curled out long tentacles, the tips spreading acid through every part of me.

"Okay." I started to close the door. "See you around, Mickey."

"Hope so."

That was a lie too.

I pushed my lips up into a smile.

He held his grin as he lifted a hand and turned away.

I didn't wait politely to close and lock the door, I did it immediately.

I turned back to the room. The recessed overhead lights were on, dimmed, but I'd normally never turn on overhead lights. I'd use lamps.

Except I didn't have any.

My feet wanted to take me to my bedroom, the bathroom there, the mirror there.

I didn't let them.

I walked to the kitchen and I did this thinking, *fuck it*.

So when I got to the kitchen, I opened a bottle of wine and poured a healthy portion into a plastic cup.

I took it out to my deck. Since moving in, I'd been out there, not much. When I got to the railing and stopped, I felt the chill coming off the sea and I liked it.

I needed deck furniture.

I needed a to-do list.

I needed a to-do list with a variety of headings, this likely ending up the length of Santa's gift list.

But first, I needed to make a decision.

Stay this low and allow myself to sink lower.

Or get my head out of my ass and pull myself together.

I'd come out to Maine to do the latter, and within a few weeks, ended up kissing my handsome, good guy neighbor, in one fell swoop killing a promising relationship of friendship and camaraderie and turning it into an awkward relationship of avoidance and unease.

I needed to talk this out and to do it, I wanted to call Robin. I wanted to tell her all that had happened and listen to her saying the things she always said to me. How sweet I was. How smart I was. How beautiful I was. How I deserved good things in my life. How I deserved to be treated properly. How I deserved to be cherished and protected and respected.

But I wasn't taking Robin's calls, only exchanging quick texts and emails, which would now be only texts since I'd sold my computer.

And I'd cut myself off from Robin.

I couldn't call Josie or Alyssa because I could tell they were close with Mickey and they'd think I was crazy, stupid, weak and lame for doing what I did.

And in the awkward relationship stakes, they'd side with Mickey. He was *their* friend. I was just a new acquaintance who was grasping onto friendship with all I had because I was so terribly *needy*.

And I knew they would, not only because they'd known me two weeks and him for ages, but because my friends who hadn't defected because I'd lost my mind after Conrad left me had defected when Conrad left me.

No.

I had to figure out what I wanted.

I had to figure out who I was.

I had to create a home.

I had to win back my children.

I had to build a life.

I had to get some self-respect.

I had to stop acting like an idiot, weak and selfish and stupid.

I had to start looking out for me.

I had to stop being so needy. I no longer had a husband to fulfill me. I had lost the children who, simply breathing, gave me all I could need. I had to find something for me that would fill those voids.

And I couldn't sink any lower. I couldn't live another day feeling like I had that day. I couldn't live another week, another month, an eternity, feeling like I had since Conrad told me across the bed we shared, the bed we made our children in, that he was leaving me for another woman.

I'd left my life behind because it was not a good life.

And I'd come to Maine to change that life.

So I had only one choice.

No matter what it took, no matter how much time, no matter that it made me bleed, no matter what it cost me, no matter that it would take everything I had and force me to find more, I had to do what I'd come to Maine to do.

I had to make a home.
I had to heal my family.
I had to find me.
I had to let go of the old.
I had to pull myself together and start anew.

5

OFF AND RUNNING

"*W*e got...a bowl."

Alyssa announced this after she pulled said bowl out of its bag and protective tissue wrap and set it on the edge of the bar of my kitchen.

I stared at the bowl.

Josie, standing by Alyssa, spoke.

"It's a nice bowl."

"We've been shoppin' all day, all over the county, and we bought...a bowl," Alyssa countered.

"Decorating an entire house doesn't happen in a day, Alyssa," Josie informed her.

"I hear that," Alyssa returned. "But you go to fifteen shops in three towns over a span of nine hours, you get more than...a bowl." Then, even though I was wandering to my kitchen dazedly, my eyes still aimed at the bowl, I knew she was addressing me when she stated, "Girl, you got a couch and a bed. You don't even have a TV. You gotta step this shit up."

I stopped in the kitchen and took my eyes from that bowl. A beautiful bowl. No, an astonishingly beautiful bowl; big, wide, squat, the outside a rough slate gray, the inside lip a lustrous blue, so blue it was nearly black cascading into a indigo that was so gorgeous, in all honesty, it took my breath away.

Thus I'd bought the bowl, the only thing I'd bought after fifteen shops in three towns.

I moved my gaze to the sun setting over the sea.

It was still light, the hues shading the clouds baby pinks and buttercreams.

But I'd looked out those windows for two and a half weeks. I knew the shades would shift and change. There would be deep peaches, soft lavenders, blazing orange-yellows, startling fuchsias, cobalt blues...all reflected in the sea.

"Amelia, are you all right?"

I heard Josie's question but I was staring at baby pink and buttercream.

"Babe," I felt a light touch on the small of my back and Alyssa's whispered words close to my ear. "You okay?"

"Syrah," I murmured.

"Say what?" Alyssa asked, not moving from me.

I turned, dislodging her hand and looked between them. "The Syrah glasses from that shop by the cove. All the reds from there. Pinot Noir, Cabernet. I didn't like their white wine glasses and the champagne flutes were abysmal. But I'm getting their red wine glasses."

"Uh...is she sayin' shit you get?" Alyssa muttered to Josie.

"She's talking about those wineglasses at the Glassery," Josie told her.

"She's gonna buy different types of glasses for different types of red wine?" Alyssa asked.

"Shh, Alyssa! I'm sensing an epiphany," Josie replied, lifting a hand and shaking it at Alyssa.

"That armchair, the beaten leather one with the tacks," I kept going as if they didn't speak. "That leather was so supple. Amazing. With the ottoman. Up on the landing." I lifted my hand and pointed across the space at the large landing opposite the kitchen. "And an eighty inch TV, mounted on the wall. Big, so you can see it from anywhere in the room."

"Gotcha. Now roll with it, roll with it, babe," Alyssa encouraged.

I focused on her. "The stoneware from Williams-Sonoma. A mixture of the orange, blue and green with the matching swirling pieces in here and there."

"Loved that shit, keep goin'," Alyssa urged.

I looked to Josie. "Those lamps from that lighting warehouse. Terrible displays but that standing one and the matching table one, in iron, looking like they're made out of loops. The standing one in the sunken area, the one on a table up top. Bringing the two areas together."

"Those were beautiful, Amelia," Josie said softly as I felt a hand again at the small of my back, gently pushing me.

"The daybed at your interior designer's showroom," I kept at it as Josie backed up and Alyssa pushed me toward the front door. "In fact, that whole area. That cream painted iron side table that looked like tiered flowers. The rug that was all pebbly. The fantastic lamp that had that pearly base that looked like it was made from the inside of shells. I want that in my bedroom on the other side of the fireplace. Oh, and those rugs. The memory foam ones. Three of them for the kitchen, sink, work area, stove."

"How much time we got?" Alyssa muttered.

"Some of the specialty shops will be closed, but we can still get to the mall," Josie replied, backing out my front door that she'd opened.

"Toss pillows," I mumbled. "Pottery Barn. Those huge downy ones with those covers in those deep colors."

"Beep the locks, bitch, we're outta here," Alyssa ordered.

I heard the locks on Josie's Cayenne beep.

Alyssa shoved me in the front seat and Josie got behind the wheel while Alyssa hauled herself into the back.

And away we went.

It took another four hours and we closed down the mall, but we got my stoneware, the kitchen rugs, the toss pillows and new towels for all the bathrooms. We also got new bed linens that would match the seating area. Further, we found a new set of bed linens for Olympia's room, a paisley of bright pinks and oranges, her favorite colors.

In fact, the Cayenne was not small, but it was stuffed full by the time we made it home.

And Josie had called her designer, reserved the items I wanted, all I had to do was go in with my credit card and arrange delivery.

The next day, I went out to do that and get the rest (what I could fit in my car, which was a single lamp and the wineglasses) and I ordered what needed to be delivered and set up, including a new TV, DVD player, receiver, Xbox, printer, laptop and desktop PC. I'd even found a table that worked with the chair for the landing, highly distressed wood planks at top and bottom, positioned and cut round, held together by swirling bands of wrought iron.

It was amazing.

The rest of the day I ran load after load in the dishwasher, cleaned and put away the wine glasses, laundered and put away the towels, the same with the linens, making the beds.

The day after that, the deliveries began, the TV mounted, the system set up, the receiver connected to the house's surround sound system (though all the components had to be put on the floor since I didn't have a media cabinet), the computer stuff set up, also on the floor in the back room.

I needed a desk.

I went out and bought a pad of paper.

I came home and made a to-do list.

Several of them.

I also spent hours taping paint chips up on the walls, changing them out, rearranging them, standing back and assessing, moving them to another area with different light.

I was off and running.

———— • ————

I WAS CRAZY.

Even knowing this, I did a U-turn on the quiet street (my fourth) and drove past the church again.

Definitely crazy.

I kept driving.

Then, like they were someone else's hands and feet, mine executed another U-turn and this time I didn't drive past the church.

I parked in front of it.

I looked up at the white building with its stained glass windows and high bell tower.

I'd never had a job. Not once. I didn't even work in a local ice cream shop as a teen just for fun.

I'd gone to college at Stanford where my father went, got a liberal arts degree, studying English Literature because even I could read.

I'd done well. I'd graduated *cum laude*. My father had been *summa*, but as I was a girl, he didn't expect much and he'd been pleased with my standing.

I didn't go to work after. Girls like me didn't work. I had a job I would fulfill, a job my mother had chosen for me: being the wife of a wealthy man, keeping his home, raising his children, continuing my ultimate role of being a Hathaway, and sitting on as many volunteer boards of appropriate charities that would have me.

Before I met Conrad, I'd lived off my trust funds and I had a good time. I absolutely did. I went out in little black dresses with my girlfriends. I drank cosmopolitans. I flirted. I dated.

I did all this appropriately. It wouldn't *do* for me to get a reputation. It wouldn't *do* for me to have the kind of fun an early twenty-something might wish to have.

So I didn't.

When I met Conrad, I'd been at a charity ball, wearing a fabulous evening gown. We'd been standing by a stone balustrade on a back balcony of a fabulous estate. I'd gone out to get away from the oppressive heat of a crush of bodies and he'd gone out to get away from the oppressive company.

For me, him so beautiful in his well-cut tuxedo, his hair slightly over-long, a quiet rebellion I found titillating, it was love at first sight.

He'd told me he'd felt the same thing.

Now I was thinking it was my cleavage and, although they weren't long, they had been shapely, my legs through the slit in my dress.

We'd dated. We'd become involved. We'd gotten engaged. We'd married. And I'd done what I was supposed to do.

I became the wife of a wealthy man, took care of his home, raised his children, and sat on every board of an appropriate charity that would have me.

In other words, I was good for nothing. I couldn't find a job outside of entry level even if I tried.

I knew it.

But I couldn't shop for furniture to fill my eternity. I couldn't bake because there was no one to eat it but me, and I loved doing it, but didn't have a taste for eating it. I couldn't read entire days, weeks, months, years away.

I needed to *do something*.

On that thought, resolutely, I pushed out of the car and walked to the church.

Once inside, I found being in a church in the middle of the day for no reason was not like it was in the movies. A well-meaning pastor didn't show up nearly instantly to sit with you in a pew, listen to your worries and share his wisdom.

Although the church was open, no one was around.

I gave it time then went wandering. Down a side hall and back, I found a small sign that said "Office" with an arrow.

I followed the arrow.

At the end of the hall, a door was opened. I turned to it and stopped in its frame.

It was definitely an office, a relatively nice one, not huge, not tiny, an official-looking desk with a small but beautiful stained glass window behind it, a woman at the side of the desk leaning over it, scribbling on a piece of paper.

"Um…excuse me," I called.

She jerked straight and turned startled eyes to me.

"Sorry to startle you," I murmured.

She shook her head as if to pull herself together and shifted to face me. "Not at all. Is there something I can help you with?"

"I'm looking for the pastor," I told her.

She nodded, her lips curving up slightly. "Reverend Fletcher, my husband, isn't here." She suddenly appeared concerned. "Was he expecting you?"

"No, no," I assured her, shaking my head. "I just popped in. Actually, I'm new to Magdalene and he doesn't even know me."

She rested her thigh against the desk, lost the concerned look, her features moving back to friendly and she asked, "Maybe I can help. Or I can leave a message for him or set an appointment, if you need to speak with him."

I took a step in, looking at the pastor's wife, knowing the woman behind such a man was probably just as good.

Or better.

"I'm thinking perhaps you can help," I said.

Her friendly look became friendlier as she invited, "Try me."

I nodded and strangely found I didn't know what to do with my hands. It was like I was at a job interview, coming there wanting, being found lacking, and I hadn't even presented my résumé.

I clasped my hands in front of me.

"Okay, as I mentioned, I just moved here, however, I'm...well..." I licked my lips, pressed them together and rolled them before I admitted, "independently wealthy."

She nodded, appearing to take that admission in stride, and said, "Welcome to Magdalene."

"Thank you," I mumbled, cleared my throat and continued, "I'm here because I thought...well, it's a church and I figured churches need volunteers and I don't work, or have to work, or really know..." I trailed off then bucked up and started again, "Anyway, I know my way around a computer and I'm really organized..." Again I had to let that hang because I couldn't think of any other skills I had. Therefore, I was forced to finish feebly, "Do you need someone to help with things around here?"

She smiled and I knew the careful, gentle way she did it meant she found my résumé seriously lacking.

"We have a small congregation, it being a small town, but we're lucky because they're also very generous. We're covered when it comes to volunteers," she told me.

I bit my lip and nodded.

"How much time to you have to volunteer?" she asked.

All the time in the world, I thought.

"I'm not really sure," I said. "Maybe two, three days a week for two or three hours?" I suggested, like she could tell me what I was able to offer.

"Are you good with senior citizens?" she asked and I felt my head twitch with surprise at that question.

"I'm sorry?" I asked back.

She straightened away from the desk and took a step toward me, slightly lifting her hands out to her sides before she grasped her opposite elbows in her fingers loosely in front of her. It was a strange stance. Strange because it wasn't cold and shut off but somehow welcoming, as if she was folding something lovingly in her arms.

"We have a nursing home run by very kind people. People who are overworked and underpaid. They do the best they can and they do it because they genuinely like their jobs. Or because for them it's not a job, it's a calling. But there's always a good deal of work and they can't seem to keep some of their staff or volunteers. Probably because they can't pay much and volunteers find the work difficult, sometimes tedious, at times heart wrenching, but all the time constant. They called a few days ago, saying that a volunteer had quit in order to go back to college and another one simply stopped showing. They asked us to keep a look out. I'm going to help until they find some people to do so and do it regularly. But if you have time and don't mind hard work, they could use your help."

I had time but I didn't know if I minded hard work. I'd never had to do any. Growing up, we had actual live-in maids and cooks and the like. The rest of my life, I'd had services take care of everything.

There were times when Conrad and I would move, before I found cleaning services, that I did the cleaning, and right then, new to Magdalene, I'd been doing it at Cliff Blue and I liked it. I didn't want to do it for eight hour days, five days a week, but it wasn't terrible. And it felt nice to accomplish something.

No, it felt nice just to *do* something. Something needed. Something real.

And I'd never thought of senior citizens but I didn't have an aversion to them. All my grandparents had loved me, so had Conrad's. They'd really, *really* loved me. In fact, anytime we were together, I'd always end up sitting with them or off somewhere with them, talking, sharing, joking, laughing. I liked my grandparents and Conrad's a whole lot better than my own parents (and, incidentally, Conrad's) and I'd been devastated as, one by one, we'd lost them all.

Maybe that was something else I had a talent with.

Still, I said to the pastor's wife, "To be honest, I would need to discuss what was needed of me but I can clean. I can cook. I can talk. I can tidy. I can organize. I can look after people. And I like doing all of that. So I'd like the opportunity to discuss it."

Her eyes slightly narrowed, not in an unkind way, but in a speculative one when she said, "I wouldn't like to introduce these people to a volunteer who isn't interested in helping out how they need it, and just as importantly, for the long haul."

"I would agree," I replied. "That's why I think I should know what I'm getting into so I can know if I can give them what they need. However, I do want to find something I enjoy doing, something that's useful, and do it for the long haul."

I drew in breath as I bought time to say the words I needed to say without lying in a house of God.

Then I said, "My children are older. They don't need me as much anymore and my husband and I are divorced so I actually don't have them all the time. I've never worked, but with an empty house, I need something to fill my life. I think I might like it filled with some elderly who are doing me a return favor by keeping me company."

She studied me a moment before she said softly, "I like that you think of it that way."

"I'm glad," I replied then introduced myself. "I'm Amelia Hathaway."

She lifted her hand and started to me, with me meeting her halfway. "Ruth Fletcher."

We clasped hands and her hold was firm and warm. "Lovely meeting you, Ruth."

"And you, Amelia," she replied.

We let go and she motioned to the desk. "How about you give me your telephone number? I'll call Dove House and we'll set up a meeting with Dela Coleman."

"Excellent," I agreed, moving with her to the desk.

I left my number, we said warm good-byes and I went back out to my car.

I didn't dally in front of the church wondering if I'd done the right thing.

I drove away, thinking volunteering at a nursing home could mean anything, and a variety of those things could be unpleasant.

But I wouldn't want to volunteer and demand that I got to read stories or oversee craft time.

I'd want to *volunteer* and do what was needed.

Which could mean cleaning up a number of messes, changing sheets, doing laundry, who knew?

And as I drove home, something strange stole over me. Something strange and new and unbelievable.

Because my mind was filled with all of the things that could be required of a down and dirty volunteer at a nursing home, and all I could think was that I hoped like heck they liked me.

Because I couldn't wait to start.

———— • ————

"Praise be to Jesus!" the woman behind the desk at Dove House called to the ceiling, her hands lifted up there, her plethora of black braids shaking. She dropped her hands and her eyes hit Ruth, sitting across the desk in a chair beside me. "Call up the good Reverend", she jerked her head my way, "and God sends a miracle."

Ruth beamed.

"I'm hardly a miracle," I mumbled.

"'Scuse me?' Dela Coleman, Director of Dove House Retirement Home, asked me. "Did you just say you didn't mind bed pans, changin' sheets, lookin' after dentures, wipin' up half-chewed food, vacuuming, dusting? Not to mention folk who call you other people's names and swear up and down for hours that you're their own child or the girl who stole their boyfriend back in the day and they might come tearin' at you, fingernails bared?"

"I did say that I didn't mind that," I confirmed.

"And did you say you could give me three days a week for three hours a day and I don't have to lay cash on your behind?" she went on.

"I said that as well," I told her.

"Then if you actually show up those three days a week for three hours a day and work and don't take off and become a no show or tell me you're," she lifted her hands and did air quotation marks, "goin' back to college at age fifty-six, then you...are...a...*miracle*."

"People do go back to college at any age," Ruth put in and Dela turned her eyes to her.

"Ruth, honey, I saw the woman at The Shack eatin' omelets and suckin' back coffees with her biddies and she did not have a laptop in front of her, workin' on coursework for her online classes to become a graphic designer," she stated bluntly. "Now, I got old folk attemptin' the great escape every day, and they may be old but they are not stupid. So it's touch and go we shut them down or we gotta go to Wayfarer's to stop them shufflin' down the aisles in their slippers. Loretta is not gonna be a graphic designer. Loretta was tired of cleaning up half-chewed food and havin' Mrs. McMurphy shout at her every time she saw her to keep her hands off her man."

I gave big eyes to my lap, doing this to stop laughing.

"I need to trust you."

I lifted my eyes when I heard Dela say this.

It was quiet, but it was full of meaning.

"You'll note you didn't have to beat off old folk with a stick in order to get in here," she carried on. "They don't wanna be here. You're here for a day, you'll know why. We do our best with this place but this is not home. This is where you go before you die if you can't take care of yourself any longer and you have no one who can take care of you. This is a sad place. We do all we can every day to make it less sad. But that's a losin' battle, Amelia. You gotta be on board with that, know it and keep a smile on your face and your commitment to me, to them, so we can all count on you. Because they need me makin' their stay here a wee bit better, not sittin' down with person after person like you who's got good intentions, and we all appreciate it, but who's gonna turn tail and go the minute it gets too much."

I squared my shoulders and kept looking right in her eyes. "Then I'll ask if you'll give me the evening to think about it. I'll consider what you said. And I won't phone you to set up an orientation if I'm not certain I can make that commitment."

She bobbed her head. "I'd appreciate that."

"And I appreciate you giving me your valuable time and considering me," I returned.

She shook her head at that, her lips curving up. "You know, if every volunteer considered what they were doin' a job they gotta apply for, interview for and earn their right to stay, world'd be a better place."

I didn't disagree so I didn't say anything.

She stood, rounding her desk and reaching out a hand to me. "I hope I get a call, Amelia."

I took her hand and gave it a squeeze. "I hope I have that call in me, Dela."

We let go and Ruth stayed behind to talk to Dela because she actually was starting to work, though she didn't need orientation since I'd learned she filled in a great deal.

I got in my car and drove home.

I got home and didn't fall into deep contemplation about whether or not I had it in me to go the distance as a volunteer in a nursing home.

I went right to my laptop, firing it up and trolling the Internet to get interior design ideas or possibly find pieces online, something I enjoyed doing throughout the evening. Though I didn't buy anything. I liked to touch and see the real thing and if I actually bought something online, it would have to be fabulous.

But I did find a few more shops I could add to the "Visit" subsection of my six page to-do list.

So I did.

———— • ————

THE NEXT MORNING, PROMPTLY AT NINE O'CLOCK, I CALLED DELA Coleman.

I took the job.

———— • ————

I WAS IN MY KITCHEN MAKING CUPCAKES FOR THE RESIDENTS OF DOVE House.

I'd gone through orientation that day. Then I'd gone out to a specialty kitchen shop and bought four cupcake carriers that moms who had little kids in grade school would own so they could cart cakes to school for their kids' birthdays.

And while I was there, I bought all new dishtowels that matched my new kitchen rugs *perfectly*.

And a KitchenAid standing mixer in an exquisite shade of blackberry.

The next day I'd start my tenure as a volunteer at Dove House.

And I was bringing the old folks cupcakes.

I was on batch two when my cell on the counter rang.

I looked from the chocolate frosting I was using to ice the vanilla cakes, saw the display on my phone and stopped moving.

My doorbell rang.

My eyes went there and I saw another body I'd know from anywhere through the stained glass.

On the phone, Dad.

At the door, Mickey.

Why me?

Mom had stopped calling a few days before and I shouldn't be surprised Dad was now up to the plate. Actually, I should be surprised it took a few days for him to make his attempt.

Mickey, however, I had no idea.

I made the difficult decision as to which might cause me the least pain, unsure if it was the correct one, ignored my phone and walked to the door.

I opened it and looked up.

It had not been long since I'd last seen him, just a week, but in that short time he'd somehow become a great deal more beautiful.

"Hey," I greeted, my voice sounding husky.

"Hey, Amy," he greeted back, his voice sounding simply like Mickey.

I looked beyond him to his house then back to him. "Everything okay?"

"Get the kids back soon and was talkin' with Ash," he told me. "She wanted me to ask you for the recipes for the shit you made for the league sale. She wants to try 'em out." He gave me his grin. "Since I don't have your number and all that shit tasted good and I don't mind my daughter tryin' her hand at givin' it to her brother and me, I'm here askin'."

"Of course," I replied, stepping out of the way. "Come in."

He came in. I shut the door. He moved out of my way so I could walk to the kitchen. When I did that, he followed me.

And through this, I found having Mickey, more beautiful than ever and being a better person than me, clearly capable of moving past my idiocy, was the wrong choice in causing the least pain stakes.

In other words, I should have ignored the door and taken the call from my dad.

"I could email them to you or print them out or both," I offered, making it to the kitchen counter where my laptop was, reaching to it, turning it to me and lifting the screen.

"Email," he muttered. "Add your number," he went on. "I'll email mine back."

Having Mickey's number.

Why did the thought of having that, knowing I could never use it for the reasons I'd want to use it, make me wish someone would kill me?

"Gotcha," I replied, sliding the on switch just as my phone, which had quit ringing, started ringing again.

"Need to get that?" Mickey asked.

I glanced at the display.

Mom was not ill-bred enough to call more than once.

Dad was arrogant enough to call repeatedly until you gave him the attention he felt he deserved.

So that was what he was doing.

"No," I answered, eyes to the laptop, waiting for the login screen to come up.

Mickey was silent.

The login screen came up and I typed my password in.

The phone stopped ringing.

"House smells like heaven again, darlin'," he noted.

I kept my attention on the laptop as I used the touchpad to bring up my email. "Cupcakes. I start volunteering at Dove House tomorrow and I'm using them to buy the old folks' affection."

"You're volunteering at Dove House?" he asked.

The disbelieving tone of his voice made me glance at him.

Yes, still amazingly beautiful.

Somebody.

Kill.

Me.

I looked back to the laptop, confirming, "Yes, three days a week, three hours a day."

"Not lookin' for a job."

My gaze went back to him to find that now *his* eyes were on the laptop and his face was impassive.

I knew why.

I'd shared a little bit of me and it was like the rest of me.

Not exactly promising.

"No," I whispered.

He looked to me and there were a lot of things I wanted from his blue eyes, but the emptiness in them right then was not one of them.

Even with that, he said, "Cool you're doin' that. My great-gran went there when her Alzheimer's got bad. They're always needin' help."

"Yes," I agreed.

He tipped his head to my laptop. "Ready for my email?"

In other words, let's get on with this so I can do the errand my beloved daughter wanted me to do and get the heck out of here.

"Ready," I told him.

He gave it to me. I typed it in then attached the recipe files and added a subject and my cell phone number in the message space.

All that done, I hit SEND.

"It's away," I said, lifting my eyes to his to see his aimed at my hips.

At my words, they cut to mine and he asked, "You had dinner?"

I stared, a little surprised that I hadn't thought of dinner and it was probably close to eight o'clock.

I made myself smile. "I'm having cupcake batter for dinner."

He stared in my eyes for long moments before he muttered, "Right," like he wanted to say more, but he didn't.

My phone rang again.

I looked to it and it was again my father. Seeing that made my neck muscles tighten, knowing he was likely getting angry and with every call he'd get angrier and more determined to find ways to share that anger with me.

"See you're not tight with your dad," Mickey noted and I tore my eyes from my phone to look at him.

"We have…issues," I admitted.

"Shame," he muttered.

"Yes," I concurred. "Are you…" I hesitated to ask, to draw his visit out, to request information that was not mine to have, then my mouth went for it, "Close with your folks?"

"Absolutely."

He answered and it was firm but it invited no further conversation.

"You're lucky," I mumbled, looking back down to my laptop.

"Absolutely," he repeated, just as firmly.

I nodded to my laptop before looking to him. "Do you want a cupcake before you go?"

His mouth tightened and I watched it do this with an unhealthy level of fascination.

I did this because it had not escaped me he had nice lips, a full lower one, captivating creases running along both the top and bottom, all this highlighted by alluring whiskers and framed by hollowed cheeks under very cut cheekbones and his squared off jaw.

Oddly, that mouth tightened in anger made it even more striking than it was normally.

Even so, I couldn't imagine why my thinly veiled attempt to give him the opportunity to escape me would cause him to feel that anger.

He untightened his mouth to ask, "Where'd you come from?"

My head twitched at his question. "I'm sorry?"

"Before Magdalene," he explained.

"La Jolla. In California," I answered.

"Know where it is, Amelia."

Amelia.

Not *Amy.*

He was angry.

Why was he angry?

"Your folks back there?" he asked.

"Yes," I told him. "I grew up there. Conrad took positions in practices in Boston and Lexington, but we landed back home before, well", I tipped my head to the side, "here."

"Practices?" he queried.

"He's a neurosurgeon," I said.

And again, Mickey's mouth tightened.

"Your family?" I asked to change the subject to something that might not make him angry. "You said they sold you their—"

"Florida," he cut me off, answering my question before I completely got it out, telling me something he told me already. Then he carried on, "Got three brothers. One in Boston, the oldest, moved the family business there. Second oldest is in Bar Harbor, he runs a subsidiary. Youngest, Dylan, lives in Vermont. He's a professor at a college."

"Oh," I murmured.

"My great-granddad was a fisherman," Mickey kept going, as usual, letting the information about him flow and doing it openly. "My granddad took his business and built it. Dad built it bigger. Big enough, he could afford a house in this neighborhood to put his woman in and raise his sons in. Big enough, that business outgrew Magdalene and Sean had to move it to Boston."

"Sean is the oldest?" I asked.

He nodded. "Sean, then Frank, then me, then Dylan."

Four Donovan brothers.

If they were half as magnificent as Mickey, it was good they didn't live in Magdalene or the entirety of the female population would have problems, just like me.

"Your dad still work?" he asked and I felt my neck get tighter.

"Yes," I told him. "He probably won't retire until Auden comes of age and he can hand over the business direct to family." This was true, and Dad had shared this with my son, but the idea of it terrified me. I obviously didn't tell this to Mickey. Instead, I explained, "My brother took his own path, lives in Santa Barbara, he's an attorney."

His mouth got hard again but he still moved it.

"What's your dad do?"

I didn't want to answer.

In fact, I wasn't really certain why he asked, he couldn't care.

In fact, I was *completely* uncertain why he was still there when I couldn't imagine that he wanted to be.

But he frequently laid it out for me and maybe this was his attempt at keeping things friendly. Know thy neighbor or something like that.

So even if I didn't want to, I answered anyway.

"He's CEO of Calway Petroleum, the family company."

His eyes flared then shut down on his, "Jesus."

This was not a surprising response. Unless, until recently, he'd lived his life on Mars, he'd know Calway Petroleum. There were Calway stations across America (and Canada, and *the world*).

There wasn't one in Magdalene but only because I noted there were only two gas stations in the whole town.

But both neighboring towns had a Calway.

My great-grandfather was a Texan. My great-grandfather had a ranch and was already scary-wealthy when he struck oil. He, then my grandfather and then my father, brilliantly, fiendishly, callously and determinedly kept the business thriving even after my great-grandfather's vast fields of proverbial gold dried up.

Now the company was deeply involved in offshore drilling.

My mother's family was in shipping, like big-time, Onassis-style shipping.

I just hoped Mickey didn't ask about her.

His eyes drifted beyond me to the wall of windows beyond which was a multi-million dollar view to the sea.

"Don't gotta work," he muttered.

I didn't reply because I knew he knew precisely why I had that multi-million dollar view, could sell off all my stuff and replace it nearly immediately and had plenty of time to volunteer at a nursing home.

I also knew he thought this was no good.

He looked back to me and proved that by declaring abruptly, "I'll pass on the cupcake, Amelia."

"Okay, Mickey," I said quietly.

"Thanks for the recipes," he replied. "Ash'll love 'em."

I nodded.

He lifted a hand and dropped it. "You can get on with what you're doin'. I'll see myself out."

I was sure he would.

"Okay," I said. "Good to see you, though."

"Yeah. You too," he murmured distractedly while turning.

I watched him move through my house, going right to the door.

He gave me his eyes before he closed it behind him, saying, "Later, Amelia."

"Later, Mickey," I returned.

He nodded, shut my door and disappeared.

I closed my eyes.

My phone rang.

I opened my eyes, grabbed my phone and turned off the ringer.

Then, because I had no choice, or none that were healthy for me, I went back to my cupcakes.

———— • ————

I HAD NO IDEA IF MICKEY GOT MY EMAIL.

I just knew he didn't reply as he said he would, sharing his number.

And I told myself that was okay with me.

But I lied.

6

NEITHER REPLIED

*a*t three-thirty the Friday my children were to come back to me, I was ready.

Mickey's words about how his ex-wife let their kids get away with anything because she was making up for her weaknesses had not been lost on me.

They'd had their first visit to settle in. Whether they did or didn't, that was their choice (though, since they were hardly there, I knew they didn't).

Now it was time to share that this was their home, I was their mother, we were a family and things were going to be a certain way.

So when I stood in the open front door watching the red Civic roll up, I was prepared to face my children and forge ahead with the healing.

The approach to the house went exactly the same way as the first one did. The kids grabbing their bags. Me greeting them. Pippa not looking at me. Auden barely paying me mind.

I let them in and closed the door behind us.

Although both of them stared with surprise into the very changed great room, they did this as they headed straight to their rooms.

I drew in courage on a deep breath and crossed my arms on the exhale.

"Hang on a second, kiddos," I called.

They stopped and turned to me almost at the mouth to the hall.

I looked between them and laid it out as I'd practiced.

"Okay, just to say, if you have plans this evening with your friends, I don't want to make you change those plans at the last minute. So I'll allow you to go out if that's what you intend to do."

Auden's lip curled. Olympia's face grew hard and she looked to the floor.

"Tomorrow," I forged on, "we're having a family dinner. If you have plans through that, you need to change them. You may do what you wish during the day and after dinner, but we're eating together. Now I'll say that, but I'll also say that eventually I'd like to meet your new friends, so I'd like you to think on having them around. And I'll also say that I don't get a lot of time with you. I miss you when you're gone. I think about you all the time. So when I do have you, I'd like to *have* you. That means after this weekend, I'll ask you to plan to be with me when you're with me and not make arrangements to be out doing something else."

That got me Pippa's eyes, which were slits, and Auden glared at me.

"If it's something special or something you don't want to miss," I said softy. "Obviously, I'll want you to do it. But if it's not, I want you to be with me."

Pippa hitched a hip, threw out a foot slightly and crossed her arms on her chest, looking to the sectional.

Auden continued glaring at me.

"On Sunday," I kept going, "I'm going to an estate auction." I threw an arm out toward the living room. "As I texted you and now you can see, I sold most of our old stuff to raise money for the town's junior boxing league. Fresh town for me, fresh start in a lot of ways, including, I hope, with you two."

I paused, watching them closely, but neither of them gave me anything, though Pippa did aim her eyes to the sea.

So I had no choice but to keep at it.

"I'm going with a new friend of mine, Josie. She's very sweet. I'd like you to meet her. I've never been to an auction but it might be fun. And there's a lot to do to make this house a home and I'd be very, *very* happy if you'd participate in that with me."

Neither of them said anything.

I drew in another breath and powered ahead.

"I've unpacked your rooms. I've also gone through your things. This weekend, I'd like you to go through the piles I've made of stuff you might no longer be able to use or want. If you can't use it or don't want it, it can be put to good use elsewhere. But if you want it, I want you to have it. So just sort that for me, putting away what you want to keep, putting what you don't in one of the extra rooms, and I'll deal with it for you. And Pippa," I called. Her eyes came to me and I smiled at my baby girl. "I have a surprise for you in your room. I hope you like it."

She said nothing.

I had nothing more to say.

My children and I stood, fifteen feet between us, thousands of miles separating us, and we did this silently.

Finally, Auden spoke, "Are you done?"

His words and tone cut deep and I felt the bleed.

"Yes," I replied. "Except to say, I made cinnamon oatmeal cookies. They're in the tin on the counter. You can help yourself."

Auden ignored that, even though those were particular favorites of his, and instead told me, "We both got plans."

I licked my lips and pressed them together as I nodded.

"So, if you're done with this, can we do that?" he asked nastily.

"As I said, honey, you can. But I want you home for dinner tomorrow night," I told him.

"Whatever," he muttered, starting to turn, Pippa moving with him.

"Not whatever," I called and did it firmly, getting their attention again. "I mean that, kids. I want you home tomorrow night for dinner."

"We gotta, we'll be here," Auden snapped.

It wasn't much, but I'd take it.

I looked to Pippa.

"Sweets?" I asked.

"Gotta do it, I'll do it," she mumbled.

That was the same, I'd still take it.

"Thank you," I murmured.

Pippa looked to her brother and rolled her eyes.

Auden looked to his sister and shook his head.

They both then delayed no further and disappeared down the hall.

Not long after, they reappeared.

But only so they could leave.

THE NEXT NIGHT, I MADE DINNER, ONE OF THEIR FAVORITES, PRIME ROAST
of beef with my fresh-made horseradish sauce, scalloped potatoes, hari-
cots verts and homemade rolls. I topped all this with one of Olympia's
favorites, my decadently moist carrot cake with its thick cream cheese
frosting.

I had plenty of time to do this considering both my children left very
early for a teenage Saturday and didn't reappear until they arrived,
precisely timed, thus meticulously planned, so neither of them had to be
with me alone, at six o'clock.

Since I hadn't yet replaced the dining room table, we ate off my new
dishes, sitting on the sectional.

Conversation was stilted, mostly muttered complaints that our dining
room table was gone as was an end table so they had to lean to the floor
to grab their drinks.

They still sat with me and I took that, telling myself it was progress,
minor progress but at least it was something.

After, when I'd hoped they'd lounge on the sectional with me and
watch a movie on our new, huge, expensive, all-the-bells-and-whistles
TV, they in unison took their plates to the sink and began to head to their
rooms.

"Kids," I called, slowing their progress but not stopping it entirely. "I
cooked," I carried on. "I think it's fair you clean."

"We'll do it later," Auden replied before being swallowed by the darkness of the hall.

Pippa said nothing, just disappeared.

I fought the urge to refill my wineglass.

Instead, I got a book and didn't read. I just sat on my sectional, the
book held open in front of me, and waited for them to come out and
again leave the house.

They didn't.

This surprised me.

Surprised me and made me hope.

If they were going to stay, maybe I could convince them to do it with
me while watching a movie. I'd take surly and I'd endure it, telling myself
it wouldn't be hard since I'd take it while all our attention was diverted

with a movie.

In order to make this attempt, I put my book aside, climbed the stairs from the sunken living room and headed down the hall.

Their doors were open. Their lights were on.

And I wasn't even at the door to Pippa's room before I heard her talking.

At her tone, which was snide, I stopped and listened.

"...have to wear sunglasses, this comforter is *so* bright and *so* butt ugly. I cannot *imagine* why she dumped my other stuff and got me *this*. I *hate* it. She's *so incredibly crazy*."

My feet moving for me, taking me in the opposite direction to where I wanted to go, they positioned me in the frame of her door.

My beautiful little girl, growing into a big one, noticed the movement there, her head jerked my way, and her eyes, *my* eyes, came right to me.

They rounded in horror.

They melted in dismay.

Then they instantly hardened in ire.

"Listen much?" she snapped.

"Don't forget the dishes, baby," I whispered.

She glared.

I reached in, caught the handle, and closed the door.

My innards tattered and dripping, my feet moved me to my son's room and he, too, was talking.

I didn't bother to eavesdrop. I leaned a shoulder against the doorframe and watched him pace his room. His back and alternately side my way, he didn't notice me.

"...*everything*, Dad, she sold *everything*. Our whole house, she sold *all of it*. Says she did it for *charity*. Totally crawling up the butts of *everybody in town*. Probably because she wants the town not to think she's a complete whackjob. But she did it selling *our whole house* for some freaking *junior boxing league*. Like she gives a crap about junior boxing. She doesn't give a crap about *anything*, and obviously not our *home* because she got rid of *everything*."

He jumped when he caught my movement in his peripheral vision as I leaned forward and grabbed his door handle.

His eyes came to me, his face paled and went slack, and I held his gaze, mine watery, as I closed his door.

I went directly to my room and closed mine.

Then I went right to my fabulous daybed that sat on its thick pebbled rug by my gorgeous freestanding fireplace and I sat on it, back to the side, knees to my chest, arms around my calves, eyes across the room to the sun setting on the sea.

My children hated me.

They *hated* me.

It took everything I had, absolutely everything, but when I burst out crying, I did it silently.

———— • ————

THE NEXT MORNING, I WOKE UP TO DIRTY DISHES.

I made coffee, cleaned them, poured a cup of java, then went back to my room, showered and got ready to face the day.

I came out and went down the opposite hall.

I knocked loudly on Pippa's door, didn't open it and called through it, "I need you up, Olympia. In the kitchen. I want a word. Now."

I walked down and did the same with Auden.

I went to the kitchen, prepared a travel mug and waited.

Sleepy, in their pajamas, looking cute and young and beautiful, my children came out and positioned themselves cautiously opposite the bar to me.

Neither of them met my eyes.

In their words, "whatever."

"As it's doubtful you wish to go to the auction with Josie and me, and I need to leave imminently, I'll be doing that. Since I won't be home, and you've made it clear neither of you wish to be here, there's no reason for you to remain here while I'm gone. You may go home to your dad's."

Both their eyes widened and Pippa looked to Auden but Auden turned his wary gaze to me.

"Before you go, I'd like you to tidy your rooms, make your beds and please go through those piles as I asked. If you don't, I'll assume you don't want any of those things and I'll donate them to charity." I looked to my daughter. "And if you truly don't like your new bedclothes, your old ones are in the first guest bedroom. Just grab them and put them in your room. I'll switch them out and deal with the new."

I drew in breath, went to the counter, shoved my phone in my purse and hooked it over my shoulder.

As I did this, neither of my kids said anything.

I moved beyond the counter and stopped, turning back to them.

"I made grave mistakes," I whispered and watched both their bodies lock. "I know this. I've admitted it. I've come here not to continue to do that but to get my family back. You're my children and I love you. I love you more than anything. I love you more than my own life. I failed you and I intend to rectify that. I understand your anger. I don't blame you for having it. All I ask is that you give me a chance. One last chance to show you that I'm sorry, to give you back the mom you love. The mom you want to be a part of your life. Because there is nothing in mine I want more than having you in it."

They said nothing.

I took that too with a nod and finished it.

"I love you, honeys. Have a good day, take the cookies with you and I'll see you in a month."

And with that, I left.

———————•———————

ALTHOUGH JOSIE KINDLY DIDN'T COMMENT ON THE FACT I ARRIVED AT THE auction without my children, it was still awkward.

But it was not the worst part of my day.

That had already happened.

In a different frame of mind, I would have enjoyed the auction.

Regardless of the fact that I was barely capable of functioning, I still found and bought a fabulous set of furniture—including a high-button-backed, leather rolling chair and a baronial desk—that would be perfect for the back room.

Not only that, I found a whimsical bedroom set that I bought for the guest bedroom. I'd need mattresses, but I envisioned a fanciful, beachy room that would give any guests I might eventually have (though few and far between, the only prospect being my brother and his family, only three of the four of them I'd actually want in my home) a tranquil, but exceedingly pretty, place to call their home away from home.

I arrived back at Cliff Blue at just after three, a couple of hours before my kids were supposed to leave me.

I also arrived back at an empty house.

They'd left the cookies.

They hadn't gone through their piles of stuff.

But Olympia had not put her old bed things back in her room.

I texted them both to make certain they were good with me donating their things and added on Pippa's that she wanted to keep her new linens.

Neither replied.

7

PICKING UP THE PIECES

*T*he next evening, I sat in my car and stared at the cineplex.

I did this concentrating.

And what I was concentrating on was not on the disastrous visit I'd had with my children that weekend.

No, I was concentrating on the fact that the auction furniture I bought would be delivered the next day and thus I could turn my mind to creating a tranquil, beachy, fanciful room that would delight the dearth of guests I would probably not be having.

I was also concentrating on my triumph that day at Dove House when I did not freak way the heck out during mealtime when Mrs. McMurphy clamped my wrist in her clawed hand, yanked me to her and looked at me with clear, light blue eyes, hissing, "I know you're a spy." Then she'd let me go only to drag a finger across her neck threateningly and declare, "I'm telling General Patton."

Further, I was concentrating on the fact that right then, instead of going out and buying a teal Thunderbird with white upholstery and driving it to the nearest cliff where I would then drive right off it— considering I'd made such a mess of my own life, that was the only option open to me—I was going to a movie.

By myself.

I'd never done anything by myself, except shopping. I'd not gone to a meal by myself. I'd never even gone to a spa for a facial by myself.

When I lost Conrad and all my other friends, Robin had come with me.

On this thought, my phone rang.

I shouldn't have pulled it out of my purse. I knew who was calling.

Though, it could be Josie and Alyssa. It seemed they actually liked me and they definitely liked decorating.

But when I looked at the display, I saw I was right.

It said "Dad."

I stared at it for a long time. Long enough for it to quit ringing. Long enough for it to bing in order to tell me I had a missed call.

Then, to my surprise, it binged again to tell me I had a voicemail.

New.

He hadn't yet left a voicemail.

Shit.

That was when I did something else I shouldn't do.

I activated my phone, went to voicemail and listened to it.

"Amelia, *call me*," Dad bit out icily.

"Shit," I whispered, dropping the phone but moving my finger over the screen, going to my text messages.

Not that I was going to text my father. I knew he was already losing his mind, frosting over, hatching plans to eviscerate me. He did not *text*. If I tried to text, he'd likely pay millions of dollars to some scientific genius to build snow bombs, have them directed at my house and bury me under an avalanche of chill.

No, I went to Robin's text string and opened it.

I'd texted her last and I'd done it two weeks ago.

But my text reply had been two days after she'd sent hers.

She was giving up on me.

I told myself this was what I wanted. I needed relationships that were healthy. If nothing else, my recent visit with my kids told me I could not veer from that path.

But I missed my friend.

I rested my hand with the phone against my thigh and dropped my forehead to the steering wheel.

Josie and Alyssa were sweet. Josie and Alyssa both made it clear they liked me. Josie and Alyssa also had made it clear that they were there to listen should I need to share.

But I couldn't share, not that, not the ugliness that I'd perpetrated against my family. I wanted them to keep liking me, not think I was the whackjob my son called me.

No, right then I needed someone who *knew* me. Who *got* me. Who understood where I'd been and where I was going.

Robin understood the first part.

The last, I wasn't sure she had that in her.

But right then, I was no longer sure I shouldn't give her the chance to try.

And right then what I was worried about was that the longer I didn't offer her that opportunity, the less likelihood I'd learn she had it in her to give it to me.

More, I had it in me to give what I could back.

"One day at a time," I whispered to the steering wheel. "One challenge at a time. One thing at a time. Keep moving, Amy."

I blinked at the steering wheel and abruptly sat straight.

I'd never called myself Amy because no one had ever called me Amy.

Until now.

"Oh God, now I'm torturing myself with absurdities," I snapped at the windshield.

What lay beyond came into focus and I remembered I was challenging myself to go see a movie. To keep building a life. To learn to be comfortable with me.

Sitting in my car, doubting myself while talking to myself meant I was failing.

Resolutely, I turned the ringer off on my phone, threw it into my purse, grabbed my bag and got out of my car.

I was in my seat in the theater when I realized none of that was hard.

In fact, it was not only easy, it was *great*.

Sure, asking for one ticket was a little tough.

But then I got to buy whatever concessions I wanted, knowing I didn't have to share. So I got myself a vat of popcorn, a box of Milk Duds and a Diet Coke so big it could quench the thirst of an army.

And when I hit the theater, I found that I didn't have to take anyone's preferences but my own into account when selecting a seat.

I didn't have to sit in the middle of the row in the middle of the theater because Auden liked close but Olympia liked far. I also didn't have to sit way at the back, where Robin demanded we sit because she enjoyed people watching more than movie watching.

I got to sit where *I* wanted to sit, behind the handicapped railings, knowing no one would sit in front of me and I could rest my feet on the railing without bothering anyone.

Okay, so it was off to the side.

But it was awesome.

I sipped. I munched. I bested nearly all the trivia that flashed on the screen and freely judged (mentally) the ridiculous ads, enjoying myself immensely, looking forward to losing myself in a movie, finding something I actually liked to do spending time with just me.

Then it happened.

The lights were already lowered, the trailers coming on, and I saw movement at the opposite entrance to where I was sitting.

I glanced that way, expecting only to glance, but I didn't just glance.

This was because the latecomers were a couple.

And one half of that couple was Mickey.

My stomach got tight, my muscles contracted, and I stared as he walked in, his arm flung around the shoulders of a very tall, very buxom, *very* pretty redhead who looked not one thing like me.

The lights were dim, I couldn't study her to get a lock on her age, but many things were clear.

She was way taller than me.

She had way better hair than me.

She was way better dressed than I'd ever be.

She was way, *way* prettier than me.

And, smiling up at a smiling-at-her Mickey, the biggest hit of all…

She was out on a date with Mickey.

I jerked my eyes to the screen, feeling like throwing up and hoping, hoping, *hoping* that he would not see me all alone at a cinema to watch a movie.

Not long after, the theater went dark and I waited. I actually counted the seconds.

When I figured the time was right, I carefully, quietly set my snacks on the floor (even though the sound system could drown out an exploding bomb). I grabbed my purse then bent double (even though the theater wasn't close to full and I wasn't obstructing anyone's view, I still made myself as miniscule as I could) and I dashed to the stairs and around, running down the side hall and out of the theater.

I forced myself to slow to a walk, a swift one, one that took me through the lobby, out of the cineplex and directly to my car as quickly as I could get there.

I got in.

I dumped my purse in the passenger seat.

I started up.

And I got the fuck out of there.

I drove home and I shouldn't have. I should have breathed deep. I should have gathered my thoughts. I should have calmed myself.

I didn't.

But by some miracle, I made it home safely.

And when I got home, I didn't want to. I'd been avoiding it. The last thing I wanted to do considering the fragility that was me was *that*.

But as had become their wont, my feet decided for me.

So I found myself in my bathroom, flipping on the lights and positioning myself in front of my mirror.

I looked at myself. I had to. I couldn't avoid it.

But I did it being absolutely certain I didn't actually *see* me.

Right then, my eyes refused not to take me in.

And it was worse than I expected it to be.

Not worse than it could be. My mother had drilled a regime into me since my fourteenth birthday, when I was allowed to wear light makeup.

So I cleansed. I moisturized (daily and nightly). I exfoliated, and twice a week did this deeply prior to slapping on a facial.

But other than that...I didn't look after me.

My shining, brunette hair had strands of gray. Silvery-gray that may, when it took over, be stunning.

Right then, it made me look like I didn't care.

I had lines at my forehead, but not many.

But my skin was sallow. My cheeks were sunken. My eyes looked huge and not in a good way. My makeup was there, but it was uninspired, doing absolutely nothing for me.

And I already knew my clothes were conservative, high-quality and older than my years. I wasn't a spry twenty-something and they were *still* older than my years.

I looked past it.

I looked like I gave not...one...*shit*.

Because I didn't.

I had not gone for a proper facial since moving to Magdalene. I had not had a manicure or a pedicure. I had not had my hair cut even before I'd moved to Magdalene. And I'd never dyed it, the gray started coming in when Conrad left me (and, incidentally, I blamed each strand on him regardless of the fact that, at my age, it was time) and I'd left it at that.

Robin had said things, cautiously, sensitively. Mother had said them too, not cautiously or sensitively.

I'd acted like they didn't even speak.

I'd let myself go.

Mickey clearly had different tastes, taller, possibly younger, trendily dressed, beautiful red hair (though his woman had big bosoms and I did too but that was the only thing we shared).

But staring at the disaster that was me, it was no wonder Jake Spear didn't even allow his eyes to wander to my hair. And it was no wonder that boxer in his gym paid no mind to me.

I was no longer young.

"But I'm not dead yet," I whispered to my reflection.

On that, I shrugged my purse off my shoulder so it fell to the counter. I dug my phone out. And I made the call I needed to make.

"Hello, Amelia, how's your evening?" Josie answered.

"I need lunch."

There was a heavy pause before, "Sorry?"

"You. Me. Alyssa. Lunch tomorrow. Emergency," was all I could force out, my eyes still glued to the mirror.

"Are you okay?" she asked, concern heavy in her tone.

"No. No, I am *far* from okay," I told her.

"Do you need me to come over now?" she went on.

"Lunch," it came out as a squeak. I was losing it. I could feel it happening. "Tomorrow. Can you call Alyssa?" I closed my eyes tight, fighting my thoughts telling me I was being dramatic, selfish, thoughtless, demanding, *weak*. Telling myself these were good women, they'd get it. If I let them, they'd get *me*. I opened my eyes, whispering, "Please, Josie."

"Anything, Amelia. Anything you need," Josie whispered back. Yes, a good woman. "I'll call Alyssa. Are you going to be okay until then?"

"Yes." It came out hoarse. I cleared my throat. "Yes. I'll be okay."

"Okay," she said as if she didn't believe me. "I'll text you with where and when."

"Okay, Josie," I replied.

"You sure you're going to be okay?"

No.

But I was sure I had to keep trying.

At least for a little while.

"Yes, I will be and Josie...?"

"Yes?"

"Thank you," I said softly.

"As I said, anytime, Amelia. Anything."

Yes, I so very much liked her.

I just hoped she would keep liking me.

"See you at lunch tomorrow," she continued.

"See you at lunch, Josie."

We said our good-byes and rang off.

Then I went directly to the garage and got some boxes, went to the kitchen and got the packing tape and went back to my bathroom.

Unless they were absolutely necessary to remain clothed for the next two days, I boxed up everything.

Everything.

Clothes. Shoes. Belts. Handbags.

I also tossed in all my makeup.

I dragged it all to the garage, took a shower, got into the only nightgown I'd left for me and got into bed.

It was early.

It took forever to fall asleep.

But I finally did it and wished I didn't.

Because when I did, I dreamed of watching Mickey marry a tall, beautiful redhead who was not me.

———— • ————

Rushing out the door before the furniture truck even pulled away after they made their deliveries the next morning, I drove hell on wheels into Magdalene.

I parked on Cross Street.

I hoofed it to Weatherby's Diner.

I immediately spied Josie and Alyssa sitting in a booth, ready for me. I knew this because they were seated on the same side and three glasses of ice water were in front of them.

And I ignored their looks of shock when they saw me walk in, makeup-less, hair pulled back in a ponytail and I knew looking pale and frantic.

I slid in across from them as Alyssa breathed, "Oh my God, honey, you look like—"

"I need a makeover," I announced.

Alyssa clamped her mouth shut.

They stared at me.

Then I jumped when suddenly Josie went flying out the side of the booth.

This was because Alyssa shoved her out.

Josie righted herself and whirled, eyes narrow, face full of fury, tone frosty. "What *on earth?*"

Alyssa, who didn't hesitate in exiting the booth she'd shoved Josie out of, waved in her face.

"No time," she muttered then looked to the long counter. "Marjorie. Three patty melts. I'll send someone from the salon to pick them up in twenty."

"I don't want a patty melt," Josie snapped.

Alyssa didn't look at her. "Two patty melts and a Reuben."

Josie got close to her. "I don't want a Reuben. I want a Cobb salad."

"Oh for ef's sake!" Alyssa clipped. "Two patty melts and a Cobb salad."

Through this, I got out of the booth too and added tentatively, "I actually wanted a chicken Caesar."

Alyssa threw up her hands but asked a waitress who was apparently named Marjorie. "Got that?"

"Got it, babe," Marjorie replied.

"And three Diet Cokes," Alyssa kept going, doing this grabbing my hand and beginning to drag me to the door.

We were out on the sidewalk and Alyssa was tugging me down it in the direction of her salon, Maude's House of Beauty (Alyssa was a hairdresser who owned her own place, this, plus Josie having a career in the fashion world, why I enlisted their support) when Josie demanded, "Can you explain why you're acting like a lunatic?"

Alyssa stopped abruptly, causing me to crash into her, but she didn't notice me.

She had eyes only for Josie.

"'Cause our girl here is beautiful," she declared.

I drew in an audible breath.

But she was not finished.

"But she's broken."

I stared at her profile and held that breath.

Alyssa went on, "I don't know why. I just know that shit is real. And every girl knows a makeover is the start of pickin' up the pieces. And I'm all over that."

She turned to me and it was then I noticed my vision had gone misty.

"You wanna share, you sock it to me," she offered. "You don't wanna give it, it's all yours to keep. But I'm doin' this and so is Josie. I get your hair. Josie gets your makeup. And both of us get your clothes."

Suddenly, she lifted up a hand sharply, palm out to Josie and turned her eyes that way.

She did this still speaking.

"I know I walk on the skank side. I like it. It's me. My baby likes it. Keeps him just like I want him to be. But I know better with our Amelia. You get the class but me havin' my part doesn't mean I'm bringin' the trash. I'm bringin' the *va-va-va-voom* 'cause with this girl's tits and ass, she can be all over *va-va-va-voom*." She turned back to me. "'Cept you're takin' off too much weight. Sister, you gotta *eat*."

And with that and not another word, she carried on charging toward Maude's House of Beauty, hauling me with her.

I was in her chair with a robe on before I knew what was happening and Alyssa wasn't done bossing.

She shoved a Surface in Josie's hands and declared, "I got a one-thirty. This doesn't leave much time but I'm gonna get her cookin'. You're gonna be surfin'. Use the salon's Wi-Fi. Password's written on a piece of paper in my top drawer. Show her what you find. Show me. Email her links.

Anything we wanna pick up at a store, we're goin' tomorrow." She curled her hand around my shoulder. "Anything you wanna buy, babe, you get home, open those links and go crazy. Now!" she cried excitedly. "I gotta go brew up some magic. I'll be back."

And she was off.

I sat in my salon robe in her salon chair staring after her.

Slowly, my eyes drifted to Josie.

She was standing beside my chair, forgotten Surface held in her hands, her eyes where Alyssa used to be.

"If you have other things—" I began.

I stopped when her eyes cut to me.

"There is nothing right now more important than what you need."

My vision again went misty.

"This is—" I started again.

"You picking up the pieces," she finished for me. "And this is us, at your side, helping."

I felt the tear slide down my cheek.

"I'm being selfish," I whispered.

Her head tipped to the side, her eyes filling with confusion. "How's that?"

"You both dropping everything so I can get a new hairstyle," I explained and shook my head. "That's me. Part of me at least. Selfish."

"May I ask, if you met me and I behaved like you've behaved since I met you, and suddenly I phoned you, making it clear you needed me, how you would feel?"

Oh God.

"Honored that you asked me," I said quietly.

"Indeed," she replied firmly.

"I've made a mess of my life," I shared.

"Join the club, Amelia," she returned instantly.

I blinked and another tear escaped down my cheek.

What was she talking about?

She was *gorgeous*. She was the most fashionable woman I'd ever seen. She was *always* turned out *perfectly*. She had Jake, who was nice and sweet and almost as handsome as Mickey and he was so into her, it wasn't even funny. Her son was adopted, but he clearly adored her beyond reason. And Jake's other two kids loved her the same way.

She had everything.

How was her life a mess?

"I didn't always have Jake and all that he brought to me," she announced, as if hearing my thoughts. "I didn't always have Conner and Amber and Ethan. I didn't always have Alyssa and Junior. I used to have next to nothing. Then," she leaned into me, her eyes holding mine, "with a good deal of help, at long last, and when I say that, I mean for me it lasted *decades*, I picked up the pieces." She reached out and grabbed my hand. "You'll note, in saying that, when I did, I did *not* do it alone."

Another tear chased down my cheek.

Josie watched it then looked back at me.

"Will you give me the honor of letting me help you not go it alone?"

Without the ability to do anything else, I nodded.

She squeezed my hand.

"Thank you," she whispered.

"Don't mention it," I whispered back, the only way I'd be able to speak.

She started chuckling.

"Back!" Alyssa cried, and Josie and I both jumped, Josie straightening away from me, my eyes going to Alyssa in the mirror. "Right, bringing you back to your original beauty *with* threads of blonde to make it exciting, just pieces throughout this mass of gorgeousness," she stated, dumping the two bowls she had on the counter in front of me and gently pulling the ponytail holder out, my hair falling around my shoulders. "But around your face", she flipped my hair forward, over my shoulders, then twitched some locks by my temples, "more blonde to highlight your pretty face. Sound good?"

I had no idea. I'd never had highlights. My mom thought highlights were common.

I didn't care.

Alyssa could do anything.

Just as long as she helped me to a new me.

"Sounds *great*," I said softly.

She smiled brightly at my reflection in the mirror, straightened from me and shouted to the room at large, "Ruby! We got a mission and we need to sustain that mission so we gotta get our order from Weatherby's. I'll owe you a bottle of tequila, you go pick it up. Tell 'em to put it on the salon account."

"The salon has an account?" a female voice I suspected was Ruby called back.

At this point, Alyssa was pulling on plastic gloves. "Tell 'em to make one."

"You offer tequila, I expect Patrón," the unseen Ruby declared.

"Whatever. Hoof it. My bitches are hungry," Alyssa returned, reaching to open a drawer filled with foils.

"On it," Ruby replied.

Alyssa started sectioning off my hair.

"What do you think of these?" Josie asked and I turned my eyes to the Surface screen.

There was a pair of silver pumps on it that were simply extraordinary.

"Maybe you should get my credit card out of my purse," I suggested.

"Size?" Josie asked, her voice smiling.

"Six and a half," I answered.

She grabbed my purse and sat in the salon chair next to me.

Alyssa twisted and clipped up my hair.

And as time wore on, I found it was astonishingly easy to pick up the pieces.

All you had to do was sit in a chair…

And have good women as company.

———— • ————

"ARE YOU READY FOR IT?"

It was hours later.

It was thousands of online shopping dollars later.

It was two sessions of makeup lessons (Alyssa's salon did special occasion makeup and had a huge trunk full of it). This done in between me "cooking" and getting my hair washed out, Alyssa taking a client, then coming back to do a cut (with my side or back to the mirror), Alyssa taking another client, then coming back to do the style.

Now I was done.

Staring at the back wall, unable to see myself in any of the copious mirrors around me, I replied on a lie because I was anxious as anything, "Ready."

She whirled me around.

I looked in the mirror and watched my face crumple.

"Girl, do *not* start crying!" Alyssa fairly shouted. "You'll mess up your makeup."

I took a breath in through my nose. I took another one in through my mouth.

And I stared at me.

Alyssa had cut in delicate layers, these making my now shining, gray-less, subtly highlighted hair less heavy. These layers were more distinct around my face where she'd feathered them down the sides and cut in a long bang that hung to my eyelashes and dipped lower at my temples. That and the increased blonde around my face giving my skin a healthy glow. And Josie's expert makeup tactics that were all about proper use of color, perfect shading, all of this packing a punch, made my eyes pop even more than they used to do.

I looked younger, not decades, but definitely younger.

Mostly, I looked like I gave a shit. I looked like I cared. I looked like I was worth something...*to me.*

Worth taking care of.

Worth spoiling.

Worth everything.

"My husband who I loved more than anything on this earth, save my children, had an affair with a nurse at his hospital, put an engagement ring on her finger before he asked me for a divorce, and married her only days after we signed the papers," I said to the mirror, my eyes on *my eyes*, something I'd thought when I was younger was my best feature.

Something that was my best feature again.

Finally.

"Oh shit," Alyssa muttered.

I felt Josie lean into me.

I didn't take my eyes from me.

"I lost it. Completely," I stated. "I went absolutely insane and made them both pay for this betrayal at every opportunity. My kids saw it. It was unhealthy. They didn't like it. It went on for years and got so bad my ex had to move across the country to escape me. He got a judge to award him my kids. They're all here and I followed them to heal my family. My husband welcomed me to Magdalene by showing at my new house, shouting it down and threatening me. And last weekend, my children made it clear they hated me."

"Amelia," Josie whispered.

Alyssa sat down in the salon chair on my other side and grabbed my hand.

I looked between them and then back at the mirror.

"I messed up," I whispered my admission.

Neither of them said anything.

"I kept doing it," I went on.

They stayed silent.

"And now I'm trying with everything I have to fix what I broke but I'm afraid I'm going to fail because they've completely lost faith in me."

My new friends remained quiet.

"I miss my family." It came out almost like a whimper.

"Of course you do," Alyssa said on a hand squeeze.

I kept going, "And I messed things up."

"Of course you did not," Alyssa declared, startling me, and I looked her way.

"I'm sorry?"

"So I take it you went batshit crazy when your husband left you," she noted.

"Yes," I confirmed humiliatingly.

"And those two, him and his new woman, don't deserve that...how?" she asked.

I stared.

"Shit happens, babe," she continued. "Marriages disintegrate for a lot of reasons. And you're sittin' in a chair that's seen a lot of ugly tales told and those include women losin' their men because those men fell outta love and into love with someone else. I don't live those feelings so I can't say if it's okay or not for that shit to happen. What I can say is that it's *not* okay for it to happen while anyone is still wearin' a wedding band."

"She's right," Josie added and I looked her way.

But I looked back to Alyssa when she again started speaking.

"I don't know what your kids saw. I can guess if it got so bad that shit is as ugly as it is for you. What I do know is that, you're right, they shouldn't see that stuff. You're also wrong. Kids gotta learn they gotta stick up for themselves. That there are consequences to actions. That you don't play with emotions. And you *never* piss on them. So it got outta hand. You're pullin' yourself together. If they're good kids," another hands squeeze, "and I *know* you got good kids, Amelia. You're a good woman, you can't have anything but. So I also know they'll come around."

"I hope you're right," I whispered.

"This is gonna sound harsh," she replied. "But they got a good mom and if they go the way of their dad and piss all over her, then it'll suck, it'll *kill*, but that's the way it is and you just keep on lookin' after you. They don't come around, it's the wrong decision, Amelia. You pulled up stakes and tucked your tail between your legs and gave it your all and if they don't have it in them to let go and let you back in, then *they'll* have consequences. And those consequences will be losing you."

"You can't say I'm much to lose because you barely know me," I reminded her.

"I know you're hangin' on by a thread," she returned instantly. "That thread is the last you got after unravelling and you got the courage and strength to hang the fuck on and not let go, and you're doin' all that for your kids. Your ex fucked up your life. *He* did that. *You* didn't. He broke your trust. He kicked your heart around. And you might have faltered along the way, but you haven't fallen yet. So you got that in you and you're still fightin' to keep your family alive, they don't wake up and see, their loss."

"Alyssa," Josie said warningly.

Alyssa sliced her gaze to Josie and sat back, letting my hand go and repeating, "Their loss."

"If the impossible happened and this happened to you, would you feel the same way about your children?" Josie asked.

"My Junior screwed me over and I spent their whole lives showin' my kids how much I loved their father, through the good times and the bad, standin' at his side, and they knew he did that to me?" She shook her head and kept going. "And after I pushed them out and wiped their asses and blew their snotty noses and cleaned up their puke and loved on them at every opportunity and dropped everything the minute they needed me, and I had a time in my life where I needed a little understanding and they bailed on me?" she asked then answered her own question. "Yes. Absolutely."

Josie touched my knee and I looked her way. "She's right, of a sort. But I believe you should give them some time."

"I am," I told her.

"That's good," she said softly.

I couldn't keep looking at her because I had fingers wrapped around my chin, forcing me to look back at Alyssa.

"You give them time. And you fight for your family. But," she forced my face to look in the mirror and dropped her hand, "that isn't a miracle, Amelia. That's us doin' what we can to remind you of what was already there. You walk outta of here not believing in what we believe, not seein' what we see, not thinkin' your kids should open their eyes and see the same thing, then all is already lost. You deserve to be happy. You deserve the people in your life that love you to want the same thing for you. But it's *you* that's gotta go out and find it. To prove to them you're worth it. To explain to them that you always knew that in your heart. That you deserve to be treated right, loved right, that you're worth it. And you may have gone a couple of extra miles too far in sharing that, but you're back to you and now you expect to get what you give."

I looked at my reflection in the mirror and I didn't know if I saw what they saw.

I did know that I didn't look anything but like me.

My hair was great. My makeup was awesome.

But all that was what Alyssa said.

It was me.

Not a new and improved me.

Just me.

With fantastic highlights and expertly shaded makeup.

"I'm buying you both a Porsche," I declared.

Alyssa burst out laughing and Josie did the same, except not as loud.

"I already have one, sweetheart," Josie said when her laughter died down.

"I don't. And I don't want no Cayenne. Turbo. Black," Alyssa put in.

I turned and grinned at her, knowing she was joking and still wishing she'd let me buy her a Porsche.

But I'd do something else.

I'd do what she wanted me to do.

I'd return the favor she extended to me.

Not fantastic highlights and a beautiful haircut.

I'd be a good friend.

———— • ————

THE NEXT DAY, ARRIVING BACK FROM ANOTHER SHOPPING SPREE WITH Alyssa and Josie with much more than a bowl, I found my front stoop littered with packages.

The results of online shopping with overnight shipping.

Nothing fit me as I found that day in the shops I was a size smaller.

I kept it anyway and I put it all away, with that day's acquisitions, taking the last of what was left of the wardrobe of my old life and shoving it in the boxes in the garage.

Then I went to my kitchen and opened a bottle of wine.

I sipped it while I made myself a nice dinner.

8

BESTED ME

*L*ate that next week, on one of the days I wasn't at Dove House, I was in town at Wayfarer's Market, doing some shopping.

I was having a cooking renaissance, starting with my baking, which the old folks at Dove House enjoyed (most specifically Mr. Dennison, who was a total flirt, and Mrs. McMurphy, who still thought I was a Nazi spy but that didn't stop her from liking my cookies).

But also, I was learning to cook for one, something that had once caused me to fall into the pit of agony I'd dug, but now I'd decided to take as a challenge.

First, there were things that I could freeze, and if I ever gave an extra hour (or two, as I was wont to do) to Dove House and came home fatigued, I could have a readymade meal that was also delicious.

Second, there were casseroles, which often tasted even better as leftovers.

In trolling for things to add to my whimsical beachy bedroom (that was coming around, I'd bought the mattresses and also found some fabulous prints for the walls that were whimsical and beachy without being trite or cutesy), I'd gone off course and started looking up recipes.

And I found one I couldn't wait to try. A hash brown casserole that, with its ingredients, could be nothing but scrumptious.

However, I was going over to Josie and Jake's that night to have dinner with them and the kids. Jake was gearing up to let his oldest son go off to college and Josie had told me he was holding up, but mostly so Conner wouldn't sense his dad was not fired up to watch his first son leave the nest. She was looking for ways to distract him at the same time give him more time with his son, which meant, in Josie's eyes, dinner party.

I was looking forward to it and not only because I liked Josie (after my meltdown we just kept getting closer) but also because I liked her husband and kids and wanted a chance to get to know them better.

Not to mention, Conner's girlfriend, and Alyssa's daughter, Sofie was going to be there and Josie told me they were *adorable* together (she'd even put the emphasis on it). Sofie was a singer and had had some singing thing the day of the house sale so I hadn't met her, or seen her with her boyfriend, so I was looking forward to that too.

But I was going to Dove House the next day and I wanted hash brown casserole for dinner the next night (perhaps with a nice pork tenderloin, which would also keep and be great for sandwiches). And since Dela hadn't found more volunteers, my three days a week at three hours a day were becoming four or five hours a day, and because I knew how much work there was to do, I'd at least pop in for an hour or two other days.

That plus doing my own cleaning, laundry, errands, grocery shopping, continuing to augment my wardrobe, wandering my new environs, hanging with my new friends and decorating my new house meant I was busy and on the go pretty much constantly.

And being busy and on the go pretty much constantly, I was in a rush that day to get the shopping done, get to the flower shop to buy a bouquet to bring with me to Lavender House (where Josie, Jake and family lived), get home and get everything put away before I had to head out. I'd asked if I could help Josie make dinner and she said Ethan was her helper but I could be an alternate sous chef while drinking wine and chatting.

That sounded fun and I didn't want to miss that opportunity.

So I was also ready for dinner at a friend's.

This meant I was in skinny jeans that were a dark wash but also had a subtle glimmer of silver. These I'd paired with a fabulous silvery-green blouse that was gathered at the waist and wrists, with full sleeves and no collar, but it had buttons down the front which could, or could not (as the case right then was) be opened to bare a little somethin'-somethin'.

My hair was blown out, bangs wispy against my eyelashes. Makeup done in browns, taupes, greens and peaches. All this much more color and flair than the neutral-only palette my mother ingrained in me, but it highlighted every good feature I had, making my hazel eyes and rounded cheekbones stand out beautifully.

And last, on my feet were the spike-heeled, criminally elegant, unbelievably trendy silver pumps that were the first thing Josie had shown me when she and Alyssa guided me back to me.

Me being dressed and ready to roll, even grocery shopping was something that would end up being *most* fortunate.

And this began when I turned into an aisle, eyes scanning the shelves for anything I needed or just wanted in my pantry, and I felt the hairs stand on end at the nape of my neck.

I looked down the aisle and froze when I saw my daughter, Olympia, with her stepmother, Martine.

I took in my pretty girl and then trained my gaze on Martine.

It had not been lost on me that my husband had a type.

Thus Martine Moss was a younger version of me.

And standing there staring at her in her fabulous outfit (but for once, mine was *so much* better) with her thick dark hair a cloud around her pixie face, her big green eyes round and pinned on me, this fact yet again did not escape me.

What also didn't escape me was that her mouth was hanging open.

As was my daughter's.

Honestly, as I'd wanted to do every time I saw Martine, my first inclination was to walk right up to her and slap her across the face.

But I'd never done that.

This time, I didn't do it either.

I also didn't do what I might normally do, which was cause an unholy scene.

What I did was stroll their way, stop and look to my daughter.

"Hey, honey," I said quietly.

With visible effort, she shifted her astonished face to bored and mumbled, "Mom."

I looked to Martine. "Martine."

She also shifted her stunned expression but hers hardened and she said nothing.

I let that go and looked back to my daughter. "Good to see you, Pippa." I tipped my head down and smiled. "Like your shorts."

She just glared at me.

I took that and kept smiling at her. "Looking forward to seeing you in a couple of weeks."

"Whatever," she muttered, casting her gaze to the floor.

I took that too and said softly, "Enjoy your day, sweets." She didn't look at me so I looked to Martine. "You too," I said and wanted to twist myself into a knot in order to pat my own back that it came out (almost) like I meant it.

Then I turned to the aisle and started pushing my cart away.

I stopped when Martine snapped, "Seriously?"

I kept facing forward but twisted their way. "I'm sorry?"

"Do you honestly believe we're gonna fall for your crap?" she asked, and she'd twisted too.

Not her body.

Her face.

I stared at her and with tardy but blazing clarity something struck me.

Not once. Not twice. Not rarely. But nearly always.

She goaded me.

She did not simper and shrink away. Even if I was only in the mood to lob spit balls, she returned fire with poisoned arrows. *She* had stolen *my* husband, and from the beginning she never hesitated once to go after me.

And right then, when I was about to walk away, she wanted me to bring it.

She *wanted* me to look like a bitch in front of my children. She *wanted* them to think I was a whackjob.

And I'd *let* her.

But right then, I had fabulous skinny jeans, fantastic hair and shoes any woman would kill for, but they were on *my* feet and I did not care what it said about me that I didn't look at this as armor. I didn't look at it as a shield. I didn't look at it as crutch.

I let it *feed* me.

"If you don't mind," I said calmly and quietly. "I'd rather not do this." I held her gaze and finished, "*Ever.*"

"Like I'm gonna believe that," she sniped at me. "Like you haven't given us a break from your venom to lull us into thinking you've changed and then you strike."

"As I said," I replied firmly, "have a nice day, Martine."

I turned my eyes to my daughter, who was watching this closely, looking confused, something that twisted my heart. But regardless that it ripped a new hole in me, all I could do was give her a soft smile, which I did.

Then I turned away and kept walking.

"You know, Con is done with you," Martine called to my back. "You slip up once more, Amelia, and he'll end it."

I said nothing. I didn't look back. I may have started shaking but I didn't think she could see it.

I just kept walking.

I also decided to meander a bit more so if they saw me again, they wouldn't think I was escaping.

And once I did that, I checked out and got the heck out of there.

I didn't have all the ingredients to my hash brown casserole but I could buy them tomorrow.

However, I would find that it was unfortunate that I'd been able to hit the wine aisle, for when I walked down the sidewalk with the handles of my brown bags in my hands and a man came charging out of the door of a shop down the walk and slammed into me, I went flying. I dropped both bags, the twenty dollar bottle of wine I'd bought to take to Jake and Josie's crashing and breaking, red wine soaking through the bag and spreading along the sidewalk.

"Watch where you're—" a harsh voice started and my back shot straight as I righted myself and turned to him, raring to go.

I was this because, first, I'd just had a run-in with Martine, never pleasant, this one the same.

Second, she'd been with my daughter, *my* daughter, grocery shopping, when my daughter would barely look at me—and didn't—and would never entertain the idea of grocery shopping with me.

She also barely spoke to me.

And last, *he* had come charging out of a shop without looking where he was going. I was already on the sidewalk. I had right of way (according to me). And *he* was not going to blame *me* for breaking my bottle of wine.

"Watch where *I'm* going?" I asked a man who was tall, dark and attractive, but he reminded me of my father.

He was also gazing contemplatively at me as he lifted a hand and swept it toward the sidewalk. "My apologies. I broke your wine."

"You absolutely did," I confirmed, stepping away from the spreading wine stain, not wanting it on my criminally awesome shoes, at the same time going into a squat to rescue the other bag.

"Allow me," he said, crouching beside me.

"Thank you, but I've got it," I returned coolly.

"No, really," he murmured and curled his fingers around my wrist, staying my movements, and at this unwelcome familiarity so soon in our acquaintance, forcing my eyes to his. "Allow me."

He wanted to do it?

He could do it.

I pulled away and straightened.

He grabbed the handles of my good bag and transferred the items of the ruined one into it, setting it aside rather than lifting it and possibly breaking it due to its new weight.

"I'll go to Wayfarer's, get another bag, replace your wine," he offered. "Are you fine to wait with your other things while I do that?"

Even though Wayfarer's was the last place on earth I wanted to be, something about him made me decline his offer.

"Again, thank you but I'll do it."

"Please," he pushed. "You were on your way before I crashed into you and I'd hate to think of the other bag breaking while you sort out something it was me that made you need to sort out."

He was right about that.

"I'm in kind of a hurry," I somewhat lied.

He more than somewhat smiled. "Then I'll be certain to hurry."

I sighed and decided discussing it with him would make this situation last even longer, not to mention mean I'd remain in his presence for longer, so I gave in by nodding.

He kept smiling and nodded back.

Then he sauntered off, appearing not in a rush at all and not bothering to ask me what the wine was he should be replacing.

I stood on the sidewalk, hoping to all that was holy that Olympia and Martine wouldn't walk out and catch me standing on the sidewalk looking like an exceptionally well-dressed, exemplarily-shod, fabulously coifed and made up daytime prostitute.

This didn't happen and within minutes, a checkout boy from Wayfarer's dashed out with a bag. He also repacked my things. Another one came out as the first one was doing this. He had a dustbin and broom and cleaned up the broken bottle and wasted bag.

They were both gone by the time the man came back with another Wayfarer's bag, this one doubled against the obviously heavy contents inside that could not be a single bottle of wine.

He approached me, again smiling. "Let me help you get this to the car."

"I'm able to carry it," I replied.

"As my way of an apology, I bought you four bottles of wine. It's heavy."

Four bottles?

I stared.

"Your car?" he prompted.

I again sighed and gave in.

"This way," I said and started walking.

He fell in step beside me, doing this noting, "I haven't seen you in Magdalene."

"No, you haven't," I confirmed.

"I'm Boston Stone," he shared and I looked up to him as I turned in front of him, causing him to stop then follow me as I moved toward the trunk of my car parked on the street.

"Hello, Boston Stone," I greeted because I had no idea what else to say.

"You are?" he asked as I put the bags to the ground and touched the button on the trunk that would open it keyless.

As it glided open, I opened my mouth, doing it uncertain if I'd share my name or continue to try to brush him off, but I didn't have the chance to decide.

I heard the word, "Babe," growled from behind me.

I turned and saw Mickey stalking our way.

Not sauntering.

Not simply walking.

Stalking.

And he didn't look happy.

"Mickey," I called tentatively as a greeting, uncertain at his demeanor.

I hadn't seen him since he hadn't seen me (I hoped) at the movies.

He was in his firefighter-not-fighting-a-fire uniform of blue khakis and tee. His eyes were moving up and down my body. He still was unbelievably beautiful (that uniform...seriously).

He didn't greet me back.

When he stopped, his gaze cut to Boston Stone and it went flinty.

"You need somethin'?" he asked incomprehensibly inhospitably.

"I was just helping this lovely lady with her groceries," Stone responded.

"I got it," Mickey stated flatly and then he got it. As in, he carefully pulled me back, grabbed the bags I was perfectly capable of picking up myself and placed them in my trunk.

He then went for the bag Stone was carrying, caught hold, but Stone didn't let go.

"I can put it in the trunk myself, Donovan," Stone clipped.

So they knew each other.

"As I said, I got it, Stone," Mickey clipped back.

Yes, they knew each other.

The handles flattened as they both kept hold and pulled.

"Please!" I exclaimed. "We already had a wine incident. The sidewalk of Magdalene has been anointed with one red, let's not anoint Cross Street with four."

Mickey instantly let go and stepped back, running into me but he didn't apologize or move away.

He stayed close, the back of his left side touching the front of my right.

It was at that point I noticed Mickey gave off a lot of heat.

Stone put the bag in my trunk, shut it and turned slowly to Mickey and me.

But he had eyes on Mickey.

"Are you two seeing each other?"

"That's your business how?" Mickey asked as reply.

"It's my business because, if you're not, I'd like to request you leave so I can ask her to dinner," Stone returned.

My head jerked as my body locked in shock.

"That's not gonna happen," Mickey growled.

My body stayed locked in shock but that didn't mean my eyes didn't fly to Mickey's stony-faced profile in *more* shock.

"So you *are* seeing each other," Stone remarked.

"Again, not your business," Mickey bit out.

Stone's expression turned shrewd. "And that's something that would lead me to believe that the beautiful woman standing behind you is free to go to dinner with me."

"You forget English?" Mickey asked. "I already answered that too."

I butted in, "I think I can speak for myself, Mickey."

He moved nothing but his head (though his torso shifted an inch) so he could look down at me.

His eyes were communicating again.

This time they were communicating the fact that he *really* didn't like Boston Stone.

Considering what I knew of Mickey, this would be something that, along with my own natural aversion to Mr. Stone, would have made me decline the man's invitation.

Unfortunately, Mickey added words to his look so this didn't happen.

"You're not goin' out with this guy."

Was he being serious?

He couldn't tell me what to do. He wasn't my father, my brother *or* my lover.

Heck, he barely knew me!

All he knew about me was that he didn't want me. I was his…"attractive" neighbor who he now did not even walk over to beg recipes from (okay, so Aisling didn't know of any other recipes I had, but whatever).

He didn't even return my email!

And he was off with beautiful, statuesque redheads, smiling at them, taking them to movies.

He couldn't tell me who I could and could not see.

"I'm not?" I snapped.

"No," he turned fully to me, an ominous fully. "You are not," he enunciated each word clearly.

"Sorry?" I asked sarcastically. "When did you become my big brother?"

He was still enunciating clearly, and dangerously, when he stated, "I absolutely am *not* your big brother."

"No, you're not," I retorted, tossing my hair, which I hoped was shining in the sun. And with my hair toss, I further hoped my fabulous highlights caught the rays and gleamed. "You're my neighbor. And if I want to go out with someone, you can't say boo to the contrary."

"This guy is an asshole," he bit off, jerking his thumb at Boston Stone.

I felt my eyes get big and I got up on my toes, leaning into him, hissing, "That's insufferably *rude*, Mickey Donovan."

"It isn't rude if it's the truth."

"You may think so but you don't *say* it in front of the man in *question*."

"You do if he's as big of an asshole as this asshole is," Mickey shot back.

My eyes got wider and I leaned closer. "Stop being nasty!" I demanded.

"You been in town, what?" he asked then answered with another question he didn't expect a reply to. "A coupla months? I lived here my whole life and trust me, I'm savin' you from a load of misery, this guy gets interested in you," he returned.

I rocked down to my stilettos. "I *am* a big girl, Mickey. All grown up and everything. I do think I can make such decisions for myself."

"You do, and they're not what I'm tellin' you to do, you'd be wrong."

I glared at him.

Then I pushed right past him, hand lifted and got in the space of Boston Stone.

"Boston," I said as he took my hand, grinning arrogantly and more than a little obnoxiously at me. "A belated nice to meet you. I'm Amelia Hathaway."

His hand tightened in mine as he murmured, "Amelia."

I pulled my hand from his, asking, "Do you know Cliff Blue?"

"Of course," he replied, inclining his head in a pompous way that actually was kind of creepy.

"I live there," I announced, doing another hair toss and powering beyond the creepy. "And I have plans this evening but I'm free tomorrow. Are you?"

"I wasn't," he replied. "But I'll be making a phone call and I will be."

"Excellent," I decreed. "Seven?" I went on to ask.

"I'd be delighted," he said softly, his eyes dancing with humor and I could see that too was relatively malicious.

I didn't care.

I'd go out with him once, just to stick it to Mickey.

Then I'd be done with Boston Stone.

And anyway, I had about seven new outfits that would be *perfect* for a date and I knew this even though I hadn't been on a date in two decades.

"I'll see you then," I said.

"You will, Amelia." He dipped his chin to me. "Looking forward to it."

"And me," I replied.

He gave me another arrogant grin then transferred it to Mickey.

"Donovan," he murmured.

Mickey didn't reply.

Stone looked back to me. "Until tomorrow, Amelia."

"Yes, Boston. And please, feel free to call me Amy."

Mickey grunted.

Boston smiled before he turned and sauntered away.

I whirled on Mickey and tipped my head to the side. "See? All grown up and able to make decisions for myself."

"What I see is a pattern here," he retorted unpleasantly.

"Oh?" I asked with mock interest. "Do tell."

Then Mickey told.

"First time I laid eyes on you, your ex was up in your face, cursing at you, threatening you, shouting right at you and acting like a total fucking dick. It's obvious he's rich and up his own ass and didn't give a shit you were alone, and because of that, you probably felt unsafe. It was just as obvious you were lettin' him use you as his punching bag. Even if no woman deserves the way he was speakin' to you, he just kept right on punching. Now, you know that guy you just made a date with is a total asshole and you made that date anyway. So that's your pattern. You open yourself up for assholes to shit all over you. And if that's the way you like it, baby, then no way in *fuck* I'm gonna get in there to show you there's another way."

Before I could retort, he turned on his boot and prowled away.

I glared at him as he did it then jerked toward my car.

I stopped dead because Olympia and Martine were standing at the sidewalk at the front bumper of my car.

Martine was staring after Mickey incredulously.

My baby girl was staring at me, her eyes big and shocked, her face ashen.

"Honey," I said softly, hurrying her way.

"Dad shouted at you?" she whispered.

I stopped at the curb. "He—"

I got no further because Martine grabbed her hand and yanked her away, saying, "Let's go, sweetie."

I didn't know what to do. I wanted to stop them. But Martine clearly didn't want to be stopped, and if I tried it might cause a scene.

So I couldn't stop them.

Thus, powerless (as usual), I stood at the curb watching my daughter's stepmom drag her away as she stayed turned, her eyes on me.

I lifted my hand and waved.

Martine pulled her into the street behind a parked SUV and I lost sight of her.

I closed my eyes, drawing in a deep breath, and opened them, turning to my car.

I got in and dug in my purse to get out my phone.

When I had it, I texted my daughter.

Just to finish, I texted, *it wasn't as bad as all that. I'm okay. Your father was just sharing the lay of the land after I arrived in Maine. It's done with and I'm good. I love you, Pippa. See you in a couple of weeks and looking forward to it, honey.*

I sent the text then decided to send more.

And it's worth a repeat that those shorts really look cute on you, sweets, I typed in.

I sent that and looked through my windshield, staring at a kid in a Wayfarer's apron hosing down the wine stain.

That just happened.

A hysterical giggle burst out of me but it was short-lived as I swallowed it down.

I couldn't believe that just happened.

First and foremost, what was the deal with Mickey and Boston Stone?

Whatever it was, he was not going to use me to work it out.

Sadly, I had stubbornly and definitely stupidly agreed to go out with a man who, with one look, I knew I wanted nothing to do with.

Well, there was nothing for it now.

And at least I'd get to wear a new outfit that it was unlikely I would wear anytime soon for the men were not beating down my door.

Except Mr. Dennison, who clearly had a crush on me. But since he was eighty-eight and confined to a nursing home without access to a motor vehicle, I didn't think we'd be able to get anything going.

On that thought, having things to do, I decided it best to move on and do them.

So I started my car, carefully backed out of my space and into the street, and did just that.

———— • ————

"I HAD A LOVELY TIME," I SHARED WITH BOSTON STONE ON MY FRONT STEP, looking up at him and hoping he didn't try to kiss me.

It was the next night.

The night before, I'd had dinner with Josie, Jake and their kids (and Sofie and Connor *were* adorable together—young love, seemingly the real kind, something I'd never seen before but it was amazing).

I did not share any of my Mickey-Stone-and-me stupidity with Josie because there was no need. I knew she was close to Mickey, I had a feeling that Jake was even closer and I didn't want to be talking about him behind his back with this friends.

It would all be over the next night anyway.

So I'd had a lovely night with the Spear family and then gone home.

I'd gotten up and went to Dove House. I flirted with Mr. Dennison, listened to Mrs. Naigle telling me about her twelve great-grandbabies, found a pair of missing dentures in the cushion of an armchair in the lounge, assisted a staffer with a profoundly unpleasant situation that was the result of way too much prune juice, and avoided Mrs. McMurphy threatening to tell President Roosevelt about me.

Then I'd gone out with Boston Stone.

I'd been right. He was a man I wanted nothing to do with.

He was also boring.

Further, he was rich and he took every opportunity, including purchasing a four hundred dollar bottle of champagne for us to drink at dinner, to make certain I was aware of that.

This was even more boring.

And now, I really wanted the night to be over so I could go in, admire myself in my dress (which even I had to admit was fabulous) before I took it off and went to bed with a book.

What I didn't want was for him to kiss me.

As was the way of my world, I didn't get what I wanted.

He leaned in and kissed me.

It was short, not deep, and only included him curling a hand around my waist. His breath smelled of champagne and mint, which wasn't all bad. And his lips were firm, which wasn't all bad either.

Last, he didn't go for tongues, which was a definite relief.

When he lifted his head, he said in a voice that I had a feeling was supposed to be sexy but missed the mark, "I'd like to see you again, Amy."

God, I should *never* have invited him to call me Amy.

"Why don't you call me?" I suggested, wishing, in all my boasting about being grown up, I was grown up enough to let a man I did not like down for any repeat dates face to face.

He pulled slightly away but not far enough for me. "I will, if you give me your number."

Shit.

Now I was giving him my number!

Well, I'd successfully avoided my mother, who had my number. My best friend, who was alarmingly no longer using my number. And my father, who was rich enough to find commandos to track me down, kidnap me and bring me back to La Jolla to tie me to a chair and interrogate me about why I didn't phone my mother.

I could avoid Boston Stone.

"Do you have your phone?" I asked.

This was a good move.

He shifted away, saying, "Certainly."

He took it out.

I gave him my number.

He punched it in then bent and gave me another brief champagne, minty kiss before he leaned away and said, "Goodnight, Amy."

"'Night, Boston," I mumbled.

Then he stood there as I let myself in my front door.

I gave him a small smile as I closed the door and I did not wait a polite time so he wouldn't hear me lock it against him.

I should have told Josie about my lunacy so I could call her and pick over that tediously boring date.

Or I should have shared with Alyssa.

Or I should have found a more mature way to deal with Robin so I could pick over *everything* with her.

Most especially the fact that, no matter how tedious, I had moved on so far that I was to the point of dating, something else which I wished I could pat myself on the back for.

On this thought, I wandered to my kitchen counter, dropped my sleek new clutch to it and pulled out my phone.

I went to Robin's text string and typed in, *Haven't heard from you in a while. All okay?* And hit send.

It was a puny attempt at communication but at least it was something.

I was staring at my phone, like Robin was hanging around waiting for me to text so she could reply immediately (when she was possibly making voodoo dolls of her selfish, thoughtless, gutless ex-friend who didn't have the courage to lay it out about the way it needed to be, and sticking pins in it, something I knew she did because I'd done it with her—repeatedly) when it rang in my hand.

I stared at the display giving me a local number I didn't recognize.

It wasn't late. Not early, after nine so really too late to call and do it politely (according to my mother, who had a cutoff of nine o'clock for some Felicia Hathaway reason).

That was, unless you were in California, got a new phone with a new number that you hadn't shared, and wanted to call your wayward daughter or friend and blast it to them.

It was hours earlier in California.

Shit.

Even on this thought, I took the call, putting the phone to my ear. "Hello?"

"You went out with that dick."

I stared at my counter.

It was Mickey.

"Mickey?" I asked to confirm.

He didn't confirm but he didn't need to.

What he did was ask, "You talk to Josie about that guy?"

"I'm not really sure how this is any of your business," I replied.

"You didn't," he stated. "You did, Josie woulda told you that that asshole tried to steal her home from her. Lavender House."

I blinked at my counter.

Lavender House, Josie's house, was beautiful. *Stunning.* And it was pure Josie, imposing and welcoming at the same time.

Further, she'd told me it had been in her family for generations.

She loved it. She loved the family in it. In all that was Josie, who was her brand of kind and sweet but still kind of a hard nut to crack, those two facts were plain to see.

"What?" I breathed to Mickey.

"Yeah. And not up front. He did it nasty. Freaked her out. Scared her shitless. Brought back family, the bad kind Josie hadn't seen in years, who not only got up in her face publicly, but also tried to break in to steal shit in the middle of the night."

"Oh my God," I whispered.

"Good people, Boston Stone," he said sarcastically and my spine snapped to.

"You could have said this to me yesterday, Mickey."

"You weren't big on listenin' to me yesterday, Amy."

"That's because you were being kind of a jerk yesterday, Mickey," I retorted.

"Kind of a jerk lookin' out for you, Amy," he shot back.

He was kind of right about that so I changed tactics.

"I'll have you know," I began, "that my daughter was standing on the sidewalk and she heard what you said about her father."

"I'm sure that's supposed to make me feel bad," he returned instantly. "But it doesn't. See, I've been tryin' to puzzle out why a woman who makes unbe-fucking-lievable cupcakes, who plays Frisbee in my back-yard, who's got so much money she doesn't have to work but she doesn't spend her time at the spa and instead spends it at a goddamned nursing home, who looks about ready to rope my kid to the chair at the fuckin' *possibility* he might do something dangerous for a living, that happening in a fucking *decade*…why that woman has only got her kids for two days of the month."

I sucked in a breath.

But Mickey was not done speaking.

"Instead, they're with your ex, who's a fuckin' dick."

"Mickey," I breathed. "Are you *spying* on me?"

"Red Civic in your drive, babe, not hard to see."

Time to give Auden a garage door opener and I couldn't believe I hadn't already.

And if my son didn't respond to a text to come get it (which he wouldn't), I'd mail the thing to him.

Mickey spoke into my silence.

"You're loaded so it can't be that you don't have the cake to hire a decent lawyer to look out for you. So not sure what it could be. 'Cept he did what dicks like him do. Especially dicks like him who think they can treat women the way he treated you. He convinced you that *you* were a piece of shit when *he* is and you went down without a fight."

Oh God.

"Mickey, please—"

He again spoke over me. "And maybe he's convinced your kids you're a piece of shit too. They're old enough to get to you if they wanna see their mom. But that Civic isn't in your drive but a coupla days a month. So maybe your girl heard me and woke up a little to the way it really is, Amy, and I gotta tell you, I don't feel bad about that shit at all."

"I...can't talk about this with you," I told him shakily, his words rattling me.

"Not surprised," he replied and then socked it to me. "Down without a fight."

I forgot about being rattled and snapped, "None of this is any of your business."

"Yeah, you've made that clear."

What did he mean with that? How did I make that clear?

No. No, I didn't care.

"Not clear enough," I returned. "Has it occurred to you with all you've said about things you know nothing about that perhaps *you* are treating me much like Conrad did?"

"Oh no," he whispered and a chill chased up my spine at the sound of it. "No, you fuckin' do *not*, Amelia," he kept whispering sinisterly. "If you were mine, no matter if you fucked me, you'd get respect from me. I know that shit because my wife sunk into a bottle, she fucked up our lives, our future, our kids, and she never gets that shit from me. You cannot tell me that whatever it is that happened between you two is as bad as you pickin' booze over your family. So you cannot tell me the way he spoke to you was what you deserved because I know that shit isn't fucking true."

Again, he was right and this time, not kind of.

This time, he was *really* right in a way that again rattled me.

"I can't imagine why we're discussing this," I said defensively. "We hardly know each other, and again, my business isn't yours."

"I figure you're right, you can't imagine why we're discussing this because even someone who gives a shit about you, we hardly know each other or not, lays it out straight with no bullshit, you're so deep in what he's taught you to believe, you refuse to see."

Again.

Right.

Again.

Rattled.

"Maybe we should stop talking," I suggested.

"Maybe," he returned.

"Like, *ever*," I went on.

"You want it that way, Amy, in your big house all alone, accepting the dregs when a woman like you should be handed everything, you got it."

Before I could reply, he hung up on me.

I took the phone from my ear and stared at it, asking, "Did that just happen?"

The phone and the entirety of my house were unsurprisingly silent.

He convinced you that you were a piece of shit when he is and you went down without a fight.

Mickey's words pummeled me so hard mentally, my entire body jerked.

Did I?

Did I go down without a fight?

It felt like I'd been fighting for years. Anytime I saw Conrad or Martine, anytime I forced them to see me, I fought.

But I didn't.

In the game they made me play against my will, each time that happened, I wasn't fighting.

I was showing them my cards.

So it wasn't a big shock that they'd bested me.

And maybe he's convinced your kids you're a piece of shit too.

My husband had cheated on me. He'd left me. *He'd* destroyed our family.

I thought we'd been happy. For years, *years*, I'd run through moments, snippets, hours, weeks, *months* and the only thing we consistently disagreed about was how he didn't want me to spoil the children. Outside of that, I'd never found a single *second* where he'd given me any indication things were going wrong.

Conrad had never sat me down and shared something wasn't working. He'd never found his time to find his way to say something I was doing upset him, troubled him, annoyed him.

He'd never said or done anything.

Heck, we'd made love, doing it most enjoyably, until the night before he told me he was leaving me!

"Oh God," I breathed, staring unseeing at my phone. "I'd showed them all my cards and they'd bested me."

I lifted my head and looked at my reflection in the glass of my wall of windows.

It was wavy but it was me.

Great highlights.

No-longer-Felicia-Hathaway dress that very much suited me.

And I knew I had elegant, stylish, strappy, high-heeled sandals on my feet.

But that was wrapping.

All of that, *all* of it, was me.

It had always been me.

And I let Conrad—*and* Martine—convince me differently.

"They bested me," I whispered, my hand curling tight on my phone. "Those assholes *bested me. All of them bested me.*"

I glared at my image in the glass.

Time to grow *the fuck* up.

On that thought, I stomped through my fabulous, multi-million dollar, Prentice Cameron house right to my unfinished den/office/whatever-I-wanted-it-to-be.

I fired up my computer on my used, massive, intricately carved baronial desk and I sat down in the officious, completely awesome, leather button-backed chair behind it.

I waited and when it was ready, I pulled up my email.

I typed my father's address in.

Dad, I wrote.

I'm aware you and Mom have been calling. I'm emailing you now to explain why I've not picked up.

Before I left, I told you I was moving to Maine in order to be closer to my children. My relationship with them the last few years has deteriorated and it's crucial I do the work I need to do to focus on healing that breach.

And I do believe you're aware that there's a great deal of work to do on that. Therefore, I've been doing what I intended to do when I moved to Maine, focusing on just that.

I don't wish to hurt or offend you by suggesting you or Mom are distractions, however, I'm sure we all can agree that Olympia and Auden, as well as myself at this current juncture, are the priorities.

I wish to assure you I'm here. I'm safe. The house is even more wonderful than I thought it would be. I've met people and made friends. I'm volunteering. And although the road has been very bumpy, I'm settling and have hope I'll find happiness here...with Auden and Olympia.

You have my sincere apologies I didn't share that with you sooner. I'm sure you were worried and I'm terribly sorry I made you feel those feelings. But I must share now that there may be lapses between you hearing from me because the work I must do must take all my attention. I'll try not to let the time go on this long before you get an update from me.

I would enjoy receiving emailed updates from you and Mom as well. I'll do my best to reply as soon as I can.

My love to you and please extend that to Mom.

-Amelia

I only read it once for typos before sending it.

I held absolutely no hope that it would stop my father from attempting to get in touch with me to lambast me verbally, but I didn't care. I was beyond caring. I was tired of being bested. I was tired of allowing myself to feel less than I was. I was tired of being what others wanted me to be and not being me.

So I did my daughterly duty.

If Dad couldn't read that message and decipher what I needed and instead demanded what he needed back from me, he could go jump in a lake.

I shut down my computer, waltzed back to the kitchen, opened a bottle of wine, poured a glass in one of my exquisite new glasses and walked to my armchair that was made of leather so supple it was buttery.

I turned on the light.

Having used up large reserves of courage I didn't know I had, I didn't curl up in my chair and call Robin like I should.

I called my brother.

It was the right thing to do.

We both bitched about our parents, Conrad, and I told him about the way my kids were behaving and the things Alyssa and Mickey had said about Conrad and Martine.

With all of those things, supportive to the last, my big brother forcefully agreed.

Alas, he was extremely angry at my children, but then again, maybe he (and I) should be.

In the end, it was exactly what I needed.

We hung up and I did it smiling.

All my life, I'd allowed myself to be beaten, even gave away the ammunition to make that so.

Right then, I was curled in my chair in my elegant shoes and pretty dress with my exquisite wineglass and I decided on yet another part that was me.

That shit was going to end.

Completely.

9

NICE DRESS

"*F*rom the gentleman down the bar...for you," the bartender said.

I looked from him down to the fresh cosmopolitan he put in front of me then down the bar at an attractive man with blond hair, a little gray at the temples, his smiling blue eyes on me.

"Holy shit," Alyssa said, sitting on a stool at a nice restaurant with a respectable bar one town over called Breeze Point.

"Lovely," Josie, sitting on my other side, murmured.

We were out "trolling" as Alyssa put it, or "having girl time with the possibility of something happening" as Josie put it.

I decided to think of it as the latter as well as an opportunity to wear another of my going out outfits.

But at that moment, when the possibility of something happening happened, I didn't know what to do. I hadn't had a man buy me a drink in so long that I forgot what I'd done when they did.

Since my current drink was running low, I lifted it to my lips, finished it and put my fingers to the stem of the glass of the new, shifting my eyes back to the man.

I smiled.

He smiled back again.

"Pure cool," Alyssa approved.

"Well done," Josie did the same.

I looked to Josie and noted, "He's only sent this because you both have huge rocks on your fingers."

They did. Although Josie's was a fair sight bigger than Alyssa's, neither ring failed to state the giver's intention that these two women were t-a-k-e-n, *taken*.

And they were far more attractive than me, both tall, both blonde and both stunning.

"You say shit like that again, I'm bitch slappin' some sense into you and don't you doubt it," Alyssa muttered.

I looked to her to see her eyes squinty on me, but I did doubt it.

Alyssa would never do that. She'd threaten it repeatedly (if needed), but she'd never do it.

"You're hot," she went on to declare.

"I'm not a tall, built blonde," I pointed out.

"No, you're a petite, beautiful brunette with big knockers, awesome gams and a great ass even though you pushed out a coupla kids and the rest of you is still too skinny," she retorted. "Now shut up or I'll bring a catfight to Breeze Point, I don't care how ritzy this place is."

"She's right, you know," Josie said and I looked her way. "There are many varieties of...hot."

Josie using a slang word, something she rarely did, made me giggle.

"Now grab that drink, sister, and get that great ass over to that hot guy," Alyssa ordered.

I looked to her in surprise.

"Me go to him?" I asked.

"He laid it out," she said by way of answer. "You got your bitches with you. Don't make him come over here and lay it out in front of your bitches. It's already hard enough to put himself out there, buyin' a drink for a beautiful woman, settin' himself up for a crash and burn seein' as he's cute but you're all that's you. Don't make it harder."

I saw her point (though I might not have entirely agreed about "all that's me") but I didn't like this.

And it struck me that I didn't like this because I was me.

I was greedy.

I wanted it all.

I wanted a man who had confidence enough in himself not to lay it out but to *lay it out*. I wanted a man who looked at me and was so drawn to me he'd put himself out there for me. He took the chance to walk over to me with my friends and show me how much he wanted me. I wanted a man who would demonstrate he wanted me so much, he'd do anything to have a shot with me.

He'd buy me a drink.

He'd walk over and speak to me.

He wouldn't give one thought to "shitting where he lived" because he was my neighbor. Instead, he'd want me so badly he'd throw caution to the wind just for a chance to be with me.

That's what I wanted.

And that was what I would get or I'd take nothing.

Shock of shocks, I was okay being alone in my big house with mostly me as my company. I wasn't going to settle for just anybody so I'd be less lonely because I was no longer lonely.

I was just alone.

And I was fine with that.

"If he wants me," I mumbled, lifting the drink he bought me to my lips and before taking a sip I finished, "He can come and get me."

"Well, batten down the hatches, babe, 'cause here he comes," Alyssa stage-whispered loudly.

My body locked.

"Ladies," a smooth male voice said.

I took my sip, luckily not choking, and swiveled on my stool.

He was right there, smiling at me then he looked beyond me. "If you'll get these other ladies a drink and put them on my tab." He looked from the bartender to me. "I'd like a moment with you to introduce myself privately."

He lifted his hand to me.

I looked into his blue eyes that were not as beautiful as Mickey's but they were still handsome.

Then I looked to his hand, which was not as strong as Mickey's, and not rough at all, but it was a nice hand.

And of its own accord, my hand lifted and my fingers curled around his.

He gripped them and helped me off my stool.

I took my drink with me as he kept hold of my hand and walked me back to where he had been sitting.

As I walked, I glanced over my shoulder to see Josie beaming and Alyssa mouthing, "Go get him, tiger."

I grinned at them and allowed myself to be led away.

His name was Bradley.

———— • ————

MY PHONE WAS RINGING AS WAS MY DOORBELL.

I grabbed the phone, seeing the number was not known but local, and since there were a lot of things happening and the call could have to do with any of these, I took the call as I rushed to the door.

"Hello?"

"Amy?"

Not Mickey.

Boston.

Shit.

It had been three days since our date.

Player move.

Boring.

"Boston," I said, unlocking the door and opening it to a man standing there in paint spattered, white coveralls. I lifted a one minute finger to him then rolled my whole hand, stepping back and inviting him inside. He came in and I kept talking, "I'm so sorry, but I'm in the middle of something and have someone waiting."

"That's too bad, but do you have time to tell me you're free tomorrow evening?" he asked.

I was.

"I'm sorry, I'm not," I lied.

"I'm out of town on Friday and I'll be gone a few weeks."

Brilliant news.

My "Oh," was noncommittal.

"I'll call you while I'm away."

Not brilliant news.

"I have some things happening, a number of them, I'm going to be very busy," I shared, and that was the truth.

"We'll find a time, Amy."

God, I really, *really* wished I hadn't told him to call me Amy.

I also wished he'd catch a hint.

"Right," I said distractedly. "I really have to go."

"We'll speak later."

"Okay."

"Good-bye, Amy."

"'Bye, Boston," I mumbled then hung up and looked at the painter who I hoped would give me a decent quote for painting my massive, multi-million dollar house.

And I smiled.

AFTER OUR DATE, I WAS ON MY FRONT STEP MAKING OUT WITH A HANDSOME blond named Bradley.

He wasn't boring. He was actually quite nice, very attentive, well-to-do enough to take me to a lovely place for dinner, including ordering a very nice bottle of wine, without hitting me over the head with all of this.

Thus I'd wanted him to kiss me.

He didn't taste minty.

He tasted like chocolate (his dessert) and warmth and this coupled with his cologne that was not overwhelming but was woodsy, I liked.

He also didn't go for a brief kiss.

He started it slow but when I liked it and showed that, he'd gone for more.

There were tongues and I was wrapped around him, enjoying myself thoroughly.

I was this until the dark against my closed eyelids was pierced with muted light and I lost some focus.

Bradley got it back.

But it disappeared completely when a faraway noise that could not be mistaken tore me right out of the moment in a way I tore my lips from Bradley's.

I looked over his shoulder to see Mickey's garage door going up, his black Ford Expedition gliding into the drive.

"Amelia?" Bradley called and I looked to him.

"Maybe we should call it a night here," I whispered.

His arms still around me, arms that felt nice and strong, gave me a reflexive squeeze but he nodded.

"How are you set for tomorrow night?" he asked.

How I was set was that Junior and Alyssa wanted a date night and so did their eldest daughter, Sofie, who usually looked after the kids when they needed her to. But now she had a boyfriend who was about to go to Boston to start his freshman year of college so she wanted all the time with Conner she could get.

Therefore, I'd told Alyssa I'd come over and watch the kids and she'd fallen on that like a man dragging himself through the dessert had just hit the water hole at an oasis.

"I'm watching a friend's kids tomorrow night. The next?" I asked.

"I have a work thing," he muttered with disappointment. Then he gave me another squeeze. "I'll call."

I smiled at him, my arms still wound around his shoulders.

"That'd be good," I said softly.

His eyes dropped to my mouth then his lips dropped there.

We didn't make out again but our kiss was hot and heavy, just brief, before he gave me a quick peck, a sexy smile (that actually was sexy), said goodnight and walked toward his burgundy Infinity.

I watched him go for a moment before I let myself in, closed and locked the doors.

I went to the kitchen and flipped the lights before I took out my phone and did what I did more than occasionally since the last one she didn't answer.

I texted Robin with, *Hey, things are happening and there's a lot to tell you. You're not replying, which has me worried. Give me a time that's good for me to call and I'll call. Love you!*

I got ready for bed, doing it a little dreamily because Bradley was a little dreamy and it was clear he liked me, but by the time I was ready for bed, I realized that Robin again hadn't texted back.

So, finally being grown up, I phoned her.

I got voicemail and left a message.

"Okay, now I'm really worried. Honey, we need to connect. There are some things I need to explain to you. Please call me."

I got a book and went to my buttery leather chair but I didn't read and slowly lost all the dreamy.

Because my friend didn't contact me.

———————————•———————————

THE NEXT MORNING, AS I WAS RUSHING INTO DOVE HOUSE, I HEARD MY phone chime with a text.

I dug it out as I pushed open the front door and I looked to Ruth at the reception desk.

I waved and said, "Hey," as she smiled at me and said, "'Morning, Amelia," and buzzed me in.

I pushed open the side door that locked the old folks in and walked through as I looked down at my phone.

I stopped dead, hearing the door click behind me.

Feverishly, I swept my finger over the screen to read the whole text.

Got the garage opener, Auden had texted. *Like your note said, I'll park in the garage. Thought you should know I got it.*

That was it.

No, *later.*

No, *bye, Mom.*

No, *love you.*

I didn't care. I'd take it.

Smiling huge, I started walking again just as I heard shrieked, "*Nazi!*"

I looked to my right to see Mrs. McMurphy sitting in the lounge glowering at me, her hand a fist above her head and lifting, her tongue lolling out, doing a signal of death by hanging.

"Good morning, Mrs. McMurphy," I called.

She jabbed a finger at me. "Got my eye on you."

I kept smiling but I walked away and started giggling.

Because Mrs. McMurphy might think I'm a Nazi.

But still, I was happy.

———————————•———————————

I WAS IN MY BEDROOM, PACKING AN OVERNIGHT BAG, DOING THIS attempting not to expire from death by paint fumes, when my phone rang.

I feared it was Alyssa, who'd shared she'd had a *very* good date night with her husband that began and ended in a motel room with a bottle of bourbon and another of chocolate sauce, thus she wanted to do it again.

Soon.

However, I'd spent that time with her kids, who were awesome, but they were rowdy and they'd done me in.

I wanted to be a good friend. I liked being around her kids. But I needed to ration that or her kids might kill me.

I saw the unknown number on my screen, but it was a number that was local and vaguely familiar, so I took the call, now hoping it was not the painters telling me the project of painting Cliff Blue would take two weeks rather than one.

They'd done my bedroom that day, painting the walls a beautiful dove gray with an elegant blue accent wall. This was why I was packing. I couldn't sleep in there, I didn't want to sleep in my kids' rooms and the guest bedroom was a wreck because the painters were moving on to that the next day. The living room had been painted the day before and still smelled, therefore the couch was also out.

So I was spending at least one night at Lavender House with the Spears.

I took the call and answered, "Hello."

"Amy," Mickey bit off.

I shot to straight at his tone and replied, "I thought we weren't talking."

"We aren't. Problem with that shit is my kids don't know we aren't and Ash's got some recipe she wants you to eat. She wants you over for dinner tomorrow night."

Disaster.

A disaster that had to be avoided.

To do that, I remarked, "I think that perhaps the fact that you and I clearly don't get along would mean that you should shield your children from that."

"I think the fact that since you're all grown up, you can be adult enough to act like you like me so my kids who like you can have you over so my girl can cook for you and my boy can talk your ear off," he returned.

It was frustrating that he was right.

"Fine," I snapped.

"Right," he clipped.

"Time?" I gritted out.

"Six," he bit off.

"Wonderful," I hissed.

"Terrific," he ground out.

With that, he hung up on me.

And with that, my head exploded and my thumb moved over my screen, not only programming his number in so I would never be blindsided again by Mickey Donovan, but also so I could tap his number and call his ass back.

Which I did.

"What?" he asked curtly as his greeting.

"I'm not fond of people hanging up on me," I shared waspishly.

"Noted," he grunted like he wished he didn't even have to make that noise while communicating with me.

"I also need to know if you want me to bring anything," I told him.

"Don't give a fuck what you do. Knock yourself out," he told me.

He could *not* be believed!

"Charming," I mumbled.

"Got a Ford and a job that means a tool belt hangs on my hips, Amy. Charm's just not in me. Not a man with an Infinity and bad manners, which means he makes out with a woman on the front step of a house in a family neighborhood."

He'd seen Bradley and me.

I felt my eyes turn to slits. "You *are* spying on me."

"Amelia, you were goin' at it *on your front step*," he returned tersely. "Not hard to see."

"Don't look," I retorted.

"Take that shit inside," he fired back.

"I will, Mickey," I snapped.

"Great," he bit out, sounding like he didn't think it was great at all. Then he continued, "Since we're havin' this loving conversation, please tell me you aren't sleepin' in that house tonight."

That confused me so I asked, "I'm sorry?"

"You are then you're not," he informed me. "You're comin' over here and sleepin' in my bed."

My heart skipped a beat and my knees went weak.

"I'll sleep on the couch," he went on. "But you aren't sleepin' in paint fumes. That shit can fuck you."

Oh God, now he was being his jerky, overbearing brand of sweet.

"I'm on my way to Lavender House," I assured him.

"Good. So now, heads up, do what you gotta do to prepare, but I'm hanging up."

Now he was just being a jerk.

"Don't be a jerk, Mickey," I snapped.

"You give me sweet, baby, you'll get it back," he retorted low, angry, and this was infuriatingly but indisputably outrageously sexy, which gave credence to the possibility I *was* a whackjob. "You ready for me to hit end?" he asked.

"I was ready five minutes ago."

"Bye, Amy."

"Good-bye, Mickey."

He hung up.

I threw my phone on the bed and it bounced on my duvet cover, which was subtle floral swirls in soft gray, porcelain blue, gentle taupe and muted apple green.

My mind conjured images of Mickey's long, big, hard body tangled up in that duvet and I shouted, "*Arrrrrgh!*" before I stomped to my bathroom to get my toiletries.

———————— • ————————

"Mrs. McMurphy sounds like da bomb," Cillian stated enthusiastically.

It was the next night and I was sitting at Mickey's dining room table, a table in a dining room I had not seen on my last visit because it was through a door on the other side of the kitchen and I had not been offered a complete tour.

It was a dining room table that was a long, farm table with ladder-back chairs that had fluffy, but trimmed, navy cushions and had been laid by Aisling for her dinner party.

It was a family table at which was seated a family.

I liked it. And I liked it even though Mickey and I had barely spoken from me arriving to that moment, when we were finishing up Aisling's delicious yellow cake with its thick layer of scrumptious chocolate butter-cream frosting. This being after we finished her delicious meal of Coca-Cola cured ham and expertly seasoned sautéed potatoes.

The food was excellent, but I was with a family and I just liked that.

This time, I had things to say, carrying on the conversation with Cillian, doing my part by sharing about the folks at Dove House, to Cillian's delight.

Mickey sat mostly silent and definitely brooding at the head, Aisling to his right, Cillian to her right at the long table that sat eight, but me, regrettably, to Mickey's left, which meant too close for comfort.

Throughout the meal, I gamely ignored him at the same time trying to appear like I wasn't ignoring him.

This was difficult. He was as handsome as ever and was wearing a dark blue, lightweight cotton shirt with the sleeves again rolled up. A shirt that did amazing things to his eyes.

He was also wearing jeans that were worn in but not worn out, and they fit his front, his back, and his long legs in a way I wish I could unsee because the vision of them kept popping up into my head at inappropriate times, in other words *constantly*.

It became less difficult because he was seated so I could no longer see his jeans.

Then it became even less difficult as I noted that Aisling was being Aisling, quiet, a little shy, solicitous, taking care of her family, but more of the former two.

I feared this was because she was not an eleven-year-old boy, who would miss the fact that Mickey and I were not speaking, but instead a fourteen-year-old girl, who *wouldn't* miss it.

And I noted that she didn't and this troubled her.

What troubled me was that I got the sense it was more. Something deeper. Something that had to do with Aisling alone and nothing to do with Mickey and me.

Something maybe to do with her mother.

"She is da bomb," I agreed with Cillian, watching Aisling at the same time trying not to appear like I was doing it and shifting my seat back, twisting to cross my legs to the side. "Though, if she were to meet you, I'd hope she doesn't think you're a Nazi."

"Me too," Cillian replied. "Maybe, when we go with you to Dove House, I'll dress as an Allied soldier so she won't get the wrong idea."

This amused me at the same time it alarmed me because he'd said "when" they went with me to Dove House.

I was about to address that when I felt something altogether too pleasant for the circumstances slinking over my legs and I felt this not after my mind conjured an image of Mickey in his jeans.

I looked to my legs then up to Mickey.

He was sitting back in his chair, one hand in his lap, one elbow on the arm of his chair, jaw resting on the backs of his curled fingers, eyes on my legs.

No, his entire *attention* was on my legs.

Completely.

I had on a pair of strappy, but casual, tan high-heeled sandals and with these was wearing a shirtwaist dress in a drifty silk with a subtle feminine pattern that had a background of deep pink. It had a belt of the same material cinching it at the waist, buttons up the front (and I'd only undone a proper few at my collarless neckline) and long sleeves. But the skirt was scalloped up at the side seams and hit above my knee.

Sitting, it rode up significantly.

So with my legs to the side, aimed toward Mickey, and crossed that way, a goodly amount of thigh was on show.

I felt a tinge of heat hit my cheeks—and, frankly, elsewhere—and I fought it back as I stared at Mickey, perplexed at the same time I resisted the urge to hide my legs under the table.

Why was he looking at my legs?

"So, when can we go?"

This question drew my attention and I looked to Cillian.

"Go where, honey?"

"With you to Dove House," he explained.

I blinked.

"That'd be cool," Aisling said quietly. "And I'm sure they could use the help. We could go one day before school starts, while Dad's at work."

"I—"

Cillian spoke over me, doing this to declare, "I'm not cleanin' up old people puke."

Aisling looked to her brother. "You won't have to. You can play checkers with them or something."

"I can't beat old people at checkers," he returned. "That'd be mean and I'm a master checker player."

"Then play something you're bad at," Aisling replied.

"Dude, I'm not bad at *anything*," Cillian retorted with a cheeky, arrogant grin.

"Why do you wanna go?" Aisling asked.

"Because Amy is *da bomb* and I want some old lady to shout at me," Cillian answered.

Aisling made a face that was not easy to behold.

But before I got a lock on why that was, she smoothed it and rebuked, "That isn't cool, Cill. She's not right in the head because she's old. You shouldn't go to a nursing home just to make fun of people."

Cillian reared back in horrified affront. "I'm not gonna *make fun of her*. I reckon everyone looks at her like she's crazy. She yells at me and calls me a Nazi, I'll march around in that stupid way they did and make her feel *not* crazy."

That was weird, but it was a weird kind of sweet.

"You go with Amy, you help Amy," Mickey entered the conversation, his voice deep with fatherly authority. "She wants you to play checkers with the folks there, you play checkers...and lose. Or you do dishes. Or you do whatever she asks."

Oh no, this couldn't happen.

I liked Mickey's kids. I liked being with them. I liked sitting at their table, chatting and eating. Even not getting along with Mickey, it felt nice to be a part of a family.

But the bottom line was that Mickey and I weren't getting along so in order for this not to trouble Aisling, or eventually be communicated to Cillian, we should curtail our together-type activities.

Not make up more as we went along.

"Just to point out but I have a two-seater car," I told them and looked to Mickey. "I can't get them there."

"I'll drop 'em off," he told me.

"I can't get them back," I replied desperately.

"I'll pick 'em up," he stated smoothly.

I glared.

He looked to my mouth and his got tight.

"Groovy!" Cillian cried and I forced myself to drop the glare and look at Mickey's boy. "When can we go? Tomorrow?"

The next words I had to say I knew might kill me.

"I need to tell Dela you're coming. She runs the place. So how about I talk to her and if she says it's okay, then I'll phone your dad and we'll set a day before you go back to school."

"Awesome!" Cillian exclaimed.

"Yeah, Amy, that'd be cool," Aisling said softly, a small smile on her lips.

I took in her smile and just getting it, I'd put up with her father.

"Look forward to *that* call," Mickey muttered, his meaning lost on everyone but me.

I shifted my legs in order to kick him in the shin.

His body jolted and his gaze cut to me.

I gave him a look I hoped was nasty.

He took it, something shifted behind his eyes, and he grinned at me.

Jerk.

I looked away.

"Can I have another piece of cake, Dad?" Cillian asked.

Mickey answered his boy, "Yeah, son."

I looked to Aisling, who was looking between her father and me. Caught, she then cast her eyes to her plate.

"Dinner was amazing, blossom," I told her softly.

She lifted her gaze to me briefly and mumbled, "Thanks, Amy."

I watched her do this and thought that, yes, something about Aisling Donovan was troubling me.

Cillian got his extra piece of cake, everyone cleared and Mickey set his kids to washing up while I explained it was time to leave.

I got good-byes from the kids and unfortunately, Mickey decided to walk me to his front door.

"I can get there myself," I said under my breath on the way.

"You can also get there with me," he said under his.

I shut up.

We reached the door and I stopped, seeing my mistake immediately as I should have stopped to the side, not in front, or I should have just quickly opened the damned door myself.

This was so, knowing Mickey would characteristically take charge (I refused to think it was gentlemanly), I wouldn't feel Mickey's hard chest and lovely heat against my back as he reached beyond me to open the door.

Furthering my mistake, when the door swung open in front of me, I had to press back into him, something he rudely didn't move out of my way to allow me room to do.

So when it was open, I made my escape.

I did this with Mickey noting softly, "Nice dress, Amy."

I whirled on him and hissed quietly, "Don't be a jerk."

His eyes went dark. "Jesus, baby, it's a nice fuckin' dress. What's your problem?"

"I'm sorry, *you* were being nice to *me?*" I asked sarcastically.

"Yeah, but now I see my mistake so, apologies, won't happen again," he answered shortly.

My heart was for some reason hammering in my chest, perhaps because maybe he *was* being nice and I hadn't been and I felt stupid and petty.

But like I couldn't stop it, to save face, I continued being so as I shook my hair, ordering, "See that it doesn't."

"Maybe you *should* date Stone," he muttered. "Match made in heaven."

I couldn't believe he just said that.

"That's a terrible thing to say," I snapped.

"Call 'em like I see 'em," he declared.

That made me even *more* angry.

Angry enough to lean into him. "It's *you* being *mean* that brings this out in me."

He bent his neck deep, getting in my face.

"I told you 'nice dress,'" he clipped. "Because it's a *nice dress*. Looks good on you. If that's mean, you definitely got a screw loose and have no clue how a man *should* treat you. Fuck, you like nasty, after I saw what your ex did to you, now I'm wondering what it took Infinity to get his tongue in your mouth. What? He tell you you looked like a whore?"

"I'm not discussing Bradley with you," I retorted coolly.

He leaned back, his eyebrows going up, and asked incredulously, "*Bradley?*"

"Yes. *Bradley*," I bit off.

"Like, he makes you say the whole thing?" he pushed.

"The whole thing what?" I asked.

"Bradley. Not Brad," he explained impatiently.

"Yes, the whole thing. He prefers Bradley," I confirmed.

He looked over my head and let out a puff of disgusted air.

"It *is* a name, Mickey," I informed him and his eyes came back to me.

"It's a name for a douche, Amy."

All right, enough.

"Are we done?" I asked.

"Probably until your phone call, yeah," he answered.

"Enjoy the rest of your evening with your marvelous children who I have absolutely no clue how they could have come from your loins," I bid him.

"And you enjoy the rest of yours in your big house all by yourself," he returned.

"I will," I gritted.

"I bet," he retorted, stepped back and shut the door in my face.

"Jerk," I whispered to his door.

Then I turned on my beautiful high heel and stomped down his walk (I couldn't go through his yard, my heels would sink in), down his drive and right to my house.

He couldn't hear me and he wasn't looking.

I still slammed my front door.

———— • ————

"Yeah?" Mickey answered.

Charming.

"It's Amelia."

"Know who it is."

"Dela said the kids can come."

"I'll alert the media."

Jerk!

"Can you drop them off at Dove House at ten?"

"Yep."

"And pick them up at one?"

"Can do."

"Excellent."

"Later."

"Bye."

He hung up.

I glared at my phone.

Then I shoved it in my purse and flounced out of Dove House, the flouncing all for me since no one was in reception so no one could admire my magnificent drama caused by a man named Mickey.

"This is gonna be so fun," Cillian whispered excitedly.

I looked to him standing by me on the walk to Dove House.

I knew no child who thought hanging for three hours at a nursing home would be fun and I wondered, even if he gave no other indications he wasn't, if Cillian was all there.

"You do what Amy says," Mickey ordered.

"No probs," Cillian assured.

"We will, Dad," Aisling mumbled.

Aisling gave her dad a hug. Cillian and Mickey bumped chests. Cillian ran inside with Aisling trailing and I looked to Mickey.

"One," he stated, turned on his foot and walked away.

The kids were one hundred percent wonderful with the old folks.

So much so it was astonishing.

Cillian was talkative, exuberant, full of energy and had all the time in the world for everybody, including staffers that asked him to help with things.

Aisling was sweet, attentive, helpful and quietly charmed everyone she met.

Mrs. McMurphy called Cillian by his name.

Mr. Dennison transferred his affections to Aisling.

And me, if I was their mother, I would throw every bottle of booze I had into the sea and do everything I could to show these two amazing beings how proud I was to say they belonged to me.

So it wasn't only me who was disappointed when I had to tell the kids to say good-bye so I could walk them out front to wait for their father. It was also the residents, who rarely had visitors, and rarer still those visitors were of the young variety.

We got outside to find Mickey was already there, parked out front and leaning against the side of his big SUV, wearing what he was wearing earlier (except now they were dusty), clothes I suspected were his construction clothes as they included construction boots, faded jeans and a snug fitting tee.

Even that outfit he made amazing.

"We're *so* doing that again, Dad," Cillian cried, rushing to his father.

Mickey pushed away from his truck, smiling at his son. "You liked it, boy, I'm *so* letting you."

"Cool!" Cillian yelled, turned to me and waved. "Later, Amy."

"Later, honey," I called.

"Yeah, later, Amy," Aisling, at my side, said softly.

I turned to her and lifted a hand to curl it light on her upper arm. "Later, blossom. Thanks for being so lovely."

She shrugged a shoulder, her head tipping that way, this gesture causing me to feel what was becoming familiar unease when it came to Aisling, before I had to let her go because she meandered to her dad's truck.

Mickey walked to me.

I looked up at him and braced.

I braced more, tipping my head far back when he got closer than was necessary.

"Seems they had a good time," he said quietly.

"They did and they charmed everybody," I replied quietly. "You've got good kids, Mickey."

"Yeah," he murmured, drew in a breath that expanded his broad chest, something that made me feel odd things, things I quit feeling when he finished, "Later, Amy."

It struck me then that his kids were supposed to call me Miz Hathaway.

But they'd been calling me Amy.

And he'd said nothing.

I didn't mention this.

I said, "Later, Mickey."

He lifted his chin and turned away.

I watched him walk, doing this taking in the natural control he had over his body, thus doing it enjoying it, and I knew I should go in. I knew I shouldn't stand out there and watch them drive away.

But I stood out there and watched them drive away.

I even did it waving and smiling.

They were making the turn onto the street when I jumped because I heard, "Your fellow is quite good-looking, Amelia."

I looked down at Mrs. McMurphy, who was wearing a bulky winter coat and standing beside me.

"He's not—" I started but stopped when she leaned into me.

"Don't let him loose. Smart woman never lets go of a good man," she advised.

I stared because I realized we were having a relatively normal conversation and she'd called me Amelia, something she never called me.

Then she shivered, even though it was a sunny, summer day, and looked to the heavens.

She then turned, smartly snapped open an umbrella that had come loose from two of its prongs, put it over her head and started walking away.

I kept staring then I jolted because Mrs. McMurphy had somehow slipped through the admittedly dreadful security keeping the old folks inside and safe, and she was ambling away in a cold thunderstorm that was not happening.

"Wait!" I exclaimed, starting after her.

She turned and brandished her umbrella at me. "Don't get near me, you Nazi!" She swung the umbrella wide and shouted, "Death to Hitler!"

I managed not to laugh as I also managed to corral a cantankerous Nazi-hating old lady back into her nice, but still slightly shabby, home for the elderly.

10

THEY SPOKE TO ME

The Friday my children were to return to me, when I heard the garage door go up, I did not rush to the door leading to the garage, open it and stand in it, waiting.

I continued doing what I was doing in the kitchen.

So when my kids came through the door, I was there, waiting for them, glad they were home, but not showing them I was waiting for them.

But I did show them I was glad they were home.

I did this looking to the side, smiling wide, and calling, "Hey, honeys."

Auden looked to me.

Olympia shuffled behind him to get out of the way of the closing door.

"Come here, would you?" I asked, rolling dough in my hands that was going to be sugar cookies with M&Ms, another of their favorites.

They moved my way but stopped well beyond the end of the counter that started the kitchen.

I let that happen and continued doing what I was doing, shifting my attention between them and the cookies and doing it speaking.

"I hope you did as I asked and didn't make plans, because tonight we're having dinner and then we're watching a movie together. *A Few Good Men.* As you can see, I got a couch so we can all sit close to the TV. *And there are tables.*"

I tipped my head toward the opposite landing to call their attention to the couch.

I also took in all I'd wrought.

The couch was an unusual online buy, but it was perfect. Low backed but very deep seated, with sweeping arms at the sides and chunky, squat wooden legs at the bottom. It was in a camel twill and it had a plethora of fabulous, scrunchy toss pillows on it, matching ones on the chair. And the couch was so long, it would easily seat both my babies even if they stretched out (and shared some space).

Further, there was a low, wide, rectangular wooden chest in front of it that I was using as a coffee table. I found it in an antique shop by the cove. And Josie's interior designer had one of her cabinetmakers custom-make a very long, low media center. It sat under the hanging TV and had shelves for all the components, some cabinets to store stuff, and more shelves to put CDs and DVDs.

And the walls had been painted a warm, but neutral oyster. There was now another end table around the sectional that was also a chest, taller and square, and a square coffee table in the middle that wasn't the same wood as the chest, but it was in the same hue, battered and beautiful.

There were wire glass candle pots and squat round pewter candle holders of varying heights with fat candles in them dotted around, mingling with the knickknacks I didn't sell because they meant something from our home in La Jolla, and framed photos, with a fabulous conglomeration of the last scattering the top of the low media center under the TV.

I needed prints for the walls and afghans to snuggle under when it started to get cold. I also still needed a new dining room table, an acquisition that was foiling me.

But it was coming together.

The effect was warm. It was rich in a way that had nothing to do with money (but still did). It was inviting. It was pleasing to the eye. It was comfortable. And even with the magnificence of the structure all around, the stylish, state-of-the-art kitchen with its cement countertops, stainless steel appliances and fabulous hanging pendant lights, the massive wall of windows, the glorious view, it was not imposing, overwhelming or in-your-face.

It said you're welcome to be there, take a seat, relax and enjoy.

It was me.

I kept rolling cookies, putting them on the baking sheet and blathering to my children.

"Tomorrow, I'm taking you out shopping." I shook my head and a doughy hand at them and went on, "Don't lose it on me, but I don't want you to have to lug bags here and back to your dad's. We're talking shampoo. Curling irons. Pajamas. Some clothes if you want. Things like that. I just want you to do what you can in the short time we have to make this feel like your home. So that's what we're doing."

I wanted that. I thought it was a good thing to do. Both of my kids liked shopping, even Auden. And I wanted them to feel when they came to me they were coming home.

I also wanted to take them to Dove House.

However, as sad as it was to admit, I didn't know if they'd be as charming and respectful of the old folks as Aisling and Cillian were.

I did know that they would not be affectionate and respectful to me and I didn't want the residents seeing that. I also didn't want it to confuse them, considering Aisling and Cillian weren't my kids and they had been both.

"We'll go out to dinner and a movie tomorrow too," I kept going. "Then, on Sunday, I found this place that does really amazing outdoor furniture. It's not close, about an hour and a half drive, but that's where we're going."

I put a ball of dough on the sheet and looked their way to see they hadn't moved. Olympia was watching my hands. Auden was watching me.

I didn't stop talking.

"I know that the weather is going to turn here soon so I probably shouldn't worry about the deck until next year." I grinned. "But I haven't had *weather* in a long time. I'm looking forward to it. And knowing what it was like in Boston and Lexington, I know by the time summer rolls around again I'll want to be ready to enjoy that deck right away."

My kids said nothing.

I still didn't quit talking.

"So that's it. Those are our plans for this weekend. Sound good?"

"Did Dad shout at you?" Auden asked tersely.

I froze at his question, except my eyes slid to my daughter to see she was shuffling her feet and rolling her lips.

She'd told her brother what she'd heard.

I looked back to Auden, not even knowing how to begin to handle this.

"Yes, honey," I answered honestly.

His jaw went hard and his Adam's apple bobbed before he bit out, "He came here and got in your face."

Even though I suspected (though I hoped not), that Martine and Conrad would throw me under the bus and did (often), that was not me.

So I didn't do that.

"I believe we're all aware that prior to me arriving in Magdalene, I gave your dad reason to be angry with me," I reminded him softly.

"You were here by yourself?" Auden asked belligerently.

"Well, yes, sweets. I didn't know anyone back—"

"You were here by yourself," he repeated, a statement this time, his tone angry.

I turned fully to them, doughy hands and all.

"Yes," I answered.

"Are you eating?" Auden asked confrontationally, a change in subject that made my head twitch.

"I'm sorry?"

"You're too skinny," he informed me irately. "Why aren't you eating?"

"I..." I shook my head. "I lost some weight but—"

"You're super-skinny, Mom," he bit out.

God.

He called me Mom.

He hadn't said my name in so long, it hurt.

Killed.

I didn't burst into happy tears.

I told him, "I was busy when I got here, honey. I lost track of what I was eating. I know I lost some weight, but I'm eating again. Promise."

After I said this, Olympia shifted a bit to her brother's side and asked like she was making an accusation, "Are you dating?"

I stared at my girl.

How could she know that?

She must have seen more of the interaction with Boston, Mickey and me than I thought.

"Well...yes," I answered carefully.

My daughter had not shared that tidbit with her brother. I knew it when his eyes got wide before his brows snapped together. "You're *dating?*"

Now how did I handle *this?*

When that question hit my brain, it struck me that my children were living with their father *and* his new wife *and* they'd been doing it for years, so they knew very well how divorced parents moved on.

They also weren't kid-kids anymore. They were old enough to know at least some of the ways of the world, especially those their father already taught them.

"Yes, I'm dating," I declared. "And it's healthy," I went on. "It's part of getting on with my life and *building* a life, enjoying it and maybe, some-day, finding some happiness for me."

"Are you dating that guy?" Pippa asked and I looked to her, worried she meant Boston Stone as she'd seen me with him and clearly seen me accept a date with him.

To confirm what she meant so she had a straight answer, I queried, "What guy?"

"The old, hot firefighter guy," she answered.

Mickey.

Funny she thought he was old. He seemed criminally vital to me.

I shook my head. "No, Pippa, I'm not dating him. He's...a friend."

"You're not dating him?" she pushed.

"No, honey, I'm not."

"He's into you," she declared.

I blinked.

"Jeez, Pip, shut up, will you? Auden muttered and ended on, "Sick."

She looked to her brother. "You weren't there. This slimy guy was hitting on Mom and he swooped in and got in his face. It wasn't sick. He's old but he's hot and that *definitely* was hot. And he wouldn't even let Mom put her groceries in the car, that's how into her he is. And he practically got in a smackdown with that slimy dude when *he* tried to put Mom's groceries in her car." She drew in a deep breath and shared, "*And* he was the one who saw Dad shouting at Mom."

Clearly, my girl had been on the sidewalk a whole lot longer than I suspected.

Auden's eyes cut to me. "Did this guy see Dad shouting at you?"

"He kind of…saved me," I told them.

Auden's eyes went stormy. "Saved you?"

"Your father was emotional," I thought it safe to say.

Auden's jaw went hard again and his eyes sliced to the wall of windows.

"So!" I said loudly, deciding that although I was beside myself with delight my children were talking to me, this particular conversation needed to come to an end. "Here we are. Your mom is moving on, dating, the house is getting shaped up and we're spending time together. Now, it'd be great if you'd dump your things, get settled, take some time to make a list of stuff we need to go out and buy tomorrow, then later, we'll have dinner and watch a movie."

They both stared at me.

"You can do that now," I prompted. "I'm going to finish these cookies."

Auden looked me up and down and asked, "Are you going to *eat* some cookies?"

I really, *really* hoped that question meant my boy was worried about me. I didn't actually want him worried, but I thought it said good things that he'd feel anything.

"Yes, baby," I answered gently.

His jaw went so hard at that, a muscle jumped in his cheek.

Then, without a word, he prowled across the space to the hall.

"Did you dump my new comforter?" Pippa asked and her voice had an edge of ugly but there was something else there that was reminiscent of my little Pippa.

"No, Pippa, you didn't put your other stuff back in your room so I got rid of your old stuff." I tipped my head to the side. "I hope that's what you wanted."

"Whatever," she muttered, turning away. "It wasn't *that* ugly."

She liked it, my stubborn baby girl who was perhaps too much like me.

I grinned at the cookies.

My children spent time settling.

Then they actually did as I asked and made lists.

We had dinner.

We watched a movie lounged in front of the TV (and they ate cookies!).

We went out the next day and spent the entire day shopping (neither of my children was averse to either of their parents dropping a load of cash on them, one thing that hadn't changed), after which we had dinner out and went to see a movie.

And Auden drove as I sat beside him, Pippa in the back seat, and we went to the furniture place. I fell in love with two lounge chairs I bought on the spot (and could tell, even though neither said much, though Pippa mumbled, "They're pretty cool," that my kids liked them too) and paid a fortune for shipping.

We stopped for lunch on the way to, and after we drove back, they went home to their father's.

Through this, they were not affectionate. They were not chatty. They sometimes were surly, but that was thankfully rare. Mostly they were indifferent or acted like they were putting up with me.

But they gave me the whole weekend.

And they spoke to me.

So I'd take that.

Oh, yes, I'd take it.

Absolutely.

11

WANT MORE

a couple of days after my children left, I was rushing to get ready for my date with Bradley.

It was our third.

And it was not working.

Yes, he was good-looking. Yes, he was interesting. Yes, he was interested in me.

But what I was trying not to admit to myself, and failing, was that he wasn't Mickey.

He wasn't so beautiful it almost hurt to look at him. He didn't make me feel so hard I lost sight of everything, even if with Mickey, much of what I felt with him was angry.

Mickey was not an option for me. He didn't find me attractive. I knew that.

And he'd still ruined me.

Also, who actually *did* make people call them *Bradley*?

That reminded me of my father, who persisted in calling my brother Lawrence, when my brother hated that and everyone, even my mother, called him Lawr and he allowed me (and my kids) to call him Lawrie.

So I was going to have to end it with Bradley, something I had no clue how to do because that, too, was something I hadn't done in decades.

Fortunately, in all the time he'd been gone, Boston Stone had only called twice, and one time I had been working at Dove House so he left me a message (that I didn't return), and the other time I'd been having lunch with Ruth and Dela so it was rude to talk to him, except briefly.

In that brief time he'd told me he was coming home imminently, so I'd have to deal with him too.

I could have worse problems, I knew, having a husband who'd ended it with me. Being on the other side of that was always the wrong side to be.

So I had to be a grownup and get on with it.

I was digging through my makeup tray trying to find the lipstick I was looking for when my phone on the bathroom counter rang.

I looked to it and my heart stopped beating.

It was Conrad.

He'd never phone unless something was wrong with the kids.

I snatched it up, sucking in breath, took the call and put the phone to my ear.

"Conrad?"

"I'll thank you to phone your brother and tell him to stop badgering me."

I shot straight and looked unseeing into the mirror.

"I'm sorry?" I asked.

"He's phoned twice, laying into me about turning my children against you, and I'll not have it, Amelia."

"Our children, Conrad."

"What?" he clipped.

"*Our* children," I repeated. "And if Lawrie's calling you and you don't want to hear from him, don't answer the phone."

"If this is your latest tactic—"

"Right," I cut him off. "We're not doing this," I declared firmly. "I had no idea Lawrie was calling you but he's a big boy. He does what he does. I can't control him. I'll phone him to ask him to stop. If he doesn't, *you* be a big boy and don't take his calls. Problem solved. What I won't do is have you blaming me for something I didn't do. And, I'll ask, since I didn't do it, that you don't bitch to our children about their uncle badgering you when calling twice is hardly badgering, and doing that bitching blaming that on me. Truly, Conrad, with *all* that's happening, you should man up and not complain to our children about the situation *you* created."

"What's that supposed to mean?" he asked hostilely.

"Think on it," I answered. "Now, I'm late preparing for a date and I have to get going. But I'll say one last thing and that is, *you* made it clear that communication between us should be curtailed *completely*. I've had you communicating with me twice while I've been in Maine, and twice it was unpleasant and unnecessary. So that goes both ways. I'll leave you to your life. You leave me to mine. And in between, we share *our* children. Now, have a good evening, Conrad."

"Amel—" he started.

I hung up and when I saw his name pop on my screen when my phone started ringing again almost immediately, I ignored it and kept digging for my lipstick.

"Yes, two. I have a reservation. Bradley Tinsdale," Bradley said to the hostess as I stood by him, holding his hand, looking into the restaurant called The Eaves that I knew was very nice because I could see it. But also because Josie and Alyssa had both squealed over it when I told them Bradley was taking me there (well, Josie hadn't actually squealed, but her excitement was clearly evident).

At that moment, it made me nervous because Bradley was taking me somewhere very nice, each date the escalation of *nice* was rising, as with each date the make out session at my door got more heated (okay, so there was only one other time, still that time was more heated).

I didn't know if he was hoping to coax me into bed by buying me increasingly more expensive meals (which wasn't happening) or if with each date he liked me more and was trying harder to impress me.

Neither was good since I was ending things with him that night (prior to any make out session happening, obviously).

This was what was consuming my thoughts when I heard the hostess say, "Please, follow me," and felt Bradley tug my hand.

I followed him wishing I hadn't used my most awesome outfit on this.

It was my first little black dress since Conrad divorced me. Simple. Skintight. Hem well above the knee (but not skanky). V at back and front, both deep, front exposing cleavage, back exposing skin all the way down to my black, lacy bra strap (which I hoped would be attractive should the V dip lower).

The dress was an Alyssa pick and it might be simple, but it was spectacular (incidentally, the lacy black bra was also an Alyssa pick, it was not simple and the jury was out on if it was skanky because it, and its matching panties, were *sexy*).

My legs were bare but I'd used this oil/lotion stuff on them that Robin had bought me for Christmas the year before that I'd never had a reason to use. But I found the results were *divine* as it gave a sheen to my skin that seemed natural, was absolutely not, but it *was* utterly fabulous.

On my feet I had black pointed-toed, slingbacks with pencil-thin heels, these covered in lace so the rim of the shoe was scalloped delicately...and amazingly.

I'd also spent a huge amount of time on my hair, arranging it in a messy side bun that took ages to pull off but I thought looked great.

Why I'd gone gung-ho, I didn't know. The outfit didn't say, "I'm ending it." It said something else entirely.

Except perhaps that night, I was using my clothes as armor.

My mind still consumed with what would happen at the end of the evening (as well as uselessly contemplating the pros and cons of my outfit, something I should have done two hours ago), it came as a surprise when I heard Cillian cry, "Amy!"

I was studying my toes in my amazing shoes moving across the carpet, so at my name, my head shot up, and at what I saw, my whole body jolted.

Seated at a table were Cillian in a white dress shirt, Aisling in a pretty pink dress, and Mickey in his own white dress shirt under a well-cut, navy blue sports jacket.

They were perusing menus.

Oh God.

Why?

Why me?

Cillian circled his hand to me as Aisling turned and looked over her shoulder, the timid smile on her face dying the instant she saw Bradley.

That troubled me but I had no time for it because Mickey looked our way.

When he did, his eyes dropped the length of me and shot up, cut to Bradley briefly, then back to me, his face turning to stone.

Seeing that, how my daughter could think he was into me, I had no idea. He obviously disliked me and I knew this because he didn't bother to hide it.

"Do you know them?" Bradley murmured, pulling me closer to him.

"They're my neighbors," I answered.

"Put the menus at our table, please. We'll be there shortly," Bradley ordered the hostess.

She nodded and swept away.

Bradley pulled me to the Donovan table.

"Hey!" Cillian cried when we got close and then announced upon our arrival, "It's my birthday."

Shit.

I didn't know.

I controlled the accusatory look I wanted to throw Mickey's way and instead smiled big at Cillian.

"First, happy birthday," I said. "And second, please assure me that you accept late gifts."

His smile got bigger. "Totally."

"Also, assure me that you provide late wish lists," I went on.

He beamed. "*Totally.*"

"Good," I said, still smiling at him. "I expect that list to be in my mailbox by noon tomorrow."

"You got it!" Cillian cried.

Bradley squeezed my hand and I quickly looked up at him, realizing I was being rude.

"Sorry," I murmured then looked to the table. "Let me make the introductions. Bradley, this is the Donovan family. Aisling, Mickey and Cillian, the birthday boy. Donovan family, this is Bradley Tinsdale."

Mickey stood and offered a hand wordlessly.

Bradley took it.

They both looked into each other's eyes and held their grip two shades too long.

I fought squirming.

"Nice to meet you," Bradley said to the table when he and Mickey finally disconnected.

Mickey seated himself, his eyes coming to me, and when they did, it felt like they were skewering me.

He was angry, plain to see.

But I couldn't imagine how that could be.

"What?" I mouthed silently, gaze on Mickey.

His eyes dipped, came up to catch mine and they narrowed.

He was communicating, I just didn't know what he was saying.

"*What?*" I mouthed again, leaning forward a little to put emphasis on my soundless word.

"Amelia?" Bradley called.

My body gave another jolt and I looked up at him to see him watching me closely.

"Yes?" I asked, trying to pretend he hadn't just caught me mouthing to Mickey.

"Would you like to go to our table or chat with the Donovans?" he asked politely, but a little stiffly.

"We should probably go to our table," I replied and looked to Mickey's family, concerned to see Aisling had righted in her seat, this meaning she had her back to Bradley and me, which was impolite for a girl who was never that way. "Wish list, kiddo. Tomorrow. Noon," I said Cillian.

"You got it," Cillian replied, still smiling.

"Aisling," I said softly, reaching out to touch her shoulder.

She glanced up at me swiftly and then away, muttering, "Good to see you, Amy."

I braced and looked at her father. "Mickey."

"Amy," he replied, drawing his brows together and again dipping his eyes before they came back to mine.

I had no opportunity to make a further fool of myself by soundlessly demanding to know what Mickey was saying because Bradley drew me away.

When we got to our table, he pulled my chair out and I sat in it. Then he sat. And thankfully we did this, ordered drinks and received them, all without incident.

We were perusing our menus when I looked across the three tables that separated us and saw Bradley's back was to the Donovans, but Mickey's side was to me and his head was turned my way, his complete attention on me.

And I could tell he was still angry.

Very angry.

That was when I had my first inkling I was in trouble.

He jerked his head in an aggressive manner that irked me.

Chancing a glance at Bradley, who was studying his menu, I looked back to Mickey, tipped my head to the side and flipped out a hand in my non-verbal, "what?"

He lifted a hand and jabbed a finger my way, tipping it slightly down, then up, then moving it to touch it to his chest.

Oh God.

Did I have something on my dress?

I looked down instantly and saw all was clear.

I lifted my head, snapped my brows together, and after another click glance at Bradley, who was still examining his menu, I looked back at Mickey and again flipped my hand out.

Her jerked his head in that aggressive way again but not toward me, in another direction.

I looked in that direction and saw there was a door to a hallway, above which it had a sign that read "Restrooms."

I looked back to Mickey's table to see he was no longer there. He was up and prowling infuriatedly toward that door, looking insanely hot doing this in his sports jacket.

God, he was killing me.

"What looks good to you?" Bradley asked.

Mickey Donovan, I did not answer.

"I need a moment," I said and his head came up, his eyes to me. "Just need to freshen up a bit. Do you mind?" I asked.

"No, Amelia," he replied, his face getting soft. "Take all the time you need."

He was a nice man.

And I was an idiot.

Even knowing that, it didn't stop me from grabbing my clutch and shooting out of my chair perhaps a wee bit too swiftly for someone who'd just insinuated she might need to use the restroom but mostly she wanted to fix her lipstick.

Then I stormed across the restaurant to the hall and down it.

It was a long hall and at the end of it, another hall led off at a T with a sign that said "Restrooms" with an arrow pointing right, "Staff Only" with an arrow pointing left.

I went right, passing the men's (why was the men's room always first?

irritating) and then the ladies', heading to the very end of the hall where Mickey was standing, arms crossed on his chest, scowling at me.

I shoved my clutch under my arm, again lifted both hands, stomping his way, but this time I asked a verbal, "What?"

I arrived at him.

Then I was not in the hall but shoved into an alcove off the side, which was quite possibly a place where they put racks to hang coats during winter months but right then was a dark space totally removed from *everything*.

"Mickey," I whispered, half in shock, half something else entirely.

"Uh...no," he said infuriatedly and bafflingly.

"No, what?" I asked, staring up at him, not believing I was in a dark area removed from a restaurant where my date was, his kids were, and I was pressed against a wall by an aggressive, inexplicably angry Mickey Donovan.

"No," he repeated but he did this shocking me to my bones by lifting a finger and gliding it from the very start of the cleft of my cleavage *over* that cleft, dipping slightly *into* my cleavage.

Even though his touch made my nipples harden instantly, I lifted my hand and snatched his finger away, keeping hold of it.

"What are you doing?" I hissed under my breath.

"Pull your goddamned dress up," he clipped under his.

"Are you *crazy*?" I kept hissing.

"That guy, fuckin' *Bradley*, is that a joke?" he asked.

I didn't know what that meant.

That didn't stop me from snapping, "No."

"Amy, even your ex, who's a dick, is not as big of a douche as that douche at your table."

Oh my God!

"Bradley is not *a douche*," I retorted.

"Bradley is *a douche* and you do not give cleavage to a *douche* who you're gonna let take you out for a couple of dinners and then dump his ass when you figure out he's a *douche*."

"For your information, I'm ending things with Bradley tonight, but not because he's a *douche*, since he's not. He's nice. Because it just isn't working for me."

Mickey's expression clouded over with sudden brotherly affront. "And you're showin' your tits to give him a look at what he's not gonna get?"

I felt my face get pink and not in ways that Mickey normally made it pink.

Because I was *furious*.

"I have cleavage because my dress has cleavage, Mickey."

"Pull up the dress, Amelia."

I looked from side to side in mock panic before looking back to Mickey, letting his finger go, and grasping frantically at his lapels.

"Oh God!" I cried. "Did I enter a time machine and didn't notice it? Are we back in 1818 where a man can drag a woman into an alcove at an eating establishment and demand she cover herself up?"

Mickey didn't answer, and him not having a ready comeback surprised me enough to pay closer attention.

And what I saw was him looking down at me, his face thunderous, his jaw ticking, looking like he could easily murder someone, painfully and bloodily.

And the closest someone was me.

"Mickey," I whispered, uncurling my fingers in order to smooth his jacket and then hopefully slide away and escape.

I didn't get that far.

He muttered a terse, *"Fuck it."*

And then he was kissing me.

Mickey Donovan was *kissing me!*

At first, I was suspended in utter disbelief.

Then his tongue touched my lips, I opened my mouth, it slid inside...

And I tasted Mickey.

He was the most beautiful taste to ever touch my tongue.

Because of that, I wanted more.

And I took it, in doing so receiving the best kiss I'd had *in my life*.

It was deep, wet, *blazing*.

So much of all that I forgot everything.

I forgot I was in a restaurant.

I forgot I was on a date.

I forgot my date was *in* said restaurant.

I forgot Mickey's kids were there.

I forgot *everything*.

Everything, but Mickey.

It consumed us both in its blistering heat to the point mouths and tongues weren't enough and we both started groping.

I was right.

He was hard and he was hot, everywhere I touched.

I *loved* it.

And his hands on me, over my clothes, did things to me I didn't know I could feel.

I whimpered against his tongue and he tore his mouth free.

But he didn't go far and I found myself pressed to a wall by the solid heat of Mickey, his fingers tangled in my hair, his other hand cupped on my behind. My arms were in his jacket, one hand clenched in the back of his shirt, the other one pressed tight against his rock-hard shoulder blade.

We were both breathing heavily.

"Two choices, Amelia," he stated in a low, throaty voice that sped right between my legs, forcing the wet already gathering there from the kiss to become soaked. "You either go out there and tell that guy to take a hike, come and sit at our table and have Cillian's birthday dinner with us or you go out there, get that guy outta here, end it with him and I'll be over later."

"It would be rude to tell him to take a hike," my mouth said for me.

"Then get his ass outta here, end it and I'll be over later."

Oh God, what was happening?

"Mickey," I whispered.

He pressed me into the wall and his fingers slid deeper into my hair, gripping my side bun as his hand at my behind clenched.

Sodden was history, now I feared I was dripping.

"Get him outta here, Amy," he growled.

"Okay, Mickey," I breathed.

His eyes dropped to my mouth and he muttered, "Right across the street, *fuck*."

"Mickey, I think—" I began.

He interrupted me, "You think for the next three hours that you're gonna think about anything but that kiss and ending it with that guy, I'm gonna kiss you again, Amy, so you won't."

He couldn't kiss me again. If he did, I'd lose thought of everything and probably end up having sex against the wall in a dark alcove in a fancy restaurant with Mickey.

"I don't think I'll forget that kiss," I told him breathily.

"Right," he bit off, sounding angry.

"Are you angry?" I asked.

"Are you gonna walk out to that guy wearing that dress?" he asked back.

"Well...yes."

"Then yeah, I'm angry."

More baffling.

"Why?" I asked.

"Reverse roles and think of me walkin' out to a woman who was wearing that dress," he clipped.

That wasn't baffling.

"Oh."

I had a feeling my fourteen-year-old daughter was right.

Mickey Donovan was into me.

"Now are you gonna be cute, which means I'm gonna have to kiss you again, which will maybe be so hot I won't be able to stop it this time so I'll have to fuck you against a wall in the hall of a restaurant while my kids are waiting for me to eat my son's birthday dinner? Or are you gonna get your ass to the table and get that guy outta here?"

I was breathing heavier when I answered, "I'm gonna get that guy outta here."

"Good call."

We stared at each other and didn't move.

This lasted long moments before Mickey noted, "You aren't leaving."

"You have to let me go, honey," I whispered.

"Fuck,' he whispered back, and the unbearable happened.

His fingers slid out of my hair, his hand glided away from my bottom, and he stepped back.

I felt like a treasure chest full of gold had been bared to me, all mine for the keeping, and then the minute I dug my fingers into the gleaming coins, it disappeared in a blink.

"Go, baby," he ordered gently.

I held his gaze, licked my lips, rolled them together and nodded.

Then I started to go but stopped when he called a soft, "Amy."

God, just my name on his lips made me even *wetter*.

I turned to him to see he'd grabbed my forgotten clutch from where it had dropped to the floor and was holding it out to me.

I took it, whispering, "Thanks."

"Go," he whispered back.

I took off, wisely going first to the bathroom to fix my hair (it didn't look near as good when I finished, then again, I didn't have a lot of time and my hands were shaking).

I also put lipstick on.

But there was no way to hide I looked like I'd been kissed. Thoroughly. My lips were swollen, my cheeks flushed, my eyes dazed. I tried to rectify it but I didn't have time enough for that either.

This would be to my fortune, though not entirely, for it would make my errand of getting Bradley out of the restaurant easy, it was just that doing it wasn't pleasant.

He'd noticed Mickey gone.

He noticed my thoroughly kissed mouth and disheveled side bun when I returned.

So when I shared gently we had to leave so we could talk, he threw an acid look Mickey's way before he tossed his napkin down, pushed his chair back, got out his wallet, flung some bills on the table and stalked away.

He didn't help me out of my seat.

He didn't hold my hand as he marched out of the restaurant.

And he went so fast, I had to hurry to keep up so I could only glance and wave at the Donovan table.

Mickey was looking at me, his look was a mix of annoyed and heated.

Cillian waved at me.

Aisling only glanced at me but when she looked away, she smiled a little smile like the cat who just got her cream.

———— • ————

I WAS PACING IN FRONT OF MY WALL OF WINDOWS, PHONE TO MY EAR.

I was also babbling.

To voicemail.

"Okay, so I know I pulled back. I know you tried to keep in touch with me. I know I had a lot of things on my mind but you were one of them and I should have let you know that and not just through texts," I said to Robin's mailbox. "But a lot was happening with me, *is* happening with me, and while that happened, I made a lot of mistakes. *Lots* of them."

I pulled in a deep breath and kept babbling.

"But later tonight, a man is going to ring my doorbell and I know in my heart I won't be making a mistake opening it to him. But I screwed up so bad picking Conrad, who I knew in my heart was the man for me, I'm scared to death because that man that's soon arriving and I...it's been rocky. It's been...Robin, it's been *really* rocky."

I closed my eyes and started winding it down.

"I'm shutting up now. And I'm hoping to all that is holy that you're not communicating with me because you're angry with me and not because something has happened with you and nobody's told me."

I turned and looked out at the sea.

"Call me," I finished. "Please, Robin, call me. And if you're angry with me, then at least text me to tell me you're okay."

With that, I ended the call.

I stopped pacing and looked out the windows.

Suffice it to say, while Bradley was wasting no time (and scaring me a little) driving like a madman to get me home and dump me at my house, he didn't mind at all that I was ending things.

He also didn't walk me to the door or even wait to reverse out of my drive and take off before I got to it.

This was beyond awkward and it made me feel like a bitchy slut, or a slutty bitch (no, actually, both).

So after I let myself inside and turned on a lamp by the TV, walked to the kitchen and flipped on the pendants over the bar, I put my clutch on the counter and dug out my phone.

Then I texted him, *There's no excuse for what happened tonight so I won't try to make one. I'll only say I'm very sorry. I enjoyed our time together and I'm sad that it ended this way.*

I said no more, not telling him he's a good man and he'll find someone, which would probably not be something he wanted to read from me. Nor did I tell him I wasn't leading him on or playing games and that things with Mickey and I were complicated, which was true but would sound banal to him and also something he wouldn't want to read. Nor did I tell him I hoped he didn't think badly about me because that was selfish and likely an impossible feat.

I kept it short and offered my apologies. It was the only thing I could do.

I fretted for a while about my behavior but the fretting drifted away and the pacing started when it sunk in completely that Mickey Donovan had kissed me.

Kissed me.

I didn't know how that could happen. I'd kissed him and he'd pulled away, told me I was…"attractive," gave no indication he was interested in me, and in fact gave lots of indication he didn't much like me.

When the fretting about that started to overwhelm me, I'd called Robin.

With that call done, now I had hours before Mickey would show at my door, possibly to kiss me again (which caused such extreme excitement I felt the urge to go straight to the toy in my nightstand drawer and make use of it). He also possibly would ask me out, which was frankly unfathomable (or had been, until he kissed me).

Or he possibly would come over in order to tell me what happened at the restaurant was a huge mistake and he thought it best we never see each other again.

Which would mean I'd lose Mickey even though I didn't have Mickey and when I did, we were fighting.

Even so, the very idea of that loss was too much to even contemplate.

It would also mean I'd lose Aisling and Cillian.

Something else I couldn't contemplate.

When these thoughts were about to send me over the edge, I decided to call my brother, who would listen then give it to me straight. And since he was a man, he might know what was in Mickey's head.

On this decision, my phone in my hand let out a chime.

I looked down at it then quickly slid my finger on the screen to get to the text.

It was from Robin and it read, *"I'm fine. I'm also pissed at you. Give me three days to hold a grudge then I'll call you. But I reserve the right for the grudge to last less time.*

That was it but it gave me relief, made me smile and was a little surprising since a three day grudge for Robin was unheard of—case in point, the grudge she had against her ex lasting five years without cooling.

Before I could send a reply, I got another text from her.

And this guy better be hot. Hot enough to make Conrad lose his mind and consider suicide. Anything less, MeeMee, and I'll be very disappointed in you.

That made me smile bigger because it was funny and because she would very much approve of Mickey. She might live for revenge against her cheating ex-husband, but that didn't mean she didn't appreciate masculine eye candy.

I texted back, *Okay, sweets, and this is the last you'll hear from me until your grudge is over. But just to put your mind at ease, Mickey is definitely hot.*

After sending that, I called my brother.

"Hey, MeeMee," he greeted.

"Hey, Lawrie. You free?"

"I'm at work but for you I'm always free."

I was not surprised he was at work, seeing as it was earlier there, not to mention the fact that, since both his boys were old enough to drive and go off and do their own things, my brother stopped working constantly and started working *constantly* in order to escape his wife.

I was also not surprised he would make himself free for me. In my life, after I'd found that Conrad didn't, Lawr was the only one who loved me demonstrably and unreservedly.

"Listen," I began. "Conrad called tonight and he asked me to ask you to quit badgering him."

I heard Lawr hoot before he replied, "Jesus, that guy's an asshole. I called him twice, MeeMee. The first call lasted two minutes before he hung up on me. The second was right after that where he answered and I shared he was a dick before I hung up on him. That's not badgering."

He would know badgering. He was an attorney.

"I figured it was something like that," I muttered, then clearer, I said, "He's blaming me, so I appreciate you sticking up for me, but I'd prefer you stopped doing it."

"He mention the kids?" Lawr asked.

"No. Why?" I asked back, my neck muscles tightening.

"I called them too."

I stared at my reflection in the window. "I'm sorry?"

"Told them to cut you some slack. Told your son that you don't have anybody since his father tore apart your family so he was up to bat and had to take care of his mother. Told your daughter she had one good female role model in her life and she was going to blow it if she lost that."

So *that* was why they spoke to me. Because their Uncle Lawrie, who they both loved, adored and respected, had called them and laid it out.

God, I loved my brother.

"Should have done that years ago," he murmured.

"They were a lot better at the last visit," I told him.

"Good," he said softly.

"Kinda shocking, you being a pain in the behind big brother for twenty years then turning out to be so cool when you're nearly fifty."

"Shut up, MeeMee," he returned, a smile in his voice.

I smiled at my reflection and asked, "Do you have more time?"

"Are you my MeeMee?"

God, *I loved my brother.*

"I am," I confirmed.

"Sock it to me, sweetheart," he invited.

That was when I started pacing again because I did. I socked it to him and told him everything—absolutely *everything*—about Mickey.

This took a while. There was a lot of pacing. I was still in my sling-backs and it would be a lot later when I would come to the happy realization I could walk that much in them and they'd still be comfortable even being new shoes I'd never worn.

When I was done telling my brother everything, I stopped, wrapped my free arm around my belly, stared at my toes and asked, "So? Is Pippa right? Is this guy into me?"

At that, I heard Lawr burst out laughing.

My head came up. "What's funny?"

"Is this guy into you?" Lawr asked my question back to me, his deep voice still vibrating with humor.

"That's the question and in my current circumstances, I don't find anything funny," I snapped.

"Right." That word sounded kind of strangled, like he was choking back laughter, and he still hadn't quite done it when he went on, "I'll confirm a fourteen-year-old girl's keen perception of the way of things with you and this guy are even though she witnessed you with him for all of five minutes. Amelia, this guy is *into you*."

I felt shivers trail over my skin at his confirmation *and* his emphasis.

But my voice was an octave higher when I asked, "How can that be? For weeks, we've hardly exchanged a pleasant word."

I barely finished speaking before Lawr launched right in. "First, a guy might see a man in a woman's face and intervene, but he will not offer to help her around the house unless he likes what he sees."

"That's impossible, Lawrie. I hadn't even had my hair highlighted then," I informed him.

Lawr ignored that and continued, "He also doesn't give a shit she's running herself into the ground doing some house sale, so he certainly doesn't ask her over for a barbeque to help her relax."

"When you do something like that with children involved, and you're interested in the woman you're inviting, it requires planning," I shared haughtily. "Mickey's invitation was near on spur of the moment."

Lawr kept ignoring me. "And if he's not interested and his daughter asks for her recipes, or wants her over for dinner, he tells his daughter to go over herself and get them and he finds a way to say she can't come over for dinner."

"He doesn't have full custody of them, Lawrie," I reminded him. "So she's not around all the time. And she's sweet. She's a hard girl to say no to."

My brother again ignored me.

"And bottom line, a man does not lose his mind every time another man is anywhere near this woman if he doesn't want her for his. He doesn't expend the energy to fight with her because if he doesn't give a shit, he wouldn't bother. But in his case, he was fighting with you instead of doing what he really wants to do with you. And he sure as fuck doesn't shove her into an alcove in a restaurant and kiss her, infuriated she's out on a date. And I'll say that also saying I know your age, I know you've been married and have kids, but I'm talking about a man shoving my little sister into an alcove and kissing her and I'm doing it under duress."

I almost smiled at that.

But I didn't.

Lawr carried on, "I'm also doing it saying that was a bold move, and commendable, if the woman he wants is stubborn and irascible, like you are, he'd reached the end of his control, and the time had come where he needed to make his play."

I moved to the window and leaned a shoulder against it, dropping the side of my head to the glass, eyes out to the dark sea, ignoring his comment about me being stubborn and irascible, because we both knew I was so there was no use discussing it.

"He told me I'm...*attractive*," I whispered.

He understood that and I knew it by the tender tone of his response. "Can't call that one, MeeMee. Maybe denial. But this guy's actions aren't speaking louder than words. They're shouting. He likes you."

I closed my eyes. "I'm a whackjob."

"What?"

I opened my eyes. "What happens when he finds out how I lost it with Martine and Conrad? How I lost my kids? If he really likes me and something happens between us, he'll eventually find out."

"That you loved someone, lost them and acted out?" Lawr asked. "MeeMee, I know Mom and Dad wanted us both to be perfectly programmed automatons, but you're human. Give yourself a break. This guy sounds like a good dad. He sounds like he's responsible. He sounds like his ex-wife put him through the wringer and he made it to the other side while guiding his kids there. He sounds like he knows practically nothing about your situation and has a better lock on it than you do. Give him a break too. Life is life and it's happened to this guy just like it's happened to you. He's going to get it. But I'll tell you this, if he learns that about you and runs a mile, that says more about him than it does about you."

"I wish you were closer," I blurted, and I really did.

I loved my brother, my kids loved their uncle, he was the only real family I had (outside my kids), and I wanted to be in a position to see him happy and do something about it.

This would mean me conniving to break him up with the witch he called a wife but I wasn't above that, absolutely not.

I'd proved I'd do anything in the name of love.

In fact, I'd wanted to fix him up with Robin for a long time. When she wasn't being scary and wreaking vengeance, she was sweet, funny, and above all, loyal. And whenever Robin and Lawrie were together, he was always being droll and hilarious, this aimed often at Robin, and she was always laughing and being suggestive, and this was aimed at Lawr but mostly it was aimed at the witch because Robin hated Lawrie's wife just as much as me.

Hmm.

"I'll come out and visit," Lawr told me.

"Thanksgiving," I said instantly.

"I'll think about it."

"Leave the witch, bring the boys," I said with no hesitancy.

I was straight with Lawr, Lawr was straight with me. He knew I didn't like her. He also knew (since he told me) that their marriage was over and he was holding it together, supposedly for the boys.

But I suspected, after telling my father to shove his billion dollar company up his ass and going into the law (a profession Lawr had always been fascinated with), he'd exhausted his rebellion, so divorce was out of the question.

"I'll think about that too."

I blinked.

Lawr had never considered something like that.

"Really?" I asked.

"Maybe experiencing my little sister fighting for happy is teaching me something."

Oh God.

That would be *wonderful*.

"I won't jump on that, push it and do it while flipping cartwheels," I promised.

"Good, because you're on the phone with me and if you did that, you'd have to do it one-handed and you might break your neck, which would mean a date with this guy would be postponed indefinitely."

A date with Mickey.

More shivers.

"Perhaps Robin is free for Thanksgiving," I mused.

"Christ, what'd you say about pushing?" Lawr asked.

"I'll stop talking," I offered.

"And I need to get back to working. Your big brother sort you out?"

I grinned even though he didn't, not entirely. I was still anxious and a bit confused.

But I was less of both.

"Yes, sweets," I replied.

"Then I'll let you go, MeeMee."

"Okay, Lawrie. Talk to you later."

"Anytime, sweetheart. Take care."

"You too."

We hung up and I rested my phone against my chin and stared out to sea.

Then I took it from my chin, activated it and saw the time.

I still had hours to wait before Mickey would come to me.

But it was after eight and thus not too late, so I opened up my texts and sent a group message to my kids.

Your Uncle Lawrie is thinking about bringing your cousins out for Thanksgiving. If you have time, text him or call him and tell him you'd like to see him. Love you, honeys.

I sent it and pushed away from the window, wondering if I should change before Mickey got there, when the doorbell rang.

I looked that way, saw the motion sensor outdoor light had been activated and Mickey's body was framed in the stained glass window.

What on earth?

It wasn't even nine o'clock. They couldn't have ordered and eaten and gotten home in that time.

I hurried to the door as my phone in my hand sounded.

Startled, I looked down and saw a short text from Auden.

On it.

Oh my God!

I was grinning and still hurrying to the door when my phone sounded again.

I was at the door, multi-tasking by unlocking and reading a text from Olympia.

Me too.

I didn't know if that was for Lawr or me or both.

I just knew it was more progress.

This made me happy.

And as I opened the door, I hoped by all that was holy what lay behind it would make me happy too.

I looked up to Mickey's face, caught his expression and froze, the happiness leaking right out of me.

He said nothing, just moved inside in a way I was forced to move back. Once he got in, he stopped and so did I.

He closed the door and turned back to me.

"Hey," he said softly.

"Hey, Mickey," I replied in the same tone.

"Gotta get back to my kids," he told me.

But, he'd just arrived.

"I—"

"Rhiannon didn't show."

I stared in shock.

His ex was supposed to be at dinner?

This knowledge forced a variety of thoughts to tumble through my head, including the fact he'd kissed me at the restaurant and one of his options after our kiss had included joining them—joining them for a dinner that would be consumed with his kids *and* ex-wife.

I also thought of something I hadn't noticed. That they were at a four-top and they'd had their menus when Bradley and I arrived.

They'd also had them when we'd left.

But the priority thought that pushed all others aside was that Cillian's mother didn't come to his birthday dinner.

"Oh no," I breathed, getting closer and lifting a hand to place it on his chest. "She was coming?"

"We have an agreement," he said shortly, looking strange, speaking strange, like he was controlling something but only barely. "So the kids wouldn't feel all the loss her bullshit could make them feel, we'd do what we could to give them their family on days that were special. Not goin' all out, shit like her sleepin' over Christmas Eve, which could give them ideas. But at the very least birthday dinners, Christmas dinner, Thanksgiving, we'd have them together. If one of us found someone, that'd be part of the deal and whoever that was would have to get that. We've been divorced a year and a half, separated a year more than that, and this has worked. She's never bailed on our kids."

"So," I started cautiously, "did she call? Explain—"

"Oh yeah, the bitch called," Mickey interrupted me to growl viciously.

His tone frightened me but I forced myself to stay in his space and keep my hand light on his chest, even though he wasn't touching me and he was holding himself in that strange way he'd been speaking.

"That doesn't sound good," I noted quietly.

"It wasn't," he confirmed. "You haven't seen it, but when she gets Cill, she fucks 'im up. He gets wound up, acts out, comes to me. Takes a day or two, but I give him what he needs, he settles in. He goes to her for her week, she unravels that, so when I get him back, he's gone again. Vicious cycle. So tonight, the longer it took for her to show, he knew, *they* knew."

"They knew what?" I asked carefully when he said no more.

"That she goes on benders."

I swallowed a gasp as Mickey kept talking.

"When we were together, I covered her ass. Told myself the kids didn't get it. That was a lie. They see everything. Worse, they feel it. Didn't happen a lot but it happened too fuckin' much for me. After the one I decided would be her last, she came home, I had her bags packed. Told her to kick the booze or get the fuck out. She told me she didn't have a problem even though she was so hungover, she looked about eighty. I told her if she didn't get her disappearing from our family home without warning for three days so she could get hammered was a problem, she needed to get her shit and get out. Then she grabbed her shit and walked right out."

I got closer and whispered, "Mickey."

"After I got shot of her, she pulled it together, never did it when she had the kids. Never left our kids to fend for themselves. Never missed a special meal. But we were at the restaurant twenty minutes before you got there, Amy, she was supposed to meet us there, and she hadn't showed. Fifteen minutes after you left, after the fourth text I couldn't hide sending the bitch to find out where the fuck she was, Cill started losing it. Then he lost it and threw a tantrum. Took him outside to calm him down, got him to do that, but he wanted to leave. We left, went to get fuckin' *burgers* for my boy's *birthday*, 'cause that was all he was up for. Got home, started to do cake and presents, the bitch called. She called Ash's phone. Cill knew it was her, grabbed it before my girl could save him that shit, and he got a birthday call from a mother who was totally shitfaced."

I felt tears fill my eyes.

Oh, Cillian.

"Honey," I whispered, getting even closer, my hand now pressing.

"He was good with her, my boy's good with his mom, but he got off the phone, went wild. Threw the cake Ash made for him against the wall and slammed into his room. We had words, he's still not calmed down, but I'm givin' him time. I gotta get back to him because I gotta shape him up and sort out Rhiannon's mess. Again."

"Okay, then go," I invited.

"We gotta talk."

That didn't sound promising.

But right then, not one thing was about me.

"I'm not going anywhere," I told him.

"Best kiss I ever had," he told me.

I drew in a sharp breath, those five words thrilling down my throat, to my belly, straight to the tips of my toes.

"Want more," he went on. "You with me?"

I nodded and just stopped myself from doing it humiliatingly enthusiastically.

"Good," he stated curtly. "We talked. I sort out my boy, we'll talk more."

"Okay, Mickey."

He bent abruptly and touched his mouth to mine.

His lips were firm at the same time soft and he wore no cologne, but he smelled heavenly.

He lifted his head but he did it also lifting his hand, and finally, he touched me.

He did this cupping my jaw and sweeping his thumb along my cheek.

He said nothing, just touched me sweetly and stared into my eyes.

I said nothing back, just stood close and let him.

Then he said, "Call you, baby."

"Okay, Mickey," I repeated.

His lips tipped up in a preoccupied grin that was still amazing before he let me go, turned to the door and disappeared through it.

12

EVERYTHING I'D EVER NEED

*W*hen I got home from Dove House the next day, I went back out and grabbed my mail.

I took it back in and went through it on the kitchen counter.

No wish list from Cillian.

I turned my head toward the front of my house like I could see through it and feel what was happening at the Donovans.

My phone in my purse rang and I quickly dug it out, hoping it was Mickey.

It wasn't.

It was Boston Stone.

I let it go to voicemail and made a decision I wasn't sure was mine to make. I was pretty sure Mickey and I were starting something and because of that, I wasn't sure what I intended to do was the right thing.

Still, I shoved my now-silent phone into the back pocket of my jeans and went to Mickey's house.

It seemed quiet and standing at the front door I reconsidered ringing the bell.

Then my hand decided for me, lifted and rang the bell.

God, I hoped I was doing the right thing.

The door was opened by Aisling.

"Hey, blossom," I greeted.

She tipped her head to the side and greeted back quietly, "Hey, Amy."

"You doing okay?" I asked.

"I'm good," she answered too quickly.

Lying.

I let that go and just nodded, asking, "Your dad home?"

She shook her head and replied, "No, he's working."

"Your brother home?" I went on.

Her answer to that was to step out of the door.

I took this as my invitation to walk in, so I did.

She shut the door behind me and mumbled, "He's in the family room."

"Okay, sweets," I mumbled back and moved that way.

I found Cillian lounged on the couch, eyes to the TV, the evidence of an unhealthy feeding frenzy littered around him, including a melting tub of ice cream on the coffee table that was not on a magazine or a mat or anything.

The mother inside me screamed but my mouth didn't.

"Hey, kiddo," I greeted, going to the side of the sectional and shifting a hip to rest on the back so I could catch his eyes.

He didn't give them to me.

"Hey," he muttered, not taking his gaze from the TV.

"I came home, checked my mail, didn't get a wish list," I remarked.

He didn't say anything.

I was used to that, just not from Cillian.

"Got an afternoon free to go shopping," I tried again.

"Don't want anything," he kept muttering.

I looked up and saw Aisling hanging close to the mouth of the hall.

She shrugged but she looked upset.

I sighed, looked around and saw no cake remains splattered everywhere, but I did see the bar had a profuse gathering of unwrapped birthday presents.

My gaze slid to Aisling. She caught it and shrugged again.

I turned my attention back to Cillian.

"So I guess it's clothes," I announced, knowing no twelve-year-old boy wanted clothes.

"Don't want anything," he repeated, still not taking his eyes from the TV.

"No kid I know and like turns twelve without me buying him something. It's a rule. I have it written in blood on a contract in my wall safe," I somewhat lied, since I didn't have any such contract.

Or a wall safe.

Cillian didn't respond.

"Underwear," I declared. "With animals on it."

I watched Cillian's nose scrunch.

Finally.

"Not something Combat Raptor," I said, not knowing because Auden was beyond that kind of thing, but thinking that was all the rage.

"I'm not *seven*," Cillian noted disgustedly.

Okay, that was out.

"A new Frisbee," I pushed.

"Got five of them," Cillian told the TV.

"So, clothes," I concluded.

"He likes paintball," Aisling offered and I looked to her.

"No way," I stated. "That's dangerous."

"Not if you have eye gear," Cillian mumbled.

Paintball eye gear.

Check.

"Those pellets can hit more than your eyes," I told him.

"Won't hurt, you got a helmet, or a vest, gloves, or pants," he told me.

Helmet.

Vest.

Gloves.

Pants.

Check.

"So it *is* clothes," I teased.

"Whatever," Cillian muttered.

"There you go. I have my mission," I announced, straightening away from the couch. "Could wait to ask your dad if someone might want to go with me," I offered that thinly veiled suggestion.

Cillian didn't reply and that hurt. He was usually so talkative, enthusiastic, energetic.

Now he was slobbing out in front of the TV, sullen and crabby.

My children could be that way and they'd never had a mom or dad that did anything but love them, support them, give them all they needed and a good deal of what they wanted. Conrad and I might have behaved badly, they might have seen it, but we'd never missed anything important or made them feel unimportant.

Heck, I even went to all Auden's wrestling matches and I disliked wrestling.

I knew two kids who needed a reality check.

I also knew that someone needed to find Rhiannon Donovan and shake some sense into her.

Since that could not be me, I could only find paintball gear.

Therefore I was going to do that.

"Okay, I'm off," I declared and started Aisling's way. "See you later, kiddos."

Cillian didn't say anything.

Aisling followed me to the door.

I stopped at it and asked quietly, "Do you know his sizes?"

She nodded and gave them to me.

I looked down the hall then to her. "Did his dad get him any of that stuff?"

"Dad faked him out with a bunch of new clothes for school. The new Xbox that's really his present is still in Dad's closet."

That was cute and sweet.

"Right, blossom." I tipped my head to the side. "You sure you're okay?"

"Yeah, I'm good," she again answered too quickly.

"You ever wanna talk, I'm across the street," I invited.

"Okay, Amy," she said in a way I knew she'd never take me up on that.

I didn't push it. Maybe one day I'd have a chance, and looking at her pretty face, I hoped that day would come.

I just said, "Okay, Aisling."

I opened the door and was through it when she called, "Amy."

I turned to her. "Yes, honey?"

"Are you...is that...?" Her eyes slid away then to my house where she kept them as she finished, "That Bradley guy you were with seemed nice."

"I broke up with him last night, Ash."

Her gaze cut to me.

I shrugged, going for casually. "We just didn't click."

"Sorry," she mumbled.

"Sometimes it works, sometimes it doesn't," I told her quietly.

"Yeah."

She wanted me with her dad.

I liked that. It felt nice.

And it was scary.

"I'm going out paintball gear shopping," I told her. "I'll see you later?"

She nodded.

"'Bye, sweets."

"'Bye, Amy."

I turned and walked to my house. When I got there, I went to my laptop and looked up where I could find paintball gear. The closest place was at a shop in a bigger town that was forty-five minutes away.

I headed there, stocked up with everything the clerks told me any paintball aficionado would need or even want and stopped by a Target on the way home to get a card and gift wrapping.

When I got home, I wrapped the gifts and took them over, handing them off to Aisling but not bothering Cillian again.

She gave me a small grin and thanked me.

I gave her a big smile and went home.

Through this, Boston Stone called again.

But Mickey did not call me.

———————— • ————————

IT WAS LATE AND I WAS ON A STOOL AT MY BAR WITH A GLASS OF WINE AND my laptop.

And Mickey still had not called me.

It was a struggle. It made me feel selfish to an extreme. I had no idea what effort you had to put into dealing with kids who were dealing with the ugly fact their mother was an alcoholic, but I suspected that took a lot of effort.

It still hurt that after all that had happened, after that kiss, Mickey hadn't found time in his day even to text me.

I sent an update, how's-it-going email to my parents, who had not replied or phoned since my last email, but I couldn't let that bother me.

It was what it was. They were who they were. I couldn't change them and I wasn't going to allow them to change me. Not anymore.

So whatever would be with that would just have to be.

I was trolling Internet sites, trying to get a lock on or even an idea of the perfect dining room table when my phone sounded.

I snatched it up then pulled up the texts excitedly to read an out of the blue text from my son.

Heads up, Pip tried out for the cheerleading squad. She didn't make it. She isn't happy.

I was elated to have news about my kids. I was beside myself my son had shared this with me without anything from me prompting him to do so.

I was upset at the news.

I didn't know much about my children but I knew Pip had been living to be a freshman cheerleader. I also knew, having her heart set on that, she'd worked at it and she liked to get what she wanted.

Not getting it, she'd be devastated.

I texted back, *Thanks for the heads up, kid.*

Then I went to an online flower site and ordered a bouquet to be sent to my daughter the next day that had a card that said, *You're awesome. Love you. Mom.*

It was all I could do, but even though it wouldn't help much, my baby girl loved flowers so I hoped it'd do something.

I was putting away my credit card when my phone rang.

Hoping it was Mickey, I snatched it up.

It wasn't Mickey. It was Robin.

Vying for best call I could get that day, I'd take that and I did.

"Hey, gorgeous," I answered.

"You have five minutes to give me ten reasons not to cut you out completely when you blew me off *almost* completely," she replied.

I drew in a breath.

Then I took far more than five minutes and gave her all I could give her. Everything about me; all my epiphanies, all I was thinking, maybe being an idiot about our friendship, Mom and Dad, Lawr, Conrad, the kids, Martine, Josie and her brood, Alyssa and her brood, Aisling, Cillian, Boston Stone, Bradley…and Mickey.

I'd drained my wine and topped it up through all this talking.

And when I was done, the wine doing nothing, I was tense at her response, which was a shocking, "You got highlights without me?"

"Er…yes," I replied hesitantly.

There was silence.

"Robin—" I began.

She interrupted me, "Girl, if you were ready to move on, I could be the bestie who moved on with you. I can do havoc. I can also *not*."

"I know, but—"

"But whatever," she cut me off. "I understand where you're coming from but you knew me before both our lives imploded. You knew you'd get anything from me that you needed."

She was right.

And I was an idiot.

"I'm sorry, Robin, I was just…I guess in all the rights I was trying to make, I made some wrongs."

"Uh, *yeah you did*," she agreed and I tensed again but found I did it for no reason when she continued, "But whatever. You're moving on. You got a hottie next door who's a good kisser and he kisses *you*. Your kids are finally pulling their heads out of their asses. And I got *huge* news for you."

I couldn't quite believe it because there it was. That was it. I explained, Robin listened and that was done.

Though I should have believed it.

She was right. She wasn't all about retribution and mayhem.

She was mostly about friendship and loyalty and that started but didn't stop when the retribution and mayhem began.

In protecting myself I'd *over*protected myself.

And once I'd figured that out and admitted it, Robin, being Robin, let that be.

I decided to do the same, settled in, grabbed my wine and before taking a sip, asked, "And that is?"

"I'm moving on too."

I nearly choked on my wine, accomplished not doing this, and sputtered, "I'm sorry?"

"Get this," she demanded. "That Pilates instructor my ex-ass left me for left him for a Pilates instructor too. And that instructor is a *she*."

I felt my eyes get huge right before I burst out laughing.

"No," I forced through my laughter.

"Yes," she said gleefully. "My ex-ass drove his tight body bitch right into the arms of a tight bodied bitch. Isn't that *fabulous*?"

"It *so* is," I agreed.

"*Everyone* is talking about it. He's so humiliated he's taken leave and is hiding at my ex-house on Coronado."

"That's brilliant, Robin," I told her.

"I know," she replied. "And I got more." Her voice changed when she said, "But this might not be so brilliant."

Oh no.

"What?" I asked cautiously.

"It's not about me, sweetie," she said.

My neck got tight. "Your kids?"

"No," she said quickly. There was a long hesitation before she went on, "You."

I felt my brows come together. "Me?"

"You're over him?" she queried softly.

Oh *no*.

"Yes," I answered carefully.

"Okay, then, this shouldn't hurt as much as it would have."

Oh God!

"Robin, *what?*" I demanded.

"Had lunch with Helena," she stated quickly. "She told me her hubs went to a conference. At that conference were some neuros who worked with Conrad in Kentucky. They got to talking and Helena's Ron mentioned Conrad and Martine and you and that Conrad and Martine moved to Maine. Since these guys worked with Conrad, at this news, they shared that his practice had been warned because Conrad was fucking every nurse in the hospital, leaving them high and dry. One got pissed and filed a sexual harassment suit and that's why you guys got your asses back to La Jolla."

I sat on my stool, wineglass in my hand, elbow to the counter, unmoving.

He'd said it was a better opportunity.

He'd said it was more money (and it was).

He'd said *not one thing* about a sexual harassment suit.

"Worse," she continued quietly. "They said that happened in Boston too and that's why you guys went to Kentucky."

I remained immobile and stared unseeing at the wine bottle.

"I know this seems bad but let's look at the bright side," Robin suggested. "If you want to get your kids back, you can dig these bitches up and—"

"Oh, I'll be digging these bitches up," I declared.

"What? Really?" she asked.

I had not fought for my kids. I thought I did. I had a good attorney. He cost a fortune. He was a shark, like my brother. My brother was sweet to me. He loved his kids. He loved my kids. But in a courtroom, he was a ferocious lion that showed no mercy.

In fact, Lawr had recommended my attorney.

But I had not let him loose. I didn't want it to get ugly. I didn't want my kids to go through that.

But really, I didn't want *me* to go through it. I was too mired in pettiness that got me nowhere to involve myself in the real fight that would have been a *far* better use of my energy.

"I'm making headway with the kids. If that continues, I'll want them more. If they want the same and Conrad doesn't agree with that, then I'm going to parade these women in front of a judge and in front of Martine and obliterate him," I decreed.

"You go, girl," she returned gleefully.

I was going to go.

God, he'd not cheated on me.

He'd screwed everything in three states while married to me!

How had I been so wrong about him?

Before I could ask that of Robin, my head snapped around because a loud knock sounded at the door.

The outside light was on and Mickey's frame was shadowed in the stained glass.

He was here.

My belly flipped.

"Oh God, Mickey's here," I breathed to Robin.

"Fabulous," she didn't breathe back.

The knock sounded again. Actually, it was banging.

Why was he banging and not using the bell?

"I need to go get that," I said to Robin, slipping off the stool and putting my glass down.

"You *so* do," she agreed.

"I'll call you soon."

"You better, and just saying, you ever try to blow me off again without telling me what's on your mind, you won't win me back so easy."

I absolutely knew that to be true.

I moved to the door quickly and said, "I wish I could tell you how happy I am you made this time easy, but Mickey's here."

"Hot guy at your door. Every woman knows that takes precedence over pretty much everything. But I'll expect a report. *Soon*," she told me.

I unlocked the door saying, "You'll get it. 'Bye, honey."

"'Bye, sweetie."

We disconnected as I opened the door and looked up.

My "hey" froze on my lips at the look on Mickey's face.

Oh no, what did Rhiannon do *now*?

I moved back when he pushed in but I closed the door and turned to him to see he'd stopped four feet away and was facing me.

"Everything okay?" I asked tentatively.

"Oh yeah," he replied, for some reason sarcastically. "My son is all good now, seein' as he's got an Xbox and about five hundred fuckin' dollars' worth of paintball shit."

I stared at him, mystified as to why this was what it was obvious he thought was a bad thing.

"Is that bad?" I asked when he didn't continue.

"Fuck no," he answered, crossing his arms on his chest. "It isn't, seein' as it reminded me why this shit isn't going to work."

On his "this shit" he threw a hand my way and then crossed it back on his chest.

And when he did that, my insides squeezed.

"This...shit?" I queried, sounding out of breathe because I suddenly found it difficult to breathe.

His big body shifted, like he was settling in, and he asked, "You know how much of a hit my parents took sellin' that house to Rhiannon and me?"

My head twitched in confusion at this odd question. "No."

"Seven hundred K and I *still* paid two hundred grand more than I could afford, and now that's a whole lot *more* than I could afford, gettin' shot of Rhiannon, who was not much but at least the bitch made a decent paycheck."

"Mickey—"

"And we don't have coastal property," he spoke over me. "That road I cross to get to your house, you know it, babe, is like crossin' tracks from houses that cost a whack to houses that cost fuckin' five million dollars *and* you got a deal because those assholes that lived here before you fucked themselves."

"I'm not certain why we're talking about this," I noted hesitantly.

"You don't buy my kids, Amelia," he stated bluntly.

I shook my head agitatedly, again confused, asking, "I'm sorry?"

"You spent more on my kid for his birthday than I did," he bit out.

"But, he—"

"You didn't ask," he clipped. "You went out and laid that load on him and what?" he asked angrily. "What's next? You and I start somethin', they get used to a woman in their life who's drowin' in money, you handin' them the world. Shit happens and it doesn't work out between us, how do they get used to not havin' someone hand them the world?"

I was seeing his point and realizing my decision of earlier that day wasn't a good one. We hadn't even started and I was making the same mistakes I made with my kids but now with Mickey's.

So I started, "You're right. I should have—"

He again didn't let me finish.

"I had one woman who I wasn't enough for her. The family we made wasn't enough for her. She needed somethin' else, found it, fell into it and it became more important than all of us. Now, you move in across the street and here I am again thinkin' about startin' something with another woman, no way in fuck I can give her what she needs because she doesn't fuckin' *need* anything, because she can get whatever the fuck she wants bankrolled by her family."

He was four feet away.

He'd still just slapped me across the face.

"So thanks for the shit you gave my kid," he clipped ungraciously. "Made his night. He's over there dressed in paintball gear, playin' games on his Xbox, havin' the time of his life, totally forgettin' his drunk of a mom is off somewhere drowning in a bottle and hasn't even been around to drop off his present. But this is not happening." He flipped his hand between us again. "I don't need that shit again and my kids sure as fuck don't need it."

"You're right," I whispered. "This shit isn't happening."

He nodded in agreement, slicing right into me, making me bleed.

"It'd be good you don't come over," he told me.

I stepped out of the way of the door. "It'd be good you returned that favor."

He nodded again, once, moved to the door, yanked it open and prowled through it.

I moved behind him, grabbed the edge of the door and called his name.

He turned back to me.

I looked right into his beautiful blue eyes.

"You have absolutely no idea what I need," I whispered. "And the sad part about that is that you didn't notice you'd already given me everything I'd ever need just letting me sit at your dinner table with your family."

And on that, I closed and locked the door.

Mickey

MICKEY STOOD AT HIS BACK DECK, STARING AT THE SHADOWS OF THE TREES, his house quiet and dark behind him.

He sucked back a pull off his beer.

You'd already given me everything I'd ever need just letting me sit at your dinner table with your family.

He felt his jaw get tight.

She hadn't been lying.

He knew by the wounded look in her big hazel eyes, Amy said those words and she hadn't been lying.

His gaze dropped and through the dark he saw the light of one of Cill's Frisbees lying in the backyard.

The Calway Petroleum heiress lived right next door and she spent her days with an old lady who thought she was a Nazi and came over to his house, ran around the backyard and played Frisbee with his kids.

Rhiannon had not pulled her shit together enough to bring her son a present.

Amy had hustled her ass to a store she probably had no clue existed until she had to find it so she could rain goodness down on his boy.

Before he kicked her out, Mickey had not had sex with his wife for eight months because at night she'd be passed out before he could try, and he didn't have the stomach to touch her any other time just remembering that shit.

He'd kissed Amy once and she'd been so hot for him, he knew he could have yanked up the skirt of that amazing dress, yanked down her panties, fucked her against the wall and they both would have got off on it.

Huge.

And something was up with his girl and when he'd phoned Rhiannon months ago to see if she'd noticed anything or could find a time to sit down and talk to her, Rhiannon had told him she had no idea what he was talking about. And when Mickey pushed it and his ex made a lame attempt to see if there was anything there, she'd reported to Mickey that all was fine and they had nothing to worry about.

Amy studied Ash in a way Mickey knew she saw it too; it just wasn't her place to do anything about it.

"Fucking shit, I fucked that up," he murmured.

Mickey had no idea why Amy didn't have her kids.

But he knew not having them was bringing a slow death and she was fighting with all she had to stay alive and kicking.

And she was into him; she'd made that clear from almost the start.

And *fuck*, he was into her. Those eyes, Jesus, they said everything. He could look into them for hours and know every thought that crossed her brain and better than that, the woman she was, he'd be interested in it.

And going head to head with her surprisingly did not suck. It got his blood pumping. It pissed him off. It made him *feel*.

He'd been going through the motions of life for so fucking long—covering Rhiannon's ass, getting shot of her, doing what he could to look out for his kids—he forgot what it was like. He forgot how it felt to be so into a woman, when she was quiet and sweet, he had to fight the urge to pull her in his arms and kiss her. When he saw her in pain, he had to fight the urge to curl her close and do what he could to take it away. And when she was stubborn and a pain in the ass, he had to fight the urge to shove her against the wall and fuck her senseless.

Not to mention Amy's tits, that ass, those legs.

But his head was so far up his own ass because the woman was fucking loaded and he'd been burned so bad, he'd protected himself by putting her off then lost control and backed her against a wall in a hall when she was on a date, for Christ's sakes, then demanded she get shot of his ass.

And she did.

For him.

For a shot at *them*.

Then she'd gone all out for his son and he'd walked over there and kicked her in the teeth.

"Fucking *shit*, I fucked that up," he bit out.

You'd already given me everything I'd ever need just letting me sit at your dinner table with your family.

She hadn't lied.

That was all Amelia Hathaway needed.

"Fucking shit," he whispered to the trees. "I fucked that shit up."

He downed the rest of his beer, walked into his house, slid the sliding glass door shut, locked it, put the pole in the tracks, dumped his bottle in the recycling bin and walked through the dark house to his empty bed.

13

WRECK YOU

I walked toward the security door at Dove House, hand in my purse, looking for my phone.

"Amelia."

I looked left and saw Mr. Dennison in an armchair, hand up, finger crooked to me.

I pinned a smile on my face and headed his way.

"Need something?" I asked.

"Closer," he answered when I stopped at his side.

I crouched so he could look down and I was looking up, something he couldn't do often considering he was stooped and further, had to walk with a Zimmer frame.

"Everything okay?" I asked.

He studied me with his fading blue eyes.

"Mr. Dennison," I called. "Can I get you something?"

Finally, he focused on me. "You ever need to talk, love, my ears are old, but they can still hear."

Well, that answered that. I was not hiding the fact that I was still bleeding from that scene with Mickey last night even if I'd finally pulled myself together enough to call Robin back, tell her all about it through silent crying hiccups and listen to her ranting about how men were all jerks and I was better off knowing sooner rather than later, like I'd learned with Conrad.

She was not wrong.

But somehow, what happened with Mickey hurt more than Conrad's betrayal, even when recent news could make it fresh.

I had no idea how this could be. Except for a shining twenty-four hours that held the promise of him, he and I never were.

It still destroyed me.

But this time, older, wiser, maybe stronger, but definitely tired of this crap, I thought I was letting it do it quietly.

Mr. Dennison didn't agree.

I grabbed his hand and gave it a squeeze. "Maybe we'll have a gab over a cup of tea when I'm back."

"You bring some bourbon, you're on," he told me.

I didn't need to bring bourbon. He had a stash his son augmented every week when he came to visit.

I smiled at him and gave his hand another squeeze. "See you later, honey."

He squeezed me back. "Later, love."

I walked to the security door, punched in the code, pushed on the bar, walked through but stopped in the vacant reception area to pull out my phone.

I activated it and scrolled through the notifications.

Bad news: another call from Boston Stone.

Good news: my attorney in California had called me back.

Unbelievably great news: Pippa had texted me.

Flowers are pretty. Thanks.

I was grinning like a fool (inside, outside, after the Mickey thing, I still couldn't do it), as I poked at the screen and sent a text back to my daughter.

Glad you got them. Chin up, kiddo. Hope you know how much your mother loves you.

I sent that, poked the screen again and put the phone to my ear. I listened to it ring, got his secretary, and considering my last name, she put me right through to my attorney.

Only then did I again start walking.

"I got the message, Amelia," Preston Middleton said in my ear. "Are you sure about this information?"

I pushed through the front door. "Not really but I'm sure enough I'd like to invest in being absolutely certain."

I walked down the sidewalk to my car, eyes to my feet, as Preston replied, "I can set a private investigator on it."

"Consider this the go-ahead to do that," I told him, looking up.

My step faltered when I saw Mickey in his hot guy dusty construction outfit leaning against my driver's side door.

Really?

What now?

What could he possibly have left to use to destroy me?

I kept my gaze on him as I made my way right to him and stopped just off the curb by my bumper.

"Is there something you're thinking in having this information?" Preston asked in my ear.

"I want my children back," I answered, gaze to Mickey, seeing his eyes in his impassive face flare at my words.

"Full custody?" Preston was sounding enthusiastic and I envisioned him rubbing his hands together and not only because of the billable hours but because he liked to get his teeth into a good fight.

"I'll not be greedy," I replied. "Every other week. My children love their father and I don't want them to lose something they love. I need some time to see where the kids are, but when I'm ready, this time I don't intend to lose. And I don't care how much it costs. I want every woman he had sex with while he was married to me contacted, deposed and ready to testify should Conrad push this to ugly."

Mickey's body slightly straightened at my "had sex with" but mostly he stayed leaned against my car, his gaze on me.

"I'll talk to my investigator," Preston said.

"Thank you," I replied.

"You're doing well?" he asked.

"I am, but I'm also on my way somewhere. I don't want to be rude but I need to go."

"Of course, I'll call you with updates, Amelia."

"Thank you, Preston."

We disconnected and instantly I asked Mickey, "Can you step away from my car?"

"You're fightin' for your kids?" he asked back.

That was none of his business.

But after what he did to me last night, he thought he could ask?

I'd answer.

"My best friend in Cali just found out that my husband didn't only fuck, and then fall in love with, and then put an engagement ring on the finger of a nurse in his hospital in San Diego, this all while still married to me," I shared. "He fucked his way through his hospital in Boston, the one in Lexington, perhaps the one in San Diego too, and he'd had at least one sexual harassment claim against him. As this is new information and I'm tired of not seeing my children, should he not agree to a more equitable custody schedule, I'm afraid I'm going to have to fight dirty."

"That's not dirty, Amy, he's dirty," Mickey said quietly.

"Thank you for your opinion," I returned tartly. "Now will you step away from my car?"

He straightened from it and turned to me.

But he didn't step away.

"We gotta talk," he told me, his voice gentle, his eyes not leaving me.

"No, you see, you're wrong about that," I replied. "We've done that and I've found it isn't much fun for me."

"I was outta line last night," he stated.

"You were," I agreed. "Is that your apology?"

"Yeah, Amy, that's my apology." His voice was still gentle.

It sounded amazing.

It didn't work on me because just standing there looking at him, I was still bleeding.

"Apology accepted. *Now* will you step away from my car?"

He shook his head not taking his eyes from me. "I'm here askin' you to give me a shot at explaining that fucked up shit I spewed last night."

"I'm not an imbecile, Mickey," I informed him instantly. "You explained it pretty clearly last night. You had a wife who you loved who did something you couldn't control. It was a betrayal against you and your kids, as sure as if she'd gone out and slept with an entire army. Being a man's man, a protective man, possibly a good man, it hurt you that you couldn't give her what she needed. I suspect you could handle that, but she hurt your kids and keeps doing it. You're now forced to tolerate that, even as it's intolerable. And being a man's man, you're not about to put yourself or your kids in the same position with another woman. Do I have that right?"

"That about sums it up," he confirmed.

"I do believe we decided that was where we stood last night so I have to admit to some confusion about why you're here today," I remarked.

"Because I fucked up last night," he returned.

"You're right. You did. And it's done. I still don't understand why we aren't moving on...*separately*."

He made as if to move to me but stopped when he saw my body lock.

His expression went as gentle as his voice, and with that look on his features, *that* was a sight to see.

It also didn't work on me.

"I'd like a chance to fix it, baby," he said softly.

"No," I returned firmly. "You see, in three months, you've made me feel unattractive, undesirable, unwanted, *unneeded* and it took two *decades* for Conrad to make me feel all that." I fought past his flinch, a flinch even as much as he hurt me I felt right to the heart of me, and concluded, "I'm not yearning for more, Mickey. So why don't we just let what never was really anything be just that."

"That's not going to happen," he declared.

"Why?" I asked.

"Because I can't do that," he answered.

"*Why?*" I snapped.

"Because we both want more."

"We did," I confirmed. "Now *I* don't."

"We got something, Amy," he returned.

"Wrong," I retorted. "We might have but then we didn't."

His jaw got hard as his patience started waning. "You know that's bullshit. There's something here. Something strong. Something I tried to fight but couldn't. Something that draws us to each other. Something we're both old enough and smart enough not to ignore. And there's something you don't even know that makes it more."

Twenty-four hours ago I would have loved knowing he thought that.

Right then, I wouldn't allow myself to.

"This might have been true but it no longer is, Mickey," I replied. "And since you aren't catching my hint, I'll say it straight. I don't wish to discuss any further what we might have had when in future we won't be having *anything*."

"You're not the only one with a legacy, Amy," he shot at me, patience definitely waning. "That fishing company my brothers run is Maine Fresh Maritime. The fillets and fish sticks you can find in the green, white and orange box in your local grocer's freezer."

My mouth dropped open.

"Yeah," he grunted. "That's why my dad could drop a shit ton on selling his house to me because that was part...*part* of my inheritance. I coulda been a part of that but I didn't want a desk job. I wanted to fight fires. I wanted to stay in Magdalene. I wanted nothin' but that and eventually a wife and kids sittin' around a dinner table. I tried to work the boats, take my stake of that legacy in a way that worked for me. Found bein' on a boat for weeks cut into my time chasin' skirt while also lookin' for a wife. So I quit and volunteered doin' what I love to do and found a way to have a life, and when the time came, take care of my family." His eyes moved to the nursing home then back to me, doing this to hammer his point home but he also did it verbally. "You get that, Amy?"

This heretofore unknown parallel of our lives was shocking.

And enthralling.

I obviously didn't share I thought that with Mickey, but he didn't give me a chance to because he wasn't finished speaking.

"I could go to Bar Harbor and walk into Frank's office, ask for a job, get it and make ten times more than I do right now just for bein' his brother. That's my choice not to do that. That's my choice not to give my kids what they could get outta that. You made another choice that's different, but it's yours. Though, don't think I know a single soul who might come close to getting me and my choices, except you."

"This is true, Mickey, I get you. But that doesn't mean one thing. That's impressive. Maine Fresh Maritime, very impressive. But I have three trust funds that I'm *not* turning my back on because I *like* the way I live and I'm *not* going to be made to feel less because I do or be judged because I do or feel pressured to be anything but what I am."

"That's not my point, Amy."

"I'm not sure I care to understand your point, Mickey."

"Tough, 'cause you're going to."

I rolled my eyes to the heavens and asked the clouds, "Why is that not surprising?"

"Babe, my point is, you got that, you live the way you want, and still you got it right about the only thing you need to be happy. And it isn't those trust funds."

I rolled my eyes back to him and narrowed them. "Don't you dare use my killshot of last night against me, Mickey Donovan," I spat.

Clearly coming to the end of his patience, he leaned toward me and bit back, "I'm usin' it to point out, last night your aim was true."

I threw out my hands and looked back to the heavens, crying, "Well hallelujah! I can die happy."

My gaze shot back to him when he asked irritably, "Why is it when you're a smartass I wanna fuck you more than I normally wanna fuck you?"

"You wanna fuck me?" I asked back, injecting these words with deep disbelief. "Shocker considering I'm..." I paused and leaned into him, "*Attractive.*"

His brows snapped together. "Wouldn't wanna fuck a woman who wasn't, Amy."

I glared at him. "Fascinating, since you didn't want *me* until I got *highlights.*"

His brows stayed knit and his eyes got dark. "You got what?"

"*Highlights,*" I snapped, jerking a pointed finger to my hair.

He looked to my hair and muttered, "Fuck, thought something was different."

I blinked.

He looked back to me. "Looks nice. Definitely like the bangs."

I blinked again.

Then I took a step his way, got up on my toes and accused, "Do not stand there and tell me you didn't notice my highlights or my new clothes."

He looked down his nose at me. "Noticed the haircut, babe, like I said, it looks nice. Definitely noticed the clothes but didn't think they were new. Thought the old shit was shit you were usin' because you hadn't unpacked all your stuff yet 'cause when you did, it was more you."

"So you're saying this newfound attraction to me isn't about my highlights and clothes," I scoffed.

"Babe, don't hand me that crap," he growled. "You're old enough to know you got it. And you're also old enough to know a man does not get in the face of another man and then offer to help around the house unless he's into the woman he's offerin' that shit to."

My heart jumped, my teeth clenched and Lawr was proved correct.

However, I could not let this get to me.

Instead, I found it was time to share something with him.

"I am aware that your preferences run to tall redheads with big breasts."

Surprise washed over his features as he asked, "What?"

"I saw you," I spat. "With that beautiful redhead at the movies."

That was when his features turned smug.

I felt pressure build in my chest, throat, but especially in my head. "You *like* that I saw you?"

"May not say much for me, Amy, but after watchin' you make a date with Stone right in front of me and make *out* with that douche, yeah. I like it that I gave you a little of that torture you handed me, seein' me with Bridget."

That torture you handed me.

That hurt him.

God, he was *into me.*

I couldn't let that get to me and leaned deeper into him in order to remind him, "I kissed you and you pulled away."

He bent his neck to get in my face and called sarcastically, "*Hello*, Amy. First, fightin' your pull because I didn't need to be fuckin' the woman across the street, and if that shit went south, puttin' myself in an awkward situation when I got my kids every other week…or puttin' myself in that situation *at all*. Second, fightin' your pull because you're *you* and you're *loaded* and I had my head up my ass about protectin' me and my family. But last, not gonna fuck some cute brunette with great tits on my couch while my kids are in their beds."

"I'm not cute," I snapped waspishly.

"No, you're not, you're fuckin' gorgeous. But when you wake up on my couch after playin' Frisbee with my kids, you're cute."

I rocked back, staring up at him, lips parted, liking too much the way all of that made me feel.

"Now, are we done givin' the residents their afternoon entertainment and you're gonna let me take you out and make it up to you or are we gonna go a few more rounds?" he asked.

When he did, in horror, I turned to look over my shoulder to see all the windows had been opened and the seniors had their faces in them. Mrs. McMurphy even had a cheek pressed to one of the bars.

It was then I realized that quite some time early in our conversation, both our voices had started rising.

Mortification seeped through me.

I slowly looked back when Mickey kept on and he didn't do it quietly.

"I'll warn you, might make me crazy, might make me a dick, don't give a shit, but I get off on goin' head to head with you. So if you feel like keepin' your gloves up, baby, bring it. 'Cause I know after doin' it for a while and then gettin' that kiss from you, you keep doin' it, when I finally fuck you it's gonna," he leaned deep into me, *"wreck you."*

I stared into his eyes and *that* got to me.

I wanted to be wrecked.

I wanted to be wrecked by Mickey.

Needed it.

Thankfully, I didn't say that because my lips wouldn't move.

"Michael Patrick Donovan, I'll be sharing your liberal use of profanities with your mother *and* Father Riley!" a female I was pretty sure was Mrs. Osborn, who wandered the home with her rosary beads daily, shouted.

Mickey ignored that and I watched his eyes change in a way that made me wish I could fall into them and swim in that blue forever.

"Have dinner with me," he whispered.

Oh God, I wanted that too.

I felt his hand curl around the side of my neck and the feel of his strength, his heat through that simple touch made me want it more.

"Amy," he prompted.

"I need to think," I whispered and watched his eyes flash and they did this with victory.

It was fabulous.

Then his hand on me tightened and he murmured, "I'll give you what you need."

I didn't lie. I needed to think.

I also needed to call Robin and discuss.

Thoroughly.

And, possibly, Lawrie.

Mickey lifted up and kissed my forehead in a way that was unbearably sweet.

Then he let me go and I felt bereft in a way that was intensely troubling.

In a haze caused by Mickey, I felt him move beyond me and whirled quickly.

"Mickey," I called.

He turned to me.

I looked at his beauty and swallowed.

Then I said softly, for only him and no audience to hear, "*If* I decide to give this a shot, before I share that with you, you need to think too. You have to have your head straight. I know you're still dealing with Rhiannon's issues and I hate that for you and the kids. But they're hers, not mine. And if you do anything like you did to me last night ever again, I'm sorry, it might not be fair, but I have to tell you, there won't be any more second chances."

"Don't have to think," he returned instantly and also quietly, only for me. "If you give me that shot, I don't know what's gonna happen. If this goes somewhere, we both gotta know that won't always be smooth. That happens, that'll be ours. But what I handed you last night that you didn't do shit to deserve, swear to Christ, Amy, I won't need any second chances."

Swear to Christ, Amy, I won't need any second chances.

That'll be ours.

Ours.

That sounded amazing.

"Yeah?" he called when I drifted away.

I focused on him. "Okay, Mickey."

"Hope you make the right choice, baby," he whispered right before he walked away.

I hoped I did to.

"Do you need to come in for a shot of bourbon?" Mr. Dennison called.

My body jolted and I looked to the windows.

"No, Mr. Dennison, thanks!" I called back.

"Is it only me who sees Nazis conspiring in the parking lot?" Mrs. McMurphy asked tetchily.

I loved that woman.

No matter what I was feeling, like right then I was feeling a lot, and even if she had no intention of doing it...

She always had me smiling.

———•———

"Oh my God, I want your life," Robin declared.

It was early that evening, we were on the phone, and I'd told her everything.

"Not sure it's as fun living it," I mumbled.

"I haven't had sex since my personal trainer moved to Vegas," she retorted.

"*Eek.*"

Yes, I made that noise out loud.

"You understand me," she mumbled.

I did.

Then again, I hadn't had sex since the night before Conrad told me he was leaving me, and I'd obviously not had sex with anyone other than Conrad for two decades.

Something else to fret about for I had a feeling Mickey hadn't abstained since he kicked his wife out.

Maybe sex was like riding a bike.

God, I hoped so.

I curled my legs deeper under me in my sectional and asked, "So what should I do?"

"Honestly?" she asked back.

"Wouldn't have it any other way," I told her.

"Okay, then honestly, if we never again took a chance on love, then our ex-asses would win. They'd beat us. Completely."

I drew breath sharply into my nose.

I'd recently realized I'd been beaten, and often, and not only allowed that to happen but had given away my power in order for it to happen.

And I'd also recently made the determination that had to stop.

"So," she continued, "if this doesn't work, it doesn't. If you have a spell where you go to your nursing home and decorate your house and go to movies by yourself, you do. If you find another guy, you try. But it would suck if we let those assholes beat us. It would suck if we let normal shit a lot of women endure and then bounce back from take us down for the count. So we shouldn't. You should ride this out. Be smart. But see where it will take you. And hopefully at the very least it will take you to out of the zone of self-induced orgasms and into a new zone that feels a whole lot nicer."

Her words were wise.

I just wondered if she heard them as she said them.

"Robin—" I started.

"Lawr isn't the only one waking up while watching you go through the tough stuff," she said quietly.

My heart settled.

Wouldn't it be great if my brother and best friend were happy?

Wouldn't it be even better if they found happy *together*?

It was too good to believe.

But I hoped for it all the same.

"Anyway, my ex-ass's wife is a lesbian and he's soon going to be paying double alimony, so if that's not a shot in the pants, nothing is," she added.

I burst out laughing.

She laughed with me.

My doorbell rang at the same time there came a pounding.

I twisted to it, heart starting to hammer, thinking I'd see Mickey in the frame and that was definitely early indication he was angry about something.

But I didn't see Mickey.

I saw two bodies, both appeared female.

I had a feeling the afternoon nursing home entertainment had made the rounds.

"I think my friends Josie and Alyssa are here," I said as the pounding kept coming and I folded out of my couch.

"Old folks talking," she muttered.

"My guess…yes," I confirmed.

"I'll let you go, but sweetie?"

"Yeah?" I asked, ascending the living room steps.

"Go for it. Don't let him shit on you. But take a chance on being happy."

I smiled at my phone as I lifted my hand to the lock. "Thanks, sweets."

"Later, darling."

"'Bye, honey."

We disconnected and I opened the door.

The instant I did, Alyssa sniped, "Seriously? Mickey? *And you didn't say anything?*"

She pushed in and did it carrying what appeared to be a chilled bottle of vodka.

I turned to Josie to see her waving toward the driveway. I looked beyond her to see Jake pulling out of my drive in his truck.

"Apparently, we're getting drunk," Josie said under her breath when she turned to me. "Jake's designated driver but he's not staying for the inebriation part."

As I moved out of her way, I thought that was a good choice, considering his company all had vaginas, he did not and the topic of conversation was undoubtedly going to be his friend who also didn't.

She came in and I closed the door, observing, "Small town, fast talk."

"You got that right, sister!" Alyssa yelled from the kitchen. "I cannot believe you didn't tell us!"

"I didn't want to be talking to you two about Mickey behind his back. You guys are friends with him," I told them.

"So?" Alyssa returned. "I'm friends with a lot of people and that doesn't stop me from talking, and listening, behind their backs. I'm a hairdresser, for God's sake, if these lips are loose," she pointed to her mouth, "clients find another maven with the mojo to beautify."

"I also wouldn't talk," Josie said, slipping onto one of my stools. "But I do appreciate you not sharing. For Mickey's sake. I wouldn't say anything to anyone else but, of course, I'd need to share with my husband and that would be awkward."

"I share with my husband too, but he's long since learned to tune that shit out when I'm yapping at him. This happened when I told him Carver Hoover had a penis ring. I start yammering," she waved a hand over her face, "Junior's *gone*."

I looked to the vodka her other hand was curled around then to her.

"I don't have mixers," I shared, if only to get us off the subject of penis rings.

"Who needs mixers when we're doin' shots?" she asked.

I looked to Josie.

Josie's eyes twinkled and she shrugged.

Alyssa started slamming through my cupboards, "Please tell me in all the buying sprees you went on, you bought shot glasses."

"I didn't," I admitted.

"Whatevs," she mumbled, pulled down some juice glasses and started pouring.

"So, apparently, there's a decision to be made."

This was surprisingly a prompt from Josie.

I looked to her. "It's a long story, but we'll just say, things with Mickey and me have been rocky."

She nodded.

"We'll get to the long story later. Decision now," Alyssa demanded, scooting glasses across the counter to us. "Have you made one?"

I took my glass and stared at it.

Then I lifted it and shot it.

I let the chill glide through me and looked to my friends.

"I'm terrified, and I'm terrified because I think I'm pretty much half in love with him already, so if I didn't at least take a chance, I'd never forgive myself," I announced.

"*Right on!*" Alyssa screeched to the ceiling then immediately did her shot.

Josie's eyes twinkled again as she lifted her glass and sipped.

When she was done, she said quietly, "He's a very good man."

I licked my lips and pressed them together.

"The *best*," Alyssa concurred.

I started rolling my lips.

"If things work, I believe he'll make you very happy, Amelia," Josie added.

I stopped rolling my lips and clenched my teeth.

"You're scared," Alyssa noted.

I looked to her. "Like I said, terrified."

"No," she replied gently. "Scared of it working."

"I—"

"And *then* collapsing," she finished.

I swallowed and nodded.

She poured more vodka in our glasses then lifted hers.

I took that cue and lifted mine.

Josie did the same.

"There is nothing guaranteed in life. But the only leaps really worth taking are leaps of faith on love. So look where you leap, beautiful, and happy landing," Alyssa toasted.

I smiled and raised my glass a smidge. They did too.

Then we all shot them back (even Josie).

Alyssa crashed hers to the bar and demanded loudly, "Now! The long story!"

I slid onto a stool and, on command, shared a long, hopeful story with my new friends.

———— • ————

I SAT IN MY NIGHTIE ON MY BED, KNEES TO MY CHEST, ONE ARM AROUND MY calves, phone in my other hand.

It was late. I was tipsy. Josie and Alyssa were gone.

And I thought it was time to call Mickey.

My mother would disagree since it was well past nine. In fact it was well past eleven.

But if I were him, I wouldn't want to have to go to sleep not knowing.

Maybe he didn't care that much.

But it seemed he did.

So he should know.

I activated my phone and slid my thumb over the screen. When I found his contact, I hit go.

I put the phone to my ear.

It rang once and then I got sweet and low, "Hey, Amy."

"Hey," I replied.

"Your posse hit the road?" he asked.

"Were your ears burning?" I asked back.

"Can take it," he muttered.

I drew in breath.

"Mickey," I called.

"I'm here," he replied.

"I like you," I whispered.

"Fuck." It sounded pained.

"Mickey?" I called again, more urgently.

"Here, Amy, and I'm glad, baby, 'cause I hope you get I like you too."

"So maybe we should go to dinner?" I suggested.

There was no pain in his voice but a smile when he replied, "Yeah, maybe we should."

"Okay," I said quietly.

"Okay," he returned. "You goin' to bed?"

"I'm in bed."

There was a pause before he said, "Let you go then, Amy."

"Okay, Mickey."

"Later, babe."

Something about this ending wasn't right. It was abrupt, not soft and sweet and gentle like it had started.

I felt funny about it but I replied, "Later."

He hung up.

I took the phone from my ear and stared at it.

God, I hoped he wasn't one of those thrill of the chase men who caught their prey and lost interest in it.

But I couldn't jump to conclusions. He had kids. They were still with him. School didn't start until next week so they could still be up and something could have happened to take Mickey's attention.

I put my phone to my nightstand, got under the covers, turned out the light and pulled the covers up to my shoulder, snuggling in.

I was wide awake.

And I was thinking I'd agreed to have dinner with Mickey but then he'd ended the call before we'd even made plans.

"Oh God," I breathed.

My doorbell rang.

My head shot off the pillow as a shiver stole over my skin.

The doorbell rang again.

My hand threw back the covers as my feet threw themselves over the side of the bed.

I hit the floor and started running. Running in my little navy satin nightie with its plum lace (an Alyssa choice, no skank, all class, very sexy) right to the front door.

The motion sensor light was activated.

Mickey was shadowed through the glass.

I unlocked it, threw it open and looked up just in time to find myself in the strong arms of Mickey Donovan, his mouth on mine, and he was kissing me.

I let him, pressed close to his heat, held on tight and kissed him back.

We made out, wet and sweet and hard and wild, on my landing in the open front door and we did it for a *really long time*.

I loved every *fucking* second.

Arm tight around the small of my back, me up on tiptoes, Mickey mostly supporting my weight, his other hand in my hair, my arms wound around his shoulders, Mickey ended it.

Slowly, my lips bruised and tingling—*lots* of things tingling—my eyes drifted open.

"Lobster Market tomorrow night at seven?" he asked, his voice thick, his eyes through the shadows I could actually *feel* were heated.

I felt a giggle of pure joy bubble inside of me, forced it down to a smile and breathed, "Works for me."

"No kids," he said. "Just you and me."

I nodded, holding on just as he kept holding me. "Just you and me."

He dipped so close that his nose brushed mine. "You made the right choice, Amy."

Current evidence was strongly suggesting I did.

"Not certain there was another choice, Mickey," I admitted and he grinned.

I had it back.

I loved that too.

He bent to put my feet on the floor and started to let me go. I figured it would be a little clingy at this juncture to hold on tight, so I let him.

With one arm still around me, he lifted his other hand and brushed my bangs out of my eyes.

"See you tomorrow, baby."

He would.

And I'd see him.

I was standing in his arm and still...

I *couldn't wait.*

"You will," I confirmed.

He grinned again, bent and kissed my nose this time and then let me go.

"Don't be polite, wanna hear the locks click behind me," he ordered.

God.

Mickey.

"All right."

I went to the door and held the edge as he walked out.

I started to close it when he turned and called, "Amy?"

"Yeah?"

That was when I got a grin and a look in his eyes I'd never seen.

A grin and a look that foretold what he had said earlier.

When he had me, and he was going to have me, he was going to wreck me.

Then he said, "Nice nightie."

I held on to the edge of the door tight so my legs wouldn't fail me.

Mickey turned and walked away.

I forced myself to close the door and lock it without chasing him, or alternate scenario, melting in a puddle.

On shaking legs, I walked back to my bed.

I got in it knowing I'd never fall asleep.

I slept like a baby.

14

EVERYTHING ABOUT ME

*T*he next night I sat beside Mickey in his truck, nearly paralytic with agonizing.

First, because this was happening. I was in Mickey's truck and he was taking me to a restaurant for a date.

In all that had already happened, *this* was our beginning.

But there were no kids, no house sale and we weren't fighting.

What if we had nothing to say?

God, what if he didn't find me interesting?

It was funny (not in a *ha ha* way, in a *terrifying* way) as well as very telling that I hadn't cared one bit about whether Boston or Bradley had found me interesting.

But I *needed* Mickey to find me interesting.

And I was terrified he wouldn't.

Second, in a frenzy that was the beginning of my agonizing, nearly upon waking I'd gone through all my new clothes and found I didn't have a single thing to wear for our date.

So I'd gone out shopping.

In store seven at the mall, I decided on a caftan dress that I thought was stunning. It looked made of scarves with a nearly Pucci print in robin's egg blue and lavender. It had a straight hem that cut at my knees, had a tight waistline under my breasts and full three-quarter sleeves.

Most importantly, through a deep V that went to the waistline, it had cleavage. I'd paired this with t-strap, light taupe suede sandals that had a high, thin, stacked wedge—four inches, no platform.

Very sexy.

I bought this because it was clear Mickey liked the dress I wore on my date with Bradley.

But the Lobster Market was not The Eaves. I'd been there for lunch with Ruth and Dela. A little black dress was not appropriate. I needed something more casual but I also needed it to say I felt this date was a special occasion because I didn't want Mickey to think he wasn't getting the best of me.

The good news was when he'd showed at my door his eyes had dropped to my cleavage and I saw them flare.

But then he'd just grabbed my hand and tugged me out of my house, waiting only briefly for me to lock the door before he quickly guided me to his truck that he'd driven across the street and parked in my drive so I didn't have to walk all the way to his place.

Which was sweet.

But he didn't say anything about the dress.

And last, I was agonizing because we were on our first date, but with all that had happened—fights, barbeques, Frisbee playing, family dinners —it felt more like a fourth or fifth date.

This, back in the day, was when I would start considering having sex.

And this, right then, might be when Mickey thought we should start having sex.

I had not had a lot of partners before Conrad, but I also wasn't a virgin. And Conrad and I had had a healthy sex life. One I enjoyed. One I thought we'd both enjoyed. One that continued not only from start to finish but didn't wane when I was pregnant or even after my pregnancies when I carried baby weight. And although during those times Conrad encouraged me to lose it and "get healthy," that didn't seem to affect his attraction to me.

And it was safe to say I wanted to have sex with Mickey.

But I was terrified because not only might he not find me a good conversationalist, worse, it had been a long time for me. I couldn't imagine you could forget how to do it but I was concerned I'd get tense or worry too much I was giving him what he needed and he might find me a terrible lover.

Then where would we be?

I just stopped myself from wringing my hands and wondering hysterically if I should have slept with Bradley just to get back in the saddle when Mickey called, "Amy."

"Yeah," I answered the windshield.

God, even my voice sounded tight!

"Ash is with some girlfriends. She'll be home by ten."

"Okay," I mumbled.

"And on our way back from the restaurant, we gotta pick up Cill, who's hanging with some buds."

"All right," I kept mumbling.

My head twitched and I looked down when I felt Mickey's hand at my elbow. I watched and experienced the tingles when it trailed down, at the same time tugging until he folded his big hand around mine.

"What I'm sayin' is, you need to relax," he went on gently. "My kids'll be home tonight so, seein' as when I have you, I intend to take my time doin' that and not fuck you on your couch and do it quick so I can get back to my kids, this is just dinner, baby. You and me and some alone time. When I can concentrate on just you, that's when we'll take this there. Until then, just sit back and enjoy."

How did he know what I was thinking?

Likely because he was thinking of having sex with me.

Just not tonight.

That was one relief.

Though, it didn't help, his comment about "taking his time," which made me want to start having sex with him immediately.

Unfortunately, that new urge was added to the other things I continued to worry about.

"You hear me?" he asked on a hand squeeze when I didn't answer.

"I heard you."

"You gonna relax?" he pushed.

"We're not fighting," I blurted, looking to him to see his eyes aimed at where we were going.

"No," he agreed.

I stared at his handsome profile.

No five o'clock shadow, he'd shaved for me.

I liked the whiskers.

I liked it more he made an effort for me.

The rest was him. Faded jeans, a lightweight cotton shirt with sleeves rolled up.

But the jeans were less faded and the shirt was an attractive plaid in beige and light blue against white that was a *tad bit* nicer than what he usually wore around me.

Yes, he'd made an effort for me.

This meant something.

So I decided to put it out there.

Tightening my fingers around his, I turned my body his way. "What if, no kids, no fighting, you find I'm not interesting?"

His hand convulsed in mine, nearly causing pain his strength was so formidable, and he did this bursting out laughing.

My comment was hardly funny.

"Mickey," I snapped.

I could tell he was forcing his laughter to chuckles when he said incredulously, "You, the Calway heiress who's busier than me, and I essentially got two jobs and am the only parent to my two kids, in that fuckin' dress, sittin' across from me with a million stories about old folks and what they get up to, not to mention what you get up to with Alyssa and Josie…not interesting?"

He made it sound like that was impossible.

"You've heard a lot of my old folks stories, Mickey," I reminded him.

"They all kick the bucket since you last told 'em?" he asked me.

My heart clenched at the thought as I forced out, "Of course not."

"Then don't worry," he muttered, slowing the truck and letting me go to keep a hand on the wheel and flip on his turn signal.

"I can't regale you all night with stories of the residents of Dove House."

"You can crack my shit up by using words like regale," he returned.

I found that surprising.

"Regale is funny?" I asked.

"Amy," he said as answer and said no more, but my name on his lips was uttered with a smile.

So I queried, "That's it? Amy?"

He looked both ways and made his turn, saying, "I'll confirm. Regale is funny."

"How?"

"How is anything funny? It just is," he replied.

"I find that strange," I murmured, not knowing if that stung or if it didn't.

He heard that too.

I knew it when he said, "I'm not makin' fun of you, babe. It's just cute. Like you can be when you're not being bull-headed and a pain in the ass."

God.

Really?

I glared at him. "You can be bull-headed and a pain in the ass too, Mickey."

He glanced at me and did it grinning. "See? We already got a lot in common."

It was in that moment I realized he was teasing and further realized it was funny and sweet. It also put us into a spot where we were familiar. This wasn't a first date to be nervous about. This was Mickey and Amy going to dinner.

That was when I felt complete relief and I was grateful to Mickey for giving me that.

I didn't share that verbally. I just rolled my eyes and faced forward but did it smiling.

And when I did it, I saw we were on Cross Street. Mickey took us down to the end, by the wharf, and found a parking spot only two doors down from the Lobster Market. It was clearly a score since the street was busy, not only with cars at the curbs angled in their spots, but with people strolling.

I figured this was an end of summer, use it before you lose it kind of thing. Living in La Jolla we didn't have seasons, so I'd forgotten how you learned to pack it all in before you lost daylight and warmth.

Once parked, Mickey got out and was at my door by the time I had it opened and had a foot to the runner. He helped me down, away from the door, which he slammed, and he beeped the locks as he led me to the sidewalk.

He held my hand as we walked and again, I thought that was sweet.

When we made it to the Market, he went in and the hostess smiled, saying, "Hey, Mickey. Got your table all ready."

She gave me a smile too before she grabbed some menus.

But I was surprised that the Lobster Market took reservations (and I was surprised in a nice way at more sweet from Mickey that he took the time to make one).

Still holding my hand, as Mickey guided us behind the hostess, I took in the restaurant and something settled inside me.

Because the Lobster Market was perfectly Mickey.

And perfectly Magdalene.

And maybe perfectly me.

I'd never been there in the evening, but I saw the lights were dimmed. And as at lunch, on the tables they had the squat glass vases filled with short buds, only two or three stems each, but it brought a bit of class. They also didn't change their blue and white checkered tablecloths for the evening. The salt and pepper shakers were glass, attractive, but not crystal.

However evening meals, I saw, did not have paper napkins like at lunch, but blue or white cloth napkins and also small, lit candles.

The view of the wharf from the big windows was amazing.

Even though it was nice, it wasn't exactly romantic.

What it was was a place that could be for anything. A date. A family dinner. Whatever you needed it to be. It wasn't fancy, it wasn't casual. It wasn't a burger joint you dropped by to grab a meal. It was a place you made special for whatever reason that might be.

It wasn't elegant and refined, however, the fare wasn't cheap but it was delicious.

It was just right for Mickey.

And, I decided, walking hand in hand with Mickey, for me.

The restaurant wasn't full, though there wasn't a lot of seating left, but the hostess led us right to a prime table at the windows so our amazing view was unadulterated.

Perfect.

Mickey seated me before he seated himself and the hostess gave us our menus. Before we could even glance at them, a busboy came with glasses of water.

After he left, I put the menu down and looked at Mickey.

"You're the Maine man, show me how to eat at a lobster joint in Maine," I challenged.

As I spoke, Mickey's eyes went from his menu to me and they were smiling.

"Anything you don't like?" he asked.

"Not really," I replied.

"Then you're on," he muttered, looking back at his menu.

The waitress came and asked for our drink orders. I ordered a sauvignon blanc and Mickey ordered a beer. We received our drinks and Mickey handed the menus to the waitress after ordering us both steamers, cups of New England clam chowder, dinner salads and full lobsters with all the fixin's.

When she left, I turned wide eyes to Mickey.

"That's a lot of food."

His gaze went guarded but even so, it didn't leave mine when he replied, "Amy, you gotta eat more, baby."

And I felt it again. That settling inside me.

This time I felt it because certain things he'd said to me, and certain ways he'd looked at me, I realized belatedly that he'd noted I'd lost weight. Not only that, but he knew why.

And he was worried about me.

"With all that was happening, I lost track—" I started to explain.

He interrupted me gently, "Things are settling, so take better care. You with me?"

He was right. Things *were* settling.

I needed to take better care.

I nodded.

And that was when the date officially began.

We started talking and it came easy.

He told me even though Rhiannon had still not shown, Cill was "back on track" and both his kids were "gearing up for school."

Then he'd made that settling feeling settle even deeper when his beautiful blue eyes got more beautiful when they became warm and intent as I shared the first real things with him about my kids; that Pippa had been upset not making the cheerleading squad and both of them were in cahoots with me to get my brother out for Thanksgiving.

"I get Thanksgiving this year," I told him happily.

And getting this information, Mickey looked just as happy.

"Close with your brother?" he asked.

"Yes," I answered. "Growing up, he could be an annoying big brother, but in our house, it was him and me. Dad was always working. Mom had other priorities. We were mostly raised by nannies who Mom thought it was her only motherly duty to find lacking, fire, then hire someone new we'd get used to right before she'd fire them. So we were smart and we were lucky, with only each other, we got close rather than stuck in our own worlds."

"Good you had somebody," he remarked and I grinned.

"Better because Lawr isn't just the one who was there. He's a good guy who cares a lot about his probably annoying little sister."

"With only brothers, always wanted a sister," he told me.

"Even having a great brother, I always did too," I replied.

Things stayed easy as we got our steamers, then ate our chowder with Mickey ordering me another glass of wine when mine got low.

Through this, he shared about his work, mostly why he disliked his boss.

This was because his boss had underbid so rabidly on projects, he'd built almost a monopoly in the county. This he was able to do providing substandard materials. He also pushed his workers to finish the job quickly, cutting corners along the way, which meant not only the materials but the labor was substandard.

And Mickey was always foreman on the roofing jobs and sometimes foreman on the construction jobs. He didn't like doing what his boss made him do. He didn't agree with doing it. But it wasn't his job to like it or agree with it. It was his job to do it.

And Mickey being the kind of man Mickey was, he liked this least of all.

So, with Mickey the face of the business for clients, he got it at both ends: the workers angry they didn't have time to do their jobs and more, they were pushed to overtime and weekend work, but also the clients who would contact Mickey and complain when things inevitably went wrong.

I made a mental note to look outside the county should I need any of this kind of work done, but other than that, I had little to say, except, "I'm sorry, honey. That sounds awful."

"Yeah, it sucks," he agreed. "But recent news, I've got it in me to take the risk, it could get better."

Since his work seemed pretty dismal, and this sounded quite exciting, I leaned slightly over my empty chowder cup, hand up with my wineglass, elbow resting on the table, and asked, "How?"

"Chief told me that the town's gonna vote on allocating more money to the fire department," he answered. "We had a development go in 'bout five years ago. Nothin' big, only twenty houses, but it's still more people and more taxes. Now, the Club has asked for planning permission to build a golf course and add houses that'll be built around that course. Members of the Club got money and pull, so this'll go through. And that shopping place is already up and running on Mills jetty, more buildings, more trade. We got enough volunteers to cover but we all know that's thin and it asks a lot of the guys to put their asses on the line and give the time needed, which for each of us is a lot."

I nodded, still not liking that Mickey put his "ass on the line," still not sharing that, instead asking, "The Club?"

"The Magdalene Club. Private bar and restaurant, moneyed, members only."

"Ah," I murmured.

When that was all I had, he kept speaking.

"So, the chief has gone to the town council with a proposal. Stay at part-time pay for a chief and full-time pay for a firefighter who'll help the chief recruit, do scheduling, training, keep volunteers sharp by runnin' drills and shit—"

"And you want to be that firefighter," I cut him off to guess.

"No, Amy, I wanna be the chief."

I blinked.

"Bobby is sixty-three," he explained. "He can't live off part-time, even if that packet is pretty decent. So he's also got a full-time and he's been our chief for eleven years. Town might be small and sleepy but shit happens and the fire department can never not be on the ball. His last vacation, he and his wife went to Tucson to look at houses. He's ready to retire. He does, he's gonna recommend me to the town council for his job. I got in the most time, got the most experience, fill in for him when he's not around. So I can do that job, take that salary and then run my own crew."

"Of firefighters?" I asked.

"Yeah. *And* of roofers," he answered and I felt my eyes widen. "Start my own business. People around here know me. I won't be the cheapest but they can expect quality, have their roof redone or fixed and know they don't have to worry about the next rain or any weather for another ten, fifteen years, depending on the materials they pay for. I know I could take Ralph's trade. Could do the same with his contractor work too. Already got the license, went for that a while ago when Ralph pissed me off more than he usually does. Just was dealin' with Rhiannon and didn't have the time to cut loose. But if I do this, I'd have to start small, build it if it works. Won't have to worry about the crew, all Ralph's boys'll come with me. With the money coming in regular from the department, I've only done the numbers in my head, but I figure things'll be really tight for about six months and then I'll start turning a profit and in the end things'll be a whole lot more comfortable for the kids and me."

"Oh my God, Mickey, that's *great*," I breathed, reaching past our chowder cups to grab his hand on the table.

He turned it and wrapped his fingers around mine, holding tight. "It would be, I can pull it off," he agreed.

"Are you a shoo-in for the chief's job?" I asked.

"Absolutely," he answered.

"And when is the chief retiring?"

"Not sure he can make it the two years he'd planned before retiring. Bobby's not just done with all the work; he's done with Maine in the winter. Could talk to him but I think he wants to get the department where he wants it and feels good to go and then he'll go."

"Then, could you start now?" I queried. "The roofing," I explained. "Not a big company, quitting your job to begin, but, I don't know, taking smaller jobs? Just so when you can really do it, you hit the ground running."

We had to separate as the busboy came and took our spent dishes and we did this with Mickey studying me and not speaking.

"Sorry," I mumbled after the busboy left, thinking I read his silence. "I don't know anything about this kind of thing."

"It's a good idea, Amy," he surprised me by saying. "Don't have a compete clause with Ralph in my contract. Could get the word out, do patch work, open a line in case of emergencies, talk to some of the boys who want to take side work, start forming a crew. Build it from there while I still got a full salary."

"Will Ralph get angry?" I asked.

"He does, he does," Mickey answered on a slight shrug. "He's got no call with the work I'm hired to do for him to fire me and he's not stupid. He knows I eat shit a lot and talk fast for him; he won't want that buffer taken away. But he gets rid of me, then I just go for it."

I smiled big.

Mickey smiled big back to me.

That also settled inside me in another way that felt good.

I lost that feeling too fast for my liking when our waitress came with our lobster.

I stared at mine, the whole thing, and I did this trying to hide my horror.

I'd had lobster. I loved lobster.

But I'd never had to take one apart to eat it.

I was still staring at it when Mickey's hand curled around it.

I looked up at him to see him looking down at my lobster, shaking his head and grinning, then twisting my lobster apart expertly, doing this muttering, "My dainty heiress, doesn't wanna get her hands dirty."

He was teasing. He was his normal handsome (and then some) teasing.

But he was also annoying.

"I've never torn apart a lobster, Mickey. If you'd just explain how to do it, I could do it myself," I declared as he put the tail on my plate.

I declared this even though I very much wanted to eat my lobster but I very much did *not* want to twist it apart.

His eyes came to me, dipped to my cleavage and came back, "And have lobster juice squirt on that dress? No way, baby."

I liked that he liked the dress.

I liked that he was taking care of me by tearing apart my meal.

I did not like that he called me a "dainty heiress."

Though, truth be told, I *did* like that he called me *his* "dainty heiress."

"I'm not a dainty heiress, Mickey," I snapped.

He dumped the claws on my plate and then he dumped the gross part on another plate the waitress had given us for that purpose, doing that as his gaze came to me.

"You drive a Mercedes. You live in Cliff Blue. You go grocery shopping and come over for a family dinner in high heels. You *so* are, Amy," he replied.

"I'll have you know I do *all* my own laundry, cooking and cleaning," I announced.

He picked up his own lobster, eyes still on me and they were dancing. "*All* of it? Wow, baby, impressive."

I glared at him even as something warm stole through me.

He was teasing and he was doing it in a way he'd get a rise out of me because he *liked* to get a rise out of me and I knew why.

Even in getting along, he wanted me to have, as he put it, my "gloves up," because he liked sparring with me, mostly because between us that was a spark that we had that when he fanned the flame with a kiss (or, eventually more), it blazed into an inferno.

That knowledge tingled someplace private, a sensation I enjoyed. A sensation I would have liked to experience a lot longer.

But I didn't.

Because suddenly, the hairs on the back of my neck stood up.

Shockingly, the instant they did, I watched Mickey tense. I also watched his head turn.

I followed his gaze and that was when I tensed.

Because being guided to a table across the restaurant were Martine and Conrad. They were moving but both had their heads turned, looking at Mickey and me.

Conrad appeared annoyed. Then again, for the last three years, that was always the way he looked at me.

Martine looked annoyed too.

Her eyes darting between Mickey and me, she looked something else as well.

Catty.

And if I could credit it, there was a hint of envy.

And there was a lot to be envious about.

She had Conrad, who was a cheat in a way he was probably still cheating, but this time, on her.

And I was sitting with Mickey, who was much more handsome, nicer, funnier and a whole lot better of a kisser.

Not to mention, my dress was far more stylish than her skirt and blouse and my shoes kicked her shoes' ass.

The hairs on my neck eased.

"Fuck," Mickey grunted.

"Honey," I called and Mickey looked to me. "Thanks for ripping apart my meal."

It was my way of saying this was him and me, our first date, our time, and Conrad and Martine were not going to ruin it.

He studied me before his eyes warmed and his face grew soft and when they did, I knew he heard me.

"Anytime, Amy."

I grinned.

Then I looked down and picked up my cracker to dig into my lobster claws.

———— • ————

I was stuffed by the time we were done, and thankful, in an effort to get me eating, Mickey didn't push dessert because I couldn't have done it.

But I would have wanted to do it.

For him.

I'd also had three glasses of wine, the meal being delicious, the company better, and I'd found that I'd been anxious all day for nothing.

There were no awkward pauses. There was no searching for conversation. There was no panic about trying to be interesting.

Mickey and I had already laid the groundwork. We knew about each other and each other's lives. He teased. I reacted. We talked about kids and jobs and family and life and it came easy. There was much to learn but it was being discovered freely and naturally.

Mickey was good company.

And most important of all, he made it clear he felt the same with me.

In fact, when I'd communicated that Martine and Conrad did not exist, they actually ceased to exist.

So the end of the dinner was just the same as the beginning.

Free and natural and all about Mickey and me.

I was surprised but not averse when, after we left the restaurant, Mickey didn't guide me to his truck but instead to the street where he walked us across hand in hand to the wharf. He then walked us down the wharf to the end.

I hadn't been there yet but I liked being there. I could smell the sea, feel the cool air calming me along with the three glasses of wine, and I could hear the tranquil, muted sounds of the bells on the buoys.

Better still was when we reached the end, Mickey turned my back to him and curled his arms around my midriff, pulling me to his heat.

"Ever think of leaving Magdalene, just walk right here and you'll think you're crazy," he murmured and his words made me relax against him.

Belly filled with delicious seafood, mind settled by a great date with Mickey, standing there with the smells and sounds, I took that moment to take in the sights.

Magdalene was built into a set of coves, the town proper in the longest of them. The coastline rose up gray and black rocky cliffs that were partially bare and dark right then, but in the light the tops were forested with trees. However, quite a bit of it was taken with homes, their faint lights in the shadowed structures giving the view a magical feel.

This was augmented by the charming lighthouse flashing its light from where the structure was built on a sharp jut of land to the north. Not to mention Josie and Jake's Lavender House, which was a feature of Magdalene's coastline. It was large and picturesque and now its windows were lit, indicating the family inside was up and active, doing things together, carrying on the tradition of love and family, why that house was built.

I couldn't see Cliff Blue, which was built up high over a small cove, so it was hidden. But I wondered then how the coastline looked from the sea.

It was likely fabulous.

There were sounds of cars driving down the street behind us, but this wasn't constant.

No, the constant was the bells of the buoys and the waves lapping against the shore and slapping against the planks of the wharf, peaceful, easy beauty.

I wrapped my arms around his at my midriff and leaned back into him. "I can see why you'd never leave."

"Want for my kids whatever they want," he stated. "I'd be happy as long as they're happy. But I hope, if they take off, when they come back and I bring them right here, wherever life took them, they'd know in their bones that standing right here was the only place that was home."

I loved what he said but feeling Mickey, looking at the view, smelling the smells and hearing the sounds off Magdalene's wharf, having lived the life I lived, it occurred to me I'd never had a home.

Not a real one.

I thought I did, with my husband, my family, until Conrad tore it away from me.

And I wanted a home.

A home that looked like that, smelled like that, sounded like that and felt like it felt to stand there in Mickey's arms.

Lulling me with that beauty, Mickey went for it.

He did it gently.

But he did it.

"You're not ready, Amy, then you decide the time. But you're eventually gonna have to share how he got your kids from you, baby."

I felt every inch of me grow solid and Mickey didn't miss it, couldn't, and his arms grew snug around me.

He also dipped his head so his jaw was no longer resting against the side of my hair and he said in my ear, "If this is not the time, it's not. But I'll say now, this is what this feels like it might be, you gotta learn there's no safer place than in my arms and when you're here, Amy," his arms gave me a squeeze, "you can give me anything."

I closed my eyes.

This is what it feels like it might be...

Maybe, just maybe, he felt the same way as me.

And if he did, he needed to know, sooner rather than later.

No safer place than in my arms and when you're here, Amy, you can give me anything.

I opened my eyes.

"I told you how things went with him and Martine."

I felt his breath whisper along my ear, then his lips, before I felt his jaw again pressed to the side of my head.

"Yeah."

I drew in a breath and let it out, saying, "When he left me, I lost it."

"Within your rights, Amy."

I stared at pure peace and beauty.

Then I decided this was important, Mickey was important, and I had finally grown up.

So there was a way this needed to go and I had to find the courage to make it go that way.

I did this, turning in his arms, lifting my hands to his biceps, and most importantly, catching his eyes.

"When I say I lost it," I whispered when he was looking down at me. "I lost it, Mickey. Like, *lost it*. I went more than a little crazy. I was hurt and I wanted *them* to hurt so I made them hurt. I went out of my way to do it. I took every opportunity to do it and if there weren't any, I created them. I did not do what I should have done, felt the pain, but powered through it for myself and my kids. I nursed it and fed from it and behaved selfishly, thoughtlessly, and worst of all, spitefully."

"He fucked and got engaged to another woman while he was married to you, babe. Again, within your rights," Mickey told me.

"For three years?" I asked.

He didn't even blink.

He asked back, "Is there a time limit for bein' pissed about betrayal?"

"My kids saw it, Mickey."

To that, he said nothing.

My heart pinched but I had to keep going.

"I should have shielded them from it. I can't say it was frequently. But it was not rare. It happened at their school events. When Conrad would pick up the kids. When I'd pick them up. They should have never seen that. And what they didn't see, they heard. I connived to find ways to get into it with Conrad and Martine, embarrass them, take my pain out on them. I went to Conrad's practice. I went to the hospital where Martine worked. I wanted everyone to know what kind of people they were. In the end, it was only me I made a fool of."

"How'd your kids know about that other shit?" Mickey asked.

"Eventually, as he went for more and more custody, Conrad shared it with them. Before they came here, they were old enough to speak with the judge and decide who they wanted to live with. I made it so they did not want to live with me."

Mickey's mouth got tight but he said through it, "He shouldn't have done that, Amy."

"I shouldn't have given him the ammunition *to* do it, Mickey," I returned and shook my head, looking to his shoulder, dropping my voice and admitting, "I don't think you understand how bad I got. How ugly I was. Petty and stupid. He had no choice but to push things with me, and in the end, move across the country to make his family safe from my ugliness."

When Mickey didn't say anything, panic started leaking into me.

I lifted my eyes to his and assured urgently, "I know this is crazy. But that isn't me anymore. If there's a lesson to be learned, any mother will learn it when her children are taken from her. I learned it, Mickey. I fell into a pit of agony that I dug myself and allowed myself to drown in it, wanting to pull everyone down there with me. And I went to extremes to do that, taking my kids with me. I didn't *deserve* to keep them because no good mother behaved like me. But the minute Conrad and Martine moved out here and took my kids with them, I knew something had to change. Months, I gave them, seeing my kids one weekend every four weeks, and I gave them that to give them a break from me. I did this planning to move out here, fix my relationship with the kids, heal my family so I could give my babies something that would be safe and healthy. So I went crazy, but I learned. I learned that was not me. That was someone else. But she was not me."

When I stopped talking and he simply continued to stare down at me impassively, I turned my head and looked to the sea, knowing he thought I was a psycho bitch, a terrible mother, and if things went bad between us, he'd be treated to the same thing.

And I lived right across the street.

This was our beginning and our end just as I knew, when he'd learned the worst in me, it would be.

I clenched my teeth as the tears threatened, but I didn't blame him.

That didn't mean I wasn't bleeding.

"You done?" he asked matter-of-factly.

My eyes shot to his.

"Yes," I answered tentatively.

"Raised by nannies," he stated strangely.

"I'm sorry?"

"Growing up, your parents give you anything?"

I knew what he was asking, shook my head, but said, "Well, they taught me I should act appropriately, which in this case was championing all my shenanigans because they also taught me a Bourne-Hathaway should demand to be treated a whole lot better than Conrad treated me."

"A Bourne-Hathaway?"

"Mom's a Bourne," I told him then reluctantly kept the information flowing. "As in Bourne-Tran Freight and Shipping."

His eyes got slightly wide as his arms convulsed around me before his gaze went over my head and he sighed.

He'd heard of Bourne-Tran.

Not surprising.

"Oil and shipping," he muttered.

Strike two.

I had a feeling I wouldn't be getting to strike three.

"You've never heard of me and we're not objects of fascination because great-granddad Hathaway was into privacy," I stated stupidly and Mickey looked down at me, expression still impassive. "He was a very smart man, so even back then he saw the way of things and decreed that any of his offspring would behave with decorum. Flash and attention and exploits were not tolerated, and he guaranteed this by putting a codicil on all Calway money that would guarantee if this ever happened, a trust fund wouldn't be awarded, and if it happened after, it would be rescinded. We lived quiet, at his command, even if he's long since dead. And Mom and Dad were perfect for each other since her family had much the same philosophy." I looked to his throat and finished, "Though, Uncle Hugh is a bit of a wild one."

"Amy," Mickey called.

I looked to him.

"So you're an oil and shipping heiress," he noted.

I nodded.

"Raised by nannies," he went on.

I nodded again.

"And you're not tight with your parents," he kept going.

I shook my head.

"Your brother?" he asked.

"Lawr barely speaks to them," I whispered then added inanely, "At least he barely speaks to Dad."

"Right," he grunted, then he said, "So you're an oil and shipping heiress with a shit ton of money who got married, had kids, then your husband fucked you over. Until then, your life had been golden and you probably had everything you ever wanted, except what was important. So when something you wanted was taken away from you, you had no clue how to deal and no foundation to keep you solid. What you did have was parents who felt you should stick it to your ex because he had the audacity to fuck over a Bourne-Hathaway."

My life hadn't been golden.

But I knew what he was saying.

"That's pretty much it," I kept whispering.

Mickey nodded once. "How long were you with him?"

"Married sixteen years. But we were together for three before we were married."

Something moved through his eyes at my answer but he didn't address that.

He stated, "So he fucked you over, you lost it, and went psycho on his ass."

Yes, there it was, he thought I was psycho.

"Yeah," I confirmed.

"And your parents didn't advise you to go psycho by hiring a really fuckin' good attorney?" he asked.

"I had that too," I shared. "I just lost sight of priorities and didn't let him fight like he wanted to because I didn't want it to get ugly for the kids."

"But they saw a different kind of ugly."

I couldn't say it aloud again so I just nodded.

"Shit happens, Amy."

I felt my lips part.

It took a while but I finally asked, "I'm sorry?"

"Honest to Christ, I'm actually shocked you had it in you to pull yourself together at all."

I was so surprised, I couldn't say anything.

Mickey didn't feel the same way and kept speaking.

"Grew up, you know I had money, not like you but in this town we were part of the elite," he told me. "Dad got offered membership to the Club. Granddad didn't because he was Irish and he was Catholic and they were assholes. They were still assholes when they offered membership to Dad, who's also obviously Irish and Catholic, but by that time, he made so much money, they felt they could lift their racist, bigoted, unwritten rule and offered it to him anyway. He took it just so he could find ways to shove it up their asses."

When he stopped speaking and didn't go on, without anything else to say, I said, "Okay."

With this prompt, Mickey continued, "So Dad went and got drunk and loud and obnoxious and loved every minute knowin' those arrogant fuckers hated it. Dad let his boys go knowin' we'd get drunk and loud and obnoxious too. We upped it by doin' that as well as gettin' into fights with any stick-up-his-ass asshole who looked at us funny, and you probably get there were a lot of them. He also probably knew we'd go all out to get whatever rich bitch pussy we could nail, which is undoubtedly why he snuck us condoms, puttin' 'em under our pillows."

I emitted a soft gasp at this but didn't respond verbally.

So Mickey kept going.

"And we did. Had my fill of spoiled little rich girl, Amy, and none of them were near as well-off as you. They grew up and some are still around, and not one of 'em has it in 'em to learn a fuckin' thing except to think they're entitled to have what they want and do whatever they wanna do and they don't give that first fuck if it's right or wrong or hurts anybody."

"I—" I started but stopped when his arms got extra tight and he dipped his face so it was close to mine.

"You stumbled," he stated firmly. "Then you picked your ass up, opened your eyes and saw what was important and started fightin' for it. So you fucked up. Now you're makin' it right. And that's the only thing that means *anything*."

I couldn't believe what I was hearing.

"Do you...really think that?" I asked.

"Fuck yeah," he answered. "The mistakes we make in life don't define us, Amy. The way we handle 'em after makin' 'em do. You made a mistake. Now you're handling it and doing it the right way and that's who you are. A mother who wants to heal her family and make them safe and healthy. So really, you got that strength in you, that's all you ever were. Your ex tripped you up and you weren't expecting it and you didn't handle it right. But that's over, so you gotta find the strength to keep handling it right now."

"I...it's hard to get over the making the mistake part."

He lifted his head away, but not far. "Yeah, what you lost makin' yours, I get that. But the root of this issue is not your burden to bear. I understand how it went down, but a cheater manipulating a bad situation *he* created, gettin' the upper hand with his kids and continuing to beat down the wife he fucked over." He shook his head. "No. You get that now, I'm seeing. But I'll repeat...no. You're right. You know it and I don't have to say it, but your kids shouldn't have seen that. But what *I* saw is this guy who shared your bed for sixteen years then tore your family apart and sent you reeling up in *your* face at *your* front door without you buyin' that shit at all, just movin' to be close to your kids. He's a motherfucking asshole, Amy, and in all this, whatever you served up to him, he bought that and deserved every second of the shit you shoved down his throat. So that...you let go. Because that's not on you."

"I shouldn't have licked my wounds, kept them fresh, torn at them more, Mickey," I told him. "I should have taken my licks, sorted myself out and moved on."

"Rhiannon was passed out every night before I could make love to her and that shit went on for months," he declared.

I stared.

But he wasn't done.

"Seein' my wife like that, sloppy drunk before she was unconscious, half the time she got to that point, she still had a wineglass in her hand. So many stains on the carpet, I had to put new in when she moved out because the carpet was a mess but more, to erase those memories for my kids and for me. So I didn't have it in me to go for it when she was sober. A man needs to fuck, Amy, and I was dry for eight months when I had a wife in my bed and I *still* never even *considered* steppin' out on her. She was my wife. Good or bad, you do not do that shit. It's bad, you end it and *then* you find ass to tap."

"Conrad made love to me the night before he told me he was leaving me," I whispered and watched Mickey's jaw go hard.

"Fuck, he's a motherfucking asshole," he bit out.

I curled my hands tight on his biceps and asked, "Does all I've admitted honestly not cause you alarm?"

"That you're human?" he asked back.

And again, Lawr was right.

"I guess," I said quietly.

"Anyone can find themselves in a place they don't wanna be, and even knowin' they don't wanna be there, they can't get out. It's findin' it in you to get out that says it all about you, Amy. So no. I'm not alarmed you're human. In fact, knowin' this shit, I went from likin' you to likin' you a fuckuva lot more."

I couldn't believe that either.

I wanted to believe but it seemed too easy.

"Really?" I asked, my voice pitched higher.

His face again dipped lower as did his voice. "Yeah, baby."

"It was ugly," I reiterated.

"Life isn't always beauty," he returned. "Most of the time it's shit. But you keep fightin' to turn it around, that says it all about you. And you're fightin'. As a fighter too, I fuckin' love that in you."

Oh God.

It *was* that easy.

My voice dipped lower too when I said, "I love it that you understand."

"I love it that you had the courage to give that to me," he replied.

Oh God!

I was going to start crying.

In case that happened, I ducked my head and shoved my face in his chest.

Mickey started stroking my back with one hand as he said into the top of my hair, "You got your face in my chest, we can't make out on the wharf for the five minutes we got left before we gotta go get my boy."

I instantly took my face out of his chest, but even though I wanted a kiss, that wasn't why I did it.

I did it to beg, "Don't go home and think on this, Mickey, think on it and decide differently. Decide I'm some whackjob, psycho, crazy lady you're worried about starting something with, worried about her being around your kids. Because I might not have known who I was before I moved to Maine, but I've spent a lot of time figuring it out once I got here, and that is *not* me."

He stopped stroking my back and used that hand to cup my cheek. "Good I got your assurance on that, but don't need it. I'm thinkin' I knew who you were before you knew, and you're worried about something that's just not gonna happen."

"Okay," I said shakily as the vision of him started getting misty. "Now I like *you* a fuckuva lot more."

I got his misty smile before he dipped his head and then I got his warm lips.

He kissed me.

It wasn't wild and hard and amazing.

It was slow and sweet and amazing.

And apparently it lasted five minutes, because when he ended it, he lifted his head and whispered, "Gotta go pick up Cill, darlin'."

I held on because I had to (slow and sweet also did a number on me) and I nodded.

He gently pulled away but held my hand as he walked me down the wharf and to his truck. He put me in. He got in. He backed out. I took deep breaths.

Then I let all that settle inside me.

I'd fretted.

I'd worried.

And Mickey made it easy.

That was when I smiled.

We drove and got Cillian, who hefted himself into the backseat, crying, "Hey, Amy!" then took up the entire conversation babbling all the way home.

Mickey didn't drive to his driveway. He drove to mine.

Then he turned in his seat and said to his son, "You can get out and run home or you can hang and I'll drive you there, but not makin' Amy walk in her shoes."

"Wiped so I'll hang," Cillian said to his dad and looked to me. "See you later, Amy."

I turned in my seat too. "Later, kiddo."

I got Cillian's grin, which also brought relief since the last time I saw him he was far from grinning.

Then Mickey and I got out and he again held my hand, right in front of his son, as he walked me to my front door.

When we got there and I got it open, he surprised me by stepping in with me.

He also surprised me by shoving me to the side.

It wouldn't be a surprise after he did this when he took me in his arms and kissed me again, this time hard and deep, but short. So I knew he shoved me to the side so not only could Cillian not see us from the drive, but if Aisling was home, she couldn't see us from their house.

When he lifted his head, he noted, "Your turn to have us over to dinner, Amy."

"Tomorrow okay?" I replied instantly and got his easy grin.

"Yeah," he whispered.

"Good," I whispered back.

"Kids wanna go back to Dove House," he told me.

I nodded. I wanted them back too, and so did the oldies.

"I'll talk to Dela and arrange it with the kids tomorrow night."

"Great," he murmured, eyes dropping to my mouth.

That was when I said something I didn't want to say.

"Cill's in the truck, honey."

His gaze lifted to mine. "Right."

I pressed closer in his arms, tightening mine still around his shoulders. "It was a good night."

"Yeah."

"Thank you, Mickey."

"We'll do it again, Amy."

We'd do it again.

I smiled.

He smiled back, dipped in, touched his mouth to mine and let me go.

I walked him to the door, stood in it and watched him walk out.

He was two steps out before he twisted his torso my way.

"Need to wear that dress when I can take it off."

Wet flooded between my legs and I latched onto the edge of the door with my hand in order to remain standing.

"Yeah, baby?" he prompted.

"Yeah, Mickey," I replied breathily.

He gave me my favorite grin of his, the one filled with heat and promise, before he turned away, lifting a hand in a short wave.

I lifted mine back before I looked to the truck and waved at Cillian.

He returned it.

Unsteadily, I closed and locked the door.

Moving into my dark house, I walked to the kitchen and turned on the pendant lights.

I looked across the space I created that was all me and I did it feeling something I'd never experienced feeling.

Light and airy, like I was floating above the ground and didn't have my feet solidly under me.

It should have felt scary.

It was exhilarating.

The weight of my life had been lifted. The weight of my upbringing. The weight of the mess I'd made of my family.

All was not right in my world, but I'd discovered me and found that I'd done something right along the way.

I'd built a support network, new and old, of people who cared about me and were generous enough to take care of me, listen to me, understand me. And I was able to build this because I was me.

And that said everything. Everything about me.

Not the me I wanted to be.

The me who had always been.

Not to mention I was walking on air because Mickey liked my dress.

As in, *really*.

15

SOARING

"*Marriage* counselling?" I asked my phone sitting on the kitchen counter beside where I was working.

Lawr was on the other end and we were talking on speaker so I could continue to make my chocolate chip cookie sandwiches stuck together with chocolate buttercream frosting. A double delight. A real winner. And something I was making because the next day was Mrs. McMurphy's ninetieth birthday, and she might think I was a Nazi, but I was going to be a Nazi bringing her birthday treats.

"Marriage counselling," Lawr confirmed.

I slathered buttercream frosting on the back of a cookie and asked, "Are you crazy?"

"No," Lawr replied with a smile in his voice.

"Okay, you think that then I'll ask, is it working?"

"I've learned she doesn't mind my working hours because, in three sessions, she hasn't mentioned them. However, it annoys her that I sometimes don't hit the laundry basket with my dirty socks. This is something I can't imagine why it would be annoying since she has a woman come in twice a week who cleans and does laundry so she doesn't even touch my socks. However, now I make certain I hit the basket with my socks."

I knew long hours. My ex-husband had worked them too. I hated it but he loved his job, had wanted to be a neurosurgeon since his uncle, who also was one, allowed him to stand in an observation room and watch a surgery when Conrad was sixteen.

Alas, now I knew that those long hours weren't all about patients.

I'd also had a cleaning lady and Conrad hadn't even bothered to throw his clothes anywhere near the hamper. I didn't really care. He worked. I didn't. I had the time to gather clothes and dump them in a hamper.

If we had marriage counselling, I might mention the work hours...tentatively.

I wouldn't give a fig about the laundry.

"Lawrie—" I started.

"It's got to be done," he told me.

I scrunched the top cookie on and set them aside, asking, "Why?"

"Because I have to tell myself, and my sons, that I did all I could do."

I shut my mouth but I did it fuming.

He was correct. He should do that so he could live with whatever came of this, but also so his boys could see him giving it one last go with their mother before hopefully he made the decision to leave his wife and find some happy.

But I hated the idea of whatever that witch would put him through in the meantime, including during those sessions.

I mean *socks*?

Really?

"So, if you're committed to this, then I take it Thanksgiving is out," I remarked, irately snatching up another cookie.

"I talked with Mariel about going. We're considering it."

I threw up a little in my mouth at the thought of the Wicked Witch of Santa Barbara tainting my whimsical, beachy guest bedroom with her malevolence.

When I powered past that, I declared, "If she's coming, I'm inviting Robin. Her ex has her kids this Thanksgiving. She'd be all over it."

"MeeMee," Lawr stated irritably.

"Mercer and Hart love Robin," I reminded him, and they did. My nephews thought she was a hoot.

"She drives Mariel up the wall," he reminded me.

"Of course she does, due to all the sexual tension that's crackling between her husband and a beautiful, vital woman who's learned how it feels to have a jerk break her heart so she'll know it's worth any effort needed to make a good man happy."

"You do realize you, *and* Robin, lost your minds when your husbands cheated on you and now you're attempting to set me up with your best friend right under my wife's nose."

I didn't care what it said about me that this didn't cause me the slightest unease.

And I explained to my brother why, "I'd have qualms about that if your wife gave indication she's still breathing. Heck, if she gave indication she was still *human*. I'm uncertain of the law, you'd know better, but I don't think you can cheat on the undead whose sole purpose on this earth is to spread evil. In fact, I'm uncertain your marriage is even valid. Can you pledge your troth to a vampire?"

"Christ, you're in a bad mood," Lawr observed, and I could hear the humor in his voice, which made me settle more firmly in my belief he needed to leave his wife. No man who still loved his spouse would allow anyone, even his little sister, to talk that badly about them.

But he wasn't wrong. I was in a bad mood.

A very bad mood.

And this was because, according to me, things with Mickey were not going very well.

And *this* was because we had not had sex, something that was admittedly hard to do since I rarely *saw* Mickey.

It started off so promising and continued that way…for two days.

The first, dinner at my house, had changed to dinner at Mickey's because Ash wanted to cook something, wanted me to help, and she knew her kitchen so felt more comfortable in it.

Of course, I went over there. It wasn't hard. It was just walking across the street.

And I'd had fun cooking with Ash.

But it was more. Me being there before her dad got home from work was me being an adult and taking some of the onus off her taking care of her family since she watched her brother while her dad was away. She also liked female company it was plain to see, and while we cooked and chatted, we bonded. She came out of her shell a little bit, lost some of her timidity, and we'd had a marvelous time.

Mickey got home and it got better, mostly because he was Mickey and he was home. But also because this wasn't a formal dinner gathering. It was an informal gathering of family having dinner. We ate Ash's meal in front of the TV, Mickey doing this sitting beside me. He was not demonstrative, something I agreed with as it was too soon for that in front of his kids, but he sat by me and it was a thrill to feel the heat of his thigh pressed to mine and have him close, even if he wasn't really touching me.

When that was done, he walked me home and we made out behind my closed front door, doing it hot and heavy.

He ended it, saying, "Gotta get back or those two'll know what we're up to."

Again, appropriate.

Again, I agreed on this propriety.

But also disappointing.

During our dinner, we'd made arrangements for the kids to go with me to Dove House the next day, which happened the way it did before: Mickey dropping them off and picking them up. The kids had been just as helpful and charming and the residents and staff again had enjoyed having them around just as much as the first time.

But this was when it started going bad.

Understandably, Mickey couldn't spend all his time with me when he had his kids or shove me down their throat constantly.

This began our days of brief phone conversations where we said absolutely nothing, their entire purpose, from what I could tell, was reminding each other we knew the other existed.

There were also texts, which were obviously briefer.

Then Aisling and Cillian went back to their mother, something that surprised me considering her behavior that week. I thought he would keep them or at least have words with her about what she'd done, warning her that couldn't happen again, especially if they were *with* her, and what might happen if she did.

Mickey didn't explain this decision to me and I didn't ask about it because it wasn't my place. It concerned me, but it wasn't my place to share this either. They were his kids not mine, and he knew Rhiannon and all the history, I didn't. So I kept quiet.

I learned the week he didn't have his kids just how crazy his life was, juggling work he hated, kids back and forth and volunteering as a fireman.

I learned this because he had no time for me.

He did most of his evening shifts at the firehouse when the kids weren't with him. He made up paid work for Ralph for day shifts he did at the firehouse both when he had his kids and when he didn't. And all this meant he had no time left over.

Since the diner was just down from the firehouse, he had asked me to meet him at Weatherby's for dinner one night that week, something I did. Something that lasted for an hour before Mickey had to get back. Something that ended with me not even getting a kiss.

And he'd had one other night off before he got the kids back. A night where we talked on the phone, even though he was on his couch in a house across the street from mine, and I was in my fabulous armchair in a house across the street from his.

We did this for half an hour before he stated, "Wiped, Amy. Gotta hit my bed."

Obviously, without demur, since he was tired, I let him go.

The kids came back and we'd actually had a family outing, all four of us going to some burger shack out in the middle of nowhere that frankly was kind of scary (the being in the middle of nowhere business *and* the restaurant, which, even without me doing a full inspection, I knew had to be making a variety of health violations).

It could not be denied, however, that the kids loved it, the burgers were delicious and I loved family time with Mickey and his kids.

But outside brief phone calls and texts, that was it for that week with Mickey.

Now his kids were gone again. It was Tuesday, *my* kids were coming that weekend and my relationship with my own offspring meant that it was too early to add Mickey to that mix.

So we wouldn't be seeing each other that weekend.

And it was nearly five and he had not called or texted all day. In fact, the last text I got from him was the day before at nine thirty in the morning that said, *Need to make plans.*

I'd replied, *We do. Do you have some time off some evening this week?*

I'd received no return text.

Nothing.

I didn't wish to be a spoiled, selfish, dainty heiress, but if I was going to have a man in my life, I wanted to have a man in my life, not the specter of a man who became real only infrequently.

And I didn't wish to allow Conrad to destroy the possibility of me finding something good and healthy (if Mickey and I miraculously found together time to actually build a relationship) by wondering what, precisely, was taking all of Mickey's time.

The fact was he'd been with *Bridget,* the tall, buxom redhead. I'd mentioned her, but he'd said nothing about her.

Were they still dating?

Was she being fit in here and there, whenever Mickey had time not working, volunteering, fathering or being with me?

It had been a long time since I'd been in the dating game, but Mickey had told me to end it with Bradley. I did. It might be an incorrect assumption but Mickey, clearly not being tolerant of me being with another man when there was not one thing between us but a lot of arguing and a kiss, would lead me to believe I could expect the same and that, although relatively new, our relationship was exclusive.

Since I'd grown up, I would have broached this subject with Mickey just to make certain we were on the same page.

Unfortunately, I rarely saw Mickey in order to broach this subject.

But obviously, that niggled at me.

Was Bridget still in the picture?

And last, there was the fact that Mickey had said straight out that men needed to fuck and I was right across the street. I didn't say it outright but it was implied I was a relatively sure thing. I liked the idea that he wanted to take his time with me but *I was right across the street.*

A man had needs.

A woman had needs.

But he was not seeing to these needs for either of us.

So what was that all about?

The only good thing that came of the last two weeks (and it was a *very* good thing) was the fact that things were progressing with my own kids. Pippa had started high school, and I was anxious to know how she was handling that. But both of them were back to school, and I was just interested to know how things were going.

So I asked.

And they answered.

Their phones.

As in, *not through texts.*

I could not say the conversations lasted for hours and included them baring their souls to me, telling me they forgive me and explaining they wished to spend more time with me.

But I called, they answered, we chatted, it was amicable and relatively informative and the more it happened, the less stilted it became.

I did not push this. I texted every day just to say something to let them know they were on my mind.

They texted back.

But I'd called them both more than a couple of times since Mickey and my first date, and they always answered.

Except once, when I got Auden's voicemail.

But then he'd called me back, getting mine, apologizing for not picking up and sharing things were going okay.

I was ecstatic, completely beside myself with joy.

About that.

But things with Mickey—being fast, heated, crazy and ending with me floating on air, only for them to stall almost completely—made me again feel leaden, carrying the weight of worry that something so exciting, so promising would end so soon after it began.

I couldn't wait to see my babies that weekend.

But things with Mickey had gone from understandable to frustrating to irritating in a way I knew I was feeling that rather than concern that what seemed to be the beginning of happy would dwindle into nothing.

"Yes, I'm in a bad mood," I told Lawr.

"Why?" he asked. "You said things were improving with the kids."

"They are."

"And you've found someone to spend time with."

"I did. And that's past tense."

"Oh fuck," Lawr muttered. "You two already broke up?"

"I'd have to *see* him to break up with him and, again, I'm uncertain of the laws, this time of dating, but I would assume you'd actually have to see each other regularly, and, oh, I don't know, maybe have sex at least once for a relationship deterioration to be considered a breakup."

Lawr was silent.

"Did I lose you?" I called.

"You haven't…" He sounded like he was being strangled. "You haven't had sex with him?"

"No," I snapped, slapping the top cookie on the frosted one and setting the sandwich aside, going on, "You're a man, tell me. You have a sure thing you pretty much know is a sure thing across the street, would you sit on your couch and talk with her on your phone for half an hour before stating you're wiped and need to go to bed? Or would you find your second wind, walk over and fuck her dizzy?"

"Maybe you should talk to Robin about this," Lawr suggested.

"Robin's not a man," I noted.

"So maybe you should talk about this to a man who is not me, a me who's your brother."

"Lawr, honestly?" I asked.

"Mariel and I have not had relations for over two months and the last time we had them it lasted ten minutes and *I* finished alone."

I made a gag face that also included a gag noise my brother heard.

Thus Lawr continued, "Do you wanna talk about sex with your brother?"

"Maybe not," I conceded.

"Right. Call Robin," he ordered.

"She's at her new Pilates class."

There was a moment of silence before Lawr begged, "Please tell me she's not—"

"She is," I interrupted him to confirm. "The lover of her ex-husband's soon-to-be-ex-wife is her new instructor. She says the class is magnificent. The instructor knows who she is. They go for chai teas after and the other one meets them. They're all bonding over mutual hatred."

"Jesus Christ," Lawr muttered.

"It's actually quite healthy."

"It's nutty, like that woman is," Lawr returned. "And she's been burned badly enough, she shouldn't court more."

"She's healing, Lawrie," I said softly. "Let her do it her way."

There was another moment of silence before Lawr said, "Right."

I scrunched another sandwich together and replied, "I should probably let you go."

And I should let him go because he had to get going.

I had an evening of nothing ahead of me.

"Yeah. I'll let you know about Thanksgiving."

"That'd be great, Lawrie. Hope the rest of your day goes well."

"Yours too, sweetheart. And MeeMee?"

"Yes?"

"Slow is not bad," he said gently.

He was right. Slow probably wasn't bad.

Crawling to a virtual stand-still wasn't all that hot, however.

I didn't share that.

I said, "Thanks, Lawrie."

"Talk to you soon."

"Back at you."

"'Bye, MeeMee."

"'Bye, Lawrie."

I hit the button to disconnect and kept at my cookies, thinking it was getting late and I'd not planned anything for dinner hoping that there might be some possibility I'd be eating whatever I'd be eating with Mickey.

After the cookie sandwiches got finished, packed up for transport the next day and I did the cleanup, I realized that was not happening and then got annoyed because I hadn't taken anything out to defrost, and I had nothing in the fridge to make.

I opened the door, stared in the fridge and saw my only choice was an omelet, which didn't sound appetizing.

But at least it was something.

Therefore I made my plans. Omelet. Wine. Book. Bath. Bed.

And no Mickey.

Before I started all that skin tingling excitement, I sent my kids their texts of the day and gave myself my only thrill of the day because I then got their replies.

I had the cheese grated, the garlic minced, the mushrooms sliced and was beating the eggs when my phone on my counter rang.

The display said "Mickey."

I glared at it and the time above it, which told me it was ten to six.

I wanted to let it ring, go to voicemail, force him to make more of an effort to get in touch with me, but that was petty.

And I was no longer petty.

So I hit the button to accept then hit the button for speaker.

"Hey," I greeted.

"On my way home from work."

What?

No.

Whatever.

"Fascinating news," I replied.

He said nothing for a few seconds before he stated, "Forgot if you had bacon on your burger."

"I'm sorry?"

"I'm at Tinker's. Picking up burgers for us for dinner. Remembered you got Swiss and mushrooms. Forgot if you got bacon."

He was picking up dinner for us at Tinker's, the scary burger joint out on route whatever?

No, he was not.

"Don't worry about me. I'm having an omelet."

"What?" he asked.

"I'm making an omelet. Right now. I'm covered for dinner."

"You're making an omelet for dinner," he said like this was beyond belief.

"I'm hungry," I replied.

"Tink's burgers are better, baby."

The edifice and its environs might be sketchy, but there was no denying the burgers would be better than an omelet.

"I'm beating the eggs now. If I don't cook them, they'll go to waste," I shared.

There was a smile in his voice when he replied, "Amy, you're a gazillionaire. Thinkin' you can probably afford to pour a coupla eggs down the sink."

"I am, indeed, quite wealthy as we've discussed *frequently*," I replied tartly. "However, that does not negate the fact people on this earth are starving so it would be irresponsible and insensitive to have food and waste it."

"Then throw in a coupla more eggs. When I get to your place, I'll eat that with you," he returned, sounding like he wanted to eat a roofing shingle between two pieces of bread more than he wanted to share an omelet.

"You can get your burger. The omelet's just for me. And you can't come over. I have plans this evening."

He didn't sound amused when he asked, "You got plans?"

"I do," I confirmed.

"What plans?" he pushed.

"I'm washing my hair," I snapped. "Now, the butter in the skillet has melted. I have to go. I'm sure I'll talk to you later…someday."

"Am—"

I hit the button to disconnect, turned off the ringer and turned my phone over so I couldn't see the display. When it vibrated, making noise against my counter, I shoved it in a drawer and picked up the remote to turn on my system across the room, bringing up Pandora and listening to my Billie Holiday station.

The day was gray and drizzling. I was eating alone. Mickey was probably still dating a redhead who was not me. And he thought he could come over whenever he could squeeze me into his life.

It was time for the blues.

I was about to slice the side of my fork through the finished omelet, and not looking forward to it, when the banging came at my door.

My head whipped that way.

Through the glass, I saw Mickey.

On no, he was *not* banging on my door like *he* was angry when *he* said we needed to make plans and *I* agreed and asked when, then *he* did not bother to reply to me.

I wasn't sitting around, anxiously awaiting his attention!

And I was not going to be the type of woman who accepted the scraps of attention from a man.

He had a busy life? He had things going on? We had to plan and be patient and time our moments together?

I could do that.

If we spoke about it, like two adults, and we both knew where we stood.

Not Mickey expecting I'd be hanging around waiting for him to decide to bring some burgers to me.

And being one of those two adults, the one *not* banging on someone's door, I decided I'd be adult enough to share that with him.

I dropped my fork, stomped across the landing, unlocked the door and threw it open.

"I have a *bell*, you know," I informed him acidly.

He moved in, his big body in motion meaning I had no choice but to get out of his way, so I did.

I watched him turn and did this shutting the door.

"Do you need something?" I asked.

"Washing your hair?" he asked back angrily.

"Yes," I returned. "Though I haven't gotten to that portion of my exciting evening yet. However, before I get to it, I'll thank you not to bang on my door, which has beautiful stained glass in it that I very much like and would prefer it stays exactly how it is. So, in future, I'll ask you to use the bell."

He planted his hands on his hips, asking, "What's this game, Amy?"

I crossed my arms on my chest and returned, "What game, Mickey?"

"Said I was comin' over tonight, I'd bring dinner. And you got somethin' up your ass and you're dishin' that shit to me for no fuckin' reason."

"You did *not* say you were coming over. I asked when you had a free evening this week. I asked that yesterday morning. Since then, I've heard nothing from you."

"Took a coupla hours to reply but I did and I said tonight and I'd bring dinner."

"You didn't."

"I did."

"You did not."

"Fuck," he leaned back and threw out his hands, "I *did*."

I glared at him while stomping to my kitchen. I had to stop glaring at him to yank my phone out of the drawer and pull up his text string.

I recommenced glaring at him when I stomped back to him, shoving my phone his way.

"You…did…*not*."

He aimed his angry scowl at my phone, his eyes narrowed, then he dug out his phone.

I crossed my arms on my chest as he ran his thumb over the screen for some time before he muttered, "Fuck, texted that to Janice Quiller."

My stomach started roiling.

"And who's Janice Quiller?" I asked.

Mickey looked at me. "Client of Ralph's."

"Oh yes?" I asked disbelievingly.

His expression turned stormy. "Yeah, Amelia. She is. And she replied she didn't understand, and I didn't understand what she didn't understand so I texted her back something about the job, which was what we *had* been texting about. Answered her question. The texting died and I didn't realize I'd fucked up."

Well, clearly there was a mistake and it was an innocent one.

But somehow, that didn't make me any less angry.

Mickey wasn't either.

I could tell when he said, "And not real big on you insinuating that Janice could be somethin' else to me."

"If that's the case then perhaps you'll take this moment to share where things stand with you and Bridget."

"Bridget?" he asked, looking perplexed, like he'd never heard that name in his life.

God!

Really?

"Yes," I returned. "You see, you made it very clear when it became clear something might be happening between you and me that I needed to get rid of Bradley. It was uncomfortable and I'd already planned to do that, but just in case you have any ongoing queries about that, I'll confirm that I ended things with Bradley. Now I'd like to know where things stand with you and Bridget."

"Went out with her twice," he told me.

"Is that your answer?" I pushed.

"Not sure what more you need," he shot back.

"Are you going out with her again?" I explained, and his stormy expression turned thunderous.

"You really askin' me that shit?"

"We've been on *a* date, Mickey," I replied. "I'm rusty with this but I do think it's within your rights not to want exclusive at this early juncture. However, I do believe it's within my rights, if you don't want that, not for you to expect that from me."

He lifted up a hand, snapped loudly twice and clipped, "Reality check, babe. You are not standin' here havin' it out with your ex. I'm," he leaned toward me, "*Mickey.*"

I felt my eyes get wide in preparation for my head to explode.

"Did you just *snap* at me?"

"Yeah, seein' as you were in the middle of a flashback, havin' a conversation with a guy who'd be asshole enough to make you end somethin' with a douche so he could start somethin' with you at the same time carryin' on with somebody else. That guy not bein' *me*."

"Well, I'm sorry I'm troubling you with this conversation, however, I'll make my apologies reminding you that we haven't actually had this conversation or *many* conversations *at all* since we never see each other."

"Amy, I work."

"I'm aware of that, Mickey."

"Got kids," he went on.

"That hadn't escaped me either."

"And give my time to the department when I got it to give."

"Which is a lot," I noted.

The thunderous went out of his face and angry, surprised wariness slid in when he asked, "That a problem for you?"

I shook my head incredulously. "You doing what you've always wanted to do?"

"I made that clear enough you know that's what I need, which makes your comment about me spendin' a lot of time doin' it somethin' that doesn't sit real good with me."

"Perhaps I made that comment since you spend a lot of time doing a lot of other things and all those other things don't really involve me," I retorted.

His expression again changed to disbelieving with a hint of repulsion. "So you're havin' a shit fit because you want your piece of me?"

"No, Mickey Donovan," I snapped. "I'm having a shit fit because I want you to give some indication you want your piece of *me*."

His upper body swung back and his voice quieted when he replied, "You know I do, Amy."

"Really? I'm sorry, that escaped me."

"Got shit on, a lot of it, and you know it."

"You're right. I do. And I understand that. And I wouldn't have a problem with it. One date we've had, I am aware that doesn't shoot me up to the top of your priority list. But I'd like some indication I've actually been scratched on it."

His face started to go hard again when he stated, "The shit in my life, I bring a woman into it, I need some understanding."

"And you'd have that," I returned. "If I knew what I was understanding."

"And you'd know that," he fired back. "If you'd fuckin' asked."

"Fine," I bit off, throwing out my hands. "Consider this my formal request."

His eyes flashed. "Jesus, you're a serious fuckin' smartass."

I lifted my brows. "Shall I take that as you declining my request?"

"Yeah, babe," he clipped while on the move toward me. "That request is declined until I can cool off and speak to you without doin' that at the same time I wanna spank your ass."

I didn't have the chance to make a dramatic gesture by opening the door for him, considering he was moving so quickly he got there before me, but I did manage to get in my final shot.

"That effort would be appreciated, Mickey."

I got that off, aimed at his back, right before he slammed the door behind him.

I glared at it.

Then I leaped to it and locked it.

That done, as Billie Holiday serenaded me, I stomped back to my kitchen, tossed down my phone and stared at the omelet on my fantastic new plate, trying to convince myself not to pick it up and throw it across the room.

Billie barely got in there before I heard banging at my door again.

My eyes shot there and I saw Mickey framed in the glass.

"This man cannot...be...*believed*," I groused as I stomped back to the door, unlocked it and threw it open, looking up to him and on a near-yell demanding, "Do not bang on my—!"

I didn't get it out because Mickey was kissing me. A hard, invasive, *shut-up* kiss that he delivered at the same time shuffling me in and closing the door with his boot.

I put my hands to his chest, pushed free and snapped, "I cannot believe—"

I didn't finish that either because Mickey's hand darted out, catching me at the back of my neck. He yanked forward and I slammed against his body right before his mouth again slammed down on mine.

I pushed back at my neck while lifting my hands to press against his chest. But he caught one wrist then swept it across and caught the other one, holding both tight in one hand between us.

This meant the only thing I could do was twist my mouth from his and order loudly, "Take your hands off me!"

He did.

I took a furious step back.

He took a furious step into me, lowering his torso and catching me in the belly with a shoulder.

Then I was up and he was stalking across the landing, taking me with him.

"Mickey!" I shouted.

He didn't reply.

I was so angry I decided a fall from his shoulder was unlikely to kill me so I rotated my body to twist away.

Being the trained firefighter he was, he simply adjusted his hold to keep me where I was and kept stalking.

Down the hall.

To my bedroom!

"*Put me down, Mickey Donovan!*" I shrieked.

He did as I asked but only after planting a knee in my bed and tossing me off his shoulder onto my duvet.

My breath swept out of me as he instantly gave me his weight.

I stared into his irate, very heated, amazingly beautiful blue eyes and it struck me immediately that I'd made them that way.

Me.

"Mickey," I whispered.

And that was again all I got out before he was kissing me. In his dusty construction clothes, his weight and heat pressing me into my bed, his mouth on mine wet and hot and demanding.

I'd given it a try, fighting him off.

I'd failed.

And if I'd learned anything, it was when to stop fighting when it was getting you nowhere and find alternate ways to get what you needed.

So I did that and kissed him back.

The second I did, he made a sexy, manly noise that drove down my throat and detonated right between my legs.

It was on.

And I was for once going to get what *I* needed.

I got it.

But Mickey helped me.

I didn't care about his dusty construction clothes. I didn't worry that I was out of practice. I didn't get tense that I wasn't going to give it like Mickey liked it.

I just took what I wanted, kissing him, touching him, ripping off his shirt.

He arched away to let me to do this then went back at me, rolling us so I was on top, then knifing up, still kissing me. I was forced to straddle him and his hands went to the hem of my top.

I lifted my arms as he tugged it off and threw it away. Then I put my hands to either side of his head and was going to dip in for another kiss, but I halted when Mickey did the dipping, trailing his lips briefly over the skin above the beige lace over the cranberry silk of my bra then, without warning, he went down and, through the lace and silk, drew my nipple in his mouth, swift and *hard*.

I arched back, grinding into his crotch.

I was wrong.

Now, it was on.

And it went wild.

He took.

I took.

He bit, licked, sucked, kissed, stroked and groped.

I bit, licked, sucked, kissed, stroked and groped.

He might argue but I had it better since there was so *much* of him to take in in *so many* ways and all of it was solid, hot and *staggering*.

Then I had nothing on but my panties, Mickey had nothing on but his jeans, our mouths were locked, our tongues tangled, our bodies sealed, I had my hand down his fly stroking something rigid and thick and long and promising, when I let out a cry because Mickey broke the kiss and hauled me up.

He settled on his back at the same time he settled me on him.

On him.

Straddling his face.

One hand yanking me down, one hand between his mouth and me

shoving aside the gusset of my panties, suddenly his tongue was buried inside.

Oh God.

Yes.

"*Mickey,*" I breathed.

He said nothing. He was busy eating.

And he ate, licked, sucked, tongue-fucked and took me high, higher, flying, before he drove two fingers inside, sucked deep at my clit and I was soaring, arching, moaning, shuddering and *coming*.

It was so big, I couldn't breathe. Whimpering and gasping, he kept sucking and finger-fucking me driving me higher until he stopped, gently pushed me off, tore my panties down my legs, whipped me to my back and covered me.

"Mickey," I whispered, still feeling it, still up in the clouds.

I also felt him doing something between my legs.

Then he whispered back, "Good?"

Good?

No.

There were no words for how it felt when Mickey sent me flying.

"Yes," I breathed.

I saw the grin hit his blazing eyes before he warned, "Get ready for more."

Before I could, he drove inside me.

Oh yes, what I'd been stroking was promising.

Rigid. Thick. Long.

Amazing.

My back curved up and my limbs curled in, cocooning him as he thrust hard, deep, fast.

"Yes," I whimpered, not having come down, I was again climbing.

"Yeah," he grunted and then kissed me.

I kissed him back, clutching him to me, gliding my hands over the muscles of his back, over his short-cropped hair, in every way drawing him in deeper, closer, wanting him to soar in the clouds with me.

I knew he was getting there, I could feel it, *taste* it, then I lost it.

But only for a second when he pulled out, flipped me to my belly, kicked my legs apart with his knee, positioned, yanked me up at my hips and reentered me, slamming me back with his fingers curled at my ribs as he powered inside.

"Yes," I repeated on a gasp, taking over, pushing back as he thrust forward.

Mickey said nothing intelligible, but the power of his grunts matched the power of his drives, and both pushed me higher.

"Mickey," I gasped as I again began to soar.

"Padded headboard," was his reply.

Too far gone, all I could do was keep rearing back and blink.

Then I wasn't rearing back.

He pulled out, flipped me again, lifted me up and walked on his knees until I crashed into the headboard and Mickey thrust back up inside me.

I looked into his blue eyes and moaned, "Honey."

"Yeah, Amy," he grunted, one arm around my waist holding me to him, the other hand slipping over my hip and in.

His thumb hit my clit right when he drove his cock deep.

"*Honey,*" I breathed and I was gone, arms curled around his shoulders, heels digging into his ass. The power of my orgasm meant I gripped his sex with mine as I clutched the rest of him to me and fought for air. So high it felt there was no oxygen left to breathe as bliss scored through me.

"Fuck, astounding," he grunted before he groaned, "*Amy,*" and fucked me wild, his face buried in my neck, as he pushed me higher, making mine last longer, score deeper, and he joined me.

The pounding gentled and slowed before he slid inside and stayed there. He glided his lips up my neck, along my jaw and up where he caught my mouth, sweeping his tongue in, kissing me, this time wet and sweet.

I held him close and kissed him back.

Still needing oxygen, it was me who tore my mouth free and pushed my face in his throat.

Mickey slid his hand from between us, over my belly, around and across my back, tightening his arms and pressing deep, giving me a sexy, sweet hug as he called, "You okay, baby?"

I was.

I absolutely was.

Even though he'd wrecked me.

He gave me a squeeze, prompting, "Amy."

"I'm good," I replied faintly.

He heard it. He read it.

He knew he'd wrecked me.

I knew he did when his body started shaking and a low satisfied chuckle vibrated up his chest, but he did this moving back. He held me to him as he shifted in a variety of ways and I would know what he was doing when he slid me off his cock, laid me down in bed and touched his mouth to the base of my throat before he murmured there, "I'll be back." He rolled away and twitched the covers he'd yanked from under us over me.

I stared at my ceiling a moment before I turned to my side, languorously stretched, then curled into myself, pulling the covers up to my shoulder.

Mickey came back from my bathroom in nothing but his jeans, his eyes on me.

I kept my eyes on him too, delighted I was not wrong.

That body was hard everywhere.

And utterly fascinating.

I was in the throes of memorizing the definition of his collarbone as he sat on the edge of the bed.

I didn't move, just shifted my gaze to look up at him.

He grinned at me as he brushed my bangs out of my eyes and slid the hair away from my cheek and over my shoulder.

"Been a while?" he asked gently.

If he hadn't just wrecked me, I might find this question annoying.

Since he had and the answer was obvious considering I'd gone wild and come two times (maybe three), I just said, "Yeah."

His grin remained as he bent to me, putting his weight into both forearms on the mattress in front of me and his face close to mine.

"Omelet on the counter, I take it you didn't have dinner," he remarked.

"Nope," I answered.

"You like Chinese?" he asked.

"Yep," I answered.

His grinning eyes moved over my face as a breathtaking mix of tenderness and amusement slid into them, something else I gave him even as he was giving it to me.

"I'll order delivery," he declared.

"Crab cheese wonton and hot and sour soup," I ordered instantly. "Surprise me with the meal."

His gaze stopped wandering, he looked right at me and said, "You do know this means we'll have to be irresponsible and insensitive to the starving nations of the world by throwing away that omelet. Eggs don't keep."

I had enough in me to narrow my eyes. "Don't piss me off, Mickey."

He pushed closer and dropped his voice low. "Think doin' that's workin' for me, baby."

Too sated to rise to the bait, I rolled my eyes.

"We'll talk while we eat," he went on after I rolled them back.

I held his gaze and whispered, "Yeah, honey, that'd be good."

He pushed even closer and kissed me lightly.

Then he moved away and, not moving a muscle, only my eyes, I watched him bend down and snatch up his shirt. I also watched him tug it on as he sauntered out of my bedroom and into the hall.

He even made tugging on a dirty tee look sexy.

I sighed.

Then I snuggled deeper into my bed, thinking that had actually gone quite well.

Mickey was no longer seeing Bridget.

Auspiciously, at this early juncture, he expected exclusivity from me and intended to give the same.

The fact he didn't text me since the morning of the day before was a simple mistake.

He was insanely phenomenal in bed.

And he liked Chinese.

Yes, that had gone quite well.

So well, naked and alone in my bed while Mickey was off ordering Chinese, I started smiling.

———————— • ————————

AFTER ORDERING, MICKEY CAME BACK TO ME AND TOLD ME HE WAS GOING over to his place to shower and get out of his dusty clothes.

He then sat at the edge of the bed again, but lifted me in his arms this time, kissing me thoroughly before he ended it, kissed my nose, placed me back in bed, got up and walked away.

I was wrecked but I'd just had sex with Mickey. We were going to have dinner together, alone at my house.

And I didn't care what I was going to do was going to say.

I wasn't wasting this opportunity.

So the minute I heard the front door close, I threw back the covers and launched myself out of bed.

I put on new undies—ecru, lacy, sexy—and a pair of loose-fitting yoga pants (that Josie disapproved of me buying, looking at them with revulsion and stating she feared yoga pants were heralding the death of fashion). I paired these with a powder pink, light cashmere sweater that had a deep dip in the back that was held together with a thin strap of cashmere across my shoulders.

I arranged my hair in a messy knot at the top back of my head, pulling out tendrils around my ears and neck that I hoped looked both adorable and appealing.

Then I dashed out of my bedroom, got rid of the omelet, did the minimal clean up and ran around lighting candles and lamps so the effect would be cozy and romantic.

I left Pandora on my Billie Holiday station. I wasn't feeling the blues but Billie Holiday worked for a variety of situations.

I was pulling down plates when Mickey came back.

I watched as he caught my eyes, grinned, then looked around the house and back to me, his grin turning smug.

I didn't care. He knew I was into him and I wanted him to know that what we'd just shared and spending time with him was important to me.

He could be smug about it. He was gorgeous.

And right then he was all mine.

The delivery guy came, Mickey paid and I brought plates, silverware and napkins down to the sectional while Mickey pulled out food. I also got myself a glass of wine and Mickey a beer (something I started stocking when the possibility of him being over became a probability, something that, until then, I'd never had the chance to offer him).

Mickey was lounged back with an eggroll over a plate and I'd torn the corner of a crab cheese wonton loose and had dipped it in some sweet and sour sauce that was resting on a scrap of the brown paper bag the delivery came in that was sitting on the couch between us.

I held the dripping wedge over my plate, my eyes to it, when I said quietly, "I like spending time with you, Mickey."

"Got that, Amy."

At his response, I lifted my gaze to him and put the wonton in my mouth.

As I was chewing, Mickey went on, "Need you to get that I like spending time with you, too, baby."

I nodded, swallowing.

"We both got busy lives," he told me. "This isn't going to be easy. We just gotta work at making it worth it."

He was right about that.

His tone had changed when he continued, "And I gotta admit that I took it for granted you'd get it without me giving it to you."

It wasn't an accusation.

It almost sounded contrite.

But I took it as an accusation. "I understand you're busy, Mickey. That's not what I'm saying. And don't take this as ugly, just me sharing, but even knowing you're busy, it doesn't feel good that in all that busy, you don't have a lot of time for me."

"Got word out that I'm takin' private roof jobs."

I held my forgotten plate with its lone, partially dissected wonton on it in my hand and stared at him.

"Already?" I asked.

His eyes warmed. "You gave me the idea. It was a good idea. I thought on it and when I did, I thought, why wait? Either I'm gonna be able to pull this off or I'm not, but either way, I gotta know sooner rather than later. So I told a few folks, talked to a few of the crew. That rain last week, had two people phone me because they had leaks and they didn't want Ralph to deal with them. They wanted me."

I smiled big and said excitedly, "That's great, Mickey."

He smiled back, popped the rest of his eggroll in his mouth, chewed, swallowed and told me, "Sent boys to do those jobs and do 'em right and also had a meet with Arnie so I could find out what I had to do legally to establish a company. Started work on that too."

"Arnie?" I asked, resting the plate in my lap to rip off another wedge of my wonton.

"Arnie Weaver," he answered. "Attorney in town. Him and his partner the only ones I've met that I actually like."

I hoped that didn't color his hopefully eventual meeting with Lawr.

I didn't remark on that.

"So you're busier than normal," I noted.

His voice lowered. "No, Amy, I'm usually busy. I'm definitely busier, but I'm always busy. Now we've had that out, though, won't take where you're at with me and what we're tryin' to build for granted."

The light feeling I was experiencing got lighter and I gave him another smile as I replied, "And in return, I'll try to be more understanding."

He smiled back but his was different. His was sexy.

"You could. Or you could get pissed, stick up for yourself, get in my face, be a smartass and earn yourself a couple of orgasms."

I felt my knees tingle in a way I knew they'd be weak if I was standing instead of sitting cross-legged, facing him on the couch.

I didn't show this reaction. I shook my head like he was annoying and kept eating my wonton.

"Though," he kept going, "after my dainty heiress went wild for me, we'll see about you gettin' orgasms on a more regular basis."

I felt a tingle elsewhere at that and the tingle traveled north to my nipples when I caught the look in his eyes that told me how much he wanted to give that to me.

And how much he wanted me to give it back.

I liked that. I wanted more.

It was frightening but I couldn't deny that, from the moment I saw him, I wanted it all from Mickey.

But in getting, I had to give.

"I appreciate you being so sweet about all this, honey," I said softly. "But I'll still try to be more patient and get that you have a lot on your plate."

"That'd be good, darlin'," he replied softly. "But I'll repeat, I get in my head or in my life and I'm not givin' you what you need, you let me know. We both got hot heads. We get into it, we do." His lips twitched. "Just as long as we make up."

I liked the variety of ways Mickey was showing that he could make up, so I shoved more wonton in my mouth and smiled at him with my eyes.

"One thing," he stated.

I swallowed and asked, "Yeah?"

"I'm not him."

I stilled and forced my mouth to say, "Mickey."

"I get he scarred you. I get that might take time to sort your head about. But I'm not him. Told you I'd never do that shit to a woman, and it's arguable, but with the one I had, I actually had cause to go lookin'. I didn't. If you need to work that out with your girls, or me, you do it. I'm here. I'm gonna make time for you, for us, because that's important. I'll definitely make time for that. Us startin' out, both of us got a lot going on, I know I'm already askin' a lot of you. But that's not gonna stop me from askin' that. I can't promise I'm gonna do everything right, and it sucks but you already know that with how we got right here." He dipped his chin to indicate us eating Chinese on my couch. "But I'd never do that to you and you gotta get that."

"Okay, Mickey," I whispered.

"Okay," he replied. "Now come here and give me a kiss."

I balanced my plate, avoided sweet and sour sauce, and leaned toward him to give him my kiss. He helped by leaning into me and lifting a hand to cup the back of my head.

It was a quick touch but I liked it very much.

I didn't move very far away before he stated, "Spendin' the night, Amy."

"Okay, Mickey," I repeated my whisper.

He leaned and touched my mouth again, let me go and settled back.

I settled back too, finished my wonton and reached for the soup.

———————— • ————————

"MICKEY," I BREATHED AND WENT FLYING.

He let me.

Then he kissed me as he kept taking me.

I descended but kept gliding as I felt him move inside me. Listened to his noises. Took him in with fingers and mouth. Moved my hips with his increasing rhythm. And helped coax him there until he slid a hand up my forearm, pushing it up over my head, linking his fingers with mine and pressing our hands into the pillow.

He squeezed hard as he thrust deep and groaned loud.

My heart took flight.

I gave that to Mickey too.

How was it that his weight was on me, his body connected to mine, and it felt like I was floating?

I knew he recovered when his hips stopped spasming between mine, he tweaked my nose with the tip of his then took my mouth in a slow, deep, tender kiss.

He ended it, brushing his lips along my jaw, as he gently slid out of me, rolled off but pulled the covers over me before he got out of bed and sauntered naked to my bathroom.

I watched, my first view of his sculpted behind a vision I enjoyed greatly, before I shifted to sitting on the side of the bed. I reached and grabbed his tee from the floor, tugged it on and straightened off the bed, nabbing my panties.

I had them up and was walking to the bathroom as he was walking out.

Mickey, naked in my bedroom, full-frontal view.

He had a great ass, an amazing back.

But his chest and other attributes were better.

He stopped to bend his neck as I stopped and got on tiptoes. My hand was light to his flat stomach as I touched my mouth to his.

He lifted away and I walked into the bathroom going direct to the drawers in my walk-in closet.

I exchanged Mickey's tee for a short, satin nightie in a dusky rose with deep edges of delicate oyster lace and thin spaghetti straps that criss-crossed at the back.

I walked out holding Mickey's tee, turned out the lights of the bathroom and walked into the bedroom.

There I saw Mickey Donovan in my bed, under my duvet, on his side, head in his hand, elbow resting in the pillow, long legs partially visible but totally tangled in my sheets, eyes on me. Eyes now telling me he really liked my nightie.

I took him in.

I had that. I'd *had* that.

That was all for me.

I wanted to cry. I wanted to jump with joy.

Instead, I dropped his tee and joined him in my bed.

He grabbed hold of me the minute I did, shoving his face in my neck, brushing it with his lips, touching it with his tongue, before his hold got tighter and he rolled this way and that, taking me with him to turn out the lights on both nightstands.

He settled us front to front, covered by my duvet, tangled in each other.

He slid the tip of his nose down the bridge of mine before he whispered, "Night, Amy."

"Goodnight, Mickey," I whispered back.

He lifted up, kissed my forehead and settled in to the bed, doing this tightening his arms around me.

I pressed closer and returned the favor.

I didn't think I'd do it.

Heck, I didn't *want* to do it.

I wanted to lie in the dark in my bed with Mickey Donovan and exalt in the feeling.

I did that.

But I did it quickly falling to sleep.

16

OPEN YOUR DOOR

$\mathcal{M}$y phone on the nightstand clattered as it rang.

I opened sleepy eyes and stared at the light coming from it as I looked at my alarm clock.

It was the night after Mickey and I connected (literally).

It was also the middle of the night.

My heart started racing because a middle of the night phone call could mean anything.

I reached out, grabbed my phone and saw the caller was Mickey.

I took the call and put the phone to my ear. "Everything okay?"

"Open your door, Amy."

My skin ignited and my body flew into action.

I threw back the covers, jumped out of bed and ran down the hall to the front door. I unlocked it and pulled it open to see Mickey, in his firefighter-not-fighting-a-fire outfit sauntering up my walk toward me.

I waited, my eyes locked to him, his eyes locked to me, the burn building with just a look, and when he was close enough, I jumped him.

He caught me, kissed me, backed me inside, closed the door and locked it, all without taking his mouth from mine.

His tee hit the top step to the sunken living room.

My nightie fell to the first set of steps that led up the hall to my bedroom.

In the morning, I'd find my panties dangling off the arm of the daybed in front of my fireplace.

But we didn't make it to the bed.

We sunk down on the rug under it and that was where Mickey fucked me.

When he was done with me, I was too replete to go searching for my nightie. So when he lifted me in his arms, deposited me in my bed, went to the bathroom to deal with the spent condom and came back to me, we slept together naked.

It wasn't one of my top things to do. I wasn't big on naked sleeping.

I didn't give it a thought with Mickey.

———————— • ————————

THE NEXT EVENING, NERVOUSLY, I WALKED ON MY SILVER PUMPS INTO Magdalene's firehouse.

As arranged, I was there to have dinner with Mickey and the boys.

It was coming clear that when he said he'd make time for me, he meant it.

It was also coming clear that when he said we were building some-thing, he'd decided not to waste any more time doing that.

Meeting the boys at the firehouse, in my opinion, was one step down from telling your children you were seeing somebody and you were all going out to dinner.

Thus, I was entering the firehouse with a stack of containers holding blonde brownies baked in cupcake tins with a wedge of Dove chocolate shoved in the top of each.

I was doing this in my silver pumps, a pair of boot-leg dark wash jeans, a filmy, blush, sleeveless blouse with understated silver threads and profuse ruffles up the front and my hair in a loose bun at my nape, curling tendrils pulled out around my face.

I jumped when I heard a male voice shout, "Hot chick on the premises!"

I looked toward the sound and saw a very big man in Mickey's fire-fighter-not-fighting-a-fire uniform standing at a bank of lockers against the wall, head turned my way, grinning at me.

"Hey," I called.

"Yo," he called back.

"Is Mickey here?" I asked.

He didn't answer.

He bellowed, "*Mickey!*"

"Jesus, Jimbo." I heard Mickey mutter loudly and my eyes went his way. He was grinning and walking to me. "Hey, baby."

"Hey," I said quietly, slightly shyly, grinning back tentatively.

He stopped in front of me and his eyes dropped to the containers.

"You baked," he noted.

I lifted them up a smidge. "Blonde brownies with Dove chocolate."

His eyes came back to mine and they were dancing. "Buyin' the boys approval with baked goods?"

I didn't deny this because it was clear I was doing just that.

"Just so you know," the man called Jimbo joined us, his gaze resting on my lower half. "You got my approval with those jeans."

I felt my cheeks flush, but I did this fighting a gratified smile.

Mickey cut narrowed eyes to his colleague.

Jimbo caught his look, lifted his hands, but said, "Bud, you asked her here and you know I'm not blind."

"I know that. But I knew it thinkin' you got manners," Mickey returned.

Jimbo looked at me. "I offend you?"

"Not exactly," I told him. "And I'm pleased you like my jeans."

He settled a bit back, remarking, "Good jeans. More what's in 'em I approve of."

My eyes got big and Mickey turned fully, and a little scarily, to his fellow firefighter.

"Seriously?" he asked dangerously.

"Mick, dude, you cannot be pissed I'm glad you scored a hot chick with a great ass who makes brownies," Jimbo returned. He looked to me. "No offense."

"Not certain I *can* take offense to you thinking I have a great ass," I replied.

He smiled big.

At that point, I found myself divested of the containers and Mickey was shoving them into Jimbo's hands.

"Take those to the kitchen," he ordered.

"Gotcha, captain," Jimbo said through his smile, took the containers and strolled away.

I moved closer to Mickey. "Captain?"

He stopped scowling at the departing Jimbo, looked down at me, hooked me with an arm and pulled me to him whereupon he laid a hard, swift kiss on my mouth.

He kept hold of me with one arm as he lifted his head and gave me a much nicer, "Hey."

"Hey," I gave it back. Then repeated, "Captain? Is that a nickname?"

"Rank," he stated.

I felt my brows draw together. "Rank?"

"I command this company."

I was no less confused. "You...sorry?"

"Chief is the Battalion Chief. He commands five houses in the five big towns we got across the county. Each house has a captain who commands the company, which is the rig and the men who work it. But also the house, which is everything to do with this department that isn't handled by the chief. We got two lieutenants as well as me. Chief schedules it so each shift, I'm on it or one of the lieutenants is on it, takin' charge of the equipment and the boys and managing shit if we go out on call, at least until the chief gets there. Don't really got enough to go around for all shifts, so we got acting lieutenants with enough experience in to take shifts if that's needed."

"Oh," I mumbled. "So you're kind of second-in-command head honcho."

His eyes again started dancing as he confirmed, "Yeah."

"That's pretty impressive," I noted.

His eyes warmed on his muttered, "Thanks, Amy."

I lifted my brows. "So your chief commands five houses?"

"Yep."

"Isn't that a lot?"

"Nope."

I tipped my head to the side. "It isn't?"

"Not really. In a bigger city, a Bat Chief would command all the houses in that city."

"Part-time?" I pushed and he gave me a squeeze.

"That would be a no."

I did not like this. I didn't like it because Mickey wanted this position and it seemed a lot more work, overseeing five fire departments in five cities across the entire county, rather than just Magdalene's.

"Want a tour before dinner?" he asked, taking my mind off this.

A tour of a firehouse?

What girl would say no?

I focused on him. "Absolutely."

That earned me another squeeze before he took my hand and guided me around.

They had a big red truck (obviously). On the lower level with the truck there was a bank of lockers down one side. They had a variety of equipment like axes, wound hoses and such mounted on the walls.

There were also pictures in cheap frames put up here and there. They depicted the crew either formally arranged for an official photo or with arms thrown around each other's shoulders in a line. There were also candid shots of everything from someone grinning while washing the fire truck or someone wearing a tee shirt that had a big "MFD" on the front and jeans, swinging a bat during a softball game.

Close to the truck there was firefighter-actually-fighting-a-fire gear (which Mickey told me was called bunker gear) set out and ready for men to jump into boots, pants and grab jackets and helmets.

They even had a shiny brass fire pole.

Which meant they had an upstairs, and although there were equipment rooms and a small bathroom downstairs, upstairs there were full showers with more stalls (Mickey called out for an all clear before we peeked in) as well as a workout room that was small and held mostly weight equipment.

There was also a dark room that had bunk beds (four of them, lined head to foot against the walls) another room with a beat up couch and a couple of even more beat up recliners, all facing a massive, old console TV I knew for certain didn't provide HD. That room also had mismatched end tables with ring stains in the top of the wood, these dotted around for easy reach.

And last, there was a kitchen that had once been new and state of the art.

In 1956.

Now it was dinged up and old.

And even though the entire house was spic-and-span (this, Mickey explained was because the new guys had to go through a period of serving the station, the men testing their mettle in a variety of ways, including the duties of keeping the entire house, rig, equipment and gear performance ready and exceptionally clean), at its age, it couldn't be anything but dingy.

I couldn't spend a lot of time upset at the fact that, although their rig and gear seemed to be in good shape, the rest of the space was an afterthought. That these men spent a lot of time there, did that without pay and did it with the possibility they'd be saving lives, property and putting their own lives on the line. And because of that, they deserved at least a nice flat screen with HD and a microwave that didn't look like it was the prototype before the prototype *before* the prototype they actually produced the year microwaves were introduced to the masses.

I couldn't spend this time because Mickey introduced me to the crew.

There was Jimbo, the driver, who I'd already met.

There was also Stan, a man I figured was around Mickey's and my age (in the dearth of communication with Mickey the last two weeks, I *had* learned during our thirty minute phone call that he was forty-eight). But Stan was shorter and losing his hair. Then there was Mark, who I'd put in his thirties, who had a gleaming wedding band, a smile almost as easy as Mickey's and really nice biceps.

And last, there was Freddy, who was young, maybe mid-twenties, but that was at a push. He had a shock of thick, dark, messy hair, a smile he knew was effective, veins that ran his forearms and biceps (Mickey had these too) and he was perhaps four inches taller than me and I was five three.

He was their recruit.

After I got my introductions and shook hands with everybody, I was offered a seat.

I noted that the contents of one of the three containers of brownies was decimated (and I bit my mother's tongue not to remind them they shouldn't spoil their dinner at the same time delighted they dug in so quickly).

I sat and saw that Freddy was making dinner with Jimbo and Stan busting his chops as he did it (Mark was more quiet and less of a ball-buster).

Freddy didn't appear to care. Freddy appeared to care solely about flirting outrageously, if innocently, with me, something Mickey didn't protest because, it seemed, it gave him fodder to join in busting Freddy's chops.

It was teasing. It was lighthearted. It was funny. It was quite an experience to have the opportunity to sit with these men who spent a lot of time together, perhaps did some harrowing things trusting each other, and had an easy camaraderie.

The dinner was sloppy joes and baked frozen tater tots with brownies for dessert.

I ate it and almost the whole time I did it smiling.

Or laughing.

When everyone was done, we lounged while the guys started busting Freddy's chops again as he did the cleanup.

Then Mickey tugged a tendril of my hair.

I turned my attention to him and he said quietly, "Time to get you on the road."

I nodded and pushed away from the table without objection. They were hanging around waiting for a call that might not come, but if it did, they couldn't have distractions.

And regardless of how clean and neat it all was, it was very much their world, their space, and although they'd all been welcoming, I got the sense that they were on their best behavior because of me and it would be better that they were free to let loose and do and say what they pleased.

Farewells were exchanged and Mickey took my hand and walked me downstairs.

We were at one of the two opened bays to the house when he gave my hand a tug to stop me.

I turned into him and pulled our hands free so I could put both mine to his chest. In return, Mickey curved an arm around me.

"You need a new microwave," I announced and he let out a deep chuckle.

But he didn't say anything.

"And a TV," I went on. "And it's shocking you have a kitchen that's surely a fire hazard situated *in* a firehouse."

His eyes were still amused when he replied, "We make do, Amy."

"I would be of the opinion that men volunteering to put their lives on the line should expect more than *making do*."

He didn't lose any amusement but I could still see a hint of serious seep into his eyes when he said, "Okay, you don't got a dick so you're just gonna have to go with me on this when I say it's okay for my girlfriend to make the guys brownies. It is *not*," his arm gave me a squeeze, "okay for you to buy us a TV."

That was precisely what I intended to do (plus a microwave) but I read the seriousness in his eyes and decided not to push that partly because I didn't have a dick, he was right. He did, it was a very good one and he knew how to use it.

But mostly because he'd called me his girlfriend and I liked that a lot.

I didn't want to appear eager and scary by sharing that fact with him so I asked, "Does the town give you *any* money?"

"Bobby'd lose his mind and the boys would not show up if our rig and gear was not all it needed to be. They keep us equipped that way, Amy. We're guys. We don't need a lot more."

"Not even a better TV?" I queried incredulously.

"Gotta admit," he mumbled, lips twitching. "That TV sucks."

"Even when Archie Bunker was watching it, it sucked," I mumbled back and he chuckled again. "Do you do any fundraising?"

He nodded. "Every year 'round Christmas, the wives and some wealthy broads in town throw a Fire and Policemen's Ball, and 'round Valentine's Day all the guys in the county step up for a Firefighter and Police Officer Bachelor Auction. But what we make on that goes into a pot to divvy out in case something happens in the line of duty."

I ignored the "line of duty" business and asked, "Bachelor auction?"

He grinned and replied, "Things keep goin' the way they are, this year, I won't participate."

This year?

I ignored that too and stated, "Oh yes you will. I'm loaded. I could go the distance to beat any woman who thought she could get her hooks in you for a dinner."

His grin got bigger as his body started shaking. "Then next year, I'm first to sign up."

I leaned closer, enjoying his humor and that I gave it to him. I still felt it important enough to push.

If gently.

"So, seeing as I'm not properly equipped to get it, but I still get it, and a direct donation from me is out, would it be unacceptable if a certain someone leaned on some local businesses that sell electronics to get them to donate a new microwave and TV? These efforts being anonymous, of course."

His eyes warmed and his arm squeezed. "You wanna put the effort into that, knock yourself out. This keeps goin' where it's goin' and you meet some of the other wives and girlfriends and wanna arrange somethin' like you did for the junior boxing league so the guys got it better when we're hangin' around waitin' for a call, that wouldn't be a problem either."

So I could get someone else to donate or raise money. But Mickey Donovan's wealthy new girlfriend was not going to become the Magdalene Fire Department's patron.

Understood.

I let that go and asked, "Do women invade the sanctity of the firehouse very often?"

"Yeah, considerin' we got one in the company."

This surprised me. Not that firefighters couldn't be women, just that what I saw appeared to be a man's domain.

"Really?"

"Yeah. She's tough. She's good. Been with us four years. Name's Misty."

A firefighter named Misty was incongruous and humorous for several reasons.

I did not smile.

I mumbled, "Misty the firefighter."

Mickey gave me one of his easy grins. "Yeah. She took a lotta shit about that girlie name while she was a recruit."

"There aren't a lot of women named Butch," I pointed out and got another chuckle. "Was she okay with that?" I asked.

"She didn't have a choice," he answered. "You take it or you get the fuck out. She gets sensitive and pissy about gettin' shit about her name, no way she has it in her to aim a hose at a wall of flame."

I didn't like the sound of that last part but I didn't let on and instead queried, "So, how about wives and girlfriends?"

"It happens. They show. Necessarily, this is a family. You're part of the family, you're welcome." He bent his neck to put his face close to mine. "But everyone knows, the men and their women, our woman and her man, there's an unwritten rule. Dinner's okay. Occasionally. Droppin' in to drop shit off or have a chat, that too. The boys may look laidback but they gotta do that bein' prepared. So we keep distractions at a minimum."

I nodded.

Then I didn't know why I did it, but I figured I did it because I had to know.

This being asking, "Have you fought a lot of fires?"

He lifted his free hand to curl his fingers around the side of my neck and used his thumb to stroke the skin under my jaw when he replied carefully, "Seen a fair few."

I let that go because I didn't want to delve deeper and changed to teasing.

"Rescue many cats from trees?"

"Yeah."

I blinked up at him in surprise.

"I thought that was a myth."

He shook his head. "Big cities do not rescue cats. You call a fire department in a city to rescue a cat, they'll tell you to call animal control. We're not a big city. We're a small community and our commitment is to serve that community. So people call us about cats in trees and we do what we can. This does not include takin' the rig out and using our ladder to rescue Fluffy. This includes sending a guy out to see what he can do to help. We also get calls about cats gone missin'. Dogs gone missin'. *Kids* gone missin'. Cats and dogs, we don't roll out. Kids, obviously, we do. Then there's domestic disturbances. Car crashes. Smoke alarms goin' off. Someone fallin' off a ladder cleanin' their gutters. Someone slicin' into their finger cuttin' tomatoes. You name it, call comes in direct or they're punted to us from 911."

"Someone slicing into their finger?"

"Me, Jimbo and our two lieutenants are certified EMTs and Freddy's doin' his training. Doesn't matter. It's protocol for the FD to be called in the event of a household accident. But in Magdalene's case, closest hospital is twenty minutes away, closest independent ambulance service is fifteen. Even with ambulances on the cruise, in most cases, our boys can get there faster. "

I blinked again. "You're an EMT?"

"Got outta high school, the next month went to firefighter school. Graduated, volunteered at MFD while goin' for my EMT. While doin' it, lived in the room over my best friend's parents' garage and worked my dad's catches for money."

Wow. Mickey *really* wanted to be a firefighter and all that entailed.

"Your dad didn't get angry you didn't join the family business?" I asked.

"Nope," he replied, shaking his head. "He paid for my training. All of it. Said if I went to college like Sean, Frank and Dylan, he'd be payin' for that so he paid for what I wanted to do. And he was proud of me. Fuckin' seriously proud of me. Proud of all his boys and showed it. He didn't want anything for me, or any of us, except to love what we're doin' and be happy."

"I think I like your dad," I murmured.

"Lot to like. Good man. Good dad. Good granddad." Mickey gave me another grin. "He'll like you too. He likes cute and smartass."

I very much liked that he seemed sure I would meet his dad but it was on the tip of my tongue to ask if his father liked Rhiannon. I stopped myself because that was a question that would change our comfortable mood to an awkward one. Not to mention it wasn't any of my business, and further she was gone, so it didn't matter anyway.

I pushed closer, saying, "I knew you were impressive because you're good-looking, a good dad and a good man. Now I know there's a lot more to be impressed with about you, Mickey."

He shifted his hand to cup my jaw and said through low chuckles, "Got my looks from my folks, Amy. That's hardly impressive."

"You don't get to look at you all the time. Trust me, it's impressive."

He kept chuckling as he bent closer and started kissing me.

It felt great but it didn't last long before he ended it and ordered in a whisper, "Go to sleep with your phone by your bed, baby."

He was coming to me.

That made me happy.

I pressed even closer and replied, "Okay, honey."

He bent in and touched his mouth to mine once before breaking contact and saying, "Go home and careful getting there."

I nodded, got up on my toes, gave him my own lip touch and then pulled out of his hold and walked away on my silver pumps.

Even though I wanted to turn, wave, see him one more time, I felt his eyes following me, I hoped he liked what he saw, so I gave that to him and just kept walking.

———————— • ————————

HAZILY I LOOKED DOWN AT MICKEY ON HIS BACK IN MY BED, HEAD TO THE pillows, while I rode his cock, shifting and angling my hips so every other stroke the head of it grazed the slick walls inside me, hopefully giving him something while I gave the same to me.

My hope was granted when he growled, "*Fuck*," knifed up and wrapped an arm around my hips, jerking me and angling me himself as he pulled me up and down, forcing me to ride him faster and harder.

His other hand trailed up the silk of my nightie at my side and in, cupping my breast, his thumb dragging hard against my nipple, using the silk as added friction.

His touch shot through me, my hips bucked and I lifted my hands to the sides of his head, whispering, "Mickey."

"Like your nighties, baby," he told me and then pinched my nipple, keeping hold and twisting gently.

That sent my hips jolting. I gasped as my sex convulsed around him, lost my rhythm and started grinding.

"Ride, Amy," he ordered gruffly, releasing my nipple but only to drag the silk and lace down, baring my breast and bowing his back to take it in his mouth and suck deep.

Oh.

Even better.

I rolled my hips and clenched my fingers on his head as I panted, "Oh my God," stuck in feeling all he was making me feel and unable to do anything but *grind*.

His mouth released my breast and his head tipped back.

"*Ride*, Amy," he demanded on a growl, his thumb dragging over the slick his mouth left at my nipple.

All I could do was glory in his cock buried deep, Mickey all around me, his thumb teasing my nipple so I didn't do what I was told. I kept grinding and my head dropped back.

"Right," he bit out and surged up, still connected, and I was on my back in the bed, Mickey on me, one hand clasped to the back of one knee, yanking it high, the other arm wound around me, holding me steady, as he drove into me.

"Oh God," I breathed.

"Work your clit," he ordered.

That clit contracted at the order.

His mouth came to mine. "Wanna feel you workin' yourself as I fuck you. Do it. Now, baby."

I shoved a hand between us and down and did it.

When I did, my heels dug into the backs of his thighs and my hips came off the bed. Not long after, my head dug into the duvet and my lips parted.

Because I went soaring.

I felt Mickey's mouth at my throat until I righted my head and then I felt his mouth on mine, the invasion of his tongue, and I loved how much Mickey kissed while he made love to me.

He quit doing that when he normally quit doing that, and I cupped my hands on the back of his head to hold him to me so his grunt of release filled my mouth.

He rode me hard through his orgasm before he rode me soft and did it with the same kind of kiss.

When it left him, he ended the kiss, but gave me another one on my nose, then my chin before he slid out, saying gently, "Gotta get ready for work, darlin'."

I held on, not clingy, just lightly, as he moved out of my arms.

I did this nodding.

It was Friday morning. My kids were going to be there after school. I would see them but I wouldn't see Mickey until they were gone.

He pulled the bedclothes over my lower half before he exited the bed.

I twisted so I could watch him saunter to the bathroom.

I curled into myself as I heard the shower go on.

This was becoming our routine.

Mickey came to me after being at the firehouse. Had sex with me.

Slept with me. Had sex with me in the morning. Showered at my place. Went to his, changed clothes and went out.

It was a routine that was working for me.

I looked to the clock.

It wasn't even six thirty.

At that, I smiled a lazy smile, liking a whole lot how Mickey was making time for me.

With my lazy smile, I lazed in bed, listening to the shower. I continued to do it when Mickey came out, short hair wet, naked body moving around and becoming clothed.

When he'd accomplished that, he sat at the end of my bed, reached out a hand and cupped my cheek.

Through this, I didn't move.

The soft way Mickey was looking at me, I knew he didn't mind.

"Lookin' forward to the kids?" he asked a question he knew the answer to.

"Definitely," I gave him that answer.

"You get time, touch base with me."

I turned my head slightly and pressed my cheek into his hand.

"Definitely," I repeated.

"Gotta head out," he said.

I nodded under his hand.

When he was about to move, I caught his wrist. He stilled and focused again on me.

I lifted up to my elbow and kept hold of his hand by his wrist, tucking it to my chest.

"I just want to say that it isn't lost on me, the effort you're making to spend time with me."

He stared at me but said nothing.

"Mickey?" I called when this went on a while.

"Babe, you wear short, sexy nighties."

That was when I stared at him.

"I'm sorry?" I asked when he didn't elucidate.

"Silky ones that feel good." He paused before he added, "With lace."

"Well..." I drew that out but trailed off, still not certain what he was saying.

"Feel good," he stated, his eyes locked to mine. "Look good. You run to the door in the middle of the night to open it for me. I get my mouth on you, that's it. You put it right out there you can't get enough of me. We fuck before we sleep. We fuck when we wake up. You're a seriously good lay. And you made the boys brownies."

"I—"

"Not a hardship," he cut me off to say. "In fact, I'm a dumbfuck for not doin' it before. Can't do that shit when I got my kids. Still, lost a week."

I grinned, his words again making my heart take flight.

"So don't thank me for makin' time to spend with you when I *like* spending time with you, Amy," he finished on an order.

"Message received, Mickey," I told him through my grin.

He kept ordering. "Now, you're up, you can get up further and kiss me before I go."

He was right.

I could do that.

I pushed up and scooted to him, wrapping my arms around him as he did the same, and I put my mouth to his.

He arched me over his arm and took over the kiss.

It was heavy and heated before he broke it, lifted a hand to the side of my head and swept a thumb over my cheek.

"Have a good visit with your kids," he murmured.

"I will, honey."

"Got mine on Monday. You're over for dinner."

I nodded, feeling happy build inside me.

"Later, Amy."

"Try to have a decent day at work, Mickey."

"Will do," he muttered, brushed his mouth to mine and laid me back in bed.

He had to know I was watching him walk away, and enjoying it (not the walking away part, the watching Mickey's body doing it part).

Still, he turned before he hit the doorway and gave me a soft look as he lifted his hand in a low wave.

I gave him a soft look and a soft smile back.

He faced forward and disappeared.

17

THEY WERE BACK

*a*t three thirty-seven that afternoon, I heard the garage door going up.

I stayed in the kitchen and continued doing what I was doing; rubbing herbed butter on a raw chicken I was going to put in to roast.

The door opened and I turned my head that way, smiling and calling, "Hey, honeys."

"Hey, Mom," Auden replied, my insides warmed then I went still as he walked right to me.

Right to me.

And when he got to me, he leaned down, kissed my cheek then looked to the chicken.

"Excellent. Mom's roast chicken. I'm starved," he declared.

I stayed still as he walked away, but my eyes watched him move out of the kitchen toward the landing.

They caught on Pippa who was standing at the end of the counter.

"Hey, Mom," she launched in when she got my attention. "I know this is Mom Time and I woulda asked earlier, but Polly only told me today that her mom's always wanted to see Cliff Blue. So she asked if she could come over some time with her mom and we could show them around. I thought she could come over tomorrow, if that's okay."

"That's fine, sweets," my mouth said for me, my tone sounding natural and calm and not how I felt.

Ecstatic and overjoyed.

"Cool," she muttered, shrugging her purse off her shoulder and digging in to get out her phone. She then started wandering away, texting, but she did it talking. "Awesome you're roasting a chicken. Haven't had your chicken in *ages*."

I stood immobile with buttery hands watching my daughter wander away texting until she disappeared down the hall.

I continued to stand immobile with buttery hands, fighting the urge to jump on my phone and text Robin, Lawr and Mickey to tell them what just happened.

I was still fighting this when Auden yelled, "Hey, Mom! Can I move the bed from the side wall to the back wall?"

I closed my eyes as euphoria swept through me.

I opened them and yelled back, "Yeah, kiddo! Hang tight, I'll get this chicken in and help!"

"I will too!" Pippa said after me.

My throat felt thick, I could feel the tears gathering behind my eyes and that was when I stood there and fought that.

It was a fight I had to win because I had to get the chicken in the oven, clean my hands and help my son move his bed in his room to where he wanted it to be.

I focused on doing the first parts, and after the chicken was in and my hands were cleaned, I walked toward my children's rooms, calling, "We get this bed moved, you know the drill! Homework done first thing so you don't have to worry about it all weekend!"

"But there's something I wanna watch on TV tonight!" Pippa called back.

I was in her door when she finished. "So watch it with your books in front of you."

"Whatever," she muttered, but she did it good-naturedly.

"Come help me with your brother's bed."

She nodded, tossed her phone on her comforter and I moved out of her doorway toward Auden's room, thrilled with the knowledge that my baby girl was following me.

———————— • ————————

"Mom, you've got nothing in your scheduled recordings," Auden announced after dinner that evening.

He was lounged on the couch across from where I was lounged in my fabulous armchair. He had the remote up and pointed at the TV.

"I don't watch that much TV, kid," I reminded him.

He looked back to the TV and started pressing buttons. "You got HBO. Showtime. Cinemax. Jeez, you got the premium package." His eyes returned to me. "You don't even wanna record movies?"

I'd been so busy, except with Mickey and his kids and when I had my kids, I hadn't thought about movies.

"That's a good idea," I murmured.

"Hey!" Pippa snapped, bouncing into the room, coming from whatever she'd been doing in her bedroom (hopefully her homework), her gaze aimed at the television. "Don't use up all the DVR space. I get half."

"You get *a third*, Pip. Mom's gonna start recording movies."

"*Whatever*, Auden. I get a third so don't use it all up," she returned, throwing herself on the couch and kicking at his legs unnecessarily to make room for herself when there was already plenty.

"Don't be a douche," Auden bit out, moving his legs back to where they were before Pippa kicked them.

"Just 'cause you're taller than me doesn't mean you get the whole couch, Auden," she retorted.

"Actually," I put in, "it kinda does." Both kids looked at me, but I looked to Pippa. "You don't need that much room, sweets. The couch is long, you have plenty. Share with your brother, baby."

She hunched back into the couch, looking to the TV and mumbling, "You always take his side."

"*I* didn't get a new comforter, Pippa," Auden returned.

Oh no.

"Do you want one?" I asked my son.

"No," he answered me. "Just pointing out she's full of it."

Pippa looked to me. "Can you get another armchair like yours that I can sit in?"

That would crowd the space and look funny.

"No," I told her gently.

"I cannot *believe* you asked Mom to buy you a *chair*," Auden said precisely like he couldn't believe it.

"That chair is awesome," Pippa retorted, making the warmth inside me snuggle deeper, which was what their bickering was doing, as crazy as that sounded.

Auden turned his attention back to the TV, clicking the remote, answering, "It is. But it'd look stupid, crammed up here with all this other stuff. And it's not like chairs grow on trees."

"I didn't say they did," Pippa returned.

"Just be cool for once," Auden shot back.

"Okay," I cut in. "I love it that you love my chair, Pip. And I love it that you're protective of my design aesthetic, Auden. But how about we make this zone," I circled my hand to indicate the space we were occupying, "a bicker free zone for ten minutes."

Pippa hunched back into the couch and Auden turned back to the TV, doing this grinning.

"Design aesthetic," he muttered, clearly amused.

Back in the day, I amused my boy often.

Right then, knowing I did, I tasted a sweet so beautiful, I knew I'd buried the memory so understanding I'd lost it wouldn't kill me.

When he did, Pippa audibly swallowed back a giggle before also muttering, "Mom's so goofy."

I drew in a silent breath and let it out.

Whackjob I hated.

Goofy I'd take since, to my kids, something they told me frequently, I'd always been goofy.

That also tasted sweet.

I'd missed it too.

The ten minutes actually only lasted about two before Pippa asked irritably, "Can we *watch something* while you schedule your bazillion programs into the DVR?"

I looked at the programming happening and wondered when my son actually intended to watch all that.

"What do you want?" he asked.

"*Something*," she answered.

Expertly, Auden changed the channel to something Pippa would accept then went back to programming the DVR.

But he did this asking, "That cool for you, Mom?"

In my son's voice (or my daughter's), "Mom" was the most beautiful word in the English language.

"Yeah, kiddo," I replied, not even knowing what we were watching.

I didn't care.

They were back.

My kids were back.

With me.

———————— • ————————

"Amy, that's fuckin' great," Mickey said in my ear through the phone while I reclined on my daybed in my bedroom.

The kids were still camped out in front of the TV, but I'd gone to my room because it was late.

It was also high time to text Lawr and Robin.

But I decided to phone Mickey.

Lawr and Robin texted back with different but equally elated responses.

Mickey was giving his verbally.

"It's actually Lawrie's doing," I told him. "He called them a while ago and gave them a talking to."

"Just a catalyst to finish the work you been doin', darlin'," Mickey replied. "Don't give away credit you should take."

That was when it happened. I didn't know why that was what made it happen. But it happened.

And my soft sob was audible.

"Fuck, Amy," Mickey whispered.

"I missed them," I whispered back, my voice husky and trembling.

"Can't imagine, don't want to, baby, but they're back. Rejoice."

"I am, Mickey. These are happy tears," I told him.

"Then I won't walk over and jimmy up your window so I can climb in and take care of you."

God, he was a good man.

And suddenly, I wished they were sad tears.

"You could still do that," I told him.

"How about we don't introduce me to your kids with the possibility of them catchin' me breakin' into your bedroom?"

I was still crying a little even as I giggled.

"That I like to hear," he murmured, that murmur underlining his words.

"So, kids DVRing a million programs, do you think that means they're going to come over and watch them?" I asked hesitantly, wiping away my tears, asking this because I wanted the answer to be a definitive yes, but I was worried it would be an uncertain one.

"Don't know your kids' habits, babe, but also do not know a kid who tapes a show they don't intend to watch. I also know, if they got a million taping, your DVR space is gonna be used up and so they're gonna have to find a way to clear it somehow, and that shit's not gonna happen comin' over once a month."

That was not definitive.

But I'd take it.

"I should let them know they're welcome over anytime," I declared.

"You haven't already done that?" he asked.

"I should repeat to them perhaps more than once over the next two days that they're welcome over anytime," I amended.

I could hear his smile in his, "Good plan."

"Are you still at the firehouse?" I asked.

"Yep," he answered.

"I should let you go," I noted.

"Yeah, but only because I went somewhere to talk privately, the guys have invaded and they're givin' me shit for talkin' to my girlfriend."

I again very much liked him referring to me as his girlfriend.

But my back went straight. "That isn't very nice."

"You got time to kill, apparently they feel in the mood to kill it tonight bein' assholes."

I had a feeling this was directed right to guys.

I also had a feeling I really should let Mickey go.

"I'll help put an end to that and say goodnight," I offered.

"Okay, darlin', check in tomorrow."

"I will, Mickey. Stay sharp."

"Always," he replied. "Later, Amy."

"Later, honey."

We hung up and stared at my unlit fireplace.

Don't give away credit you should take.

There was no denying that their Uncle Lawrie calling and sharing he felt they needed to shape up helped.

But Mickey was right.

It was mostly me.

I'd been in the battle of my life, the stakes the most important there were.

And I'd won.

On that thought, feeling like I was floating for a different reason, I got up and walked to my bed. I put my phone on the nightstand and went to my bathroom. I got ready for bed, turned out the lights, slipped between the sheets.

And I fell asleep easily.

———— • ————

I was at the kitchen counter, clicking through my laptop, when I saw movement.

I looked up and saw Auden wandering in wearing a navy tee snug across his broad (and getting broader) chest and a loose pair of plaid pajama bottoms.

"Hey, kiddo," I called. "You want breakfast?"

"Yeah, Mom," he replied, wandering my way, still looking sleepy. Half boy. Half man. All my son. "Waffles?" he requested as he came to a stop at the end of the counter.

"Sure," I replied, straightened away from my laptop and turned to the kitchen.

It was Sunday morning.

Our Saturday had been just as good, if not better, than our Friday night.

I met Polly and her mother, Sherry, when they came over to get a tour of Cliff Blue.

I liked Sherry unreservedly. She was what I was learning most of Magdalene was. Nice, open and friendly. We got along immediately.

I wished I could say the same about Polly.

She was a pretty little thing, not as pretty as my daughter, but still very attractive.

She also had an air about her that put me on edge.

Conceited. Snooty.

And the way I grew up, I could call conceited and snooty from twenty paces.

Further, it was clear she was queen bee and my daughter was her minion. She didn't overtly treat Pippa as such, but it was communicated anyway.

Olympia might like her, but I suspected Polly held some position at school that Pippa wanted to be close to and so she was serving her queen.

I felt badly about thinking this about Polly, especially considering Sherry was so lovely. I was also troubled about witnessing this from Pippa.

These feelings didn't get any better when Auden interacted with the girls, openly reluctant to be in the presence of Polly in a way that he was clearly trying to hide his aversion to her.

During their visit, we all decided to go out to lunch, with Auden deciding not to join us (this being because he was a teenage boy, not because he didn't like Polly). He hooked up with his friends, and I enjoyed spending time with Sherry but, alas, this time with Polly only cemented my opinion of her.

For one, she was openly catty about the people around us (mostly the females, their hair, outfits, anything she could note and say something mean about). Sherry attempted to curtail this but didn't put a lot of effort into that, probably because she didn't want to embarrass her daughter by remonstrating her in front of her friend and her friend's mom.

And further, Polly was almost entirely negative about absolutely everything; the food, the temperature of the restaurant, the service.

After we parted ways, I decided it was too soon in my reparation efforts to broach this subject with my daughter, so I didn't.

I didn't do this also with the hope that she'd sort herself out. She was a good kid. A smart one. She had good friends back in La Jolla, they were close, had been friends a long time and they were all great kids. She'd been in Magdalene awhile, but she still was in a new place finding her way, and now, doing that her first year of high school.

I just had to trust she'd find the right way.

We came back, had a family dinner and I let them go out with their friends last night.

I got a knock on the door when Pippa got home, through which she'd called, "Mom! I'm back!" and I'd replied, "Good. Hope you had fun!" to which she said, "I did! Goodnight."

Auden didn't knock on my door but I stayed up until he got home.

Now, it was morning and, except for Polly, the weekend had been a smashing success and I was still flying.

"What's this?" Auden asked.

I turned from getting the pancake batter mix down and saw him looking at my laptop.

"Just some research I'm doing on a possible fundraiser I'm thinking about," I told him.

That was the truth.

However, the specifics included me attempting to find what I thought should be easy to find, though I'd never looked for such things. They were still public records. These being the town of Magdalene's financial accounts.

I didn't know what was driving me or if I'd make any sense of what I found when I found it.

I still wanted to know what they allocated to the fire department.

The town was clean. There were flowers decorating Cross Street and the boardwalk. The 4th of July decorations had been effusive but attractive. The roads were nice. There was a small police station that resembled the fire station in its age, size and quaintness. They had an extensive recycling program.

But there was also money in that town. Coastal properties that I knew from experience cost a good deal. Shops that were not inexpensive in the slightest that stayed in business because someone was patronizing them regularly. Very nice restaurants.

Everyone paid taxes and with property tax alone, there had to be money in the coffers for more than flowers, holiday decorations, decent roads (which might not be the town's responsibility at all but the county's or the even the state's), recycling and street sweeping.

"It was cool what you did for those kid boxers."

My thoughts about the town's finances flew out the window as my eyes shot to my son.

His voice was strange.

Not sleepy.

Regretful.

When I caught his eyes, I saw that tone reflected in them and felt my heart squeeze.

Auden went on, "My friend Joe and his little brother are both in that league, though Joe's in the young adult portion. But Joe's family isn't rolling in it. They can't afford gloves and shorts and all the other stuff they need. Same as wrestling, I guess, it not being fun to put on sweaty headgear a hundred other guys have used before you, even if it is cleaned."

I looked to my son feeling a great deal but saying nothing.

"Joe was freaking ecstatic you raised all that money. He's into that. Boxing. Been in that league for five years. Says this year, because of that money, it'll be the best one yet."

"Well, now I'm happier I did it than I was before," I replied.

"It was cool," he repeated softly.

Instead of weeping, I gave him a gentle smile.

"Been a dick," he whispered.

Our conversation had turned to a place I did not want my son to go.

My nose started stinging and I whispered back, "Auden. Don't."

"Thinking on it, you had your reasons," he said.

"I did," I agreed. "But I should have shielded you from it."

"I guess," he muttered unconvincingly.

I slid closer to him and stated, "We're all moving on. That's done. Behind us. Now is now. And now is good. So let's stick in the now, honey."

His head tipped to the side, his gaze evading mine, and it looked like he wanted to say something but he didn't say it.

He said, "I can stick in the now."

"Good," I replied.

He caught my eyes. "Are you happy?"

I gave him a reassuring smile. "I'm doing great, kiddo. Really, really good. And yes, happy." I gave him that. It was no lie. But I had to get him out of the place he was in. "Now do you want waffles, or what?"

His lips quirked and he asked, "Where's the iron?"

"Cupboard to the side of the sink," I answered.

I got to work. My son got the waffle iron out for me. Then he grabbed some juice and sat on a stool.

"Be cool I come over and hang, watch some of my programs?" he asked and my heart leaped as he went on, "Martine's got a bunch of crap taping, so Pip and I miss a lot of things."

Selfish, DVR-hogging Martine.

But he'd just mentioned her without being tense about it so that was indication he trusted I was over it so he could.

Which meant everything.

"Sure," I told him casually. "Just give me a heads up you're coming over."

"Cool," he muttered.

I was pouring the first waffle on the iron when Pippa wandered out of her room in much the same outfit as my son's except the top was a pale yellow camisole and the bottoms were a yellow, green and peach plaid.

"Morning, honey," I called. "Want waffles?"

She stared dazedly at the iron as she made her way to the kitchen and hiked her behind on a stool.

Only then did she say, "Yeah."

I dropped the top and just contained myself from doing a whirl.

"You gonna get a dining room table, or is that space reserved for you to set up your Buddhist meditation space?" Auden teased.

I grinned at him. "The dining room table is foiling me."

"You'll need one, Uncle Lawrie, Mercer and Hart come for Thanksgiving," Auden pointed out.

This was very true.

It was time to make the dining room table a mission.

"Just so you know, I talked with your Uncle Lawrie and they're considering it, but Aunt Mariel might also be coming."

Both kids did not look delighted with this news. Then again, having a soulless, emotionless vampire as an aunt to your favorite uncle was not something my kids liked either.

Pippa powered through first and suggested, "We can hit some stores today."

I jumped on that trying not to appear like I was jumping on that. "You're on."

"God, furniture shopping," Auden mumbled.

"Lobster at the Lobster Market for lunch, you come with your sister and me," I bribed my son.

"Auden'll do anything for lobster," Pippa chimed in.

She didn't have to tell me. I knew that.

"Add lobster chowder on top of lobster and I'm in," Auden negotiated.

"Then we have plans," I said.

Pippa looked sleepily excited.

Auden looked resigned but not surly.

And I was floating on top of the world.

———— • ————

"THIS IS TOTALLY YOU," PIPPA DECLARED.

I looked to my daughter who was holding up a bottle of perfume.

We were in Sephora. Dining room table shopping had been a bust. The Lobster Market had been a blast. And we were at the mall because Pippa wanted to go and because Auden's friends were already there hanging.

So he was with his friends, and Pippa and I were dinking around shopping, something we'd done a lot before I'd lost my mind and my kids. Something we liked doing.

"Sock it to me," I said and Pippa grabbed a paper strip, spritzed the perfume on it, waved it and then stuck it out to me.

I smelled it.

It was fresh and clean with a delicate floral background and hints of vanilla to mellow it out.

It was no Chanel N° 5, but then again, that was the perfume to end all perfumes and nothing was.

But there was something about the scent my daughter chose for me that I loved. Subtle. Mellow. Fresh. But still complicated.

"Grab a bottle of that, sweets," I said after sniffing it.

She smiled and did as asked.

We drifted away and she shared, "I need more mascara."

"We'll grab a tube," I replied. "Have you experimented with bronzer yet?"

"No," she told me.

I grinned at my girl. "Let's go play."

She grinned back.

Then my baby girl and me played with makeup.

———————— • ————————

I HIT THE GARAGE DOOR BUTTON AND STEPPED OUT OF THE DOOR THAT LED to the garage after waving at my kids as they backed down my drive.

It closed on me and I wandered to the kitchen.

Smiling, I grabbed my phone and started alternately texting Lawr and Robin to share all the news of my first good weekend with my kids in over a year.

While doing this, my phone in my hand rang.

It was Mickey.

I answered it, "Hey, honey."

"It's after five. They gone?" he asked.

"Yes," I answered.

"Today good?" he asked.

He knew yesterday was, I'd reported it to him through texts.

"It was great, honey."

"Right, then get your ass over here. Makin' you dinner and it's almost ready."

My toes curled, my belly flipped and my soul took flight.

"I'll be right over."

"Amy?" he called before I could say good-bye, ring off and race over to his house (without looking like I was racing, obviously).

"Yes?"

"Bring a nightie."

My knees wobbled, my belly dipped and my heart soared.

"Okay, Mickey."

"See you in a minute."

"You will. 'Bye."

"Later."

We hung up.

I dashed to get a nightie.

I shoved it in my purse with my phone, a small travel bag of facial cleanser and moisturizer, as well as an extra pair of panties.

Then I went over to Mickey's.

18

PATH THAT WAS
DARK AND FORBIDDING

"*B*aby."

I kept working Mickey's cock.

"*Amy.*"

That was a growl.

I kept bobbing and sucking.

His hand cupped my cheek.

"Amy, baby, fair warning."

Each word was a groan.

I slid him up, kept the tip in my mouth as I rolled it with my tongue and looked up his fantastic torso to his burning blue eyes.

That was mine. I gave him that.

Me.

Holding those eyes, I slid down, taking him deep.

His head fell back to the arm of my daybed and watching it, I felt a rush of wet hit between my legs.

Then I went for it, gave it, gave it good, and swallowed the evidence of the last.

I licked him clean then made my way up his body, kissing his stomach, his chest, his neck, and only when his arms closed around me did I settle, skin against skin on Mickey.

I caught his eyes and when I did, he muttered, "She's cute, a smartass, makes great brownies and swallows."

"Is this a stamp of approval?" I asked.

His hand slid down and clenched my behind. "Like you don't know a man gets off on a woman who takes *all* of him in her mouth."

I grinned and I could tell it was smugly.

His gaze narrowed on my mouth right before he surged up. I cried out. Then I was down, head to the pillow on the other side of the daybed and Mickey was on top of me.

"Payback," he whispered.

And without hesitation, he commenced working his way down my body until he threw my legs over his shoulders, dipped his face to me and proved that payback Mickey Donovan style was, one hundred percent, *not* a bitch.

———————•———————

IT WAS SEPTEMBER, THE WEATHER HAD COOLED, THOUGH NOT THAT MUCH. But I had a fireplace in my bedroom. It was easy to light and it was romantic. So, in front of said fire, after I gave it to Mickey with my mouth and he returned the favor, we laid under my new, fluffy, soft afghan, naked and silent on my daybed, sometimes stroking but mostly just holding each other and watching the fire.

It was Wednesday after my kids left me and Cillian and Aisling were at friends' houses, Cillian hanging, Aisling doing some school project.

This meant we had time.

It was just time that was going to end.

"When do you have to go get Cill again?" I asked.

"Eight thirty," he answered.

I stayed as connected to him as I could and reached to the closest thing that would give me what I needed, this being his phone. I pressed the button on the bottom and saw it was just going eight.

I dropped the phone and snuggled back into him, muttering, "Half an hour."

"Come away with me."

My head jerked against his chest before I lifted it and looked at him. "I'm sorry?"

"Got the kids this weekend. Next weekend I don't, and you don't have yours. And Jimbo's got a hunting cabin that his wife took over to make it a cabin-cabin. It doesn't have a lot, but it's got everything you need. Jimbo uses it when he hunts but she uses it to hang around and read while he hunts. Been there once. It's a nice place. Not much, bed, kitchen, stereo, no TV. If he's not usin' it, wanna take you there."

I didn't care if it was filthy and decorated in dead animal heads, Mickey wanted to take me there, I wanted to go.

"Okay," I replied.

"Like I said, it's not much," he said. "But it's far away. No kids. No exes. No fire department. No old folks. Just two days, you and me."

That sounded *fabulous*.

"I'd love to go, Mickey."

He took one arm from around me and ran his knuckles down my jaw, dipping his voice to say, "It's pretty basic, Amy. But they got heat and light, a fridge, a stove," he tilted his head to the fire, "a fireplace." He rubbed his thumb along my lower lip. "We can be naked the entire time and you won't even notice where you are."

I loved he wanted to go away with me.

I loved that he was being so sweet.

I loved how he was touching me.

I did *not* love all that his words were saying to me.

"You do know, although I was born with a silver spoon in my mouth, that filthy rich people don't spontaneously combust when they step foot over the thresholds of such places as hunting cabins."

His hand dropped away and his eyes narrowed on me. "Just want you to be prepared for what you'd get when you got there."

"I kinda got what I was going to get when you said Jimbo has a hunting cabin. Since Jimbo shared that for his regular job he's a mechanic at a local dealership, I would not expect to go to said cabin and find you having a personal valet and me having the opportunity to boss around a chef."

His eyes stayed narrowed as he growled, "Tame the smartass, Amelia."

"I will, *Michael*, when you come to terms with the fact that I have money," I snapped.

"Think we had a drama witnessed by the residents of a nursing home that saw the end of that shit," he returned.

"Really?" I asked my question but kept right on speaking. "Then why would you need to assure me we could be naked and I wouldn't even know where I was?"

He clamped his mouth shut and his jaw went hard.

"Yeah," I whispered.

He unlocked his jaw to reply, "Maybe we shouldn't go."

I slid myself up his chest, my pique increasing at his words. "Oh no you don't. You're not allowed to be sweet and lovely, offering to take me away from it all, then rescind that offer."

"I do if you turn into a smartass and hand me shit."

"I *want* to go away to a hunting cabin with you," I told him.

"Then you shoulda just said *that*, not *handed me shit.*"

"I did," I reminded him.

"You did then you handed me shit."

I looked to the fire and mumbled, "Forget I said anything."

"Amy," he called.

"What?" I asked the fire.

"Babe, fuckin' look at me."

I turned squinty eyes to him. "Yes?"

"Tell me, how is it you just gave me the best blowjob of my life, capped that by takin' my cum, I asked you to go away for a weekend with me, and I'm this pissed?" he demanded.

"How is it that you went down on me, gave me only the *fourth* best orgasm of my life, the first two were our first time, the third one the time on the rug by my bed, you asked me to go away with you, and *I'm* this pissed?" I retorted.

"Fuck," he growled. "I don't have enough time to fuck you properly in order to fuck that sass outta you before I gotta get my kid."

"Then do it *improperly*, Mickey," I challenged.

I barely got his name out before I was on my back, Mickey looming over me, his hands at my ankles forcing my knees bent and my legs wide, and just with that, I was breathing heavy and speeding near orgasm.

It was then, his phone rang.

We both looked down to it but only Mickey clipped, "Fuck me."

He lowered himself between my spread legs, resting some of his weight on me, and reached a long arm out to his phone. He nabbed it, turned a heated scowl to me, something I ignored entirely, wrapped my legs around his thighs and rested my hands to his chest as he took the call and put the phone to his ear.

"Coert, swear to fuck, this better be good," he ground down the phone.

He listened for less than a minute before he was up, seated on the daybed, and he'd arranged me straddling him.

His eyes were to the fire, but they saw no romantic fire blazing by a marvelous daybed.

They were far, far away.

I watched with some awe, and admittedly some unease, as whatever was happening far, far away began to piss Mickey off.

To extremes.

"What do I want you to do?" Mickey asked the unknown Coert, his voice low, rough and filled with such fury, I felt it vibrating all through me. "It's cool you called me, and just sayin', she doesn't have the kids, they're with me. But I'm not owin' a favor this time. I want that bitch's DUI on record."

I tensed.

It wasn't even eight thirty and Rhiannon was drunk driving?

And...*this time?*

"Yeah," he grunted. "Yeah," he grunted again. "Right. Thanks, Coert."

He disconnected and tossed his phone to the afghan.

"Goddamn shit," he muttered to the fire.

"Mickey," I whispered.

"*Goddamn fucking shit!*" he roared, surging up, but planting me gently on my feet before he did something that was sweet— unbelievably sweet in the circumstances—and bent, tagging his tee and handing it to me.

He then went after his boxers as I pulled his tee over my head and when I had it on, I saw he had his boxers up and was nabbing his jeans.

"She's done this before?" I asked carefully.

He shoved his foot in one leg, answering, "Yeah." He shoved in the other one and tugged them up then he looked at me. "That was what happened before the thing that happened before the bender that happened when I got shot of her ass."

"Oh, Mickey," I said softly, wishing words were magic and I could find the right ones to make that magic work.

He started pacing.

"Maybe she's..." I started, stopped, then tried, "Maybe all these things are happening and she's going to hit bottom and—"

He twisted his head to face me and snarled, *"She's not doin' that shit with my kids."*

I stood there staring at him thinking I'd never seen anyone that angry.

In all my antics, I'd made Conrad spitting mad.

But he'd never been as angry as Mickey was right then.

Somehow, in the face of his rage, I felt no fear.

I just murmured soothingly, "Of course not, honey. You wouldn't let it."

"Loved her," he spat and I flinched. Not at his words, at his emotion. "Only bitch I tagged more beautiful than her is you. Lookin' back, I knew it was gonna be her the minute I laid eyes on her. Knowin' that, from the second I met her, treated her ass like gold. I had it to give to her, I gave it. We had it good. She gave me babies. It didn't happen fast, her sinkin' into the bottle. It went slow. Can you imagine, Amy, day after day, no matter how hard you held on, watchin' someone you love slip right through your fingers?"

"No, baby," I said gently, again feeling the bleed inside.

This time, though, I was bleeding for Mickey.

"Does she love them?" he asked suddenly.

"I'm sorry?" I asked back in confusion.

"Ash and Cill," he bit out. "'Cause, she does, I don't get it. She didn't love me. Told her to get sober or get out. We fought. She swore she didn't have a problem, told me *I* had a problem. Comin' back to me and our family smellin' like stale booze and lookin' like shit, and *I* had the problem. Then she got out. That meant she chose the bottle over me. That's not love. That the same thing with my kids?"

"I don't know anything about addiction, Mickey, but I would guess she does, and she loved you too. But she's not in control. The addiction is."

"That's weak," he clipped.

"You're angry," I said softly, moving to him, getting close, but not touching him. "I know you know better. Sickness isn't weak, and alcoholism is an illness."

He clenched his jaw, looked away and I watched a muscle dance in his cheek.

He knew.

I took a chance and invaded his space. When he didn't pull away, I burrowed closer, wrapping my arms tight around him and resting my cheek against his chest.

It took him a few moments, but he finally curled an arm around me, cupped the back of my head with his other hand and held my cheek against his warm skin.

"Hunting cabin is out 'cause I'm thinkin', she doesn't sort her shit, I'm not givin' the kids back to her," he said over my head.

I nodded, my cheek sliding against his chest, wondering but not asking why he'd given them back after her last escapade on Cillian's birthday.

"And that fuckin' sucks," he went on.

It did but I didn't agree verbally, I just held him tighter.

"She's still fuckin' me over. She can't hold her shit together means I can't have time with you."

"We'll find our times."

He gave a noncommittal grunt before he stated, "Maybe shit'll settle, the kids'll be good in a coupla months and Josie and Jake'll take 'em while we go up for a coupla days."

I held on and replied, "That'd be good."

I felt Mickey's chest expand with the deep breath he took and then felt his sigh when he let it out.

His hand slid to my jaw and he tipped my head back.

When he got my gaze, he said, "Gotta have my tee so I can go get my boy."

I nodded, rolled up on my toes and Mickey met me halfway for a lip brush.

I rolled back and he let me go. I went to get my robe, pulled off Mickey's tee, pulled on the robe and took it back to him.

He had his boots on by the time I returned. Straightening from the daybed, he reached out as I handed him his shirt.

When he had it on, he pulled me back into his arms. I wrapped mine around him.

"You're gonna have to store up some smartass so I can fuck it outta you," he remarked and I smiled at the same time I tingled.

"I don't think that'll be difficult," I assured him.

"For you, no," he teased.

I grinned at him then tipped my chin down and kissed his chest over his shirt.

He cupped my head to keep my face there, and I kept it there for him, rubbing my nose against his chest then turning my head and pressing my cheek to it again.

"Sorry this fucked our night," he said quietly.

"No night is fucked when I'm with you," I replied.

"Christ, Amy." This came out as a groan right before I felt his lips at the top of my hair.

We held each other for long moments before I pushed my head back, his came up, and I caught his eyes.

"You gonna be okay?"

"Got no choice, but yeah, baby. I'm always okay."

I hoped he wasn't lying but to do my bit (the only thing I could do), I gave him a reassuring smile and a gentle squeeze.

He dipped down and touched his mouth to mine before he let me go but grabbed my hand and walked me to the front door.

I got another lip brush before he was out the door on his, "Talk to you tomorrow, babe."

I stood in the door and replied, "Okay, Mickey." I watched him take five steps away from me before I called, "Mickey!"

He turned to me.

"You're a great guy, a wonderful father, and walking away from just you, she made the worst decision of her life. Walking away from your family, it's mean to say, but that's just crazy."

In the outside lights I saw his face go soft before he ordered, "Don't be sweet and make me wanna make out with you to the point I'm fuckin' you in your foyer when I gotta go get my boy."

"My apologies," I said through a smile.

"Now get outta the fuckin' door wearin' only that robe," he kept ordering.

"No one can see me, Mickey."

"Babe?" he called.

"What?" I asked.

"Get outta the fuckin' door."

I squinted my eyes at him and got out of the door.

But before I fully closed it, I stuck my face through and blew him a kiss.

Thus, the last look I had of Mickey was him shaking his head wearing a grin that might not have been easy, but at least I'd managed to give it to him.

———— • ————

LATE THE NEXT MORNING, I WALKED INTO MAUDE'S HOUSE OF BEAUTY AND went right to the pedicure chairs.

I bent to touch cheeks with Alyssa, who was working on Josie's toes, gave a "Hey," got a "Yo, babe," back and then moved to do the same with Josie.

"Careful, her fingers are still wet," Alyssa warned.

I was careful as I gave Josie her greeting then lifted up the arm in the next chair and climbed into it.

"How's Jake doing with Conner gone?" I asked Josie.

She tipped her head to the side, sadness seeping into her eyes and answered, "Amber and Ethan aren't good. They miss their big brother. So he has his chin up for them." She drew in a breath and lowered her voice. "But I found him in Con's room the other day, just sitting by himself on Con's bed. I left him to it and didn't mention I found him there. But I know he's melancholy."

I nodded. Having lost my kids in my own way, I understood Jake and it didn't thrill me that I got them back just in time to have Auden for two years before I'd be going through the same thing.

"How's Mickey?" Alyssa asked.

I shook away my thoughts and smiled down at her. "He's good."

"I'm sure he's good, havin' a hot neighbor who puts out," Alyssa returned (incidentally, they were my friends, I didn't go into details—much to Alyssa's despair—but they knew how things were progressing with Mickey and me). "But I'm not talkin' about that. I'm talkin' about his ex gettin' hauled in for drunk driving," Alyssa went on.

I stared at her in horror. "How do you know that?"

"Babe," she replied, then threw out a hand holding the brush of a bottle of nail varnish.

I took in the salon, mumbling, "Right."

"He's probably used to it," Alyssa said, turning her attention back to Josie's toenails.

He wasn't used to it.

I looked to Josie. "Do you know about Rhiannon?"

She looked apologetic as she answered, "I've never met her but Jake's told me about her, and I've...heard things."

"Small town," I noted.

"Yes," Josie agreed.

"If I were Mickey, I'd haul her ass in front of a judge," Alyssa remarked.

"I don't want to share Mickey's business," I told them. "But I'll say he isn't happy."

"I'll bet," Alyssa muttered.

"Are his kids okay?" Josie asked.

"No," I answered. "But they have Mickey so they cope."

"Very sad," she said softly.

"Yeah," I agreed.

I heard my phone in my purse chiming to tell me I had a text, so I dug it out and looked at it, the pall of our conversation lifting when I saw it was Auden.

Can I come over tonight, hang and catch some of my shows?

I texted back, *Of course. Do you want me to make dinner?*

To that I received, *That'd be cool.*

To which I sent, *Is your sister coming with you?*

And while Alyssa announced to Josie, "You're done. Don't move. I'll sort you after I get started on Amelia," I got a return text.

Don't know. I'll ask her. Gotta go to class.

Thus I replied, *Okay, kiddo. Talk to you later,* and got back, *Yeah. Bye.*

I set my phone aside as Alyssa grabbed my hand armed with a cotton ball and polish remover.

She started going at my polish and I shared, "That was Auden. He's coming over for dinner and to watch TV."

I got two beaming smiles from two beautiful blondes as well as Josie's, "That's fabulous, Amelia," and Alyssa's, "Right on, sister!"

They were correct.

It *was* fabulous.

It was just sad that my life with my family was shifting to fabulous while Mickey's seemed to be careening down an unknown path that was dark and forbidding.

Josie stayed while we did girl talk and I got my mani-pedi. Then Josie and I left and she took me to The Shack on the wharf, which was just that. A dilapidated shack that I'd noticed when Mickey walked me down the wharf weeks ago. With Josie, I found during the day it served coffee, breakfast and lunch, and it was run by a friend of Josie and Jake's, a man named Tom who was all Magdalene: warm and friendly.

He also brewed excellent coffee.

Josie went her way, I went mine, mine being to Dove House.

But before I went in, I took out my phone and rang Mickey.

"Hey, baby," he answered.

"Hey, honey, do you have a quick sec?" I asked.

"Sure," he told me.

"I mean, a quick sec for not great news," I shared carefully.

"Fuck," he muttered then louder, "Sure."

I launched in because he was working and also because not great news was always best delivered quickly.

"I had a mani-pedi at Alyssa's with Josie this morning and Alyssa had heard about Rhiannon," I informed him.

"Babe, not a surprise," he replied surprisingly calmly. "Told you a long time ago, small town. People talk. Word gets around and fast. Especially that kind of word. Everyone knows about Rhiannon. The only one who doesn't is Rhiannon."

"Oh, right," I mumbled.

"Thanks for heads up, though."

"I was just worried that maybe the kids would hear."

"They will," he confirmed. "Since that's the case, sat down with both of them last night. Shared it. It didn't go down too great, but at least some kid says somethin' they heard their parents say, they won't be blindsided."

God, I could not imagine having to do that with my kids. It had been hard enough sitting, traumatized and brokenhearted, with Conrad, sharing with our children that their father was moving out and we were getting a divorce.

The looks on their faces was the catalyst to my crazy behavior.

They'd looked shattered. Confused. Devastated.

And the seed was planted.

"Talked to Coert," Mickey went on. "First offense on record, blood alcohol level wasn't that high, bail was low. She bonded out last night. Don't know what's gonna happen from here. She 'fesses up, may get a slap on the wrist but at most, Coert says it'll be community service. I called her. She was pissed I called but I told her we had to talk. Took some doin' since the last talk we had before I gave her the kids back after she pulled that shit on Cill's birthday wasn't taken all that great. But she agreed to meet tonight. Goin' to her before I go home to my kids."

That was surprising.

"You talked to her after Cillian's birthday?" I asked.

"Not gonna send my kids back to her if she's still on a bender," he replied.

"You didn't..." I hesitated, wondering if I should go on but since I'd started I decided I'd better, "tell me."

"Amy, you had your own shit goin' down with your family. We'd just got on track. Not the time to drag you down in my shit. Never is really the time to drag you down in my shit, but Rhiannon isn't in my life and still, seconds away from fuckin' you, doin' it hard because you're bein' a smartass and both of us lookin' forward to it, get a call from the sheriff with her draggin' both of us down in her shit."

I didn't really have a good feeling about Mickey not thinking he could share things with me.

I also didn't think it was the time to go over that with him.

Instead, I invited, "Auden is coming over tonight for dinner and to watch TV. But I'd like it if you'd phone me to let me know how your meeting went." I said that but quickly added, "I mean, if you want to."

"I get home, get my kids fed and sorted, I'll do that, baby."

At least that was good.

"And fuckin' great news your boy is comin' to you just to hang."

That made me grin. "Yeah."

"Right, aren't you at Dove House?" he asked.

"Outside, about to go in," I told him.

"Hope Mrs. McMurphy doesn't hand you your ticket to Nuremberg."

That had me giggling through which I said, "I think I've bought some immunity with her birthday cookie sandwiches."

"Only Nazi I know who could do that is you, though, sayin' that, those cookies were the shit."

He would think so. He'd had three after we'd had Chinese.

"I should probably get in," I said.

"I should probably get back," he replied, though his was a lot less enthusiastic than mine.

I really hoped his roofing business took off.

"Okay, I'll let you go."

"Talk to you later, Amy."

"Yeah, Mickey…" and I made a sudden choking noise because I had to physically stop myself from ending that, *Love you.*

It was a natural conclusion to a conversation with someone you cared about.

But we weren't anywhere near there.

Or, at least, I figured Mickey wasn't.

Me, as crazy as it was, I was near there the instant I clapped eyes on Mickey months ago.

"Babe?"

He heard it.

"Just…something caught in my throat. Later, honey."

"Bye, Amy."

We rang off. I went in, and within half an hour found my immunity with Mrs. McMurphy had expired when she said matter-of-factly to me, "Too bad you're a Nazi. When you're hung, who's going to do the vacuuming?"

It was late-ish that evening, after dinner with my son, and Auden was on the couch on the landing, watching TV with his books around him.

I was not being creepy Mom sitting with him watching programs I had no interest in. I was down on the sectional with my laptop, giving him space and sending an update email to my parents (who were still incommunicado with me, something I was alternately thankful for and found concerning).

Olympia had not come. She was over at Polly's.

I hit send then went back to the website that had the dining room table that was intriguing me. A small shop in New Hampshire. Everything was handmade from local woods. It was amazing. It was pricey. And shipping would be crazy.

But I was thinking I loved it.

Staring at it, I still had that feeling as my phone lying on the seat beside me rang.

I looked to it and saw it was Mickey calling.

I snatched it up, my eyes going to the landing to see nothing. The TV was on and Auden was lounging.

I took the call and put the phone to my ear, setting the laptop aside, saying, "Hey."

"Hey back. Your boy still there?"

"Yes," I told him.

"He spendin' the night?" Mickey asked.

"No," I replied.

"When he's gone, text me. When my kids are down, I'll text you and want you over here."

Oh no. That didn't sound good.

"Is everything all right?" I asked.

"Not even a little bit."

He sounded unhappy.

"Okay, I'll...we have a plan."

"Right, and just sayin', things are tightenin' up with your kids, you think about when you can introduce them to me so I don't lose you when you have them, and if I call, you don't gotta talk to me like you barely know me."

Yes, he was unhappy.

"We'll discuss that," I promised.

"Yeah, we will. Text," he ordered.

"Okay."

"Later," he said then hung up.

I took the phone from my ear and looked back to the couch.

Auden hadn't moved.

I set the phone aside, grabbed my laptop and sent an email to the New Hampshire furniture people. Then I set it aside and went up to do the dishes.

I'd barely started before Auden called, "You want help?"

I looked to him to see he was up and looking over the back of the couch.

My handsome boy, my good kid, no longer my baby.

"Finish your program. There isn't much to do here. I'm good," I called back.

He nodded and disappeared again.

I did the dishes. Auden finished his program, deleted it and gathered his books. He told me he had to go and I walked him to the door to the garage.

When we were there, I looked up into his light brown eyes. "Tell your sister I said 'hey.'"

"Will do, Mom. Be back to catch more, yeah?" he asked.

"Anytime, sweets. This is your home too."

He grinned at me then bent to give my cheek a kiss and he left.

I watched him drive out, saw the garage door going down then I moved into the house, right to my phone.

Auden's gone, I texted Mickey.

I got no text back for some time before I got, *Cill's down but Ash's still up. Hang tight.*

I hung tight, more time elapsed and finally it came.

Come over now.

I didn't waste a lot of time getting over there now.

I'd not made it to the curb on my side of the road before I saw Mickey's front door open with Mickey shadowed in the frame.

I was about to step up on his front stoop when he noted, "You didn't wear a jacket."

"It's right across the street."

He didn't reply. Just looked annoyed, reached to me and grabbed my hand. He pulled me in and closed the door then tugged me to the side where there was a coat closet. He let me go to yank the door open.

"Mickey," I whispered.

"Deck," he whispered back.

The reason I needed a coat.

He grabbed a huge canvas coat and handed it to me. I shrugged it on, and drowning in it, with Mickey wearing only one of those attractive sweatshirts with the high collar and zip at the throat, he found my hand under the long sleeve, tugged me through the house and out to the back deck.

He stopped us at the railing close to the grill. The night dark, the air chill, we were as far away from his sleeping kids as we could get, and I was very uneasy.

"What's going on?" I asked, still whispering.

"Told you I talked with Rhiannon after Cill's birthday went south," he said.

He did.

Belatedly.

I didn't mention the last. I just nodded.

"Told her then that was uncool, and I was not good with it or what it might mean. Told her she had to give me a really fuckin' good reason why that shit happened, reason enough not to keep our kids home and safe with me."

"And she said?" I prompted when he stopped speaking.

"If you can believe this shit, shit that was unbelievable then but it's more unbelievable the day after she got a DUI, she said that she had some work thing she had to go to. Someone at her job was leaving. She'd had too much to drink so she didn't want to get in her car. Said she texted Aisling that when Ash didn't say any of that shit to me, and she would, and my girl checked her phone about seven hundred times when we were at The Eaves."

The only thing I could come up with to say was, "Oh, Mickey."

He took that lameness and kept giving me the ugly, "When I asked her to explain why she didn't contact our son after, she said she had a big late birthday thing planned for when he got back to her and she didn't wanna ruin it. And she did do a big thing. Though if she had it planned before I got in her face or not is anyone's guess."

"Excuses," I murmured.

"Absolutely," he agreed. "Now tonight, I called her on the DUI, askin' what the fuck is up that this shit is goin' on and leakin' into our kids' lives. And she fuckin' told me that I needed to call my buddy off. She wasn't likin' that I was handin' her this crap, makin' her out to be the bad guy in an attempt to steal our kids from her."

I stared up at him, dumbfounded, and asked, "What?"

He nodded shortly. "That's what the bitch said."

"Your buddy?"

"Coert," he bit off. "He's the sheriff and he's a friend of mine. Good friend. We've known each other awhile and we're pretty tight. But he wasn't the one who pulled her over. He *was* the one who didn't slap a DUI on her the last time she pulled that shit, because that was her first time, but also because he's my fuckin' *buddy*, but I'm guessin' she forgot that part."

"So...so..." I stammered. "So she's making this out to be you targeting her in an attempt to get custody of your children when you had nothing to do with her being picked up for drunk driving?"

His mouth got hard but he still forced through it, "That's what she's makin' it out to be. Called it my 'grand scheme.' Said her blood alcohol level was negligible, just over the edge, proves I'm out for her and roped Coert into that shit, and if they try to put that on her permanent record, she's fightin' it. Also said I started this scheme even before we split. Said if I didn't back down, stop maneuvering, she was gonna fight me tooth and nail. And she said if I tried to keep the kids from her, she'd have me arrested for kidnapping."

"Oh my God," I breathed.

"Yeah," he grunted.

Now I understood why he was so unhappy.

"Mickey," I grabbed his hand and held tight, "I don't know what to say."

"What's there to say?" he asked, lifting our hands and pressing mine against his heart as he shifted closer to me. "I'm stuck. Called Arnie again. The attorney?"

I nodded.

Mickey continued, "He said this is a case of declaring her unfit to raise our children. I'd have to call CPS. They'd have to inspect. I'd have to have evidence. I'd have to have witness testimony. The DUI on record is something but it isn't enough. And at the kids' ages, they're old enough to be deposed. They could get dragged in. Have to talk smack about their mother."

"It isn't smack if it's true," I shared carefully.

"You're right. But would you want your kids to sit with some fuck they don't know and share their dad is a cheating asshole?"

No, I would not want that.

I shook my head.

"No," he bit off. "So I got two choices, keep my kids from her and brace for whatever shit she throws at me. And she was pissed, Amy. She's got her back up and she's so deep in denial, it's a wonder she's breathing. Or let my kids go to her and wait for the other shoe to drop, maybe this bein' something that scars my kids in some *new* way I won't be able to heal."

I moved closer to him and pointed out the obvious, "You're between the rock and the hard place."

"I am. 'Cept I got one more option, this comin' from Arnie. Sit down with my kids and see if they wanna live with me, makin' 'em say they don't wanna live with their mom. And they might not wanna live with her, but I don't wanna *make* 'em share that shit."

No. That wasn't easy. I knew it. I wasn't with my children when they had to make that choice and say it out loud, but I'd seen the way they couldn't look at me afterward. The sorrow on their faces. It was agonizing.

And it was the beginning of my recovery.

Even though that would be promising in the case of Rhiannon, who clearly needed to be shaken out of her delusion, it was not something to take lightly.

"I would cautiously advise that's a last resort, honey," I told him.

"Yeah," he agreed.

"So, what are you thinking of doing?" I asked.

"Only one real choice," he answered. "Wait until she fucks up again. Keep track of shit. Keep an eye on my kids. I don't, I keep 'em away from her, she's gonna go at me and then they'll be dragged in and there'll be nothin' I can do to stop it."

Suddenly, I hated yet another person I'd never met.

I'd hated Martine before I even knew her name. I just knew my husband had fallen in love with someone else.

And now I hated Rhiannon.

"What do you need from me?" I asked.

"You, keepin' an eye on my kids. Droppin' by. Comin' around more often. Givin' Aisling a good woman to be with. Givin' my kids healthy."

I nodded. "I can do that."

"And I want you in my bed tonight."

My head jerked back and I blinked.

"But—"

He cut me off, "I'll get you home before they get up. Not a fan of sneakin' and won't ask you to do it often. But I had a shit day. I'm gearin' up to face a shit time I don't know how long it'll last or how bad it'll get. Right now, I wanna go in there and sit on my couch with you, relax, drink a beer then go to sleep smellin' your hair."

"I can do that too," I said immediately.

Then I held my breath as I watched Mickey close his eyes and turn to face the dark of his backyard.

I pushed closer, pressing my hand in his at his chest, and called, "Mickey."

He opened his eyes but kept them to the yard.

It took time and I gave him that time before he looked at me. "What if she gets behind the wheel with my kids in the car and she's shitfaced?"

"You talk to them," I answered firmly. "Do it trying not to bring Rhiannon into it. But Ash is a freshman. High school kids, they do stuff. They party. You could couch it in a warning they have to be smart about that, tell Cillian you're talking to him at the same time to save time or something, and you do this inflexibly so they get your meaning."

"They're not dumb. They'll get my meaning. My *whole* meaning, Amy."

Regrettably, I had a feeling they would.

"Then be certain they know at *any* time with *anyone*, if someone wants them to get in a car with a driver who's inebriated, then they can call you to come and get them and there will be no recriminations."

"My son doesn't have a phone," he told me. "Rule is, they gotta hit fourteen."

"Maybe you should break your rule, Dad," I said, giving him a weak grin and a weaker tease.

Mickey stared down at me, a muscle ticking in his cheek, unsurprisingly not ready to lighten the mood.

Then he growled, "Could strangle that bitch."

I pushed even closer.

"I thought I'd scarred my own kids beyond healing, honey," I told him. "And tonight my son came over of his own choice just to have dinner with his mom and watch TV. Proves you give them good, they'll respond. You said it yourself, they're not dumb. Yes, all this is terrible. But one day they'll see how hard you worked to give them safe and healthy, and they'll appreciate it. But you just *giving* them safe and healthy, you'll get them through."

Mickey again stared down at me for a while before he sighed, lifted his free hand, cupped the back of my head and pressed my cheek against his chest.

I wrapped my free arm around him and gave his hand in mine a squeeze.

I allowed us to stay that way for a bit before I pushed my head against his hand and looked up at him.

"Gotta get my guy a beer," I said softly.

He didn't respond except to bend his neck, touch his forehead to mine then he went in for a lip brush.

After that, he pulled away but kept hold of my hand.

We went inside. Mickey got a beer. We lazed on the couch while he drank it and we watched *Letterman*.

Then he closed down the house and silently, he guided me to his bed.

19

FLASH

I sucked hard at Mickey's thumb in my mouth and I did this so I wouldn't pant.

It was very early the next morning.

We were in Mickey's bed.

We were spooning.

Mickey had his face in my hair.

And I had my hips tilted, Mickey's finger at my clit, and I was taking his cock.

Suddenly, his thrusts increased in power and velocity, the pressure of his finger magnified, and his mouth was at my ear.

"Fuckin' get there, Amy," he growled.

He was close.

But I was too, and his growl shivered down my neck, my shoulder, across my breasts, belly, then gathered between my legs, and with his cock and his finger, I sucked his thumb deep and went soaring.

"Thank fuck," he gritted, buried his face in my neck, his cock deep and groaned against my skin.

I felt nothing but my orgasm and all that was Mickey, his heat, his strength, the power of his body tensed with his own orgasm.

Then mine glided from me and I relaxed against him and lapped at his thumb.

I knew his had left him too when he slid it out of my mouth and ran it along my lower lip.

His mouth came back to my ear. "You on the Pill?"

"Yes," I breathed against his thumb.

"You fuckin' anyone but me?"

I grinned at his ridiculous question.

"No."

"You trust I'm not takin' anyone but you?"

I felt my body stiffen because that was huge.

But this was Mickey.

So I whispered, "Yes."

His fingers at my jaw dug in and I knew he knew what I gave him was huge.

But he didn't dwell on it.

He asked, "Then you good with ungloved?"

"Yes, Mickey."

"Thank Christ," he muttered. "Condoms are history."

I relaxed into him, sliding a hand up his sinewy forearm and wrapping my fingers around his wrist.

He twisted it, caught my hand and pressed both gently to my throat.

He settled in and I felt his breath stir the top of my hair.

We lay connected for glorious moments before he said, "Thanks for stayin' the night."

"You need me, I'm here," I replied.

I heard the lightness in his tone when he went on, "Thanks for takin' my cock."

"You need me, I'm here," I repeated.

I felt his chuckle and squeezed his hand.

"My heiress wanna loaf in bed while I take a shower?"

I didn't know what my other choices were, other than get up, get dressed and go home before he had to get his kids up.

Or shower with him.

But truly, a waking-up-being-made-love-to-after-getting-about-five-hours-of-sleep orgasm was maybe the only thing that would encourage me to "loaf" in his bed rather than be naked with him in his shower.

"If I've got time, I'm gonna loaf."

"You got it," he murmured, kissed my shoulder then slid out of me and the bed.

He pulled the covers up before he walked to the bathroom.

I watched him walk to the bathroom, heard the toilet flush then the shower go on.

I'd been in his room once before, the night I spent there when my kids last left me. I didn't need to peruse it.

I knew it was nice. Manly. Rhiannon, if she'd ever been there in the decorating scheme, was g-o-n-e *gone* from there in a way it looked like she'd never existed.

His room, like mine, took up one whole end of his house. It included a big master bathroom toward the backyard that had a double basin, separate shower and the toilet was in its own little room. There was a walk-in closet, only one, but it was huge. The fixtures weren't old, it had been renovated and that was done sometime relatively recently. Perhaps not last year but if I had to guess, in the last five. If I didn't have the bathroom to beat all bathrooms and three trust funds that meant I could create any bathroom I wanted, it would have been amazing.

The walls of the bedroom were painted a slate gray that worked with the wood baseboards and amazing tongue and groove ceiling, the wood so dark it was nearly black. He had a fireplace too, one with a stone hearth like the others in his house. That was situated against the wall across from his king-sized, mission-style bed.

He had slate gray sheets that had a sateen sheen. He also had a duvet with a cover, his in dark gray with a hexagon pattern, the lines making the design burgundy.

Between bed and bathroom, there was a large hunk of floor space that he'd filled with two matching club chairs. They shared an ottoman, a sturdy but attractive end table and a standing lamp made in brass. The chairs were covered with clothes (apparently, Mickey didn't hit the laundry hamper with his clothes either, it looked like he hadn't done laundry since I met him).

It was clean, though not tidy, exceptionally masculine...and all Mickey.

I loved it.

So I lay happily tangled in his sheets in that room, still feeling Mickey between legs, loafing, snoozing and floating.

"Babe."

I wasn't asleep, exactly.

But my eyes were closed.

I opened them to see Mickey in clean work clothes standing beside the bed.

"Time for me to go?" I asked languidly.

"That, right there," he stated.

I studied him, unsure of his statement, his tone or the intense look on his face.

I began to push up and Mickey ordered, "Don't fuckin' move."

I stilled but held his gaze and whispered, "What's going on, Mickey?"

"I walked out of my bathroom to that every morning for sixteen years, no way in fuck I'd walk away from it."

I drew in a sharp breath and remained unmoving as that cut through me and I felt the release.

It wasn't a bleed.

It was like opening an aching blister to get the fetid ooze out.

"He doesn't know. He might never know," Mickey carried on. "But do *you* know how fuckin' stupid he is?"

"No," I replied. "But I do know how fucking lucky *I* am right now."

I watched his reaction to that flash in his eyes, but he remained distant until he took the last two steps to the bed and leaned over me.

He brushed the bangs out of my eyes and said softly, "Gotta get you up and dressed. I'll walk you home and come back and take care of my kids."

I nodded.

He let his fingers trail down my hairline before he straightened and walked away.

I got up, got dressed and Mickey walked me to my house.

He kissed me in my opened door.

And I watched him walk several steps away from me before I closed it behind him.

* * *

THE TEXT CAME MID-MORNING.

Can Polly and I come after school and hang?

Olympia.

I returned, *If you hang while doing your homework and getting some of these recorded shows off my DVR, then yes.*

She replied, *Deal. Pick us up?*

I thought of my car and while I did, I decided to buy an SUV.

Then I returned, *Sure, if we take turns. Can't fit you both in my car.*

To which I received, *You need a new car Mom. I'll ask Auden to bring us.*

I sent, *Do that, sweets. Am I making dinner?*

And got, *Dinner! Yummy!*

My kids liked my cooking. Then again, I cooked like a mom and could do that freely now that Conrad wasn't around.

I replied, *Dinner. Check.*

A few hours later, I got a text from Auden that said, *Drop Polly and Pip off after school. Pick them up at nine.*

To which I sent, *Thanks, kid. And I'm thinking of a Cayenne.*

And got back, *Land Rover. White. Totally you.*

I grinned.

Then I changed the girls' plans when they got there (a change of plans they were ecstatic about) and before homework and dinner, we went out and test-drove Land Rovers.

———— • ————

"YOU BUY A FUCKIN' CAR WITHOUT ME, AMY, IT'S GONNA PISS ME OFF," Mickey said in my ear.

My daughter and her friend were gone. It was late. Now, I was in bed saying goodnight over the phone to Mickey.

I'd also, obviously, shared my plans to purchase a new vehicle.

"Do you want to test-drive it?" I asked.

"I want you not to get fucked over buying it," he answered.

"Mickey, car salesmen hardly screw over women anymore," I scoffed. "They freely screw over everybody."

"You're wrong, Amy."

"It's not 1968, Mickey."

"Right, you go in, get the best deal you think you can get, then walk away. I'll go in after and get the best deal I can get, text you, you come in and we'll see about that shit."

"You're on," I snapped.

"Tomorrow?"

"Perfect."

"You pissed?" he asked.

"Yes," I answered.

"Because you know you're goin' down," he declared.

"Whatever," I mumbled.

He chuckled.

I changed the subject. "The kids okay?"

"Tonight, we had the drunk driving talk. They got me as in *got me*. Tomorrow, before I show you car salesmen are still assholes, I'm goin' in and havin' all my teeth pulled without Novocain. Figure that'll be a whole lot more fun."

"Oh, Mickey," I said quietly.

"It's done. They get me. All I can do. Movin' on," he stated.

"Okay," I said and decided it was time to change the subject again. "So, I was thinking, the kids coming over and things going better, this keeps up for a little while, when they both say they're coming over together, I can tell them about you. Then, the next time they're over together, you'll be here. We can see how it goes when they get here. A quick meet and greet or you casually stay for dinner."

"Let me know, I gotta rearrange some shit, I'll do it."

He'd rearrange some shit for a chance to meet my kids.

And again I was floating.

"Thanks, honey," I whispered.

"No problem, Amy. Now hate to cut this short, but wanna check on Ash. She's been quieter than her normal lately and has been in her room all night. Gotta check on my girl."

That didn't sound good at all.

But it wasn't surprising.

"Okay, I'll let you go."

"Sleep tight, babe."

"I will, Mickey. See you tomorrow."

"Yeah. And plan to be over for dinner. We'll get your car, come back and hang out."

I couldn't wait.

"Sounds good. 'Night, honey."

"'Night, baby."

We hung up. I read a bit.

Then I went to sleep.

———————— • ————————

MICKEY WAS RIGHT.

Car salesmen still screwed over women more than men. He got my Land Rover (I got black, Auden would just have to deal) for several thousand less than I could negotiate the deal.

Cillian and Aisling came with us and hung with me while I tried my hand at the negotiations. I asked for their company because I thought this was added incentive—kids in the mix—that would make the salesmen less inclined to screw me.

I was wrong.

Cillian gloated with his dad.

Through this and all the time I spent with her that day, I found Mickey was right, but it was more.

Aisling was quieter than normal to the point that she was unusually sullen.

It also looked like she wasn't washing her hair.

This alarmed me.

But I didn't have a chance to say anything about it until after we had dinner, Ash had retreated to her room and closed the door, and Cill had commandeered the TV to play some game on Xbox.

This forced Mickey and me to lounge on the loveseat on the deck in our jackets.

"She's not good," I noted.

"Nope," Mickey replied, rocking the loveseat with me beside him, curled into him, legs up under me, one of his arms around me, the other hand around the neck of a bottle of a beer he took a tug from after he answered.

"Does she open up to you?" I asked.

"Got no clue how to talk to an almost fifteen-year-old girl with a drunk for a mom," he replied.

"Is she...does she have *moods*?" I pressed carefully.

"If you mean, has she started her period? Then yes," he told me. "That happened last summer. Her mom took care of that. She comes home with boxes of shit Rhiannon gets her. I saw Midol on her dresser, made sure there was more in the bathroom. Didn't have any sisters but did have a wife for fourteen years, so I got a clue when those kinds of moods strike. Ash gets 'em. This is not one of those."

"I'm not sure I'm at that place where it's okay for me to talk to her," I noted.

"I hear you," he muttered.

"But we can keep an eye on the situation and if she doesn't open up to you, regardless if I'm at that place, if you want me to, I'll go in."

His arm tightened around me, tucking me closer. "That'd be good."

He wanted me to.

That made me snuggle even closer.

I did that and took a sip of my wine before I asked, "Do you think they know what's happening with you and me?"

"On the deck havin' a drink with you and you're over a lot. Close with the Gettys that live next door because they moved in when I was eight and never left. They're welcome here any time. The kids love 'em. But I don't walk them home, sit close to them on the couch or out on my deck at night, havin' a beer."

"Do you think that's what's troubling her?" I went on, even though, in the early stages, she seemed to hope her dad and I would get together.

"Again, no clue," he said.

"You want to meet my kids, Mickey, perhaps you should think on sharing what's happening with Cill and Ash in an official way," I suggested. "If it's out in the open, you can discuss it with her."

"Great. My Sunday plans look only slightly better than my Friday night plans did."

I grinned, lifted my head from his shoulder and looked to his jaw. "It's not like we're not used to this road being rocky."

He didn't look down at me.

He said to the dark night, "You're right. The fuck of it is, you grow up thinkin' things are gonna be a certain way and then they end up mostly fucked with moments of decent and flashes of really fuckin' good."

I snuggled my cheek to his shoulder, hating that.

Mickey had a boss he did not respect, a job he didn't like doing that bought him taking a lot of complaints from angry people about decisions he did not make.

He'd had a wife he loved who'd become an alcoholic right before his eyes. He lost her and now she was making him live in fear for his kids not only when they were with her but what her effect was on them when they weren't.

He needed to become fire chief.

He needed to get his business off the ground.

And Rhiannon needed to sort herself out.

As for me, I needed to do what I could to give Mickey as many flashes of really fucking good as I could.

Mickey read my mood but he read it wrong.

"Sorry, baby, you don't need my bitching."

"Actually, I do," I returned. "Because if you don't lay it on me, it'll eat you up inside and your kids need you whole, standing and fighting. So I'll take whatever you got. It isn't hard. So you have that and you have what you need to take care of your babies."

Mickey was silent and the night was still. This lasted so long it made me tense.

"Mickey?"

"Sixteen years. Fuck, that asshole blew it."

I relaxed against him.

"I spoiled our kids," I admitted. "Gave them everything they wanted."

"Yeah, got a dose of that," he returned.

"Conrad didn't like it. He talked to me. I didn't listen."

"God, fuck, sorry. You're right. It's a wonder your kids are functioning instead of in inpatient therapy. Now I get it. You spoiled your kids. That guy had every reason to step out on you."

There was lightness to his voice but just to be sure, I asked, "Are you joking?"

"Fuck yeah, Amy. Shit," he answered, his voice shaking.

I pressed my cheek into his chest and also started shaking.

Then audibly giggling.

Mickey audibly chuckled with me.

When I stopped, I lifted my glass and took a sip of wine.

When Mickey stopped, he did the same with his beer.

We fell silent and sat in the dark.

But I did it hoping it was one of Mickey Donovan's moments of decent.

Or maybe even a hint of a flash of happy.

———————•———————

THE NEXT AFTERNOON, MY PHONE ON MY KITCHEN COUNTER RANG.

I saw it was Mickey calling and I snatched it up, glanced at my landing, saw the TV on and bits of both my kids' limbs. Neither of them looked my way, so casually, I took the call while walking to the hall and heading toward my bedroom.

"Hey," I answered.

"Hey back. Havin' a good day?"

"I think so, although I'm a little concerned about what appears to be evidence that suggests my kids have a serious television habit."

"They're there again?"

I made it to my room, silently shut the door and went to my bed to sit on it, saying, "Yes. It's Sunday but they texted this morning around ten, were here within the hour. We had lunch. We took the Rover out for a spin. And we're having dinner."

"This is good, Amy."

"It is, Mickey. So good. Amazingly good. But a little freaky."

"Kids watch TV, babe."

"I know. But something about this isn't right."

"How's that?"

"One minute they're barely speaking to me. And it wasn't like the next minute they were. We worked up to it, got over the hump, skidded down the other side." I crossed my legs under me on my bed. "But now we're speeding. They're here a lot and I *want* them here a lot. I want them here for good. I'd take them here forever. But there's something about this change that makes me think that either they're escaping their dad's or Martine is perpetuating cruel and unusual punishment by not allowing two teenage kids to DVR *anything*."

"Maybe they saw they were bein' hard on you and they're tryin' to make up for it," he suggested.

"Maybe," I mumbled.

"Go with it. Build on it. And just have this good without makin' it dark when you don't know if there's anything to worry about."

That was good advice.

"I'll do that."

"Good," he said. "Now, speaking of kids."

"Oh boy," I muttered.

"Yeah. Ash and Cill know their friend and next door neighbor, Amy, is Dad's girlfriend."

The girlfriend again.

It felt nice again.

But I was still braced.

"And?" I prompted.

"Cill's cool with it. Not straight up, he looks after his mom, had questions about what this means for me and his mom and it wasn't real fun to share that there was not ever gonna be a me and his mom again. He came to terms with it without throwin' a shit fit, which was a surprise but it was good. Ash didn't have much of a reaction except to say, 'No kidding, Dad?' which started to set Cill off because he thought she knew something he didn't know and he isn't big on that."

"But it's all okay now?"

"Woulda had you over for dinner tonight, but don't think spendin' the day with you yesterday then havin' you back tonight would be good. But I do think, if we keep easin' them into it, they'll get there."

I smiled at the phone. "That's good."

"So, tomorrow and Tuesday, I'm at the firehouse. That means phone on your nightstand."

"Right," I agreed, still smiling.

"Wednesday, your kids aren't with you, I'm takin' you to dinner and a movie."

Me and Mickey in a dark movie theater.

That sounded fantastic.

"I'd love that, Mickey," I told him. "But we're taking my Land Rover."

"Fine. I drive."

"You drive?" I asked. "But it's mine."

"I strike you as a man who rides?"

"Jimbo drives the fire truck," I pointed out.

"Jimbo doesn't have a vagina."

My back shot straight. "Really?"

"Your ass is in my Expedition in the passenger seat or in the same place in your Rover," he declared.

"It's a new car, Mickey. I love it. It took everything I had to allow Auden to take it for a spin today. I wanna drive."

"Drive around the next coupla days. Wednesday night, you know your choice."

He was lucky he was so fabulous for the times when he was *so* annoying.

"You need to get checked," I snapped. "You clearly have an overabundance of testosterone in a way it's harmful to your health."

"Not sure that can even happen," he replied smoothly.

"The harmful to your health part is me murdering you."

"You take me out, it's back to that toy in your nightstand and I'm thinkin' you don't want that."

My head twitched as I asked, "Have you been snooping?"

"Single woman who goes hot quick, babe, took a guess, I was right and I don't consider it snooping. More like investigating just in case I'm in the mood to shake things up. Any man has gotta have the tools he needs to get the job done."

That gave me a shiver along with the premonition of an aneurysm.

"Amy?" he called when I didn't respond.

"Quiet. I'm trying to think if I've seen any Internet cafés I can go to to anonymously order poison off the Web."

"Toy comes out tomorrow night," he muttered.

Another shiver.

"Are you done annoying me?" I asked.

His smile was in his voice. "For now."

"Fine. See you tomorrow night."

"Charge it up, Amy."

God, he couldn't be believed.

The problem was I was thinking I loved that about him.

Along with a variety of other things.

"Whatever. Have a good night."

"'Night, baby."

With the call with Mickey done for the night, I tossed the phone on my bed and went back out to my kids.

———————•———————

"Yes," I breathed, I came, Mickey slid my vibrator away and then he slid inside me. "*Yes,*" I repeated.

We were on our sides, face to face and I had my leg thrown over Mickey's hip. Even though it lasted a good long while, Mickey let me finish coming before he kissed me, fucked me and again sent me flying.

Condoms being history, after, it was me cleaning up, slipping on a nightie and back into bed with Mickey where he tangled us together and held me close in the dark.

I was snuggled deep, warmed by his body, replete and half asleep before he spoke.

"See, my heiress likes the way I shake things up."

I opened my eyes and saw his shadowed throat.

"Shut up, Mickey."

"Think I'm a year older, you came so long."

I tipped my head back and glared at him through the dark.

"Shut *up*, Mickey."

He bent his head and kissed me. It lasted longer than my orgasm, *a lot* longer and ended with us tangled up tight, his hand on my behind and me pressed so close it was like I wanted him to absorb me.

"Now, go to sleep, baby," he ordered when he stopped kissing me.

I tucked my face back in his throat and told him, "You're most annoying."

"Good you get off on that."

He was correct.

I decided silence was in order.

I was as close as I could be without Mickey being inside me.

He still pulled me closer.

"Flash," he whispered.

"What?" I asked sleepily but still managed to inject tartly.

"Of really fuckin' happy."

I wasn't going to cry.

I was *not* going to cry.

I didn't cry.

I pushed even closer, kissed my guy's throat and whispered, "'Night, honey."

"'Night, Amy."

I closed my eyes, settled into Mickey, and experiencing my own flash, I fell asleep.

———————•———————

MICKEY AND I WERE ON OUR WAY BACK FROM THE MOVIE WHEN HE SAID, "Both your kids came to you last night, so I talked to a coupla buds. They're good with bein' on call should I need them at the firehouse."

He had my hand in his resting on my thigh and he was stroking the side with his thumb.

He also was gently reminding me he wanted to meet my kids.

I liked that but I was nervous about it.

"Next time they come again together, I'll give them the talk," I promised.

We'd already had the dating discussion and they were absolutely not under the impression their father and I would get back together.

But Mickey was right. Although I didn't see them on Monday, they both came over after school the day before and stayed well past dinner. And they didn't even watch a program they DVRed. We all watched a movie on HBO together.

And it was good. It was easy. It was normal. It was what we had three years ago and it was this way like those three years hadn't happened.

Of course, Auden and I had our brief discussion and it wasn't a surprise that Olympia didn't address it. She shied away from confrontation (except when she was fighting with her brother). Not only her own but others. Something that made what I did make me feel even guiltier because she'd seen a lot of that between Conrad, Martine and me.

She wouldn't broach it. She'd let it lie and move on.

And Mickey was also right that I should rejoice, build on it, let it be and not worry.

But I was a mother, and as removed from my children as I was, I knew them.

Something else was happening.

Until my last breath I wanted them to feel I was their safe harbor.

I just wanted to know, if that's why they needed me, what I was harboring them from.

Mickey drove to my place, hit the garage door opener and drove right in. I sat beside him, taking my mind from my thoughts by thinking my house was perfect. In that moment, I was thinking that because it had a two-car garage as well as a smaller one-car one next to it that you could get to with its own opener and through a door from the bigger one to the smaller one inside.

The one-car one was perfect for my Mercedes.

The Rover and my son's Civic got the big one.

See?

Perfect.

He parked. We got out. We went in.

I was wandering to the kitchen, flipping on the pendant lights, asking Mickey, "Do you want a beer?" when the doorbell rang.

I stopped and looked to it.

Mickey, a few paces behind me, had also stopped and he was twisted to it.

The outdoor light was on and I knew the body shaded in the glass.

Conrad.

What was he doing here at this hour?

Or at all?

"Shit, that's Conrad," I whispered.

Mickey stayed twisted toward the door, but slowly, his head turned to me.

I caught his look, which meant I caught my breath, and that was unfortunate because I had to focus on breathing and was too late in *acting*.

This meant Mickey was swiftly prowling toward the door before I got my body to move and my mouth to call, "Mickey, let me."

He stopped at the door, aimed that dangerous look at me and said one word.

"No."

Then he turned back to the door, unlocked it and threw it open.

I was five feet away but had a good view of Conrad on my doorstep scowling up at Mickey.

"You do not get to do this," Mickey growled as I got to him, pressed to the side of his back and put a hand to its small.

Before I could say a word, Conrad looked to me.

"Call your Neanderthal off, Amelia."

Mickey went solid beside me and I was right there with him.

"Don't speak about Mickey that way," I snapped.

"Why?" Conrad bit back. "You felt free to aim your venom at Martine."

"Yeah, but she isn't fuckin' me with your ring on her finger. You got no leg to stand on with that one so get past it, asshole," Mickey ground out.

Conrad turned angry eyes to Mickey. "You have no idea what you're talking about."

"I do and part of what I know is your woman knew you had to scrape off your wife before she got her own ring from you so she doesn't have a leg to stand on either," Mickey returned. "Now, again, get past it and if you got somethin' to say, say it and then get the fuck outta here."

Conrad looked back to me. "This man doesn't know me, he has no call to curse at me."

"Man, you're here at ten at night uninvited and unwanted and you rang the bell the minute we got in, so you been layin' in wait for your attack," Mickey shot back. "I opened the door and you brought it. You brought it and blew any respect you *might* have gotten from me. This isn't your home. You got no rights in this situation. And advice. Fuckin' grow a pair. No call to curse at you?" he taunted. "Fuckin' sissy."

Conrad's face was hard and his fury was palpable when he turned that to me.

"I'll thank you to adhere to the custody agreement ordered by the judge," he stated.

"I'm not kidnapping the kids and forcing them to watch TV here, Conrad," I replied. "They ask to come. This is their home. They can come anytime they please."

"If they're asking to come, as ordered by the court, you should explain you've got them one weekend a month and you'll see them then."

What a pompous ass.

And further, it could not be believed that he actually *wanted* to keep our children away from their mother when *they* wanted to spend time with me.

God! How had I ever been in love with this man?

"I can't say I read every word, Conrad," I retorted. "But I don't think it says anywhere in the court documents that if the children wish to spend additional time with me, I'm not allowed to let them do that."

"I'll have my attorneys scour them and if that's not the case, perhaps I'll move to see them amended," Conrad volleyed.

"You do that," I invited.

"You don't want to go in front of the judge again, Amelia," he warned.

"You're wrong," I told him. "I so do. I really, really do."

"You have a very short memory," he sneered.

"I could say the same thing," I returned.

"What? A few months of behaving yourself? That won't go very far," he scoffed.

"I'm sorry, my mistake. I'll take one moment to mention that it actually *hasn't* been *a few months*, but over *a year*. But to the point, it isn't just your short-term memory that's lacking. It's your long-term."

"My relationship with Martine is no longer a weapon you can use against me," he declared.

"Perhaps. Though, her and Gail Conway might get me somewhere."

Gail Conway, the instigator of the sexual harassment suit in Lexington and a woman who had since moved on but who still very much disliked Dr. Conrad Moss.

Conrad blanched.

Bulls-eye.

"If that isn't enough, I'll add Hillary Schmidt," I went on.

Ms. Schmidt did not file a suit, but she wasn't too happy Conrad slam-bam-thank-you-ma'am'ed her while he was also wooing Martine, this going on for *six months*.

I couldn't say I was overjoyed to see the fear flash across his face.

But it didn't suck.

"And Erin McIntyre," I kept going.

Obviously, I'd had a report from my attorney.

And he had a very good investigator.

"I would refrain from trying to get to them," I advised. "They've already agreed to be deposed. Jumped at the chance, actually. They aren't real big fans of yours."

His face twisted and, really, how had I ever been in love with him?

"So this is your new tactic?" he bit out.

"No. This is *your* warning," I replied. "You do not keep my children away from me. You allow them to come when they please," still standing close to Mickey, I leaned into Conrad, "without one *peep*." I leaned back. "And when I speak to them about making that a regular thing, suggest sharing custody and they agree, you'll not only also agree, you'll fucking *champion* it. Other than that, you'll keep your mouth *shut*. You'll also keep your wife's mouth shut. Or we *will* be back in front of a judge, Conrad. But this time, I'll *eviscerate* you."

"The Hathaway comes out," he sniped.

"At least they gave me something," I fired back.

"You'll regret this, Amelia," he threatened.

On this, clearly, not liking me being threatened, Mickey shifted a little so he was between Conrad and me.

When he did this, I fell a little more in love with Mickey Donovan.

And I was falling in love.

Tumbling.

Head over feet.

Unfortunately, I couldn't feel all the goodness of that. Conrad was there being an ass.

"Too late," I replied. "I'm already deep in regret that I wasted twenty-two years on you when you weren't worth a minute." I delivered that, peering around Mickey's arm to do it.

"You're done," Mickey stated right after I was done speaking and right when Conrad opened his mouth to retort.

Conrad's eyes jerked to Mickey.

Then he jerked them right back to me. "You share any of the dirt you dug up on me with our children—"

"I could bang my chest and drag you to your truck by your throat," Mickey suggested and Conrad's eyes flew back to him. "That way, you might get me."

"You touch me, I press charges," he warned.

Mickey looked down at me. "I feel some grunts comin' on. You wanna go get my club?"

I started giggling.

"Fuck you," Conrad spat.

Mickey looked to him and lifted his brows. "Now who's cursing?"

Conrad looked ready to explode but he had no choice but to scowl, turn and stomp away.

Mickey backed up and with our proximity he took me with him. He shut the door and locked it.

He then turned and again looked down at me.

"Babe. Seriously. You're a fun date."

I burst out laughing.

While I kept doing it, Mickey's arms stole around me.

I put my hands to his chest, slid them up and curled them around the sides of his neck.

However, when I sobered, I saw Mickey didn't find anything funny.

"You okay?" he asked.

"Yep," I answered.

He studied me closely.

I snuggled into him and assured, "I'm fine, Mickey."

"He's not a dick, Amy. He's a motherfucking *dick*."

"Yep," I repeated.

He looked to the door and back to me. "You gonna get any blowback from that?"

I shrugged. "I have no idea. If I do, I'll deal. He's already done his worst, I survived and now I'm standing in my fabulous house in a magnificent man's arms. He no longer has any weapons that could harm me."

His arms convulsed on "magnificent man," but when I was done talking, he warned, "Watch your shit with that guy. He's a man with a little dick but he still likes to swing it."

I hadn't really thought about it but having a man as endowed as Mickey, it occurred to me this was quite accurate.

"I'll watch my shit," I promised.

"Good," he muttered then asked, "We done with that?"

"Yeah, Mickey."

He was back to muttering. "Excellent." He let me go, grabbed my hand and tugged me across the landing, announcing, "You owe me a hard fuck on that weird couch by your fireplace, baby."

I absolutely did.

"It's a daybed," I informed him.

"Whatever. It's sturdy."

I thought it was fabulously stylish but Mickey wasn't wrong.

It was sturdy.

I knew this already but Mickey and I put it to the test.

It passed.

20

COMPARING DICKS

*T*he next day, feeling proud of myself, I walked out of Bertram's Electronics Store phoning Mickey.

"Hey, baby," he answered.

"Hey, guess what?" I replied.

"Don't know but I hope whatever it is is good."

I grinned as I beeped the locks on my Rover. "It isn't good. It's fantastic."

"Right, then lay it on me," he said with a smile in his voice.

"Tomorrow, someone in the firehouse needs to be available to accept delivery on a new microwave."

Mickey didn't say anything so I was open to give him the grand finale.

"And a sixty inch flat screen TV!" I cried, pulling open the door to my SUV.

"Don't know what to say," he muttered, not sounding nearly as happy as I expected him to be.

I hauled myself up into the driver's seat and closed the door, suggesting, "You could say, 'That's awesome, Amy!'"

"That's awesome, Amy," he repeated after me, doing it by rote.

"Um…did you hear the part about the TV being sixty inches?" I asked, confused by his reaction.

"I did. And I hesitate to get into this with my heiress, but I gotta ask. The folks at Bertram's donate that shit?"

I stared at my windshield.

"Amy?" he called.

"I didn't buy it, Mickey," I told him. "You asked me not to."

"Just bein' sure," he told me.

"They donated it," I confirmed, feeling deflated.

He heard the deflation and explained, "It just seems too easy, baby. You get a wild hair, go to a store and, just like that, they donate an expensive TV?"

"Well, not *just like that*," I replied. "They did remember me from when I came in months ago and bought a bunch of stuff. Your firefighters on duty will also need to stand in front of the TV and shake hands with the delivery guys so they can take a photo to put up in the front of their store. I also got them to donate one to Dove House and Dela and some of the residents have to do the same thing."

"I hope you get I had to ask," he said.

"I'm not sure why," I returned. "You told me you didn't want me purchasing it, I didn't purchase it. You told me it's okay to get it donated, I got it donated."

"Been played before, babe," he said, his tone moving from careful to irritated.

"So you've dated another heiress who rained goodness on your fire-house?" I asked sarcastically. "Sorry, I didn't see the evidence of that when I was there. Or did she purchase the rig?"

"In this conversation there's no call for you to be a smartass, Amelia. You know real fuckin' well I had a wife who descended into a bottle, and shit like that happens, games are played. She took cash outta our bank account so she could buy wine without me seein' the credit card receipts when I did the reconciliations. She fed me bullshit about where she was and what she was doin'—"

I interrupted him to declare, "You're not Conrad and I'm not Rhiannon."

"Asked a simple question, Amelia."

"A question that was offensive, *Michael*."

"Right, that picture gets taken I know I can trust you and I won't have to ask again."

I gritted my teeth, which meant my next sounded forced.

"Regardless of the fact that my husband was a cheat, our marriage still disintegrated and *you* know that I spent a lot of time agonizing over that. Including thinking on what *I* could have done to make it go wrong. In my case, I found out later that it was the simple fact my husband was a cheat. But looking back, there were things that were important to him that he communicated to me that I ignored. Feel free to feel elated that *you* have the Amelia Hathaway that learned that lesson and isn't about to make the same mistake again."

"You sayin' I had a hand in my wife fucking our marriage?" he asked incredulously.

I made a disbelieving sound and answered, "I'm talking about *me*, Mickey. *You and me.*"

He was done with our conversation and shared this by stating, "I got shit to do and part of that shit is not fightin' with you."

"Then I'll let you go," I shot back. "You and the boys enjoy your *donated* microwave and TV. Good-bye, Mickey."

"Later," he bit off and hung up on me.

I stared at the electronics store through my windshield, gave a moment's thought to how all that could have gone so bad and came up with one answer: Mickey. Then I emitted a muted, frustrated scream.

After that, I started up my new Rover and drove away.

———————— • ————————

IT WAS LATE. I WAS IN MY BATHROOM IN MY NIGHTIE, CLEANING MY FACE when the doorbell rang.

I looked to the mirror, grabbed my hand towel, dried my face and nabbed my robe off its hook before I walked out.

I wanted not to answer.

But unfortunately I was grown up.

I was home. He probably knew I was home. So it was mean-spirited not to answer.

I swung the robe on as I walked down the hall and inspected the body shadowed in the stained glass before I went to the door, opened it and looked up at Mickey in his firefighter-not-fighting-a-fire uniform.

"Can I help you?" I asked coldly.

"I'm a dick," he replied.

Unfortunately, as I'd spent the day gearing up to hold a Robin-style grudge against him (the new Robin, the one who held a grudge for twenty-four hours, not eternity), his words delivered a direct hit to that determination.

I held on to enough to share, "You can be."

"We both been through the wringer. You got shit left over to process and get past with your ex. I do too."

He was correct about that and my determination took another hit.

This time, I decided on no reply.

His brows went up. "Gonna make me stand on your doorstep sayin' this shit?"

"You have an ongoing issue with my wealth, Mickey," I informed him.

"Workin' on that," he informed me, but he didn't deny it.

He might be working on it but he was obviously failing.

"I am who I am. I have what I have. And frankly, before things progress further between us, we need to discuss it so this doesn't fester in a way that it wreaks devastation at a later date."

"Agreed, but I'm takin' a break from the house to come do this so I don't have the time to do that now."

"We'll schedule that meeting," I said tartly.

His face softened as did his tone when he replied, "Amy, let me in. Let me give you a kiss. And let me go knowin' you're good and we'll sort this out when we got time."

I was no match for Mickey's soft looks.

So I sighed as I reached out, bunched his t-shirt in my hand and pulled him in.

He made it easy and, once close, wrapped his arms around me, bent his neck and I lifted up on tiptoes to offer my mouth.

His kiss was deep and sweet and when he broke it, he lifted a hand to sweep the hair off my shoulder before curling his hand around the side of my neck.

"Phone by your bed," he murmured.

"Okay," I replied.

He looked relieved and it was troubling that we'd had the fight we had and the possible reasons behind it that I experienced deep relief just seeing his relief.

"See you later tonight."

"Okay, Mickey."

He gave me a squeeze, let me go and walked out of my house.

I was watching as well as closing the door when I stopped because he did and he turned.

"I am who I am. I have what I have. And one of the things I got that I wanna keep is you."

I licked my lips, pressed them together and held his eyes.

"We'll sort it, baby," he finished.

I nodded.

"Sleep good," he said.

"Stay alert," I replied.

He smiled, lifted a hand, turned and walked to his truck.

I closed the door thinking I knew top on the list of things that could kill a relationship was money.

And the kind of money that sat between Mickey and me was serious.

And Mickey was the kind of man that was Mickey.

I liked that he wanted to keep me. I wanted to keep him.

I just worried that one day something that was obviously disturbing him because he brought it up so frequently would make him rethink that.

I WAS ON MY KNEES, FACE IN THE PILLOWS, TAKING MICKEY'S COCK, DOING it moaning and whimpering.

He was giving it to me hard and rough.

He'd arrived after his shift at the firehouse and it had been what it always was. I opened the door; it started insanely good and progressed even better.

But this time, it was different.

Mickey didn't talk much during sex, but I said things.

Both of us were silent.

But still, something was being communicated.

I didn't get it and I had my mind on other, vastly more pleasant things, so I didn't attempt to figure it out.

But I felt it.

Mickey knew what he wanted in bed. This was commanded sometimes verbally but mostly physically. He let me do things. He let me take things from him. But mostly he guided it and I followed his lead. He could get rough. He was strong enough to move me around, position me, so far as arrange me. We made love and there was always a sense of the tenderness to that, even when we were fucking.

Now, we were fucking.

But we were just *fucking*.

It was rough, fast, connected physically (obviously) yet disconnected emotionally, close and distant and there was something about it that was freeing at the same time vaguely alarming.

I couldn't think on that either, whether it was good or bad how completely I was getting off on it.

I couldn't think because I was close, reaching for it, when Mickey pulled out, flipped me, ran his hands up the backs of my thighs, positioning them up his chest. Then he clamped his fingers on my hips and reentered me.

I dug my heels into his shoulders and was powerless to do anything but watch his face, his eyes, hard and dark and stormy, as he fucked me.

He watched me too, his gaze moving over me, then he bent his neck and watched his cock thrust into me.

When he did, his hips started pistoning.

And when his hips did that, I lifted my arms up and pushed against the headboard so I could drive myself into his thrusts.

Digging my head in the pillows, eyes closed and focus entirely on taking his cock, loving what he was doing to me, I was losing it at the same time I was losing the disconnection and distance.

It again became Mickey and me connecting in every way this could be, becoming what was always but *always* perfect between Mickey and me, and I begged, "Yes, baby, *fuck me.*"

He fucked me harder.

"*God, yes, Mickey. Fuck me,*" I moaned.

I was there again, nearly soaring, when he pulled out and whipped me back around so I was on my belly. He lifted me up with an arm wrapped around the chest, walked us forward on our knees and let me go to grip me tight on the inside upper thighs at either side of my sex.

He pulled me up, I tilted my hips, he drove back in and I grasped onto the headboard with both hands.

He shifted a finger and tweaked my clit.

That was it, taking his cock, feeling that touch, experiencing the power of Mickey, my body started spasming as I cried, "Mickey!" and then I took flight.

His grunts filled the room as he went at me harder, faster, his finger still pressing my clit and rolling.

"*Baby,*" I panted, still coming.

He kept at me.

"*Mickey,*" I pleaded, not knowing why and still coming.

His grunts became physical things against the skin of my neck and my body started shuddering.

I was still coming as he spoke.

"You had it this good?" he growled in my ear.

"No," I gasped.

"You ever had it this good, Amy?"

His question was about more than our fucking.

I gave him the truth.

"Never, Mickey," I rasped.

His finger at my clit moved, his hand sliding up so he could wrap his arm around my belly, he drove me down on his cock and groaned against my neck, "Fuckin' right, Amy."

I kept coming through his orgasm because he had it grinding into me. Finally I started gliding, soft pants whispering past my lips and I felt Mickey coming down with me.

I shifted and he surprised me by ordering roughly, "Don't move."

I stilled.

He slid his knees between my legs, settled me in his lap, still connected, and lifted his arm to wrap it around my chest, holding me to him there and at my belly, his breath warm on the skin of my shoulder.

"I can't give you much, but I can give you this," he stated thickly.

"Mickey, no—" I started, his words cutting deep, their meaning that all he had to give was good orgasms very much not sitting well with me.

"Shut it, baby, and listen," he said and since his tone was tender, I let the words slide and did as he asked.

"I made the decision to be my own man a long time ago but that man is based on the man my father taught me to be. I'm a provider. And it isn't lost on you that I'm strugglin' with the fact that I'll never be in a position to provide for you."

Oh God.

"Mi—"

His arms gave me a squeeze. "Amy, shut it."

I closed my mouth.

"But I can give you this," he said.

"You're more than just a fuck, Mickey," I snapped.

"Baby," he shoved his face in my neck and tightened his arms around me, "*feel*."

I felt Mickey holding me, Mickey all around me, Mickey inside me.

I still didn't get it.

"Honey—"

He again cut me off, "Tonight, you gonna sleep alone?"

I closed my eyes and relaxed in his hold.

I got it.

He felt it.

"Yeah, Amy. This is what I got to give. This progresses, your money, we're gonna have to have ground rules. But whatever those are, however we work it out, the way this feels with you even after I fucked up, forced a stupid fight, hurt your feelings, what we got, you can only get it from me. Even disconnected, we connected. Even upset, you opened your door to me. Twice. Means what we got means somethin' to you and no matter what obstacles we face or put up ourselves, you're gonna work on it with me. I just gotta come to terms with the fact that all I'd want to give you, I can't give. But you got something from me that you want and you can only get it from me."

Suddenly, a future with Mickey struck me with blinding clarity.

I had Cliff Blue. I'd paid for it in cash. I'd made it all me.

But Mickey lived in his childhood home he worked hard to keep. It was older, more worn, more lived in, friendlier, more welcoming. It was a family home in a very good neighborhood.

My home was a multi-million dollar show home that I'd made suitable for a family.

If this worked, if we had a future, the decision would have to be made and Mickey wouldn't want to give up his home, where he grew up, a home he worked a job he hated to provide for his children, and then move them all in with me.

That was just the beginning. Life was life but some of the ways life could sock it to you, I would never feel.

If I had a leak in my roof, I'd hire someone to fix it. If a storm washed half of Cliff Blue into the sea (God forbid), I wouldn't blink at rebuilding in so far as flying Prentice Cameron from Scotland to oversee it was done correctly.

There were birthdays and Christmases and special occasions where I'd have to curb my generosity and my ability to give it. And if we blended families, this would not only be for him and his children, but to keep things fair, my children as well.

And each time, he'd know. He'd feel it. He'd understand to keep an even keel, my kids would feel it.

And that would eat at him.

It was then I understood why people like me partnered with people like me. Why my mother drilled it into my head at every opportunity just what kind of man I needed to find.

Conrad had fit that bill not only because he was a neurosurgeon who made an excellent salary, but because he came from money. His family was not as wealthy as mine but they were far from hurting. Like me, he'd lived a privileged life and had his own trust fund. He started his practice without crippling student loans to repay because his parents had paid for every penny of his education.

Before I made the decision to move on with Mickey, I needed to know down to my soul that I could give him what he needed and I could accept what he could give me.

It was then I thought of waking up in his bed in his masculine bedroom in his family house in a very nice neighborhood, doing it with Mickey making love to me.

Sure, his fireplace was not as stylish as mine and my daybed would not match his furniture.

But I'd go to sleep in Mickey's bed with Mickey and wake up with Mickey. A Mickey I hoped was falling in love with me. A Mickey who would never cheat on me. A Mickey who teased me and annoyed me and got me deals on cars I didn't need because I could afford to overpay. A Mickey who protected me, and even when we were fighting and the sex started rough and distant, it was fabulous and we ended up connected in more ways than just physically.

I had had the partner I was supposed to have and he nearly destroyed me.

And it shook me tremendously to understand that if the good I got from Mickey kept going, got better, I'd give up everything to keep it.

This shook me because the problem with all of that was convincing Mickey to believe it and getting him past any concerns he had about sacrifices I was willing to make to have a man at my side who truly cared, who looked out for me, who I enjoyed annoying me, who made me laugh, made me happy and who was phenomenal in bed.

"Amy," he called when I didn't speak.

"Do you understand that will always be just what I need?" I asked.

"I think that's dawning on me."

"If this works," I whispered, "I get to go all out for Christmas. Birthdays, we keep it real. I don't want to one-up you or make you feel anything but good about what we give the kids and I don't want you competing with what we give each other. But Christmas, just Christmas, I get to go crazy and we can say it's from Santa."

"Crazy in the sense checkin' off more than a few items on a wish list is a crazy where I can deal. Crazy in the sense you buy each kid a Porsche and take us all on a family cruise of the Caribbean on the staffed yacht you buy me, no."

"Do you want a yacht?"

"Do you know how steep Magdalene Harbor slip fees are?"

"No."

"Just sayin', no, I don't want a yacht or even a dingy, I gotta pay slip fees and it sits there with me not usin' it because I'm busy working, with my kids or fuckin' my woman."

I started giggling but stopped abruptly and called, "Mickey?"

He didn't answer. He just tightened his arms around me.

So I kept going.

"I have a lot. I can have most anything I want. But there are only five things in the world that mean so much to me I'd do anything to keep. Auden. Olympia. Lawrie. Robin. And now...you."

He moved then, sliding me off his cock and shifting to fall back at the same time turning me so when he was on his back in the bed, my weight was on him, chest to chest.

He slid his hands into my hair on either side to hold it away from my face.

"She didn't," he whispered.

"I'm sorry?" I asked.

"She didn't do anything to keep me."

I lifted a hand to his stubbly cheek and said softly, "Mickey."

"Do not take from that I got feelings for her. I don't. But she burned me, Amy. I heard you about it bein' an illness but in her case, it's her that had to find the strength to beat back the symptoms, even if she'll never have a cure. Already told you I had a woman I couldn't give what she needed, now you get how deep she scarred me. And I guess it's eatin' me I got one I like havin' that needs nothing from me."

I stiffened on top of him and said, "Mickey, I think I told you—"

"You did, baby," he said gently. "But that shit has to sink through scar tissue that's tough and runs deep. So you gotta keep gettin' in my face, kickin' my ass and makin' that statement until it digs through."

I glared at him, shifting my hand to his neck and declaring, "I think I'd rather kick *her* ass."

"Please don't do that, Amy. You do, she'll think it's part of my grand scheme."

I said nothing even though I was happy to see Mickey was grinning.

Considering his mood seemed to have improved, I demanded, "Do I get Christmas?"

"You get Christmas," he agreed.

"Thank you," I snapped, though, I was not only glad he gave me Christmas, I was glad we both thought we'd be together at Christmas, that "we" including Mickey.

He kept grinning. "Told the guys. They're pretty happy about the new shit that's coming."

"Of course they are," I returned. "It's a sixty inch TV. A woman is happy with six inches. For a man to get happy, it has to be sixty."

He burst out laughing.

"Do I speak truth?" I asked.

His brows shot up. "You'd be happy with six inches?"

"I was happy with less than that for sixteen years so I guess the answer is yes."

He kept laughing but started doing it so hard the bed shook.

In the face of his hilarity, I started grinning and said, "It was amusing, honey, but *not* that amusing."

He sobered but not entirely, and replied, "Knew that guy had a small dick."

"Without extensive study, I would hazard to guess that it was average and you're...not."

He kept smiling, doing it big, as he returned, "Guess I can give you somethin' else you can only get from me."

"Like you didn't know you were endowed," I scoffed.

"Never got out a ruler and do my best not to compare."

"Guys do that all the time," I told him.

"Uh...no they don't," he told me. "And I'm in a rare situation where a guy is doin' that shit, he gets a look from me he knows if he doesn't mind his own fuckin' business, he's gonna find his nasal passages at the back of his skull."

My focus shifted to his ear as I mumbled, "I find this interesting."

"You thought guys stood around comparing dicks?"

I focused back on him. "Actually, yes."

He grinned at me. "My heiress and her perverted fantasies about guys comparing dicks."

"It's not a fantasy, Mickey."

"Good you got one that's a winner."

I narrowed my eyes at him. "Can we stop talking about this?"

Suddenly, he pulled me close to his face and sobered entirely.

"I'll try my best not to be a dick, not to bring it up, not to hurt your feelings or make you worry about it. I hate that I made somethin' good you did that you were excited about, that *I* should have been excited about, into a fight. I may stumble along the way, Amy, but you got my word I'll work on it."

That, just that, was all I needed.

I melted into him, glided my hand to his jaw and slid my thumb along his lower lip, replying, "All I can ask, honey."

He pulled me even closer, touched his lips to mine and then pushed me an inch away.

"Clean up," he ordered quietly. "Get in one of your nighties and come back to me. Need sleep."

"Okay, Mickey."

I bent and gave him my own touch before I lifted up and again glided my thumb over his lower lip. After that, I rolled off, cleaned up, donned a nightgown and went back to him.

Mickey turned out the lights and tangled himself up in me.

I was almost asleep when Mickey mumbled, "My heiress thinks men compare dicks."

My eyes shot open and I snapped drowsily at his throat, "Stop teasing me when I'm half-asleep."

He gathered me closer. "You got it, baby."

I sighed loudly, closed my eyes, snuggled into his heat and fell asleep tangled up in Mickey.

21

STAMP ME APPROVED

"*Truth be told!*" Mrs. Porter shrieked at the TV.

"Jesus, what is that?" Lawrie asked in my ear as I moved away from the lounge at Dove House with my phone.

"Mrs. Porter. *Wheel of Fortune.*" I shared. "She got it on only the *r.*"

"Impressive," he replied. "But are your ears bleeding?"

I grinned. "Since they got a TV they can actually see, *Wheel of Fortune* gets extreme. And you don't want to be anywhere near the lounge during *Jeopardy.*"

I heard Lawrie chuckling.

My grin turned into a smile as I got into a much quieter hall, leaned against a wall between two residents' rooms and gave him my attention.

"Why are you calling, big brother?"

"The invitation still stands, I'm coming for Thanksgiving."

I felt joy.

Then I felt fear.

"Mariel?" I asked.

"Only me."

I felt more fear. "Not the boys?"

"It's time they got used not having me around, even on special occasions."

Oh no.

"Lawrie," I whispered. "Marriage counselling isn't working?"

"Our counselor never touches us," he told me. "Never even looks like she's going to. Last session, she grabbed Mariel's hand for no purpose except, my guess, to see if she had a pulse."

I didn't laugh. His words were funny but the tone he delivered them in was not amusing.

I pushed away from the wall and wandered further down the hall saying, "I'm so sorry."

"I wanted to know."

I stopped and braced because now he was being quiet but fierce.

"Wanted to know what, honey?" I asked softly.

"What went wrong," he answered instantly. "What I was doing that took her away from me. I wanted to know. I didn't care what it was. How big. How small. How petty. If she'd mentioned some bracelet she had to have that I didn't notice she'd asked for and I didn't get her. If she was hurt I stopped telling her she was beautiful. I wanted to know so I could change it. I wanted to know what took away the girl I fell in love with so I could get her back. The girl who made me laugh. The girl who'd ruin a complicated soufflé and toss it in the trash without giving that first shit and pull out Chips Ahoy and slather them in Cool Whip for dessert. Rather than that being something that heralded an ice storm the boys and me would have to endure for a week. The girl who wanted nothing more than to stay in bed naked all day with me. I wanted to know how she became our mother. I wanted to know why she surpassed that until we had nothing."

I closed my eyes and leaned a shoulder against the wall at hearing my brother's pain.

"During your counselling, she gave you nothing?" I asked.

"Once the dread sock situation was outed, she's hardly said anything in our sessions. Once a week she sits there barely moving with her arms crossed on her chest and her eyes to her knees. Her expression doesn't even change. I lay it out. I even throw out the ugly just to see if I can get her to react to *something*. Nothing, MeeMee. It's so bad even our counselor suggested a trial separation, and I think she did in an effort to put me out of my misery. The fuck of that is it's humiliating. In fact, the whole fucking thing is humiliating."

I hated that.

I hated that for my glorious big brother Lawrie.

He was not short like me. He was tall and straight and lean and commanding, like my dad.

But he had great, thick, dark hair that now had silver in it that was attractive (which was like mine, without the dye job and highlights, obviously).

And we shared our hazel eyes.

He got my father's cut, angular, masculine bone structure that started forming and defining when he was fifteen. So since then, to when he met Mariel, he'd had to beat them off with a stick.

He loved his sons.

He was the youngest attorney in the history of his firm to make partner.

He made a ton of money and just *had* a ton of money.

He was smart. He had a great sense of humor.

And I remembered. I remembered the way he used to be with her. How she'd walk into the room and everything about him would change. The way he told her she was beautiful, and it wasn't a throwaway compliment she could settle into, but he did it, each time I heard it, like he meant it and he wanted it to mean something to her.

I also remembered the way he stood at the altar at the church and watched her walk to him with this look of happy, expectant certainty like he just *knew* their lives would be beauty from that day until they left the earth.

This was why I hated her.

Because she became my mother when he did *not* become our father, and then she became worse than my mother and doing it, proved him wrong.

"You're welcome, with the boys, without them, with her, or without," I assured him. "You're welcome anytime, Lawrie."

"Thanks, MeeMee."

"And I'm so sorry," I repeated.

"I lived for years stupidly hoping she'd snap out of it or just snap. Let fly what was causing her to be the way she was being. And maybe I should give it longer. But I'm not twenty-five. It isn't that I didn't try to talk to her. Take her away for the weekend. Adjust things I was doing in case I hit on the right one. She gives no indication it's anything but over. The boys are old enough to get it and the fuck of that is, I think for them it'll be a relief. They love their mother but she isn't what I want for them because she gives them less than Mom gave you and me. And that's my biggest fuck up, MeeMee. I should have gotten them away from that a long time ago."

"Hindsight is twenty-twenty," I told him.

"And hope is as blind as love," he told me.

God, but the two men I loved most in this world had taken a licking by the women they gave their hearts to.

I straightened from the wall at that thought because I'd admitted to myself I was falling in love with Mickey.

I'd never admitted I was there.

Since in that moment my brother needed my attention, I shook this off and said, "Come for Thanksgiving and let me, Auden and Pip take care of you."

"I'll be there, MeeMee, and I'll let you know what Mariel and I decide about the boys."

Whereas I couldn't wait to have my kids with me for a holiday, she'd probably shrug and say, "Whatever you think is best, Lawrence."

Lawrie took us off that subject by asking, "Since you brought up Auden and Pip, things still going good with that?"

They were. It had been three days since Mickey and my fight. It was now Monday, his kids were back and as for my kids, the TV visits were continuing. Not to mention Pippa and Polly had a sleepover on Saturday night at my place (Pippa having a sleepover I was happy about, her bringing Polly, who, when she wasn't being negative she was being mean, not so much).

And that evening, both of my kids were coming over and Auden had said they were spending the night.

We were definitely back. Things were Mom and Kids. It was a different brand of Mom and Kids that meant they had two homes and a divided family, but it was working for us.

I still had concerns there was something not right about it, but they didn't seem to be cagey about anything. It was just like they wanted to spend time with their mom.

So I was taking it.

I shared all that with Lawrie and ended it, asking, "By the way, have you heard from Mom and Dad?"

"Mom called this weekend. She wanted to know when Mariel was taking her next spa weekend so she could come up. Since every other weekend is a spa weekend for Mariel and we've hit that rotation, she's coming up on Friday. Why?"

Mom and I agreed on very few things. Our mutual dislike of Mariel was one of them. And a shocking twist to this, we both disliked her for the same reason.

Not that Mariel wasn't the appropriately styled, turned out and behaved wife to a prominent attorney who also was a Bourne-Hathaway (because she was).

But that she didn't make Lawr happy.

Mom avoided Mariel like the plague.

"I haven't heard from them for a while. I've been emailing but I get nothing," I explained.

"Neither of them are big on email," Lawr reminded me.

"I know but they also haven't phoned or anything. Not in weeks, or, Lawr, maybe even *months*."

"They disagreed with you moving across country, MeeMee. Maybe this is your penance. But I'll talk to Mom when she's up this weekend. See if I can find out where she's at with that."

I knew he'd get nowhere with that. If Mom didn't feel like sharing, and with her silence she obviously didn't, she wouldn't share.

I still said, "I'd appreciate it."

"Consider it done."

I smiled and asked, "You going to be okay?"

"In the stages of grief, I'm past denial, anger and bargaining. I've hit depression. One more to go and I'm good," he joked.

I didn't laugh.

"I'm here, anytime you need me, Lawrie," I told him.

"I know, sweetheart," he replied.

"I've gotta get back to the residents. *Jeopardy* is after *Wheel of Fortune* and the staff try to stick close in case a fight breaks out."

I was relieved to hear the smile in his voice when he said, "I'll let you go."

"Lawrie?"

"Hmm?"

"I love you lots and lots," I whispered words I'd say to him when he was there for me when we were kids. Putting a Band-Aid on my arm or calamine lotion on my poison ivy or listening to me after a boyfriend broke up with me. In that house with zero love and affection, he was the best brother there could be.

"Love you lots and lots back, MeeMee."

"See you soon."

"You will. 'Bye, sweets."

"'Bye, Lawrie."

We disconnected and I stared unseeing out the windows of the fire doors at the back of the hall.

I wanted to invite Robin to Thanksgiving.

I knew it would be too soon, maybe for both of them.

So I couldn't invite Robin to Thanksgiving.

That didn't stop me from really, *really* wanting to.

Then, suddenly, I found my hand lifting and my finger sliding across the screen of my phone.

I put it to my ear and heard it ring twice before I got, "Hey, baby."

"Hey back," I greeted Mickey then blurted, "I wanna go away with you."

"Uh...what?"

"Whenever, wherever for however long you want to go. I don't care. I want you to know I want to go with you. I want to take Pop Tarts and squirtable cheese and crackers, and other food we don't have to cook that we can eat with our fingers so we can stay in bed naked all day together. I want to go, whenever, wherever, and I want it to be just about you and me."

There was a moment of silence before he replied gently, "I love that, Amy, I love that you gave that to me. But gotta ask what brought it on."

"My brother's marriage is disintegrating."

"Shit, Amy," he muttered.

"So you need to know I want that. Not this weekend. Or next. No pressure. Whenever we can do it. Whenever we can fit it in. Whenever we have a day or two or five where we can do that. I just need you to know I want that. I want that with you."

"We'll find our time, darlin'," he told me.

"And," I swallowed, gathering the courage to go on, "if this keeps growing, I don't ever want you to forget no matter how many weeks or months or years pass, all you need to do is tell me to pack a bag and I'll do it, happy to go away with you."

"Love that too, Amy," he said softly and he sounded like he did. He sounded like he loved that.

And I loved that sound.

I closed my eyes. "Okay."

"You okay?"

I opened my eyes. "I hurt for my brother," I told him. "But I'm fine."

"Life sucks. But if he's getting out of a bad situation, it's his first step to finding some happy."

"I hope so."

"It'll happen. Won't know when it will happen. But mine moved in right across the street."

I drew in a sharp breath.

Mickey kept talking like he didn't just gift me with something precious.

"I got work, babe. Hate it when you're hurtin' for your brother, but I gotta go."

"Okay, Mickey. I'll let you go."

"Talk to you later."

"Yeah. Later, honey. 'Bye."

"'Bye, babe."

We disconnected and I drew in another breath.

Mine moved in right across the street.

I let the breath out, smiling.

"*Bonnie and Clyde!*" I heard shouted in two voices.

Then I heard, "I said it first!"

"You did not!"

"Tell her, Ellen! I said it first!"

"I knew on the *n*. I didn't even *need* the *d*!"

"Then you should have said it on the *n*!"

"Ladies—" I heard Mr. Dennison say calmingly.

"Shut it, Charles!"

At that, knowing with brief but alarming experience it was time to take action, I stopped thinking about Lawrie, Robin, Mickey and Thanksgiving and rushed to the lounge.

⸻•⸻

"IT'S ALL RIGHT."

That came from Auden.

"I think it's the bomb. Get it, Mom."

That came from Olympia.

We were in the back den, gathered around the PC and I was showing them the dining room table I was considering purchasing from the New Hampshire furniture company.

When they replied to my email, I found they had a small showroom but none of those pieces, although lovely, were big enough for the space I had. And the one I'd seen on their site had been purchased and was unavailable.

Mostly, however, they did custom designs and builds and the one we were viewing was a build that the people who ordered it had reneged on.

If I wanted it, it would be all mine.

"It works. It's perfect," Pippa went on. "And you need to get something. Uncle Lawrie is coming and Thanksgiving is just around the corner."

I had time but my girl was right. We weren't going to eat Thanksgiving dinner sitting on the sectional.

"Okay, I'll get it," I decided.

"Great. Can I stop looking at furniture now?" Auden asked.

He wasn't in a surly mood. He was just a boy who didn't give a fig about dining room tables.

"No," Pippa answered for me. "We need to look at couches. And Mom, you need to get hopping on the other guest bedroom and get a pullout for in here so Hart and Mercer don't have to share a room."

I was looking at her, thinking she was right. I had the desk and chair but there was vast amounts of space in that room that needed filling and the whole room needed decorating.

However, when she quit talking, I reminded her, "Sweets, I explained the boys might not be coming."

"If they have a choice between Uncle Lawrie and Aunt Frosty, they'll *so* be here," she returned.

My kids called my brother's wife "Aunt Frosty."

It was funny.

But it wasn't nice.

"Aunt Frosty isn't nice," I rebuked gently.

She didn't look contrite. "It isn't but it's real."

I couldn't argue that.

I still didn't want my daughter being mean.

"Sometimes we should be careful about calling them as we see them," I advised. "And especially when Lawr, or if the boys, come. They may be at the beginning of going through something you know from experience is unpleasant, so let's help them do that better than we got through it, shall we?"

That was when she looked contrite, licked her lips and rolled them together.

"I care less about the guest bedroom, couches and pullouts," Auden put in. "So *now* can I stop looking at furniture?"

I rolled my chair slightly back so both kids, gathered around me, moved back too.

After I did this, I said, "Actually, I need you for another little bit to talk to you about something."

They both donned expressions of wary.

I ignored that and launched in.

"A while ago, we had a discussion about me dating."

"Yeah, and now you're dating some Neanderthal," Pippa declared. "We know."

My back went straight as I fought a quick retort and instead asked, "How do you know?"

"Dad told us," Auden answered and my eyes looked to him to see his expression was now carefully blank. "Said we should know in case we see you two in town."

"And your father called Mickey a Neanderthal?" I queried, my voice thin.

Pippa looked out the window.

Auden shifted but held my gaze and said, "Yeah."

I fought the itch that was covering every inch of my skin, screaming to get scratched, me doing that meaning I marched to my car, got in it, drove to Conrad's and shrieked at him for being such a huge...fucking...*dick*.

But that was the me he made me.

Now I was just me and he was not going to push me into going back.

"Mickey isn't a Neanderthal," I told them firmly. "Mickey is a good man who I've come to care about quite a bit. I enjoy spending time with him. He feels the same about me. This is something that we both feel is important and we're both building on that. So since he's important to me and *you're* important to me, I'd like you to meet him."

"Cool," Pippa said casually.

I stared at her, shocked at her non-response.

Or, more precisely, her not negative one.

"You should make your pulled barbeque chicken when he comes over. With your homemade coleslaw," Auden suggested.

I moved my stare to him.

Then I asked, "I...that's it? Do you have questions? Anything you want to ask me about Mickey?"

"No, why?" Auden asked back.

"It's about time," Pip stated before I could answer my son. "You've always been pretty and those highlights kick butt. So it's no surprise you hooked up. And it's good you have somebody."

Could it be this easy?

"Pippa, sweets, you should know, it's that firefighter you saw that day on the street."

She grinned. "Awesome. He was hot."

I blinked.

She bent over the computer and commandeered the mouse, saying, "Now, I was looking and I totally dig the whole thing you got going in the other guestroom. I found this bed that was like *yin* to that *yang*. From the beach straight to the forest!" she declared and started clicking.

Oh my God.

My daughter had been looking for furniture for the home she shared with me.

And *oh my God*, my kids didn't mind that I was dating and wanted them to meet somebody.

I felt something strange and my eyes drifted from my daughter clicking the mouse to my son.

The instant I caught his gaze, he looked away and mumbled, "I approve of everything so don't bother asking me."

He then strolled out.

"Look, Mom, here it is! Isn't this the bomb?" Pippa cried.

I looked at a four-poster bed that looked made of logs.

It was absolutely "the bomb."

I rolled forward, ordering, "Scooch, kid, let me see."

Pippa scooched.

Fifteen minutes later, I'd ordered a log bed off the Internet.

Twenty minutes after that, I'd ordered all the linens for that bed.

And an hour after that, my girl sitting on a stool she'd dragged from the kitchen bar (I really needed more furniture in the den) and I were still online furniture shopping.

———— • ————

"DON'T STAY UP TOO LATE, KIDDO. I'M OFF TO BED," I SAID TO AUDEN WHO was lounged on the couch in front of the TV, surrounded by schoolbooks, notebooks and his tablet.

It was late. His sister had gone to bed half an hour ago. Auden was still doing homework. The TV was on, but as only kids could do, he was sitting in front of it with it blaring but most of his attention was on his work.

I put my hands to the arms of the chair I was in and started to push up when Auden's eyes came to me.

"He fucks you over, you get rid of him."

I froze.

"Auden," I whispered.

"The minute he fucks you over, Mom, get rid of him," he ordered, his voice low and there was a tremor of emotion that cut deep.

I rested my behind back to the seat and kept my focus on my son.

"First," I said quietly, "I'm not fond of your language."

Auden didn't reply, he just continued staring at me.

"Second," I went on, "is there something you want to share with me?"

"Dad screwed you over and it messed you up," he declared instantly.

God, direct hit.

"I know, kiddo, and I'm sorry I made that so easy for you to see."

He shook his head forcefully. "No. That's not what I mean. Dad screwed you over and it messed you up, Mom. You're good now. You got through it. But you know better than me that guys can be dicks. Don't let this guy be a dick to you."

"I learned something from what happened before, sweets," I assured him. "And whatever's in my future with a man, or even getting a hangnail, I'm not going to allow that to happen again. And by that I mean I'm not going to fall apart."

He stopped lounging and leaned toward me. "*No*," he repeated emphatically. "Just don't let this guy be a dick to you."

I stared at my boy and tried to read anything I could that he wasn't giving to me verbally.

When I couldn't find it, even though I sensed it was there, I started, "What happened between me and your father—"

Auden interrupted me, "I had no control over that. But I will over this. If I see this guy being a dick to you, then I'm doing something about it."

"Auden," I began cautiously, "is there something you aren't telling me?"

That was when he broke my gaze, still looking toward me but now doing it beyond me. "Just that I'm not letting anyone be a dick to my mom."

That felt nice. Incredibly nice.

I still sensed that wasn't it.

"If you have something you need to talk about, I hope you know you can talk to me," I told him earnestly but solemnly, hoping he didn't also read my anxiety.

Auden didn't say anything.

"Mickey's a really good man, honey," I shared. "He's got two kids of his own and he's a great dad." I leaned his way and dropped my voice. "He makes me laugh and he takes care of me and he makes me happy. And I hope you know I wouldn't put you through introducing you to somebody who I didn't think would be around for a good long while."

Auden again looked right at me. "I'm glad he makes you laugh and you're happy. But if he's a dick to you, Mom, he's gone."

I again tried to read my son.

I again sensed something there that I couldn't read.

And he obviously didn't want to share it.

So I said, "I think that's a fair deal."

Auden nodded and looked back at the TV.

I decided to end it there, got up and went around the back of the couch. When I was in position, I leaned deep and kissed the top of his head.

"Love you, my baby boy, forever and ever," I whispered.

"Love you too, Mom," he mumbled in return.

I closed my eyes, throat getting clogged, swallowed to clear it and straightened away.

"Sleep tight," I said as I moved toward my room, snagging my phone off the kitchen counter on the way there.

"Yeah. You too," Auden called back.

I got behind closed door and instantly called Mickey.

Within a couple of rings, just like Mickey, he picked up.

I told him the good news, that Auden and Olympia were open to meet him.

I did not tell him my ex referred to him to my children as a Neanderthal. He'd done that to Mickey's face and Mickey didn't like it. He didn't need to get upset about Conrad saying it to my kids.

Then I told him the not-so-good news about the intense conversation I just had with my son.

I ended this with, "What do you think that was about?"

"Haven't met your boy, babe, don't know anything about him but what you've told me. But if my dad did my mom the way his dad did his, I may have gotten caught up in the hurricane and its aftermath, but when things settled down, I'd be thinkin'. Men look to our fathers to show us the man we should be. He's at an age where that's gonna be some intense scrutiny. And I'm thinkin' he doesn't like what he's seein'."

"I don't want that for him," I said uneasily.

"Could just be him mannin' up," Mickey added. "He's of an age to do that too. His mom is dating. She got fucked over. He wants you to know he's lookin' out for you. I'd do that for my mom too. Any good son would look after his mother."

I liked that idea better.

"He said the f-word, Mickey."

Mickey started chuckling.

I didn't find it funny.

"*Twice*," I stated.

"Bet he says it a lot more around his buds."

This did not make me happy and I looked to the door.

"Babe, advice," he went on. "Seriously. Listen to this shit. Back off. He's findin' the man he's gonna be. You gotta give him space to let him."

"He should respect his mother and not curse," I declared.

"Do you honestly give a shit about cursing?" he asked incredulously.

"You doing it as a grown man, no. Auden doing it at sixteen, yes."

"You call him on it?"

"Carefully."

"Then make it be known that in your house and to you and your daughter, he shows you that respect. After that, back off. That is, unless he keeps doin' it."

"Right," I mumbled.

"Brady Bunch action is definitely gonna take time," he stated, and I knew he meant by this that it would be only him for dinner. We'd do the blending of kids at a later date, which was a relief. "So this dinner has gotta happen next week after the kids go to Rhiannon. Scheduled off at the house on Tuesday. See if they can make it then."

"I'll talk to them, Mickey. Do you like coleslaw?"

"Yeah. Why?"

"Because Auden placed his order for dinner with the man Mom's dating and it includes coleslaw. I already know you like barbeque chicken, which is the other menu item he selected."

"Totally a sixteen-year-old boy. His mom tells him she's got a new man, he's worried about what he's gonna eat."

That made me smile and settled other things inside me.

Mickey kept talking, "But you don't have a grill."

"Slow roasted barbeque pulled chicken," I told him.

"Shit, it's after ten and now I'm hungry."

And another smile.

"You goin' to bed?" he asked.

"Yeah."

"Wish that was happening beside me," he muttered.

And with that, *everything* settled inside me.

"Me too," I told him quietly.

"Monday," he said.

That seemed a long way away.

"Monday," I agreed.

"Right, Amy. Lettin' you go. Sleep good, baby."

"You too, Mickey. 'Night."

"'Night."

We rang off and I got ready for bed.

Once in it, I tossed and turned and didn't sleep.

I wanted to believe that the fierceness coming from my son was a protective instinct for me. I would even like to know if Mickey was right about Auden looking at his father and wondering if he'd become that man.

But I didn't think it was either.

I thought it was something else.

Something that drove both my kids from their father to me.

Something I was going to have to find a way to figure out.

For them.

Not me.

———— • ————

"I'm not liking this," I said two days later, standing in Jake's office at the gym, watching through the window, Jake and Mickey in the ring sparring.

"I know," Josie, standing next to me replied. "Actually, I *don't* know. Jake never loses. To anyone. Even Mickey, who's quite formidable, but still, he's only second best in the league. Jake was once a professional boxer so you shouldn't feel any less of Mickey. Jake fought pay-per-view. He was quite something. Thus, I can't say I know how it feels that Mickey's losing."

I couldn't even think of Mickey losing. And I didn't suspect anyone was losing since they were only sparring with a throng of young men from age eleven to eighteen standing around watching.

The junior boxing league signups and gear handouts. The reason I was there. So I could watch the boys get fitted for the gear that I'd made it so they could have for their season.

No, I was thinking that I hated the idea that Mickey boxed. I could barely watch my son roll around on a mat struggling to pin his opponent.

I hated watching Jake punch Mickey even if Mickey was punching back.

I'd hate it more if they were doing it to win.

But what I hated most of all was the heretofore unknown knowledge that Mickey was a member of the adult league which, like the junior league, was again starting its season.

Now, how *exactly* was Mickey going to do all he did *and* train to box *and* actually *box*?

"He has two jobs, two kids, a girlfriend and he's starting his own company," I stated. "How on earth is he going to find time to train so he doesn't get his ass kicked?"

"Jake owns two businesses, has three children and a wife. He does it."

I looked to Josie. "One of his businesses is a boxing gym."

She looked to me. "Yes, but someone must *run* it. He can't train all the time."

Even though I didn't think Jake had it as bad as Mickey, I asked, "Okay, so how does he juggle all that?"

"He found himself a wife."

A thrill shot through me.

Interrupting this thrill, a cheer came from the gym and Josie and I looked that way.

Jake was spitting out his mouth guard and Mickey was leaning on the thing at the corner of the ring, his guard already out, and he was using his teeth to pull open the Velcro grips on his gloves while Jake started addressing the boys.

I studied Mickey thinking it could not be denied, in his loose track pants with his skintight, short-sleeved shirt, leaning casually against a corner thing of a boxing ring, that he looked exceptionally hot, even with his headgear on.

I still hoped he didn't want me to go watch him beat someone up while taking a beating.

"I hope he doesn't ask me to his fights," I muttered this thought aloud.

"Oh yes you do."

Josie's strange tone of voice made me look at her. "Why?"

She visibly tore her eyes from her husband and looked at me. "Fight night."

I felt my brows draw together. "I'm sorry?"

"Fight night starts with the fight but it ends in far more pleasant activities," she explained.

The look on her face, it was dawning on me.

But she kept going.

"Win or lose, though as you know I don't know about losing, but Alyssa does, and I'm very aware that even when Junior loses, Alyssa's favorite night of *any* night is *fight night.*"

"So they..." I trailed off.

"Yes," she stated firmly.

"And after a fight, they can—?"

"*Absolutely.*"

"Better than other—?"

"The *best.*"

My voice was pitched higher when I asked, "Really?"

"I find it awkward to share how Jake is as a lover. However, I will tell you that he's excellent even when we must be quick. It's always good. I love that about him...amongst many other things. But fight night is different. Unique. And quite honestly, I'd watch him lose every single time just so I could be there, however he needed me, once the fight was over."

"Wow," I breathed.

"Precisely," she replied, studying my face then stating, "So, I'll be certain that at every fight, you have your seat with Alyssa and me."

I wasn't looking forward to that at the same time I was.

Mickey...*better?*

My legs started trembling.

We heard a shrill whistle and we both looked into the gym to see Jake taking his fingers out of his mouth to wave us his way.

"That's our cue," Josie murmured and started moving.

I moved with her and we barely cleared the door before Jake announced, "Right, you know we've struggled to get you boys good gear. But this year, Mrs. Spear, and especially Miz Hathaway, who donated a bunch of really good crap to be sold for the league, raised enough that not only do we have all new gear this year, but you'll be fighting your matches in the big ring in Blakeley."

We had all the boys' attention on us as we came to a stop at the back of the group.

At this news there were some open mouths and a sweep of excitement glided through the space before Jake concluded, "So give it up for the ladies."

I felt my cheeks warm as the boys let out a collective whoop.

In all my years of raising money, not once had I personally faced a single soul who benefited from that.

Taking in those happy faces and their cheer, I found it felt *great*.

"Now, line up at the scale," Jake ordered. "We gotta class you then we'll get you your gear. After that, get your trainer assignments, introduce yourself to your trainer and get your training schedule."

The boys started milling about and Josie and I stepped out of their way so they could do this.

And my night got better when Cillian walked by with one of his friends.

He was grinning at me.

I was grinning back.

And his friend was saying to him, "Bonus to being a fighter. You get hot chicks."

"Yeah," Cillian replied, looking away from me. "The short one's my dad's girlfriend."

"Whoa, *nice*," his friend said, eyeing me as they jockeyed for position in a line that led to one of those upright scales that Junior was attending.

It was at that from Cill's friend that it just wasn't my cheeks that were warm but other parts of me, primarily the region around my heart.

The last time I was in this gym, I felt old, unattractive and past my prime.

Now, I had the approval of twelve-year-olds.

It wasn't much but it was something, and having Cillian's approval of me for his father was even better.

Then the night got *better* when I felt weight around my shoulders, looked up and saw Mickey had claimed me with his arm around me.

"Hey," he said on an easy grin.

"Hey back," I replied.

"This feel good?" he asked.

I nodded.

"Good," he muttered.

"Mr. Donovan." I heard and looked up to see a bruiser who might be seventeen or eighteen standing close to us.

"Joe," Mickey greeted.

The boy looked at me. "Hey, uh...you're Auden's mom, right?"

I straightened and regarded my son's friend, Joe, who was not seventeen or eighteen but sixteen, which was shocking. He looked like he could be a Marine. And he was very cute.

"Yes, Joe. I'm Ms. Hathaway." I offered my hand. "Nice to meet you. Auden's talked about you."

He took my hand briefly then let it go, looking this way and that shyly, as he said, "Yeah. Cool. He's a good guy."

"He is," I agreed.

"Anyway, thanks for doin' this." He threw out a hand. "Totally cool."

"Happy I could help," I told him.

"Right. Great. Anyway, later," he muttered and moved to the line.

"Later, Joe," I called after him.

Mickey's lips came to my ear. "You and Josie gotta get the fuck outta here or the situation is not gonna be good."

I pulled my head back so I could catch his eyes and he lifted his so he could give them to me.

"Why?" I asked.

"'Cause your boy's friend just met his friend's MILF of a mom and Josie is pure MILF too. So you two better take off so the league doesn't grow three times its size just so boys can get a look at the possible ass they'll be tapping when they're old enough to know what to do with their dicks. Ass they'll tap because they were smart enough to train to be a fighter."

I reared away, not getting far as Mickey's arm around my shoulders tightened, but that didn't stop me from exclaiming, "Mickey! *Really!*"

"Babe, I used to be sixteen," he returned. "Mrs. Getty next door is now seventy-five but she once was forty-five and she saw a lot of sock time."

I leaned into him. "I think I just threw up a little in my mouth."

"Think of what poor ole Joe is thinkin', he's gotta go to school tomorrow and face his friend with the hot mom."

"Stop talking," I ordered sharply.

Mickey burst out laughing.

"Stop laughing," I demanded hotly.

He didn't.

What he did was bend to me and touch his mouth to mine *still laughing*.

I didn't pull away because there were people around, but I did glare at him when he was done.

"This, right here," he said. "Again, all you. What you gave the boys, one of 'em my son, the way I feel standin' beside you with the way you look and what you did for this league. Another flash of happy."

I instantly stopped glaring.

"Thank you, baby," he whispered.

I pressed my lips together so they wouldn't tremble.

"You gonna cry?" he asked.

"No," I mumbled, but even one syllable, it was shaky.

"Best not kiss you again," he noted.

"If you say one more gross thing, I'm not having sex with you for a week."

I got another easy grin. "Like you can hold out that long."

"Whatever," I muttered.

"Amy?"

"What?" I snapped.

"You're the best woman I've ever met."

I stared into his beautiful blue eyes, seeing those words reflected there and knowing since the moment I clapped eyes on him, one of the things I wanted most was to see that look aimed at me.

It wasn't "I love you."

But it was the next best thing.

"Great, now I wanna make out with you," I griped under my breath to hide how his words made me feel.

Mickey was again grinning.

"So, Tuesday is on with Auden and Olympia?" he asked a question he knew the answer to but I knew he asked it to change the subject.

I nodded as I moved into him, excited and anxious about this first meeting, but hoping, my kids being *mine*, they'd see Mickey. They'd see how he was with me. They'd see he made me happy. And it would all go great.

"Lookin' forward to it, Amy."

That was when I smiled up at him but while doing it, I felt a shiver slide up my neck.

I looked to the side and saw Cillian edging up the line with the other boys being weighed. His neck was twisted. His eyes on his dad and me.

He looked reflective.

I braced and did it further when he caught me looking at him. But then he waved a little man's version of a big man wave, grinned and turned away.

Not embarrassed to wave at me in public.

Not turning sullen at his dad touching me, talking to me, laughing with me.

Bragging to his friend I was his dad's girlfriend.

This meant, if Cillian had a stamp, he could press it into ink, come to me and stamp me approved.

And this made me happy.

Very, *very* happy.

22

ROUGH NIGHT

"*P*ip, light the candles, sweets, would you?" I called and right on the heels of that, "Auden, do me a favor. Pull up Pandora. A good station, down low, nothing techno or anything like that. Dinner music." And right on the heels of that, "Pip, when you're done, set the bar. Placements. Plates. Cutlery. Water glasses." And on the heels of that, "*Ouch!*" that last because I'd burned my finger on the chicken.

"Chill, Mom," Pippa said quietly and I looked to her to see her in the drawer where she could get the long handled lighter. She was looking at me. "It's gonna be cool. We're gonna like him."

She then grabbed the lighter, shut the drawer and took off to light the candles.

Needless to say, it was the next Tuesday and Mickey was going to be over imminently.

Also needless to say, I had lost all excitement about this meeting and was a complete and total wreck.

For the past week, life had been good with Mickey. I'd had dinner and then hung out at his place three times when the kids were still with him and we'd spent all day Saturday together, dinking around at the shops at Mills jetty then going out for dinner.

Cillian had definitely approved me. He was relaxed, at ease, open to being what boys his age were: part goofball, part young man.

Alarmingly, Ash was getting worse. Her hair definitely had not been washed in, my guess, several days. And I'd realized that I'd never really noticed her clothes, because they weren't noticeable. However, with the hair thing, taking in her full appearance, I noted them along with the fact that her hair was not only not washed, it needed a cut, she didn't put on makeup and her clothes were bulky and oversized, not quite hiding the fact that she was putting on weight.

Unlike my mother, I was not of the opinion that every female should be stick thin, wear makeup and spend huge chunks of time on their appearance, unless they enjoyed doing that kind of thing.

But Ash's timid quietness moving to awkward near-silence and the total deterioration of her appearance at her age was alarming.

Mickey had a lot on his plate but I felt it was too important not to mention. Therefore, when we'd met at the diner for dinner the night before, I'd brought it up.

It had not escaped him. He was extremely concerned. He also was a man and had no idea what to do. Further, he shared that he'd brought this up with Rhiannon some time ago and she didn't agree there seemed to be an issue, but she did have a conversation with Aisling and declared all was well.

As Mickey did not agree with Rhiannon's assessment, he'd shared with me that over the past few weeks he'd tried to broach the subject with Aisling. He'd since backed off due to the fear that his efforts were making her retreat further and get worse.

Clearly all was not well. But now, Mickey and Rhiannon didn't have the relationship where he could discuss this with her so her mother could step in and as her father, he was at a loss of how to broach it.

"Next time she's with me, I'll try one more time. See what I can do. That doesn't go well, I gotta ask you, baby, if you'll step in," he'd said.

I didn't feel I was at a place with Ash where I could do this. We'd had together time and we'd done some bonding making dinner weeks before, but we weren't close and in all the time I'd spent with Mickey's family since we officially got together, we didn't get any closer. This was mostly because whenever I was over, she had dinner with us but then would disappear in her room and I'd only get a, "Later, Amy!" shouted back when Mickey shouted that I was leaving.

This in itself was alarming. She hadn't shared with me in any open way or even in girl code that she liked me with her father. But still, in the beginning, even if she didn't make it plain, she'd communicated that to me.

Also in the beginning, even before Mickey and I got together officially, Aisling seemed to settle in to the shifting Donovan family unit, a unit that included me. We'd been connecting, gradually, but that had been the path we were on.

Now there was nothing.

But I didn't care. If the father-daughter talk didn't go well, I was going in.

Thus I'd replied, "Whatever you need."

Mickey didn't hide his relief, which told me precisely how concerned he was about the situation.

However, that conversation happened last night.

Right then, I had other things on my mind.

Things that included the fact that I'd just gotten my kids back and now I was introducing Mickey into the mix.

The way the current mix was didn't seem volatile and after the last few years, my mother's antennae to something like that was tuned to extremes.

But outside of Conrad showing and being a jerk, the kids had decided their own custody schedule, and since our hostile conversation, Conrad hadn't said a thing. They'd even both brought clothes to keep at my place because they were at Cliff Blue as often as they were with Conrad and Martine.

I liked floating on those calm seas. I didn't want to rock that boat.

I kept telling myself that Mickey was a good guy and there was nothing even in my wildest conjuring he was likely to do to make my kids not accept him.

That didn't mean I wasn't worried.

I fought down the urge to phone Mickey, call dinner off and reschedule in six months as I finished pulling the chicken, mixed it with the barbeque sauce and put it into the oven to keep warm.

I turned to take in my house and heard soft music playing. It wasn't my choice of dinner music, it was rock 'n' roll, but the John Mellencamp type of rock 'n' roll that wouldn't put you to sleep and sounded good turned down (though, that didn't mean it didn't sound better turned up).

I also saw the bar was set. I'd contacted the furniture company and the dining room table was coming, but it wasn't going to arrive until later that week, so we were eating at the bar. Pippa had done as I'd asked and even filled my pretty new pitcher with ice water.

The candles were lit. The lighting was a shade up from romantic.

All was perfect.

Except I should have bought flowers.

"I should have bought flowers," I mumbled.

"Not sure, but since your dude is a dude, he probably doesn't give a crap if you bought flowers," Auden, sliding on the stool opposite me, told me.

He was right.

I smiled at him, lifting a hand to tuck my hair behind my ear.

It was then I realized I'd forgotten to put earrings in.

"Shit! I forgot earrings!" I cried, this exclamation being far more dramatic than the situation warranted.

"According to the microwave you have two minutes to accomplish that mission, Mom," Pippa teased. "Since your jewelry isn't in Calcutta, thinking you can pull that off."

I gave her a look that was half smile, half glare as she grinned at me then I moved, saying, "I'll be right back."

Auden got in on the act, calling to my back, "We'll try to survive without you."

I hoped they'd have to wait years before they had to do that.

I hurried down the hall but I'd nabbed my phone before I left the kitchen in the unlikely event Mickey called me, told me he had 24-hour pneumonia, but not to worry, Florence Nightingale had resurrected to care for him personally, though, alas, he could not come to dinner with me and my children.

This didn't happen.

But after the third pair of earrings I put on (the first, diamond studs, they were big thus too flashy and too expensive; the second, long hoops that nearly reached my shoulders that Alyssa had talked me into buying, they were too disco; the last, a fall of beads and tiny gold leaves, just right), my phone rang.

I looked down at it on my bathroom counter and my neck muscles got tight when I saw it was Conrad.

Considering he might know what tonight was for Pippa, Auden, Mickey and me, and if he did the odds that he was calling was to ruin it for me were high, I didn't answer.

However when I'd decided on earrings number three and did a mini-spritz of perfume (that day, I decided on the one Olympia had chosen for me) and I heard my phone chime it had a voicemail, curiosity got the cat.

I picked it up, went to voicemail and listened to Conrad's message.

"Amelia," he said tightly. "I'm hoping this call came in prior to your evening's...*festivities*."

He knew what tonight was for the kids and me.

"However," he kept talking, even on voicemail sounding like he was doing it while having his nails pulled out by the roots, "things are busy at the moment and I had some time to call. There are some things we need to discuss. If you'd please call my secretary, we can set a meeting. Have a...good evening."

He then rang off but as I was listening my phone chimed with a text. This too was from Conrad and it was his secretary's name and number.

I stared at it wondering what we needed to discuss. I also wondered why whatever that was needed to be discussed face to face. And last, I stared at it thinking that we actually *didn't* have anything to discuss face to face and I would share that via text the next day after I survived the trauma of the next few hours.

I walked out of my bathroom and was heading down the hall when the doorbell rang.

My steps faltered as I experienced a mini-heart attack.

"I got it!" Auden called.

I then experienced a not-mini-heart attack.

Even in the throes of a life emergency, I rushed down the hall seeing Auden strolling to the door and I did this feeling my pulse jumpstart and do it way too quickly.

I got to the mouth of the hall and stopped dead because Auden had the door open and Mickey was standing there looking all that was Mickey, wearing another nice shirt, this one plaid in a muted red and brown against a cream background, jeans and boots.

He was also carrying an enormous bouquet of flowers.

Again, my heart stuttered as my cheeks flushed and I fell a little bit deeper in love with Mickey.

I did it wondering how that saying came about considering falling in love didn't feel like falling.

It felt like soaring.

"Hey," Mickey greeted, not having looked at me, his focus was on Auden.

My son puffed up his chest a little and straightened his back, not yet as tall as Mickey and I didn't know if he would get there, but he was claiming all the height he had in the face of all that was Mickey.

"Hey," Auden replied.

"Flowers!" Pippa exclaimed happily, skip-dashing toward the door before she stopped, turned to me and beamed.

My girl liked her flowers and Mickey thinking of them was a good thing.

But Mickey bringing a bouquet that huge, to Pippa, was a major statement that spoke volumes.

"You wanna let him in, kiddo?" I suggested to Auden, forcing my body to move forward as Mickey looked from Pippa to me.

He smiled, big and beautiful.

I smiled back, hoping I gave him the same thing.

Auden stepped out of the way and Mickey walked in, coming right to me as I met him halfway.

When we stopped, he put a hand light to my hip and bent deep, touching his mouth briefly to mine.

When he lifted away, he murmured, "Hey."

"Hey back," I replied quietly.

His eyes kept smiling then he took his hand from my hip and turned to the kids.

"Okay, I think we all know each other but let's make that official," I suggested. "Auden, Pippa, this is Mickey. Mickey, these are my kids, Auden and Olympia."

I did hand gestures along the way as Auden pushed in first, offering his hand to Mickey.

"Hello, sir," he said formally, which made Pippa widen her eyes and look at me.

I pressed my lips together, giving her wide eyes back, as Mickey took my son's hand and replied, "Mickey's fine, Auden."

"Right," Auden muttered as he let go.

"Hey!" Pippa cried brightly, hopping toward him, beaming up at him and offering a hand.

I watched her do this, allowing myself a brief moment of sheer joy that my girl was back.

Mickey took her hand and replied, "Hey."

They separated and Pippa tipped her head to the flowers and offered, "Do you want me to take those? I can put them in water for Mom."

Mickey lifted the massive bouquet of green hydrangeas, peach roses and red gerbera daisies to Pippa and said, "Sure, darlin'. Thanks."

She took them in both hands, pulling them to her chest, before she beamed at me and skipped away.

"Can I get you a drink, Mickey?" Auden asked.

"Yeah, thanks. A beer," Mickey answered.

Auden nodded and moved away.

I looked to Mickey. He looked to me. Then he moved in close, sliding a hand to the middle of my back.

"You doin' okay?" he asked under his breath.

"I'm a wreck," I told him under mine.

"Don't mean to freak you, Amy, but you aren't hiding that."

"Great," I mumbled and he grinned.

"It's cute."

"It doesn't *feel* cute."

"Relax," he replied. "I already know you got good kids. This is gonna go fine."

It seemed so far he was right. I just hoped it kept up that way.

"The flowers were a nice touch," I shared.

"Got that. Your girl is as easy to read as you."

I felt my face get soft.

"Uh...Mom," Pippa called. I jumped and looked her way. She was smiling broadly. "You sold all the vases."

"Crap," I muttered.

Auden came out of the fridge with Mickey's beer and asked him, "Do you want this in a glass?"

"Bottle's good," Mickey answered.

"I know!" Pip exclaimed. "I'll pour the ice water in the glasses and use the pitcher."

"Good idea, sweets," I told her.

She jumped to the pitcher, setting aside the flowers.

Auden approached with Mickey's beer, handed it to him and asked me, "Do you want a glass of wine?"

"That'd be great, kid," I replied.

He nodded, all man of the house, and moved away.

I watched my kids handling this situation so splendidly, better than I was, and suddenly was overwhelmed with an enormous feeling of relief. Relief that I'd done such a good job raising them (admittedly with Conrad also being a good father). Relief that they survived the "hurricane" as Mickey described it and its aftermath and then settled right back into the great kids we'd raised.

This was coupled with the hope that if my kids could survive a stormy breakup of their parents and move on the way they did, that Mickey's kids would do the same.

And taking this in, I was no longer a wreck. I was a woman in the warm, friendly home I'd created for my family, *with* said family and my handsome wonderful boyfriend having dinner.

I looked up at Mickey. "You want to take a seat while the kids and I start putting dinner together?"

"Rather help out," he replied.

I beamed up at him.

His beautiful blue eyes moved over my face before I saw warmth and pride shine out and he lifted a hand to run his knuckles briefly along my jaw before he dropped it and asked, "What can I do?"

"Mickey, you can help me grill the buns and we'll get the fries in the oven," Pippa bossed. "Mom, you cut up the pickles. Auden, get out the cheese platter and coleslaw. And make sure you grab a serving spoon for the slaw."

We all hopped to, moving around the kitchen doing our assigned tasks. While Mickey and Pip did theirs, he asked how she was liking high school and that was all he had to do. In mile-a-minute speak, Pippa answered, telling him even more than what I knew about how she felt about high school (in summary, it was *awesome*).

We got dinner together and were seated, Mickey at the end of the bar, me, Auden and Pippa down the front, and Mickey told my son that I'd told him Auden wrestled.

"Yeah," Auden confirmed.

"You any good?" Mickey asked.

"Made all-county and won regionals last year," Auden answered, his tone bordering between proud and humble.

My good son.

"You're good," Mickey muttered, took a forked-up bite of his pulled chicken sandwich (the only way you could eat it since it was piled high with cheese and slaw). He swallowed and his eyes slid to me. "And *this* is good."

I grinned at him. "Thanks, honey."

He gave me a moment to take in his eyes dancing before he looked back to Auden. "Obviously, you're gonna wrestle again this year."

"Yeah," Auden replied. "We've already started conditioning." He looked at me and teased, "You don't have to come, Mom."

I rolled my eyes at him and shoved a forkful of sandwich in my mouth.

"Why wouldn't you go?" Mickey asked me.

"Mom hates wrestling," Auden answered for me.

I quickly chewed, swallowed and denied, "I don't hate wrestling. I just hate watching people wrestle *my son*."

"It's a sport. No one gets hurt," Auden returned.

"I know," I replied, falling into a conversation we'd had several times before. "But I'm a mom. This is a feeling you'll never feel so you'll never understand it so you just have to let me feel it and deal."

"I usually pin them," Auden pointed out.

"This, and the fact you're my son and I'd go even if you didn't, is why it doesn't drive me totally crazy. Just borderline crazy."

Auden shook his head, his lips quirking.

"You don't like your kid wrestling, you're gonna be a basket case at my fights," Mickey remarked.

I looked to him. "Probably. But if you ask me, I'm still going."

Mickey appeared surprised before his attention turned to Auden who asked, "You fight?"

Mickey nodded. "Adult league."

"Wow. Cool," Auden murmured.

"I'm sooooo...*totally*...going to the junior league fights," Pippa declared.

"You are?" I asked, stunned at her declaration.

"Totally," she confirmed.

"Totally because she's got a thing for Joe," Auden muttered.

"Auden!" Pippa snapped.

My son raised his brows. "Do I not speak truth?"

"No," she bit out.

Auden ducked his face to his plate, and before tossing a fry into his mouth, mumbled, "Full of it."

Before Pippa could explode, I shared, "Met Joe at the league signups. He seems very nice." I looked to my girl. "And very cute."

Pink hit her cheeks and she looked away to concentrate on her meal.

"Too bad Polly's got a thing for Joe too," Auden added.

This did not make me feel good things, especially when Pippa's head jerked Auden's way.

"She does?"

Auden looked to his sister, to me, to Mickey then said to Olympia, "She's kinda big on anything you're big on."

They were friends. That would be the case.

However, this should not include boys.

Pip looked a little startled, a little confused as she turned her attention back to her plate and before I could wade in and change the subject, Mickey, clearly noticing Pippa's discomfiture as well, did it for me.

"So, Auden, you gonna be a doctor like your dad or you thinkin' you got other plans?"

This was so smooth, his mention of Conrad in a casual way, no nastiness, not even a tinge of ugly to his tone, I wanted to grab his head, yank him to me and kiss him.

Both kids caught it too. I knew it when both looked his way appearing surprised.

But Auden, my good boy, followed Mickey's lead and went with it.

"Dad's job is awesome but I'm not thinking it's for me. My uncle Lawrie let me observe him in court once, and he ruled. It was freaking cool. So I don't know, I got some time to decide, but I might be an attorney."

Mickey gave no indication he comprehensively disliked that profession and replied, "Big plans. You already thinking of colleges?"

Auden answered his question and thus began easy chatting while eating that Mickey skillfully guided, mostly with the kids showing he was interested in them in a natural way that wasn't nosy or eager to please.

As for me, I ate, listened to the casualness of their getting to know each other and just felt the happy.

I was feeling this when I also felt Mickey's knee brush my knee and I turned my head his way.

His lips hitched up very slightly but it was his eyes that were communicating.

They said, *See? It's going fine.*

I pressed my knee against his and hoped I gave him the message back that I agreed and it was making me happy.

Dinner done, the kids cleared and rinsed the dishes, putting them in the dishwasher as Mickey got out the dessert plates and I got out the apple pie and ice cream.

Conversation was still flowing but it was at this juncture that it occurred to me that Mickey inserting himself into dinner activities rather than sitting on a stool, drinking beer and being removed, was another skillful move. He'd been to my house often. He was welcome at my house any time I could get him there. I couldn't say we made dinner together or ate together there but he really wasn't a guest in my home. He was part of my life and thus part of my home.

And he didn't cast himself in the role of guest in my home when my children were present either. Something they couldn't miss and something that again Mickey made easy.

I was grinning to myself at how smart Mickey was when his phone in his jeans pocket rang.

I didn't think much of this, didn't even look at him until I felt the shiver trill down my spine.

My head snapped his way to see his focus completely on his phone, his lips muttering, "Sorry, gotta take this," and his legs moving him out of the kitchen.

I had one eye on Mickey wandering across the landing, one hand on the handle of the knife I was pulling out of the block and half a mind on my daughter who was asking me, "Mom, you want me to nuke the caramel sauce?" when Mickey stopped, turned and started back our way.

"Right. There in ten," he stated, took his phone from his ear and looked to me. "Gotta go, babe. Fire on the jetty."

My body stilled completely.

Mickey's didn't. His long legs brought him in my space where he bent quick, hand cupped on the back of my head to tilt it, and he brushed his lips against mine so briefly, it was a memory while it was happening.

"Sorry," he muttered.

"That's okay," I forced out.

He let me go and looked between the kids. "Sorry to cut this short. Good meal. Cool to meet you."

"No probs," Auden replied as Mickey moved swiftly to the door. "Cool to meet you too."

"Be safe!" my daughter, far more together than me, called as the door was closing on Mickey.

I stared at the door.

There in ten.

I kept staring at the door.

Fire on the jetty.

"Mom, you okay?"

Mickey was off to fight a fire on the jetty.

"Hey, Mom, you okay?"

I blinked and saw Pippa in my space.

"There's a fire on the jetty," I whispered and watched my daughter watching me and then I saw her face twist.

Fear.

For Mickey, maybe.

For me, that was the bigger possibility.

I'd proved to both my kids that I couldn't handle extreme situations.

She thought I was going to lose it.

So I had to pull myself together for a variety of reasons.

For my daughter, who, like my son possibly was with his father, had me to look to to learn how to cope with life and all it could throw at you.

For Mickey, who loved being a firefighter and wanted me in his life so I had to prove I had it in me to deal when something like this happened. He fought fires. He didn't need to do it at the same time worried his woman was at home falling apart with worry.

And for my son, who possibly was manning up, thinking he had to take care of his mom, and who also didn't need to worry about his mother falling apart.

Mickey was trained. Mickey was experienced. Mickey had done this before.

I had to trust in him and in the fates that brought him to me. And I had to trust that having him, thus having happiness, the fates wouldn't then sweep it all away.

I drew in breath and focused on my daughter.

"Okay, do we want pie? And I didn't ask, did you guys get your school-work done? This was a big night for us and we were all busy preparing. But now there's time so you can hit it without having to stay up until midnight."

Pippa stared at me in blank surprise.

"I got stuff to do," Auden shared.

I looked to my son. "You want to do it eating pie?"

He was examining me closely.

He stopped doing that, gave me a gentle grin and asked, "Am I Auden Moss?"

"You are," I confirmed, grinning back. It might be forced but damn it, I did it.

"Then...totally," Auden answered about the pie.

"Okay. I'll get pie," I said. "You get your books." I turned my attention back to Pippa. "Sweets? How about you?"

She kept staring at me a moment before she snapped out of it and told me, "I have a paper to write."

"Oh God, I hope it isn't a long one," I mumbled.

"It'll go faster with pie," she declared.

I winked at her and replied, "Gotcha. Need my laptop?"

"I have mine."

"Okay. Let's get on it," I said, moving back to the pie.

I was quaking inside and I let that happen.

Outside, I was holding it together.

Maybe one day I'd be able to completely deal.

Maybe not.

It didn't matter.

This was working.

THE TV WAS PLAYING. THE KIDS WERE ON THE COUCH WATCHING IT. I WAS IN my armchair with a full glass of wine I hadn't touched in an hour and a half.

My eyes were to the television but my mind was on my phone, which was sitting at the base of my wineglass on the table beside me.

I was still quaking inside and now it was worse. It was lucky I was sitting down because I could give the appearance of relaxed lounging when I was not relaxed in the slightest.

It was after eleven. And it was precisely three hours and forty-two minutes since Mickey rushed out to fight a fire on the jetty.

How long did it take to fight a fire?

My phone rang and I couldn't contain my jump, which I fancied sent me inches into the air in my chair.

I sensed my kids jumping with me.

I looked to the phone and felt a sweet release when I saw on the display that it was Mickey.

I snatched it up and leaped from the chair as I took the call and put the phone to my ear.

"Hey," I greeted.

"Hey back," he replied as I walked the landing in front of my wall of windows.

"Everything okay?" I asked.

"Fire's out," he answered.

"Everyone's fine?" I pushed.

"We're all good, baby," he said softly, but he sounded tired.

I felt my shoulders slump as I stopped, dropped my head and kept the phone to my ear.

"Good," I whispered then suddenly lifted my head, twisted and gave a thumb's up and a reassuring smile to my kids, both of whom were looking over the couch at me.

Pippa clapped silently and Auden gave me a relieved grin.

I turned my attention back to my feet. "Was there a lot of damage?"

"Four shops gutted, fire and smoke damage to the rest of the jetty. It wasn't good, Amy. Had to call all the rigs in all over the county."

"Oh my God," I breathed.

"Yeah. Haven't had anything this big in at least ten, eleven years. We're waitin' for the cool down so the chief and captains can go in, have a look.

But this is a new build. Chief did the inspections himself. No way this shoulda gotten this out of control."

This did not make me feel great but I was talking to Mickey who sounded tired but obviously was alive so I pushed past that and asked, "What are you saying?"

"I'm sayin' by the time I got here, there were three rigs here and three shops were already gone. Buildings that are less than a year old made of modern materials, fire alarms and state-of-the art fire protection systems."

"Are you saying—?"

He cut me off. "Right now I'm sayin' we'll finish this later. I just wanted you to know all was good. Most of the shops were closed, civilians that were around got out. No one hurt. We're hosin' it down, makin' sure all the sparks are out. Gonna be a while before I get home."

"I'll have my phone on my nightstand."

"What?" he sounded distracted.

"I'll have my phone on my nightstand," I told him. "Call me, text me, whatever before you come home. I just want to see you before you go to sleep. I'll run over and just...see you then let you go in and crash. Would you mind doing that?"

I had his full attention when he replied, "It's late and it's gonna be later when I get home, Amy."

"You know I don't mind late when it comes to you."

I got a soft, sweet, "Right. Then I'll get in touch, darlin'."

"Okay, Mickey. I'll let you go."

"Thanks, babe. Later."

"'Bye, honey."

We rang off and I turned to my kids.

"So he's okay?" Auden asked for confirmation.

"He is," I nodded, moving back to them. "Everyone is. It's all good. I mean," I positioned my behind over the chair and fell into it, "not the jetty, which sustained a lot of damage. But the important part. The people."

"Bummed," Pippa murmured then jerked her head and assured me, "Not about Mickey. Totes happy he's good, Mom. Just that there are a lot of awesome shops on the jetty. I hope the good ones didn't get toasted."

"Olympia Moss, ground zero on new mental illness. Shopping on the brain," Auden said, his tone having an edge of nasty but it was this in subtle rebuke, stating in his big brother way he thought she'd been insensitive.

"Auden! Shut up!" she snapped.

Auden opened his mouth but I got there before him, doing it straightening out of the chair I'd just collapsed in, taking my wine with me.

"Okay, kiddos, no fighting. I know Pip didn't mean anything by what she said. But Mom's had a rough night. The meeting of her beloved children with a man she cares about who is officially now in *all* of our lives and that man racing off to fight a fire before having his pie. I need to sip wine in a hot bath and then go to sleep. Can I do that without you two killing each other in front of the TV?"

"With Pip as my sister, I have tons of experience curbing murderous tendencies," Auden declared.

"With Auden as my brother, I have *more*," Pip added irately.

"Wonderful. I'll wake up to my house as I like it and not the aftermath of a blood bath," I said while walking in front of the couch and stopping. "Now, hugs for your mom who had a rough night seeing as you could be eighty and give me hugs and that'd fortify me through anything."

To my delight, neither hesitated before they got up and gave me hugs.

Pippa's was tight and swift.

Auden's was longer and included a kiss on the cheek.

As they settled back in, I wandered away, the quake inside gone, good to get in my bathtub, soak, finish my wine and wait for Mickey's call.

I did my wandering, saying, "Don't stay up much longer."

"Won't, Mom," Auden replied.

"Going to bed soon," Pippa told me.

"Okay, kids, 'night."

I got return "'nights." I walked to my room. I took my bath. I sipped my wine. I did both of these extremely glad that night was over and proud of myself that I'd found it in me to hold myself together.

Out of the bath, I lotioned and put a spritz of perfume, a pair of fleecy yoga pants, a shelf-bra camisole and a cardigan that was soft and pretty but was also warm.

I lit my fire, got my book, set my phone on the side table and was about to lay on the daybed snuggled under my afghan waiting for Mickey's call when my eyes drifted to the door.

Mickey was fine. The night went well. All my loved ones were safe.

But one thing happened that night that was niggling me, and after the success of the evening, my kids showing they were good kids, I thought it might be time to do something about it.

I walked out of my room and down the hall to see the living room dark, the TV off.

I kept walking and saw no light coming from under Pippa's door.

But there was one coming from under Auden's.

I knocked softly at my son's door and called, "Hey, kid, you still up?"

"Yeah, come in, Mom," he called back.

I opened the door, took a step in and stopped.

I had not found a cleaning lady yet because I still was enjoying the feeling of accomplishment when I cleaned my own house.

But with the kids back, I enjoyed it more, picking up rooms they'd made their own because they spent time in them.

Auden's bed worked much better no longer against the side wall but the back wall and facing his windows to the sea. He had band posters up plus blood-guts-and-glory type inspirational posters, these he'd started putting up years ago, I suspected to psych him up constantly, if sometimes subconsciously, to be a good competitor.

He needed to tidy. He was like his dad dropping his clothes every-where. And there was tons of stuff all over his dresser, his desk. This I never touched, thinking he probably knew how to find whatever he needed. But it was a sixteen-year-old boy's room, lived in and Auden's, even if it was that in a multi-million dollar show home.

I liked this.

But I was hesitant about the conversation we needed to have.

"Everything cool, Mom?" he asked, prompting me out of my study of his room, and I gave my attention to him.

He was across the room, standing in his pajamas but he had his tablet in his hand, and when I'd opened the door, he'd been sticking his head-phones in it.

"Just wanted to bend your ear a second about something that's trou-bling me," I told him.

"What?" he asked.

I stepped in, shut the door and leaned into it. "What's your read on Polly?"

His face went guarded.

"I'm not being—" I started to assure him quickly.

"She's a phase," he cut me off to say.

"I'm sorry?"

"For Pip. She's not Pippa's normal kind of friend. But Polly knows everybody. She's real social. Big on that. And Pip coming to a new school, Polly latched on. Pip having money and nice clothes and being pretty and stuff..." he trailed off and shrugged, though he didn't need to finish that, I knew what he was saying. Then he continued, "I think she's a phase."

"So you don't care for her all that much," I guessed.

"Won't have to think anything once Pip finds her place in high school and Polly's history."

That was his hope.

He did not like Polly.

It was also my hope because as awful as it was to say, I didn't either.

I nodded. "Okay, Auden. I didn't want to put you on the spot but I also got the sense she wasn't Pippa's kind of friend. That said, it's clear Pip likes spending time with her so I didn't want to bring it up with your sister and upset her."

He nodded too. "Yeah. But we're just back at school, Mom. Freshmen settle in. She'll find it."

"Okay, kid," I replied.

"Don't worry. Pip's a good girl. It'll turn out okay."

I loved my son.

I smiled. "You're right. It will. But mothers worry."

He smiled back. "Well, you can stop worrying about that."

Very, *very* much loved my son.

"Okay, I'll leave you to your music."

"Right, Mom. 'Night."

"'Night, kiddo."

I gave him another smile before I went out the door, closed it behind me and walked back to my room.

Feeling better about all that, only then did I settle into my daybed to read and wait for Mickey's call.

* * *

My body jolted as my cell rang.

I sat up, my book crashing to the floor, and snatched the phone up.

"Hey," I said into it.

"Hey back," Mickey replied. "Almost on our street."

"Okay, honey, I'll be over at your place. Quick kiss then you can hit the sack."

"See you there."

We rang off and I stared a little guiltily at the fire I'd left burning and fell asleep in front of (though, who would have imagined I could ever fall asleep waiting for Mickey coming back after fighting a fire). I shut off the gas, waited for the flame to die out then slid my feet into my slippers that looked like they were made of sweater material, with sequins on the knit and a fluffy trim of fake fur. They were warm but they also had a plastic sole with traction.

Then I took off, dashing down the hall and out the front door.

I slowed my step as I made my way down the walk.

I speeded it up as I saw the lights of Mickey's SUV coming down the street.

I darted in a half-jog, half-walk up Mickey's drive, doing this following his SUV.

I slowed again as he got out of his truck but only because I was nearly upon him.

I didn't wait for him to close the car door before I threw myself in his arms.

As mine closed around him, his wrapped tight around me and I could feel his breath stirring the hair on top of my head.

"Fuck, you smell good," he murmured.

"Took a bath before bed to relax," I replied to his chest.

"Mm..."

I felt his sound through my cheek and it vibrated deep in my belly.

We held on a while and when Mickey stated gently, "I'm good, Amy," I tipped my head back to catch his eyes.

"Yeah," I whispered.

He cupped my jaw with a hand. "You worried."

"I was terrified out of my mind," I told him the absolute truth but did it in a quip and then delighted in his chuckle.

He thought I was joking.

And he would think that, forever.

I would never lie to Mickey about anything else.

But so he could do what he loved to do to protect the citizens of Magdalene without a thought of the worry it caused me, I'd hide that from him for as long as he gave his time to the MFD.

Then he said something to me that, not with his words but with the strength he assumed I had in sharing them, was one of the biggest compliments he could give me.

"It was arson, Amy."

I stared up at him. "Really?"

"Chief's callin' in an investigator. We don't have one workin' for the county because we don't need one. But it was not one fire that spread. We found fire origin in three of those shops. We saw it. We know it. Bobby wants someone to make it official so Coert's got everything he needs."

"Who would do that?" I asked.

"No clue," he answered. "Could be some issue with those shops or that development. Could be we got a fire bug."

Oh, God. No.

I hid the panic at the very idea of that and what it would mean to the boys of the MFD, primarily Mickey, when I saw the fatigue gathered around his eyes and said, "Okay, honey. It's out now and all's good. But it's late so I need to let you go so you can get some rest."

"Okay, baby, kiss first."

I nodded, rolling up on my toes as he bent into me and we shared a quick, sweet kiss that was a little wet since, during it, he touched his tongue to mine.

I rolled back and whispered, "Glad you and all the guys are safe, Mickey."

"Me too, babe."

I gave him a squeeze and ordered, "Go to bed."

"Right," he muttered, bending in for another lip touch before I pulled away and moved away so he could get out of his car door and close it.

"Sleep well," I told him, grabbing his hand and leaning back into him.

"Will do. You too."

"Will do. 'Night, honey."

He tightened his hand in mine before letting it go on his, "'Night, Amy."

I grinned, turned and walked away only to stop and turn around when he said loudly with great humor, "Jesus, darlin'."

"What?" I asked.

"Only my heiress would have fluffy slippers with sequins on 'em."

I loved it that with the night he had, he was smiling and I'd done something to make him do it.

Thus I went for more.

"There's not much I do to keep up the Bourne-Hathaway name, but I feel it's a moral imperative to wear appropriate heiress slippers."

He shook his head and ordered, "Go home."

"You got it," I replied, turned and strolled back to my house.

This time, I didn't do it letting Mickey watch me in my yoga pants and sequined slippers.

I did it turning once and waving hard, with a big smile.

He also had a big smile and he jerked up his chin.

I didn't hear the garage door go down and I would see as I was closing my front door that Mickey waited at the rear bumper of his SUV for me to get home safely even though I lived right across our usually sleepy but at that hour, now totally comatose street.

My guy was a good guy.

I locked the door and then jumped a mile when I heard, "Mom."

I turned, hand to my chest, heart hammering, to see Olympia in the shadows.

"Honey, you scared the dickens out of me."

Suddenly, I found my daughter in my arms, the side of her head pressed to the side of mine and she was squeezing the breath out of me.

Just as suddenly as she threw herself in my arms, she said, "Glad Mickey's okay," let me go, turned and hurried away.

She'd heard me make plans to go see he was all right.

She'd waited up with me.

And maybe, (I didn't put it past my girl, she could be nosy) she'd watched through the guestroom window as I ran across the street to make sure he was all right.

I had a feeling Mickey had already earned my baby girl's stamp of approval.

Just because he meant something to me.

And fortunately, even though she'd waited up, obviously she hadn't heard her brother and me talking about Polly.

I smiled to myself as I turned away from the door, wandered down the hall, took off my cardigan and threw it on the arm of the daybed, kicked off my sequined slippers and climbed into bed.

Then I, Amelia Hathaway, who'd grown up not learning how to deal and never having a solid foundation, after a very rough night, fell right to sleep.

23

MY UMBRELLA

I was Pledging my fabulous new dining room table that looked *perfect* in its place in my great room and better, the bowl I'd bought that began my new beginning looked *perfect* in the middle of the table, when my phone rang.

I wandered to it, thinking I needed a rug under it and wondering if I'd be able to find that, and arrange for Mickey—and perhaps Junior and Jake, with the help of Auden—to come and move the huge, heavy table in order to put the rug under it.

This was a happy thought, which made the announcement on the display even more annoying than it normally would be, considering it obliterated my happy thought.

I sighed and wondered if I should perhaps not be grown up all the time as I took the call and put the phone to my ear.

"Conrad," I greeted.

"You didn't phone my secretary," he replied.

No hello. He didn't even say my name in greeting.

This was not starting out great.

"I'm sorry. You called during an important evening and it slipped my mind," I somewhat lied.

He ignored my mention of the important evening and asked, "Now that I have you, when can we meet?"

"Perhaps first you can tell me *why* we're meeting," I suggested.

"We need to talk," he said shortly.

"I could guess that. But about what?"

"This situation with the children isn't working."

"I'm sorry you feel that way but it's working for me"

"I can imagine it is. But it isn't for Martine."

Like I gave a crap.

He had to know I felt that way so I didn't tell him that.

"They're of an age they can decide where they want to spend their time," I informed him of something he knew, since he'd forced them to make that decision in a legal way. "But more, it would seem from their demeanor that they enjoy that freedom. I think, as their parents, having put them in a position where they have to divide their time between us, giving them the ability to do that as they wish is something we should allow."

"The way things are, Amelia, Martine doesn't know if they're going to be home for dinner. If she'll need to pack lunches for them. This affects grocery shopping—"

I interrupted him, "I face the same thing. However, I do find it's easy to cope with making last minute adjustments. And they aren't six and eight, Conrad. They can pack their own lunches, something they do at my house."

"Martine likes to be certain they eat healthy," he returned. "You would find it easy as they're *your* children so you'd make those adjustments as a matter of course. We can't forget that they *aren't* Martine's children, their home is her home, and the mingling of that has to be managed. This is not managed well."

The mingling of that has to be managed?

This entire thing was making me uneasy.

"Conrad, I don't need to remind you that your wife chose to pledge her troth to a man with children. Thus she had a readymade family, which I'm sorry if you disagree, but it's my feeling *she* would need to adjust to fit within that family, make our children comfortable in the home she shares with them, not *her* home, *all of your* home, and do what's best for them. If this means she has to endure the horror of cold cuts going bad because someone isn't eating them, I'm sure she'll eventually find it in her to survive."

"There's no need to get ugly," he clipped.

"You're taking my time to share the fact that your wife is annoyed she can't predict what groceries she needs to buy for the week, Conrad. I'm busy. I have a life. I don't have time for these trivialities. Honestly?"

"Our children aren't trivialities, Amelia," he snapped.

"We aren't discussing our children," I shot back. "We're discussing your wife. And to me, she *is*. Now, unless there's some *real* reason that this situation with the children cannot continue as it stands that you wish to discuss, the discussion is over. Things remain as they are and Martine has to find it in her to deal."

"Fuck, why did I think you'd give that first shit about managing an issue with our kids?"

"Because this *isn't* an issue with our kids," I whispered my reply. "You have an issue at home with your wife." That was a guess but with this ridiculous conversation, with the way I now knew my children were escaping that house and with what I knew of my ex-husband, it was a guess I suspected was correct. "You're making this *my* issue because you can't sort it yourself. I do not factor in your life, Conrad. I do not *want* to factor in your life. I will not be dragged into issues you have in your home with your wife. So do not *ever* call me when things are not going well for you unless that *genuinely* involves our children."

"I'm assuming this is your way of telling me that even though you've at long last settled down and pulled yourself together, you don't wish to participate in a team effort in the raising of our children."

How could he take that from what I said?

"Am I speaking English?" I asked.

"Go fuck yourself, Amelia," he retorted and hung up on me.

God, what a *dick*.

I stared at my phone now knowing things were not good with Conrad and Martine.

I didn't give a crap about that.

I was worried about my kids.

Shit.

LATER THAT MORNING, I PUSHED OPEN THE DOOR TO DOVE HOUSE AND MY eyes went right to the reception area where I saw Ruth sitting.

"Hey," I greeted.

I was surprised she was there. Ruth was still volunteering but sporadically, mostly because my three days a week, three hours a day had morphed into four days a week, four to five hours a day, and since I was there so often Dela didn't really need another volunteer who may or may not be in it for the long haul (the last part was what she really didn't need).

We always needed help, though, so Ruth filled in here and there, but it was no longer regular.

"Hey, Amelia," she replied.

"Good to see you," I said, shrugging off my jacket.

"You too," she returned. "But, um...Dela wants to see you too. In her office."

I focused more closely on her and saw her usual pretty, benevolent features were shadowed with something.

"Is everything okay?" I asked.

"Dela wants to speak with you, hon," she repeated.

I stared at her, nodded and went to the door that led to the administration wing. I didn't have to punch in the code because Ruth buzzed me in.

I walked down the short hall to Dela's office, jacket over my arm, purse over my shoulder, and stopped in her opened office door. I knocked on the jamb, and when her head came up and she looked at me, I said, "Hey, Dela. Ruth wanted me to check in with you?"

"Yes, Amelia, come in, would you? Have a seat."

She swept an arm to the chairs in front of her messy desk, and cautiously, I moved to one, feeling funny.

I'd been working there a while. I knew the lay of the land. I knew my duties. I knew when to pitch in, where and how. I knew the chain of command. I took tough stuff and easy stuff. Unless they thought I was a Nazi, all the residents liked me. I thought I did a good job.

I could not imagine I'd done something wrong.

Studying Dela's face as I sat and tucked my purse and jacket into my lap, I couldn't get a read on if it was saying I was in trouble or something else.

I just knew whatever it was saying wasn't good.

"What's going on?" I asked once I'd settled.

"Amelia, honey, worst part of this job but I have bad news for you, girl."

I tensed.

She gave it to me.

"Mrs. McMurphy passed away last night."

My lips parted and my throat started burning.

"I'm sorry, Amelia," she went on, sounding like she absolutely was. "You were real good with her and I know she liked you, even if she thought you were a Nazi. This is tough news to hear and I hate havin' to give it to you."

"But, she was okay yesterday," my mouth said for me, my voice sounding far away in my head.

Dela shrugged, keeping kind eyes on me. "Happens. Sometimes outta the blue like that. One minute their accusin' you of bein' in cahoots with Hitler. The next minute, peace." She got up, walked around her desk, sat in the chair next to me and leaned in to grab my hand. She held it between us and said softly, "First one's always the hardest, girl. Gotta say, plain truth, second one isn't a whole lot better. We know 'em. We care for 'em. We give 'em what we can to make their time with us as best as it can be. It isn't easy for them to be in here. And one thing we give 'em that they don't know they're gettin' is how hard it is to find it in us to be able to say good-bye."

I heard her. She was saying the right things.

But I looked to the window, wondering how on earth I could spend my days at Dove House without Mrs. McMurphy.

It was raining outside, gray, cold and windy, but I didn't see that.

I saw Mrs. McMurphy walking down the front walk in her coat with her umbrella on a sunny day.

It was no longer funny.

Right then, it pierced my heart and made it bleed.

I felt a tug at my hand and my eyes drifted to Dela.

"You with me?" she asked.

"They'll all go." My mouth was still speaking for me in that distant way.

"Eventually, we all go, honey."

She was right.

Mrs. Osborn.

Mrs. Porter.

God. Mr. Dennison.

"Not many folk have gifts like you and me."

I focused again on Dela at her words.

"We get it," she said, still gentle, but also now firm. "We got the strength others don't have not ever to show to them we know they'll go but we'll suffer the good-bye. We just keep on givin' 'em the good. That's our job. That's our gift. You with me?"

Somewhere in my dazed brain I understood she was challenging me.

And somewhere in my dazed brain I wondered if she actually saw that strength in me or if she wanted me to reach for it, believe in me, grab hold and give that to the folks I helped look after.

Perhaps the Amelia Hathaway my parents raised wouldn't actually have that gift Dela was talking about.

But the Amelia Hathaway I'd become in spite of that definitely had it.

So it wasn't just my mouth that replied, "I'm with you, Dela."

I saw relief flash in her eyes, knew then she thought this sad event, like it had probably with others, would have me leaving.

But truly, if I did, who would Mr. Dennison flirt with?

I tipped my head toward the wall. "Are they upset?" I asked.

Her hand clenched in mine before she let it go and sat back. "The ones who been around awhile, they're dealing. The new ones, not so much."

"I better get out there," I told her.

"Yeah," she replied.

"Thanks for being so kind in telling me."

"Practice," she murmured like she wished she didn't have it.

I figured she didn't want that practice (because who would?) as I gave her a smile that I hoped reassured her, got up and went to the door.

I turned in it to see she was up and rounding her desk.

"Do you have any idea why she thought I was a Nazi?"

Dela lifted her eyes to me as I spoke and shook her head after I was done. "No clue. The woman thought I was Rosa Parks. Every time she saw me she congratulated me on the courage I showed on that bus. Now I've seen a fair few pictures of Ms. Parks and not in one of them did the woman have braids. But didn't matter. Mrs. McMurphy lived in her own world and until the end it was a safe world. Somethin' else we can give. Somethin' she got."

Yes. That was something we gave. Even as a Nazi, she never feared me. So that was something she got.

"Thanks, Dela," I said.

"Not a problem, honey," she replied.

"Are you okay?" I asked.

"Long time ago, I learned what was important to give and through that, how to deal."

I nodded, gave her a wave and walked out of her door to get to the residents.

I spent part of my time there seeing to things that needed to get done, but most of it I spent being with the resident, taking their pulse, being sensitive and as business as usual in the circumstances as I could be.

It was not a fun day.

And at the end of it, I did something that was probably not right.

But I didn't care.

I went to Mrs. McMurphy's room, stole that broken umbrella and took it home with me.

I didn't know why I wanted it.

What I did know was that it would always be with me.

———— • ————

I STOOD AT MY WALL OF WINDOWS, THE DOUBLE-PANED GLASS SURPRISINGLY warm on the inside when I knew the day, still gray, damp and windy, was chill.

I stared at the stormy sea and thought I needed some kind of seating up there. The landing was wide, two people could walk across it comfortably. Maybe three. A nice seating arrangement or chaise lounge that you could relax in, watch the sea and brood when you had really crappy days that no book or TV would help would be just the ticket.

My phone chimed and I looked over my shoulder to it sitting on the kitchen counter.

I wanted to continue to mope about Mrs. McMurphy but it was the Wednesday after the week Mickey met my kids. My kids weren't over that night and Mickey had texted that morning to say we should get together if they weren't coming since both Cillian and Aisling had something going on at friends' houses.

Since it might be Mickey, I went to the phone, picked it up and saw it was a text from Auden.

I opened it. It said, *Found it* and it had a web link.

I touched the link and a page on the official Magdalene site came up with the title of "Town of Magdalene: Budget, Financials and Annual Reports."

In continuing to search but not finding the information, I'd asked Auden to help and obviously he'd done it.

I looked at the web address and saw that this information was buried under "About Magdalene" then "Meet the Town Council" then "Our Administrative Staff" and finally "Other Information."

No wonder I couldn't find it.

I went back to my texts, thanked my son, and forwarded it to Robin, telling her, *Auden got it. Here it is. Can you look and report back?*

She knew what it was about because I'd mentioned it. And I was asking for her help because once, in a very brief period of deciding that perhaps her life was more than wreaking havoc on her ex, she'd decided to become an accountant (part of this, admittedly, was to be around accountants in order to find a new man because, "Amelia, sweets, a boring accountant wouldn't have it in him to cheat").

This had started with bookkeeping classes. And even though she switched back to wreaking havoc on her ex, it included her finishing those classes as during one of their clashes he'd baited her about them, telling her she'd never finished anything she started.

She finished those. Two years of them.

But even before that, she was good with numbers.

Roger wilco.

That made my mouth curve up.

Five minutes later, I was back to moping at the same time considering cueing up a movie in order to take my mind off things.

I was considering this because I could be brain dead doing it. I actually should be going over some of the online paperwork I'd told Mickey I'd fill out for him in order to file it so he could establish his new company. I also knew I should check email because, in his stead, I'd requested some insurance quotes for his new enterprise and I knew those would be coming in imminently.

I'd done this after Josie had told me that in order to cope with a busy life, Jake had found a wife.

I was not Mickey's wife but that didn't mean I couldn't help. And when I'd offered, I knew the extent of his gratitude just with the way he looked at me.

So I was on it, and although it was a slow process, I was getting there.

But at that moment, in the doldrums, I didn't think I had the brain capacity.

These were my mental meanderings when my phone rang.

It was Mickey.

"Hey," I greeted.

"Hey back," he replied. "Listen, babe, Ash's plans changed. She's home tonight. Thought you could come over for dinner."

To my surprise, I didn't like this idea.

If it was just Mickey, I'd take time with Mickey. I'd be with Mickey anytime I could.

Except right then, with Ash.

It was nothing against Ash. It was just that I felt I had to be upbeat around her, keeping things light, keeping myself open should she wish to bond or unload or anything with me. She hadn't been back at Mickey's house long enough for Mickey to have another try at a sit down so it wasn't that.

It was that both of us moping I didn't think would be a good thing. I knew I didn't have it in me to be upbeat. And Ash was such a concern I didn't want to introduce any kind of bad mood that she might catch, making her even worse.

"Why don't you have some time with Ash, Mickey? I'll stay home and let you have that."

There was a moment of silence before, "You okay?"

"Not really," I told him.

"What's going on?" he asked.

"Conrad called this morning. He was a dick to me, but reading between the lines, something's up with him and Martine and he's taking that out on me," I told him.

"Fuck," he growled.

"More importantly, Mrs. McMurphy died last night."

"Babe," he whispered.

Then it happened. Like it had happened the time I talked to him when my kids came back to me.

And as a repeat, my sob was audible.

Mickey heard it. "Amy, baby."

"I haven't cried yet," I sniffed.

"Have at it, then," he offered.

It was a lovely offer, so very Mickey, but I didn't "have at it."

I wiped my face, took a deep breath and said, "Maybe it's good that tonight I just hang at home, watch a movie…"

I trailed off, thinking of myself clutching Mrs. McMurphy's umbrella and watching *Cocoon*.

Maybe I *should* mope with Ash at Mickey's.

Mickey spoke my thoughts. "Not sure that's a good idea."

"I won't be good company, Mickey. I'll be okay and I'll come over another night."

"Amy—"

"I'll be okay."

He didn't respond immediately and when he did, it was, "Hang on."

I hung on.

He came back. "Shit, got a patch job that's come through. After work, gotta go see to that."

"See?" I asked. "This is not our night."

"Right," he replied. "Touch base with you later."

"Okay, Mickey."

"Keep your chin up 'til then."

"I will, honey."

"Later, babe."

"'Bye, Mickey."

We hung up and I pulled myself together, getting some hummus and tortilla chips and camping out in front of the TV *not* watching *Cocoon* (or *The Notebook* or *Fried Green Tomatoes*). Instead I watched *Rock of Ages* and did it hoping Cillian didn't see it because emulating Tom Cruise from that movie might make Mickey's head explode.

I was channel surfing after the movie when I jerked and lifted up, looking over the back of the couch toward the door because the bell rang.

I didn't have the best view but I still could see it was Mickey through the stained glass.

"Touching base," I mumbled to myself, liking that I had a guy who would do that in person after I got really bad news that ruined my day.

I rolled off the couch, went to the door, unlocked it and tipped my head back.

"Hey," I greeted.

"Hey back," he replied then pushed a handled, glossy bag my way. "That the right shit?"

I stared at him, brows drawn, before I took the bag, opened it and saw inside a bottle of my cleanser and another of my moisturizer. These were rattling around with a toothbrush in its plastic.

I didn't use stuff you got at Walgreen's.

My stuff was expensive and you got it direct from the salon or at the mall.

He'd gone to the mall for me.

Slowly, I lifted my head and, not knowing what else to say, said, "Yes."

"Right," he replied, pushed past me, walked to the kitchen, nabbed my purse, snatched up my phone then came right back to me. "Keys in your purse?"

"Yes," I repeated.

He handed my purse to me. "Get 'em out."

"Mickey, I—"

"Let's go, babe. I'm starved and Ash has dinner ready." My mouth dropped open as his eyes moved to the TV. "Fuck. That's on. I'll get that."

He then sauntered to the TV, turned it off and then turned off all the lamps I had lit.

After that, he came back to me.

"Keys?" he prompted.

"Are you saying...am I...am I spending the night at your place?" I stammered.

"You had a shit day," he replied. "You lost someone you knew. Don't know how tight you were with her. Do know it fucked with you. So you're not gonna sit over here alone and you're not gonna sleep alone. You're comin' over. Broke the news to the kids that we lost Mrs. McMurphy today. They're not feelin' good about it, just like you. So we're gonna have dinner and hang and then you're gonna sleep beside me, mostly so I can sleep beside you and know you're okay. The kids know you're spendin' the night. They get why in more ways than one. And they want you over. So, keys out, Amy, so we can lock up and get home so I can eat."

I felt tears hit my eyes again.

"Babe," he said impatiently, "cry over at my place. We'll hole up in my room. But at least after I get you through that, all I gotta do is walk to my kitchen so I can stuff my face."

I licked my lips, rolled them and took a breath through my nose.

Then I bent my head, dug out my keys and walked out the door.

Mickey followed me.

I locked my door.

Mickey grabbed my hand and walked us to his place.

We didn't hole up in his room.

By the time we got there, I'd pulled myself together.

So when we got there, there was no delay in Mickey stuffing his face.

———— • ————

LIKE MICKEY DID WITH MY KIDS, BUT WITH MORE PRACTICE, ME AND THE Donovans cleaned up the kitchen after dinner.

Through dinner, I could tell the kids were a bit stunned by the news, but since they'd only met her a couple of times, mostly they were cautious and watchful over me.

It was sweet.

It wasn't until we had the kitchen cleared and we were camped out in front of the TV that Cillian stated loudly, "Okay. I'm just gonna say it. She was a nutty old lady and she was funny. Why can't we think about the funny? If she was right in the head and here right now, wouldn't she want us to think of her and how funny she was?"

"Cill," Ash, who had elected not to close herself in her room that evening, snapped.

"I'm being serious," he shot back. "I mean, I didn't know her when she was right in the head, but if I ever got not right in the head I'd want people to think I'm funny instead of worrying about me and bein' sad. And after I'm gone, I'd want them to remember me that way. That's a whole lot better than bein' sad."

"Maybe Amy feels like being sad," Aisling retorted. "She knew her better than you."

"I stole her umbrella," I announced into this discussion.

All three pairs of Donovan eyes came to me.

"Come again, baby?" Mickey asked cautiously.

I told them the story of her taking a stroll in the cold rain on a warm sunny day and then shared, "So before I left today, I went into her room and stole that umbrella." I looked to Cillian. "I had no idea why I did it until you said what you said, kiddo. Now I know I did it because when she did what she did, it made me smile. But I'd wanted to laugh. And I wanted to remember that about her. I took that umbrella because I never want to forget her and I always want to remember how she made me want to laugh."

"See?" Cillian said to Aisling.

Before Ash could retort, I told them something they knew. "She thought I was a Nazi."

And then I started giggling.

Uncontrollably.

"She told me you had a poison pill in your tooth," Cillian shared through my giggles, smiling at me. "And you better use it because she'd told the Office of Strategic Services on you."

I started laughing harder.

"She told me your cell phone was some secret Nazi coding machine and you were sending messages direct to Joseph Goebbels," Aisling added.

At that, I was forced to fall sideways because Mickey's arm curved around me and he pulled me into him as I started laughing hysterically.

"One thing can be said, the woman knew her history," Mickey observed drolly and I curled my face into his chest to mute my cackles.

And I loved to feel his chuckles, hear them and his children laughing with me.

It took a while and I was just sobering when Ash asked, "I'm pretty sure Mrs. McMurphy liked Rice Krispie treats because *everyone* likes Rice Krispie treats so we should celebrate her life with Rice Krispie treats. Who's with me?"

"Totally!" Cillian cried. "With peanut butter."

"No, darlin'," Mickey put in and I shifted my face so my cheek was to his shoulder as he went on, directing this at his daughter, "Chocolate chips."

"Chocolate chips *and* peanut butter," Cillian bargained.

Mickey sent an easy grin to his boy. "Good compromise, son."

"Cill, you're on marshmallow duty," Aisling ordered, pushing out of the couch.

Cillian didn't push out of the couch. He vaulted over the back.

Mickey's arm around me gave me a squeeze and I tipped my head to look up at him. I also noticed how he grabbed his girl's hand as she walked by him and gave that a squeeze too. And through this, I didn't miss her looking down at her dad and giving him a sweet smile.

When she was gone and the kids were in the kitchen making Rice Krispie treats, he turned his attention to me.

"Better?" he asked.

I loved him.

Totally loved him.

I mean, how could you *not* love a man who helped you end a day where the world lost a soul that had touched your heart, doing it guiding you to it giggling with his family and eating peanut butter, chocolate chip Rice Krispie treats?

"Better," I whispered.

He dipped in and touched his mouth to mine.

Then he turned his eyes back to the TV.

I stayed tucked close, rested my cheek back to his shoulder and did the same.

It was late, hopefully Donovan family bedtime because I was tired, and I was coming back from the bathroom when I ran into Ash in the hallway.

"Hey, blossom, going to bed?" I asked.

"Yeah," she answered.

I stopped and thought twice but decided to go for it, reaching a hand her way and brushing the back of hers with my fingertips before I said quietly, "Thank you for helping make me feel better tonight."

She ducked her head, shrugged a shoulder and replied, "Not a problem, Amy."

I didn't like that but I didn't push it. The night had been a good night. She'd been Ash of old (or the old I knew). Hanging with her family. Being quiet-ish but not gloomy. It wasn't the time to push it.

"Okay, kid, I'll let you go to bed. Thanks for a good dinner," I said, giving her a small grin and moving past her.

"Amy?" she called.

I stopped and turned back, seeing her in the open door to her bedroom.

I was only two feet away.

"Yes, honey?" I asked.

"Mom bought that candle. The one on the coffee table."

At her words, words delivered apropos of nothing but whatever was in Aisling's head, I braced.

"Okay," I said when she spoke no more.

"It was on what she called our first 'big girl shopping trip,'" she told me. "I was seven. I picked the sand."

"It's a pretty candle, Ash," I remarked when she stopped talking.

"She brought it home," she carried on like I didn't speak. "Dad teased her like he always teased her when she bought candles. Saying no wife of a fireman had candles. But he didn't really care. What she liked, he'd like because he liked her."

"Aisling," I whispered.

She lifted her chin. "She took it. When she left. She took it."

I nodded.

"I stole it," she declared. "I stole it and brought it back."

"Right," I said gently.

Her chin trembled and she stared at me.

"Ash—"

"It's my umbrella," she whispered.

Then she disappeared behind her closed door.

Which was good since I had to put my hand to the wall to hold myself up, she'd cut me so deep, the blood was pouring out of me.

———— • ————

"Fuck me," Mickey murmured, his head turned to the side.

He had his back against his headboard, knees cocked, gray flannel pajama bottoms on. I'd never seen him in pajama bottoms (or anything of the like). Then again, when Mickey and I spent the night together, it didn't involve children in the house.

I was cross-legged beside him, wearing his tee.

I'd just told him Aisling's candle story.

"Mickey—"

He looked to me. "She brought it back. I noticed. I didn't say anything because she was weird about it and it was clear she didn't want me to say anything."

"That was probably a good call," I replied.

"For her, that candle's good times. Before her mom got lost in the bottle. When things were good between her mom and me. Good in the family."

I nodded.

Mickey looked away and repeated, "Fuck me."

I gave him a moment, doing it because he needed it but doing it hating to watch him bleed for his baby, before I advised gently, "You should leave it, honey."

"Yeah," he told his duvet.

"Mickey?"

He looked to me. "Yeah?"

I looked at him. I looked in those beautiful blue eyes that were now bruised. Worried about his girl. Wanting to fix things. A provider. A protector. Powerless against ugly memories that were still being made.

I wanted to tell him I loved him. I wanted those words to be the magic words I could say that would sweep away the pain. If even for a brief flash of happy, take it all away and send him soaring.

But it was too soon. Neither of us had gotten anywhere near that. In our one-step-at-a-time relationship that included us building it at the same time taking our positions in each other's families, which would ultimately lead to blending those families, I was spending my first night in his bed under his roof with his kids there.

That was enough for now.

So I gave him that, pushing forward and putting my hands to him, then my weight to him as I kissed his chest, lifted up and kissed the base of his throat and finally snuggled close.

He curved his arms around me.

"The good news is she opened up to me. That means, maybe I can see where that will lead and get more," I remarked.

"Yeah, that's the good news."

He didn't seem fired up about it.

Then again, he had to see that candle every day probably dozens of times a day and do it knowing what it meant.

I decided to change the subject.

"Thanks for taking care of me tonight."

He straightened his legs and turned, drawing me closer before he tangled us together, one of his hands gliding up and into my hair to cup the back of my head so he could press my face to his throat.

When he was done doing that, he muttered, "Somethin' else I can give you."

"Something you're good at giving," I told him. "It was a terrible day. But it was good night."

"Yeah."

"Though, in all honesty, you don't get all the credit. Peanut butter Rice Krispie treats with chocolate chips did a fair amount of the work."

I heard the smile in his voice when he asked, "A fair amount?"

"However, I must admit to being alarmed Mrs. McMurphy knew about my secret coding machine."

His body started shaking with his chuckles.

I cuddled closer and kissed his throat.

I settled in and shared, "But you did help. A little bit."

"Good I could help…a little bit," he replied, still lightly chuckling.

"And you may be the only man on earth who notices toiletries and has the courage to brave the cosmetics section of the mall to buy his girl-friend moisturizer," I remarked.

I felt him shift and tipped my head back to see him looking down at me.

"Selfish," he stated.

"I'm sorry?" I asked.

"Break this seal, can't be resealed. And it'd suck for you since you're gonna be in my bed a lot to have to drag your shit back and forth all the time. So now that won't suck for you."

Oh my God, he was right.

The seal was broken and now…now…

Now I got more time with Mickey.

His tone lowered when he noted, "Nighties, you can tuck in your purse then shove in my drawer."

He was okay with my shoving stuff in his drawer!

I shivered even as I smiled, *big*.

He saw the smile but I knew he felt the shiver when he said, "Fuck you in the morning, baby, when I know the kids are out."

"Okay, Mickey."

"Now kiss your guy so I can turn out the lights."

"Okay, Mickey."

I did as ordered. It didn't get hot and heavy, but like any kiss with Mickey, I liked it a lot.

Then he turned out the lights and re-tangled himself with me.

I lay in his arms in his dark room in his bed and realized he had really good mattresses.

Mine were good too.

But I could be happy sleeping on those mattresses.

Very happy.

Doing it sleeping with Mickey.

24

OBVIOUSLY

"*N*ada. Zero. Zilch. Zip. *Nothing.*"

Robin was reporting back on what she'd found after studying Magdalene's finances.

"No discrepancies?" I asked, rushing around my bedroom, finishing getting ready for the evening's festivities. "Nothing fishy?"

"Nothing fishy," she answered. "I did some research. You know, found towns of the same size, in the same region with around the same wealth distribution. Even looked up job descriptions and salary structures. It's all copasetic. Except maybe Magdalene's Fire Chief has a slightly elevated pay packet. But then again, as a coastal town and county, your wealth distribution is higher, as is cost of living, so that isn't surprising."

She'd really done the work. I was impressed.

I was also let down.

I didn't know why, because I didn't know what I expected to find.

Perhaps all the firehouses in towns like Magdalene had crappy microwaves, outdated kitchens and old TVs (until someone got new donated, that was).

Even though I didn't know what drove me to check, I was glad I did it if only to know there actually wasn't anything suspicious about it. That said, I wouldn't have minded if there was something meaty to sink my teeth into so the guys could demand a decent kitchen.

But it was what it was.

And therefore I'd give it some time seeing as there hadn't been much since my last efforts bore fruit. Then I'd get some of the other MFD wives, girlfriends and husband-boyfriend (as the case may be with Misty) together to sort out a fundraiser for a new kitchen.

All we needed were appliances and cabinets. With Mickey's foreman skills, the boys could do the fitting.

And with my skills at fundraising, that would be easy.

"Thanks, sweets," I said to Robin.

"Major letdown," she replied. "I was hoping for something juicy. Amelia Hathaway exposes corruption in a small town in Maine."

"Personally, I'm glad there *is* no corruption in a small town in Maine since I live here."

"I hear you," she replied, and when she did I heard the smile in her voice. Then she asked, "Hey, since I got you, Lawr called me while I was at Pilates. I'm gonna call him after I get off with you, but do you know why he's calling?"

At her news, my heart skipped a beat.

"I...can't imagine," I lied.

"Maybe he's coming to town," she said absently. "Usually when he comes to town, you're here so I know through you and you set up the fun. Now you're not here."

"Maybe," I hedged.

"Hope he's coming and I love it that if he is, he thought of me even without you being here. He's one of the three good ones, the other two being my dad and, hopefully, your hottie."

I loved it that she loved that, and I loved it that she thought that about Lawrie.

"My bestie and my big bro, getting together even without me. Love that too," I stated benignly but, if only to myself, leadingly.

"I just hope he doesn't bring the ice queen," she mumbled.

I decided not to reply.

"Anyway, I'll give him a buzz," she finished.

"Good, sweets. Now I gotta go. Plans with Mickey and his kids."

"Wonderful, darling. I'll let you fly."

"All right. Talk to you later."

"You too. Have fun," she bid me.

"Thanks. Let me know what Lawr says."

"Will do. Later."

"Later, Robin."

We rang off. I grabbed a scarf from a shelf, the jacket I wanted from a hanger and dashed out of my walk-in in order to grab my purse and keys, lock up and run over to Mickey's.

"ALL RIGHT, WE'RE OFFICIALLY RUNNING LATE!" I CALLED.

"I'm coming! I'm coming! Two seconds!" Cillian yelled from the bathroom.

I was standing at the end of the hall at Mickey's, staring at my watch. I turned my head, however, when I heard a door open.

I saw Aisling step out. "Go without me, Amy."

She then stepped back in and closed the door.

Shit, we were supposed to leave that very minute. Now, what was I going to do with Aisling?

I wondered this even though I wasn't surprised about Ash's decision not to join us.

Mickey, with what he'd hoped was good timing—Aisling coming out to be with the family and take care of me on Wednesday night—had taken the opportunity to try to have his sit down with her the night before, Thursday.

This did not go well. There'd been a drama with some shouting, some, "There's nothing bothering me," which, after Mickey pushed, segued to, "*You'd never get it, Dad!*" more shouting and some slammed doors. She'd then calmed down but when she did she'd clammed up.

I knew all this because Mickey had given me a full report.

Now, I was taking the kids into town to attend the town council meeting, which would hopefully end with a vote approving a full-time firefighter. This being the first step toward Bobby feeling the department was in good shape, thus he was okay to leave, making Mickey the chief.

Mickey wasn't at home with us because he was at a meeting at the firehouse. The fire inspector's report had come in, disturbingly confirming that the fire at Mills jetty was arson. It was not the MO of any other such fires in Maine, but upon sheriff Coert receiving the report, he'd investigated and found that similar fires were started in Nevada, Colorado, Wyoming and Minnesota.

Thus, there was possibly an arsonist in Magdalene and the boys at MFD were getting a full briefing from the chief and the sheriff and we were joining Mickey in town for the council meeting, something which all the members of the department (save the ones on duty) were attending.

Something, in order to get there in time to settle in and get seats, we should be seeing to.

I stared down the hall, trying to come up with a game plan, when Cillian walked out of the bathroom.

My body jolted at the sight.

"What do you think?" he asked, pointing to his head, which had hair that looked wet but all of it stuck up on end like he was in the middle of a cartoon electrocution.

"Uh..." I mumbled, not knowing what to say since what I thought wasn't good.

"It's got the wet look now but it'll calm down when it dries," he informed me.

I had experience with this, considering my son went from not caring about his appearance to being all about it, this in the expanse of about two weeks. Thus I knew that men's hair with product that was going to dry did not stick up on end like that.

"How much did you use?" I asked as he sauntered toward me, his gait like his dad's, except cute rather than hot.

"About half a pudding cup," he answered.

Oh dear.

"Just to say, kiddo, you're supposed to use about the size of a dime."

He'd stopped in front of me, and at my words, his eyes got big. "Seriously?"

"Yeah. You use as much as you did, it's gonna dry just like that." And take about three washings to get it out, something I decided not to inform him of at that time since we should be leaving.

"Crap!" he yelled, turned and ran back down the hall.

"Cillian!" I called after him just as the bathroom door slammed. "We need to leave!"

"Two secs!" he shouted back.

"Shit," I whispered, deciding Aisling first, Cillian second, when the doorbell rang.

"Get it, Amy!" Cillian hollered.

Nothing from Aisling.

"Shit," I repeated, moving to the door.

I opened it and saw on the stoop a pretty, petite, curvy woman with dark blonde hair who was perhaps five years older than me. She wore attractive clothes, had a great handbag and was staring at me like a deer caught in headlights.

"Hi. Can I help you?" I asked politely.

"You're Amy," she replied strangely breathily, like she was winded because she showed up at Mickey's door after a five K run.

My head twitched at the knowledge she had that knowledge and I confirmed cautiously, "Yes."

She continued to stare at me, taking me in, then looked away only to look right back and announce, "I'm Rhiannon."

Oh *shit.*

"Um…hi," I repeated.

"Is Mickey here?" she asked.

"No, he's in town. Meeting at the firehouse. I'm taking the kids in to join him for the town council thing."

"Right, right. I forgot," she mumbled, shifting, fidgeting. She then dropped her keys, bent quickly to pick them up and straightened, not looking at me. "I'll call him."

"Do you want me to tell him you came by?" I asked.

"Yes, yeah, that'd be good," she answered, making as if to turn but not doing it and instead saying to me. "Um…thanks."

"Do you want to say hi to the kids?" I offered quietly.

She looked beyond me, pain gathered in her features, released and she glanced at me before she looked to my shoulder. "No. I don't want to delay you. I'll call them too."

"It's no problem," I lied, since it was considering we were already late.

She looked to her watch then to my shoulder. "Council meetings begin at six thirty so I'd probably just make you late. That's okay. I'll see them soon."

"All right," I said, still quietly.

"Um…yes, well…" She shifted again as if to turn away, shifted back, didn't reach my eyes, and said, "Well, 'bye."

"'Bye, Rhiannon. Nice to meet you."

That was when she looked me right in the eyes and I again saw the pain.

That didn't sit great with me not only because of what might be behind it but because it wasn't fun seeing she had it.

"Yeah, Amy. Nice to meet you too."

I forced a smile.

She attempted to force one back but before she succeeded, she turned and hurried down the walk toward her car in the drive.

I watched her, rattled by that encounter, but only for a second before I closed the door, partly so she wouldn't catch me watching her, mostly because I *really* needed to get the kids moving.

I dug my phone out of my purse and texted Mickey, *Running late. Will text when we're on our way.*

I gave him only that. The news about Rhiannon could wait.

I sent that and I hurried to Aisling's door.

It had a poster of a band on it and the good news about that was it was not a boy band. In fact, it shared the knowledge she had excellent taste in music.

I knocked, put my hand to the knob and opened it, poking my head in.

I'd never seen her room. The door was always closed.

Now I saw it had been a little girl's room, all pink and purple and flowery, but that evidence now lay beneath a lot of clutter, a bunch of spent clothes strewn everywhere, a TV with piles of DVD boxes all around, an unmade bed and a liberal coating of more band posters.

However, there was one other poster. A movie poster. A movie poster that, in its aloneness as a movie poster in Aisling's room rather than it being one of many, concerned me.

The poster was for the River Phoenix, Lili Taylor movie that had come out decades before.

Dogfight.

My eyes swept back, taking in a plethora of makeup and hair stuff on top of her dresser, all of it coated with a visible layer of dust, and I saw her in bed amidst the mussed sheets (as well as discarded clothes), back against the headboard, book in her hands.

Before I could say a word, she told me, "Dad won't mind."

I stepped in but not far. "I think he will, blossom. This is a big night for the department and I'm thinking that your dad would never ask you kids to go to a boring town council meeting unless it meant something to him. And anyway, we're getting dinner after."

"I can get something to eat here," she told me.

"You can but my guess is we're not only going out to dinner after because we're all together and it'll be too late to cook anything, but because he's hoping to have something to celebrate."

"You and Cill and Dad can do that without me," she replied.

I took another step further into her room, doing it carefully, but not very successfully, to avoid the layer of clothes covering the floor. "We can, but your dad won't want us to. He'll want you there."

She lifted her chin. "Am—"

Abruptly, I jerked my head to the movie poster. "Have you seen that movie?"

Her eyes darted to the poster, to me, then to my stomach. "Yeah. Own it."

"An old movie for you to be into," I prodded.

"Yeah, well, my brother wants to be a fighter pilot because of an even older movie," she pointed out accurately. "We're a movie family."

This could not be denied.

"Something in that movie that speaks to you like Tom Cruise speaks to your brother?" I pushed, but did it on a smile, hoping that would work to get her to open up to me, but doing that not thinking it was a probability.

I was correct.

Her gaze came to mine. "Well, yeah. *Obviously.*"

It was far from obvious to me.

She said no more.

This was not good.

"What, honey?" I queried. "What does that movie say to a girl like you?"

She looked away.

My phone in my hand chimed.

I looked down at it and saw Mickey's return text, *Got it. See you soon.*

I looked back to Ash. "Ash—"

"Here it is! Better?" Cillian asked from behind me.

I twisted and watched as he leaped into the room, landed right on clothes (and didn't care) and threw his arms out.

His hair was now slicked back like an Italian movie gangster.

"Much better," I lied.

He looked to his sister. "Right. Let's go."

"Not goin', Cill," she replied.

He stared at her. "You are."

"I'm staying," she told him.

"You're goin'," he told her.

"No, I'm not," she returned.

"Yes, you are," he shot back then snapped, "This is a big thing for Dad."

"I'm—" she began.

But I cut her off. "Going. Up, Ash. Now, blossom. We shouldn't keep your father waiting."

"But I—"

"Please, honey," I whispered. "He trusted me to get his kids there and now I'm asking you to please help me do what he asked of me."

It was a complete gambit, me playing the new-girlfriend-being-tested card. Mickey would never do that to me.

But I was hoping she cared enough about me, me with Mickey, and her dad to think that it was *me* who wanted to make sure I gave her dad what he wanted and she'd go along.

"All right, whatever," she mumbled, pushing away from her headboard.

I hid my sigh of relief.

"I get shotgun in the Rover!" Cillian cried and raced out the door.

She trudged toward me and I watched her do it, wondering what was crushing Mickey's pretty girl.

I wouldn't find out that night but I had to do something.

So I caught her hand and held it firm so she stopped trudging and looked up at me.

"Something's up with you and I don't want to make something that's obviously bad any worse, but I do want you to know it's worrying your dad. It's worrying me. He wants to help you get beyond that something and I want the same thing. I told you once you can talk to me about anything. I'll say it again. Anytime, Aisling. Anything. You need me, I'm there."

"Okay, Amy," she replied and I knew she did it just so I'd shut up.

I still nodded like we had an understanding and gave her a small smile. "Let's get going."

"Guys! Hurry!" Cill shouted from the front of the house.

"Coming!" I shouted back, walking out of Aisling's room, feeling Mickey's girl following me.

• ———

We hit the Town Hall late, so at a bad time. Most everyone had taken a seat and it was clear the meeting was about to begin.

Mickey hadn't taken a seat. When we walked in, he was standing off to the side at the back talking with a tall, very handsome man wearing a sheriff shirt complete with badge, this paired with jeans.

Like he could sense our presence, we'd barely entered before Mickey looked to us.

He lifted his chin. I smiled and he looked back to the man he was with. They spoke a few words, clapped each other on the arm in a way I knew, if either of them had done that to me, I'd have a bruise, then Mickey broke off and sauntered our way.

He looked amongst us but his gaze stopped on his son.

Then when he arrived at us, he asked, "You got an offer I can't refuse?"

"What?" Cillian asked back.

Mickey gave his boy an easy grin, curled a hand on the side of his neck, tugged him side to side and answered, "Nothin'." He let Cill go and looked to Ash. "Hey, baby."

She looked to him then to his arm. "Hey, Dad."

He looked to me.

I gave him big eyes.

He took them in, bent and touched his mouth to mine.

"Hey," he said when he'd moved away.

"Hey back," I replied.

"Does my son have a tommy gun in the Rover?" he asked and I smiled.

"This hairdo is better than the first, trust me," I replied.

His eyes started dancing.

"If we can all take seats, we'll begin," someone said over a microphone.

"Let's move," Mickey ordered, shifting out of the way for us to precede him then following us.

As a pack, we moved down the center aisle of the angled bench seating that looked like a church but was much smaller and had zero decoration except a couple bulletin boards covered in fliers informing Magdalene residents of various happenings.

We shifted into a bench, Ash then Cill, me then Mickey.

We sat down and the minute we did, an older man who sat in the bench in front of us and had been watching our progress turned fully to Mickey. He had short cropped, metal-gray hair that was thinning on the top and red cheeks like Santa Claus.

"Mick," he greeted.

"Bobby," Mickey greeted back, lifting an arm and stretching it along the seat behind me. "You haven't met Amy."

Bobby turned smiling brown eyes my way and said, "Nope, but I licked the crumbs outta one of those plastic things, which gave me a hint of what has now become legendary brownies to the MFD."

I loved that and showed him by smiling brightly and promising, "I'll make more for Mickey to bring in when you're around." I lifted my hand to him. "It's good to meet you, chief."

He reached over the back of the bench and squeezed my hand, replying, "Likewise." He let me go and his focus went to Mickey. "Quick question, son. You into somethin' with Boston Stone?"

I felt my body get tight as I felt Mickey's eyes move to me.

I turned my head, caught his, licked my lips and rolled them together.

"I see," Bobby muttered and we both looked back to him.

"What's up?" Mickey asked.

Bobby couldn't answer because we heard, "The Magdalene Town Council Meeting is now in session."

"Later," Bobby mouthed before turning back around.

I turned my eyes to Mickey. "Honey," I called.

He looked down to me. "Douche," he stated. "Don't worry, Amy." He then gave his attention back to the front where there was a panel of five seated behind a long, tall, official-looking bench desk.

The one in the middle was saying something, but I was thinking that I was under the impression, considering I hadn't heard from him in some time, that Boston Stone finally got the hint and stopped calling me. We'd had one date. We'd had one kiss (well, one and a half).

What we had not done was make avowals of love.

So whatever he was up to that had to do with Mickey couldn't be about me.

Surely.

A variety of business was swiftly brought up and voted on without any comment from members of the public. This was not surprising since the room was not quite half full, and I suspected attendance was greater that night because the volunteers of the MFD were there.

Clearly, the town of Magdalene didn't involve themselves too much in town business and from how very boring it was, I didn't blame them.

Ash and Cill were playing games on their phones (due to the Rhiannon situation, Cill now had his own) when the issue of additional town resources allocated to the Magdalene Fire Department was raised.

Evidently, the head honcho sitting in the middle thought it would be voted through without demur because when he asked for public comment, he missed movement in the room and immediately started, "Right then we'll vo—"

"One moment, Councilman Whitfield," a smooth voice I knew called out.

I looked to the side, my neck muscles tensing, and watched Boston Stone strolling arrogantly (and you could stroll arrogantly, he was proof) up the center aisle.

"Boston, of course, take the podium," the head honcho, apparently Councilman Whitfield, invited.

Boston did just that, lifting an attractive, slim leather briefcase in front of him to rest it on top of the podium and pulling out papers.

Once he had them, he started, "I can only assume with this referendum being raised, our town council members aren't aware that, nationwide, the incidence of fires is on a dramatic decline and has been for the past decade." He then raised the papers he'd gotten out and shook them officiously.

The inference the council had not done their homework was not lost on any of them, they didn't like it and they showed it.

"We are aware of that, Boston," Councilman Whitfield retorted, sharing this verbally.

"Then I must admit to being curious, since that's the case, as to why you'd be allocating more funds to a city service that should, in fact, be getting less," Boston replied.

Mickey straightened beside me and both his children looked up from their phones.

On my part, I found my hands forming fists.

"Due to their function and its importance to public safety, I can't imagine anyone would begrudge the current funds the MFD receives," a female council member off to the left stated.

"I'm a citizen of Magdalene and I'm doing just that," Boston returned.

"I would assume you're in the minority," she retorted.

"Please don't assume, Louise," Boston replied condescendingly, shifting some papers. "To that end, I'll present you with a requested action, voted approved by the members of the Magdalene Club, that this referendum be deferred until further research into the need of fire services and the funds allocated to that need are thoroughly researched. After which we call for a report to be offered to the citizens prior to an open public vote on this issue."

Bobby twisted his neck, gave Mickey a dour look, mouthed, "Asshole," and turned back.

Councilman Whitfield held up his hand resignedly and invited, "I'll have a look at that if you don't mind, Boston."

"Not at all," Boston murmured into the microphone in front of him, moved from the podium, presented the papers to Whitfield and returned to the podium. "As you'll see in the addendum attached to that paper that a goodly number of businessmen and women in this community, who voted that action, are concerned about this issue."

"In other words, the rich folk, thinkin' they're high and mighty and their money should get them attention, wanna throw a fit about somethin' none of us get but if they get their way, could put us in danger," a man called from the gallery.

Whitfield looked from his study of the papers over the reading specs he'd slid on in the direction of the voice. "Tom, if you have something to say, we ask you say it during your turn at the podium."

"And make me listen to this crap in the meantime?" Tom, who I saw was the Tom who ran The Shack on the wharf, returned.

"Everyone has a voice in this meeting and if a citizen takes their time to share their thoughts with this council, as servants to this town, it's our duty to listen," another council member replied.

"Not if their thoughts are full of it and it isn't worth your time," Tom shot back.

There was a titter and I caught Mickey grinning at his lap.

"Tom—" the council member started but was interrupted when someone else spoke up.

"This is crazy. The boys at the MFD volunteer. And just last week, they put their asses on the line, makin' sure the entire jetty didn't go up in flames like it could have."

"I'd ask you to refrain from using coarse language, Jeff," the council woman named Louise requested firmly.

"What else would you call it?" Jeff asked. "Straight up fire or fire damage closed down that whole shopping area and if the worst happened, those same things coulda took *out* the folks fightin' it. I call that puttin' your ass on the line. Now, no disrespect, Louise, but I didn't hear about you in your gear fightin' that blaze. I sure as hell didn't hear about Stone doin' it."

That got another titter.

"They aren't all asking for salaries," someone else called loudly. "They want one salary for one guy. Town's over two hundred years old and we never paid a single firefighter. Only pay a chief and he acts for the whole county so we don't even pay his full salary. Think it's about time we did that. Shoot, if it was up to me, they'd *all* get paid."

"Yeah," Jeff said.

"I agree," a woman piped up.

"How about that," Tom put in, standing. He looked around. "Who's for a deferral of the vote so the council can take a look at this referendum and find some blasted money to pay *all* our boys who wear a fire helmet?"

"Me!" Jeff shouted.

"That's got my vote," the woman yelled.

"Me too!" a new man called, standing up to do it.

"I'm in too!" a woman added, also standing up and doing it continuing to speak. "We don't do this, what's next? We ask all the sheriff's officers to do their jobs volunteer too? That's crazy!"

A gavel banged and Councilman Whitfield called, "Quiet!"

Tom wasn't quiet.

He looked to Boston and remarked, "You know, Stone, just because a pretty girl prefers a firefighter to you doesn't mean all the boys at that firehouse need to suffer for you bein' jilted. Far's I know, you got served this lesson at least once before. Learn, son. You may actually land a girl one day if you stop actin' like an ass."

Oh God, he was referring to Mickey and me.

Small town.

Someone *kill me*.

I felt my cheeks flush as I sunk in my seat because several eyes turned Mickey and my way.

Yes.

Somehow they all knew.

Someone...*kill me*.

"Cool, Dad," Cillian stated under his breath but under it for a boy his age, which meant he did it loudly. "You beat out Boston Stone for Amy? Awesome!"

"Right! Quiet! Order!" Whitfield commanded on another bang of his gavel.

Before anyone could disobey, he trained his eyes again over his specs on Boston and continued speaking.

"I've had a quick read of this, Boston, and I'm sorry to say that the current referendum we're discussing was communicated to the citizens of Magdalene for their examination four months ago via our usual procedures, which means anyone could access and study it thoroughly. That time allowed plenty of opportunity for any resident of this town to share with the members of this council their concerns or to be present at this meeting to have their voice. The names on this document represent a negligible percentage of the inhabitants of our town and thus, I must say, it really carries no sway during these proceedings."

"Have you had a close *look* at those names, Whitfield?" Boston asked threateningly.

"I have indeed," Whitfield retorted immediately, flicking the papers to his side so the woman sitting to his left could take them. "And I'll take this opportunity to share with you news I hadn't intended to announce until the next election, but Sue and I are moving to Florida next year. I won't be seeking reelection. However, your implication that the names on that document, some of whom donated to my past election campaigns, would sway me while I'm sitting in this seat is *most* unwelcome."

At his tone, a tone that said it was more than unwelcome, it was insulting, slanderous and entirely unacceptable, meant everyone quieted and those standing sat.

"I meant nothing of the sort," Boston returned.

"You most certainly did," Whitfield bit out.

I smiled, deciding I liked our head honcho Councilman.

He kept talking.

"Now, if you have nothing further, I'll ask you to vacate the podium so if someone else has something they wish to say, they can do so." He looked beyond Boston and through the gallery. "I'll state, however, that you all have also had an opportunity to study the referendum prior to attending this evening's meeting. We will not entertain a delayed vote or an alternate resolution to be put to the vote. If you feel the town should consider compensating the entirety of the members of our fire department, request a new referendum to be researched by the council and presented for discussion and vote at a future meeting. I'll warn you, however, this town relies *heavily* on the goodwill and generosity of time and skills from our firefighting force and we're all aware of it. If we could have afforded to pay them, we would have. But if this town is content with increased taxes in order to see to that, that also can be discussed."

"We just want one boy, Whit!" Bobby shouted. His head turned the way of a woman who was highly attractive, had great hair, and I could tell was definitely fit even only seeing her shoulders and head. She was sitting one bench in front of him and down, looking over her shoulder at him, appearing miffed. Then he finished, "Or a girl! Whatever!"

Well, there she was; firefighter Misty.

"Then let's see about getting you that," Whitfield replied. His eyes went back to Boston. "Boston, please step down."

Boston glared at him then turned, and without a glance at anyone he stalked down the center aisle. He didn't wait for the vote. He walked right out of the room.

I couldn't believe that Boston connived to put the entire town in danger because he was angry I was with Mickey.

But apparently, it was because he was angry I was with Mickey.

Which meant Mickey was even *more* right than I thought he was that day when he told me not to date the guy.

Brilliant.

"Anyone else have something to say?" Whitfield invited.

There was a low murmur of noise but no one moved to the podium.

"Excellent, then we'll put it to the vote," Whitfield declared. "All in favor of allocating further resources to the Magdalene Fire Department to hire a full-time salaried firefighter, say aye!"

There were five ayes.

I grinned.

"No nays, the resolution passes," Whitefield announced. "Now, the next order of business..."

"So, now how you feelin' about not takin' my advice about that asshole?" Mickey muttered in my ear.

He didn't sound angry.

He sounded teasing.

And patronizing.

I snapped my eyes to him and narrowed them.

He gave me an easy grin before he gave me a quick kiss.

I was still glaring at him when he finished, which set him to chuckling.

"Heard through the grapevine he had somethin' up his sleeve," Bobby whispered as Whitfield kept talking and both Mickey and I looked to him to see him again turned to us. "Good news, that's done. Better news," he smiled, "task force of the county councilmembers have full hiring authority when it comes to the fire chief. Nothin' comes to a vote. And they do this volunteer themselves so they aren't gonna spend months goin' through some hiring process, which will end with them goin' for whoever I recommend in the first place. This means, when I put you forward, you're in, son."

"Yeah, Bobby, that is good news," Mickey replied.

Bobby slid his eyes to me. "You seriously dated Stone?"

"No. It was only one date. And I did it before Mickey and I were together because I was angry at Mickey who was, at the time, being annoyingly bossy," I shared.

"Seems good reason," he uttered these words as the obvious lie they were.

"I'll have you over for dinner, explain the entire thing to your wife, then let her explain it to you," I stated.

His eyes twinkled and he murmured, "Ah."

"That's done, Bob, gotta feed my family," Mickey put in, already shifting like he was going to exit the bench.

"Right," Bobby said to Mickey then looked back to me. "Nice meetin' you, Amy. Lookin' forward to that dinner invitation and my brownies."

Staring into his kind eyes, I was looking forward to dinner too.

"We'll plan through Mickey," I said, shifting after Mickey.

"Right. Later, sweetheart."

"Later, Bobby," I replied.

Bobby looked to Cillian who was moving down the bench behind me. "Boy," he greeted.

"Uncle Bobby," Cillian replied, giving Bobby a high five when Bobby raised his hand.

Next came Ash. "You walked by me once without givin' your Uncle Bobby a kiss, pretty girl. Don't do it again."

"Uncle Bobby," she muttered, bending in to give him a quick kiss then moving fast to follow us.

Together, we walked down the aisle, out of the room, out of the Town Hall and Mickey stopped us on the sidewalk.

I looked up at him. "Happy?"

He smiled down at me. "Oh yeah."

"So cool, Dad! You're gonna be fire chief!" Cillian shouted, jumping at his dad, and Mickey caught his boy in his arms, giving him a squeeze Cillian gave back.

"Totally cool, Dad. Happy for you," Aisling mumbled when Cillian moved away. She slunk in, ducked her head but gave her dad a sideways hug that was genuine.

"Thanks, baby," he murmured against the top of her hair, obviously not caring it was greasy. He didn't let her go far, keeping her close to his side with his arm around her shoulders, asking all of us. "Lobster Market, Breeze Point, the Boathouse or Tink's?"

My choice was Lobster Market or the Boathouse because the former was wonderful and I'd never been to the latter but I'd heard it was good.

Cillian shouted, "Tink's!" just as Aisling said, "Tink's." So even not voting, I was outvoted.

"Amy, babe?" Mickey asked me.

"Absolutely," I replied. "Tink's."

Cillian raced toward my car, yelling, "I ride with Amy!"

Mickey turned his daughter around but did this stretching out a hand to me. I took it and Mickey got to walk with both his girls close as we made our way to our vehicles.

The only thing that happened during this brief trek was seeing the tall, good-looking sheriff Mickey had been talking to standing with his back to us between a car and an Explorer decorated in sheriff colors with a county sheriff insignia on the driver's side door.

He was on his phone and I heard him asking tersely, "Trouble follow you from Denver?" and before whoever he was talking to could possibly reply, he demanded, "Answer me!"

I looked up at Mickey as we kept walking. He felt my eyes and gave his to me.

I lifted my brows.

He gave a shrug.

I let it go and we went to Tink's, Cillian riding with me, Aisling riding with Mickey.

The burgers were again phenomenal.

But the place still scared me.

———————•———————

"Yeah. Right." Pause. "Yeah, I get it. You forgot. That's okay. I appreciate you showing."

Mickey was pacing his room in nothing but a pair of pajama bottoms (these flannel also, but navy), his broad chest and cut abs bare.

Usually, I would watch this with great fascination.

But since I'd told him Rhiannon had come over and he was speaking with her while I sat cross-legged on his bed in one of my nighties, I decided to give them a modicum of privacy.

I did this tearing my eyes away from my guy, giving my attention to my own phone, and texting Robin.

Did you call Lawrie?

I sent that and then reached for the moisturizer Mickey bought me that was sitting on his nightstand.

I was rubbing it in when she texted back.

I finished rubbing before I grabbed my phone again and read, *Yes. He's coming to town. Wants to get drinks.*

My hand curled around my phone and I just stopped myself from pumping my arm in victory.

Instead I texted back. *Lovely, are you going?*

To which she quickly replied, *Of course, he's Lawrie.*

Fabulous!

"Okay, Rhiannon. That'd be good. Like I told you this morning, the scene with Ash didn't sit great with me," Mickey said and I looked up at him. "Right. It'll be good you do that." Pause. "Okay. Later."

He took the phone from his ear and sauntered around the bed to his nightstand.

I looked to my phone and swiftly texted, *Good. Have fun! Now going to bed. Talk to you later.*

Then I looked to Mickey. "All that okay?"

He nodded. His phone was on his nightstand and he was throwing back the covers.

He got in, settled with his back to the headboard and gave his attention to me.

"Like I said after you told me she came 'round, I ended our détente this morning to give her the info on the scene with Ash. She says she's also noticed the deterioration, came by to check in, talk to me, maybe speak with Ash. She forgot about the council meeting. Now she says, when she gets her back, she's gonna give it a go."

"That's good," I whispered, my phone chiming.

I looked to it and saw, *'Night sweets. Cuddle your hottie for all the single ladies.*

I grinned, set the phone on the nightstand, but stopped grinning when I turned back to Mickey.

"Have you seen the movie *Dogfight?*" I asked.

"Nope, it new?" he asked back then offered immediately, "You wanna see it?"

I adjusted myself so I was facing him fully, feeling my features soften at his offer but also in preparation for what I had to do. "No, baby, it's an old movie. Ash has a movie poster for it on her wall."

His eyes went unfocused before they refocused on me. "Try not to pay too much attention to her room. Place is a sty."

It was and a strict-ish dad should probably do something about that but I didn't address that.

I asked, "Do you know what a dogfight is?"

His brows drew together. "Everyone does, Amy."

"No," I replied quietly, leaning toward him putting my forearms in the bed between us. "A dogfight in regards to a nasty game a pack of boys play on a girl."

His entire body stilled and his eyes started burning into me.

"You know," I whispered.

"Do not fuckin' tell me..." he trailed off like he couldn't finish.

"I don't know. I brought it up with Aisling, didn't get very far. I asked if that movie spoke to her and she just said 'obviously.' I didn't get more out of her before Cill interrupted us."

Like the words were difficult to say, he ground out, "If some fuckwads played that game with her, you're a chick, you think she'd have that poster on her wall?"

I shook my head. "I don't know. If it was me, no. I wouldn't want the reminder. But, Mickey, in that movie, the boy falls in love with the girl. He goes to war and he comes back to her."

"I'm not—"

"My fear, honey, is that she identifies with the plain, overweight girl in that movie and maybe looks at it in a twisted way as hope for her future. I'll say that saying that the actress in that film is extraordinary and she was beautiful in so many ways. But my concern is, Ash doesn't see *all* of them."

"Been worried about her weight," he muttered.

"Don't. That's not the issue," I stated firmly. "She carries extra weight but not that much. And she's pretty, she's sweet. She's a little shy, but it's cute. And she's probably *supremely* aware of her weight when she's far from obese. You mentioning it at this juncture would not be a good thing. From you, she has to feel she's nothing but beautiful no matter what. The issue is that's one symptom in many and some of those include overall not caring about her appearance. For a girl her age, that concerns me. It isn't that she has to cake on the makeup and spend an hour doing her hair every day. But I don't think she's showering, Mickey."

"Yeah, me mentioning that was when things blew up last night," he reminded me.

I nodded. "I hope Rhiannon can get through to her. But I'd like to hang out with you guys this weekend, just in case I have another shot."

"Then you're here, babe, happy for that for more than the fact you wanna look after my girl."

I smiled at him.

He didn't smile back but lifted his hand and sifted his finger through my bangs.

"You didn't say much about meeting Rhiannon, Amy," he noted after his hand dropped.

"It went fast and was a surprise for both of us," I told him.

"And she was cool with you?" he asked, even though I'd already told him she was.

I nodded again.

"She's worried about our girl," he said. "Think that's a good sign. Maybe she's gettin' her shit together."

"Worry about your kids can kick a mom's ass right into gear," I reported.

That got me a grin. "Yeah."

"If my crew can go through what they did and bounce back, Mickey, then really, anything can happen."

His grin died as he repeated unconvincingly, "Yeah."

"Yeah," I stated more firmly.

He changed the subject.

"You gonna sit there all night like that, or you gonna get in bed with me?"

"Get in bed with you."

"Then do it."

I sat up. "You do know that kind of thing forced me to go on a date with the slimy Boston Stone."

He stared at me and asked disbelievingly, "Now that shit's my fault?"

"It was always your fault," I retorted haughtily then I cried out when he reached out and yanked me to him.

I landed on his chest. He curved an arm around me as he rolled into me and yanked the covers from under me. He then flicked them over, moved to his back and turned out the light, then rolled my way and gave me his weight when he reached out to turn out mine.

He then arranged us tangled in the middle of the bed.

"I take it discussion of Boston Stone is over," I remarked.

"That name said in this bed again gets my woman spanked."

I shut up.

For a second.

Then I asked, "Can we finish this discussion in *my* bed?"

I heard the smile in his voice as he muttered, "Smartass."

I smiled right into his chest as I cuddled there.

We were snuggled, quiet and I was drooping when Mickey called, "Amy?"

"Yeah, honey?"

"You find out boys did that to my girl, you don't tell me that shit. You sort it. You dig deep in there with her and you dig it out. You get her to share it with her mother. But you do not bring that to me."

I knew what he was saying.

"Mickey," I whispered.

"She's beautiful," he stated.

"I know," I replied.

"Gotta be responsible. That'd make me not be able to be responsible."

Yes, I knew what he was saying.

"Okay, Mickey. But, just to say, honestly, I don't think that poster would be on her wall if that actually happened."

"Right," he grunted.

"Right," I repeated.

"Okay, Amy."

"Let that go and go to sleep, baby."

He drew in breath, drawing his arms closer around me as he did.

He let the breath go but not me.

"'Night, babe."

I kissed his chest and replied, "Goodnight, Mickey."

It took me a lot longer to get droopy because I spent a lot of time hoping in all that was happening with Rhiannon and Aisling that I hadn't lied and the Donovan family could bounce back.

And be happy.

25

LUCK O' THE IRISH

*T*he next day, late morning, I knocked on Ash's door.

"Yeah?" she called.

I opened it and stuck my head in, seeing her on her side in her bed, earbuds in, book open in front of her, still in her shapeless PJ's, thus no shower.

At her dad's call, she'd come out for breakfast, ate it with us, then went right back in.

"Hey," I started. "We're about to go outside to toss around the Frisbee. It's chilly but it'll be fun. Wanna join us?"

"Naw," she replied. "I'm into this book and I'm almost done."

I looked to the book she was reading and saw this was not a lie.

I looked back to her. "Okay, blossom. But you get done, come and join us if you feel like it."

"Okay, Amy. If I feel like it."

She wasn't coming.

"Right. Hope to see you outside."

She didn't reply.

"Enjoy the book," I bid her.

She nodded, touched her iPhone likely to restart her music playing and looked back down at her book.

Since I wasn't blind, my eyes again took in her room before I closed the door. But when the door latched, a thought came to me.

My daughter, too, had a pretty little girl room (hers had been peaches and pinks). Starting at eleven, she'd begun begging for an update, and because I was me, but also because we were in the first throes of divorce, by the time she hit twelve, I'd given it to her.

This thought made me move down the hall. I saw Cillian's door partially open, knocked, didn't get an answer, so I stuck my head in.

Seeing it for the first time, I learned he'd had a bent toward careening down the highway to the danger zone even prior to seeing *Top Gun*. I knew this from the motif of airplanes that was in his room.

But it was little kid airplanes for a little boy. They weren't cool. They were primary colors and cartoony.

His room was also untidy but nowhere near the mess of his sister's.

I pulled my head out and moved swiftly down the hall to the back room where Mickey was standing alone behind the sectional, an MFD sweatshirt on to go out and play Frisbee, but eyes aimed to the college football game on TV.

"Hey, where's Cill?" I asked.

He looked to me. "Bathroom. Ash coming?"

I shook my head.

His handsome face turned worried and his eyes drifted to the hall.

I got close. "Before Cill comes back, can I ask something?"

He looked back to me and invited, "Shoot."

I got closer. "It'll be asking a lot, honey. And you can say no."

"Is it about Ash?"

I nodded.

"Then shoot."

Yes, worried.

But such a good dad.

I nodded again and spoke. "When I went in to talk to her, I noticed she still had her Aisling-as-a-little-girl decoration in her room under all that mess. And I remembered when Olympia hit eleven she started wanting something more grown up. So I just wondered if you might have a teeny-tiny budget," I lifted my hand to do a thumb and forefinger inch, "that we could use to update her room. Go to Target. Get a new comforter. Maybe a lamp or two. Buy some paint and she and I can paint her walls. Nothing extravagant, just a new look."

"You think she hates her room?" he asked.

"I think she's growing up and it might be nice she knows you have a mind to that. But mostly, I just want to see if I can get her excited about something."

He appeared keen about this idea before that slid out of his features.

"Do it for one kid, babe, gotta do it for both. Can give you the money for Ash but with all that's goin' on, not sure I'd wanna push that to doin' it times two."

"I agree," I replied. "But if she wants that and then Cill asks for it, you can tell him he can have it when he hits Ash's age."

"Good plan," he muttered on a nod.

"So, can I suggest that? You can give us a budget."

He looked to the hall again then to me. "Yeah, Amy. Good idea. Run with it."

I smiled up at him.

He lifted a hand to wrap it around the back of my neck before he leaned into me and touched my mouth with his.

He moved back an inch and asked, "You gonna get your jacket?"

"Yeah."

"Go," he ordered.

Since he'd agreed to allow me to do some decorating, I decided not to take him to task for being high-handed and went to get my jacket.

⸺ • ⸺

LATE AFTERNOON, AFTER ASH DIDN'T COME OUT AND PLAY FRISBEE, I WAS back at her door.

"Yeah?" she called at my knock.

I stuck my head in. "Hey. You finish your book?"

She clearly had or had given up. She was now on her stomach facing the foot of her bed, still in her PJ's, and I could see on the small TV on its stand at the end that a movie was paused.

"Yeah," she replied.

"Any good?" I asked.

"Yeah," she answered and gave me no more.

I stepped fully into her room, announcing, "Listen, your dad and Cill dragged the fire pit to the deck. They're out getting firewood and hitting the grocery store. My mission is to start dinner. We're going to have dinner and do s'mores outside later."

"Sounds good," she said.

At least that was something.

I tipped my head to the side and asked her, "Wanna help me make dinner?"

Her eyes drifted to the TV. "Kinda in the middle of this movie."

I wanted to push.

I didn't push.

"Okay, kiddo." I then looked around the room trying to pretend it was nonchalantly before I turned back to her and teased, "Under the mess, your room is cute."

She shrugged.

I shifted through the clothes and touched a daisy decal on the wall, continuing to tease, "Not sure Imagine Dragons goes with daisies."

"Yeah, well," she stated and stopped talking.

"Hey!" I cried, like the idea just struck me. "Bet we can talk your dad into updating this place." I threw out a hand. "I'm almost done decorating my place and I'd love to help. Throw up some paint. Hit Target and get a new lamp or two. Make it Imagine Dragons worthy."

She gave me no indication she found this exciting. "Not sure Dad'll go for that."

I moved slightly toward her. "He loves you to bits, blossom. And he knows you're growing up because he leans on you to look after Cillian when he's not around. I bet he'll be happy to do it."

"Seems like a lot of work and money when I don't really care there's still daisies."

I studied her wondering if perhaps her decorations reminded her of her mother or if she worried about the state of her father's finances and how much of a hit that would be if he did that for her.

I saw no emotion on her face, discomfort, hurt or even hesitancy.

She just didn't really care.

What girl didn't care about her room?

"Can I ask your dad anyway?" I requested.

She looked back to the TV then to me, making a mute point that she wanted to get back to her movie, and replied, "Sure. But I'm not really big on that kind of stuff."

I wanted to know what she was big on, outside of losing herself in books, movies and music. Not that any of that was bad or unusual for a teenage girl.

It was just that I couldn't use any of it to get in there.

Another idea struck me and I moved to her dresser. I ran a finger along a bottle tipped sideways and not righted, scoring a line through the dust.

Then I looked back to her and grinned. "See you're not big on makeup either."

"What's the point?" she asked.

"I hear you," I replied. "You're so pretty, it really isn't needed."

Her eyes, having drifted away, shot to me.

Telling.

Sad and telling.

God, I needed an in!

I glanced at the makeup before looking back to her. "You've got a lot of it for not being into it."

"Mom made a big thing of it when I turned fourteen," she told me. "She and Dad agreed I could wear it when I did, so she took me out and bought me a bunch, had some of her friends over. They all showed me how to use it, made it into a party."

"That sounds really sweet," I said softly, and it did. Rhiannon had done that up right.

She shrugged again.

"Do you wear it when you're at her place?" I asked.

"Not really," she answered.

She was giving me nothing and I was beginning to feel like I was encroaching on her time and space, and maybe being a bit creepy, so I started to make my way to the door.

"Okay, then, enough chitchat, I gotta get on making dinner." I stopped with my hand on the door and looked to her. "You get done with your movie, honey, jump in the shower and put on some clothes so you'll be warm when we have s'mores time. And I hope it finishes early. I cook by myself a lot. I like to have company."

I was a mom. I had kids. I was a master at subtle mom-guilt manipulation.

"'Kay, will do if it finishes early," she said.

She wasn't coming out until dinner. I knew it.

Even oblivious to guilt manipulation.

This was bad.

I beat back a disappointed sigh and instead smiled. "Right, blossom.
Enjoy the movie."

She nodded and looked back to the TV.

But being Ash, I didn't hear it go back on until I'd shut the door.

———•———

An hour and a half later, after Mickey shouted dinner was ready
then went back outside with Cillian to tend the fire, Aisling wandered out.

She was no longer in her PJ's but she still hadn't showered.

I said nothing about this and instead beamed at her. "Great news!"

She gifted me with her eyes twinkling and her lips quirking at my
excitement before she asked, "What?"

"Your dad said we could redecorate your room. We don't have a
massive budget, but I'm sure we can get some paint, some new
bedclothes, maybe some new rugs for the floor. Not that I know if you
have rugs on your floor since I can't *see* your floor," I ended on a tease.

The twinkling stopped as she hauled herself up on a stool and replied
without enthusiasm, "Cool."

"So, when you come back from your mom's, you wanna go out with
me?" I asked.

"Maybe," she answered. "I'll let you know."

"Ash—" I started but was interrupted when Cillian threw open the
sliding glass door and did it speaking.

Or, actually, yelling.

"She lives!"

Ash didn't have much of a reaction to that either, not even a retort to
her brother's teasing.

"You missed Frisbee," he informed her, sauntering in, straight to his
own stool.

"You're the Frisbee king, Cill," she replied. "I'm the movie queen."

"Whatevs," he muttered then looked to me. "Dinner ready, Amy?"

"It is, kiddo." I looked between them. "You guys wanna help me with plates and stuff?"

"Sure," Cill answered.

Aisling said nothing but she did slide off her stool.

"I'm gonna eat mine out by the fire," Cillian announced.

"It's freezing out there, honey. It'll get cold," I told him.

"I eat fast," he told me.

This was true.

The sliding door opened again and I looked to it to see Mickey coming in.

His eyes went from me to Ash and back to me before he raised his brows.

I shook my head.

The worry slithered through his features again before he hid it.

We got dinner together. We ate it in front of the TV (except Cill, who ate his outside by the fire) and Mickey did this sitting close to his daughter instead of me. He also did it teasing her by bumping her foot with his or elbowing her until she cried out in a way she didn't mean, "Stop it, Dad!" to which he replied fake innocently, "Stop what?" To that she gifted him with rolled eyes and a smile she tried but couldn't hide, and as Mickey continued to do it, she started sighing audibly and heavily, but said no more.

It was cute.

But it didn't work.

After dinner, we did the cleanup. Then everyone got bound up in jackets and scarves and we went out and made s'mores.

Aisling had three.

Then she went back inside to her room to watch a movie.

———— • ————

I LAY NAKED IN MY TUB LEANED BACK AGAINST MICKEY, WHO WAS, obviously, naked with me. He had his arms around me, his knees cocked beside me as I drifted the bubbly water with my hands and stared out to the sea.

It was Sunday. A Sunday where my hopes of trying new ploys with Aisling were foiled when she announced at breakfast that some of her friends wanted to go to a movie then do some hanging, and that one of her friends' parents had agreed to do the carting around. Mickey said she could go.

The good news about this included Aisling showering before she went.

The bad news included me not being able to try new ploys.

Not long after, Cillian announced one of his friends wanted him over for a day of gaming, which also included his friend's mom offering to come pick him up and bring him home.

Mickey agreed to that too but both his kids had the caveat that they were home for dinner so he could make sure they were both done with homework and ready for next week's school. I figured he also agreed because he was losing them for a week and he wanted them home for one last dinner.

In the meantime, my kids had texted me and said they'd be over for dinner and to spend the night and Auden had added, *We're staying until Wednesday, if that's cool with you.*

It absolutely was so I'd agreed.

This unexpectedly gave Mickey and me the whole day to be together.

But it was me who suggested we do it at my place and we do it naked.

I did not have to twist Mickey's arm.

"Freaky, like we're floating," he muttered, his hand sliding soothingly up and down my side through the warm water.

"Amazing, isn't it?" I asked.

"That Cameron guy knew what he was doin'," he replied.

He did, which caused me some dejection because everything was pointing to the hopeful, marvelous fact that we were going to have a future together.

But that meant I'd lose Cliff Blue and I loved Cliff Blue.

However, I loved Mickey more than my house so I'd let it go.

"Thanks for trying with my girl," Mickey said in my ear, his hand gliding through the water along my belly then back to curve again at my side.

"I'm not surprised she didn't open up upon me sharing an interest in her makeup usage and bare her soul to me. It'll take time. It's just a bummer I started my work right when she was going back to her mom."

"Maybe Rhiannon'll get in there."

"Maybe she will."

And I hoped she would. If Rhiannon was pulling herself together, three adults who loved Aisling and were looking after her were far better than one, that one being a father who loved her but he was also a guy who was uncertain what he was doing.

"Got somethin' to talk to you about," Mickey announced.

I stared out at the day, which didn't know whether to be gray or sunny so it treated us to both at thirty to forty-five minute intervals (at that moment, it was gray).

He sounded serious. Relaxed but serious.

And I didn't know what could come from Mickey Donovan when he was relaxed but serious.

Realizing I hadn't said anything, I invited, "Go for it."

"Last week, Mom and Dad called," he told me.

This was not a huge revelation. He spoke of his parents often. They had a great relationship. They doted on their grandchildren. Even from far away, they liked to be in the know about their son and his kids, but they weren't intrusive. However, they did contact Mickey regularly, always when he had his kids and in the evenings so they had a chance to talk to everyone.

"Okay," I prompted, wondering if he'd told them about me and hoping he had, he'd shared it was serious and going somewhere and now they wanted to come up and meet me.

Then I didn't hope that because that meant me meeting them and Mickey was so close to them, I'd need to make a good impression. And even if they were also rolling in it, I worried that the heiress next door might not go over too great.

"Told Dad about my plans," Mickey said into my thoughts.

"Your plans?" I asked.

"Quittin' Ralph, goin' into business for myself."

"Oh," I mumbled.

"He's excited about it."

I smiled at the view. "He would be. It's exciting."

"He wants to invest."

I twisted my neck to look up at him and Mickey adjusted so he could look down at me.

"Really?" I asked.

"Yep," he answered.

"I...that..." I shook my head slightly. "What do you think of that?"

"Dad lived here near on his whole life too, that bein' 'near on' only because he moved to Florida. Still knows practically the whole town. Him and Mom are friendly, they come back, see people, while they're gone, they stay in touch. They know Ralph's reputation and not just from me bitchin' about workin' for him for the last fifteen years."

"Okay," I said when he stopped talking.

"What I'm sayin' is, he's heard folks complaining about Ralph too. He thinks, if I go into business, I'll hit faster than I thought I would."

"That's great," I remarked.

"He's also still a member of the Club. He knows he can get them to entertain a bid from me but he thinks he could even get them to consider me as the contractor for that whole project. Their golf course development."

I felt elated.

Then I deflated.

"I hesitate to mention this, but Boston Stone is also a member of that Club," I reminded him.

"Yeah, babe, but that Club is about a lot of things and legacy is a big one. They might be racist and Stone's family may have been in Magdalene awhile, but the Donovans have lived in this town for six generations."

"That didn't stop him from getting whatever he presented to the town council signed," I noted.

"I seriously doubt he shared that whatever-that-was was about him losin' out against me for you. If he did, they would have laughed in his face."

This was likely correct.

Mickey kept going, "Not sure I could start out by takin' on a huge project like that. But I figure I could do some sub-contracting. Roofs on those houses at least. Maybe other shit. You know it wouldn't be hard for me to put together a crew. If I quit Ralph sooner rather than later, get a few jobs, start to establish a reputation, that could happen."

I began to get excited again.

"That would be wonderful," I shared quietly and he grinned.

"Yeah, it would."

"Are you...okay with taking your dad's money?" I asked carefully.

"As an investor, yeah," he replied. "He started by sayin' he'd give me the rest of my inheritance early, cash flat out that he says is mine. Said he wouldn't mind seein' me do something with it, enjoy it while he was still alive. To me, it felt like a handout so I refused. An investment, he has a stake in the company, we arrange it so I can buy him out when I can afford it, that might work."

I twisted so I was facing him more fully. "What does this mean?"

"Means I got the cake in the bank to quit and get going. You filed the papers. And thank you for that, baby," he finished softly, giving me a sweet, easy grin.

"You're welcome, Mickey." I gave him what I hoped was a sweet, easy grin back, knowing he didn't have to thank me. I'd go to the end of the earth for him.

His arms squeezed before he continued, "We got the insurance stuff mostly sorted. Just need the company officially founded, decide on which insurance we're going with. Get letterhead. Business cards. Payroll software. Employee handbook. Get the word out for hires. Line up jobs. Pull together my crew. It's a lot of work but if I can quit and see to it with cake in the bank to cover my family, that shit'd go a lot faster."

"And I can help, anything you need," I offered.

"That'd be awesome, Amy," he whispered.

"This is really wonderful," I told him.

He drew me nearer. "Yeah. Rhiannon seems to be getting her head out of her ass. We'll be hirin' a full-timer at the department soon, which puts me close to chief, which'll be more income to cover me as I get the business off the ground." His voice dipped low. "Got you."

I melted into him.

He kept speaking, "'Cept whatever's up with my little girl and every day havin' to go to a job I hate, the rest of life is good."

The rest of life was good.

We had to get Mickey out of that job and work on finding out what was troubling Aisling and fix it.

Then the *entirety* of life for Mickey would be good.

And that was the kind of life the kind of man that was Mickey should have in an everyday kind of way.

Life being good.

"I think you should do it," I told him.

"Even with capital, it's still a risk," he told me.

"Yes. I'm sure. And there'll be worries about that. But I believe in you. Your dad believes in you. Even not having a company set up yet, all those people who call you for patches believe in you. You have all the connections you need. You have an offer of the financial backing you need. Everything is pointing to you doing this, honey. I think you should listen to what the world is telling you and go for it."

"It fails, nothin' I can go back to, Amy," he replied. "Ralph's pretty much the only game in town and it isn't lost on him that I'm doin' those patches. He hasn't said anything but that keeps goin' and growin', he's gonna get pissed. I quit and compete, he's not gonna like that. I go down, he won't take me back."

"Even if you do patch jobs by yourself and do the chief job, it's better than you having to go to a job you hate every day for the next fifteen years."

His eyes strayed to the view.

I slid a hand up his wet chest, his neck, to cup his jaw and regained his attention.

"And it won't fail," I told him firmly. "You won't let it. This means something to you. And I've noticed something about you, Mickey Donovan. If something means something to you, you go all out. No fear."

His eyes dropped to my mouth. "Go all out."

I shifted against him and repeated, "Go all out."

"No fear," he muttered.

"No fear," I reiterated, my own gaze moving to his mouth, hoping he'd kiss me.

He didn't.

He shifted me so I was again leaning my back against him.

But then his hands moved.

His lips at my ear, he said, "My heiress needs to hone her organization skills. I got groundwork to lay before I put Ralph's shit in my rearview and I could use your help."

If I'd go to the ends of the earth, I'd find him payroll software.

I didn't give him that information. I didn't have the concentration (not that I thought we were at a place for me to share that information).

"Like I said," my words were breathy because his hands were still moving but with intent, "whatever you need."

"Whatever I need," he murmured, one hand dipping low, one hand up and curving.

"Mickey," I whimpered.

"Need my heiress to come in her kickass tub for me."

"I think…I can…do that," I stuttered, pressing my hips into his hand.

He rolled his finger on my clit then slid it down so it filled me.

My head dropped to his shoulder.

The fingers of his other hand pinched my nipple.

I gasped.

Mickey started finger fucking me.

Oh God.

So good.

"What about you?" I whispered.

"You're gonna blow me in your bed after we get outta the tub."

I absolutely was.

But first, it was my turn.

Mickey didn't disappoint. He pinched and rolled and rubbed my nipple as he kept finger fucking me. Then he moved his hand to the other nipple and went back to my clit as his mouth started working at my neck.

I squirmed and ground and arched and whimpered, clutching at his thighs, the warm water swirling, the beautiful view forgotten.

"That…keep doing…*that*," I begged as he added more pressure with some twitching and tugged at my nipple.

"Baby, wanna come in your mouth, stop dickin' around," he teased against my neck, but his words were growly and I could feel his hardness at my back.

The idea of that with all I was feeling drove me over the edge and with a gasped, "*Oh God*," I was soaring.

I barely got my feet back to the ground before the water surged with Mickey pulling us both out of the tub. He did a half-assed towel down of me and the same with him before he tugged me into my room.

He wasted just enough time to light my fire before he pulled me to the bed and on it.

He lay on his back, head and shoulders to the headboard, knees again angled, his beautiful cock rigid, long and thick, lying on his flat belly and I felt a shudder that was like a mini-orgasm just looking at all his power and beauty laid out before me.

I let myself have that then I "dicked around" no further, curling up between his legs, wrapping my hand around his cock and shifting it to my lips.

My eyes went to his.

Heated.

Impatient.

Hungry.

That look in his beautiful eyes all for me.

I slid him deep and lost his eyes as he closed them. I watched his head push into my headboard, his jaw clench, the muscles in his neck tense, the veins bulge as I felt his legs tighten at my sides.

God, he was so beautiful.

He gave me what he gave me in the tub and he gave me that.

So I gave him more.

And I did not mind in the slightest when his hands that had swept up my hair at the sides so he could better watch me go down on him, cupped my head and pushed me down to taking him deep when I heard his groan and he shot down my throat.

When his hands relaxed, I stroked him with my mouth, licked him clean then released him, kissing my way up his chest until I was at his neck.

He wrapped his arms around me, rolled us and covered me with his body.

He lifted his head and looked into my eyes.

"Want lunch?" I asked.

"You still hungry after that?" he teased.

I grinned, lifted up and kissed him.

He kissed me back, it started sweet and got deep before he ended it and belatedly answered my question.

"Definitely could eat."

"Finger foods," I whispered.

"What?" he asked.

I looked beyond him to the alarm clock then back to him. "We have four hours until my kids get here, around the same until yours get back. Finger foods we eat in this bed. No muss. No fuss. No preparing. No cleaning. So we have more time, just you and me. It's no hunting cabin," I grinned, "but it'll have to do."

His eyes warmed on me. "Sounds perfect, baby."

It absolutely did.

I lifted up to touch my mouth to his and when I was done, he took his cue, rolled off and grabbed my hand to help me out of bed.

He pulled on his jeans. I pulled on my robe. We went into the kitchen, raided it and took back crackers and cheese, chips and salsa, grapes, sodas and napkins. We undressed, got under the covers, munched, kissed, groped, sipped, talked then set aside the food and kept talking but did it with more groping and kissing until we were making love.

And after we finished making love, tangled up together, we started whispering.

Me and Mickey, in bed all day naked, nothing I wanted more.

And the way he did it with me, I had a feeling he felt the same.

A flash of happy for me that lasted an entire day.

Then again, with Mickey, I didn't get flashes of happy.

He gave that to me regularly.

———— • ————

"Okay, this place is crazy scary but these burgers are freaking *amazing*," Pippa declared.

It was the next Tuesday evening and Mickey and I were at Tink's with my children.

It was Mickey's idea. So when the kids got to my place Sunday night, I chanced telling them Mickey had invited us all out to dinner, taking them to a place his kids enjoyed.

Delightedly, they'd been all for it. Both of them had heard of Tink's but had not yet been (not surprising, it was not Conrad's kind of place, though Auden could have given it a go since he had a car, he just hadn't gotten around to it yet).

So now we were at Tink's.

The night had gone great. The kids were very welcoming of Mickey and seemed comfortable with him. He was Mickey so he was comfortable back. Conversation was not lacking mostly because Mickey was interested in everything they said and because Auden was more than interested in talking about the fire at the jetty (something I didn't like discussing but I didn't let on). Pippa was equally interested in that but mostly in wanting to know when Mickey thought the shops would reopen.

That was to say it had gone great...until then.

"Jeez, Pip, can you be cool for once?" Auden snapped, clearly taking her comment as an insult to Mickey's family's favorite eatery.

"I didn't mean anything," she snapped back, but I could see the pink hit her cheeks.

She was embarrassed.

"Kids—" I started.

Pippa interrupted me by saying ardently to Mickey, "The burgers *really* are good. Like...the best I've ever eaten."

"Glad you like 'em, darlin'," Mickey said unperturbedly before he lifted his own burger and sank his teeth in, showing he was not offended in the slightest at her comment.

Pippa gave *so there* eyes to her brother.

When his face went hard, I gave him a gentle kick under the table, got his attention and mouthed, "It's okay. Don't worry."

He drew in breath then looked to Mickey. "Uh...Mickey?"

Mickey swallowed and looked to him. "Yeah, bud?"

"I was talking to Joe and, you know, since we both know you're seeing Mom, we were talking about how cool it was you guys were seeing each other."

Hallelujah.

I didn't call out my exultation because my son was not done speaking (and for other reasons as well).

"We were also thinking that maybe, it's cool if it isn't okay, but we thought it'd be pretty sweet if we could hang at the firehouse with you one night. Maybe, if you get a call, do a ride along with you."

Oh God, no.

"First, it's gotta be cool with your mom," Mickey told him.

It absolutely was not. Having my guy out on a call was one thing. He was an adult. He was trained. He knew what he was doing.

He still was in danger.

Having him *and* my son near a blazing inferno?

No way.

"That'd be okay with me," I chirped.

Mickey studied me, his lips twitched, he knew it wasn't okay with me but he also knew—for me to give my son indication I knew he was growing into a man—it had to be.

He looked back to Auden. "Then all I gotta do is clear it with the chief, make sure the guys don't mind, which they won't, we've done it before, and we'll set it up."

"Totally cool," Auden said like it was. Absolutely.

"Just sayin', buddy," Mickey started, his voice lower to add weight to his words. "We'd dig you hanging around. But we get a call and you do ride along, you gotta do what you're told and stay clear. You might be there but only to observe. That gonna be okay with you?"

Auden nodded and he couldn't quite inject the cool.

He was excited.

"Right, then, you want, you can give me your number and when I talk to the chief and clear it with the guys, we'll plan," Mickey offered.

"Okay," Auden replied.

My phone chirped.

My bag was beside me on the nicked, warped, splinters-assured (though I'd never gotten one) picnic table (this being inside the ramshackle building). So I dug my phone out because we were at Tink's and nothing was rude at Tink's.

I glanced at the display and smiled.

I dropped the phone back in my purse to reply later and looked at my kids.

"Uncle Lawrie is coming for Thanksgiving," I announced.

"Awesome!" Auden said excitedly.

"So cool, Mom," Pippa agreed then asked, "Mercer and Hart coming?"

As the text said, *I'll be there Thanksgiving. Boys with their mom.* That was a no.

"Sorry, honey," I said as a gentle answer.

"Bummer," she muttered.

"Pip," Auden snapped again and with that, my attention became acute on them.

They could bicker. They could also fight.

But mostly, my son had a lot of patience with his little sister. She was a girl. Now she was a teenage girl. She could be flighty. She was admittedly a little spoiled (my doing, but she was also daddy's little girl so Conrad had a hand in that too).

Mostly, she was sweet and kindhearted and her brother knew it.

This was uncharacteristic and I wondered if he was being the way he was for fear of what Mickey would think of her (when she'd really not said anything that could offend Mickey and further, Mickey was a pretty laidback guy and didn't give any indication he was easily offended).

"What now?" she snapped back.

"I think we're good with Uncle Lawr," he chided. "We haven't seen him in almost a year and a half."

"I didn't say we weren't good with just him," she retorted. "It's just if they *all* came, we could be us. We could be awesome. And we could show them there's life after divorce, it isn't all that bad and eventually everyone could end up happy."

My hand darted out and curled around Mickey's thigh as I stared at my baby girl.

We could be us. We could be awesome. And we could show them there's life after divorce, it isn't all that bad and eventually everyone could end up happy.

I was about to burst into sloppy tears of joy when Mickey's hand curled around mine and held it at his thigh.

That gave me the strength to draw in breath and control the tears.

But it didn't stop me from saying, "I love you, baby girl."

Olympia's eyes shot to me, her face went soft, her chin started quivering, then she licked her lips and rolled them together before releasing them to say bashfully, "Love you too, Mom."

I smiled at her and turned my smile to my boy. "Since I'm being gushy, I'll say I love you too."

"It okay I don't look like a dork and get all weepy and say it back?" Auden asked jokingly.

"Yes, if in your memoirs you share with the world your deep adoration for your mother," I allowed.

"Whatever," he muttered, but he did it grinning at his burger before he picked it up and took a huge bite, this indication of how much he liked it because wrestling weigh-ins were soon and around that time, things got dicey for Auden to maintain the weight he needed.

Perhaps this was why he was short-tempered with his sister.

Having experience with Auden and his weigh-ins, I put it down to that.

Back on good footing with my kids, the rest of the night went great. Even when we got back and the kids talked Mickey into "hanging out awhile" whereupon Pippa took that opportunity to point out we'd all be a lot more comfortable if we had another chair up there. Auden didn't even rise to the bait. But this could be because we sat comfortably with Auden in what had become my chair, Pippa at one end of the couch, me in the middle, Mickey at the other end.

Mickey and I even did some minor cuddling and the kids didn't blink an eye.

However, with the kids there and the stained glass window in the door, we only got to whisper goodnights and give lip touches rather than make out, which was disappointing.

That was the only disappointment. The rest was all good. We all had enjoyed it. And Pippa had even asked Mickey back around so she could cook for him.

A success.

Which meant more happy for me.

And by the way he was acting, more importantly, for Mickey.

———— • ————

I GOT THE NEWS BY TEXT THE NEXT DAY THAT MICKEY HAD GOT THE GO-ahead from everyone for Auden and his friend Joe to hang at the fire-house on Friday night.

The boys had gladly given up any Friday night activities, including the high school football game, to go hang with the guys of the MFD.

I had been a wreck until I got a text from Mickey at midnight that said, *They're asleep in bunks. It's all good, babe.*

I got more the next morning when Auden came home (that was to *my* home as in *our* home), full of talk about how he and Joe thought Mickey and the guys were "the bomb" and they couldn't wait to do it again.

This "do it again" business did not fill me with glee. Mickey had told me the last major fire they'd been called to before the one at the jetty had been during a heat spell that came with a drought that had meant some

4th of July fireworks had taken a house with it, this happening three years before. They'd had many minor incidents, but no major ones.

I still fretted about my son liking hanging in a firehouse and what that might mean.

But he was discovering who he was and what he wanted to be. As Mickey told me, he had to have the space to do that and I had to find the strength to let him.

So I did.

And anyway, he was doing it with Mickey. He liked him. He respected him. And he wanted to spend time with him.

So that worked for me.

———— • ————

I WAS WANDERING THROUGH WAYFARER'S NOT PAYING A LOT OF ATTENTION to my grocery shopping because I was texting back and forth with Robin about her drinks with Lawrie.

To her *Did you know he asked the ice queen for a divorce?*

I sent, *I did know things were coming to a head*, and I did this thinking I really needed to phone my brother. I had no idea it had gone that far.

This got me, *He's staying there, separate bedrooms, looking for a house. He's close to offering on one.*

Definitely needed to phone my brother.

I replied, *Wow. Things have progressed. But did you guys have fun?*

She returned, *Of course. He's Lawrie. We were out for hours and laughed all night.*

I tried not to be bad and hope all night meant *all night* and sent, *That's good. So glad.*

That was when she thrilled me by saying, *I told him I'd planned on going up to Solvang. Do some wine tasting. The vault is low. He said if I drive up and stop in Santa Barbara after Thanksgiving, he might be able to show me the new house.*

She loved Solvang. There was little not to love. The town was great. The wineries were fabulous.

But she'd been up there tons of times. She knew what she liked. She could order what she liked and have it shipped. She didn't have to drive up there.

This was promising.

I liked it.

You should go, I replied.

I think I will, she returned.

That was when, wandering down an aisle, leaning on my cart and texting, I heard, "Amy."

It was not Mickey, Aisling or Cillian saying it.

My head snapped up and I saw Boston Stone in the aisle with me.

I went cold, completely, inside and hopefully he saw it on the outside.

"Boston." Ice dripped from his name.

His eyes narrowed at my tone. Then again, he didn't look happy before I sent him the ice.

Then, if it could be believed, he stated, "You are aware that at our ages, teenage antics are no longer appropriate. Say, when a man shows interest in you and phones you, if you don't share those feelings, instead of ignoring him, you say that directly with him."

I stared up at him knowing in that moment that the blow he wanted to land on Mickey was a blow he hoped to land on Mickey that was really directed at me.

Why were some people such assholes?

I stared coolly into his eyes. "And you should be aware that when a woman shows little enthusiasm for your calls, has no time for you, and stops answering, that's her way of saying that she's not interested. A gentleman would leave it at that without pushing her to doing more, which is always awkward and uncomfortable. But just to say, Boston, we'd had a single date. Frankly, I didn't owe you anything."

"I disagree," he retorted.

"You've made that clear," I assured him.

He looked down the aisle and back to me. "I guess there's nothing more to say except have a good day."

"The same to you."

He didn't mean it.

I didn't either.

He nodded and walked down the aisle.

I didn't nod and walked down my aisle thinking that perhaps I should start going to a different grocery store. Wayfarer's was a gourmet market.

I could get things a lot cheaper if I drove to the big supermarket in the next town.

The problem was, I liked Wayfarer's and what was the point of being filthy rich if you couldn't shop at expensive places that you liked?

When I had the groceries packed in the back and I was in the Rover, I called Mickey and told him what happened.

I did this hesitantly, thinking he might be mad that Boston confronted me.

He burst out laughing.

When I could get a word in he might hear, I asked, "You think it's funny?"

"Hilarious," he confirmed.

"Well..." I trailed off, not knowing if I liked that or not.

He heard my hesitation and explained, "Babe, you can stick up for yourself. My heiress is no doormat."

I knew I liked that.

And in hearing it, I thought of that encounter and I thought about how I'd handled it. I didn't go all Felicia Hathaway polite. I didn't cower under the confrontation. I didn't apologize about something I had no reason to apologize for.

I stuck up for myself.

I *was* no doormat.

This made me happy.

"I guess it was kinda funny," I told him.

"Fuck, I hope that asshole finds a woman. I'll feel bad for her but once he finds someone to put his dick in regularly, he might let the rest of the hot chick population of Magdalene out of their misery."

To that, I giggled.

And soon after, we rang off.

I drove home in my Rover doing it *not* a doormat.

I had a firefighter boyfriend and I could cope with the danger of his job (outwardly, inwardly was my business). I had a position as a volunteer in a nursing home where part of the role was losing people I'd come to care about, this being regularly and without warning. And I had two kids that I'd forced to become estranged who were back with me, one bragging about how we were happy after all that had happened.

I was not a doormat.

I was not an heiress.

I was not a doctor's wife.

I was me.

Amy.

And the best part about that?

I was pretty awesome.

•

"Erm...*what*?" I asked Mickey.

We were in his bedroom the evening of the Boston Stone incident. It was Thursday. He had his kids back.

And he'd just told me that Aisling had told him that she wanted me to go shopping to decorate her room.

The twist was that she wanted me to do this with her *and* Rhiannon.

And the twist to *that* was, Rhiannon had agreed.

So far, it had been a good week in a variety of ways. One of which was the discovery that Aisling was now showering regularly.

This was positive but not exactly surprising. Rhiannon had phoned Mickey and told him they'd had not one but three chats. The first one was reportedly dramatic, much like experienced by Mickey. The second one was surly.

Rhiannon didn't give up and the third one was beneficial.

Apparently, Aisling wasn't adjusting to high school very well. There were some girls she didn't like, who she never really liked, but it was difficult to avoid them like she used to do as unfortunately they shared a number of classes. Classes that, also unfortunately, Aisling's friends didn't share so she had no one "at her back."

According to Ash, "it wasn't that big of a deal" and that "they just don't get me, I'm not into the same crap as they are."

Rhiannon then cottoned on to the fact that they were possibly picking on her and pointed out that she should give them less to pick on, in other words, having a shower and taking care of herself better.

She also asked if she and Mickey needed to contact the school.

Aisling had flatly refused this and before any headway that was gained could be lost, Rhiannon backed down. However, she asked for Mickey to keep an eye out when he got the kids back just to make sure that Aisling was still improving.

It seemed she was. She not only showered, she also helped me with dinner. She wasn't back to her quiet but present self, but it was something.

Mickey was relieved. Mickey also communicated this to her, taking every opportunity to do that he could, without making it obvious or overbearing.

He'd also started calling her his "pretty girl" or his "gorgeous girl," things he used to say but he said them now still infrequently but with greater regularity.

These were from her dad, not some cute boy, but it was plain to see she was responding. When he said them, her face would change in a way that was good, not bad. Or she'd hunch her shoulders like she was trying to hold the subtle compliments to her.

It didn't hurt that Cillian, as if he sensed all this was happening (when, at his age, I was sure it was flying right over his head), got in on the act. He praised her cooking. And the first time she said she was going to watch TV with us instead of slinking to her room, he'd cried, "All right! What should we make Dad and Amy watch, Ash? I'm totally thinking *Arrow*."

"Someone kill me," Mickey had murmured, and both his kids had laughed (both of them!).

We'd watched *Arrow*. I'd never even heard of it but it was pretty good, even if I wasn't into superhero kinds of things.

What was great about it was that Cillian and Aisling kept up a running commentary, catching us up on back stories we could have no idea about.

And Aisling was almost as into this as Cillian.

So the efforts of the three adults in Ash's life were obviously working. It wasn't a miraculous change but the silence, isolation and gloom seemed to be lifting.

And now she wanted me to go shopping with her and her mother.

"She's not drinking," Mickey announced rather than repeating the insanity of me shopping with his daughter and ex-wife.

"I'm sorry?" I whispered.

"She isn't drinking."

I stared.

"Ash told me. Not the whole week she had them. Not a drop. And when Rhiannon wasn't around, Ash looked and there's no liquor in her house. Not wine, which is what she drinks, but not anything and she keeps other shit there for when she has company."

"Oh my God," I breathed.

This was incredible.

"I don't know," Mickey stated. "Don't got my hopes up, don't want my kids' up. But she's spoken to me on the phone and I can tell, in the evenings, when she's slidin' toward gone, slurrin' her words, losing track of the conversation. She's all there. She hasn't been all there in ten years. Now, she's all there."

Could it be that *everything* was going to turn out right?

Mickey kept going, "So, Ash wants you and Rhiannon to bond. Rhiannon knows this and she wants our daughter to have this. She said you were cool when you answered the door. She knew it was a surprise for you when she showed, not a good one, but you were nice to her. Offered to let her see the kids. Told her it was nice to meet her. It wasn't good why we got divorced and we didn't agree on why we got divorced. What we agreed on is that we'd do what we could to make us bein' apart as easy as possible for the kids. She's nice. Doesn't have a mean bone in her body, unless she's in denial and fuckin' up her life. That means she will not do you dirty. I don't suspect she wants you in her crew. I think she just wants her daughter to have somethin' solid and real. Folks around her who give a shit and also get along. And babe," he moved closer to me, "it'd mean a fuckuva lot you did this for me too."

Shit, I had to do this.

Shit, I had to *do this.*

"I'll do it."

His grin was not easy.

It was warm and beautiful and utterly amazing.

"Thanks, Amy," he whispered.

For that grin, I'd do anything.

Then again, I'd do anything for Mickey.

And Aisling.

"Do anything for your girl, Mickey," I replied.

That got me more grin until I lost it when he was kissing me.

"You guys gonna stay in there until Armageddon or what?" Cillian shouted and Mickey broke the kiss. "Spaghetti's ready!"

"Cill! Shut up!" Ash yelled on the heels of Cillian shouting.

"Comin'!" Mickey bellowed on the heels of Ash yelling.

Then he took my hand, pulled me out of his room and we had spaghetti.

———— • ————

"This is beautiful," Rhiannon decreed.

"I like it," Aisling said quietly, but from the look on her face, she didn't like it. She loved it.

It was late Saturday morning. Rhiannon had come to Mickey's to pick up Ash and me. It was awkward for Rhiannon and me from the get-go but I was working, and knew she was too, at hiding this from Aisling.

I just hoped we were succeeding.

We were now in Bed Bath and Beyond, our first stop.

And I was staring at bed linens that were sophisticated and grown up and I wouldn't mind having them in my house.

The problem was that I worried they were expensive.

The comforter was a muted green with an equally muted sheen, two wide strips of pretty beading up the sides. The sheets were cream. The green euro pillow shams also had a wide strip of beading down the middle. The standard shams had two strips to the sides. The toss pillows included a neckroll in an embroidered cream, a green rectangle with two stripes of beading to its sides, and a square with beading at the corners.

"We're getting this," Rhiannon announced and Ash turned wide, happy eyes to her. "All of it. Even those toss pillows and the euros."

I started panicking.

"To get it all, we'll need another cart," Rhiannon decided as I sidled to the shelves behind the bed display in order surreptitiously check the prices. "Can you go get one, honey?"

"Sure," Ash agreed, giving her mom a small smile, giving me one, then moving away.

I looked to the price tags on the shelves where the linens were. I did a quick calculation and continued to panic.

Mickey had given us a budget. It wasn't excessive, it wasn't skimpy.

But if we bought the entire ensemble, it would be more than half of what he gave us.

The linens would clash in her room now with all its other accoutrements. So we needed paint. We needed new lamps (all her lamp bases or shades were purple or pink). Her floors were wood and it was highly unlikely under that layer of clothes that the rugs were green or cream or beige or mushroom or oyster or anything that would work with the sophistication of those linens.

The decorator in me screamed. The mom in me screamed louder. Blowing more than half our budget on bedclothes meant the job would end up not right, half-assed, and Aisling would have to live in that until it could be sorted. Christmas was weeks away and I probably could get away with a lamp, a rug, or maybe some knickknacks, but Mickey wouldn't want me to go all out.

This meant we'd have to piecemeal her redecoration efforts and that didn't say, *We love you. We know you're growing up smart and responsible and beautiful and we want you to have space that reflects that.* It said, *We're doing what we can do. Deal with it.*

"Isn't it pretty?"

The question came from Rhiannon.

I looked to her and I didn't know what to do. I couldn't contribute to the cause because that might upset Mickey. I couldn't allow us to blow the whole budget on sheets, comforter, shams and toss pillows because that would mean we'd either have to get super cheap stuff for the rest or defer it. And I couldn't say Aisling couldn't have it because Rhiannon already told her she could and it was obvious Mickey's girl loved it.

"You don't like it?" Rhiannon asked, reading my face.

"I…well…" I drew in a deep breath. "It's gorgeous. She loves it. So I'm really sorry to say this but this stuff is going to blow half our budget and this is the first store we've been to. I'm worried about—"

"This is from me."

I wasn't thinking that was any better.

She read that too, turned her face away and it looked like she was deciding something.

I let her, watching her and seeing Mickey did have a type.

His type was me.

Sure, Rhiannon had dark blonde hair, but she also had hazel eyes, a pretty face, she was my height (maybe an inch taller) and she was very curvy in a nice way. She wore classy clothes that were a bit edgy. She took care of herself.

In fact, watching her, I noted that now, miraculously, she didn't look five years older than me. She looked my age. Her skin brighter, healthier, the flush from the cold outside still on her cheeks.

She interrupted my musings on Mickey's type when she looked back to me and declared, "It's time for honesty."

Oh God.

We'd been together for less than an hour, Ash was off getting a cart, I wasn't ready for honesty.

I braced.

She noticed it and her voice softened. "Not bad honesty, Amy. But honesty for me, after a while where I wasn't honest at all, is a good thing."

"I...okay," I said, not knowing what else to say and not saying what I wanted to say, which was that I didn't know what she was going to say but I still wished she wouldn't say it.

I didn't get my silent wish.

She started talking.

"I know it seems weird, me buying my daughter sheets and stuff for her room at her dad's. But I have a feeling Mickey's told you about me so I have a feeling you know I haven't been mother of the year. Not this year, or the last, or any for a while."

When she meant honesty, she wasn't kidding.

I decided it best not to respond, however, I kept my expression open for her to continue.

She did.

"I have a problem," she declared.

I fought against my mouth dropping open.

Was she saying what I thought she was saying?

"I'm working on it," she went on. "I'll be working on it forever but at least I've started working on it. When they were with me, the kids were talking about you and I knew the way you were around, knowing Mickey, that you meant something. I didn't...that didn't..." her voice dropped to a whisper, "that upset me."

"Rhiannon." I was whispering too.

She lifted her chin slightly. "They liked you. I...you were...it seemed

KRISTEN ASHLEY

like you were making a family. And I...I..." she shook her head, "I didn't handle that very well. Then I missed Cill's birthday—"

"Mickey and I weren't even together then," I told her quietly.

"Yes you were," she replied.

We were. We were in the throes of a bizarre mating ritual but we were into each other. I just didn't know it and he was fighting it.

I made no reply.

"That was..." she held my eyes, "a mother doesn't do that, Amy. Miss her boy's birthday."

"No," I agreed carefully.

She straightened her shoulders. "So I missed Cill's birthday. Ash was slipping. And I was wallowing. Mickey and I got into it and I didn't even know how some of the stuff I was saying was coming out. I knew he wasn't like that. I knew he'd never do the stuff I was accusing him of doing. And when he gets angry," she smiled a melancholy smile, "I'm sure you know, he lets loose. So, even still angry at me, when he phoned about his scene with Aisling it was dawning on me I had to wake up. Everyone was being adult about the situation, even the kids. The only one who wasn't was me. Then I came to the house and saw you."

I kept eye contact, unsure of what was coming.

She kept speaking.

"You were nice. You seemed comfortable there. That didn't sit well with me either. It hurt. But you were nice. You weren't cold or mean. You were...you were...*nice*."

"I'm divorced too, Rhiannon, I have kids. I know it's important to try to keep things good with all involved, doing that for the children. Saying that, my ex and I haven't actually accomplished that feat," I admitted.

"Well, I'm sorry," she replied. "I hope that gets better. I'm actually surprised to hear it because I walked away from meeting you and I thought, if that woman could stand in the home that used to be mine and be friendly and welcoming, which had to be hard considering all that was going on, but it would always be awkward, and you did what you could not to make it that way, then what was wrong with me?"

"Rhiannon—" I started.

"I went right from there to Reverend Fletcher."

I blinked.

She continued, "There's a meeting at the church, Wednesday nights. I started going."

Oh my God!

She *was* saying what I thought she was saying!

She shook her head, looked over my shoulder, then back at me. "It's not enough. But there's a community center in Fullham. It's a drive but they have meetings on Monday evenings and Saturday afternoons. I don't have a sponsor yet or anything, but there are folks who go who've been in recovery a lot longer than me who have given me their numbers so I can call if things get...if they get...*hairy*."

I held my breath.

"I haven't had a drink since I met you that Friday," she announced.

Oh my God.

How fabulous!

"Rhiannon, that's wonderful," I told her, wanting to reach out and grab her hand but knowing that wasn't where we were so I didn't.

"It's hard. Seriously hard. The hardest thing I've ever done," she told me.

"I'm sure," I said quietly.

"But it's the best thing I ever did, except making beautiful babies."

I nodded.

She was so right.

"Are you...have you...do the kids know?" I asked.

"Mom isn't pouring and I figure they noticed it. But officially, not yet," she answered.

"Mickey?" I asked.

"I don't want to ask you to keep secrets but I'd like to tell him myself. I intend to do this soon so it isn't like you have to keep it from him forever. I just wanted some time and to stay on track for a while before I shared." She took a breath and carried on, "And the important thing right now isn't me. It's seeing to Aisling. When things are better with her, I'll explain the process to the kids."

I nodded again. Though I thought that her sharing that might help things get better with Ash, it wasn't my recovery and it wasn't my place to give my opinion.

And I wasn't entirely certain why she was telling me and intended to wait to tell those a far sight closer to her. But it was hers to give to who she thought it was right to give. This had to be a process and she didn't seem to be winging it. Maybe I was step one, a person who was on the edges of her life who, not in a bad way, didn't really matter. Maybe I was a practice run. The beginning of the rest.

And if that was the case, I had to make it as smooth and positive as possible.

"I'm happy for you. For the kids. For Mickey even," I said and gave her an encouraging smile. "This is really great, Rhiannon."

"I want to make sure, to be good for a while, just in case I...I don't want to get their hopes up."

That I understood.

"I get you," I told her.

"So it isn't much but my Ash having nice bed stuff to make her smile, it's something."

We were full circle and it was quite a journey to take unexpectedly in Bed Bath and Beyond.

But I was honored to be on it.

Even so, I had to note, "You're right. It's just...Mickey."

I said no more but she knew Mickey so she understood me.

"I'll call him so he knows we're sticking to his budget and the bed stuff is from me."

"That's a good plan."

"I'll do that now," she murmured, bending her head and digging into her purse. She got her phone out and looked to me. "I'll just wander and do that. When she gets back, you'll help Aisling get her stuff? Two sets of sheets. It's no good for laundry day with just one."

"We'll take care of it," I assured her.

She nodded and gave me a small smile before she wandered off, phone to her ear.

I started amassing the stuff Aisling would need, piling it on the bed display. Surprisingly, it took some time before Aisling arrived with another cart.

I looked to her. "Hey, blossom."

"I'm sorry. I stopped because I saw these." She lifted up a plastic tray, one of several she had in her cart. "I know it isn't decorating so I'll use my own money to buy them, but I thought they'd be good to organize my makeup. You know, to get it off my dresser."

I smiled at her, wishing I could buy them for her and thinking, next time something like this happened, I'd get a budget from Mickey as to how much he'd let me splurge to spoil his girl. Even if it was twenty dollars, I'd get to have fun and I'd get to give her something.

But bottom line, it was brilliant she was interested in what we were doing and going so far as to consider adding organizing to our project.

"Great idea," I said. "Those'll be perfect."

Her lips tipped up and her eyes wandered. "Where's Mom?"

"Getting the go-ahead from your dad to spoil you with fabulous bed linens."

Her eyes shot back to me. "Do you think he'll mind?"

"Not even a little bit," I told her. "But, they should be on the same page with this project, don't you think?"

That settled her in a variety of ways. I knew it from the look in her eyes, the expression on her face and even in her body language.

She liked her mom and dad talking. She wanted them on the same page. She wanted more, to go back in time and have what they had before life tore their family apart.

But she'd take this.

"Yeah," she agreed.

"Okay, help me load this up," I said. "And you don't have euros so we'll have to go to the pillow section. Your mom walked that way. If she's not back, we'll meet up with her there."

"Cool," she mumbled.

We loaded up. We got euro pillows. Rhiannon met us in that section with the news Mickey okayed Rhiannon's contribution. After we made our purchases and were headed to Lowe's for paint, in the car, I texted Mickey and asked if I could have a budget.

He texted back, *My heiress has gotta spoil my girl. You got fifty bucks.*

Which meant I bought a fabulous lamp for her nightstand at Pier 1.

When we got home and the boys helped us cart the massive stash in, Mickey and Cillian teased Aisling about just how much it took to redo a girl's bedroom. She gave a lot of "shut ups," but she did this smiling.

Then Mickey gently laid down the law that if Aisling wanted him to corral his buds to help paint her room while she was at her mom's, the place had to be picked up, packed up (so they could move things easily) and cleaned.

She'd agreed.

Through this, Rhiannon and I sat at the kitchen bar, sipping tea and chatting.

It wasn't entirely comfortable, it wasn't uncomfortable.

What it was, was real.

And good.

For the kids.

And for Mickey.

So it worked for me.

———————— • ————————

I DIDN'T TELL MICKEY ABOUT RHIANNON'S EFFORTS AT RECOVERY. HE already sensed she was no longer drinking.

But that was hers to share.

And since we exchanged numbers "just in case," when I texted her after she left to let her know that was my decision, she'd texted back, *Thank you, Amy. I promise I won't take too long.*

I didn't know if she even knew my name was Amelia.

But I didn't mind that Rhiannon called me Amy.

She was a part of the family.

———————— • ————————

"YOU WET?"

I was sitting beside the boxing ring with Alyssa and Josie.

The question was from Alyssa.

The answer was a breathy, "Yeah."

To which I received, "Season delayed this year. Seemed to take an *eternity.*"

It was the Saturday night after my foray shopping to decorate Aisling's room with Rhiannon.

The day had been a success.

Mickey was right. Rhiannon didn't want me in her crew. But she did want something healthy between all the adults in her children's lives and obviously, I was all for that too.

In fact, things as a whole were going swimmingly, no longer just for me, but also for Mickey.

The papers had been filed for Mickey's company. I'd found a graphic designer who was designing his logo. His dad had wired him the money and Arnold Weaver had drafted the papers they were going to sign for their investment agreement. Someone had requested that Mickey put in a bid for a full roof they wanted on before the weather got too crazy. And Mickey, Bobby and Jimbo were going to start interviewing the fire-fighters for the salaried position next week.

Last, Mickey and I agreed, then took it to our kids and they agreed, that we would start the blending of families on Thanksgiving.

Mickey had said they had a pact to share those days and it was Rhiannon's turn to have them to her place for Thanksgiving. But before he asked his kids, he'd told her what we wanted to do and she'd agreed to giving up the meal if she got time with them in the evening.

Something I thought was *very* kind.

So they would be going to Rhiannon's after dinner to share family time. That meant he and his kids would come over, have dinner, but none of the kids would be forced to spend all day getting used to each other.

And with that, there was cooking and football and Lawr would be there, and he was great with kids. It wouldn't be going out to dinner, making them converse, the focus being solely on the meet and greet. There'd be tons of distractions.

It was perfect.

As perfect as it was, it scared the heck out of me.

But I did my best to set that aside and turn my attention to glorying in the fact that it was clear my guy was getting more than just flashes of happy.

And I was right then at my first fight of Mickey's.

No. I was watching Mickey, sweaty and focused, wearing white satin boxing shorts with a green shamrock on the side that really, *really* did not look even the slightest bit foolish being worn by all that was Mickey.

And he was beating the absolute *shit* out of some guy in a boxing ring.

Last, I was doing this thinking I was orgasming.

This was inappropriate. Not only were Alyssa and Josie sitting with me, Cillian, Aisling and Ethan were also with us.

But I still was pretty sure it was happening.

"You got back from Junior really quickly after his win." I heard Josie, sitting to one side of me, note softly to Alyssa, who was on my other side.

"Went back. Blew him real quick. He's good until I see how our girl here becomes a fight fanatic," Alyssa replied, also quietly so the kids sitting beyond Josie couldn't hear. "Once Mickey kicks ass, I'll hang around and make sure she doesn't rush the ring and rip his trunks off. Then we'll hit the motel that does an hourly rate on the way home and he can rock my world."

I heard these words.

I didn't tear my eyes away from the ring.

They only fought three rounds and these seemed to last two seconds of sheer exhilaration and goodness before the referee had to stop the fight because Mickey got a technical knockout.

I burst from my chair, and much like Alyssa did when Junior had won the fight before (except with less foul and suggestive language), I screamed, "*Way to go, baby! You rock!*"

Mickey's glove held up in the air, still sweaty and fabulous, his eyes dropped to me.

That was when I got an easy grin.

Yes, very much like orgasming.

It was then I realized that having the kids on fight night was not that great of a thing.

And it was then I realized that next Saturday, he wouldn't have his but I would have mine as Pippa already told me she was having Polly for a sleepover, and maybe another girlfriend. Further Auden had shared he and his buds were going to camp out in from of my big TV to watch football all day after he was done with conditioning.

With all those kids there, kids of two different sexes, they needed chaperoning, so I didn't think it was a good idea to leave.

So when Mickey had his kids back, I'd have to either finagle his kids doing sleepovers somewhere else, the same with mine, or I'd have to wait for my *real* fight night to come and it might take *weeks*.

This was disappointing.

But it was helped when we went back to the locker rooms and I could give Mickey a lip brush before Cillian took over for his blow by blow with his dad about the fight.

This was cute because Cillian was excited and his blow by blow included much reenactment. This meant he did a lot of fake punching of his dad, who fake punched back, still sweaty but with his gloves off, his hands taped, warm in his boy's excitement.

Though, in Mickey's case it wasn't cute. It was sweet-dad-cute-*hot*.

Alas, we separated in the parking lot. I had brought the kids there but Mickey, not having showered but in workout pants pulled over his boxing trunks and a zip up jacket, was taking them home.

And we were all going home to houses across the street from each other, me alone to my empty house, Mickey with his kids to his.

This was what we did and the whole way I tried to come up with ways to suggest he find sleepovers for his children when he had them again in two weeks.

I was in my nightie, standing by my nightstand, moisturizing, and I still had not come up with how I would suggest this to Mickey when my cell on my nightstand rang.

My pulse zinged when I saw it was Mickey.

I snatched it up, took the call and put it to my ear.

"Hey." It came out as a breath.

"Door," he growled.

My entire body zinged. I dropped the phone back to the nightstand without even disconnecting, and sprinted to the door.

I threw it open.

Mickey, still in his track pants and jacket, crowded me. His arm going around me, he backed me in, kicked the door closed and shifted me, backing me toward the dining room table.

"Tell me your kids didn't decide to spend the night," he ordered.

I shook my head. "No, baby. It's just me."

Then I was up right before I was down, ass to the table then back to it as Mickey leaned into me.

His mouth to mine, his eyes staring into mine through the shadows, he didn't kiss me.

He just looked into my eyes as his hand yanked up my nightie then dove right in my panties.

My lips parted and my back arched.

His eyes flamed through the dark. "Fuck, you're wet."

"Yes," I whispered.

"Ready?" he asked.

"Yeah, honey."

He moved away only to tear my panties down my legs and I whimpered.

Then he came back, I felt him working at his pants between my legs and then he was inside me.

I pushed my hands up his jacket to touch him but ended up clawing at him as he fucked me hard and relentlessly, his mouth brushing mine, his eyes to mine, his breaths harsh and assaulting my lips, his eyes blazing.

He slid one hand up my side, my arm, pulling it from around him and wrapping his fingers around my wrist where he pinned it to the table over my head.

I shivered and pressed the insides of my thighs tighter to his sides in order to hold him to me and use him to lift me up so I could get more of him.

He groaned and drove deeper.

God, amazing.

"You like fight night?" he rumbled low.

"Oh yeah," I gasped.

"You always gonna want your fight night fuck?"

"*Absolutely*," I breathed.

He fucked me harder and took my mouth in a hot, deep, brutal kiss.

That was it for me.

Then again, I'd had three rounds of foreplay so that was all I needed.

I moaned my orgasm down his throat.

He kissed me through it and kept contact when he groaned his orgasm down mine.

He was still inside me and we were both still breathing heavily when he ordered thickly, "You leave the kids in their seats next fight. They can come back after I fuck you in the locker room."

"Okay," I agreed immediately.

He ground his hips into mine as indication he approved of my response and I mewed against his lips.

"Love you, Amy."

I stilled completely.

He felt it.

"I don't care if that's too soon for you," he announced. "You do with it what you want. Keep it and hold it to you and hope like fuck you give it back when you're ready. But you gotta know, it's yours."

I stared at him through the dark.

"Now, I gotta get back to my kids," he muttered, shifted to touch his mouth to my jaw then slid out gently.

He pulled me to my feet and held me while I got my legs solid under me. Then he bent and nabbed my panties. He kept a hand to me to steady me as I tugged them on.

After that, he grabbed my hand and led me to the door.

Without a word, he took me in his arms and gave me a long, soft, sweet kiss that went on forever and it was still too short.

He ended it and said, "Talk to you tomorrow, baby."

He then set me back so he could open the door and he was through it before I called, "Mickey!"

He turned to me.

"You gotta know too," I said.

He stood there, almost right where I'd first seen him, looking more beautiful than ever.

Because he was mine. All mine. Truly mine.

Every inch.

Straight down to his heart.

"You gotta know I love you too," I went on. "You're the best man I've ever met, honey. A great dad. A good man." I smiled. "The *best* neighbor *ever.*"

I watched his eyes dance at the last but I wasn't done.

"There was no better day than the day Conrad showed up and started shouting at me, because it brought you to me."

His lips curled up. "Only time I was glad some asshole was in a woman's face."

My lips curled up too.

Then they started trembling so I pressed them together.

"Right across the street," Mickey whispered.

I pressed my lips together harder and nodded.

He gave me an easy grin, "Luck o' the Irish."

I started giggling.

His eyes kept dancing.

Then they warmed and he ordered, "Get inside, baby. Get warm. Talk to you tomorrow."

Like I wasn't already warm.

Through and through.

"Okay, Mickey. Goodnight."

"'Night, babe."

It was then I realized I didn't mind "babe" at all. Or "darlin'." Or "baby."

I'd take anything from Mickey.

Because he meant it.

I lifted my hand to touch it to my lips and drifted it out to him.

Then grinning at him like an idiot (and not caring), I closed the door on the man who loved me.

AWESOME HOLIDAY

"*I* should believe it. I really should. But I don't believe that man."

I was in my kitchen, banging around bitching.

This was because it was eleven thirty Thanksgiving morning and the kids were supposed to spend the night last night at my place, seeing as Lawr had arrived yesterday morning. But also so they could help me get things ready for the day.

Conrad had spoken to them and, for some reason, which I could read was not great, they'd changed plans and said they had to spend the night at their dad's.

However, they promised they'd be at my place by ten because the day had been precisely timed.

The house was clean, that wasn't a worry.

But there was cooking and baking and table laying to do. They were supposed to help me get most of that sorted so when Mickey and his kids showed up at twelve thirty, we could watch football and relax without too much running around. However, there wouldn't be much of that since dinner was supposed to happen at two so it wasn't a rush since they were going to Rhiannon's at four.

It was perfectly timed. Football on, something to take folk's attention but things to do together to give opportunities to mingle. Then good food with good company. And before it went on too long, Mickey and his brood had to go to Rhiannon's so everyone could be let off the hook and they could relax (which I hoped wasn't necessary but I felt it necessary to plan).

The kids being that late was throwing me off. In fact, the kids not spending the night had thrown me off. I could have no idea but I wouldn't put it past Conrad to know what was happening with Mickey this Thanksgiving, or that Lawr was going to be there, so he was trying to ruin it for me.

I didn't like Auden's tone when he phoned and said they needed to stay with their dad. He didn't share much and seemed distracted but he also seemed something...*else.*

I just couldn't get a lock on it.

And again, he didn't share it with me.

I'd asked but he'd said, "We'll talk later, Mom," in a way he needed me to talk with him about it later.

So I decided, for my boy, to let it go.

Now, it was worse not only because they were late but also, except for a quick text from Auden that said simply, *We're gonna be late. Sorry.* I'd had nothing. I gave it half an hour then I'd texted. I'd phoned.

I'd received no reply.

My kids were not impolite. Since our reunion, this kind of thing didn't happen. They might not reply immediately, but they replied.

Knowing they were late, they'd reply at the very least so I wouldn't worry.

I snatched up my cell, declaring, "I'm gonna call *him.*"

"Sweetheart," Lawr said, reaching out a hand to wrap it around my wrist. "Don't."

I looked up at him. "There are pies to be baked!" I snapped.

He lifted his brows and looked down at the pie crust he was rolling out (always there for me, my big brother Lawrie).

"We need to bake three of them, Lawrie," I reminded him.

"And they'll get baked," he replied.

I looked to the crust and mumbled, "I should have made them yesterday."

And I should have, though I didn't know how I could have, what with spending half the day baking and decorating Thanksgiving-themed cupcakes to take to Dove House, where, after Mickey left, Lawr, the kids and I were going.

That part of the day I wasn't nervous about. I was just excited. The kids were finally going to meet the residents and I was going to get to show them and Lawr what I did that meant so much to me.

And bonus, I got to spend time with my old folks on Thanksgiving *with* my family (or most of it, but maybe next year I'd get to take Mickey, Cillian and Aisling).

"MeeMee," he called and I looked back to him. "If he's playing some game, you don't want to lose it and fall into his plans. You also don't want the kids, who know they should be here and are already probably stressed out that they aren't, to be *more* stressed with you phoning and texting. Give them another half an hour. If they don't show, call Auden again. If he doesn't answer, call Conrad just to be sure they're okay. In the meantime, try to relax."

Relaxing was an impossibility.

I was a wreck.

Lawrie read it.

"MeeMee, sweetheart, I know this is a big day. It's a big day for the kids too. But *you* have to guide it. Get in that space. Okay?"

What he meant was that I had to pull myself together.

Again.

Because of Conrad's antics.

Again.

But I had made up my mind that he would never again best me.

So I nodded.

The doorbell rang.

I tensed.

I didn't recognize the shadow in the glass, which was concerning.

As I studied it, Lawrie said, "This is ready. Get it in the plate and pour that gunk in it. I'll get the door."

He gave me no opportunity to reply, he walked toward the door.

I rolled the crust on the rolling pin and was spreading it out over the pie plate when I heard, "Signed delivery."

That surprised me.

Who did signed deliveries on holidays?

I kept spreading as I watched Lawr sign then take the envelope with an expression of gratitude before he closed the door and turned to me.

He was walking and examining the envelope.

He got to the end of the counter and lifted it up. "Mom and Dad's attorneys."

I relaxed.

"I have Preston amassing information I can use against Conrad in case he feels the need to get ugly in the future," I told him something I'd shared previously.

Lawrie didn't think this was a suitable explanation. I knew it by the puzzled expression on his face as he studied the envelope.

I crimped the crust as I said, "It's probably something to do with that."

"Special delivery on a holiday?" Lawrie asked.

I shrugged.

"Can I open it?" he queried.

"Go for it," I invited.

I kept crimping and had moved on to pouring the pumpkin in the crust when he growled, "Son of a bitch."

My attention snapped to him.

He looked angry.

No, he looked *enraged*.

I tensed again but not much. It was likely Conrad had done some other horrible thing while we were married and Preston's investigator had found it.

But except for today's situation, Conrad had been quiet and not annoying me. So even though it was good to have all the ammunition I might need, so far he hadn't done anything to make me consider using it.

"If this is going to annoy me, considering Conrad is already pissing me off today, if you could just take that to my room and shove it somewhere the kids can't see, I'll look at it later."

Lawrie gave his eyes to me. "It isn't from Preston. It's from Addison."

I stared at him.

Addison Hillingham was my parents' attorney at the firm. He was a managing partner.

He was also the executor of the Calway trusts.

"I'm sorry?" I asked my brother.

"Put that in the oven" he ordered.

"Lawrie—"

"Get it baking, Amelia."

Oh God.

He called me Amelia.

He *never* called me Amelia unless something was happening where he had to go all big brother, like I was doing something stupid after Conrad dumped me, he'd heard about it and he called me to tell me to stop it and pull myself together.

I quickly put the pie in the oven then turned back to Lawrie.

"What?" I whispered.

"I'll preface this by saying this is bullshit." He waved the expensive, thick-stock paper in the air. "Clearly you've delivered some perceived slight to Mom and Dad and this is their way of communicating who holds the power."

Oh *God.*

"*What*, Lawrie?"

He drew in a deep breath.

Then he gave it to me.

"They've petitioned Addison to examine the terms of your Calway trusts, both the one they set up for you and the one all Calway heirs receive. This request is in regards to your behavior after Conrad left you. They've shared with Addison you acted in a manner unbefitting a Calway heir, which breaks the terms of the trusts, and they've asked him to consider revoking them."

I stared at my brother thinking I just *knew* something was up with them.

"They can't do this," Lawrie continued. "I was there on more than one occasion where they encouraged you to communicate your distaste for Conrad's desertion, doing this with what is for them not a small amount of glee. I know Robin was too. We'll both prepare statements and send them to Addison. If you're truly in danger, and you're not, the terms of the trust state that it can be revoked only if behavior garners public attention, which yours did not, then Dad's in the same position because he encouraged you to do so."

I kept staring at him, unable to speak.

"Regardless, Addison's firm gets a retainer from the trust, not Mom and Dad, and he's a good man," Lawrie reminded me. "He'll do what they ask but he'll adhere to the letter of the trust. This is just posturing and the timing of this delivery is not lost on me. They're making a point, just like Mom and Dad." He tossed the papers aside. "Forget it for today. I'll phone Robin tomorrow and get to work on your rebuttal."

"They can have it," I whispered.

"Pardon?" Lawrie asked.

I focused on him. "They can have it. I have the Bourne trust they can't touch. It's twenty-five million dollars. I don't live a lavish lifestyle. I don't intend to live a lavish lifestyle. But I can easily live a relatively lavish lifestyle off the interest from that trust."

This was not wrong.

Of course, I could probably not afford to sell off all my belongings, redecorate the entirety of a massive five-bedroom show home, replace my entire wardrobe and buy whatever car I wanted.

But I could get Aisling the expensive blender she was eyeing at Bed Bath and Beyond for Christmas (if Mickey approved, that was).

"You're not going to lose your trusts, MeeMee," Lawrie reiterated.

"No, probably not," I replied. "But I'm not going to phone them and give them the reaction they want to this. Either being angry or being apologetic or," I threw out a hand, "whatever they want from me. If they push this, fine. They can have the money. They can disinherit me from the piles they'd have given me when they stop breathing. I don't need that either. I just hope they don't punish Auden and Olympia with this kind of nonsense. Now *that* would make me angry."

"All right, if you don't give a shit about this, I do," Lawr said angrily. "What's up their asses?"

"I didn't take their calls when I first moved here because I was trying to sort my head out about how I'd been behaving, and I needed to focus on setting up a home, a life, and winning back my kids," I told him. "This lasted awhile but I did email them. In fact, I've been emailing them regularly for months. It isn't like I cut ties with them completely."

"That's it?" he asked.

"It could be even more trivial, Lawrie. You know them," I answered. "They don't need much."

Lawr looked down at the papers.

I moved to him and touched his arm.

He looked back to me.

"I really don't care," I told him honestly.

"It's fucking Thanksgiving, MeeMee, and they knew because you didn't have them last year that you have the kids. Even if they didn't, that's likely something you shared in your emails." He reached out a hand and pushed at the paper. "And they give you this?"

"It's them," I reminded him.

"It isn't right," he reminded me.

"No. It isn't. But it's them. And if you, or I, rise to the bait, we're doing what they want. Instead, if we let this go, see what Addison finds, which as you say will not be in their favor, we're being *us*. We're being who *we* are. We are not being what they want to *make us be*."

Lawr's jaw clenched.

"They'll get over it," I told him. "It's too ill-bred to hold a grudge."

He studied me a minute before he burst out laughing. And he did this pulling me into his arms.

I wrapped mine around him too.

We held on and I gave it time before I asked, "Do they know you're divorcing Mariel?"

"Come Christmas Day, I expect my letter from Addison to arrive."

That meant he told them and they were frosting him out.

I leaned my head back and caught his eyes.

"They're home, alone, no kids, no grandkids, stewing." I gave him a squeeze. "Where are we?"

"Together, making pies," he replied quietly.

I grinned.

"Maine made you smart," he remarked.

I glared. "I've always been smart."

"Yes. Sorry. You're right. Sitting around watching you and Robin drink vodka and connive to slash Conrad's tires. Brilliant. What was I thinking?" he teased.

I pulled away, mumbling, "A phase."

"Yeah," he replied.

It was time to move on.

"You have another crust to roll out and I have to finish the apples, Lawrie."

"Right, boss," he said briskly but this was also jokingly.

He went to his crust.

I went to the apples.

The apple pie was in with the pumpkin, and Lawr was working on the crust for the pecan pie when my phone chimed.

I looked to it, saw the text from Pippa and snatched it up.

Sorry, Mom, super sorry. We're still at Dad's. But we'll get there as soon as we can. Promise!

I gritted my teeth but replied, *Okay, kiddo. Do me a favor and text when you're on your way so Uncle Lawrie and I won't worry.*

And I knew I'd done the right thing when she quickly replied, *You're the greatest! And we will!*

My baby girl thought I was the greatest.

I could ride on that for eternity.

So it'd easily take me through another hour.

Unfortunately, it didn't.

But it wasn't Conrad or my parents who would turn Thanksgiving into a disaster.

———————————— • ————————————

My phone chimed.

I was basting the turkey, but I turned my head to Lawrie who was standing at the opposite counter, his eyes cast down to my phone.

"Auden," he said, looking to me. "They're on their way."

I sighed in relief and kept basting.

The turkey was looking fabulous. The pies were done. The potatoes were peeled. The ingredients for the rolls were churning in the bread-maker, the dough would be done in fifteen minutes so I could form the rolls and they had time to rise. My homemade cranberry sauce was already done. The sweet potato casserole was assembled and ready to go into the oven. The green bean casserole would take no time to do so it could join it. The table was laid.

It was twenty past noon. As was my life, with Lawrie's help, and even from afar without any help from my parents, I was in a good place.

And I'd hit a certain Zen because it occurred to me that Mickey had good kids, so did I, and even though Ash was shy, I figured Pippa would do what she could to pull her out of her shell, and both of my kids would love Cillian.

It was all going to be okay.

I couldn't imagine in my wildest dreams how it would go wrong.

But it did.

Spectacularly.

———— • ————

THE DISASTER DIDN'T START AT TWELVE THIRTY-FIVE WHEN I HEARD THE garage door go up, announcing my kids were there, and Mickey had not yet shown.

In fact, it started swimmingly when my kids came in, saw their Uncle Lawrie and pounced on him with sheer glee.

It took a turn for the worse when, with a mother's keen eyes, I saw something festering under that glee that was troubling.

It didn't help matters that Pippa pretended it wasn't there, and after turning from Lawrie and giving me her hug and kiss and happy Thanksgiving, she just said, "Gonna go dump my purse and jacket in my room and I'm all yours, Mom."

Auden, however, didn't pretend and when he hugged me he said in my ear, "We'll talk after Mickey leaves. Is that okay?"

It would have to be.

I nodded and he went off to get rid of his own jacket.

The kids were just in their rooms when the doorbell rang.

I was a bit jittery but I was okay. The house smelled great. Dinner was under control. The table looked beautiful laid with my fabulous stoneware, a low harvest-colored floral arrangement with candles in the middle that spread side to side at least three feet. The kids were safe from whatever was happening with their dad and they were with me. My brother was there, and even in the unlikely event things started to go awry, he'd guide them back and he'd have help. Mickey would make sure to do that too.

I would too.

Kids were resilient. Kids were better with change than grownups.

And all had been going so well, moving straight toward happy, that I knew in my heart it was all going to be *great*.

So I moved to the door quickly, opened it and smiled huge at the Donovan family.

"Happy Thanksgiving!" I cried.

Mickey gave me a grin that his kids reciprocated.

I gave out hugs and also gave Mickey a swift kiss, doing this at the same time ushering them in.

I closed the door and Lawr was there.

"Right, take off your jackets as I start introductions," I ordered. "Mickey, Cillian, Ash, this is my big brother, Lawr Hathaway. Lawr, meet the Donovan family."

Lawr was taking coats, shaking hands and exchanging nice-to-meet-yous at the same time explaining to a curious Cillian what kind of name "Lawr" was when it happened.

Lawr and Mickey had just started greeting each other. I was smiling at it, my two best (adult) guys in the whole world shaking hands, then I saw Aisling bump into her father.

My eyes went to her and my head jerked at the look on her face.

The Donovans had come looking dapper in the way they would do it for a family Thanksgiving.

Mickey was in a nice sweater and jeans. Cillian had on a nice long-sleeved shirt and jeans.

As for Ash, she'd been quiet, as usual, but open. Her hair was gleaming, beautiful and clean and it even looked like she curled it. She had on a pretty tan skirt and a nice sweater in a soft pink, both fit her figure, pronouncing the curves she had in a lovely way, and she had on a great pair of boots. She'd also put on a hint of makeup.

Upon arrival, she'd seemed okay. Better than okay.

Now, suddenly, she seemed pale and wary and even afraid.

"Ash?" I called and her eyes darted to me.

"I thought her name was Olympia," she whispered bafflingly.

"I'm sorry, blossom?" I asked.

"Her name is Pippa," she told me.

I looked over my shoulder and saw Auden and Pippa there. They were hanging back, awaiting their time to come forward for introductions.

Auden appeared curious and welcoming.

Pippa looked much the same as Aisling except pale and...

Guilty.

"Pip?" I called uncertainly.

"Pippa?"

This was fairly shrieked by Cillian.

My eyes whipped back to him to see him glaring with supreme malevolence at Pippa.

And my mouth dropped open when he pointed an incensed finger at her aggressively and shouted, "You suck!"

"Cillian," Mickey growled, moving to his son to put his hand on his shoulder.

Cillian snapped his head back to look at his dad. "She *sucks*! She's *mean*! She and her *stupid friends* say crap to Ash." He looked back to Pippa as my heart stopped beating. "You're a stinking, ugly, loser *bully*."

Oh no.

No!

"That is uncool," Auden said low, moving closer to his sister and slightly in front of her.

"It's true!" Cillian yelled at Auden. "I saw it! *Twice!*" He jerked his head back to look at his dad. "Ash won't let me say anything. She doesn't want you worrying."

I looked to Pippa and my stomach twisted so much I thought I'd be sick.

"Dad, can I go home?" I heard Aisling ask her father.

"Please tell me this isn't true," I said to my daughter.

"It is. She's the worst. She's a freaking *mean girl*," Cillian answered for Pippa.

I didn't take my eyes off my daughter. "Pippa, honey, answer me."

She looked wild-eyed and about to bolt.

But knowing there was nowhere to go, those eyes came to me and she whispered in a horrible voice, "You didn't tell us their names. You just called them Mickey's kids. I didn't know it was Ash Donovan that was coming. There are three Donovans in school. You didn't even say she was in the same grade as me."

"Yeah." I heard Cillian say and felt him move, knowing with the way his movement was curtailed that Mickey pulled him back. But that didn't stop him from talking. "I bet you wouldn't like that. Fat, ugly, Ash Donovan coming over to your house for Thanksgiving."

My stomach twisted again. Viciously.

"Pippa—" I began.

"You don't know," Cillian stated, it was an accusation and it was directed to Pippa. "You don't know how my sister has to hang with me all the time when Mom and Dad are working. How she has to make us dinner. *You don't know* how our mom is a big, fat *drunk* and Ash's always there to take care of me. You don't know when you're mean to her and make her feel like garbage how totally *awesome* she is."

Oh God.

The room went even more tense and I saw my daughter's face blanch further and my son wince.

"Cill," Mickey murmured.

Auden moved more in front of his sister and suggested to me, "Maybe we can talk somewhere else, just you and Pippa and me?"

I noted my son's movements.

But my attention didn't stray from my daughter.

"Have you been saying those things to Aisling?" I asked.

"Mom—" she started, her face a horrible thing for a mother to see.

"*Answer me!*" I shrieked.

She quailed and her brother pulled her behind his back.

"Don't lose it, Mom," he snapped at me.

"Auden, you are not in this," I snapped back and gave my attention to Olympia again. "Have you been cruel to kids at school?"

"Polly's the one who says stuff," she defended lamely.

"That doesn't stop you from laughing," Cillian put in.

"Son, enough from you," Mickey growled.

"You laugh?" I asked my daughter.

"I…it's…"

She said no more.

"It's what?" I hissed.

"Mom, can we *talk* somewhere *else*?" Auden bit out.

"Absolutely not," I clipped then back to my daughter. "I cannot believe this. I didn't raise a *mean girl.*"

Pippa, not good with confrontation and on the spot in a *very* bad way, didn't retreat.

She came out guns a'blazing.

"Oh yeah you did," she retorted angrily. "All the stuff you did to Martine?"

My body started burning and I instantly leaned back, asking sarcastically, "So, she stole your homework out of your locker and passed it off as hers?"

"Mom—" Auden began.

"No," Pippa snapped.

I kept with the sarcasm. "Oh, so she stole your boyfriend. Is that it?"

She leaned angrily around her brother toward me. "Don't pretend you don't understand what I'm saying."

"So sweet, pretty, quiet Ash destroyed your world? Knowingly and willfully participated in behavior that meant you lost everything. The man you'd loved for two decades. The home you'd made together for your children. The future you were looking forward to. Is that what happened?" I asked,

"Please, Mom—" Auden tried again.

"You know it isn't," Pippa spat.

"Your father and stepmother did that to me," I retorted. "If your father found someone else he loved, after committing his love to me, that was not okay. But there was a way to go about handling that. How he did it was *not* that way. I reacted and they had consequences, frankly, that they deserved. I shouldn't have allowed you children to see that but that's the *only* thing I did wrong. The rest, they bought that. They bought it. You betray someone, you have no choice but to live with the beast your betrayal created. What you're doing to Ash, she didn't buy that."

"Uncle Lawrie," Auden beseeched.

"Your sister did this, pal, it is *not* good. So she also answers for it," Lawrie said firmly and calmly, but there was disappointment in his voice.

Auden's face set.

"This is not my girl," I stated, my eyes never leaving my daughter.

"I had to move from my school. I had to find friends. Polly's popular and she's nice to me," she returned, strangely not blaming me for them having to move but I didn't have a mind to that.

"Polly is totally a bitch." I whirled at Aisling entering the conversation. Surprisingly, she wasn't done speaking. "Everyone knows it. And to be a friend, you have to be a bitch too. And she's not popular. She's feared."

I whirled back to my daughter, raising my brows. "Is that what you want? Do you want to be feared?"

"Mom, come on. Lay off," Auden ground out.

"Polly's history," I declared.

"Mom!" Pippa shouted.

"*My* girl does not hang with *mean girls*," I informed her.

"Mom, goddammit, *lay off*," Auden clipped.

My gaze shot to him. "Language," I snapped.

"You're losing it," he returned.

"Of course I am," I replied. "I'm dealing with my daughter who I cannot wrap my head around the fact she's been a bully at all, much less to a girl I care about deeply," I retorted.

"You need to calm the fuck down," he shot back.

"*Language!*" I bit out.

"Fuck you! Fuck that! Fuck this!" he suddenly shouted and my back shot straight.

"Auden," Lawrie growled, coming close to me.

"Do not speak to your mother that way," Mickey waded in, coming to my other side.

"Fuck you too!" Auden ignored Lawr and said to Mickey. "You can't tell me *shit*."

"*Enough!*" I screeched and the room stilled. I turned eyes to my son. "Give your Uncle Lawrie your car keys."

"What?" he asked sharply. "Why?"

"Do it…now," I whispered, my voice trembling.

"I'm not—" he began.

"Keys, pal, you're not going to make your mother ask again," Lawrie stated, moving to my son with his palm up.

I turned and caught sight of Aisling and Cillian, anger and horror and sadness searing through me that all this time *my daughter* was a part of Aisling fading.

"I'm so sorry," I whispered.

Tears formed in her eyes.

Cillian shuffled protectively closer to his sister.

Seeing that, I stomped to my phone on the kitchen counter. I snatched it up, slid my finger on the screen and put it to my ear.

It rang once.

"Are the kid's all right?" Conrad asked in greeting.

He sounded very concerned.

That did not dawn on me.

"Auden's grounded," I announced. "He cursed in my home even after I told him not to and then he did it directly to both me *and* Mickey."

"Shit," Conrad muttered, a surprising response but one that was lost on me.

"And our daughter is a bully. She's hanging with bullies and she defends her position that she doesn't say cruel things, but she doesn't deny she participates by not only egging it on by laughing but also not doing what she can to stop it or remove herself from it," I shared.

"Jesus Christ." Conrad was still muttering but now doing it sounding angry.

"She further defends herself by saying *I* taught her that garbage with what happened between you and me and Martine."

"That's ridiculous," he bit out and that got to me, making my body jerk.

"What?" I asked.

"It's ridiculous. What happened with you and Martine is not that. There's no excuse for bullying."

I didn't know what to make of his shocking show of support but at that juncture I had no choice but to roll with it.

"I want you to come and get them. I don't know what you and Martine have planned for Thanksgiving but I will not have my children under my roof behaving this way. They can come back after Olympia apologizes to Aisling and ends her association with Polly, who's the ringleader of the mean girls. As for Auden, *he* must apologize to Mickey and me."

"We're not going back there, Mom," Auden called and I turned to him.

"You'll do what I say. I'm going to rescue Thanksgiving for my brother and the other man in my life who's never treated me like dirt and his kids who are *good* kids who are also unfailingly *kind* and *sweet*. And as much as it pains me to admit, *my children* being present will negate those efforts."

Auden opened his mouth but I turned away when Conrad said in my ear. "I'll be there as soon as I can."

Of course he would.

"That would be appreciated," I said acidly then hung up.

I whirled around. "Your father is coming. Go get your jackets," I ordered.

"We're not going back there," Auden repeated.

"You most certainly are," I returned. "Get your jackets."

Now Pippa was cowering into Auden in a way that didn't sit well with me but I couldn't pay attention to that because Auden looked to Mickey.

"I'm sorry. I was out of line. It'll never happen again," he declared.

I drew a sharp breath into my nose.

"'Preciate that, bud, but you gotta turn that to your mother," Mickey replied like Lawrie, firm, but calm, and disappointed.

Auden looked to me. "I'm sorry, Mom. I shouldn't have said those things, but we had a really bad morning and last night wasn't great either and we've both had enough."

Other things were beginning to trouble me at his words but before I could latch on, Lawrie spoke.

"Whatever that is, Auden, you don't take out on your mother."

My son nodded and muttered, "I get that. I messed up."

"I didn't know about your mom."

That came from Pip and I saw her looking at Aisling.

"So?" Cillian returned. "That doesn't matter."

Pippa bit her lip and pressed closer to her brother.

"High school is hard," Auden put in lamely.

"It is," I shot back. "It's also when you begin to learn who you are, who you want to be and how to do the right thing." I looked to my girl. "What you've done, I hope to God somewhere inside you, Olympia, you knew was the wrong thing."

"If I went against her, she'd turn that on me," Pippa told me, her voice shaky.

"I can imagine and that would be awful." I swung a hand out to Aisling. "Ask Ash. She can tell you all about it."

"I'm trying to explain." Pippa's voice was rising.

"And what your mother is telling you is that there is no explanation for that behavior," Lawrie shared.

She turned eyes to her uncle, the tears forming. "Uncle Lawrie—"

He wasn't immune. His face softened.

Even so, his lips said, "There's no excuse, Pippa."

Her lower lip started trembling and a tear slid down her cheek. It killed me to stay where I was but I had to. This lesson had to take from now until eternity.

However, I allowed her brother to put his arm around her.

When he did, heartened, she looked to Ash.

"I've been a bitch. You're totally not anything Polly said you were. We even talk about it when she's not around. It's just that Kellan liked you last year and she liked Kellan and it all got...it got...she got..." She faltered then finished quietly, "Nasty."

"Oh my God, Kellan liked me?" Aisling whispered.

My eyes shot to Mickey to see his brows drawn dangerously and he was staring at his daughter.

"Yeah, totally," Pippa told her, lifting a hand to wipe the tears from her face. "He still does. Whenever Polly has a go at you and he's around, he tells her to knock it off. Which, you know, obviously makes her target you more."

"Kellan, like, Kellan Buckley?" Cillian asked.

"Yeah," Pippa answered.

Cillian looked to his dad and shared excitedly, "Oh my God, Dad! He's like, the best of his weight class in the league." He looked to Aisling. "Now you *gotta* come to our matches."

I turned from Cill to Mickey to see Mickey looking at the ceiling, not looking happy for what I knew was now a different reason.

"And he's a *sophomore!*" Cillian went on loudly. "Total score!"

"I think I'd rather keep talking about Polly and her posse bullying me," Aisling muttered, shifting and casting her eyes anywhere a human wasn't.

But I felt the crushing weight of all that had just happened lessen because she had it in her to make a joke.

"Mom, can you call Dad and tell him not to come?" Auden asked and my attention went to him. "We apologized. We meant it. Seriously. We did." He pulled his sister closer.

"We did," she agreed then she looked to Aisling. "I was...it was mean and it didn't..." She shook her head, pulled in a breath and stated, "It never felt right. And I...I know Polly's totally going to target me but," she straightened her shoulders, "whatever. She's always complaining about everything and it's a drag. So I won't have any friends. It isn't like that hasn't happened before, like when I moved here."

"It's not like Polly has *everyone* in her bitch posse," Ash said like Pippa was a dim bulb and I'd give her that...considering.

Mickey was not of the same mind as me.

"Ash," he said low with warning.

"It's true," she muttered. "It's just that the rest of us aren't the cool clique. Which some people should learn isn't death by high school."

Again, Pippa looked whipped.

"Ash," I called. "Will you come with me a second?" She appeared afraid of this idea so I hastened to add, "It's okay, honey. Just want a word in private. If you want your dad and brother with you, though, they can come with us."

She hesitated then moved to me, saying, "I'll come with you."

"Mom," Auden called. "About Dad—"

"We'll deal with that in a second," I told him, moving to Aisling then guiding her down the hall to my room.

When she got into it, she said, "Wow. Awesome room."

"Thanks, blossom."

I closed the door.

She looked to me and I went for it.

"This is not a lie, cross my heart," I did the motions that went with my words, "your decision will have no ramifications. You mean a lot to me, honey, and I want you comfortable with me and in my home. Pippa's apologized. She had a tough time out there she deserved. But if you're not okay with having Thanksgiving with her, then her father takes her home. And," I grabbed her hand when her eyes blanked against me, "I'm being serious. This *is* serious and Pippa has to learn that. I'm not putting you on the spot. If you want to leave and be safe at home, that's your choice. If you want Pip to leave and be here with your dad and brother and my brother and me, that's your choice too. If this is too big of a decision for you, I'll make the choice and I'll send my kids home."

"It's not her," she stated.

"I'm sorry?" I asked.

"She helped make school suck, but it's not her. She told the truth. She never said anything. Cill's right, she did laugh, but she never said anything. So it's not her who did it. Not fun, going to school and having them make it suck. It was more not fun going home when we were with Mom and watching her drink until she was passed out on the couch. Getting her to bed. Trying not to let Cill see it or hear it. And when we were with Dad, it was just a week away, going back to that. It's not Pippa. It's Mom and it's you."

"Me?" I whispered, again my stomach twisting, at all her words, including the last one.

"We messed up and told Mom about you. It got worse. I didn't wanna make Cillian feel bad because he didn't get it so he kept talking about you. So I know why she missed Cillian's birthday and got caught drunk driving. Because of you."

"I...don't know—" I started.

She waved her hand, appearing flustered. "It's not you. I don't mean it's you." She looked into my eyes. "But it's you." She seemed intent on my answer when she asked, "Do you get what I mean?"

I squeezed her hand. "I get what you mean."

"But she's not drinking now, which she's never done, and I don't get what that means. But, whatever." She shook her head, dismissing her mother's efforts at recovery and I again thought that it might be a good idea for Rhiannon to share. "I took advantage of her being, you know, *just her* so when she was all, you know, *there* she could meet you when we went out shopping and see you're really cool and it could all be good. Does that make sense?"

I nodded. "It does, blossom."

"Polly's never going to stop picking on me," she went on. "Even if Pippa isn't at her back acting like she's the greatest thing since Beyoncé. She's going to keep coming at me because that's how she is. She picks on people who have things she can pick on. Like me being fat."

"You're not fat," I told her.

For once, she held my eyes steady.

"I'm fat, Amy," she whispered.

"You're *not* fat," I stated firmly on another hand squeeze. "I mean that. You're beautiful and I don't think this Kellan whoever-he-is would like you and defend you to the resident Queen Bee Meanie if you weren't."

She looked away. "I didn't know about him."

"Now you do," I said and she looked back at me. "So if you don't believe me, which you should, or your father who thinks you're gorgeous, or your brother who loves you like crazy, then believe in some sophomore junior boxing league prizefighter who wants to go out with you."

Her eyes twinkled with teenage girl thrill at that very idea.

Now, *that* was what I liked to see.

I lifted our hands out to our sides, swayed back and gave her skirt a glance. "Too bad he isn't here to see how cute you look in that skirt."

She lifted a shoulder in a slight shrug, which was the first time I thought it was cute and not troubling.

Then her hand tightened in mine and she gave me her eyes. "If Pippa breaks with Polly, it's gonna be extreme."

I held her eyes. "That's not your issue."

"You were…" She looked to my closed door then back to me. "You were tough on her out there."

God, Mickey's girl was sweet.

"She needed that lesson."

"Maybe. But seriously, Polly can be really bad."

"*Dogfight*," I said.

She stared at me then looked at my shoulder and said, "She gets the cute guy."

"She did but his name isn't Kellan," I replied.

She looked back to me.

There was a knock on the door but before I could call out, Mickey came in and closed it behind him.

He looked to me then his eyes went to his daughter and stayed there. "You okay?"

I let her go as she answered, "Yeah, Dad."

"You wanna go home?" he asked.

She flipped a hand out to me. "We were just deciding that."

Mickey looked to me and I felt the weight of all that had happened start crushing me. "Should take my kids home, babe."

I nodded. "Of course," I mumbled.

Without hesitation, he turned to Aisling. "Let's go, baby."

Ash glanced at me and back to her dad. "Maybe we should—"

"Amy's family needs to sort themselves out without an audience."

She did a mini-shrug that was not cute before looking to the floor and muttering, "Okay, Dad."

Mickey turned his eyes to me. "Call you later."

"Right," I whispered.

He moved to Ash, threw an arm around her shoulders and guided her out of the room.

Feeling leaden, I followed them.

"We don't need it from you too!"

This was shouted angrily from Auden and even still heavy with the weight of the day, I went faster and so did Mickey and Aisling.

When we got out to the great room, I saw my son facing off against his father inside my closed door.

Lawr moved right to me.

Mickey, however, did not.

And more weight crushed me.

"Don't buy yourself more than your mother dished out, Auden. You're already grounded for two weeks. You keep going, I'll make it three," Conrad returned.

"We sorted things with Mom." My son looked to me. "Tell him, Mom."

"We need to let Mickey and the kids—" I started.

"You cursing at your mother, her friend, and your sister bullying kids at school?" Conrad asked over me. "I hardly think you can sort that out in ten minutes."

"We did," Auden snapped.

"Auden—" I began again.

"That's three weeks, son. Keep going," Conrad retorted.

It was then my beautiful boy leaned into his father and his face twisted in such pain and rage, every nerve end I had zapped painfully and it took herculean effort not to go running to him.

"Like I give a crap what you do to me," he snarled. "Like I give a crap about you at all. You're a fu...loser *cheat*."

"Oh no," I whispered.

"Jesus Christ," Lawr muttered.

"I think—" Mickey started.

"No," Auden bit out, his eyes going to Mickey. "You should know. You should know what you saved my mom from."

"Auden." I moved forward. "Honey, let Mickey and his kids—"

"He's moving again, Mom," Auden announced and I stopped dead. "He's got custody of us and he's taking us with him. *He thinks*. He wanted us *with him* yesterday," his face twisted further, this time in disgust on the "with him," "because Martine moved out yesterday because they're getting a divorce because he's a loser *cheat*." Auden looked to his father. "You know I was there when that woman came to our house."

"Oh no," I whispered.

"Jesus Christ," Lawr ground out.

"I explained that," Conrad snapped.

"Yeah, and you *lied*." Auden retorted. "Do you think Pip and I can't hear you two fighting all the time? And Martine isn't the only one who's loud. You *shouted* at your *wife*. Is that what I should do to my wife when I get one, Dad? Is that what Pippa should take from her husband? What you did to Mom? What you did to Martine?"

"We should discuss this elsewhere, Auden," Conrad said coldly.

Auden leaned back and crossed his arms on his chest. "Why? Pippa got laid out in front of everyone to learn her lesson about going with the wrong crowd. How are you going to learn your lesson when you go your own way, having a blast, and you drag us along with you, *not* having a blast? Hunh, Dad? Who's going to teach," he uncrossed his arms to jab an angry finger at his father, "*you?*"

Conrad was losing control, I could see it in his face getting red and the way he leaned toward his son. "I'm an adult and *your father* and I'll not have you speak to me that way *ever,* but absolutely not *in company.*"

Pippa was edging around them and I lifted my arms her way.

She ran into them.

I wrapped her close to me.

Lawrie got closer to us both.

"I'm not going with you," Auden announced. "Pippa's not going with you. And when I mean that, I mean *now* and I also mean to Texas. We talked in the car on the way here and we decided in like *two seconds* we're staying here with Mom. So you go to Texas and be with whatever woman you're gonna cheat on later there. We're staying home with Mom."

"This will be discussed later between your mother and me," Conrad declared.

Auden looked at me. "Straight up, I want to live with you because I like your house, you and Mickey actually like each other and aren't screaming all the time. Mickey's decent and you love us enough to come to us, not jerk us around all over the effing *country.*"

"I wanna stay with you too, Mom," Pippa whispered.

Conrad looked to his little girl, his little baby, his daughter who was always at his side, and the anger vanished.

His look was now beaten.

"All right, this is done," Lawrie announced. "Con, the kids are staying with Amelia. You and she can sit down and have a talk when cooler heads can prevail. Right now, we've had a lot of drama and we need to calm things down and I'm afraid your presence here is not helping."

"I—" Conrad started.

"Con, please. Go," Lawr said low. "I can understand you don't want to leave it as it is but quite honestly, it's the kindest thing you can do at this juncture."

My ex-husband stared at my brother and he wasn't angry or nasty. He seemed dazed.

Then he looked to me. "We'll talk?"

I nodded. "We will, Con," I said quietly.

His eyes went to Olympia and came back to me.

"I fucked things up again, MeeMee," he whispered.

Conrad calling me MeeMee?

Yes, completely dazed.

I pressed my lips together.

"Dad, Uncle Lawrie asked you to go," Auden declared, moving to the door and opening it.

Conrad jerked and looked to his son. It took him a moment but he nodded and moved to the door. He gave Auden another look but Auden just scowled up at him.

He turned to us all and mumbled, "Enjoy your Thanksgiving."

Then he walked out the door.

Auden slammed it behind him.

And I was shaking. Shaking uncontrollably.

Finally, I couldn't hold it back anymore and I burst out laughing.

It was hysterical.

I didn't care.

"En-en-en-enjoy your..." I gulped then cried out, "*Thanksgiving!*" and I kept holding on to my girl and giggling.

"Yeah, right," my daughter said, her voice shaking too. "Maybe next the bird will have salmonella and we'll all get food poisoning."

I held her tighter and laughed harder and *louder*.

"It really sucks what my sister did to you, Ash," Auden said tersely, and I tried to control my laughter as Pippa and I turned eyes to him. "And it sucks more your mom has a problem. But as you can see, our dad's a real peach."

"Our dad would *so* never cheat," Cillian declared. "I was with him when he was playing poker with his crew. A jack had fallen on the floor in a suit he could *totally* use and he saw it and he *totally* coulda scooped that up but he didn't. He called for a re-deal."

At Cillian's words, I kept laughing.

"I think, Cill, they mean—" Ash started.

"Same thing, Ash, just a different game, baby," Mickey said gently to his daughter.

At his voice, I sobered and looked to my guy.

I wiped under my eyes and kept hold of my girl, starting to announce, "Okay, Mickey, Ash and—"

"Are freaking hungry," Cillian interrupted me. "You got any of those horse do-overs?"

I blinked at Mickey's son.

Mickey started chuckling.

I swung my gaze his way and blinked at him.

"Can I...Ash, would you come to my bedroom with me so we can talk?" Pippa asked.

I tensed.

Ash regarded her and then she nodded.

Pip gave me a squeeze and whispered, "I'm good, Mom."

I looked to my girl. "You sure?"

She nodded. "Yeah."

"Fix that." I kept whispering, referring to Aisling.

She knew what I meant and nodded again.

I let her go.

"This way," she said to Ash and she moved.

Ash followed.

"Right, kid, you like cheeseballs?" Lawr asked Cillian.

"The puffy kind or the crunchy kind?" Cillian asked Lawr.

"The stick a knife and spread it on a cracker kind," Lawr told Cillian.

Cillian's eyes got big. "With the nuts on the outside? Like, on Christmas?"

"Christmas has come early this year," Lawr replied.

"Right on!" Cillian cried.

"Let's go lay it out," Lawr suggested. "Kitchen."

They moved.

I looked to Mickey.

He was watching his son and my brother.

I licked my lips and pressed them together, so deep in watching him watching his boy with Lawrie, I jumped when, from close, Auden said, "Mom."

I looked to him.

"Need to take a walk."

I turned fully to him. "Auden—"

"Just to blow off some steam. Get my head straight. I know we haven't helped at all but—"

"Go. Walk," I said. "But don't be long, kiddo." I lifted my hand and cupped his jaw. "And we'll talk more later about all that's been happening. Okay?"

Something I didn't like but couldn't quite read flashed through his eyes before he asked, "I gotta know now, you'll let us stay with you?"

I told him the straight up truth that would never change from that day until eternity.

"My home is your home until the day I die, honey. You don't even have to ask."

He looked like his face was about to crumble before his jaw went hard, he nodded, looked beyond me then he turned and walked toward the hall, probably to get his coat.

"Amy."

I jumped again and turned the other way.

Mickey was there.

He was staring down at me.

And again, I could get no read.

"I'm so sorry that—"

"Baby." He grinned and my heart leaped. Then he gathered me in his arms and my heart melted. "You give good date. You give fuckin' *awesome* holiday."

And again, I burst out laughing.

———— • ————

MY PHONE ON MY NIGHTSTAND RANG.

Sitting in bed, staring into space, I jumped, turned my head to it then grabbed it immediately.

I took the call and put it to my ear.

"Hey," I greeted.

"Hey back."

The weight had come back even though we'd managed to have a semi-decent meal (all because of Cillian, Lawrie, Mickey and, I was proud to say, me). The food was delicious and by the time the drama was all done and we ate, it was nearly time for Mickey and his kids to meet Rhiannon.

They left half an hour early.

That was when the weight settled hard on me.

"You hit Dove House?" he asked.

"Yeah," I answered. "It was a good diversion. Hard to be in a bad mood around folks who were left behind on a holiday and were delighted with any company." I paused, "And cupcakes."

He didn't chuckle or give me anything to lift the weight.

He queried, "You chat with your kids?"

"Yeah," I repeated. "Before Dove House. Not much more there than what you already heard. Martine is gone. She's filing for divorce. Conrad has been offered a position in Austin that he's considering taking, Auden says to get away from Martine, but there's also another reason. Auden shared that they came to Maine because Conrad followed this woman who came to the house. This he learned during Conrad and Martine's fights. She's a neurologist and she's moving to Texas. Conrad wishes to leave behind the mess he made of his marriage with Martine and follow her."

"Jesus," Mickey muttered.

"They both want to stay behind with me because they're pretty ticked at their dad but also because they're in school and they already had to move once, get the lay of the land, make friends. They're not excited about another move."

"I'll bet," he said.

"That's it," I told him. "Obviously, I've told them I want them with me. I phoned Conrad and we made a date to have lunch tomorrow."

"You want me there?"

Oh God.

God.

The weight started shifting.

I closed my eyes.

"Thanks, Mickey," I whispered and opened my eyes. "I think I should do this just him and me."

"I'm on call, you need me."

"You sure?" I asked.

"Fuck yeah," he answered. "Why wouldn't I be?"

"Ash and Pippa," I told him hesitantly.

"Baby, I can't say I don't got an issue with your girl. But the way you laid her out, thinkin' things are gonna change at school on Monday. Ash shared. Whatever went down in your girl's room, she's actually more worried about your daughter than she's pissed or fucked up about what she did. She says this Polly kid is a fuckin' mess, a freshman and she rules the school, within months of it starting, through sheer venom, which was apparently the way in junior high too. She's gonna strike at Olympia and it isn't gonna be pretty."

"Wonderful," I mumbled.

"Girl like that needs a lesson more extreme than the one you delivered to your daughter, babe," he told me. "She hands it out, you go to the administrators. This shit needs to be stopped. I talked with Ash about that too. She said that would not be good in the way of the high school world, but I don't give a fuck. Kids don't dictate the way it is. This isn't *Lord of the Flies*. Shit goes down that's unacceptable, adults step in. This little bitch doesn't back off Ash and steer clear of Olympia, she can't continue her bullshit. She doesn't do both those things, her rule is over."

"They seemed to be getting along okay during dinner," I noted hopefully. "I mean, Ash isn't super talkative and it was a little awkward. Pip was obviously embarrassed and didn't know how to behave because she's usually really social but that wouldn't be appropriate. But it wasn't the Antarctic."

"Don't wanna hurt you, Amy, but I'm not thinkin' those two are gonna be in the same crew. Ash told me her friends think your girl is a bitch by association so her eyes may have been opened to the way of things but it's not likely they're gonna open arms to her."

"Right," I murmured.

"She'll find her way with better guidance from a mom who gives a shit than a dad who's all about his dick."

That, I hoped, would be true.

"Just to say, not to take any of the blame off Pippa, who deserves it—" I started.

"You kinda made that clear," he interrupted me and I heard humor in his tone, which gave me hope.

"Yeah, I definitely did that," I agreed. "But anyway, during our chat in my bedroom, Ash shared that the struggles she's experiencing aren't just about being picked on at school. It's about her mom."

"No offense, but no shit, Amy."

I took no offense and soldiered on, hesitantly, "Also looking after her mom in the way you did when you were married, hiding it from Cillian."

There was a moment's silence then a soft, wounded, "Fuck."

I hated to have to go on but this was his girl so I couldn't hold back.

"And me."

"Come again?"

"The reason for the shopping trip. The change in your circumstances your ex-wife who you loved, who also loved you, would react to." I explained.

"Fuckin' great," he muttered.

"I think Rhiannon is adjusting to that," I told him, thinking I didn't want to go back on my promise to Rhiannon but I could no longer hold back in sharing what could give the Donovans some hope after all that had spilled out that day.

So I was setting up to tell him his ex had made the colossal step toward recovery...for her kids.

"You guys sittin' at my bar, drinkin' tea, think you're right," he agreed.

"Ash wanted her mom to know I was cool," I kept explaining. "I think she wanted her to know that everyone was moving on and it was good and she was trying to make it so her mom moved on with the rest of us."

Mickey didn't say anything.

"Anyway, how was the visit with Rhiannon?" I asked, hoping he'd give me a natural lead in to share about his ex-wife.

"Get this, the woman is in AA."

My mouth dropped open before I used it to ask, "I'm sorry?"

"Obviously had to have a word with her to tell her what was up with Ash and the shit Cillian spewed. Took her out outside to chat. Told her what went down and what was said. Thought that would be yet another fantastic conversation for this stellar Thanksgiving."

I closed my eyes again.

I opened them when he went on, "She then tells me she's been in AA for a while, it's goin' good, she hasn't had a drink since the night of town council meeting, and if I'm good with it, we can share that with the kids."

This was *great*.

"Did you?" I asked.

"Yeah. Cillian didn't know what to do with it and neither of them did cartwheels, but Rhiannon didn't expect that. She knows she's got things to prove and that's gonna be a long haul. But it was somethin'. She never admitted to having a problem. Now the woman's in AA?" He paused before finishing, "It was definitely something."

"I should tell you," I began carefully. "She shared this with me at Bed Bath and Beyond."

"Say again?"

"She told me she was in recovery. She didn't put pressure on for me not to tell you but she did say she wanted to do it herself. Since it's hers, I agreed."

He was silent a second.

I fretted that second.

Then he said, "Since you and me got a future, you two gotta establish your own relationship and with that comes trust. Sucks she put you in that position but you probably made the right decision for her."

I liked his mention about us having a future but I still asked, "Was it the right decision for you?"

"Guess if your ex came and shared somethin' important with me that affects you and your kids that he didn't want to share with you. Somethin' I know might strain things between him and me when we all gotta try to keep shit loose and good. Somethin' I know might strain things between you and me. I got no good choice. Then he shares it with you a few weeks later. If that ever happens, I'll be able to answer if it was right or not."

"Are things...strained?" I pushed.

"Babe, you didn't keep her secret for eternity." I could hear the grin in his voice. "Relax."

"Hard to relax after this day," I told him.

"No shit," he replied.

"Are we okay?" I asked.

"Amy." He said my name, said nothing for very long, terrifying moments, then he gave me what I needed. "I love you. I told you that. I meant it. I meant it in a way you needed to know so you'd know I want a part in your future, which means you definitely got your part in mine. You gave that back to me, tellin' me you want the same thing. We had a rocky day. We're fucked if we can't get through the first rocky day we have together and do it whole."

I slid down the bed and rolled to my side, curling up like I could curl his words into me.

"Amy?" he called when I didn't say anything.

"I'm here."

"Are *you* okay?"

"Your ex-wife is in recovery. My ex-husband has outed himself for the loser cheat he is and the kids want to live with me. There is no longer any mystery around all the things Aisling is coping with, which means those who care about her can focus on helping her through them in a more directed way. I know why my kids were escaping their father. And you and I survived all that because I love you and you love me. It seems I actually *do* give awesome holiday."

He burst out laughing.

I stayed curled up and listened.

When he stopped laughing, he asked softly, "So you love me, Amy?"

"I *so* love you, Mickey."

"Trial by fire today, baby. The extremes we waded through today proves we'll get through anything."

I curled deeper into myself, curling that knowledge to me, that he believed it and him doing that made me believe it, and replied, "Yeah."

"More good, your brother is fuckin' cool."

Mickey liked Lawrie.

I loved that.

I smiled. "Yeah."

"You got a good son," he stated, surprising me. "He did what he did, gettin' in your face, to protect his sister who took some hits from their dad before they got to you."

I hadn't thought of it that way but thinking it then, I knew what I already knew.

I *did* have a good son.

He didn't go about it the right way but at least he tried.

"Yeah," I repeated.

"And your girl's got courage. You laid her out like that, no mercy, your brother backin' you, she's got nowhere to turn. She pulls it up to ask Ash to talk. Says a lot, Amy. She's gonna make it."

She would.

God, I hoped she would.

"Yeah," I said.

"We'll all be okay," he promised me.

I hoped that too.

"I'd be better now with your arms around me," I told him.

"We'll arrange that, soon's we can."

I sighed.

"You in bed?" he asked.

"Yeah," I answered.

"Go to sleep. I'll call in the mornin' to check how things are goin'. Then I want you to call me after you have your meet with your ex."

"Okay, Mickey."

"Right, love you, baby."

I sighed again through my, "Love you too, Mickey."

"'Night."

"'Night."

We disconnected and I reached out to put my phone to the nightstand.

I stared at it.

I did not go to sleep.

I got out of bed, put on my robe and walked to my daughter's room.

I knocked and got no answer, so I went in.

The room was dark.

I moved to her bed, sat on it and gently slid her hair off her neck.

"Love you, baby girl," I whispered.

She turned her head so she trapped my hand against her neck.

"Love you too, Mom," she whispered back.

I gave her neck a squeeze, slid it away then bent and kissed her cheek.

I left her, closed the door and went to my son's room.

At my knock, he called, "Yeah?"

I opened it and went in.

His room was dark but I closed the door behind me and moved to where he was lying in bed.

"Just wanna say goodnight, my handsome boy."

He shifted so he was sitting and looking up at me.

"'Night, Mom. Sorry the day was all drama. Mickey probably thinks we're all whacked."

"It's over and tomorrow's another day."

"Yeah, you and Scarlett O'Hara are all over that."

I decided to take that as a compliment.

I bent, took his hand and held it tight.

"You did right, trying to protect your sister after what had gone on with your dad. You went about it wrong, but the impulse was right."

"'Kay," he muttered, sounding embarrassed.

"Mickey was the one who pointed that out to me," I shared.

He sounded incredulous, but in a good way, when he asked, "Really?"

"Yes, kiddo."

"He was pissed I cursed at you," he noted hesitantly.

"He likes me. Like you with your sister, he was protecting me."

"It won't happen again," he promised.

"That'd be good."

His fingers gave mine a squeeze. I took it and took the hint, letting him go and moving to the door.

"Mom?" he called.

In the doorway, hand on the handle, I turned to him.

"Yeah, honey?"

"I knew about Polly. Everyone at school knows about Polly. That's why I wanted to talk to you alone. Just Pip, you and me. Ash isn't right. She's living her own thing. I didn't know who she was. Not being mean, but she's a freshman. Junior guys don't pay a lot of attention to freshman girls. I would see her in the hall but had no idea she was Mickey's girl and never saw Polly go at her. But I've seen Polly pulling her crap and the freshmen might live in fear of her, but the upperclassmen think she's a pain in the butt. There's gonna be a takedown, thinking as a freshman she can lord over the school, and that's gonna happen soon. I've been trying to talk to Pippa about her to get her out of target range, but she wasn't listening. We've been going around about it for a while. It's been ticking me off."

Yes, my son was a good kid.

And perhaps I had an explanation of why his patience was shorter with his sister lately.

Further, it appeared a small town didn't extend to the bubble of the high school world.

"Okay, Auden," I said when he stopped talking.

"That's why I wanted to talk alone," he continued. "I figured, you and me both having a go at her about Polly, she might actually listen. It sucks she had to go through that today, but you were right not to back down. If she's in on it, that's not cool. But it's still a good thing it happened because she needs to be far away from Polly when the *real* mean girls make their move to show that girl her place."

I forgot how many political minefields there were in high school.

This was a good reminder. I had two kids in it and three and a half years left of guiding them through it.

I felt badly for Polly, and her mom, who I liked, who would be next in line to deal. But Polly needed to learn a lesson too.

I just hoped the timing was right that my baby girl didn't get caught in the crossfire.

Then again, if her past association drew her in, I had a feeling her brother would be at her back.

"You make me proud," I told him. "You being you but also you looking out for your sister."

"She isn't a bully," Auden told me, his voice softer, telling me my compliment meant something to him. "Pip and me talked after you went to bed and she told me Ash didn't know Pip was your daughter because her name is Moss, not Hathaway. And she didn't know Ash was Mickey's, because, well, no one knows who kids' parents are until they meet them or see them with them."

"I should have probably shared more information with you before the meeting," I admitted. "I was just nervous. I've never done this before. It didn't even occur to me they were in the same grade and might know each other. My main focus was it all working out, you all getting along, making it safe for you, *all* of you, my two and Mickey's two, when we tried blending. It's a big thing, honey," I said softly. "It means a lot to me, to Mickey, to all of us. So I guess I didn't think beyond that."

"It isn't your fault, Mom," he assured me. "We get that. This isn't about you messing up. What I'm trying to say is Pippa was tight with her friends back home in California. She missed them. Dudes they adjust. New guy, they take him in. She's a girl and it's hard to find your way into a posse and they got so many games going on, it's harder to know which is the right one. *She* messed up. Now she knows that and she'll get it together."

"I know she will," I replied.

"Yeah," he said.

"Thanks for sharing all this with me."

"No probs, Mom."

I waited to see if he had more and when he didn't say anything, I said, "Okay, kiddo. I'm gonna leave you alone. Goodnight, sweets."

I started to turn the door handle when he called, "Mom?"

"Right here, Auden."

"Love you."

The weight that had been lifting since Mickey called disappeared completely and I was again walking on air.

"Love you too, baby," I replied and shifted out the door, closing it behind me.

I moved through the hall of my house toward my bedroom and did it shouting, "'Night, Lawrie. Love you."

"'Night, MeeMee," he called from the log room (more masculine, I'd put him in the beach room when he was there after he hooked up with Robin). "Love you too. Now stop shouting!"

I heard a giggle from Pippa's room, a loud snort from Auden's.

And my world was again happy.

27

STEM THE BLEED

I was in my kitchen in slouchy, drawstring, gray yoga pants and a soft green lightweight sweater that drooped off my shoulder and had sleeves so long they had a hole in them that I could hook over my thumb.

It was an outfit I bought over the Internet that Josie had never seen to cast her disapproval.

I loved it. It was perfect for wearing it in my kitchen with my boys with me.

Or, two of them.

Though, I'd never wear it to the diner for lunch with Josie. She was the fashion queen and she'd shared her wisdom with me. It wouldn't do to fly in the face of that. She might stop sending me links to fabulous shoes (etc.) if I did.

It was the next morning and Lawr was leaning against the counter wearing track pants and a tight long-sleeved wicking shirt. He was sipping coffee. His silvered dark hair was wet around his neck and ears because he'd had his morning run, come back and done his sit ups and pushups out on the deck.

This was why he was lean and I was curvy.

My son had just gotten up and he was in pajama pants, a long-sleeved tee, his hair was a mess and his eyes were still drowsy.

He was also sipping coffee.

This was a new thing for him since I moved to Maine.

My boy was definitely growing up.

This caused me to feel a strange euphoric melancholy. It was good and it was bad.

It was also life.

I was getting breakfast orders, walking on air that I had a house full (almost) of people I loved and I got to make breakfast for them when the doorbell rang.

My eyes went to it and I saw the shadow through the glass telling me it was Mickey.

"Looks like Mickey, Mom," Auden said, his voice still as drowsy as his face.

"Want me to get it?" Lawr offered.

"I'll get it," I replied, hurrying to the door because Mickey was there.

I unlocked it, opened it and looked up at my guy wearing his construction outfit.

"Hey," I whispered.

His eyes smiled. "Hey back."

I leaned into him and tipped my head back. He put a hand light on my waist and bent to me, brushing his lips against mine.

I kept whispering and didn't move even as he lifted away a bit, "You need a key."

I watched his eyes flare then soften as he replied, "Back at you."

I grinned and stepped away, moving in but out of the way so he could come in behind me.

"Morning, Mickey," Lawr called.

"Lawr," Mickey said as he walked into my house, me at his side. He looked to Auden. "Mornin', Auden."

Auden held his gaze only a second before he muttered to his coffee. "Mornin', Mickey."

"You want coffee?" I asked and Mickey looked down at me.

"Yeah, babe, but can't stay too long. Just checkin' in to see you're all okay."

That was why he hadn't called yet that morning. He decided to do it in person.

"I'm good," I told him, gave him another grin, reached out and took his hand for a quick squeeze. Then I let him go and went to the cupboard with the coffee mugs.

I was in the process of taking one down when Auden declared, "I know you think I'm a dick."

I turned and froze when I saw Auden looking up at Mickey who was leaning back against the counter two feet away from me.

"Don't think you're a dick, bud," Mickey said low, his eyes leveled on my son.

"I don't blame you seeing as I *was* a dick," Auden replied.

"Your mom's filled me in, Auden, so I get it," Mickey told him.

"Okay, well, that's cool," Auden returned. "But just so you know I'm actually not the dick I acted like last night. And it's not like I'm the school's most righteous dude, but I think people know not to mess with me. And I didn't know her before. I also didn't know what was going down. But now that I've met Ash, I'll look after her."

Something was coming from Mickey and I continued not to move as I felt it and watched him staring at my son.

Finally, he spoke.

And when he did, his voice was gruff.

"Can't be there to look after my girl. Would mean a lot, you do it."

Auden held my guy's eyes, his chest puffing up, and he nodded.

I looked to Lawrie to see him gazing at my son, the pride I felt inside shining on my brother's handsome face.

It was in that glorious moment, with unfortunate timing, Pippa wandered out of the hall in her wrinkled PJs, her hair an attractive mussed bedhead, her eyes to her feet.

"Hey, kiddo," I called.

She looked up, caught sight of Mickey and stopped dead.

"Come on over and take a stool," I invited like nothing was amiss. "I'm making breakfast."

I then turned to get Mickey his coffee, black, one sugar.

"Mornin', Uncle Lawrie." I heard her say timidly.

"Morning, pretty girl," he replied.

"Yo," she went on.

That I knew was for Auden.

"Yo," Auden returned.

I turned to Mickey with his coffee when I heard her say, "Uh, hey,

Mickey."

"Hey, Pippa," Mickey responded.

I looked and saw her leaning heavily against her uncle, his arm around her, but her eyes were aimed at the cupboards under the kitchen sink.

"Okay, let's get breakfast going," I suggested. "Who wants what?"

"You probably hate me."

I stopped moving and looked at my girl who was looking at Mickey from under her lashes.

Shit, Mickey was getting it.

I just didn't know how to intervene to make it easier on him or my kids.

I found out Mickey didn't need me to.

But I should have known.

"I don't hate you, darlin'," Mickey said gently.

"I'd hate me," she mumbled to his shoulder.

I looked to Mickey just as he said, "Come here, Pippa."

She shrunk back but didn't get far when Lawr moved his arm from around her shoulders to put his hand in the small of her back. He gave her a light push and she crept Mickey's way.

When she got close, Mickey leaned her way, grabbed her hand and pulled her closer before he wrapped his arms around her loosely.

I held my breath as my daughter tensed in his hold.

Mickey bent his head and said quietly to the top of hers, "You got it extreme last night. You took it. You had the guts to apologize. That was big. It was appreciated. I appreciated it. My girl appreciated it. And once someone apologizes, no other move you got except to move on. You hold bad feelings, that makes you the bad guy. It's over, darlin'. If it stays over at school, then it's totally over. Let it go. Yeah?"

She relaxed in his arms somewhat and tipped her head back. "Is Ash gonna let it go?"

"Not gonna let my girl turn into the bad guy." He gave her a grin. "We didn't all have the greatest start. But one thing about that, it can't get worse."

Her eyes got wide with surprise and she let out a stifled giggle.

"It's gonna be okay," he said gently.

She nodded. "Okay, Mickey."

"Now give me a hug and tell your mother what you want for

breakfast."

She wrapped her arms around him and gave him a quick squeeze. If I saw it correctly, he gave her a quick squeeze back. Then they separated and she looked to me.

"Cheesy eggs, Mom," she ordered but added, "I'll help."

"Thanks, kiddo," I replied, smiling at her, again walking on air wondering if anyone could see the cloud of love I had for the four people around me at my feet lifting me up. "Grab the eggs from the fridge."

"You gotta stay for cheesy eggs, Mickey," Auden invited. "They're more cheese then eggs."

"Sounds like somethin' I can't miss," Mickey replied, glancing at his watch.

"If you've gotta go, honey, then I'll make them some other time when you're with us," I offered.

He looked to me, sliding his eyes to Auden then to Pip, who was coming out of the fridge with eggs and milk, and finally back to me.

"Got time for eggs, Amy."

He had to go.

But he was staying because my kids were worried that he didn't like them and he wanted them to know it was all good.

I wanted to declare my love for him again right then and there.

I had to do it with a look.

Mickey gave me that look back.

"Mom, you want me to grate the cheese?" Pip asked.

I tore my attention from my guy and gave it to my daughter. "Yeah, Pippa."

She dashed back to the fridge, and I was going to go for a bowl when I caught sight of Lawrie now studying Mickey who was sipping his coffee.

He didn't look proud.

He looked like he approved.

As he would do.

Mickey was the greatest.

This still made me happy.

———— • ————

I SAT AT A TABLE BY THE WINDOW AT THE LOBSTER MARKET.

Not the table I shared with Mickey, one closer to the front door.

I was sipping iced tea when Conrad, fifteen minutes late, walked in.

I watched his eyes move around the room until they found me and he came my way.

He was in work clothes, a very nice, very expensive suit that had not been tailored for him but made for him. His hair was trim and kept in place with minimal product. It was a style that suited him. He looked like a very successful businessman who used his money to take care of himself.

Or he looked like a talented neurosurgeon who did the same.

Studying him, it didn't surprise me I no longer found him the least bit attractive. Harkening back, I tried to figure out how I ever did. This made me think about him coming outside during that ball.

The prince meeting his future princess, it had seemed to me at the time.

But he was a toad.

It just took me years of kissing him to find that out.

Continuing to regard him as he came to me, I didn't take my eyes from him as he stopped at our table.

"Amelia," he greeted.

"Conrad," I replied.

He took his seat.

The Lobster Market was my idea. Not that I wanted to pollute my memory of being there with Mickey. Nothing would pollute that. But my ex-husband was not going to take me to some diner to have a chat, which was likely to be something I would not enjoy, and get away with an inexpensive diner bill.

He was going to buy me lobster.

"I'm sorry I'm late," he muttered, his attention on putting his napkin on his lap. "Consultation ran long."

I was used to that from our marriage. However, there was a high likelihood that many of those consultations running long were times he was fucking nurses.

I said nothing.

The waitress came with waters and Conrad ordered a coffee.

Before she went away, Conrad looked at me and stated, "You've been here before. Do you know what you want? Because I do."

He wanted this to go fast.

I was in agreement.

I turned and ordered immediately, "Lobster and steak Oscar. Steak, medium rare. Salad rather than potatoes. But I'd like the roll."

Her eyes got a little big because that was a lot for lunch but I just smiled because it was the most expensive thing on the menu.

"For you?" she asked Conrad.

"The lobster chowder. Bowl. Salad. No roll," Conrad ordered.

Still healthy.

Quite boring.

Mine sounded tons better.

She slid away and Conrad looked to me. "You look well."

God, he was going to try to be polite.

But I knew I looked well.

I looked better than that.

I looked amazing.

Alyssa still did my hair and it still looked marvelous. I got weekly manicures and bi-monthly pedicures. And right then I was wearing gray cords that had a silvery sheen, spike-heeled Jimmy Choo ankle booties with ink-blue suede at the front and black leather at the heel and a black loose-fitting cashmere sweater with a deep V that showed a hint of cleavage that I'd cinched at my waist with a magnificent draping belt.

He couldn't see my bottom half, of course, but it didn't matter. I knew it was there. I knew it was fabulous. And I knew he'd fucked up letting go of all the magnificence of me.

Even if he never understood that, which, frankly if he didn't was even worse for him.

I didn't return the compliment.

"I'm sure you don't have a lot of time so perhaps we can begin?" I suggested.

"I had my secretary clear a few afternoon appointments," he told me.

Perhaps he didn't want this to go fast, which was surprising.

I still did.

"Okay then, I'll say I don't have a lot of time because Lawr is in town and I'd like to spend time with him while he is. So can we begin?"

His jaw went hard as he turned his head and looked out the window.

The waitress came with his coffee and he didn't say thank you or even look her way.

I thanked her for him and was about to prompt him when his attention came back to me.

"I've thought about it and I've decided not to move to Austin."

I was annoyed for me. Him in Texas would be a good thing.

I was happy for my kids. They'd get over being upset with him and they needed their dad close. They also needed lives where they weren't getting on a plane and flying across country every three weeks.

"I think that's the right decision," I told him.

"Tammy doesn't agree," he muttered.

Ah.

The new one was called Tammy.

"Nothing changes," I remarked, but it was frustrated, not annoyed. "You worry about what this unknown Tammy would think and not your current wife."

His eyes narrowed on me. "There's no reason to make this ugly, Amelia. That's one of the reasons why I asked you to lunch, so we can bury the hatchet and try to find some middle ground in order that we're not always at each other's throats. It's not good for the kids. And this is more important now that I'm staying in Maine."

"You're correct," I agreed. "However, I will point out that the woman parade isn't good for the kids either."

"That's hardly any of your business," he told me.

"I'm afraid it is when my boyfriend and his kids are there, as well as my brother, watching along with me as my son loses his mind and rips into his father."

He said nothing, just focused on preparing his coffee. He took no milk unless it was skim and one sweetener.

Again, boring.

"I can't tell you to keep it in your pants," I went on and he lifted his eyes and scowled at me. "But I *can* ask you not to involve our children in your varied romantic entanglements."

"It's likely Tammy and I will be ending things. She's definitely going to Austin, and I have a practice and two children so a long distance relationship won't work for me. I'm losing her. The last couple of days haven't been easy on me, Amelia, and that's just the icing on the cake. It would be nice if you'd have a mind to that as you sit across the table from the crippled soldier and aim your gun his way. I know you've been dying for this opportunity but I'll still request you holster your weapon."

He was comparing himself to a crippled soldier?

Really?

"This was a bad idea," I whispered irately to the table. Definitely irately. Frustration was a memory.

"How is it not a surprise that I'm asking you to be grown up and you can't manage that?"

I looked back to him. "You are *not* a crippled soldier, Conrad. You're a grown man who treats women like dirt."

"There is a reason I went looking when I had you," he replied coolly.

I had to admit, I was curious. Just that, curious. I didn't really care why but I'd always wanted to know what drove him from me. Not that it meant anything anymore but at least I'd have some answers.

So I sat back and flipped out a hand. "There is? Do tell."

"You were boring."

I stared.

I was boring?

"You didn't want anything," he went on. "You did your fundraisers and you went out with your friends and you doted on the kids but you had no ambition. No drive. You had a degree from arguably the best university in the country and you didn't do anything with it. Even when the kids got older and you had more time, you just spent more time with your charities, raising money. Martine is a nurse. She has ambition. She was studying to be a nurse practitioner when I met her. She became one. She wants something out of her life."

"Good for her," I replied calmly. "However, for me, it might have come early, but I actually *had* everything I wanted from life. I grew up in a cold home where there was nothing for me but Lawrie. And early on I found a man I loved with everything I had, we made babies, and I had a home we built that was warm and affectionate and loving. I'm sorry you had a problem with me being good with just that until the day I died, Conrad. But that's your problem. I didn't hide these were my life's desires. You knew what you were getting into when you married me because I shared this with you. So frankly, you're full of shit."

He looked again to the windows.

I kept addressing him, "And I take it Martine's out because there's not much further you can go as a nurse but the sky's the limit for Tammy the neurologist? Or is she going to be ousted when you meet some woman who wants to be president?"

He didn't look back to me.

I lowered my voice and leaned into the table. "What I'm saying, Con, is that this is a pattern. These women in your life, they have feelings. They hook their star to you and you scrape them off and that has consequences I *know* you understand."

His eyes slid to me.

I kept talking.

"The issue here is *you*. Not me. Not all the women you banged when you looked for something exciting that wasn't your boring wife. Or your new boring nurse of a wife. And it won't be when you do it with your brand new inevitably to become boring neurologist of a whatever-she-comes-to-be. It's *you*."

"Amel—"

I cut him off, "And our son looks to you."

He snapped his mouth shut.

"He doesn't like what he sees," I told him truthfully. "And this is not meant to be a blow, just a wakeup call, but I'm getting the sense he *does* like what he sees in Mickey."

Conrad's jaw got hard again and he looked to the window.

He knew Auden had gone to the firehouse. He might even know that Auden looked up to Mickey.

And he didn't like it.

"*You should know what you saved my mom from*," I repeated our son's words of the day before and I saw his flinch even in profile. "That's what Auden said to Mickey right in front of you. How that couldn't sink in, I have no clue. But you have to sort yourself out, Conrad. If you need whatever you get from these women, do it privately so our kids don't see. Trust me, I know the harm it can cause when you show your children you're weak. Learn from me. But don't learn too late and don't take too long. They're coming to realize that the devastation that was wrought in our lives was not down to my antics but was all about you. You're a surgeon. You know when there's a bleed that you need to stem that bleed before you do *anything*. Your relationship with your children is bleeding. *Stem the bleed*."

He continued to stare out the window and I watched him do it.

When he kept doing it, I took a sip of my iced tea, replaced it and gazed around the restaurant.

This went on for some time so I decided to put an end to it.

"I want good things for our children, Con. So I'm happy you're staying in Maine because they love you and it's tough on them to travel in order to be with one of their parents. They're both in high school now, which brings us to the unfortunate time in our lives of having to prepare to lose them soon. So we should do everything in our power to make the waning time we have with them the best it can be. *For them.* To that end, I'll do what I can to make the relationship we have left work in order to make things easy on our kids."

Finally, he looked at me. "That would be appreciated."

I nodded.

"I'll do what I can as well," he carried on.

"That would be good," I said softly.

He hooked his coffee cup, took a sip, put it back and addressed my fork, "This man you're seeing, he spends time with the kids, you've introduced them to his kids." He lifted his gaze to me. "I take it that means you're considering a future with him?"

"This man is called Mickey and yes. We both are," I declared.

"He's a fireman, Amelia," he told me.

I tried not to react negatively. It wasn't scathing but it was condescending.

"He's a contractor and roofer, Conrad. And he's starting his own company."

He kept sharing things I knew. "You're the Calway heiress."

"And he's one of four of the Maine Fresh Maritime heirs."

Conrad's eyebrows shot up.

He was impressed.

How that was a measure of a man when he knew Mickey had nothing to do with the company outside being an heir, I couldn't fathom. But to Conrad, it was.

Yes.

Boring.

"He went his own way. He's his own man," I informed him. "But even if he didn't come from serious money, he'd still be perfect for me."

"Your parents might not agree," he retorted.

"I'm forty-seven, Conrad. I'm well beyond caring what my parents think of my decisions. I know what's right for me."

He took another sip of coffee.

I took one of iced tea.

"Perhaps we should discuss the situation of Pippa bullying," he suggested.

I relaxed.

That was his business. Mickey was too, considering Mickey spent time with his children. But he'd given me no choice with Martine (or this Tammy) so it also wasn't. He had to trust I'd choose well.

But I gave him the brief info he needed on Mickey because I was a grown up and I wanted this to work.

Now, we could discuss our daughter.

Which we did. Surprisingly, he agreed with my reaction and the plan going forward, that being barring all connection with Polly. We also both agreed to carry forward with Auden's two weeks of being grounded from his car. I felt my son had learned his lesson but I didn't feel that backing down on a punishment earned was the appropriate message to send. Conrad felt the same.

We had lunch. It was tense and not enjoyable.

But we managed it.

I only ate half my meal.

Conrad paid and he was polite enough to walk me to the door.

We parted ways on the sidewalk.

I made my way to my Rover alone, got in, started it up to get the heat going, grabbed my phone and called Mickey.

"Hey," he greeted.

"Hey back," I replied.

"You done with him?"

"Yes."

"It go okay?"

"For me and Conrad, it went swimmingly. It was still not an hour packed with fun."

Mickey chuckled.

I enjoyed listening to it for a few seconds before I shared, "He's decided not to move to Texas, Mickey."

He spoke my thoughts. "Good for the kids, sucks for you."

"Yeah," I mumbled and turned our conversation to brighter horizons. "Lawr's here. Your kids are with Rhiannon. Any chance you'd be able to go out to dinner with us tonight?"

"Seein' as your brother's around and that doesn't happen often, I could talk to a guy, get him to take my shift at the house."

"I'd like that Mickey," I told him softly.

"Then it's done, Amy," he replied, also softly. "Now, gotta go. I'll come over after I get home and shower. Be there around six."

"Okay, honey."

"Later."

"'Bye."

We rang off.

I went home to report about the lunch to Lawrie and then hang with him and my kids.

Mickey came over at around six and we all went out to dinner, Auden and Pippa declaring we just *had* to introduce Lawrie to Tink's.

Lawrie had no problem with the establishment at all. He enjoyed the burgers. He enjoyed being with his little sister, her kids and the man she loved.

Pippa ended our evening by begging Mickey to come over the next night for a dinner she was going to cook for him and her uncle.

Since his shift at the firehouse was during the day, he agreed.

Thus before Lawr was on the road in his rental to go back to the airport on Sunday, he'd had a good dose of the life his little sister was leading.

And after he gave the kids their tight hugs and good-byes, when he hugged me, he said in my ear, "Really fucking good to see you this happy, MeeMee."

I tilted my head back and caught his eyes. "Happy to be this happy, Lawrie. I'll be happier when you officially separate from Mariel and ask out Robin."

He sighed.

I smiled.

And with my kids standing beside me in the drive of our fabulous home, we waved away their Uncle Lawrie.

28

DO WHAT I GOTTA DO

"*O*kay, *what* is your *problem?*" Alyssa asked me, brushing varnish on my nails.

I focused on her. "I'm sorry?"

"Babe, you're here but your mind's so far away it's a wonder you aren't drooling," she told me.

My eyes shifted to Josie sitting next to me in her pedicure chair.

"We've been chatting for fifteen minutes, you haven't said a word, and Alyssa called your name three times," she said. "You didn't even blink."

"Oh God, I'm so sorry," I mumbled, horrified.

"So, what's goin' on with you?" Alyssa asked.

I looked to her. "Tonight, the kids and Mickey are all spending the night at my house. Movie night and together night. They live across the street but Mickey feels we're heading toward *that time* where they're gonna have to get used to an *us* that's *blended*, so he's renting a bunch of movies. We're having a pig out fest of crappy foods while lazing around the TV. And since I have two guests rooms instead of his one, his kids are staying over." I paused for the dramatic affect the next words needed. "With Mickey sleeping with me."

"Oh my," Josie whispered.

"Big shit, sister," Alyssa decreed.

It was.

The good news was that it said a lot, Mickey pushing for this (and he'd pushed).

It said a lot in a variety of ways.

It was close to Christmas. The last three weeks had been bumpy, though not for Mickey and me.

It began with what we expected coming true.

Polly had not taken Pippa's defection well.

She especially didn't take it well when she learned that Ash and Pippa's dad and mom were dating, which meant they shared an association.

Thus, her bullying went into overdrive with specific targets, both Aisling and Pippa.

The surprise came when this had the positive effect of Ash and her posse taking Pippa in.

Mickey had been wrong about that. But then again, from reports I demanded from Pip, Polly had not thrown her abuse up a notch, more like fifteen. It was relentless and it was ugly. Ash got it too. Her friends saw it. The whole school saw it. And Auden reported things were "simmering" and about to blow because it was hitting extremes.

Polly was not stupid enough to do this when Auden or his buds were around, for Joe (to Pippa's delight) had seen the tail end of one episode and waded in, making it clear to Polly he didn't want to see it again.

This didn't delight Polly, Joe defending Pippa, and only served to heighten the madness when Polly was safe to let loose.

Polly also had learned not to be stupid enough to do it when Kellan was around.

But she was doing it and my baby girl was shaken. She was holding up but I knew that was taking a lot.

Along with her other reports, Pippa shared that Aisling was taking an interest in certain things, these being dressing better, doing her hair and adding some makeup.

I had a feeling I knew why and I was proved correct for Pippa also reported that Kellan had noticed.

"He's still into her, Mom," Pippa had said.

This was also positive.

It would turn out to be a negative when Polly got wind of it and ratcheted things up to full throttle. This meaning my girl came home anxious, jittery, and she was never one to hop out of bed, shouting her joy at having to go to school, but it became a near impossible task to get her going in the mornings.

This meant Mickey *and* I had to sit down with both the girls. During this Mickey informed them he, along with me, Rhiannon and Conrad (who I'd told all this and he'd in turn shocked me by telling me we had his full support "with whatever you need, Amelia"), would be going to the school to put a stop to it.

The girls freaked out and Auden stepped in and shared he thought it best to let nature take its course without parents getting involved. He'd also promised it would.

Mickey gave Auden's assessment, "Two days, bud. Then, sorry, we're steppin' in."

It didn't take two days.

The next day in the high school parking lot on their way to Auden's car (since they lived across the street from each other, he was now taking his sister, as well as Ash and Cillian to and from school), Polly unleashed holy hell on the girls.

Auden wasn't around yet, but unfortunately for Polly, some of Kellan's friends were.

They got Kellan. He came running. Auden heard word. He came running.

And two older boys, both good-looking, both popular, shared in no uncertain terms Pip and Ash were off limits.

Polly didn't like that, shared it back and that was when the *real* mean girls, watching this from not very far, swung in.

According to Pip, Ash and Auden, who reported this to me sitting around my bar (while Cillian was hoovering through some homemade sugar cookies), they'd decimated Polly.

It was so bad that she didn't go to school after that for two days.

When she came back, the new status quo had been established.

The bully had become the bullied.

Polly's "friends" all defected, attempting to establish themselves with Ash and her crowd, who were not very accepting.

Auden wasn't exactly arrogant about his call of the situation, but he did get in a few comments the like of, "Knew this would happen."

However, as Polly was receiving her comeuppance, Kellan had finally drawn up the nerve to ask Aisling out.

Aisling was stunned and quietly thrilled.

Pippa was openly beside herself with glee.

The same could not be said for Mickey.

His first reaction was to flatly refuse to allow this.

Aisling was crushed, shared that with her mother and me, and both Rhiannon and I double-teamed him to relent.

He did.

Of a sort.

They could meet, being dropped off (since Kellan couldn't drive yet) to have dinner at the diner. They had two hours. Then they were getting picked up separately.

However, this could not happen until during the Christmas break.

What Mickey didn't know was that Kellan was walking Aisling to class, holding hands with her, and his posse was eating lunch with her posse.

Pippa shared this with me.

I did not share this with Mickey.

During this time, my kids had not quite made up with their father. He was trying and they were not rebuffing, but they stayed full-time with me.

Naturally, through all this, so much going on in such a short time at the same time preparing for Christmas, there had been an intermingling of families. The kids were getting used to each other. Auden was taking the lead as a big brother of sorts to all, including Cillian who wasn't at his school.

So Mickey thought it was time.

Which meant it was our next step but a step that said everything.

Because if he wanted our children to get used to all of us under one roof, what happened next?

Only one thing.

Us being under one roof.

Permanently.

I loved this idea, obviously. And after a very shaky start, the kids were bonding beautifully.

It still scared the heck out of me.

"What if they fight over the remote or don't agree on movies?" I asked.

"Listen to yourself, Amelia," Alyssa replied. "*All* families fight over the remote and don't agree on movies."

She was right.

I was being an idiot.

"It's weird," I whispered. "My kids knowing I'm going to bed with Mickey."

"Why?" Josie asked. "I'm under the impression you've been spending the night at Mickey's. Have I missed something? Do *his* children mind?"

"No," I answered.

"And, just pointin' out," Alyssa added. "Your two got some experience, their dad havin' another wife."

"This is true," I mumbled.

"It'll all go great," Josie assured, patting me on the arm.

"Can't go worse than Thanksgiving," Alyssa muttered.

They of course knew all about our stellar holiday.

"Alyssa," Josie hissed.

Alyssa raised her brows "Do I lie?"

"No, but still," Josie returned. "I'm sure Amelia would prefer not to be reminded."

"It's okay," I cut in. "You're both right. Heck, if Mickey has his kids, they're all together before school for Auden to take them and after school when they come back and we're almost always having dinner together."

"Families under one roof, your room a mile away from their wing of that place, means you'll finally get laid," Alyssa remarked.

This was a bonus.

Mickey and I had hit a dry patch because, me having my kids full-time, he couldn't spend the night and I couldn't either.

This meant no nights.

And no mornings.

He was gearing up to quit Ralph and keeping his regularly crazy schedule so there wasn't time for us to meet somewhere to have quickies. And even though I was supposed to leave the kids behind and go to the locker room for fight night, every Saturday *all* the kids had come, Pippa, Ash, Auden and Cillian, even bringing their friends, and it wasn't easy keeping a huge crew away from the cool dad who'd just won his fight. And, of course, my kids were with me so he couldn't come over and fuck me on the dining room table.

This meant no sex but *a lot* of phone sex, which Mickey did really well.

But it wasn't the real thing.

Thus, my guess, Mickey pushing the blending of families under one roof.

The last of the variety of reasons.

And another good one for me.

I was still nervous.

"Yeah, definite bonus," I said to Alyssa.

"Amelia," Josie called me.

I looked to her.

"I had no mother and a terrible father," she told me. "All I had was my Gran. So I can say with some authority that if kids have two moms or two dads, all who care a great deal and want more than anything for those children to be happy, this is not a bad thing."

She was very right.

And there it was. Just what I needed.

"Thanks, Josie," I whispered.

"Don't mention it," she replied.

"Now that Amelia's sorted, we gotta talk," Alyssa announced, eyes to my nails, but I had a feeling she was talking to Josie. I would know this to be true when she went on, "Sofie told her dad and me last night that Conner invited her down to Boston for the weekend. You know I'm as liberal minded as the best of them, but no way in fuck her father *or* me are lettin' her go spend the weekend with her college boyfriend."

I listened to Josie whole-heartedly agreeing and I was there. I wasn't far away. They'd helped work the things out that were taking control of my thoughts.

But I listened to them thinking La Jolla was one of the most amazing places on earth. It was beautiful and the weather was divine.

However, in all the time I'd spent there, outside of my children, I'd never gotten anything I needed.

No, I'd needed to move all the way across the country to a small town in Maine to find what I needed.

And I'd done that.

So finally, after forty-seven years, the Calway heiress didn't want for anything.

On this thought, there was movement the like it would take your attention at the windows in front of Maude's House of Beauty. Josie and Alyssa stopped talking as all eyes went there.

When they did, we saw a woman with long, thick auburn hair pulled back by one of those wide, wooly headbands that kept your ears warm. She also had on a puffy vest over an attractive turtleneck, a great pair of jeans that did wonderful things for her behind and a fabulous pair of high-heeled boots.

She'd whipped around and her rosy-cheeked face was screwed up in adorable anger as she jabbed her pointed finger at someone and shouted, "You no longer know me, Coert!"

At that moment, the handsome sheriff I'd seen at the town council meeting (a friend of Mickey's I had not yet met) came walking into view. He stopped, planted his hands on jeans-clad hips, his profile was supremely annoyed, and he said something that only could be heard as a deep murmur.

"Kiss my ass!" she shouted, turned with her rich, beautiful auburn hair flying and flounced off.

Coert didn't move, just stood there with hands on hips, muscle flexing in his jaw, watching where she went before he turned and prowled the other way.

Alyssa instantly snapped her head back to us.

"You know about that?" she asked Josie.

"No," Josie answered.

Alyssa looked to me. "*You* know about that?"

"Nope," I answered.

Her eyes drifted back to the windows. "We gotta find out about that."

"Yep," Josie and I both said at the same time.

We looked at each other, Alyssa looked to me, and we all burst out laughing.

Doing it, I knew I was right.

The Calway heiress finally had everything she needed.

———————————— • ————————————

Mickey wandered in from my bathroom while I was sitting in bed screwing the cap back on my moisturizer.

I turned my eyes to him and smiled.

My kids in the house. His kids in the house. And Mickey, his pajama bottoms, his chest and all the rest of him in my bedroom with me.

Happy.

"Hey," I called. "Went good tonight."

It did. I'd had nothing to worry about. The kids were like they were when they were hanging at my bar eating my baked goods or shuffling around Mickey's kitchen making dinner.

His eyes came to me and I saw they were distracted, but he answered, "Yeah."

It was then I noticed that he'd walked in but he didn't continue walking in. He was one step into the room and not moving.

"Everything okay?" I asked.

His head gave a slight jerk and he focused on me.

"Yeah," he repeated.

I studied him and from my study, I was forced to push, "You sure?"

"Yep," he muttered, moving around the bed to his side.

I shifted my lower body to pull the covers out from under me. I unfolded and yanked them over me as Mickey pulled his side back and slid in.

I rolled to face him.

He rolled to face me and got up on an elbow. "Cill and Auden are in Auden's room playin' some game. Think the girls are out, but my kids are in new beds. May take them time to settle. Until I know they're down, not gonna fuck you, babe."

I agreed because this was always our way when we were at his house, but the deadpan way he shared this made me uneasy.

"All right, honey," I whispered.

He dropped to his back then twisted to reach to his light.

It went out.

I stared at him as he settled on his back.

Then I forced myself to reach to my light. I turned it out and settled myself, also on my back.

I stared at my ceiling.

My bed was big and for the first time ever with both of us in it, there felt like miles between us.

And Mickey didn't reach out to me.

What was happening?

Before I could ask, he did. Pulling me to him, tangling us up, and I stifled my sigh of relief.

"You ever get anything back from your folks?" he asked.

I blinked at his throat in the dark.

Where did that come from?

"Well…" I started hesitantly. "Yes and no. They sent something through their attorneys but it's just their way. They do stuff like that. It makes no sense. They're angry with me for not taking their calls but that was months ago. They'll chew on it awhile and get over it. Though," I said with a smile, "the way it is *with* them in my life, it's awful to admit, however true, that I'm kinda liking the reprieve."

"Yeah," he replied like he didn't exactly believe me.

"It'll be okay, Mickey," I assured him. "They'll get over it and then they'll come out because it's what you do, you spend time with your daughter and grandchildren. You'll meet them. They'll heartily disapprove of you. I'll share that you're Michael Patrick Donovan of the Magdalene Donovans who own Maine Fresh Maritime and they'll stop heartily disapproving of you and start simply disapproving of you. Then Dad will attempt to talk Cillian out of his dreams of being a fighter pilot and into a role at Calway, which will drive you up a wall. In the end you'll beg me to do something that will get us six more months of peace."

I was joking.

He wasn't laughing.

He just repeated, "Yeah."

This troubled me at the same time the mention of Cillian being a fighter pilot reminded me that the first day the kids were off school, Mickey was taking them on a Christmas vacation to Phoenix. Something that was happening imminently.

He had not asked me to come, maybe because he knew I couldn't considering my kids were with me. But we'd be separated for a week. We'd talked about planning some late Christmas celebration with all of us after they returned but we hadn't nailed anything down.

I cuddled closer. "This night went so great, we should plan when we're gonna do our belated family Christmas, honey."

"After we get back. First day I have off when I got the kids. Your kids at my place."

Decision made with no input from me.

His strange, highly unusual mood meant I didn't challenge that.

Mickey was quiet.

I was worrying.

Mickey ended his silence.

"This goes the distance between us, my kids and me move in to Cliff Blue."

My head tilted back instantly. "I'm sorry?"

He didn't repeat himself.

He said, "You got enough rooms where the kids each can have their own space and you got that den for a guest bedroom just in case your brother or my folks come. I'll sell my place, give you the profit. But I pay all utilities when we move in."

"I…but…you…that's…I don't know—" I stammered but never finished the thought I didn't quite get around to having.

Mickey interrupted me, "This market, I could make eight, nine hundred K off my house. That's not a fifth of this place so I take over utilities so I feel I'm doin' what I gotta do."

"How about, when we get there," I began carefully, "that we share things equitably? What you can do a percentage of what—?"

I stopped that time because his arms gave me a squeeze and his mouth added, "Don't finish that, Amy."

I said nothing further.

"Do what I gotta do," he stated.

"Okay, Mickey," I agreed but only because he was being so strange and it was scaring me.

"And not tough. Kids love this place. It's nice. It's big. You love it. And the tub doesn't suck."

That sounded more like Mickey so I again settled in and replied, "All that's true."

"Yeah," he muttered.

I fell silent and in doing so, listened to Mickey fall asleep. No brush of the lips. No goodnight.

Nothing.

It took me longer but I fell asleep with him.

Mickey woke me with his mouth on mine, his hands pushing my nightie up my back and his lips saying, "Did a walkthrough. They're all out."

Then he kissed me.

Even half asleep, it was a kiss from Mickey so I kissed him back.

And thus commenced Mickey making love to me.

This was a surprise. We had not had any kind of intimacy that wasn't shared through cell towers for weeks. I thought it would be intense and fast and astounding.

It wasn't. It was slow and reverent and sweet.

We'd taken our time before. We'd enjoyed each other lengthily and thoroughly. I loved it when Mickey guided it to that, just as much as I loved it when we went at each other like teenagers.

But when he finally let me finish and then I took him there, he tangled us together, murmured "'Night, Amy," and I again listened to my guy drift off to sleep.

I didn't sleep myself.

Not a wink.

Because I'd been made love to like that before. Not as good, but Mickey was better with everything.

It had been the night before Conrad left me.

So no, I didn't sleep.

Not a wink.

———————— • ————————

"Okay, *what is your problem?*"

I jerked out of my reverie at Alyssa's question.

She, Josie and me were sitting together having lunch at Weatherby's. It was two days after Christmas. Mickey and his kids were returning the next day. My kids had ended their rift with their father and went to him the afternoon of Christmas day (as was his turn) and with my blessing had been staying with him since.

So I had been suddenly and unusually alone.

Alone enough to finally come to terms with what was happening.

The last real conversation I'd had with my guy, he'd shared that if what we "went the distance" he was moving his family into Cliff Blue with me.

But it bore repeating, *that was the last real conversation I'd had with my guy.*

He'd been gone for a week in Phoenix with his kids but even before he left, he had removed himself from me.

And after he left, I heard more from Cillian and Ash than I did from

Mickey, not only through their constant communications with my kids via texts and calls, but directly to me (via mostly texts).

All I got from Mickey was such as, "Phoenix is great," and "Cill kicked it in the flight simulator," and "Yeah, I know we need to plan our Christmas thing. We'll talk about it when we get back."

There were no, "You'd love it here," or "You should have seen Cill in that flight simulator," or "Can't wait to have our thing, baby, love you."

In fact, there were no "love yous" at all.

I said it when we were disconnecting and his reply would be, "Yeah. Same."

Yeah. Same.

He was pulling away and I had no idea why.

I focused on Alyssa. "I think Mickey's gonna break up with me."

"*What?*" she shrieked and I saw heads turn and this was probably because Josie added her own unusually loud, "Pardon me?"

"Shh," I hissed, leaning into the table to do it.

Alyssa, across from Josie and me, leaned back and Josie leaned toward me.

"What?" she repeated.

"He's pulling away from me," I told them.

"As it might feel, Amelia," Josie stated. "He's an entire continent away."

"He hasn't said 'I love you' in nearly two weeks."

"Fuck," Alyssa muttered.

She got it.

Josie didn't.

"He may be in company and not desirous of sharing this depth of emotion in front of his friends. You *did* say they were staying with someone he grew up with, a man who's a fighter pilot in the armed services, thus a man's man and with both, his friend might tease him about such things. Perhaps he feels private sentiments should remain private and he hasn't had a chance to gain that privacy."

"That would include *before* he was with his friend Chopper and his family," I told her.

Her eyes slid to Alyssa, which meant she had no reply to that.

"We talk…about everything," I shared. "We call each other all the time. We touch base. We keep in the know. He's hardly calling me at all."

Josie looked back to me. "He *is* on vacation, honey."

"That isn't Mickey," I whispered.

She sat back and her pretty blue eyes turned worried.

I pressed my lips together to stop myself from crying.

When I succeeded in this endeavor, I told them, "No matter what, for months, we talk before we go to sleep. We haven't done that since he left. I asked him about it, him being away, and he says it's the time difference."

"They are hours behind us," Josie said gently. "They could be busy."

"You love a bitch, you find the time," Alyssa snapped.

I looked at her.

Oh yes. She got it.

"I don't know what happened," I said.

"I don't either," Alyssa returned. "But you should call his ass on it and set up a meet to find out what's *up* his ass the minute he gets back."

Confronting Mickey Donovan. Not high on the things I found exciting.

No, I did find it exciting because that was our thing.

I just didn't find it exciting now if, in doing it, he broke up with me.

"If he's done, he's going to be done," I said, sitting back, shoulders slumping. "He's Mickey."

"He owes you an explanation," Alyssa retorted.

He did.

I just wasn't sure I wanted to hear it.

My eyes drifted to the salad I'd barely touched.

Since we got together, nothing, not anything, not in all that had happened gave indication that this wasn't heading to something real. Something permanent. Something *forever*.

Mickey giving me a happy life and more importantly, me having the opportunity to give the same to Mickey.

There had been extreme craziness, the kind that could tear people apart, and it had all ironed out. Alcoholic ex-wives. Dirtbag ex-husbands. Troubled kids. Crappy jobs.

Heck, Mickey's business was all set to go. He had two big jobs lined up to start on his return (contracting work, which was more money) and he was quitting Ralph his first day back to work.

I couldn't imagine what had gone wrong.

Except in all that goodness, I was still me.

Boring Amelia Hathaway, no job, no drive, no ambition, spending her time baking and decorating and volunteering at an old folks' home.

"Amelia," Josie called.

I glanced her way, mumbling, "I'm not hungry. Do you mind if I take off?"

"Think you should stick with your girls, baby," Alyssa told me gently.

I looked to her. "You have to get back to work and so does Josie."

I, however, did not. It was one of the few days I didn't go to Dove House.

With my kids at Conrad's, I had exactly nothing to do.

"I'll juggle an appointment," Alyssa offered.

"I make my own hours, Amelia," Josie reminded me.

I shook my head, digging in my purse at my side to pull out some bills. I took out a lot of them and threw them on the table.

"Lunch on me," I said, not looking at either of them and sliding out of the booth.

"Amelia, stay," Josie cajoled as I grabbed my jacket off the hook that was on a high bar that led up from the end of each booth.

I looked to her. "Really, I just need some alone time to think."

"Babe, you should—" Alyssa started.

"Later," I interrupted her, and pulling on my coat while juggling my bag, I made my escape.

I went to my house, walked in from the garage and stopped by the glorious dining room table on top of which, weeks before, Mickey had fucked me.

Then right there, he'd told me he loved me.

There were no used pop cans or cake plates with crumbs or cookie tins with the top askew along with no kids at my bar.

There *was* a fabulous chaise lounge with standing lamp and a table on a magnificent rug on the landing by the windows, this courtesy of a good find by Josie's interior designer.

The space was huge.

Huge and beautiful.

Huge and cold and empty.

And I found myself standing there, staring at the beauty I created, thinking that I hoped when my kids went to college that they did it far away and never came back to Magdalene.

Because after Mickey ended it with me, once they were gone, I was moving from my show home across the street from the Donovans.

I didn't know where I'd go. I didn't even know if I'd survive those years living across from Mickey and his kids.

I just knew I'd be gone.

━━━━━━━━━━ • ━━━━━━━━━━

I WAS ON MY CHAISE LOUNGE UNDER AN AFGHAN WITH MY BOOK, AND I WAS taking a sip from a glass of wine when my phone rang that evening.

I looked down at it on the table beside me, saw who was calling, set aside my wine and took the call.

"Mickey," I greeted.

There was a pause before he said, "Hey."

I said nothing.

"You there?" he asked.

"Yes," I answered.

"You okay?" he asked.

"Perfect," I lied.

"The kids with you?" he went on.

"No," I told him.

He fell silent.

I didn't jump in.

He ended the silence with, "We're back tomorrow."

"I remember."

"Early flight here, get back late there."

"Yes."

A pause before he asked, "You sure you're okay?"

"Why wouldn't I be okay?"

"You don't sound right."

I wasn't.

I was head over heels in love with a man who no longer wanted me for no reason at all.

"I'm fine," I lied again.

"You don't sound fine."

"Well, I am."

"Amy, what the fuck? Talk to me," he ordered.

Now, after weeks of me gently trying to get him to talk, *he* wanted *me* to talk to *him?*

"About what?" I asked.

"What's up your ass," he answered irately.

I would not rise to the bait. I couldn't imagine why he wanted a reaction from me, but he couldn't have it because I didn't have it in me.

"Nothing's up my ass, Mickey. I was having a glass of wine and reading when you phoned. And it isn't exactly early here."

"It's nine thirty," he stated.

"Yes. And I'm relaxed and was into a book. I had lunch with the girls today. No Dove House. Not a big day. Nothing to report. I'm mellowed out and am probably going to go to bed soon except I'm into this book so it might keep me up reading."

He took a moment as if to digest that while assessing its veracity (and there was absolutely no veracity) before he said, "Then I'll let you get back to your book. But I gotta ask you somethin' tough and that is, keep your kids at your ex's tomorrow. Once I get us home and the kids settled in, I'm comin' over. We gotta talk."

So he wasn't wasting time.

"Text me when you're on your way over," I told him.

"Will do. Now I'll let you go."

"Okay. Enjoy your last few hours of cactus and sunshine."

"Sun went down already, baby."

There was humor in his tone. I hadn't heard that in over a week.

It pained me.

"Then enjoy your last few hours of cactus and warmth."

"Will do that too. Later, Amy."

"Good-bye, Mickey."

I didn't hang up.

He didn't either.

"Babe?" he called.

"Yes," I answered.

"That it?"

What could he possibly want?

"Sorry, was juggling wine, didn't hit the button," I lied. "Anyway, 'bye again, Mickey. See you tomorrow."

Then I hit the button and set the phone down.

I stared at it. I did this a long time.

It didn't ring.

So that was it. I knew it then.

Mickey didn't call me back.

He should have because I disconnected without telling him I loved him.

But he didn't care because it was over between him and me.

Why, I had no clue.

Except I was me and when shit like this happened, I'd learned there didn't really need to be a reason.

———————— • ————————

THE NEXT EVENING AFTER EIGHT, MY PHONE CHIMED.

I looked to it and saw it was Mickey.

On my way.

Swiftly, I snatched it up and replied, *Door is open.*

I was in the kitchen making tea.

As he lived right across the street, my torture in waiting for him didn't last long.

The door opened.

Jeans. Sweater. Boots. He looked tired around his eyes from all the travelling but he still looked all Mickey.

The weight I was carrying pressed down further.

"Hey," I called, opening the paper around my teabag.

"Hey back," he replied, closing the door and moving toward me.

"Want tea?" I asked the mug I was putting the bag in.

"Babe, you know I don't drink tea."

I looked to him. "A beer?"

He stopped at the end of the counter.

God, not even getting in my space.

I looked away, crumpling up the paper from the teabag and frantically trying to think of something I could do to keep my hands busy.

I could do this. I could lose him. I could live my life without my head in the clouds experiencing the bright flashes of happy he consistently gave to me.

I could do it.

I might even find contentment (one day, in about twenty years).

But it would take everything.

So I'd never do it again.

Mickey was it for me. He had my heart in a way I never wanted it back, not even if he didn't want it anymore.

I'd go to movies alone. I'd go to bed alone. I'd watch my kids grow up and move away (alone).

I'd find a way to live my life alone.

But I'd never put myself out there again. I'd never give my heart to anyone else.

Because it wasn't mine to give.

It was Mickey's.

"Seriously?"

I looked to him again. "I'm sorry?"

"Been away a week, Amy," he told me.

"As you just returned, I do remember that, Mickey."

His eyes narrowed and his voice lowered. "Something *is* up your ass."

I stared at him, stunned he appeared angry.

"As I shared last night, nothing is up my ass," I returned.

"Then what the fuck?" he asked.

"What the fuck what?" I asked back.

"Last night you answer the phone like I'm the guy you hired to paint your kitchen. You hang up without sayin' you love me. Now I get to you after I'm gone a week and you don't come to me and kiss me and you barely even look at me?"

Was he insane?

"Why would I kiss you?"

His expression went from annoyed disbelief to stormy in a flash.

"Why would you kiss me?" he whispered sinisterly.

"You know, Mickey," I threw out a hand, "just do this. Don't draw it out. It doesn't help anything when you draw it out. Clean cut. Surgical. That's the way to go."

"Clean cut. Surgical." He was still whispering.

The kettle whistled and I moved to it, taking it off its flame.

"Yes. If you would, please," I requested, not looking at him and moving back to my mug.

"All right then, Amy. I did it," he stated.

I poured my tea. "Did what?"

"Took my inheritance."

I set the kettle with a crash to the cement countertop as my eyes flew to him.

"What?" Now it was me who was whispering.

He didn't answer me.

He turned and walked away, disappearing into the hall that led to my bedroom.

I stood wooden where he left me staring at where I last saw him. This must have lasted some time because by the time I came unstuck and was about to move into the hall, I saw him prowling back down it. He did this in a way that I quickly backtracked, walking backward.

I stopped in the kitchen.

He stopped at the end of the counter and threw what he was holding on top of it.

I looked at it and saw it was the letter from Addison Hillingham that I'd shoved in a bathroom drawer I didn't use so the kids wouldn't see it.

I'd forgotten all about it.

"Forget to tell me something?" he asked.

Again, my eyes flew to him.

"Mickey—"

"You're not gonna live any way than what you're used to living. They yank your money out from under you, I cannot give you that. So I set about makin' it so I could give you that as best as I can. Called my dad. Had a chat. He already wanted to do it so he was all over it. He talked with Sean, Frank and Dylan and they were all in. Then he went to his accountants to finagle whatever the fuck they gotta finagle so the IRS wouldn't take a huge fuckin' chunk outta what my dad wanted me to have. They did their conniving, got it sorted, Dylan was on board, so Dad gave both him and me fifteen million dollars. We signed away any claim to the company, that's Sean and Frank's. I can't touch the money unless there's an emergency but I get the interest. When I die, it's split and my kids get it. The interest is a fuckload. And it might not be what you had, but you aren't the kinda woman who needs that anyway. It'll still be better than what I could give you without it. So I did what I had to do to make it so you don't feel the hurt your parents wanted to lay on you for whatever fucked up shit they got in their heads that made them strike out and make their daughter bleed."

And again, I stood completely still, staring up at him, speechless.

He kept going.

"When we get married, I sell my house, pay back Dad's investment, the company is ours free and clear to make a go of or fuck up, however that goes down."

When we get married.

That rattled around in my brain and it was no surprise, since that was happening, I continued to be incapable of speech.

"I get home after spendin' a lot of my vacation on the phone with my dad, mom, brothers, gettin' Fed Ex'ed shit to sign, goin' over papers and emails, I come to my woman and she doesn't even fuckin' kiss me?" he asked and before I could answer (not that I was yet able to do so) he demanded, "So, tell me again how nothin' is up your ass."

"It's a ploy," I forced out and his stormy expression turned thunderous.

"What's a fuckin' ploy?" he bit out.

"That." I made my arm move to indicate the letter from Hillingham. "It's a ploy. It's Dad and Mom's way of saying they're pissed at me. Trying to get me to react. Playing their games. I'm not going to lose my trust funds. Hillingham called me a week ago saying he's shared that with my parents and I have nothing to worry about."

Mickey scowled at me.

"You didn't have to take your inheritance, Mickey."

"Why didn't you tell me that shit went down?" he asked, also tossing out an arm to indicate the letter.

"Because it was a nuisance," I replied. "It didn't mean anything. I got it on Thanksgiving and obviously that day other things took my attention. And to be completely truthful, I forgot all about it."

Mickey drew breath in through his nose and looked over my head.

I stared at him.

He took his inheritance for me.

I kept staring at him.

He took his inheritance for me.

"All I need is you," I said softly.

His eyes moved down to me.

Do what I gotta do.

He'd found that letter when he'd spent the night the first time all our kids were together.

And he'd done what he had to do.

"First, I have the Bourne trust fund, Mickey," I began gently. "Prior to me turning thirty, if I did something that the board or my parents petitioning the board meant they could withhold it from me, they could have withheld that money permanently. Once I receive it, there are no caveats. It's irrevocable. And that has enough money in it to live on comfortably."

A muscle ticked in his cheek.

"Second," I went on, "it could all go up in a puff a smoke and I wouldn't care. Yes, I might eventually want better countertop appliances when we moved in together, but even that wouldn't matter and not because I have my own. Because I'd have you. I'd have you and Auden and Pippa and Ash and Cill. If I had all that, since that would be having it all, what else would I ever need?"

"I got here, you barely looked at me," he returned.

"You've been pulling away," I shared. "I thought you were going to end things with me."

His face again went stormy. "Are you fuckin' *crazy*?"

"Think about it," I returned. "Our conversations have been perfunctory. And *you* didn't say you loved me *once* since you were in Phoenix."

"That is not fuckin' true," he growled.

"'Same here' is *not* 'I love you,' Mickey."

"It fuckin' is, Amy, especially when Chop's around. We been best buds since we were five. He takes every opportunity to bust my ass about anything and he's good at it 'cause he's had a lot of practice. Makes the boys at the firehouse look like amateurs. Then again, he gives me shit because I give it back. It's what we do. And with me, Ash and Cill yammerin' on about you, he knows what you mean to me, he's lookin' forward to meetin' you, but that doesn't mean he didn't take his opportunities, and he got a lot in. He made a point of hangin' close when I'd call you just to get the chance to give me shit. I wasn't gonna give him more openings. And it may sound fucked, but I'd never hear the end of it. And seein' as that would be about me tellin' the woman I love that I love her, it might piss me off. I didn't take my kids to Phoenix to visit a man who's like a brother to me and then spend that time bein' pissed off. "

So Josie was right.

Shit.

And they'd "yammered on" about me?

That felt *great*.

"Did you consider explaining that to me?" I asked hesitantly.

He threw both hands out in a gesture of frustration.

"Amy, I've been dealin' with all this shit for you and the fact that once I tell my kids we're loaded, Cill's gonna want me to build him his own personal paintball arena. And hangin' with *your* girl and *you*, suddenly *my* girl is into clothes and decorating. She's linin' up babysitting jobs to feed that need. She found some print online that she wants for her wall that she *has to have* in her room and that shit costs a hundred and fifty dollars. She knows I got cake, no tellin' now what *she's* gonna want."

I found that funny and wonderful news. Mickey having a daughter who liked clothes and expensive pictures for her wall were much better problems than Mickey with a daughter who had to play mother to his son because her mother was a drunk at the same time she's bullied at school.

I didn't share that.

I asked, "So it was just that your mind was on other things?"

"Yeah," he answered tersely. "All that and the conversation I'd have to have with my kids about leavin' their home and the hit it would be about lettin' that place go. Not to mention, me talkin' you into lettin' your kids hang with their dad so when I worked out my notice with Ralph and before my crew got started on their new jobs, I could give the kids to Rhiannon and take you to the Keys so I'd get a shot at you bein' in a bikini when I asked you to marry me."

I took a step back.

His scowl grew dark as it snapped to my feet.

It a flash, it snapped back to me.

"Now what?" he clipped.

"You've had a lot on your mind," I noted.

"Uh...*yeah*," he replied sarcastically.

"Why didn't you share any of it with me?" I asked.

"Like you shared that with me?" He again threw out a hand to the paper from Hillingham.

"Mickey, as dire as it sounded, it didn't *mean* anything."

"Well, you're fuckin' tidy," he shot back strangely. "Had shit to put away in your bathroom and so it wouldn't crawl up your ass I fucked that up, I opened a drawer, saw that, figured you were hidin' it from a variety of people, one of them *me*. And it bein' worthy of hidin', I couldn't know it didn't mean anything."

"Well it doesn't, but you could have shared you found it before you went off and took your inheritance," I returned. "And in so doing, got stuck in your head about a lot of stuff that was clearly weighing on you that *you* didn't share with *me*."

"Fucks with the grand announcement I wanted to lay on you when I got it sorted and to a place I could tell you I could take care of you."

That was sweet but I felt it necessary to reiterate, "You were *already* taking care of me."

"In the way you're used to, Amy," he returned heatedly.

"Yes, to repeat, you're *already* taking care of me in the way I'm used to, Mickey. The only way I need it to be."

"Right, so that shit happens," *again* with flipping his hand to the letter, "and you got a wild hair to buy a Rover and you gotta wait to save for it, if you can get it at all, rather than headin' out and buyin' it with cash, that's not gonna bother you?"

God, why was he not getting this?

"Mickey, *I love you!*" I was now yelling.

"And I love you," he ground out. "Since that's the case, I want you to have it all."

I threw up my hands. "I have all I need."

"I want you to have," he planted his hands on his hips and leaned toward me ominously, "*it all.*"

"Why?" I asked shrilly. "When I have everything I need."

"Because you're worth it."

I snapped my mouth shut.

Do what I gotta do.

Oh my God.

Because you're worth it.

Oh. My. *God.*

"No comeback?" he taunted.

"I love you," I whispered.

"I know that," he returned. "That all you got?"

"No," I replied. "That's it. Just I love you."

Mickey shut *his* mouth.

I stared at him and it was a surprise when I felt the tear slide down my cheek.

"All my life," I whispered, "I was the girl who everyone thought had everything or could get it. But the only thing I ever wanted was a man like you. You're the best man I've ever met, Mickey Donovan." I felt another tear and the words trembled when I finished, "And you're mine."

"Get the fuck over here, Amy."

I didn't hesitate an instant.

I ran into his arms.

I held him tight and burrowed in, pressing my cheek to his chest as I felt more tears trailing down my face.

He moved to cup a hand on the side of my head and whispered, "Baby, think I made it clear I want a kiss and not sure that's gonna work with you tryin' to fuse your face to my chest."

Immediately, I tipped my head back, got up on my toes and moved my own hands so I could clamp them on either side of his head and pull him down to me.

Our mouths met and we kissed, at first hard and heated, but since it went on for a long time, it shifted to soft and sweet.

When Mickey finally broke the kiss, I slowly opened my eyes and looked into his beautiful ones, seeing at the surface, and all the way down deep, the love he had for me.

It went on forever.

"So now that you're loaded, this means I get to go whole hog on birthdays too," I declared.

I watched Mickey blink those beautiful eyes.

This was right before his arms convulsed around me and he burst out laughing.

He kept his arms tight and continued to laugh even as he said, "Now that stupid shit is done, if you can get over any concern you might have at the starving nations of the world needing tea, you can toss that crap, get your shit and get your ass over to my house. The kids miss you."

Stupid shit?

Starving nations needing tea?

I swallowed the quick retort that was on the tip of my tongue.

Not because he didn't deserve it.

But because he loved me. He wasn't breaking up with me. He took his inheritance for me.

And his kids missed me.

So I rolled up on my toes again, touched my mouth to his and broke free of his arms so I could toss the tea and get my shit.

This, I did.

Then we went over to Mickey's.

EPILOGUE

BUCKLE UP, BABY

"*I*'m going."

"No, I'm going."

"Oh for goodness sakes, *I'm* going."

Mickey and I were bickering about who was going to pick Ash up from her date with Kellan.

Rhiannon had come around for the aftermath girlie discussion, which was also why Pippa was there with me.

Auden and Cillian were virtually attempting to kill unknown kids somewhere else on the planet on some online game they were playing on the Xbox in Mickey's family room. And from their shouts, they were succeeding.

Mickey wanted to pick his daughter up in order to give her date the evil eye.

I was not about to subject Aisling to that.

Rhiannon, who already had her coat and was at the door, agreed with me.

"I'll be back in twenty minutes," she declared and before Mickey could reply, she walked out.

"I hope he kisses her," Pippa said dreamily.

I felt a wall of flame come from Mickey.

"Pip!" I snapped, looking to her to see she was gazing as dreamily as her voice at the door, which was when I felt Mickey's pain for Pippa was going to be next.

She looked to me. "What?"

"Gross! Kissing Ash!" Cillian shouted, showing that clearly the loud explosions coming from the TV weren't drowning out our conversation.

Or he was listening.

"Not gross, dude. She's cute," Auden replied.

Mickey turned menacing eyes to me.

"Auden doesn't lie, honey," I said gently.

He stormed off and not long after he disappeared down the hall I heard the fridge open and close then the sliding glass door open and close.

He was drinking beer and brooding about his daughter becoming a woman.

I grinned.

"He's hot when he's all dad-who-doesn't-want-his-daughter-dating," Pippa observed and I looked to her to see her gaze aimed at the hall.

She was right.

She looked to me and grinned. "He's a total score, Mom. All the girls at school say it. They even get in heated debates about who's the hottest dad. Amber Spear's or Aisling Donovan's."

"Obviously, it's Aisling Donovan," I stated haughtily.

"Totally," she agreed, still grinning.

My eyes drifted back to the hall as I mumbled, "Maybe I should go to him."

"Maybe you should let him get used to it," Pippa advised, shifting up to sit on her knees on Mickey's couch in his front living room. "He's gonna have to. Kellan is into Ash *big time*. They're both movie freaks. She knows all about boxing. They watch the same TV shows. For high school, all that is *serious*. They sit with us at lunch but they're totally into each other and never stop talking."

The idea of Ash never stopping talking was one I couldn't wrap my head around.

But I loved that she found a boy she could open up to.

"Anyway, I want some ice cream. Do you think Mickey would mind if I had some ice cream?" she asked.

"No, kiddo. Just ask to see if the boys want some too."

"Okay, Mom," she replied, got up and bumped into me playfully as she passed me.

I watched her disappear in the hall and heard her talking to the boys about ice cream and even heard her opening the sliding glass door to make her request for ice cream officially of Mickey. When it was granted, I also heard her asking him if he wanted some too.

When I heard the door close again, I wandered into the hall but stopped at the baby picture of my guy.

I stared at it wondering if his parents knew what a remarkable man he would become.

I moved away from it knowing from experience with Auden and Pippa that they absolutely did.

Five minutes later, the sliding glass door opened and I looked from helping Pip scoop ice cream to the door.

Mickey was about to step in when, eyes never leaving the TV, Cill called, "Get this, Dad! If Ash marries Kellan we'll have a Kellan *and* Cillian in the family. Isn't that hilarious?"

Mickey didn't answer. He swung right back out the door and slid it shut.

I would have made it if I hadn't heard Pippa snort.

Since she snorted, I didn't make it.

So I had to dash to the dining room so Mickey wouldn't hear me burst out laughing.

———————— • ————————

"HEY, AMY?"

I was wandering down the hall to Mickey's room where he had moved his brooding after the aftermath girlie discussion took epic proportions and lasted hours (and may have diverted onto other paths, like online shopping on Ash's tablet).

Auden and Cillian were still attempting to kill people in the family room.

Rhiannon was gone.

As far as I knew, Pippa was still ensconced in Ash's bedroom, carrying on the aftermath girlie discussion the two moms couldn't hear.

Now, just Aisling's head was out her door and she was looking at me. "Yeah, blossom?"

"Dogfight," she whispered then grinned a small, sweet grin. "I win."

After delivering that, she closed the door.

Needless to say, the date went great.

Mickey was in his bedroom brooding.

I was headed that way smiling.

———— • ————

I WINCED EVEN AS AUDEN FLIPPED HIS OPPONENT TO HIS BACK.

"Good, bud! Stay at him!" Mickey, sitting beside me, shouted.

"Don't let up!" Cillian, sitting beside Mickey, yelled.

"Ash and me are gonna go get some sodas," Pippa, sitting next to me, announced.

She and Ash got up from the bleachers as I looked to them then, with a mother's sense, turned my head the other way and looked across to the end of the bleachers in the gymnasium.

Kellan was loitering there, eyes to Aisling.

Pippa was Ash's cover.

They moved in front of us, but Ash abruptly stopped when Mickey's hand darted out and caught her wrist.

I looked to him to see his head tipped back, eyes on his girl.

"Go to your boy but I don't lose sight of you, hear me?"

"All right, Dad," she huffed resignedly and irritably.

He let her go.

Pip aimed an amused grin at me.

I returned it.

The girls took off.

I jumped when Mickey shouted, "That's it! You got it!" and the rest of our side started clapping.

I looked to my son on the mat just as the referee slapped his hand down and yelled, "Pin!"

Auden took his feet to more applause and Cillian jumping up and down on our bleacher, yelling "Right on! Auden rules!"

At this moment of victory for my son, I felt the hairs stand on end a the back of my neck. I turned my head just in time to catch Conrad looking away from me.

He was alone. No Martine. No Tammy.

A good choice.

It was sad but it was his lonely bleacher he'd made for himself.

I turned to Mickey who was grinning at the mat and clapping.

"You do know you're going to have to back off this Ash and Kellan thing," I advised.

He stopped clapping *and* grinning and looked to me.

"She's fifteen, she gets more freedom. She's fourteen, she does not."

"She's fifteen next month," I told him something he knew better than me.

"Then she doesn't have long to wait," he retorted and looked away, toward the boys in their clutch patting Auden on the back.

He took it then his eyes went to his dad. After that, they came to me.

I gave him a thumb's up and some silent clapping.

He shook his head and rolled his eyes but did it grinning.

Then he started pulling on his track suit.

"Look at those mooks," Cillian stated disgustedly, staring at the two boys now wrestling on the mat. "Auden is the best...*ever*."

Mickey slid an arm along my waist and kept it there.

I endured the bone-crushing boredom of watching another bunch of boys—these I didn't know and love—wrestle, doing this fortified by Mickey's arm around me.

Then, thankfully, it was over and we all went home.

⎯⎯ • ⎯⎯

I KNOCKED ON THE DOOR TO THE LOCKER ROOM.

It flew open and I found myself flying in because Mickey's hand latched onto my wrist and he pulled me in.

He looked out the door he had his other hand on.

"Kids in their seats?" he asked the hallway.

"Yes, Mickey," I breathed.

He slammed the door, locked it and shoved me against the cinderblock wall.

Then, in his boxing trunks and shoes, upper body bare and still slicked with sweat, he dropped to his knees in front of me.

"Mickey," I panted.

His hands taped from the fight he just lost to Jake, he pushed up my pencil skirt.

"Are you okay?" I asked, noting (in what I had to admit was a distracted way) the red welling on his cheek.

He didn't answer.

He ripped down my panties.

I sucked in a breath.

He tipped his head back, sliding a hand up the side of my high-heeled Jimmy Choo boot.

"Like these boots, baby," he whispered.

"I…good," I mumbled.

He slid his hand back down, grasped my ankle, tossed it over his sweat-glistened shoulder and dove right in.

My head hit cinderblock and I buried my hands in his hair.

He ate me, hungry, voracious, no mercy until I came in his mouth (and again I had to admit, this didn't take long).

Still soaring, he was up, I was up, and he was fucking me against cinderblock.

I came again while he was kissing me, moaning into his mouth, tasting me and Mickey.

He followed me while I was kissing him, groaning into my mouth, tasting only me.

When he was done, he stayed buried inside me, shoved his face in my neck and held me against the wall.

I stroked his hair and his back and stared unseeing at the locker room.

"I love fight night," I whispered.

Mickey pulled his face out of my neck and looked at me.

Grinning.

⸻•⸻

"Babe."

"This is not happening."

"Amy."

"No," I snapped, pacing my bedroom and sliding my hand on the display of my phone.

I found what I wanted, tapped it and put the phone to my ear.

"Amy, this is not a good idea," Mickey growled. "Shit like this, you don't get involved."

I glared at him just as Lawrie said in my ear, "Hey, MeeMee."

"You're dating someone who isn't *Robin*?" I snapped.

He didn't reply for a loaded moment before he asked, "How did you find out?"

"We have mutual friends, Lawrie, and I'll add one of them is *Robin*."

"She heard about Tara?" he asked, sounding concerned.

"Tara?' I asked. "*Tara?*" I demanded peevishly.

"Did Robin hear about it?" he clipped.

"No." I tossed a hand to the laptop on my nightstand that he couldn't see. "I just read an email from Melly."

Perhaps it was my fevered mind but I could swear I heard a sigh of relief before he told me, "Sweetheart, I can't date your best friend."

"Why not?" I queried sharply.

"What if it doesn't work out?"

"Are you worried she'll turn whackjob on you?" I returned, and before he could answer I went on, "Because if you are, don't worry. That's for cheaters. Everyone knows that. And if you could stay with Mariel for as long as you did and not stray, you have nothing to worry about."

"That's not it."

"What *is* it?"

"You two are very close and if—"

"She makes you laugh."

"She does, but—"

"She's beautiful. Stylish. She has her own money."

"This is true, but—"

"She thinks you're handsome. She loves spending time with you. *You* make *her* laugh."

"That means a lot, MeeMee, however—"

"However *nothing*," I snapped. "We girls, we need it. We need the grand statement. We need to know that nothing else matters, nothing, *not one thing* but the shot you're willing to take at you making us *yours*. You'd risk anything. You'd do anything. Logic and manners and her living right across the street and sisters as best friends don't factor. Nothing does. Caution is thrown to the wind and you'd go against everything you believe in just for that one chance. That one chance to start building something. So if you do that in the beginning, when life happens, we know you'd do whatever you gotta do to keep us happy." I paused before I finished, "This, of course, does not include if all this happens while you're married. But that's the *only* exception."

Lawrie was silent.

"Lawrie," I hissed. "Did you hear me?"

"I'm hanging up now."

"You are *not*," I bit out.

"If I don't, how can I call Robin?"

I rocked to solid then tore my phone from my ear and hung up on him.

"You need the grand statement?"

My eyes cut to Mickey who was standing on his side of my bed in his pajama bottoms, looking at me.

"Don't ask questions you know the answer to, Mickey Donovan. You're the king of the grand statement."

His face got soft right before he stated, "Buckle up, baby."

"I know," I agreed. "Robin *is* a whackjob, just the good kind, but this isn't going to go easy because Lawrie has his own baggage too."

"Not what I mean."

"What do you mean?"

He moved from his place by the bed across the room, past me, to his jacket he'd thrown over the arm of the daybed. He shifted it, dug into it, pulled out some tri-folded papers and walked to me.

He then held them out to me.

I took them but didn't look at them.

"Itinerary," he declared. "Shit's sorted. Even called Conrad. He's takin the kids and in two days, we're goin' to the Keys."

I blinked.

"How big a rock he buy you?" he asked.

"Three and a half carats," I answered automatically.

"Then prepare to drag your hand around, darlin', 'cause you know I'll have to best that shit and do it soundly."

At that, I dropped the paper, threw myself in his arms, pushing back until we hit bed and went down on it, me bouncing on Mickey.

Then I was all over him.

"Babe, don't know if the kids are asleep," he told me (my kids, his were at Rhiannon's).

"They won't hear."

"What if they—?"

I lifted my head, my brows knit and glared at him. "Are you about to whisk me away to the Florida Keys and ask for my hand in marriage?"

"Well...yeah."

"Then we're fucking to celebrate."

His mouth twitched. "Fucking?"

"Fast, hard, rough," I dipped closer, "and *quiet*."

My breath left with the swiftness of him rolling on top of me.

"To be quiet, I gotta do all the work," he declared. "You get on top, you moan and do it loud."

That was okay by me.

I grinned.

My guy kissed me.

Then he fucked me.

We were as quiet as we could be.

After, me cleaned up and back in my nightie, Mickey in his pajama bottoms, we were tangled up in the dark in my bed.

"Love you, Mickey Donovan," I whispered.

"Love you too, soon-to-be-Amelia Donovan," he whispered back.

Amelia Donovan.

God.

I closed my eyes and pressed deep into his body.

His arms convulsed around me. "Shit, you like that."

"Happy," was all I could say.

"Yeah," he agreed.

I tipped my head back and looked at his face in the shadows. "A flash?"

He slid his hand up my back, over my shoulder to cup my cheek. "No, baby. See, 'bout nine months or so ago, give or take a few weeks, this spitfire brunette moved in across the street and those flashes became history. Now I live life blinded and that is not a bad thing."

That moved through me, setting me soaring, and I bent my neck and shoved my face in his chest so he wouldn't see me crying, even in the dark.

He felt it since I was shaking uncontrollably (and might have let out a sniffle) and he gathered me closer.

"Don't like my woman crying in my arms."

"Ha-ha-happy tears."

"Cut it out anyway, Amy. Yeah?"

My head tipped back again and I declared, "You can't order me to stop crying happy tears, Mickey."

"I just did."

"That doesn't mean it's gonna happen."

"It already did, seein' as you're layin' into me and no longer crying."

I glared at him through the dark because he was right.

"Fuck," he muttered, "I can actually feel that angry heat and now I wanna fuck you again."

"I don't actually have anything pressing on my schedule for the next oh, I don't know, eight to nine hours, Mickey."

"Jesus, you're a smartass."

"Bitching about me being a smartass is not fucking me, Mickey."

I ended that on a gasp because I ended that being flipped to my stomach then Mickey's hand was yanking up my nightie right before it dove right in my panties. It curled, I spread my legs to give him better access and he found me.

"Where's the smartass now?" he murmured in my ear.

He didn't allow me to answer. My clit, still sensitized from earlier, got a tweak from his finger and I had to concentrate on that while my hips twitched.

"Yeah," he growled with satisfaction.

"You're annoying," I breathed, squirming.

"Challenge, Amy. Repeat that when you're sittin' on my face in five minutes."

Oh God.

I kept squirming.

He swept the bedclothes off me.

"Lift your hips, baby. Wanna see that ass working for me."

Oh *God.*

I lifted my hips.

Mickey kept at me until he was done with that and he dragged me onto his face.

It took a while to get to the fucking but it was a pleasurable while, and when we were again clothed and tangled under the covers, I had no smartass left in me.

So I fell asleep in the arms of my guy knowing soon we'd be lazing around in the sun of the Florida Keys and I'd be doing it wearing the huge-ass rock he was going to give me.

I WALKED INTO MY HOUSE, PAST MY BELOVED DINING ROOM TABLE, STRAIGHT to the kitchen.

I put my purse and bag on the counter, turned to go to the fridge to assess dinner options and stopped dead.

I stood and stared.

It took a while for me to reanimate my body. But when I did, I shuffled sideways, my gaze glued to the wall beyond the dining room table.

Blindly, I dug into my purse until I found my phone. I activated it without looking at it and continued not to look at it as I did what I had to do by rote, lifted it to my mouth and demanded, "Call, Mickey."

I put it to my ear.

"Hey," he greeted after one ring.

"Hey back," I whispered.

He said nothing.

I stared at the wall.

On it was my Mother's Day present.

Mickey in cahoots with the kids had arranged for a photographer to come to the house when the bluebells had taken over.

Mickey had been right. When they bloomed they were so profuse it looked like Cliff Blue was floating on a cloud of flowers over the sea.

It was the physical manifestation of my world. The home I shared with my loved ones suspended in beauty.

We'd all got dressed up (kind of, the girls did, the boys wore nice shirts and jeans) and the photographer had taken our picture in front of the house. Mickey and me in the middle pressed close, his arm around my shoulders, mine around his waist. His other arm was around Pippa. My other one was wrapped around Cillian's chest. He was standing slightly in front of me (something he couldn't do now since he'd had a growth spurt in the time that had past and was now taller than me). Ash was beside me. She'd been caught laughing, her eyes to the camera, her cheek to my shoulder, her arms around my middle. Auden was standing close on the other side of his sister, holding her hand.

Outside Ash, who was laughing, we were all smiling.

Happy.

Now, printed huge, beautifully framed with two lovely sconces arching over it to make it an even bigger feature than it already was, that picture hung by the dining room table, pictorial evidence I had everything a woman could need.

Me and my family floating on a cloud of blue, blinded by a flash of happy.

Mickey ended the silence.

"You saw it."

"I love you," I whispered.

"Same here."

I smiled and fought back the tears.

It took some time, Mickey gave me that time, and when I succeeded, I asked, "Have a taste for anything for dinner?"

"I'll get Tink's, bring it home," he answered.

"Then we'll eat Tink's at the dining room table."

His voice was soft when he replied, "Works for me."

It worked for me too. He had his kids. I had mine.

So it worked perfectly.

"See you later, honey," I said.

"Yeah, baby. See you."

We hung up.

I walked to the picture and flicked the new light switch that now had five dimmer controls. One for the chandelier over the dining table. One for the kitchen lights. One for the kitchen pendants. One for the living room lights.

And one for my picture.

It was daytime. I didn't need that light.

But from that day forward, whenever I was home, that picture was lit.

Every day.

Reminding me, even though I knew it down to my soul, that I had all I needed.

———————— • ————————

I WANDERED DOWN THE HALL TO THE DEN, AND ONCE I HIT IT, I WENT RIGHT to the desk and dumped the bags and my purse on top. I slid the envelope out of one then dug in the other and pulled out the tissue wrapped parcel. I unwrapped it unveiling the pretty frame I'd bought at the reopened shop on the jetty.

I was about to put the picture I'd had printed at Walgreens in it when my phone in my purse rang.

I set aside the frame and picture, dug my phone out, looked at the display and took the call.

"Hey," I greeted.

"Hey back," Mickey replied. "Listen, babe, you do payroll?"

I looked to the computer on the desk.

The den was the den.

It was also another guest bedroom now that the other side of the room was taken up with a massive, slouchy sectional with a pullout.

Further, it was a family room where Auden and Cillian played Xbox when they were at my place since the girls (and Mickey *and* I) weren't big fans of them hogging the TV in the great room.

It also now had shelves on every wall not taken up with windows or the TV, beautiful walnut ones Mickey had put up with the help of Jake (and Cillian and Auden).

And last, it was the office for Donovan Roofing and Contracting.

I was Mickey's office girl. I did payroll, returned calls (or picked them up when I was at the desk), scheduled Mickey to meet with clients, typed up quotes, ordered materials, sent invoices, dealt with receivables and played bookkeeper (with tutoring from Robin).

Mickey's business had taken off.

Ralph beat him on some bids but those who paid attention to referrals and online reviews went with Mickey. Not to mention, he'd gotten the roofing contract for the build around the golf course at the Magdalene Club. A huge job. A real coup. Thirty houses and not little ones. Mini-mansions.

In fact, there was so much work Mickey had twenty-eight employees. And his business wasn't even a year old yet.

I didn't get a salary. This was because Mickey's house was on the market and we were getting married in a small, harvest-themed wedding (reception to be held at Lavender House) the day before Halloween, so what was his was going to be mine very soon anyway (as per me, we'd had words but Mickey gave in eventually).

And I loved doing it. I loved helping. I loved watching Mickey's business flourish. I loved seeing him happy in his job. I loved knowing when he started his work day he was doing something he enjoyed, something that was *his*.

Since Mickey's house was on the market, even though our wedding wasn't for three months, when it sold, even if we weren't yet married, they were moving in.

Then again, they were there most of the time already.

If they weren't, I, and if I had my kids, all three of us were over at Mickey's.

Total Brady Bunch.

It was fantastic.

"Yeah, honey, I run it every Thursday morning before Dove House," I told him something he knew. "Direct deposits will be in accounts tomorrow."

"Shit," he muttered.

"Why?" I asked.

"Jerry fucked up his timesheet. Forgot some overtime I asked him to do."

"Tell him he can just submit it with the next one and we'll make the alteration then."

"Says he needs the money, baby. The divorce."

One of Mickey's crew, Jerry, was in the throes of an ugly divorce that included an ugly custody battle. His attorney's fees were out the roof.

"Right," I said, snatching up a pen and sliding a pad of Post-its my way. "Give me the hours. I'll run another payroll and he'll have two deposits the second one is the overtime. But he needs to give you the timesheet to bring home tonight so I can have it on file."

"Will do," he replied and gave me the hours. I wrote them down while he asked, "Your day been good?"

I looked to the frame and the picture sitting beside it, ready to be inserted.

Then I looked to the shelves.

There were DVDs, CDs, books, picture frames and knickknacks in them. There were a lot of shelves and they were new so they were far from filled. But I figured when Mickey and his kids moved in, that would happen easily.

All of them had something in them, though.

But one of them had only one thing.

A broken, black, folded up umbrella.

My heart squeezed.

"No," I answered Mickey's question.

"What's up?"

I looked away from the umbrella.

"Nothing," I mumbled. "We'll talk when you get home."

His voice dipped when he repeated, "What's up, baby?"

He heard it in my voice even if I was trying to hide it. He read it. Now he was worried.

I dropped my eyes to the picture on the desk and reached out a hand to touch it with my finger.

"Amy?" Mickey called.

"Mr. Dennison passed this morning," I whispered, my voice suddenly clogged.

"Fuck, Amy," Mickey whispered back.

I stared at the picture of Mr. Dennison and me. He was sitting in a recliner in the lounge at Dove House. I was sitting on the arm, leaned in and kissing his cheek. He was looking at the camera, smiling.

It was a selfie.

I was getting good at them.

I'd learned after Mrs. McMurphy, and now I had tons of pictures on my phone of the residents, Dela with the residents, the staff with the residents, the kids, me, even Mickey with the residents.

"Peaceful," I said.

"That's good," he replied gently.

I made the noise as the tears came.

"Shit, baby," Mickey whispered, then louder and more firm, "Comin' to you. Got somethin' to do, then I'll be there. Home in an hour. I'll run Jerry's shit, don't worry about it. You relax. I'll text the kids. We'll order pizza. Quiet night at home with the family. Yeah?"

Quiet night at home with the family.

That could cure anything. Even help balm the hurt of losing Mr. Dennison.

I sniffled and agreed, "Yeah, Mickey, sounds good. But I'll run Jerry's thing."

"Okay, Amy. Be home soon."

He'd be home soon.

That, alone, could cure anything.

"All right, Mickey. See you."

"Love you, darlin'."

I smiled as a tear slid out of my eye. "Love you too."

"Later."

"Bye."

We hung up, I rounded the desk and made short work of running an additional payroll so Jerry could get his money.

Then I put the picture of me and Mr. Dennison in the frame. I took it to the shelf with the umbrella and set it up.

I took a step back and stared at it, allowing more tears to fall.

Then I swiped them away, turned and left the room knowing, as the years passed, that shelf would get filled with frames.

I'd only ever have one umbrella. I'd eventually have masses of frames.

But I'd have thousands of memories.

—————— • ——————

I WAS CLEANING THE HOUSE WHEN I SAW IT.

The weekend before, after Mickey closed on his house, he and his kids had moved in.

Although it was bittersweet, the Donovans saying good-bye to their home, it was not traumatic.

Then again, for months, they'd had two homes and a big family so they were used to me, my kids and our space.

Ash and Cillian had elected to keep the bedroom furniture I had in the guestrooms, Cillian doing this stating an excited, "I feel like a lumberjack in that bed! Totally cool. And I'm *so* lumberjacking when I'm not going Mach three."

Lumberjacking, which included axes and chainsaws, as a hobby did not thrill me, but I kept my mouth shut.

Much of Mickey and his kids' stuff was dotted here there and everywhere with some of his furniture filling in empty spaces. But most of it I'd taken pictures of and now it was in a storage unit awaiting me selling it on *Craig's List*.

The move had been such a huge project, I hadn't thought of it until right then, when I was in Ash's room, vacuuming.

She'd kept the beachy feel of the room but switched out the bed linens and added her knickknacks and posters, making the room hers.

The candle didn't fit in it.

And further, the candle was too important to be hidden in her room.

I probably should have asked but I didn't. I didn't because I didn't want her to think she had to be nice and thus say no.

The statement had to be made.

So I turned off the vacuum and grabbed the candle.

I moved my fabulous bowl to the corner of the kitchen counter.

I put the candle in the middle of the dining room table.

It worked perfectly.

I made a mental note to chat with Rhiannon before she came over again so she wouldn't be blindsided by seeing it and possibly hurt.

I then went back to cleaning.

I was at the desk in the den when the kids got home from school.

"Drop off, Mom!" Auden shouted. "I'm going to Lacey's."

I blocked out the second part of what he said because I was even less of a fan of my son dating than Mickey was of his daughter doing it.

"Okay, kiddo!" I shouted back.

"What's for dinner?" Cill yelled.

"Cheesy chicken!" I yelled back.

"Awesome!" he returned.

"*Oh my God!*" Pippa screeched. "Did someone erase my *Vampire Diaries?*"

"It's right there, Pip, jeez!" Cillian told her loudly.

"Homework, Pip!" I shouted.

"I *know*, Mom!" she shouted back.

I had my eyes to the computer but turned them to the door when I sensed something there.

Aisling was leaning against the jamb, hair curled, understated makeup making her pretty face even prettier, her curvy body encased in a cute short skirt, tights, cuter low-heeled boots and a pretty sweater.

"Hey, blossom," I called.

"Love you, Amy," she replied quietly.

She'd seen the candle.

Sitting at the desk, working, suddenly I was flying.

"Love you too, kiddo," I returned.

She gave me a small smile and disappeared.

I drew in a deep breath so I could get my feet closer to the ground in order to concentrate on work.

When I accomplished that, I turned back to my computer and went back to work on the invoices.

————————— • —————————

"I'M GONNA VOMIT," ROBIN mumbled.

"You're not gonna vomit," I retorted.

"If she doesn't vomit, I'm gonna vomit," Alyssa stated.

I looked to Josie, who was standing with the rest of my girls in our klatch.

All my girls together.

Happy.

I saw Josie was looking at me and when I caught her eyes, she said, "It *is* nauseating."

I gave my attention back to what was happening across the room, this being my mother and father fawning over Mickey's mother and father.

We were at Mickey and my rehearsal dinner in the back room of The Eaves. A grand spectacle dripping with flowers and free-flowing cham-

pagne with the dress code my mother decreed as *strictly cocktail*, something that didn't bother me or anybody but the guys.

I liked dressing up.

And it meant I got to give Mickey his own personal LBD.

Mom could decree this since she and my dad were paying for everything, the food, the flowers, the hostess gifts (two expensive crystal champagne flutes for everyone, except the kids who got boxes of imported
Belgian chocolates) and the open bar.

Needless to say, my parents' freeze out had ended. This happened
when Lawr told them I was marrying into the Maine Fresh Maritime
family. In fact, it wasn't just that the freeze had ended, they were beside
themselves with delight.

This was because Mickey's family had more money than Conrad's and
they felt this move on my part was me again toeing the line.

Mickey's family didn't have as much money as my family did (and this
wouldn't do, the Bourne-Hathaways always had to have the upper hand).
Not to mention, Mickey didn't work in the family business.

But surprisingly, this last didn't bother Mom and Dad.

"Runs his own business," Dad had stated arrogantly over the phone
during the official end of the freeze out call he'd made to me months
before. "There's a lot to be said about a man who's his own man."

I already knew that so I'd said nothing.

They'd arrived the day before, and since their arrival they'd spent
nearly all of their time crawling right up Mickey's family's asses.
Including Mickey's brothers.

Genteelly, of course.

Mickey's family was great, just like Mickey. Friendly. Teasing. Affectionate. Loving.

Mine, not so much.

"It's just their way," I said to the girls.

"How you and Lawr are of their loins, I'll never know," Robin replied.

Since I agreed with this statement, I had no comment.

But at hearing it, I looked through the room to find Lawr standing
talking with Jake, Jake's son Conner and Conner's girl, Sofie. Conner had
his arm around her and was holding her close. She was comfortable there.
Safe and content and happy.

They'd survived the first year of college apart and now Sofie was down in Boston with him.

Although Junior and Alyssa were happy she got into a good school, during a mani-pedi session prior to her move south, Alyssa had declared, "If my girl comes up pregnant her freshman year, it's gonna suck, seein' as I'll have to help raise the kid because her dad'll be doin' life for killin' the kid's baby daddy."

I didn't want to think of these goings-on, so I didn't. Auden was dating. Ash was still with Kellan (who could now drive, which meant car dates, which in turn was driving Ash's father 'round the bend) and my daughter was also dating (serially, she'd been out with four different boys since school started, all this impatiently awaiting Joe asking her out, something she hoped he would do, something, being tight with Auden, he wasn't doing).

No, I absolutely did not want to think of these goings-on.

So, I didn't.

Whatever happened, I'd survive. So would Mickey. That had been proven beyond a doubt.

Instead, I watched my big brother's eyes move around the room, catch on the woman beside me, and warm.

Robin and Lawr were no longer dating. Robin and Lawr were now an item.

It was serious.

They couldn't make any big moves since her oldest was in college but her youngest was still a junior and she didn't want to be far away. They had to wait a couple of years before she moved up to Santa Barbara to be with Lawrie permanently, but that was the plan. Now every other week, she was up there with my brother and it was working.

Splendidly.

I knew it would and, of course, rubbed that fact in at every available opportunity.

Like right then, when his attention shifted from Robin to me and assumed a superior look to which he shook his head, his lips twitching and turned his focus back to Jake.

"Gonna steal her."

I jumped slightly at hearing Mickey's murmur and turned just in tim for him to slide my glass of champagne out of my hand and set it on the table.

"Of course," Josie murmured.

"If I wasn't taken and you weren't seriously taken, as evidenced by the proceedings," Robin said to my guy. "I'd want you to steal me."

My best girl liked my guy.

And I liked this.

Mickey gave Robin a smile, and I gave Robin a fake glare as he took my hand.

While he was moving me toward the door, I felt a hint of chill and glanced my mother's way to see her aiming that chill at me as Mickey pulled me into the main restaurant.

"We're sitting down to dinner in a few minutes, honey," I told him as he guided me through the tables.

"Can't do that without us," he replied.

"This is why we can't leave," I pointed out.

He said nothing.

I didn't either when he led me to the hallway that took you to the bathrooms.

My belly started to warm and my legs started to get shaky as he turned right at the end of the hall then took us past the bathrooms.

At the end of that hall, he shoved aside the coats (I *knew* it was a cloak area) and pushed me to the back wall.

It was dark.

It was quiet.

There was likely going to be a hostess invading our space to hang up a coat at any second.

I didn't care about any of this when Mickey put his hands to my hips.

Weird how a coat closet was our place.

But it was.

This was not where it began.

But it was where it *began*.

And I loved Mickey Donovan even more for taking me there the night before he was officially going to make me his and I was going to make him mine.

His eyes were down, taking me in through the shadows.

Then they lifted to mine. "Nice dress, baby."

There I was again.

Soaring.

Though, these days, I'd learned how to live with my head in the clouds.

"God, I love you," I whispered.

That got me one of his easy grins.

Yes, I absolutely loved him.

"Good, means you'll make out with me in the coat closet," he replied.

"My mother will be displeased," I noted.

"Only reason we're goin' back at all is so I can save *my* mother from yours."

I moved into him, sliding a hand up his chest. "I'm sorry, Mickey. They're—"

He interrupted me, "Relax, Amy. They don't care. They know people like that. They know how to deal with people like that. They know you're not like that. They like you and they like your kids. That's what matters."

It was.

This meant it was time to relax.

It was also time to make out.

I tipped my head to the side. "So, are we gonna make out or what?"

I felt the heat from his eyes before I felt his lips take mine.

I slid my arms around his shoulders.

He slid one hand to curl it around the back of my neck, the other one he curved around the cheek of my ass.

At the intimate touch, I gasped against his tongue.

Mickey pressed me into the wall.

Thus, we made out at our rehearsal dinner in the coat closet, and we did it a long time.

Long enough to totally piss off my mother (something she didn't show, except for the glacial looks she aimed at me), which was fabulous.

And long enough to get me hot and bothered so, much later, when my cell on my nightstand chimed, waking me from a restless sleep, and I took the call to hear Mickey growl, "Door," I'd run to the front door (but I probably would have done that anyway).

He, at my mother's demand due to "tradition" was staying with Cillian and Auden at Jake and Josie's.

He, obviously, had the key.

So he was through it before I got there.

But the warning call was seriously sexy.

And last, we'd made out long enough for Mickey to get so hot and bothered he'd fairly dragged me down the hall to my room.

We'd fucked on my daybed.

Then he'd kissed me deep and sweet at our front door and gone back to Lavender House because it was bad luck to see the bride on the wedding day.

And even though the time said it technically *was* our wedding day, I decided it didn't count because the sun hadn't yet gone up.

So I ignored that and just slid into Mickey and my bed, put my head to the pillows and fell back to sleep.

But I did it with my head still in the clouds.

———— • ————

Mickey

MICKEY LAY NAKED IN THE BED, THE FIREPLACE BLAZING, HIS EYES TO THE kitchen, waiting.

She walked to him wearing her sequined fuzzy slippers and a short robe, carrying a tray.

"I have squirtable cheese and crackers," she announced. "I also have a can of whipped cream and vanilla wafers. I have a fresh beer. Thus I have on my magical tray the makings of dinner *and* dessert, no muss, no fuss, no cleanup."

He had no idea what she intended with that whipped cream but he knew what he was going to do with it.

He watched as Amy placed the tray at the end of the bed, moved to her side, slid off her slippers, shrugged off her robe and he took in the curves of his wife's naked body as she joined him under the covers.

He rolled into her.

Her arms slid around him even as she warned, "You're gonna knock over the beer, Mickey."

He moved away from her, grabbed the beer, leaned into her to put it beside her glass of champagne and the bottle in its bucket on her night-stand before he went back to her.

He took in her soft skin, her fresh floral scent, the warmth in her pretty hazel eyes.

And he saw it there.

Ten hours ago, with her kids standing with her and his kids standing with him, they were married in Reverend Fletcher's church.

They'd had two parties after.

One, a big, fancy one that Josie and Alyssa threw at Lavender House.

The other, a small, quieter one the old folks threw at Dove House.

His kids went to Rhiannon.

Her kids went to her ex.

And Mickey took his new wife to Jimbo's hunting cabin for their three day honeymoon.

She had no idea where they were going.

When they parked outside it, they hadn't even got out of his truck before he had to piss her off to stop her from crying.

That took no effort but she lost the pissed real quick when he carried her over the threshold.

If he still had any question, which he didn't, her reaction to their honeymoon destination would have told him everything he needed to know.

His new wife needed his body beside her in their bed.

And anything else life threw at them, she would deal.

Then again, she was dealing with a five carat diamond on her finger.

"Finest woman I ever met," he whispered.

Her hand cupped his jaw. "Mickey."

"Love you, Mrs. Donovan."

She closed her eyes and it swept through her face, something he'd seen countless times, something that never failed to move him, and fuck, *fuck*, he gave her that.

He gave it to her.

And each time he did, he got it.

She didn't need fifteen million dollars.

She didn't need all her money.

She needed to feel that feeling.

That was all she needed.

And it was only him who could give it.

She opened her eyes.

"Same here, Mickey."

He grinned at her before he kissed her and he did that a lot for three days (and beyond).

Then he made love to her and they did that a lot for three days (and beyond).

After, they ate squirtable cheese and did good things with whipped cream.

They also slept together and they woke up together.

And last, they spent three days naked together in that bed (also in the shower).

And that was all either of them needed.

The End

Spend more time in Magdalene with

The Time In Between

Cady and Coert's story.

LEARN MORE ABOUT
THE TIME IN BETWEEN

After a painful loss, Cady Moreland is coming to Magdalene to start the next chapter in her life. A chapter that began eighteen years ago but had a heartbreaking ending. The time in between was full of family and friendship, but Cady could never get the man she fell in love with all those years ago out of her heart.

Coert Yeager has learned to live without the girl who entered his life right when she shouldn't and exited delivering a crippling blow he never would have suspected. The time in between was full of failing to find what he was missing…and life-altering betrayal.

But when that girl shows up in Magdalene and buys the town's beloved lighthouse, even if Coert wants to avoid her, he can't. A fire in town sparks a different kind of flame that won't be ignored.

As Cady and Coert question the actions of the two young adults they once were thrown into earth-shattering circumstances, can they learn from what came in between and find each other again?

ABOUT THE AUTHOR

Kristen Ashley is the *New York Times* bestselling author of over eighty romance novels including the *Rock Chick, Colorado Mountain, Dream Man, Chaos, Unfinished Heroes, The 'Burg, Magdalene, Fantasyland, The Three, Ghost and Reincarnation, The Rising, Dream Team* and *Honey* series along with several standalone novels. She's a hybrid author, publishing titles both independently and traditionally, her books have been translated in fourteen languages and she's sold over five million books.

Kristen's novel, *Law Man*, won the *RT Book Reviews* Reviewer's Choice Award for best Romantic Suspense, her independently published title *Hold On* was nominated for *RT Book Reviews* best Independent Contemporary Romance and her traditionally published title *Breathe* was nominated for best Contemporary Romance. Kristen's titles *Motorcycle Man, The Will*, and *Ride Steady* (which won the Reader's Choice award from *Romance Reviews*) all made the final rounds for Goodreads Choice Awards in the Romance category.

Kristen, born in Gary and raised in Brownsburg, Indiana, was a fourth-generation graduate of Purdue University. Since, she has lived in Denver, the West Country of England, and she now resides in Phoenix. She worked as a charity executive for eighteen years prior to beginning her independent publishing career. She now writes full-time.

Although romance is her genre, the prevailing themes running through all of Kristen's novels are friendship, family and a strong sisterhood. To this end, and as a way to thank her readers for their support, Kristen has created the Rock Chick Nation, a series of programs that are designed to give back to her readers and promote a strong female community.

The mission of the Rock Chick Nation is to live your best life, be true to your true self, recognize your beauty, and last but definitely not least, take your sister's back whether they're at your side as friends and family or if they're thousands of miles away and you don't know who they are.

The programs of the RC Nation include Rock Chick Rendezvous, weekends Kristen organizes full of parties and get-togethers to bring the sisterhood together, Rock Chick Recharges, evenings Kristen arranges for women who have been nominated to receive a special night, and Rock Chick Rewards, an ongoing program that raises funds for nonprofit women's organizations Kristen's readers nominate. Kristen's Rock Chick Rewards have donated hundreds of thousands of dollars to charity and this number continues to rise.

You can read more about Kristen, her titles and the Rock Chick Nation at KristenAshley.net.

facebook.com/kristenashleybooks
twitter.com/KristenAshley68
instagram.com/kristenashleybooks
pinterest.com/KristenAshleyBooks
goodreads.com/kristenashleybooks
bookbub.com/authors/kristen-ashley

ALSO BY KRISTEN ASHLEY

Rock Chick Series:

Rock Chick

Rock Chick Rescue

Rock Chick Redemption

Rock Chick Renegade

Rock Chick Revenge

Rock Chick Reckoning

Rock Chick Regret

Rock Chick Revolution

Rock Chick Reawakening

Rock Chick Reborn

The 'Burg Series:

For You

At Peace

Golden Trail

Games of the Heart

The Promise

Hold On

The Chaos Series:

Own the Wind

Fire Inside

Ride Steady

Walk Through Fire

A Christmas to Remember

Rough Ride

Wild Like the Wind

Free

Wild Fire

Wild Wind

The Colorado Mountain Series:

The Gamble

Sweet Dreams

Lady Luck

Breathe

Jagged

Kaleidoscope

Bounty

Dream Man Series:

Mystery Man

Wild Man

Law Man

Motorcycle Man

Quiet Man

Dream Team Series:

Dream Maker

Dream Chaser

Dream Bites Cookbook

Dream Spinner

Dream Keeper

The Fantasyland Series:

Wildest Dreams

The Golden Dynasty

Fantastical

The Rising Series:

The Beginning of Everything

The Plan Commences

The Dawn of the End

The Rising

The River Rain Series:

After the Climb

After the Climb Special Edition

Chasing Serenity

Taking the Leap

Making the Match

The Three Series:

Until the Sun Falls from the Sky

With Everything I Am

Wild and Free

The Unfinished Hero Series:

Knight

Creed

Raid

Deacon

Sebring

Wild West MC Series:

Still Standing

Smoke and Steel

Other Titles by Kristen Ashley:

Heaven and Hell

Play It Safe

Made in the USA
Las Vegas, NV
30 November 2023

81865336R00350